The

War of the Ancients
Archive

The
WARCRAFT®
War of the Ancients
Archive

RICHARD A. KNAAK

POCKET BOOKS
NEW YORK LONDON TORONTO SYDNEY

Pocket Books
A Division of Simon & Schuster, Inc.
1230 Avenue of the Americas
New York, NY 10020

First Pocket Books trade paperback edition December 2007

POCKET and colophon are registered trademarks of Simon & Schuster, Inc.

For information regarding special discounts for bulk
purchases, please contact Simon & Schuster Special Sales
at 1-800-456-6798 or business@simonandschuster.com.

Manufactured in the United States of America

10

Cover art by Glenn Rane

ISBN-13: 978-1-4165-5203-1
ISBN-10:   1-4165-5203-0

These titles were previously published individually by Pocket Star Books.

CONTENTS

FOREWORD

BY RICHARD A. KNAAK

Azeroth, the *World of Warcraft*, is a realm in as much flux as our own . . . and sometimes more. When I was first contacted by Simon & Schuster to write *Day of the Dragon*, the first ever full-length novel based on it, the incredible depth of background material passed on to me by Blizzard showed the care and devotion of the creators. It also well presented the reasons for *Warcraft*'s astounding growth and and even more astounding success; Azeroth was truly a living, complicated place filled with the mystery and adventure that had drawn not thousands to it but *millions*.

Chris Metzen, Vice-President of Creative Development and one of those most passionate about the legacy of Azeroth, became an invaluable partner and friend from the very beginning. Well-versed with my previous Dragonlance work and a writer himself, Chris brought forth ideas that blended so well with my own that it almost seemed that we had been working together for years. The synopsis for *Day of the Dragon* quickly fell into place. In *Day*, we tried to introduce readers—both those familiar with *Warcraft* and those not—to elements that would steer them toward the coming *WoW* online game, and begin tightening the history as forthcoming plans for Azeroth demanded. The success of that first novel—in which we also developed more fully the great dragon Aspects—then paved the way for a much more complex and certainly exciting project: *War of the Ancients*.

Bringing to life what was the foundation of the conflict forever after engulfing Azeroth was a fantastic venture. As with our history, that of Azeroth's volatile past was an amazing collection of notes and legends—sometimes contradictory (also like our own history)—that together enabled us to build a breath-taking panoramic vision. Details not previously developed fell into place and, with a few necessary corrections, the trilogy began to take its final shape. Such is the vividness of *Warcraft* that throughout the writing process I could see everything that was set down as if it was actually happening. The battles, the intrigues, the desperate quests . . . I lived each alongside characters I came to know and love—or, in some cases, looked forward to see getting their comeuppance.

When it was finally released, *War of the Ancients* achieved all that we hoped it would. It gave further depth, further life, to Azeroth. It answered questions long wondered at and, of course, added a few intriguing ones of its own. It introduced readers to not only new characters but some of those only mentioned previously in the legends. We meet a young Malfurion Stormrage just coming into his own powers; his turbulent brother Illidan; their friend Tyrande Whisperwind; the woodland demigod Cenarius; the vain and ambitious Queen Azshara; and, naturally, such dread names from the Burning Legion as Mannoroth, Archimonde, and . . . their lord, Sargeras. There are races well-established in *Warcraft* mythos, such as the Tauren and the Earthen. Thrust into this upheaval in time are two characters familiar to those who have read *Day*—the rebellious wizard Rhonin, and his mentor Krasus, the latter of whom will find repeating history particularly unnerving. Among those making their debut are the sinister Xavius—Azshara's counselor—the young guard officer Jarod Shadowsong; the sadistic Varo'then; and certainly not least, the intrepid and loyal orc, Brox, himself, like Rhonin and Krasus, lost in time due to the desperate machinations of the great Aspect, Nozdormu.

The three volumes included in this collection—*The Well of Eternity, The Demon Soul,* and *The Sundering*—could neither have existed nor proven so successful without the loyalty of *Warcraft* fans everywhere, and to all of you I am most grateful. In addition to my own offerings, I have gotten to watch others add to Azeroth's legacy, and the diversity of stories just continues to amaze me. The novels have been published worldwide, including in such countries as Spain, Korea, the Czech Republic, Turkey, and China. They have been translated into German, French, Russian, and many other languages. Readers from many of these countries have contacted me and I marvel at how united they are in their enjoyment of *Warcraft* in all its incarnations. The list of publishers and countries continues to grow, as do the offerings. In the past year, I completed the first introductory manga for *Warcraft*—*The Sunwell Trilogy*—whose elements, like those of my previous works, are now being incorporated in *WoW*. There are intentions of proceeding with another set. There are certainly more novels on the horizon, with some interesting surprises in store.

I have been pleased to be a small part of such a phenomenon and hope that both those of you who are for the first time delving into *War of the*

Ancients and those who are returning to it will enjoy this special collection. With *The Burning Crusade* expansion already opening up new vistas, and other fantastic plans being prepared down the pipe, we can all look forward to many, many exciting adventures on Azeroth, some of which I hope to share with you.

A special thanks should also go to those who not only put together this latest archive but are in great part responsible for the series of novels beginning in the first place. Of course, there is Chris. I also thank Marco Palmieri and the rest at Pocket Books/Simon & Schuster.

And with that said, let the adventure begin!

The Well of Eternity

The Whistler

For Martin Fajkus and my readers
throughout the world.

ONE

The tall, forbidding palace perched atop the very edge of the mountainous cliff, overlooking so precariously the vast, black body of water below that it appeared almost ready to plummet into the latter's dark depths. When first the vast, walled edifice had been constructed, using magic that melded both stone and forest into a single, cohesive form, it had been a wonder to touch the heart of any who saw it. Its towers were trees strengthened by rock, with jutting spires and high, open windows. The walls were volcanic stone raised up, then bound tightly by draping vines and giant roots. The main palace at the center had originally been created by the mystical binding of more than a hundred giant, ancient trees. Bent in together, they had formed the skeleton of the rounded center, over which the stone and vines had been set.

A wonder to touch the hearts of all when first it had been built, now it touched the fears of some. An unsettling aura enshrouded it, one heightened this stormy night. The few who peered at the ancient edifice now quickly averted their gaze.

Those who looked instead to the waters below it found no peace, either. The ebony lake was now in violent, unnatural turmoil. Churning waves as high as the palace rose and fell in the distance, crashing with a roar. Lightning played over its vast body, lightning gold, crimson, or the green of decay. Thunder rumbled like a thousand dragons and those who lived around its shores huddled close, uncertain as to what sort of storm might be unleashed.

On the walls surrounding the palace, ominous guards in forest-green armor and wielding lances and swords glared warily about. They watched not only beyond the walls for foolish trespassers, but on occasion surreptitiously glanced within . . . particularly at the main tower, where they sensed unpredictable energies at play.

And in that high tower, in a stone chamber sealed from the sight of those outside, tall, narrow figures in iridescent robes of turquoise, embroidered with stylized, silver images of nature, bent over a six-sided pattern written into the floor. At the center of the pattern, symbols in a language archaic even to the wielders flared with lives of their own.

Glittering, silver eyes with no pupils stared out from under the hoods as the night elves muttered the spell. Their dark, violet skin grew covered in sweat as the magic within the pattern amplified. All but one looked weary, ready to succumb to exhaustion. That one, overseeing the casting, watched the process not with silver orbs like the rest, but rather false black ones with streaks of ruby running horizontal along the centers. But despite the false eyes, he noted every detail, every inflection by the others. His long, narrow face, narrow even for an elf, wore an expression of hunger and anticipation as he silently drove them on.

One other watched all of this, drinking in every word and gesture. Seated on a luxurious chair of ivory and leather, her rich, silver hair framing her perfect features and the silken gown—as golden as her eyes—doing the same for her exquisite form, she was every inch the vision of a queen. She leaned back against the chair, sipping wine from a golden goblet. Her jeweled bracelets tinkled as her hand moved and the ruby in the tiara she wore glistened in the light of the sorcerous energies the others had summoned.

Now and then her gaze shifted ever so slightly to study the dark-eyed figure, her full lips pursing in something approaching suspicion. Yet, when once he suddenly glanced her way, as if sensing her observation, all suspicion vanished, replaced by a languid smile.

The chanting continued.

The black lake churned madly.

There had been a war and it had ended.

So, Krasus knew, history would eventually record what had happened. Almost lost in that recording would be the countless personal lives destroyed, the lands ravaged, and the near-destruction of the entire mortal world.

Even the memories of dragons are fleeting under such circumstances, the pale, gray-robed figure conceded to himself. He understood that very well, for although to most eyes he resembled a lanky, almost elven figure with hawk-like features, silvering hair, and three long scars traveling down his right cheek, he was much more than that. To most, he was known as a wizard, but to a select few he was called *Korialstrasz*—a name only a dragon would wear.

Krasus had been born a dragon, a majestic red one, the youngest of the great Alexstrasza's consorts. She, the Aspect of Life, was his dearest companion . . . yet once again he dragged himself away from her to study the plights and futures of the short-lived races.

In the hidden, rock-hewn abode he had chosen for his new sanctum, Krasus looked over the world of Azeroth. The gleaming emerald crystal enabled him to see whatever land, whatever individual, he desired.

And everywhere that the dragon mage looked, he saw devastation.

It seemed as if it had only been a few years ago when the grotesque, green-skinned behemoths called orcs, who had invaded the world from beyond, were defeated. With their remaining numbers kept in encampments, Krasus had believed the world ready for peace. Yet, that peace had been short-lived. The Alliance—the human-led coalition that had been the forefront of the resistance—had immediately begun to crumble, its members vying for power over one another. Part of that had been the fault of dragons—or the *one* dragon, Deathwing—but much had simply been the greed and desire of humans, dwarves, and elves.

Yet, even that would have passed with little concern if not for the coming of the Burning Legion.

Today, Krasus surveyed distant Kalimdor, located on the far side of the sea. Even now, areas of it resembled a land after a terrible volcanic eruption. No life, no semblance of civilization, remained in those areas. It had not been any natural force, however, that had rent the land so. The Burning Legion had left *nothing* in its wake but death.

The fiery demons had come from a place beyond reality. Magic was what they sought, magic they devoured. Attacking in conjunction with their mon-strous pawns, the Undead Scourge, they had thought to lay waste to the world. Yet, they had not counted on the most unlikely alliance of all . . .

The orcs, once also their puppets, had turned on them. They had joined the humans, elves, dwarves, and dragons to decimate the demonic warriors and ghoulish beasts and push the remnants back into the hellish beyond. Thousands had perished, but the alternative . . .

The dragon mage snorted. In truth, there had been *no* alternative.

Krasus waved long, tapering fingers over the orb, summoning a vision of the orcs. The view blurred momentarily, then revealed a mountainous, rocky area farther inland. A harsh land, but one still full of life and capable of sup-porting the new colonists.

Already, several stone structures had risen in the main settlement, where the Warchief and one of the heroes of the war, Thrall, ruled. The high, rounded edifice that served as his quarters was crude by the stan-dards of any other race, but orcs had a propensity toward basics. Extrava-gance to an orc was having a permanent place to live at all. They had been nomads or prisoners for so long that the concept of "home" had been all but lost.

Several of the massive, greenish figures tilled a field. Watching the tusked, brutish-looking workers, Krasus marveled at the concept of orc farmers. Thrall, however, was a highly unusual orc and he had readily grasped the ideas that would return stability to his people.

Stability was something the entire world needed badly. With another wave of his hand, the dragon mage dismissed Kalimdor, summoning now a much closer location—the once proud capital of his favored Dalaran. Ruled by the wizards of the Kirin Tor, the prime wielders of magic, it had been at the forefront of the Alliance's battle against the Burning Legion in Lordaeron and one of the first and most prized targets of the demons in turn.

Dalaran lay half in ruins. The once-proud spires had been all but shattered. The great libraries burned. Countless generations of knowledge had been lost . . . and with them countless lives. Even the council had suffered badly. Several of those Krasus had counted as friends or at least respected colleagues had been slain. The leadership was in disarray and he knew that he would have to step in to lend a hand. Dalaran needed to speak with one voice, if only to keep what remained of the splintered Alliance intact.

Yet, despite the turmoil and tribulations still ahead, the dragon did have hope. The problems of the world were surmountable ones. No more fear of orcs, no more fear of demons. Azeroth would struggle, but in the end, Krasus not only thought it would survive, he fully believed it would thrive.

He dismissed the emerald crystal and rose. The Dragon Queen, his beloved Alexstrasza, would be awaiting him. She suspected his desire to return to help the mortal world and, of all dragons, she most understood. He would transform to his true self, bid her farewell—for a time—and depart before regrets held him back.

His sanctum he had chosen not only for its seclusion, but also for its massiveness. Stepping from the smaller chamber, Krasus entered a toothy cavern whose heights readily matched the now lost towers of Dalaran. An army could have bivouacked in the cavern and not filled it.

Just the right size for a dragon.

Krasus stretched his arms . . . and as he did, his tapering fingers lengthened farther, becoming taloned. His back arched and from near the shoulders erupted twin growths that quickly transformed into fledgling wings. His long features stretched, turning reptilian.

Throughout all these lesser changes, Krasus's form expanded. He became four, five, even ten times the size of a man and continued to grow. Any semblance to a human or elf quickly faded.

From wizard, Krasus became Korialstrasz, dragon.

But—in the very midst of the transformation—a desperate voice suddenly filled his head.

Kor . . . strasz . . .

He faltered, all but reverting to his wizardly form. Krasus blinked, then stared around the huge chamber as if seeking the source of the cry there.

Nothing. The dragon mage waited and waited, but the call did not repeat.

Shrugging it off to his own uncertainties, he commenced again with the transformation—

And again, the desperate voice cried *Korialstra* . . .

This time . . . he recognized it. Immediately, he responded in kind. *I hear you! What is it you need of me?*

There was no response, but Krasus sensed the desperation remaining. Focusing, he tried to reach out, establish a link with the one who so badly needed his aid—the one who should have needed no aid from any creature.

I am here! the dragon mage demanded. *Sense me! Give me some indication of what is wrong!*

He felt the barest touch in return, a faint hinting of some distress. Krasus concentrated every iota of his thoughts into the meager link, hoping . . . hoping . . .

The overpowering presence of a dragon whose magic dwarfed his own a thousandfold sent Krasus staggering. A sensation of centuries, of great age, engulfed him. Krasus felt as if Time itself now surrounded him in all its terrible majesty.

Not Time . . . not quite . . . but he who was the Aspect of Time.

The Dragon of the Ages . . . Nozdormu.

There were only four great dragons, four Great Aspects, of which his beloved Alexstrasza was Life. Mad Malygos was Magic and ethereal Ysera influenced Dreams. They, along with brooding Nozdormu, represented creation itself.

Krasus grimaced. In truth, there had been *five* Aspects. The fifth had once been called Neltharion . . . the Earth Warder. But long ago, in a time even Krasus could not recall clearly, Neltharion had betrayed his fellows. The Earth Warder had turned on them and in the process had garnered a new, more appropriate title.

Deathwing. The Destroyer.

The very thought of Deathwing stirred Krasus from his astonishment. He absently touched the three scars on his cheek. Had Deathwing returned to plague the world again? Was that why the great Nozdormu would show such distress?

I hear you! Krasus mentally called back, now more than ever fearful of the reason for the call. *I hear you! Is it—is it the Destroyer?*

But in response, he was once again buffeted by an overwhelming series of astonishing images. The images burnt themselves into his head, making it impossible for Krasus to ever forget any.

In either form, Krasus, however adaptable and capable, was no match for the unbridled power of an Aspect. The force of the other dragon's mental might flung him back against the nearest wall, where the mage collapsed.

It took several minutes for Krasus to push himself up from the floor and even then his head spun. Fragmented thoughts not his own assailed his senses. It was all he could do for a time just to remain conscious.

Slowly, though, things stabilized enough for him to realize the scope of all that had just happened. Nozdormu, Lord of Time, had been desperately crying out for aid . . . *his* aid. He had turned specifically to the lesser dragon, not one of his compatriots.

But anything that would so distress an Aspect could only be a monumental threat to the rest of Azeroth. Why then choose a lone red dragon and not Alexstrasza or Ysera?

He tried once more to reach the great dragon, but his efforts only made his head swim again. Steadying himself, Krasus tried to decide what to do instead. One image in particular constantly demanded his attention, the image of a snow-swept mountain area in Kalimdor. Whatever Nozdormu had sought to explain to him had to do with that desolate region.

Krasus would have to investigate it, but he would need capable assistance, someone who could adapt readily. While Krasus prided himself on his own ability to adapt well, his species was, for the most part, obstinate and set in its ways. He needed someone who would listen, but who could also react instantly as unfolding events required. No, for such unpredictable effort, only one creature would serve. A human.

In particular, a human named Rhonin.

A wizard . . .

And in Kalimdor, on the steppes of the wild country, a grizzled, aged orc leaned close over a smoky fire. Mumbling words whose origins lay on another, long-lost world, the moss-green figure tossed some leaves upon the fire, increasing the already thick smoke. Fumes filled his humble wood and earth hut.

The bald, elderly orc leaned over and inhaled. His weary brown eyes were veined and his skin hung in sacks. His teeth were yellow, chipped, and one of his tusks had been broken off years before. He could scarcely rise without aid and when he walked, he did so stooped and slow.

Yet, even the hardiest warrior paid him fealty as shaman.

A bit of bone dust, a touch of tannar berries . . . all part of a tried and true tradition resurrected among the orcs. Kalthar's father had taught him all even during the dark years of the Horde, just as Kalthar's grandsire had taught his father before that.

And now, for the first time, the withered shaman found himself hoping he had been taught well.

Voices murmured in his head, the spirits of the world that the orcs now called home. Normally, they whispered little things, life things, but now they murmured anxiously, warning . . . warning . . .

But of what? He had to know more.

Kalthar reached into a pouch at his waist, removing three dried, black leaves. They were almost all of what remained from a single plant brought with him from the orcs' ancient world. Kalthar had been warned not to use them unless he deemed it truly necessary. His father had never used them, nor his grandfather.

The shaman tossed them into the flames.

Instantly the smoke turned a thick, swirling blue. Not black, but blue. The orc's brow furrowed at this change of color, then he leaned forward again and inhaled as much as possible.

The world transformed, and with it the orc. He had become a bird, a huge avian soaring over the landscape. He flew over mountains without a care. With his eyes he saw the tiniest animals, the most distant rivers. A sense of exhilaration not felt since his youth almost overwhelmed Kalthar, but he fought it. To give in would risk him losing his sense of self. He might fly forever as a bird, never knowing what he had once been.

Even as he thought that, Kalthar suddenly noted a wrongness in the nature of the world, possibly the reason for the voices' concern. Something *was* that should not be. He veered in the direction that felt correct, growing more anxious as he drew nearer.

And just within the deepest part of the mountain range, the shaman discovered the source of his anxiety.

His learned mind knew that he envisioned a concept, not the actual thing. To Kalthar, it appeared as a water funnel—yet one that swallowed and disgorged simultaneously. But what emerged or sank into its depths were days and nights months and years. The funnel seemed to be eating and emitting time itself.

The notion so staggered the shaman that he did not notice until almost too late that the funnel now sought to draw *him* in as well.

Immediately, Kalthar strained to free himself. He flapped his wings, pushed with his muscles. His mind reached out to his physical form, tugging hard at the gossamer link tying body to soul and trying to break the trance.

Still the funnel drew him forward.

In desperation, Kalthar called upon the spirit guides, prayed to them to strengthen him. They came as he knew they would, but at first they seemed to act too slow. The funnel filled his view, seemed ready to engulf him—

The world abruptly twisted around the shaman. The funnel, the mountains . . . everything turned about and about.

With a gasp, Kalthar awoke.

Exhausted beyond his years, he barely kept himself from falling face first into the fire. The voices that constantly murmured had faded away. The orc sat on the floor of his hut, trying to reassure himself that, yes, he now existed whole in the mortal world. The spirit guides had saved him, albeit barely in time.

But with that happy reassurance came the reminder of what he had witnessed in his vision . . . and what it meant.

"I must tell Thrall . . ." he muttered, forcing weary, aged legs up. "I must tell him quick . . . else we lose our home . . . our world . . . again . . ."

TWO

An ominous portent, Rhonin decided, vivid green eyes gazing at the results of his divining. *Any wizard would recognize it as so.*

"Are you certain?" Vereesa called from the other room. "Have you checked your reading?"

The red-haired mage nodded, then grimaced when he realized that of course the elf could not see him. He would have to tell her face to face. She deserved that. *I pray she is strong.*

Clad in dark blue pants and jacket, both gold-trimmed, Rhonin looked more like a politician than a mage these days, but the past few years had demanded as much diplomacy from him as magic. Diplomacy had never been an easy thing for him, who preferred to go charging into a situation. With his thick mane of hair and his short beard, he had a distinct leonine appearance that so well matched his temper when forced to parlay with pampered, arrogant ambassadors. His nose, broken long ago and never—by his own choice—properly fixed, further added to his fiery reputation.

"Rhonin . . . is there something you have not told me?"

He could leave her waiting no longer. She had to know the truth, however terrible it might be. "I'm coming, Vereesa."

Putting away his divining instruments, Rhonin took a deep breath, then rejoined the elf. Just within the entrance, though, he paused. All Rhonin could see was her face—a beautiful, perfect oval upon which had been artfully placed alluring, almond-shaped eyes of pure sky blue, a tiny, upturned nose, and an enticing mouth seemingly always halfway to a smile. Framing that face was a rich head of silver-white hair that, had she been standing, would have hung nearly to the small of her back. She could have passed yet for a human if not for the long, tapering ears jutting from the hair, pointed ears marking her race.

"Well?" she asked, patiently.

"It's . . . it's to be twins."

Her face lit up, if anything becoming more perfect in his eyes. "Twins! How fortuitous! How wonderful! I was so certain!"

She adjusted her position on the wooden bed. The slim but curved elven ranger now lay several months pregnant. Gone were her breastplate and leather armor. Now she wore a silver gown that did not at all conceal the imminent birth.

They should have guessed from the quickness with which she had shown, but Rhonin had wanted to deny it. They had been wed only a few months when she had discovered her condition. Both were concerned then, for not only had their marriage been one so very rare in the annals of history, but no one had ever recorded a successful human-elven birth.

And now they expected not one child, but two.

"I don't think you understand, Vereesa. Twins! Twins from a mage and an elf!"

But her face continued to radiate pleasure and wonder. "Elves seldom give birth and we very, very rarely give birth to twins, my love! They will be destined for great things!"

Rhonin could not hide his sour expression. "I know. That's what worries me . . ."

He and Vereesa had lived through their own share of "great things." Thrown together to penetrate the orc stronghold of Grim Batol during the last days of the war against the Horde, they had faced not just orcs, but dragons, goblins, trolls, and more. Afterward, they had journeyed from realm to realm, becoming ambassadors of sorts whose task it had been to remind the Alliance of the importance of remaining intact. That had not meant, however, that they had not risked their lives during that time, for the peace following that war had been unstable at best.

Then, without warning, had come the Burning Legion.

By that time, what had started as a partnership of two wary agents had become a binding of two unlikely souls. In the war against the murderous demons, the mage and the ranger had fought as much for each other as for their lands. More than once, they had thought one another dead and the pain felt had been unbearable to each.

Perhaps the pain of losing each other had seemed worse because of all those other loved ones who had already perished. Both Dalaran and Quel'Thalas had been razed by the Undead Scourge, thousands slaughtered by the decaying abominations serving the dread Lich King, who in turn served the cause of the Legion. Entire towns perished horribly and matters were made worse by the fact that many of the victims soon rose from the dead, their cursed mortal shells now added to the ranks of the Scourge.

What little that remained of Rhonin's family had perished early in the war. His mother had been long dead, but his father, brother, and two cousins had all been slain in the fall of the city of Andorhal. Fortunately, the desperate defenders, seeing no hope of rescue, had set the city ablaze. Even the Scourge could not raise warriors from ash.

He had not seen any of them—not even his father—since entering the ranks of wizardry, but Rhonin had discovered an emptiness in his heart when the news had arrived. The rift between himself and his kin—caused in great part because of his chosen calling—had vanished in that instant. All that had mattered at the time was that he had become the last of his family. He was all alone.

Alone until he realized that the feelings he had developed for the brave elven ranger at his side were reciprocated.

When the terrible struggle had finally played out, there had been only one logical path for the two of them. Despite the horrified voices emanating from both Vereesa's people and Rhonin's wizardly masters, the two had chosen to never be parted again. They had sealed a pact of marriage and tried to begin as normal a life as two such as they could possibly have in a world torn asunder.

Naturally, thought the mage bitterly, *peace for us wasn't meant to be.*

Vareesa pushed herself from the bed before he could help her. Even so near the time of birth, the elf moved with assured swiftness. The elf took hold of Rhonin by the shoulders.

"You wizards! Always seeing the dire! I thought my own people were so gloomy! My love, this will be a happy birth, a happy pair of children! We will make it so!"

He knew that she made sense. Neither would do anything that would risk the infants. When the two had realized her condition, they ceased their own efforts to help rebuild the shattered Alliance and settled in one of the most peaceful regions left, near enough to shattered Dalaran but not too near. They lived in a modest but not completely humble home and the people of the nearby town respected them.

Her confidence and hope still amazed him, considering her own losses. If Rhonin had felt a hole in his heart after losing family he had barely known anymore, Vereesa surely had felt a gaping chasm open in her own. Quel'Thalas, more legendary and surely more secure than even the magic-ruled Dalaran, had been utterly ravaged. Elven strongholds untouched by centuries had fallen in mere days, their once-proud people added to the Scourge as easily as the mere humans. Among the latter had been included several of Vereesa's own close-knit clan . . . and a few from her very family.

From her grandfather she had heard of his desperate battle to slay the ghoulish corpse of his own son, her uncle. From him she had also heard how her younger brother had been ripped apart by a hungering mob of undead led by their own elder brother, who later had been set afire and destroyed along with the rest of the Scourge by the surviving defenders. What had happened to her parents, no one yet knew, but they, too, were presumed dead.

And what Rhonin had not told her . . . might never dare tell her . . . was of the monstrous rumors he had heard concerning one of Vereesa's two sisters, Sylvanas.

Vereesa's other sister, the great Alleria, had been a hero during the Second War. But Sylvanas, she whom Rhonin's wife had sought to emulate her entire life, had, as Ranger General, led the battle against the betrayer—Arthas, prince of Lordaeron. Once the shining hope of his land, now the twisted servant of the Legion and the Scourge, he had ravaged his own kingdom, then led the undead horde against the elven capital of Silvermoon. Sylvanas had blocked his path at every juncture and for a time, it had seemed that she would actually defeat him. But where the shambling corpses, sinister gargoyles, and gruesome abominations had failed, the dark necromancy granted the traitorous noble had succeeded.

The official version had Sylvanas dying valiantly as she prevented Arthas's minions from slaying Silvermoon's people. The elven leaders, even Vereesa's grandfather, claimed that the Ranger General's body had burned in the same fire that had devastated half the capital. Certainly there had been no trace left.

But while the story ended there for Vereesa, Rhonin, through sources in both the Kirin Tor and Quel'Thalas, had discovered word of Sylvanas that left him chilled. A surviving ranger, his mind half gone, had babbled of his general being captured, not killed. She had been horribly mutilated, then finally slain for the pleasure of Arthas. Finally, taking her body up in the dark temple he had raised in his madness, the prince had corrupted her soul and corpse, transforming her from heroic elf into a harbinger of evil . . . a haunting, mournful phantom called a banshee that still supposedly roamed the ruins of Quel'Thalas.

Rhonin had so far been unable to verify the rumors, but he felt certain that they had more than a grain of truth. He prayed that Vereesa would never hear the story.

So many tragedies . . . small wonder that Rhonin could not shake his uncertainty when it came to his new family.

He sighed. "Perhaps when they're born, I'll be better. I'm likely just nervous."

"Which should be the sign of a caring parent." Vereesa returned to the bed. "Besides, we are not alone in this. Jalia aids much."

Jalia was an elder, full-bodied woman who had given birth to six children and midwifed several times that number. Rhonin had been certain that a human would be leery of dealing with an elf—let alone an elf with a wizard for a husband—but Jalia had taken one look at Vereesa and her maternal instincts had taken over. Even though Rhonin did pay her well for her time, he very much suspected that the townswoman would have volunteered anyway, so much had she taken to his wife.

"I suppose you're right," he began. "I've just been—"

A voice . . . a very familiar voice . . . suddenly filled his head.

A voice that could not be bringing him good tidings.

Rhonin . . . I have need of you.

"Krasus?" the mage blurted.

Vereesa sat up, all cheer vanishing. "Krasus? What about him?"

They both knew the master wizard, a member of the Kirin Tor. Krasus had been the one instrumental in bringing them together. He had also been the one who had not told them the entire truth about matters at the time, especially where he himself had been concerned.

Only through dire circumstance had they discovered that he was also the dragon Korialstrasz.

"It's . . . it's Krasus," was all Rhonin could say at the moment.

Rhonin . . . I have need of you . . .

I won't help you! the mage instantly responded. *I've done my share! You know I can't leave her now . . .*

"What does he want?" Vereesa demanded. Like the wizard, she knew that Krasus would only contact them if some terrible trouble had arisen.

"It doesn't matter! He'll have to find someone else!"

Before you reject me, let me show you . . . the voice declared. *Let me show both of you . . .*

Before Rhonin could protest, images filled his head. He relived Krasus's astonishment at being contacted by the Lord of Time, experienced the dragon mage's shock when the Aspect's desperation became evident. Everything Krasus had experienced, the wizard and his wife now shared.

Last of all, Krasus overwhelmed them with an image of the place the other believed the source of Nozdormu's distress, a chill and forbidding chain of jagged mountains.

Kalimdor.

The entire vision lasted only a few seconds, but it left Rhonin exhausted. He heard a gasp from the bed. Turning, the wizard found Vereesa slumped back on the down pillow.

He started toward her, but she waved off his concern. "I am all right! Just . . . breathless. Give me a moment . . ."

For her Rhonin would give eternity, but for another he had not even a second to grant. Summoning the image of Krasus into his head, the wizard replied, *Take your quests to someone else! Those days are through for me! I've got far more important matters at stake!*

Krasus said nothing and Rhonin wondered if his response had sent his former patron searching for another pawn. He respected Krasus, even liked him, but the Rhonin the dragon mage sought no longer existed. Only his family concerned him now.

But to his surprise, the one he expected most to stand by him instead suddenly muttered, "You will have to go immediately, of course."

He stared at Vereesa. "I'm not going anywhere!"

She straightened again. "But you must. You saw what I saw. He does not summon you for some frivolous task! Krasus is extremely worried . . . and what worries *him* puts fear into *me.*"

"But I can't leave you now!" Rhonin fell down on one knee next to her. "I will not leave you, or them!"

A hint of her ranger past spread across Vareesa's face. Eyes narrowing dangerously at whatever mysterious force would separate them, she answered, "And the last thing I would wish would be for you to thrust yourself into danger! I do not desire to sacrifice my children's father, but what we have seen hints at a terrible threat to the world they will be born in! For that reason alone, it makes sense to go. Were I not in this condition, I would be right at your side, you know that."

"Of course I do."

"I tell myself that he is strong, Krasus is. Even stronger as Korialstrasz! I tell myself that I let you go only because you and he will be together. You know he would not ask if he did not think you capable."

That was true. Dragons respected few mortal creatures. That Krasus in either form looked to him for aid meant a great deal . . . and as an ally of the leviathan, Rhonin would be better protected than anyone.

What could go wrong?

Defeated, Rhonin nodded. "All right. I'll go. Can you handle matters until Jalia arrives?"

"With my bow, I have shot orcs dead at a hundred yards. I have battled trolls, demons, and more. I have nearly traveled the length and breadth of

Azeroth . . . yes, my love, I think I can handle the situation until Jalia arrives."

He leaned down and kissed her. "Then I'd best let Krasus know I'll be coming. For a dragon, he's an impatient sort."

"He has taken the burden of the world upon his shoulders, Rhonin."

That still did not make the wizard overly sympathetic. An ageless dragon was far more capable of dealing with terrible crises than a mere mortal spell-caster about to become a father.

Fixing on an image of the dragon mage as he knew him best, Rhonin reached out to his former patron. *All right, Krasus. I'll help you. Where should we rendez—*

Darkness enveloped the wizard. Off in the distance, he heard Vereesa's faint voice call out his name. A sense of vertigo threatened Rhonin.

His boots suddenly clattered on hard rock. Every bone in his body shook from the impact and it was all he could do to keep his legs from collapsing.

Rhonin stood in a massive cave clearly hollowed out by more than simply the whims of nature. The roof was almost a perfect oval and the walls had been scorched smooth. A dim illumination with no discernible source enabled him to see the lone, robed figure awaiting him in the center.

"So . . ." Rhonin managed. "I guess we rendezvous here."

Krasus stretched one long, gloved hand to the left. "There is a pack containing rations and water for you, just to your side. Take it and follow me."

"I barely had a chance to say good-bye to my wife . . ." grumbled Rhonin as he retrieved the large leather pack and looped it over his shoulders.

"You have my sympathies," the dragon mage responded, walking ahead already. "I have made arrangements to see to it that she is not without aid. She will be well while we are gone."

Listening to Krasus for just a few seconds reminded Rhonin how often the ancient figure made assumptions about him without even waiting for the young wizard's decisions. Krasus had already taken the matter of Rhonin's agreement as settled.

He followed the tall, narrow figure to the mouth of the vast cave. That Krasus had moved his lair since the war with the orcs Rhonin had known, but exactly where he had moved was another question. Now the human saw that the cavern overlooked a familiar set of mountains, ones not at all that far off from his own home. Unlike their counterparts in Kalimdor, these mountains had a majestic beauty to them, not a sense of dread.

"We're almost neighbors," he remarked dryly.

"A coincidence, but it made bringing you here possible. Had I sought you from the lair of my queen, the spellwork would have been much more deplet-ing and I have every wish of retaining as much of my power as possible."

The tone with which he spoke drained Rhonin of all animosity. Never had he heard such concern from Krasus. "You spoke of Nozdormu, the Aspect of Time. Have you managed to contact him again?"

"No . . . and that is why we must take every precaution. In fact, we must not use magic to transport ourselves to the location. We will have to fly."

"But if we don't use magic, how can we possibly fly—"

Krasus spread his arms . . . and as he did, they transformed, becoming scaled and taloned. His body grew rapidly and wide, leathery wings formed. Krasus's narrow visage stretched, twisted, becoming reptilian.

"Of course," Rhonin muttered. "How silly of me."

Korialstrasz the dragon peered down at his tiny companion.

"Climb atop, Rhonin. We must be off."

The wizard reluctantly obeyed, recalling from times past the best manner with which to seat himself. He slipped his feet under crimson scale, then crouched low behind the dragon's sinewy neck. His fingers clutched other scale. Although Rhonin understood that Korialstrasz would do his best to keep his charge from slipping off, the human did not want to take a chance. One never knew what even a dragon might encounter in the sky.

The great, webbed wings flapped once, twice, then suddenly dragon and rider rose high into the heavens. With each beat, miles fell away. Korialstrasz flew effortlessly along, and Rhonin could feel the giant's blood race. Although he spent much of his time in the guise of Krasus, the dragon clearly felt at home in the air.

Cold air assailed Rhonin's head, making the wizard wish he had at least been given the opportunity to change into his robes and travel cloak. He reached back, trying to draw his coat up—and discovered his garment now had a hood.

Glancing down, Rhonin found that he did indeed wear the dark blue travel cloak and robes over his shirt and pants. Without so much as a word, his companion had transformed his clothing to something more suitable.

The hood drawn over his head, Rhonin contemplated what lay ahead. What could distress the Lord of Time so much? The threat sounded both immediate and catastrophic . . . and surely much more than a mortal wizard could handle.

Yet, Korialstrasz had turned to him . . .

Rhonin hoped he would prove worthy, not only for the dragon's sake . . . but for the lives of the wizard's growing family.

Impossible as it seemed, somewhere along the way Rhonin fell asleep. Despite that, even then he did not tumble from his seat to certain death. Korialstrasz certainly had something to do with that, although to all appearances the dragon appeared to be flying blithely along.

The sun had nearly set. Rhonin was about to ask his companion if he intended to fly through the night when Korialstrasz began to descend. Peering down, the wizard at first sighted only water, surely the Great Sea. He did not recall red dragons being very aquatic. Did Korialstrasz intend to land like a duck upon the water?

A moment later, his question was answered as an ominous rock appeared in the distance. No . . . not a rock, but an island almost entirely bare of vegetation.

A feeling of dread swept over Rhonin, one he had felt before while crossing the sea toward the land of Khaz Modan. Then it had been with dwarven gryphon riders and the island they had flown over was Tol Barad, an accursed place overrun early on by the orcs. The island's inhabitants had been slaughtered, their home ravaged, and the wizard's highly attuned senses had felt their spirits crying out for vengeance.

Now he experienced the same kind of horrific, mournful cries again.

Rhonin shouted to the dragon, but either the wind swept away his voice or Korialstrasz chose not to hear him. The leathery wings adjusted, slowing their descent to a gentle decline.

They came to a halt atop a promontory overlooking a series of shadowed, ruined structures. Too small for a city, Rhonin assumed them to have once been a fort or perhaps even a walled estate. In either case, the buildings cast an ominous image that only reinforced the wizard's concerns.

"How soon will we be moving along?" he asked Korialstrasz, still hoping that the dragon only intended to rest a moment before moving on to Kalimdor.

"Not until sunrise. We must pass near the Maelstrom to reach Kalimdor, and we will need our full wits and strength about us for that. This is the only island I have seen for some time."

"What's it called?"

"That knowledge is not mine."

Korialstrasz settled down, allowing Rhonin to dismount. The wizard stepped just far enough from his companion to catch one last glimpse of the ruins before darkness enveloped them.

"Something tragic happened here," Korialstrasz suddenly commented.

"You sense it, too?"

"Yes . . . but what it was I cannot say. Still, we should be secure up here and I have no intention of transforming."

That comforted Rhonin some, but even still he chose to remain as near to the dragon as possible. Despite a reputation for recklessness, the wizard was no fool. Nothing would entice him down into those ruins.

His gargantuan comrade almost immediately went to sleep, leaving a much more wound-up Rhonin to stare at the night sky. Vereesa's image filled his thoughts. The twins were due shortly and he hoped that he would not miss their coming because of this journey. Birth was a magic unto itself, one that Rhonin could never master.

Thinking of his family eased the mage's tensions and before he knew it, he drifted off to slumber. There, Vereesa and the as-yet-unborn twins continued to keep him loving company even though the children were never quite defined as male or female.

Vereesa faded into the background, leaving Rhonin with the twins. They called to him, beseeched him to come to them. In his dreams, Rhonin began running over a countryside, the children ever more distant shapes on the horizon. What started as a game became a hunt. The once-happy calls turned fearful. Rhonin's children needed him, but first he had to find them . . . and quickly.

"Papa! Papa!" came their voices.

"Where are you? Where are you?" The wizard pushed through a tangle of branches that only seemed to tangle more the harder he pushed. At last he broke through, only to find a towering castle.

And from above, the children called again. He saw their distant shapes reaching out to him. Rhonin cast a spell to make him rise up in the air, but as he did, the castle grew to match his efforts.

Frustrated, he willed himself up faster.

"Papa! Papa!" called the voices, now somewhat distorted by the wind.

At last he neared the tower window where the two waited. Their arms stretched, trying to cut the distance between Rhonin and them. His fingers came within a few scant inches of theirs . . .

And suddenly a huge form barreled into the castle, shaking it to its very base and sending both Rhonin and his children tumbling earthward. Rhonin sought desperately to save them, but a monstrous, leathery hand snatched him up and took him away.

"Wake up! Wake up!"

The wizard's head pounded. Everything around him began swirling. The hand lost its hold and once more he plummeted.

"Rhonin! Wherever you are! Awaken!"

Below him, two shadowy forms hurried to catch him . . . his children now trying to save *his* life. Rhonin smiled at the pair and they smiled back.

Smiled back with sharp, vicious teeth.

And just in time, Rhonin *did* awaken.

Instead of falling, he lay on his back. The stars above revealed that surrounding him now was a roofless ruin of a building. The dank smell of decay assailed his nostrils and a horrific, hissing sound beset his ears.

He lifted his head—and looked into a face out of nightmare.

If someone had taken a human skull, dipped it in soft, melting wax and let that wax drip free, that would have come close to describing the gut-wrenching vision at which Rhonin stared. Add to that needle-shaped teeth filling the mouth, along with red, soulless orbs that glared hungrily at the wizard, and the picture of hellish horror was made complete.

It moved toward him on legs much too long and reached out with bony arms that ended in three long, curved fingers that gouged into the already ravaged stone. Over its macabre form it wore the ripped remnants of a once-regal coat and pants. It was so thin that at first Rhonin did not think it had any flesh at all, but then he saw that an almost transparent layer of skin covered the ribs and other visible areas.

The wizard scrambled back just as the monstrosity grabbed at his foot. The slime-encrusted mouth opened, but instead of a hiss or a shriek, there came a childlike voice.

"Papa!"

The same voice in Rhonin's dream.

He shivered at such a sound coming from the ghoul, but at the same time the cry sent an urge through him. Again he felt as if his own children called to him, an impossibility.

An earth-shaking roar suddenly filled the ruined building, eradicating any urge to fling himself into the deadly talons of the fiend. Rhonin pointed at the creature, muttering.

A ring of fire burst to life around it. Now the pale monstrosity shrieked. It rose as high as its ungainly limbs would enable it, trying to climb over the flames.

"Rhonin!" Korialstrasz shouted from without. "Where are you?"

"Here! In here! A place no longer with a roof!"

As the mage replied, the gaunt creature suddenly leapt through the fire.

Flames licking its body in half a dozen places, it opened its maw far wider than should have been possible, wide enough to engulf Rhonin's head.

Before the wizard could cast another spell, a huge shadow blotted out the stars and a great paw caught the ghoulish beast square. With another shriek, the still-burning horror flew across the chamber, crashing into a wall with such force the stones caved in around it.

A breath of dragon fire finished what Rhonin's own spell had begun.

The stench almost overwhelmed the wizard. Holding one sleeve over his nose and mouth, he watched as Korialstrasz alighted.

"What—what was that thing?" Rhonin managed to gasp out.

Even in the dark, he could sense the leviathan's disgust. "I believe . . . I believe it was once one of those who called this home."

Rhonin eyed the charred form. *"That* was once human? How could that be?"

"You have seen the horrors unleashed by the Undead Scourge during the struggle against the Burning Legion. You need not ask."

"Is this their work?"

Korialstrasz exhaled. Clearly he had been as disturbed as Rhonin by this encounter. "No . . . this is much older . . . and even more unholy an act than the Lich King ever perpetrated."

"Kras—Korialstrasz, it entered my dreams! Manipulated them!"

"Yes, the others sought to do the same with me—"

"*Others?*" Rhonin glanced around, another spell already forming on his lips. He felt certain that the ruins swarmed with the fiends.

"We are safe . . . for the time being. Several are now less than what remains of yours and the rest have scattered into every crevice and gap in these ruins. I believe there are catacombs below and that they slumber there when not hunting victims."

"We can't stay here."

"No," agreed the dragon. "We cannot. We must move on to Kalimdor."

He lowered himself so that Rhonin could climb aboard, then immediately flapped his wings. The pair rose into the dark sky.

"When we have succeeded with our mission, I will return here and end this abomination," Korialstrasz declared. In a softer tone, he added, "There are already too many abominations in this world."

Rhonin did not answer him, instead taking one last glance down. It might have been a trick of his eyes, but he thought that he saw more of the ghouls emerging now that the dragon had left. In fact, it seemed to him that they gathered by the dozens, all of them looking up hungrily . . . at the wizard.

He tore his gaze away, actually happy to be on the journey to Kalimdor. Surely after a night such as this, whatever awaited the pair could hardly be worse.

Surely . . .

THREE

Korialstrasz reached the shores of Kalimdor late in the day. He and Rhonin paused only to eat—the dragon imbibing in fare away from the wizard's sight—and then set off again for the vast mountain chain that covered much of the western regions of the land. Korialstrasz flew with more and more urgency as they neared their goal. He had not told Rhonin that every now and then he attempted to contact

Nozdormu . . . attempted and failed. Soon, however, that would not matter, for they would know firsthand what had so distressed the Aspect of Time.

"That peak!" Rhonin shouted. Although he had slept again, he hardly felt fresh. Nightmares concerning the sinister island had haunted his dreams. "I recognize that peak!"

The dragon nodded. It was the final landmark before their destination. Had he not seen it at the same time as his rider, he would have nonetheless sensed the wrongness in the very fabric of reality . . . and that meant something terrible indeed awaited them.

Despite that certainty, the leviathan only picked up his pace. There was no other choice. Whatever lay ahead, the only ones who might stop it were him and the tiny human figure he carried.

But while the sharp eyes of man and dragon had sighted their destination, they failed to notice eyes that had sighted them in turn.

"A red dragon . . ." grumbled the first orc. "A red dragon with a rider . . ."

"One of us, Brox?" asked the second. "Another orc?"

Brox snorted at his companion. The other orc was young, too young to have been much use in the war against the Legion, and he certainly would not have remembered when it had been orcs, not humans, who had ridden such beasts. Gaskal only knew the stories, the legends. "Gaskal, you fool, the only way a dragon'd carry an orc these days would be in his belly!"

Gaskal shrugged, unconcerned. He looked every inch the proud orc warrior—tall and muscular with a rough, greenish hide and two good-sized tusks thrusting upward from his broad lower jaw. He had the squat nose and thick, bushy brow of an orc and a mane of dark hair trailing down between his shoulders. In one meaty hand Gaskal hefted a huge war ax while with the other he clutched the strap of his goatskin backpack. Like Brox, he was clad in a thick, fur cloak under which he wore a leather kilt and sandals wrapped in cloth to preserve heat. A hardy race, orcs could survive any element, but high in the mountains even they required more warmth.

Brox, too, was a proud warrior, but time had beaten at him as no other enemy could. He stood several inches shorter than Gaskal, part of that due to a slight but permanent stoop. The veteran warrior's mane had thinned and started going gray. Scars and lines of age had ravaged his wide, bullish visage, and unlike his youthful companion, the constant expression of eagerness had given way to thoughtful distrust and weariness.

Hefting his well-worn war hammer, Brox trudged through the deep snow. "They're heading for the same place as us."

"How'd you know that?"

"Where else would they be going here?"

Finding no argument, Gaskal quieted, giving Brox the chance to think about the reason that had sent both of them to this desolate place.

He had not been there when the old shaman had come to Thrall seeking an immediate audience, but he had heard the details. Naturally, Thrall had acquiesced, for he very much followed the old ways and considered Kalthar a sage advisor. If Kalthar needed to see him immediately, it could only be for a very good reason.

Or a very bad one.

With the aid of two of Thrall's guards, withered Kalthar entered and took a seat before the towering Warchief. Out of respect for the elder, Thrall sat on the floor, enabling the eyes of both to meet at the same level. Across Thrall's folded legs lay the massive, square-headed Doomhammer, bane of the Horde's enemies for generations.

The new Warchief of the orcs was broad-shouldered, muscular, and, for his position, relatively young. No one doubted Thrall's ability to rule, however. He had taken the orcs from the internment camps and given them back their honor and pride. He had made the pact with the humans which brought about the chance for the Horde to begin life anew. The people already sang songs of him that would be passed down generation after generation.

Clad in thick, ebony plate armor etched in bronze—handed down to him along with the huge weapon by his predecessor, the legendary Orgrim Doomhammer—the greatest of warriors bent his head low and humbly asked, "How may I assist you who honor my presence, great one?"

"Only by listening," Kalthar returned. "And by *truly* listening."

The strong-jawed Warchief leaned forward, his startling and so very rare blue eyes—considered a portent of destiny by his people——narrowed in anticipation. In his journey from slave and gladiator to ruler, Thrall had studied the path of the shaman, even mastering some of the skills. He more than most understood that when Kalthar talked so, he did with good reason.

And so the shaman told Thrall of the vision of the funnel and how time seemed a plaything to it. He told him of the voices and their warnings, told him about the wrongness he had felt.

Told Thrall what he feared would happen if the situation was left unchecked.

When Kalthar finished, the Warchief leaned back. Around his throat he wore a single medallion upon which had been inscribed in gold an ax and hammer. His eyes revealed the quick wit and intelligence that marked him as a capable leader. When he moved, he moved not as a brutish orc might, but with a grace and poise more akin to a human or an elf.

"This smells of magic," he rumbled. "Big magic. Something for wizards . . . maybe."

"They may know already," returned Kalthar. "But we cannot afford to wait for them, great Warchief."

Thrall understood. "You would have me send someone to this place you saw?"

"It would seem most prudent. At least so we may know what we face."

The Warchief rubbed his chin. "I think I know who. A good warrior." He looked to the guards. "Brox! Get me Brox!"

And so Brox had been summoned and told his mission. Thrall respected Brox highly, for the older warrior had been a hero of the last war, the only survivor of a band of brave fighters holding a critical pass against the demons. With his war hammer Brox himself had caved in the skulls of more than a dozen of the fiery foes. His last comrade had died cleaved in two just as reinforcements had arrived to save the day. Scarred, covered in blood, and standing alone amid the carnage, Brox had appeared to the newcomers as a vision out of the old tales of his race. His name became almost as honored as that of Thrall.

But it was more than the veteran's name that garnered the respect of the Warchief and made him Thrall's choice. Thrall knew that Brox was like him, a warrior who fought with his head as well as his arm. The orc leader could not send an army into the mountains. He needed to trust the search to one or two skilled fighters who could then report their findings to him.

Gaskal was chosen to accompany Brox because of his swiftness and absolute obedience to orders. The younger orc was part of the new generation that would grow up in relative peace with the other races. Brox was glad to have the able fighter at his side.

The shaman had so perfectly described the route through the mountains that the pair were well ahead of the estimated time the trek should have taken. By Brox's reckoning, their goal lay just beyond the next ridge . . . exactly where the dragon and rider had vanished.

Brox's grip on his hammer tightened. The orcs had agreed to peace, but he and Gaskal would fight if need be, even if it meant their certain deaths.

The older warrior forced away the grim smile that nearly played across his face at the last thought. Yes, he would be willing to fight to the death. What Thrall had not known when he summoned the war hero to him had been that

Brox suffered from terrible guilt, guilt that had eaten at his soul since that day in the pass.

They had all perished, all but Brox, and he could not understand that. He felt guilty for being alive, for not dying valiantly with his comrades. To him, his still being alive was a matter of shame, of failure to give his all as they had done. Since that time, he had waited and hoped for some opportunity to redeem himself. Redeem himself . . . and die.

Now, perhaps, the fates had granted him that.

"Get a move on!" he ordered Gaskal. "We can reach 'em before they get settled in!" Now he allowed himself a wide grin, one that his companion would read as typical orc enthusiasm. "And if they give us any trouble . . . we'll make 'em think the entire Horde is on the rampage again!"

If the island upon which they had landed seemed a dire place, the mountain pass in which they now descended simply felt *wrong*. That was the best word Rhonin could use to describe the sensations flowing through him. Whatever they sought . . . it should not be. It was as if the very fabric of reality had made some terrible error . . .

The intensity of the feeling was such that the wizard, who had faced every conceivable nightmare, wanted the dragon to turn back. He said nothing, though, recalling how he had already revealed his uncertainties on the island. Korialstrasz might already regret summoning him.

The crimson behemoth arched his wings as he dropped the final distance. His massive paws sank into the snow as he sought a stable landing area.

Rhonin clutched the dragon's neck tightly. He felt every vibration and hoped his grip would last. His pack bounced against his back, pummeling him.

At last, Korialstrasz came to a halt. The reptilian visage turned the wizard's way. "Are you well?"

"As well—as well as I could be!" gasped Rhonin. He had made dragon flights before, but not for so long.

Either Korialstrasz knew his passenger was still weary or the dragon himself also needed rest after such a monumental trek. "We shall remain here for a few hours. Gather our strength. I sense no change in the emanations I feel. We should have the time to recoup. It would be the wisest choice."

"I won't be arguing with you," Rhonin answered, sliding off.

The wind blew harshly through the mountains and the high peaks left much shadow, but with the aid of some magic and an overhang, the wizard managed to keep warm enough. While he tried to stretch the kinks out of his body, Korialstrasz strode along the pass, scouting the area. The behemoth vanished some distance ahead as the path curved.

Hood draping his head, Rhonin dozed. This time, his thoughts filled with good images . . . true images of Vereesa and the upcoming births. The wizard smiled, thinking of his return.

He woke at the sound of approach. To Rhonin's surprise, it was not the dragon Korialstrasz who returned to him, but rather the cowled, robed figure of Krasus.

In response to the human's widening eyes, the dragon mage explained, "There are several unstable areas nearby. This form is less likely to cause them to collapse. I can always transform again should the need arise."

"Did you find anything?"

The not-quite-elven face pursed. "I sense the Aspect of Time. He is here and yet he is not. I am disturbed by that."

"Should we start—"

But before Rhonin could finish, a horrific yowl echoed harshly through the mountain chain. The sound set every nerve of the wizard on edge. Even Krasus looked perturbed.

"What was that?" asked Rhonin.

"I do not know." The dragon mage drew himself up. "We should move on. Our goal lies not far away."

"We're not flying?"

"I sense that what we seek lies within a narrow passage between the next mountains. A dragon would not fit, but two small travelers would."

With Krasus leading, the pair headed northeast. Rhonin's companion appeared unbothered by the cold, though the human had to enhance the protective spell on his clothes. Even then, he felt the chill of the land upon his face and fingers.

Before long, they came upon the beginning of the passage Krasus had mentioned. Rhonin saw now what the other meant. The passage was little more than a cramped corridor. Half a dozen men could walk side-by-side through it without feeling constricted, but a dragon attempting to enter would have barely been able to get its head in, much less its gargantuan body. The high, steep sides also created even thicker shadows, making Rhonin wonder if the two might need to create some sort of illumination along the way.

Krasus pressed on without hesitation, certain of their path. He moved faster and faster, almost as if possessed.

The wind howled even harder through the natural corridor, its intensity building as they journeyed. Only human, Rhonin had to struggle to keep pace with his former patron.

"Are we almost there?" he finally called.

"Soon. It lies only—" Krasus paused.

"What is it?"

The dragon mage focused inwardly, frowning. "It is not—it is not exactly where it should be anymore."

"It *moved?*"

"That would be my assumption."

"Is it supposed to do that?" the fiery-haired wizard asked, squinting down the dark path ahead.

"You are under the misconception that I know perfectly what to expect, Rhonin. I understand little more than you."

That did not at all please the human. "So what do you suggest we do?"

The eyes of the inhuman mage literally flared as he contemplated the question. "We go on. That is all we can do."

But only a short distance ahead, they came across a new obstacle of sorts, one that Krasus had been unable to foresee from high up in the air. The passage split off in two directions, and while it was possible that they merged farther on, the pair could not assume that.

Krasus eyed both paths. "They each run near to our goal, but I cannot sense which lies closer. We need to investigate both."

"Do we separate?"

"I would prefer not to, but we must. We will each journey five hundred paces in, then turn back and meet here. Hopefully we will then have a better sense of which to take."

Taking the corridor to the left, Rhonin followed Krasus's instructions. As he rapidly counted off paces, he soon determined that his choice had potential. Not only did it greatly widen ahead, but the wizard thought he sensed the disturbance better than ever. While Krasus's abilities were more acute than his, even a novice could sense the wrongness that now pervaded the region beyond.

But despite his confidence in his choice, Rhonin did not yet turn around. Curiosity drove him on. Surely a few steps more would hardly matter—

He had barely taken more than one, however, when he sensed something new, something quite disturbing. Rhonin paused, trying to detect what felt different about the anomaly.

It was moving, but there was more to his anxiety than that alone.

It was moving toward *him* . . . and rapidly.

He felt it before he saw it, felt as if all time compressed, then stretched, then compressed again. Rhonin felt old, young, and every moment of life in between. Overwhelmed, the wizard hesitated.

And the darkness before him gave way to a myriad flaring of colors, some of which he had never seen before. A continual explosion of elemental energy filled both empty air and solid rock, rising to fantastic heights. Rhonin's limited mind saw it best as a looming, fiery flower that bloomed, burnt away, and bloomed again . . . and with each blooming grew more and more imposing.

As it neared, he finally came to his senses. Whirling, the mage ran.

Sounds assailed his ears. Voices, music, thunder, birds, water . . . *everything.*

Despite his fears that it would overtake him, the phenomenal display fell behind. Rhonin did not stop running, fearing that at any moment it would surge forward and envelop him.

Krasus surely had to have sensed the latest shift. He had to be hurrying to meet Rhonin. Together, they would devise some way in which to—

A terrible howl echoed through the pass.

A massive, eight-legged lupine form dropped down on him.

Had he been other than what he was, the wizard would have perished there, the meal of a savage, saber-toothed creature with four gleaming green eyes to go with its eight clawed limbs. The monstrous wolf-creature brought him down, but Rhonin, having magicked his garments to better protect him from the elements, proved a hard nut to crack. The claws scraped at a cloak it should have readily tattered, only to have instead one nail snap off.

Gray fur standing on end, the beast howled its frustration. Rhonin took the opening, casting a simple but effective spell that had saved him in the past.

A cacophony of light burst before the creature's emerald orbs, both blinding and startling it. It ducked back, swatting uselessly at flashing patterns.

Dragging himself out of reach, Rhonin rose. There was no chance of flight; that would only serve to turn his back on the beast and his protective spell was already weakening. A few more slashes and the claws would be ripping the wizard to the bone.

Fire had worked against the ghoul on the island and Rhonin saw no reason why such a tried and true spell would not benefit him again. He muttered the words—

—which, inexplicably, came out in reverse. Worse, Rhonin found himself moving backward, returning to the wild claws of the blinded beast.

Time had turned in on itself . . . but how?

The answer materialized from farther in the passage. Krasus's anomaly had caught up.

Ghostly images fluttered by Rhonin. Knights riding into battle. A wedding scene. A storm over the sea. Orcs uttering war chants around a fire. Strange creatures locked in combat . . .

Suddenly he could move forward again. Rhonin darted out of the beast's reach, then turned to face it again. This time, he did not hesitate, casting his spell.

The flames burst forth in the form of a great hand, but as they neared the monstrous creature, they slowed . . . then stopped, frozen in time.

Swearing, Rhonin started another spell.

The eight-legged horror leapt around the frozen fire, howling as it charged the human.

Rhonin cast.

The earth beneath the abomination exploded, a storm of dirt rising up and covering the lupine creature. It howled again and, despite the intense forces against it, struggled toward the mage.

A crust formed over the legs and torso. The mouth shut tight as a layer of rock-solid earth sealed it. One by one, the inhuman orbs were covered by a film of dust.

Just a few feet from its victim, the creature stilled. To all appearances, it now seemed but a perfectly cast statue, not the actual monster itself.

At that moment, Krasus's voice filled Rhonin's head.

At last! the dragon mage called. *Rhonin . . . the disturbance is expanding! It's almost upon you!*

Distracted by the fearsome beast, the wizard had not glanced at the anomaly. When he did, his eyes widened.

It filled a space ten times higher and, no doubt, ten times wider than the pass. Solid rock meant nothing to it. The anomaly simply passed through it as if it did not exist. Yet, in its wake, the landscape changed. Some of the rock looked more weathered, while other portions appeared as if newly cooled from the titanic throes of birth. The worst transformations seemed to take place wherever the edges of the fiery flower touched.

Rhonin did not want to think what would happen to him if the thing touched him.

He started running again.

Its movement and growth have suddenly expanded much faster for reasons I do not understand, Krasus went on. *I fear I will not reach you in time! You must cast a spell of teleportation!*

My spellwork doesn't always work the way it should! he responded. *The anomaly's affecting it!*

We will stay linked! That should help strengthen your casting! I will guide you to me and we can regroup!

Rhonin did not care to teleport himself to places he had never seen, the inherent risk being that of ending up encased in a mountain, but with Krasus linked to him, the task would be a much simpler one.

He focused on Krasus, picturing the dragon mage. The spell began to form. Rhonin felt the world around him shift.

The fiery blossom suddenly expanded to nearly twice its previous dimensions.

Only too late did Rhonin realize why. It was reacting to the use of magic . . . his magic. He wanted to stop the spell, but it was already too late.

Krasus! Break the link! Break it before you're also—

The anomaly swallowed him.

Rhonin?

But Rhonin could not answer. He flailed around and around, tossed about like a leaf in a tornado. With each revolution he flew faster and faster. The sounds and sights again assailed him. He saw past, present, and future and understood each for what it was. He caught a glimpse of the petrified beast as it flew wildly past him into what could only be described as a whirlpool in time.

Other things flew by, random objects and even creatures. An entire ship, its sails tattered, its hull crushed in near the bow, soared by, vanishing. A tree on which still perched a flock of birds followed. In the distance, a kraken, fifty feet in length from tip of head to end of tentacle, reached out but failed to drag Rhonin along before vanishing with the rest.

From somewhere came Krasus's faint voice. *Rhonin . . .*

He answered, but there was no reply.

The whirlpool filled his gaze.

And as it sucked him in, Rhonin's last thoughts were of Vereesa and the children he would never know.

FOUR

He sensed the slow but steady growth of the leaves, the branches, and the roots. He sensed the timeless wisdom, the eternal thoughts within. Each giant had its own unique signature, as was true with any individual.

They are the guardians of the forest, came his mentor's voice. *They are as much its soul as I. They* are *the forest.* A pause. *Now . . . come back to us . . .*

Malfurion Stormrage's mind respectfully withdrew from the gargantuan trees, the eldest of the heavily wooded land. As he retreated, his own physical surroundings gradually reappeared, albeit murky at first. He blinked his silver, pupilless eyes twice, bringing everything back into focus. His breath came in ragged gasps, but his heart swelled with pride. Never before had he reached so far!

"You have learned well, young night elf," a voice like a bear's rumbled. "Better than even I could have expected . . ."

Sweat poured down Malfurion's violet countenance. His patron had insisted that he attempt this next monumental step at the height of day, his people's weakest point of time. Had it been at night, Malfurion felt certain that he would have been stronger, but as Cenarius pointed out again and again, that would have defeated the purpose. What his mentor taught him was not the sorcery of the night elves, but almost its exact opposite.

And in so many ways, Malfurion had already become the opposite of his people. Despite their tendencies toward flamboyant garments, for instance, Malfurion's own were very subdued. A cloth tunic, a simple leather jerkin and pants, knee-high boots . . . his parents, had they not perished by accident years before, would have surely died of shame.

His shoulder-length, dark green hair surrounded a narrow visage akin to a wolf's. Malfurion had become something of an outcast among his kind. He asked questions, suggested that old traditions were not necessarily the best, and even dared once mention that beloved Queen Azshara might not always have the concerns of her subjects foremost on her thoughts. Such actions left him with few associates and even fewer friends.

In fact, in Malfurion's mind, he could truly only count three as friends. First and foremost had to be his own twin, the equally troublesome Illidan. While Illidan did not shy away from the traditions and sorcery of the night elves as much as he, he had a tendency to question the governing authority of the elders, also a great crime.

"What did you see?" his brother, seated beside him on the grass, asked eagerly. Illidan would have been identical to Malfurion if not for his midnight blue hair and amber eyes. Children of the moon, nearly all night elves had eyes of silver. Those very few born with ones of amber were seen as destined for greatness.

But if greatness was to be Illidan's, he first had to curb both his temper and his impatience. He had come with his twin to study this new path that used the power of nature—their mentor termed it "druidism"—believing he would be the quicker student. Instead, he often miscast spells and failed to concentrate enough to maintain most trances. That he was fairly adept at traditional sorcery did not assuage Illidan. He had wanted to learn the ways of druidism because such unique skills would mark him as different, as nearing that potential everyone had spoken about since his birth.

"I saw . . ." How to explain it even to his brother? Malfurion's brow wrinkled. "I saw into the hearts of the trees, the souls. Not simply theirs, either. I saw . . . I think I saw into the souls of the entire forest!"

"How wonderful!" gasped a female voice at his other side.

Malfurion fought to keep his cheeks from darkening to black, the night elf equivalent of embarrassment. Of late, he had been finding himself more and more uncomfortable around his other companion . . . and yet he could not think of himself far from her, either.

With the brothers had come Tyrande Whisperwind, their greatest friend since childhood. They had grown up together, the three, inseparable in every way until the last year, when she had taken the robes of a novice priestess in the temple of Elune, the moon goddess. There she learned to become attuned to the spirit of the goddess, learned to use the gifts all priestesses were granted in order to let them spread the word of their mistress. She it had been who had encouraged Malfurion when he had chosen to turn from the sorcery of the night elves to another, earthier power. Tyrande saw druidism as a kindred force to the abilities her deity would grant her once she completed her own training.

But from a thin pale child who had more than once bested both brothers in races and hunting, Tyrande had become, since joining the temple, a slim yet well-curved beauty, her smooth skin now a soft, light violet and her dusky blue hair streaked with silver. The mousy face had grown fuller, much more feminine and appealing.

Perhaps too appealing.

"Hmmph!" added Illidan, not so impressed. "Was that *all?*"

"It is a good start," rumbled their tutor. The great shadow fell over all three young night elves, stifling even Illidan's rampant mouth.

Although over seven feet tall themselves, the trio were dwarfed by Cenarius, who stood well above ten. His upper torso was akin to that of Malfurion's race, although a hint of the emerald forest colored his dark skin and he had a much broader, more muscular build than either of his male students. Beyond the upper body any similarity ended. Cenarius was no simple night elf, after all. He was not even mortal.

Cenarius was a demigod.

His origins were known only to him, but he was as much a part of the great forest as it was of him. When the first night elves had appeared, Cenarius had already long existed. He claimed kinship with them, but never had he said in what way.

Those few who came to him for guidance left ever touched, ever changed. Others did not even leave, becoming so transformed by their teachings that they chose instead to join the demigod in the protection of his realm. Those were no longer elves, but woodland guardians physically altered forever.

A thick, moss-green mane flowing from his head, Cenarius eyed his pupils fondly with orbs of pure gold. He patted Malfurion gently on the shoulder with hands that ended in talons of gnarled, aged wood—talons still capable of ripping the night elf to shreds without effort—then backed away . . . on four strong legs.

The upper torso of the demigod might have resembled that of a night elf, but the lower portion was that of a huge, magnificent stag. Cenarius moved about effortlessly, as swift and nimble as any of the three. He had the speed of the wind, the strength of the trees. In him was reflected the life and health of the land. He was its child and father all in one.

And like a stag, he also had antlers—giant, glorious antlers that shaded his stern yet fatherly visage. Matched in prominence only by his lengthy, rich beard, the antlers were the final reminder that any blood link between demigod and night elf existed far, far in the past.

"You have all done well," he added in the voice that ever sounded of thunder. Leaves and twigs literally growing in his beard, his hair shook whenever the deity spoke. "Go now. Be among your own again for a time. It will do you some good."

All three rose, but Malfurion hesitated. Looking at his companions, he said, "You go on ahead. I'll meet you at the trail's end. I need to talk with Cenarius."

"We could wait," Tyrande replied.

"There's no need. I won't be long."

"Then, by all means," Illidan quickly interjected, taking Tyrande's arm. "We should let him be. Come, Tyrande."

She gave Malfurion one last lingering glance that made him turn away to conceal his emotions. He waited for the two to depart, then turned again to the demigod.

The descending sun created shadows in the forest that seemed to dance for the pleasure of Cenarius. The demigod smiled at the dancing shadows, the trees and other plants moving in time with them.

Malfurion went down on one knee, his gaze to the earth. "My shan'do," he began, calling Cenarius by the title that meant in the old tongue "honored teacher." "Forgive me for asking—"

"You should not act so before me, young one. Arise . . ."

The night elf reluctantly obeyed, but he kept his gaze down.

This made the demigod chuckle, a sound accented by the sudden lively chirping of songbirds. Whenever Cenarius reacted, the world reacted in concert with him.

"You pay me even more homage than those who claim to preach in my name. Your brother does not bend to me and for all her respect of my power, Tyrande Whisperwind gives herself only to Elune."

"You offered to teach me—us—" Malfurion responded, "what no night elf has ever learned . . ." He still recalled the day when he had approached the sacred wood. Legends abounded about Cenarius, but Malfurion had wanted to know the truth. However, when he had called out to the demigod, he had not actually expected an answer.

He had also not expected Cenarius to offer to be his teacher. Why the demigod would take on so—*mundane*—a task was beyond Malfurion. Yet, here they were together. They were more than deity and night elf, more than teacher and student . . . they were also friends.

"No other night elf truly wishes to learn my ways," Cenarius replied. "Even those who has taken up the mantle of the forest . . . none of them has truly followed the path I now show you. You are the first with the possible aptitude, the possible will, to truly *understand* how to wield the forces inherent in all nature. And when I say 'you,' young elf, I speak entirely in the singular."

This was not what Malfurion had remained to talk about and so the words struck him hard. "But—but Tyrande and Illidan—"

The demigod shook his head. "Of Tyrande, we have already spoken. She has promised herself to Elune and I will not poach in the Moon Goddess's realm! Of your brother, however, I can only say that there is much promise to Illidan . . . but I believe that promise lies elsewhere."

"I—I don't know what to say . . ." And in truth, Malfurion did not. To be told so suddenly that Illidan and he would not follow the same path, that Illidan even appeared to waste his efforts here . . . it was the first time that the twins would not share in their success. "No! Illidan will learn! He's just more headstrong! There's so much pressure upon him! His eyes—"

"Are a sign of some future mark upon the world, but he will not make it following my teachings." Cenarius gave Malfurion a gentle smile. "But you will try to teach him yourself, will you not? Perhaps you can succeed where I have failed?"

The night elf flushed. Of course his shan'do would read his thoughts on that subject. Yes, Malfurion intended to do what he could to push Illidan further along . . . but he knew that doing so would be a harder task. Learning from the demigod was one thing; learning from Malfurion would be another. It would show that Illidan was not first, but second.

"Now," added the forest lord quietly, as a small red bird alighted on his antlers and its paler mate did so on his arm. Such sights were common around Cenarius, but they ever left the elf marveling. "You came to ask of me something . . ."

"Yes. Great Cenarius . . . I've been troubled by a dream, a reoccurring one."

The golden eyes narrowed. "Only a dream? That is what troubles you?"

Malfurion grimaced. He had already berated himself several times for even thinking of distracting the demigod with his problem. Of what harm was a dream, even one that repeated itself? Everyone dreamed. "Yes . . . it comes to me every time I sleep and since I've been learning from you . . . it's grown stronger, more demanding."

He expected Cenarius to laugh at him, but instead the forest lord studied him closely. Malfurion felt the golden orbs—so much more arresting than even his brother's own—burrow deep within him, reading the night elf inside and out.

At last, Cenarius leaned back. He nodded once to himself and in a more solemn voice said, "Yes, you are ready, I think."

"Ready for what?"

In response, Cenarius held up one hand. The red bird leapt down to the offered hand, its mate joining it there. The demigod stroked the backs of both once, whispered something to them, then let the pair fly off.

Cenarius looked down at the night elf. "Illidan and Tyrande will be informed that you are staying behind for a time. They have been told to leave without you."

"But why?"

The golden eyes flared. "Tell me of your dream."

Taking a deep breath, Malfurion began. The dream started as always, with the Well of Eternity as its focal point. At first the waters were calm, but then, from the center, a maelstrom rapidly formed . . . and from the depths of the maelstrom, creatures burst forth, some of them harmless, others malevolent. Many he did not even recognize, as if they came from other worlds, other times. They spread in every direction, fleeing beyond his sight.

Suddenly, the whirlpool vanished and Malfurion stood in the midst of Kalimdor . . . but a Kalimdor stripped of all life. A horrible evil had laid waste to the entire land, leaving not so much as a blade of grass or a tiny insect alive. The once-proud cities, the vast, lush woodlands . . . nothing had been spared.

Even more terrible, for as far as the eye could see, the scorched, cracked bones of night elves lay strewn everywhere. The skulls had been caved in. The stench of death was strong in the air. No one, not even the old, infirm, or young, had been spared.

Heat, horrific heat, had assailed Malfurion then. Turning, he had seen in the distance a vast fire, an inferno reaching into the heavens. It burned everything it touched, even the very wind. Where it moved, nothing . . . absolutely nothing . . . remained. Yet, as frightening as the scene had been, it was not that which had finally awakened the night elf in a cold sweat, but rather something he had sensed *about* the fire.

It had been *alive*. It knew the terrors it wrought, knew and *reveled* in them. Reveled . . . and hungered for more.

All humor had fled Cenarius's visage by the time Malfurion finished. His gaze flickered to his beloved forest and the creatures thriving within. "And this nightmare repeats itself with every slumber?"

"Every one. Without fail."

"I fear, then, that this is an omen. I sensed in you from our first encounter the makings of the gift of prescience—one of the reasons I chose to make myself known to you—but it is stronger than even I ever expected."

"But what does it mean?" the young night elf pleaded. "If you say this is an omen, I've got to know what it portends."

"And we shall try to discover that. I said, after all, that you are ready."

"Ready for what?"

Cenarius folded his arms. His tone grew more grave. "Ready to walk the *Emerald Dream.*"

Nothing in the demigod's teachings so far had referred to this Emerald Dream, but the manner in which Cenarius spoke of it made Malfurion realize the importance of this next step. "What is it?"

"What is it not? The Emerald Dream is the world beyond the waking world. It is the world of the spirit, the world of the sleepers. It is the world as it might have been, if we sentient creatures had not come about to ruin it. In the Emerald Dream, it is possible, with practice, to see anything, go any-where. Your body will enter a trance and your dream form will fly from it to wherever you need to go."

"It sounds—"

"Dangerous? It is, young Malfurion. Even the well-trained, the experi-enced, can lose themselves in the Emerald Dream. You note I call it the *Emer-ald* Dream. That is the color of its mistress, Ysera, the Great Aspect. It is the realm of her and her dragon flight. She guards it well and allows only a few to enter it. My own dryads and keepers make use of the Emerald Dream in their duties, but sparingly."

"I've never heard of it," Malfurion admitted with a shake of his head.

"Likely because no night elf save those in my service has ever walked it . . . and they only when they were no longer of your race. You would be the first of your kind to truly take the path . . . if you so desire."

The idea both unnerved and excited Malfurion. It would be the next step in his studies and a way, perhaps, to make sense of his constant nightmare. Yet . . . Cenarius had made it clear that the Emerald Dream could also be deadly.

"What—what might happen? What might go wrong?"

"Even the experienced can lose their way back if they become distracted," the demigod replied. "Even I. You must remain focused at all times, know your goal. Otherwise . . . otherwise your body might sleep forever."

There was more, the night elf suspected, but Cenarius for some reason wanted him to learn on his own—if Malfurion chose to walk the Emerald Dream.

He decided he had no other recourse. "How do I start?"

Cenarius fondly touched the top of his student's head. "You are certain?"

"Very."

"Then simply sit as you have for your other lessons." When the slighter figure had obeyed, Cenarius lowered his own four-legged form to the earth. "I will guide you in this first time, then it is up to you. Lock your gaze in mine, night elf."

The demigod's golden orbs snared Malfurion's eyes. Even had he wanted to, it would have taken mammoth effort for him to pull his own gaze away. He felt himself drawn into Cenarius's mind, drawn into a world where all was possible.

A sense of lightness touched Malfurion.

Do you feel the songs of the stones, the dance of the wind, the laughter of the rushing water?

At first, Malfurion felt no such thing, but then he heard the slow, steady grinding, the shifting of earth. Belatedly, he realized that this was how the stones and rock spoke as, over the eons, they made their way from one point in the world to another.

After that, the others became more evident. Every part of nature had its own unique voice. The wind spun around in merry steps when pleased, or in violent bursts when the mood grew darker. The trees shook their crowns and the raging water of a nearby river chuckled as the fish within it darted up to spawn.

But in the background . . . Malfurion thought he sensed distant discord. He tried to focus on it, but failed.

You are not yet in the Emerald Dream. First, you must remove your earthly shell . . . the voice in his head instructed. *As you reach the state of sleep, you will slip your body off as you would a coat. Start from your heart and mind, for they are the links that most bind you to the mortal plane. See? This is how it is done* . . .

Malfurion touched at his heart with his thoughts, opening it like a door and willing his spirit free. He did the same with his mind, although the earthly, practical side of any living creature protested at this action.

Give way to your subconscious. Let it guide you. It knows of the realm of dreaming and is always happy to return there.

As Malfurion obeyed, the last barriers slipped away. He felt as if he had sloughed off his skin the way a snake might. A sense of exhilaration filled him and he almost forgot for what purpose he was doing this.

But Cenarius had warned him to remain focused and so the night elf fought the euphoria down.

Now . . . rise up.

Malfurion pushed himself up . . . but his body, legs still folded, remained where it was. His dream form floated a few feet off the ground, free of all restraints. Had he so desired, Malfurion knew that he could have flown to the stars themselves.

But the Emerald Dream lay in a different direction. *Turn again to your subconscious,* the demigod instructed. *It will show you the path, for that lies within, not without.*

And as he followed Cenarius's instructions, the night elf saw the world change further around him. A hazy quality enveloped everything. Images, endless images, overlapped one another, but with concentration Malfurion discovered that he could see each separately. He heard whispers and realized that they were the inner voices of dreamers throughout the world.

From here, you must take the path by yourself.

He felt his link to Cenarius all but fade. For the sake of Malfurion's concentration, the demigod had been forced to pull back. However, Cenarius remained a presence, ready to aid his student if the need arose.

As Malfurion moved forward, his world turned a brilliant, gemlike green. The haze increased and the whispers became more audible. A landscape vaguely seen beckoned to him.

He had become part of the Emerald Dream.

Following his instincts, Malfurion floated toward the shifting dreamscape. As Cenarius said, it looked as the world would have looked had night elves and other creatures not come into being. There was a tranquillity to the Emerald Dream that made it tempting just to stay forever, but Malfurion refused to give in to that temptation. He had to know the truth about his dreams.

He had no idea at first where his subconscious was taking him, but somehow suspected it would lead him to the answers he desired. Malfurion flew over the empty paradise, marveling at all he saw.

But then, in the midst of his miraculous journey, he felt something amiss again. The faint discord he had sensed earlier increased. Malfurion tried to ignore it, but it gnawed at him like a starving rat. He finally veered his spirit form toward it.

Suddenly, ahead of him lay a huge, black lake. Malfurion frowned, certain that he recognized the foreboding body of water. Dark waves lapped its shores and an aura of power radiated from its center.

The Well of Eternity.

But if this was the Well, where was the city? Malfurion eyed the dreamscape where he knew the capital should have been, trying to summon an image of it. He had come here for a reason and now he believed that it had to do with the city. By itself, the Well of Eternity was an astonishing thing, but it was the source of power only. The discord the night elf felt originated from somewhere else.

He stared at the empty world, demanding to see the reality.

And without warning, Malfurion's dream self materialized over Zin-Azshari, the capital of the night elves. In the old tongue, Zin-Azshari translated into "The Glory of Azshara." So beloved had the queen been when she had made her ascension to the throne that the people had insisted on renaming the capital in her honor.

Thinking of his queen, Malfurion suddenly beheld the palace itself, a magnificent structure surrounded by a huge, well-guarded wall. He frowned, knowing it well. This was, of course, the grand abode of his queen. Even though he had at times made mention of what he believed to be her faults, Malfurion actually admired her more than most thought. Overall, she had done much good for her people, but on occasion he believed Azshara simply lost her focus. As with many other night elves, he suspected any problem there had to do in part with the Highborne, who administered the realm in her name.

The wrongness grew worse the nearer he floated down toward the palace. Malfurion's eyes widened as he saw the reason. With the summoning of the vision of Zin-Azshari, he had also summoned a more immediate image of the Well. The black lake now swirled madly and what appeared to be monstrous strands of multicolored energy shot up from its depths. Powerful magic was being drawn from the Well into the highest tower, its only possible purpose the casting of a spell of impossible proportions.

The dark waters beyond the palace moved with such violence that to Malfurion they seemed to be boiling. The more those within the tower summoned the might of the Well, the more terrible the fury of the elements. Above, the storm-wracked heavens screamed and flashed. Some of the buildings near the edge of the Well threatened to be washed away.

What are they doing? Malfurion wondered, his own quest forgotten. *Why do they continue even during weakness of day?*

But "day" was only a term, now. Gone was the sun that dampened the night elves' abilities. Even though evening had not yet come, it was as black as night above Zin-Azshari . . . no, even blacker. This was not natural and certainly not safe. What could those within be toying with?

He drifted over the walls, past stone-faced guards ignorant of his presence. Malfurion floated to the palace itself, but when he sought to enter, certain that his dream form would pass through something so simple as stone, the night elf discovered an impenetrable barrier.

Someone had encased the palace in protective spells so intricate, so powerful, that he could not pierce them. This only made Malfurion more curious, more determined. He swooped around the structure, rising again toward the tower in question. There had to be a way in. He had to see what madness was going on inside.

With one hand, he reached out to the array of protective spells, seeking the point that bound them all together, the point by which they could also be unbound—

And suddenly pain unimaginable wracked Malfurion. He screamed silently, no sound able to voice his agony. The image of the palace, of Zin-Azshari, vanished. He found himself in an emerald void, caught within a storm of pure magic. The elemental powers threatened to rip his dream form into a thousand pieces and scatter them in every direction.

But in the midst of the monstrous chaos, he suddenly heard the faint calling of a familiar voice.

Malfurion . . . my child . . . come back to me . . . Malfurion . . . you must return . . .

Vaguely the night elf recognized Cenarius's desperate summons. He clung to it as a drowning person in the middle of the sea might cling to a tiny piece of driftwood. Malfurion felt the woodland deity's mind reach out to him, guide him in the proper direction.

The pain began to lessen, but Malfurion was exhausted beyond measure. A part of him simply wanted to drift among the dreamers, his soul never returning to his flesh. Yet, he realized that to do so would mean his end and so he fought against the deadly desire.

And as the pain dwindled away, as Cenarius's touch grew stronger, Malfurion sensed his own link to his mortal form. Eagerly he followed it, moving faster and faster through the Emerald Dream . . .

With a gasp . . . the young night elf awoke.

Unable to stop himself, Malfurion tumbled into the grass. Mighty yet still gentle hands picked him back up to a sitting position. Water dribbled into his mouth.

He opened his eyes and beheld Cenarius's concerned visage. His mentor held Malfurion's own water sack.

"You have done what few others could do," the stag god murmured. "And in doing so, you almost lost yourself forever. What happened to you, Malfurion? You went even beyond my sight . . ."

"I . . . I sensed . . . something terrible . . ."

"The cause of your nightmares?"

The night elf shook his head. "No . . . I don't know . . . I . . . I found myself drawn to Zin-Azshari . . ." He tried to explain what he had witnessed, but the words seem so insufficient.

Cenarius looked even more disturbed than he, which worried Malfurion.

"This does not bode well . . . no. You are certain it was the palace? It had to be Azshara and her Highborne?"

"I don't know if one or both . . . but I can't help feeling that the queen must be a part of it. Azshara is too strong-willed. Even Xavius can't control her . . . I think." The queen's counselor was an enigmatic figure, as distrusted as Azshara was loved.

"You must think about what you say, young Malfurion. You are suggesting that the ruler of the night elves, she whose name is heard in song each day, is involved in some spellwork that could be a threat not only to your kind, but the rest of the world. Do you understand what that means?"

The image of Zin-Azshari intermingled with the scene of devastation . . . and Malfurion found both compatible with each other. They might not be directly linked, but they shared something in common. What that was, though, he did not know yet.

"I understand one thing," he muttered, recalling the perfect, beautiful face of his queen and the cheers that accompanied even her briefest appearances. "I understand that I must find out the truth wherever that truth leads . . . even if in the end it costs me my very life . . ."

The shadowed form touched with his talon the small, golden sphere in his other scaled palm, bringing it to life. Within it, there materialized another, almost identical shadow. The light from the sphere did nothing to push back the darkness surrounding the figure, just as on the other end the sphere used by the second form also failed. The magic cast to preserve each one's identity was old and very strong.

"The Well is still in the midst of terrible throes," commented the one who had initiated contact.

"So it has been for some time," replied the second, tail flicking behind him. "The night elves play with powers they do not appreciate."

"Has there been an opinion formed on your end?"

The darkened head within the sphere shook once. "Nothing significant so far . . . but what can they possibly do save perhaps destroy themselves? It would not be the first time one of the ephemeral races did so and surely not the last."

The first nodded. "So it seems to us . . . and the others."

"All the others?" hissed the second, for the first time some true curiosity in his tone. "Even those of the Earth Warder's flight?"

"No . . . they keep their own counsel . . . as usual of late. They are little more than Neltharion's reflection."

"Unimportant, then. Like you, we shall continue to monitor the night elves' folly, but it is doubtful that it will amount to much more than the extinction of their kind. Should it prove to be more, we shall act if we are ordered to act by our lord, Malygos."

"The pact remains unbroken," responded the first. "We, too, shall act only if commanded by her majesty, the glorious Alexstrasza."

"This conversation is over, then." With that, the sphere went black. The second form had severed the link.

The other rose, dismissing the sphere. With a hiss, he shook his head at the ignorance of the lesser races. They constantly meddled in things beyond their capabilities and so often paid fatally for it. Their mistakes were their own to suffer, so long as the world as a whole did not suffer with them. If that happened, then the dragons would have to act.

"Foolish, foolish night elvesss . . ."

But in a place between worlds, in the midst of chaos incarnate, eyes of fire turned in sudden interest, the work of the Azshara's Highborne having also reached them.

Somewhere, the one who gazed realized, somewhere someone had called upon the power. Someone had drawn from the magic in the mistaken belief that they and they alone knew of it, knew how to wield it . . . but where?

He searched, almost had the source, then lost it. It was near, though, very near.

He would wait. Like the others, he had begun to grow hungry again. Surely if he waited a little longer, he would sense exactly where among the worlds the casters were. He smelled their eagerness, their ambition. They would not be able to stop drawing from the magic. Soon . . . soon he would find the way through to their little world . . .

And he and the rest would *feed*.

FIVE

Brox had a bad, bad feeling about their mission.

"Where are they?" he muttered. "Where are they?"

How did one hide a dragon, the orc wanted to know. The tracks were evident to a point, but then all he and Gaskal could find afterward were the footprints of a human, possibly two. Since the orcs were near enough to notice if a dragon launched itself into the air—and they had seen no such astonishing sight—then it only made sense that the leviathan had to be nearby.

"Maybe that way," suggested the younger warrior, his brow furrowed deep. "That pass."

"Too narrow," growled Brox. He sniffed the air. The scent of dragon filled his nostrils. Almost masked by it was the smell of human. Dragons and wizards.

Treaty or no treaty, this would be a good day to die . . . if Brox could just find his foes.

Kneeling down to study the tracks better, the veteran had to admit that Gaskal's suggestion made the most sense. The two sets of tracks led into the narrow pass while the dragon's simply *vanished*. Still, if the orcs confronted the other intruders, the beast would surely come.

Not giving his companion any sign as to his true intentions, the older warrior rose. "Let's go."

Weapons ready, they trotted into the pass. Brox snorted as he looked it over. Definitely too narrow for a dragon, even a half-grown one. Where *was* the beast?

They had only gone a short distance when from farther in they heard the monstrous howl of a beast. The two orcs glanced at each other, but did not slow. No true warrior turned at the first sound of danger.

Deeper they went. The shadows played games, making it seem as if unnatural creatures lurked all around them. Brox's breathing grew heavier as he sought to keep pace with Gaskal. His ax weighed heavily in his hand.

A shout—a human shout—echoed from only a short distance ahead.

"Brox—" the younger orc began.

But at that moment, a monstrous vision filled their view, a fiery image like nothing either had ever seen.

It filled the pass, overflowing even into the rock. It did not seem alive, but nonetheless moved as if with purpose. Sounds—random, chaotic sounds— filled the orcs' ears and when Brox stared into the center, he felt as if he stared into Forever.

Orcs were not creatures subject to easy fear, but the monstrous and surely magical vision overwhelmed the two warriors. Brox and Gaskal froze before it, aware that simple weapons would hardly turn it aside.

Brox had desired a heroic death, not one such as this. There was no nobility in dying so. The thing looked capable of swallowing him as readily and without notice as it would a gnat.

And that made his decision for him. "Gaskal! Move! Run!"

Yet Brox himself failed to follow his own command. He turned to run, yes, but slipped like an awkward infant in the slick snow. The huge orc tumbled to the ground, striking his head. His weapon fell just out of reach.

Gaskal, unaware of what had happened to his comrade, had not fled back, but rather darted to the side, to a depression in one of the walls. There he planted himself inside, certain of the protection of the solid rock.

Still trying to clear his head, Brox realized Gaskal's mistake. Rising to his knees, he shouted, "Not there! Away!"

But the cacophony of sounds drowned out his warning. The fearsome anomaly moved forward . . . and Brox watched with horror as Gaskal was caught on its very edge.

A thousand screams escaped the stricken orc as Gaskal both aged and grew younger simultaneously. Gaskal's eyes bulged and his body rippled like liquid. He stretched and contracted . . .

And with a last ungodly cry, the younger orc shriveled within himself, contracting more and more . . . until he completely vanished.

"By the Horde . . ." Brox gasped, standing. He stared at the spot where Gaskal had stood, still somehow hoping that his companion would miraculously reappear unharmed.

Then it finally sank in that he was seconds from being engulfed by the same monstrosity.

Brox turned, instinctively seized his ax, and ran. He felt no shame in it. No orc could fight this. To die as Gaskal had died would be a futile gesture.

But as fast as the orc ran, the fiery vision moved faster. Nearly deafened by the countless sounds and voices, Brox gritted his teeth. He knew he could not outpace it, not now, but he continued to try . . .

He managed only two steps more before it swallowed him whole.

Every bone, every muscle, every nerve in Krasus's body screamed. It was the only reason the dragon mage finally stirred from the black abyss of unconsciousness.

What had happened? He still did not quite know. One minute, he had been trying to reach Rhonin—and then somehow despite not being near it he, too, had been swallowed by the anomaly. His mental link to the human wizard had literally dragged Krasus along.

Images flashed through his befuddled mind again. Landscapes, creatures, artifacts. Krasus had witnessed time in its ultimate aspect, all at once.

Aspect? That word summoned another dread vision, one he had thankfully forgotten until now. In the midst of the swirling chaos of time, Krasus had glimpsed a sight that left his heart and hope shattered.

There, in the center of the fury, he had seen Nozdormu, the great Aspect of Time . . . *trapped* like a fly in a web.

Nozdormu had been there in all his terrible glory, a vast dragon not of flesh, but of the golden sands of eternity. His glittering, gemlike eyes, eyes the color of the sun, had been open wide, but had not in turn seen the insignificant figure of Krasus. The great dragon had been in the throes of both battle and agony, ensnared yet also fighting to hold everything together—absolutely *everything*.

Nozdormu was both victim and savior. Trapped in all time, he also held it from falling apart. If not for the Aspect, the fabric of reality would have collapsed there and then. The world Krasus knew would have disappeared forever. It would never have even existed.

A new surge of pain tore through Krasus. He cried out in the ancient tongue of the dragons, momentarily losing his accustomed control. Yet, with the pain came the realization that he still lived. That knowledge caused him to fight, to force himself back to full consciousness . . .

He opened his eyes.

Trees greeted his gaze. Towering, lush trees with green canopies that nearly blotted out the sky. A forest in the bloom of life. Birds sang while other creatures rustled and scurried through the underbrush. Vaguely Krasus registered the setting sun and soft, drifting clouds.

So peaceful a landscape, the dragon mage almost wondered if he had after all died and gone to the beyond. Then, a not so heavenly sound, a muttered curse, caught his attention. Krasus looked to his left.

Rhonin rubbed the back of his head as he tried to force himself up slightly. The fiery-haired human had landed facedown only a few yards from his former mentor. The wizard spat out bits of dirt and grass, then blinked. By pure accident, he looked in Krasus's direction first.

"What—?" was all he managed.

Krasus tried to speak but all that came from his own mouth at first was a sick croak. He swallowed, then tried again. "I . . . do not know. Are you . . . are you injured in any way?"

Flexing his arms and legs, Rhonin grimaced. "Everything hurts . . . but . . . but nothing seems broken."

After a similar test, the dragon mage came to the same conclusion concerning himself. That they had arrived so intact astonished him . . . but then he recalled the magic of Nozdormu at work in the anomaly. Perhaps the Aspect of Time had noted them after all and done what he could to save the two.

But if that was the case . . .

Rhonin rolled onto his back. "Where are we?"

"I cannot say. I feel I should know it, but—" Krasus stopped as vertigo suddenly seized hold of him. He fell back onto the ground, closing his eyes until the feeling passed.

"Krasus? What happened?"

"Nothing truly . . . I believe. I am still not recovered from what happened. My weakness will go away." Yet, he noted that Rhonin already appeared much better, even sitting up and trying to stretch. Why would a frail human better survive the anomaly's turmoil than he?

With grim determination, Krasus also sat up. The vertigo sought to overwhelm him again, but the dragon mage fought it down. Trying to take his mind from his troubles, he looked around once more. Yes, he certainly sensed a familiarity about his surroundings. At some point, he had visited this region, but when?

When?

The simple question filled him with a sudden dread. *When . . .*

Nozdormu trapped in eternity . . . all time open to the anomaly . . .

The thick woods and the growing shadows created by the vanishing sun made it virtually impossible to see enough to identify the land. He would have to take to the air. Surely a short flight would be safe. The area seemed bereft of any settlement.

"Rhonin, remain here. I will scout from above, then return shortly."

"Is that wise?"

"I think it absolutely necessary." Without a further word, Krasus stretched out his arms and began transforming.

Or rather, he *tried* to transform. Instead, the dragon mage doubled over in agony and overwhelming weakness. His entire body felt turned inside out and he lost all sense of balance.

Strong arms caught him just as he fell. Rhonin carefully dragged him to a soft spot, then helped his companion down.

"Are you all right? You looked as if—"

Krasus cut him off. "Rhonin . . . I could not change. I could not change . . ."

The young wizard frowned, not comprehending. "You're still weak, Master Krasus. The trip through that thing—"

"Yet, you are standing. Take no offense from me, human, but what we passed through should have left you in a far worse state than mine."

The other nodded, understanding. "I just figured that you spent yourself trying to keep me alive."

"I am afraid to tell you that once we entered it, I could do no more for you than I could for myself. In fact, if not for Nozdormu—"

"Nozdormu?" Rhonin's eyes widened. "What's he got to do with our survival?"

"You did not see him?"

"No."

Exhaling, the dragon mage described what he had seen. As he did, Rhonin's expression grew increasingly grim.

"Impossible . . ." the human finally breathed.

"Terrifying," Krasus corrected him. "And now I must tell you also that, even if Nozdormu did save us from the raw forces of the anomaly, I fear he did not send us back to where we came from . . . or even *when*."

"You think . . . you think we're in a different time?"

"Yes . . . but as to what period . . . I cannot say. I also cannot say how we will be able to get back to our own era."

Slumping back, Rhonin gazed into empty space. "Vereesa . . ."

"Have courage! I said I cannot say how we will be able to get back, but that does not mean that we will not try! Still, our first action must be to find sustenance and shelter . . . and some knowledge of the land. If we can place ourselves, we might be able to calculate where best to find the assistance we need. Now, help me up."

With the human's aid, Krasus stood. After a few tentative steps, he decreed himself well enough to walk. A short discussion on which direction to take ended with agreement to head north, toward some distant hills. There the two might be able to see far enough over the trees the next day to sight some village or town.

The sun fell below the horizon barely an hour into their trek, but the pair continued on. Fortunately, Rhonin had in one of his belt pouches some bits of travel food and a bush they passed supplied them with a few handfuls of edible if sour berries. In addition, the smaller, almost elven form Krasus wore required far less food than his true shape. Still, both were aware that come the next day they would have to find more substantial fare if they were to survive.

The thicker garments used for the mountains proved perfect to keep them warm once darkness reigned. Krasus's superior vision also enabled them to avoid some pitfalls in their path. Still, the going was slow and thirst began to take its toll on the pair.

Finally, a slight trickling sound to the west led them to a small stream. Rhonin and Krasus knelt gratefully and began to drink.

"Thank the Five," the dragon mage said as they drank. Rhonin nodded silently, too busy trying to swallow the entire stream.

After they had their fill, the two sat back. Krasus wanted to go on, but neither he nor the human clearly had the strength to do so. They would have to rest for the night here, then continue on at first light.

He suggested as much to Rhonin, who readily agreed. "I don't think I could go another step," the wizard added. "But I think I can still create a fire if you like."

The idea of a fire enticed Krasus, but something inside him warned against it. "We shall be warm enough in our garments. I would prefer to err on the side of caution for now."

"You're probably right. We could be in the time of the Horde's first invasion for all we know."

That seemed a bit unlikely to Krasus considering the peacefulness of the woods, but the centuries had produced other dangers. Fortunately, their present location would keep them fairly secreted from most creatures passing near. A rising slope also gave them a natural wall to hide behind.

More out of exhaustion than agreement, they stayed where they were, literally falling asleep on the spot. Krasus's slumber, however, was a troubled one in which his dreams reflected events.

Again he saw Nozdormu struggling against that which was his very nature. He saw all time tangled, confused, and growing more unstable each moment the anomaly existed.

Krasus saw something else, too, a faint, fiery glare, almost like eyes, gazing hungrily on all it saw. The dragon mage frowned in his sleep as his subconscious tried to recollect why such an image would seem so terribly familiar . . .

But then the slight clink of metal against metal intruded, ripping apart his dreams and scattering the bits away just as Krasus was on the verge of remembering what the burning eyes represented.

Even as he stirred, Rhonin's hand clamped over his mouth. Early in his long, long life, such an affront would have made the dragon teach the mortal creature a painful lesson in manners, but now Krasus not only had more patience than in his youth, he also had more trust.

Sure enough, the clink of metal again sounded. So very slight, but to the trained ears of either spellcaster, still like thunder.

Rhonin pointed upward. Krasus nodded. Both cautiously stood, trying to see over the slope. Hours had clearly passed since they had fallen asleep. The woods were silent save for the songs of a few insects. If not for the brief, unnatural sounds they had heard, Krasus would have thought nothing amiss.

Then a pair of large, almost monstrous shapes materialized beyond the slope. At first they were unrecognizable, but then Krasus's superior vision identified them as not two creatures, but rather *four*.

A pair of riders atop long, muscular panthers.

They were tall, very lean, but clearly warriors. They were clad in armor the color of the night and wore high, crested helms with nose guards. Krasus could not yet make out their faces, but they moved with a fluidity he did not see in most humans. Both the riders and their sleek, black mounts journeyed along as if little troubled by the darkness, which made the dragon mage quickly caution his companion.

"They will see you before you clearly see them," Krasus whispered. "What they are, I do not know, but they are not of your kind."

"There's more!" Rhonin returned. Despite his inferior vision, he had been gazing in just the right direction to catch another pair of riders approaching.

The four soldiers moved in almost complete silence. Only the occasional breath from an animal or metallic movement gave any sign of their presence. They looked to be involved in an intense hunt . . .

Krasus came to the dread conclusion that they were looking for Rhonin and him.

One of the foremost riders reined his monstrous, saber-toothed mount to a halt, then raised his hand to his face. A small flash of blue light briefly illuminated the area around him. In his gauntleted hand the rider held a small crystal, which he focused on the dark landscape. After a moment, he cupped the artifact with his other hand, dousing the light.

The use of the magical crystal only partly bothered Krasus. What little he had seen of the hunter's scowling, violet countenance worried him far more.

"Night elves . . ." he whispered.

The rider wielding the crystal instantly looked Krasus's way.

"They've seen us!" muttered Rhonin.

Cursing himself for a fool, Krasus pulled the wizard with him. "Into the deeper woods! It is our only hope!"

A single shout echoed through the night . . . and then the woods filled with riders. Their fearsome yet agile mounts leapt nimbly along, padded feet making no sound as the beasts moved. Like their masters, they had gleaming, silver eyes that enabled them to see their quarry well despite the darkness. The panthers roared lustily, eager to reach the prey.

Rhonin and Krasus slid down a hill and into a thicket. One rider raced past them, but another turned and continued pursuit. Behind them, more than a dozen other riders spread out through the area, intending to cut off their quarry.

The two reached the denser area, but the lead rider was nearly upon them. Turning about, Rhonin shouted a single word.

A blinding ball of pure force struck the night elf square in the chest, sending him flying back off his steed and into the trunk of a tree with a resounding crash.

The powerful assault only served to make the others more determined to catch them. Despite the harder going, the riders pushed their mounts on. Krasus glanced to the east and saw that others had already made their way around the duo.

Instinctively, he cast a spell of his own. Spoken in the language of pure magic, it should have created a wall of flame that would have kept their pursuers at bay. Instead, small bonfires burst to life in random locations, most of them useless as any defense. At best, they served only as momentary distractions to a handful of the riders. Most of the night elves did not even pay them any mind.

Worse, Krasus doubled over in renewed pain and weakness.

Rhonin came to the rescue again. He repeated a weaker variation of the dragon mage's spell, but where Krasus had received for his efforts lackluster results and physical agony, the human wizard garnered an unexpected bounty. The woods before their pursuers exploded with hungry, robust flames, driving the armored riders back in complete disarray.

Rhonin looked as startled at the results as the night elves, but managed to recover quicker. He came to Krasus's side and helped the stricken mage retreat from the scene.

"They will—" Krasus had to gasp for breath. "They will find a path around soon! They know this place well from the looks of it!"

"What did you call them?"

"They are night elves, Rhonin. You recall them?"

Both dragon mage and human had spent their part in the war against the Burning Legion near or in Dalaran, but tales had come from far off of the appearance of the night elves, the legendary race from which Vereesa's kind was descended. The night elves had appeared when disaster had seemed imminent and it was no understatement to say that the outcome might have been different if they had not joined the defenders.

"But if these are night elves, then aren't we allies?"

"You forget that we are not necessarily in the same time period. In fact, until their reappearance, it was thought by even the dragons that their kind had become extinct after the end of—" Krasus became very subdued, not at all certain he wanted to follow his thoughts to their logical conclusion.

Shouts erupted nearby. Three riders closed on them, curved swords raised. In the lead rode the one who wielded the blue crystal. Rhonin's flames illuminated his face, the handsomeness typical of any elf forever ruined by a severe scar running down the left side from near the eye to the lip.

Krasus tried to cast another spell, but it only served to send him to his knees. Rhonin guided him down, then faced the attackers.

"*Rytonus Zerak!*" he shouted.

The branches nearest the night elves suddenly clustered, forming a weblike barrier. One rider became tangled in them and slipped from his mount. A second reined his protesting panther to a halt behind the one caught.

Their leader sliced through the branches as if cutting air, his blade leaving a streak of red lightning in its deadly wake.

"Rhonin!" Krasus managed. "Flee! Leave!"

His former student had as little intention of obeying such a command as the dragon mage would have in his place. Rhonin reached into his belt pouch and from it drew what first looked like a band of glowing quicksilver. The quicksilver swiftly coalesced into a gleaming blade, a gift to Rhonin from an elven commander at the end of the war.

In the light of the wizard's blade, the haughty expression of the night elves' leader transformed into surprise. Nonetheless, he met Rhonin's sword with his own.

Crimson and silver sparks flared. Rhonin's entire body shook. The night elf nearly slipped from the saddle. The panther roared, but because of his rider could not reach their foe with his razor-sharp claws.

They traded blows again. A wizard Rhonin might be, but he had learned over his life the value of being able to fight by hand. Vereesa had trained him so that even among seasoned warriors he could hold his own . . . and with the elven blade he stood a good chance of success against any one foe.

But not against many. Even as he kept both night elf and beast at bay, three more riders arrived, two manipulating a net. Krasus heard a sound from behind him and glanced over his shoulder to see three more coming, also bearing a huge net.

Try as he might, he could not get the words of power out. He, a dragon, was helpless.

Rhonin saw the first net and backed up. He held the sword ready in case the night elves tried to snare him. The leader urged his mount forward, keeping Rhonin's attention.

"B-behind you!" Krasus called, the weakness overcoming him again. "There's another—"

A booted foot kicked the weakened mage in the side of the head. Krasus retained consciousness, but could not focus.

Through bleary eyes, he watched as the dark forms of the night elves closed in on his companion. Rhonin fended off a pair of blades, chased back one of the huge cats . . . and then the net caught him from behind.

He managed to sever one section, but the second net fell over him, entangling Rhonin completely. Rhonin opened his mouth, but the lead rider moved up and struck him hard across the jaw with his gauntleted fist.

The human wizard dropped.

Enraged, Krasus managed to pull himself partway from his stupor. He muttered and pointed at the leader.

His spell worked this time, but went astray. A bolt of golden lightning struck not the target in question, but rather a tree near one of the other hunters. Three large limbs ripped free, collapsing on one rider and crushing both him and his mount.

The lead night elf glared in Krasus's direction. The dragon mage tried futilely to protect himself as fists and boots pummeled him into submission . . . and finally unconsciousness.

He watched as his subordinates beat at the peculiar figure who had, more by chance than by skill, slain one of their own. Long after it was clear their victim had lost all sense, he let his warriors take out their frustration on the unmoving body. The panthers hissed and growled, smelling blood, and it was all the night elves could do to keep them from joining in the violence.

When he judged that they had reached the limits of safety, that any further beating would jeopardize the life of their prisoner, he gave the command to halt.

"Lord Xavius wants all alive," the scarred night elf snapped. "We don't want him disappointed, do we?"

The others straightened, fear abruptly appearing in their eyes. Well they might fear, he thought, for Lord Xavius had a tendency to reward carelessness with death . . . painful, lingering death.

And often he chose the willing hand of Varo'then to deal out that death.

"We were careful, Captain Varo'then," one of the soldiers quickly insisted. "They will both survive the journey . . ."

The captain nodded. It still amazed him how the queen's counselor had even detected the presence of these unusual strangers. All Xavius had said when he had summoned faithful Varo'then was that there had been some sort of odd manifestation and that he wanted the captain to investigate and bring back anyone unusual discovered in the vicinity. Varo'then, ever sharp-eyed, had noticed the slight furrowing of the lord's brow, the only hint that Xavius was more disturbed about this unknown "manifestation" than he hinted.

Varo'then eyed the prisoners as their bound bodies were draped unceremoniously over one of the panthers. Whatever the counselor had expected, it surely did not include a pair such as this. The weak one who had managed the last spell looked vaguely like a night elf, but his skin was pale, almost white. The other one, obviously a younger and far more talented spellcaster . . . Varo'then did not know what to make of him. He was not unlike a night elf . . . but was clearly not. He looked like no creature the veteran soldier had ever seen.

"No matter. Lord Xavius will sort it all out," Varo'then murmured to himself. "Even if he has to tear them limb from limb or flay them alive to get the truth . . ."

And whichever course the counselor took, good, loyal Captain Varo'then would be there to lend his experienced hand.

SIX

It was a troubled Malfurion who returned to his home near the roaring falls just beyond the large night elven settlement of Suramar. He had chosen the site because of the tranquility and untransformed nature around the falls. Nowhere else did he feel so at peace, save perhaps in Cenarius's hidden grove.

A low-set, rounded domicile formed from both tree and earth, Malfurion's simple home was a far contrast from those of most night elves. Not for him was the gaudy array of colors that bespoke of his kind's tendency to try to outshine one another. The colors of his home were those of earth and life, the forest greens, the rich, fertile browns, and kindred shades. He tried to adapt to his surroundings, not force them to adapt to him as was his people's way.

Yet nothing about his home gave Malfurion any sense of comfort this night. Still fiercely clear in his mind were the thoughts and images he had experienced while walking the Emerald Dream. They had opened up doors in his imagination he wished desperately to shut again, but knew would be impossible.

"The visions you see in the Emerald Dream, they can mean many things," Cenarius had insisted, "no matter how true they might look. Even what we think is real—such as your view of Zin-Azshari—may not be so, for the dreamland plays its own games on our limited minds . . ."

Malfurion knew that the demigod had only been trying to assuage him, that what the night elf saw had been truth. He understood that Cenarius was actually as concerned about the reckless spellcasting taking place in the palace of Azshara as his student was.

The power that the Highborne had been summoning . . . what could it be for? Did they not sense how stressed the fabric of the world had grown near the Well? It was still unfathomable to him that the queen could condone such careless and possibly destructive work . . . and yet Malfurion could not shake the certainty that she was as much a part of it as any of her subordinates. Azshara was no simple figurehead; she truly ruled, even when it came to her arrogant Highborne.

He tried to return to his normal routine, hoping that would help him forget his troubles. There were but three rooms to the young night elf's home, yet another example of the simplicity of his life compared to that of others. In one stood his bed and the handful of books and scrolls he had gathered concerning nature and his recent studies. In another, toward the back, was the larder and a small, plain table where he prepared his meals.

Malfurion considered both rooms nothing more than necessities. The third, the communal room, was ever his favored place. Here where the light of the moon shone bright at night and the glistening waters of the falls could be seen, he sat in the center and meditated. Here, with a sip of the honey-nectar wine so favored by his kind, he looked over his work and tried to comprehend what Cenarius had taught him the lesson before. Here, by the short, ivory table where a meal could be spread out, he also visited with Tyrande and Illidan.

But there would be no Tyrande or Illidan this evening. Tyrande had returned to the temple of Elune to continue her own studies and Malfurion's twin, in what was another sign of their growing dissimilarities, now preferred the raucousness of Suramar to the serenity of the forest.

Malfurion leaned back, his face agleam in the light of the moon. He shut his eyes to think, hoping to calm his nerves—

No sooner had he done so, though, when something large moved across the field of moonlight, briefly putting Malfurion in total darkness.

The night elf's eyes snapped open just in time to catch a glimpse of a huge, ominous form. Malfurion immediately leapt to the door and flung it open.

But to his surprise, only the rushing waters of the nearby falls met his tense gaze.

He stepped outside, peered around. Surely no creature so large could move so fast. The bullish Tauren and ursine Furbolgs were not unknown to him, but while they matched in size the peculiar shadow, neither of the two races was known for swiftness. A few branches rustled in the wind and a night bird sang somewhere in the distance, but Malfurion could find no sign of his supposed intruder.

Simply your own nerves, he finally chided himself. *Your own uncertainties.*

Returning inside, Malfurion seated himself again, his mind already caught up once more in his troubles. Unlike his phantom intruder, he was certain that he had not imagined or misread anything concerning the palace and the Well. Somehow, Malfurion would have to learn more, more than the Emerald Dream could at present reveal to him.

And, he suspected, he would have to do it very, very quickly.

He had almost been caught. Like an infant barely able to walk, he had almost lumbered right into the creature's lair. Hardly a worthy display of the well-honed skills for which a veteran orc warrior was known.

Brox had not worried about his ability to defend himself had the creature caught him, but now was not the time to give in to his own desire to meet a glorious finish. Besides, from what he had seen of the lone figure, it would hardly have been a good match. Tall, but too spindly, too unprotected. Humans were much more interesting and worthy opponents . . .

Not for the first time his head throbbed. Brox put a hand to his temple, fighting the pain. A swirling confusion reigned in his mind. What had happened to him in the past several hours, the orc still could not say with complete certainty. Instead of being ripped apart like Gaskal as he had expected, he was catapulted into madness. Things beyond the comprehension of a simple warrior had materialized and vanished before his eyes and Brox recalled flying around in a swirl of chaotic forces, all while countless voices and sounds had assailed him almost to the point of deafness.

In the end, it had all proven too much. Brox had blacked out, certain he would never wake.

He had, of course, but it was not to find himself safely back in the mountains or still trapped in the insanity. Instead, Brox discovered himself in an almost tranquil landscape consisting of tall trees and bucolic rolling hills for as far as the eye could see. The sun was setting and the only sounds of life were the musical calls of birds.

Even had he been dropped into the midst of a horrendous battle rather than this quiet scene, Brox could have done nothing but lay where he was. It had taken the orc more than an hour to recover enough to just stand, much less travel. Fortunately, during that anxious waiting time, Brox had discovered one miracle. His ax, which he thought lost, had been swallowed with him and deposited but a few yards from the orc. Not yet able to use his legs, Brox dragged himself to the weapon. He had not been able to wield it, but clutching its handle had given him some comfort while he waited for his strength to return.

The moment he was able to walk, Brox had quickly pushed on. It did not pay to stay in one place when in a strange land, no matter how peaceful it looked. Situations always changed even in the most peaceful places and, in his experience, generally not for the better.

The orc tried to understand what had happened to him. He had heard of wizards traveling by means of special spells from one location to another, but if this was such a spell, then the mage who had cast it surely had to be insane. Either that, or the incantation had gone awry, certainly a possibility.

Alone and lost, Brox's instincts took over. No matter what had happened so far, Thrall would want him to find out more about the inhabitants of this place and what their intentions might be. If they were responsible by accident or design for reaching out with magic to the orcs' new homeland, they posed a possible threat. Brox could die later; his first duty was to protect his people.

At least now he had some notion as to what race lived here. Brox had never seen or heard of a night elf before the war against the Burning Legion, but he could never forget their unique looks. Somehow, he had landed in some realm ruled by their kind, which at least opened to him the hope of returning home once he gathered what information he could. The night elves had fought alongside the orcs in Kalimdor; surely that meant that Brox had merely ended up on some obscure part of the continent. With a little reconnaissance he was certain that he would be able to figure out which direction the orc lands were and head to them.

Brox had no intention of simply going up to one of the night elves and asking the way. Even if these were the same creatures who had allied themselves with the orcs and humans, he could not be certain that those of this land would be friendly to an intruder now. Until he knew more, the wary orc intended to remain well out of sight.

Although Brox did not immediately encounter any more such dwellings, he did note a glow in the distance that likely originated from some larger settlement. After a moment's consideration, the orc hefted his weapon and pushed on toward it.

Barely had he made that decision, however, when shadows suddenly approached from the opposite direction. Pressing flat against a wide tree, Brox watched a pair of riders approach. His eyes narrowed in surprise when, instead of good horses, he saw that they raced along on swift, gigantic panthers. The orc gritted his teeth and readied himself in case either the riders or their beasts sensed him.

But the armored figures hurried past as if determined to be somewhere quickly. They appeared quite comfortable traveling in little light, which made the orc suddenly recall that night elves could see in darkness as well as he could see in day.

That did not bode well. Orcs had fair night vision, but not nearly as good as that of the night elves.

He hefted his ax. Perhaps he did not have the advantage in terms of sight, but Brox would match himself against any of the scrawny figures he had so far come across. Day or night, an ax in the hands of an orc warrior skilled in its use would make the same deep, fatal cut. Even the elaborate armor he noted on the riders would not long stand up to his beloved weapon.

With the riders out of view, Brox continued on cautiously. He needed to find out more about these particular night elves and the only way to do that was to spy on their settlement. There he might find out enough to know where in relation to home he now wandered. Then he could return to Thrall. Thrall would know what to make of all this. Thrall would deal with these night elves who dabbled in dangerous magic.

So very, very simple—

He blinked, so caught up in his thoughts that he only now saw standing before him the tall female figure clad in silver, moonlit robes.

She looked as startled as the orc felt . . . then her mouth opened and the night elf cried out.

Brox started to reach for her—his only intention that of smothering the scream—but before he could do anything, other cries arose and night elves began appearing from every direction.

A part of him desired to stand where he was and fight to the death, but the other part, that which served Thrall, reminded him that this would achieve nothing. He would have failed in his mission, failed his people.

With a snarl of outrage, he turned and fled back in the direction he had come.

Yet, now it seemed that from every huge tree trunk, from every rising mound, figures popped into sight—and each let out the alarm at the sight of the burly orc.

Horns blared. Brox swore, knowing what such a sound presaged. Sure enough, moments later, he heard feline growls and determined shouts.

Glancing over his shoulder, he saw his pursuers nearing. Unlike the pair he had hidden from earlier, most of the new riders were clad only in robes and breast plates, but that hardly erased them as a threat. Each was not only armed, but their mounts presented an even more dire danger. One swipe of a paw would slice the orc open, one bite of the saber-toothed jaws would rip off his head.

Brox wanted to take his ax and sweep across their ranks, chopping away at rider and mount alike and leaving a trail of blood and maimed bodies behind him. Yet, despite his desire to lay waste to those who threatened him, Thrall's teachings and commands held such violence in check. Brox growled and met the first riders with the flat of his ax head. He knocked one night elf from his mount, then, after dodging the cat's claws, turned to seize another rider by the leg. The orc threw the second night elf atop the first, knocking the air out of both.

A blade whistled by his head. Brox easily smashed the slim blade to fragments with his powerful ax. The night elf wisely retreated, the stump of his weapon still gripped tightly.

The orc took advantage of the gap created by the retreat to slip past his pursuers. Some of the night elves did not look at all eager to follow, which raised Brox's spirits. More than his own honor, Thrall's pride in his chosen warrior continued to keep Brox from turning and making a foolish last stand. He would not let his chief down.

But just as escape looked possible, another night elf materialized before him, this one dressed in shimmering robes of brilliant green with gold and ruby starbursts dotting the chest. A cowl obscured most of the night elf's long, narrow visage, but he seemed undaunted by the huge, brutish orc coming up on him.

Brox waved his ax and shouted, trying to scare off the night elf.

The hooded figure raised one hand to chest level, the index and middle fingers pointed toward the moonlit sky.

The orc recognized a spell being cast, but by that time it was already too late.

To his astonishment, a circular sliver of the moon fell from the sky, falling upon Brox like a soft, misty blanket. As it enshrouded him, the orc's arms grew heavy and his legs weak. He had to fight to keep his eyelids open.

The ax slipping from his limp grasp, Brox fell to his knees. Through the silvery haze, he now saw other similarly clad figures circling him. The hooded forms stood patiently, obviously watching the spell's work.

A sense of fury ignited Brox. With a low snarl, he managed to push himself up to his feet. This was not the glorious death he had wanted! The night elves intended that he fall at their feet like a helpless infant! He would not do it!

Fumbling fingers managed to seize the ax again. To his pleasure, he noted some of the hooded figures start. They had not expected such resistance.

But as he tried to raise his weapon, a second silvery veil settled over him. What strength Brox had summoned vanished again. When the ax fell this time, he knew he would be unable to retrieve it.

The orc took one wobbly step, then fell forward. Even then, Brox tried to crawl toward his foes, determined not to make their victory an easy one.

A third veil dropped over him . . . and Brox blacked out.

Three nights . . . three nights and still nothing to show for our efforts . . .

Xavius was not pleased.

Three of the Highborne sorcerers stepped back from the continual spellwork. They were immediately replaced by those who had managed to replenish their strength with some overdue rest. Xavius's false black eyes turned to the three who had just finished. One of them noticed the dark orbs gazing their direction and cringed. The Highborne might be the most glorious of the queen's servants, but Lord Xavius was the most glorious—and dangerous—of the Highborne.

"Tomorrow night . . . tomorrow night we shall increase the field of power tenfold," he declared, the crimson streaks in his eyes flaring.

Unable to meet his gaze, one of the other Highborne nonetheless dared say, "W-with all due respect, my Lord Xavius, that risks much! Such an additional increase may destabilize all we have already accomplished."

"And what is that, Peroth'arn?" Xavius loomed over the other robed figures, his shadow seeming to move of its own accord in the mad light of the spell. "What *have* we accomplished?"

"Why, we command more power than any night elf has ever commanded before!"

Xavius nodded, then frowned. "Yes, and with it, we can squash an insect with a mountain-sized hammer! You are a shortsighted fool, Peroth'arn! Consider yourself fortunate that your skill is demanded for this effort."

Clamping his mouth shut, the other night elf bowed his head gratefully.

The queen's counselor looked with disdain upon the rest of the Highborne. "What we seek to do, we need perfect manipulation of the Well to accomplish! We must have the ability to slay the insect without its even realizing the death until after the fact! We must have such precision, such a fine touch, that there will be no question as to the perfect execution of our final goal! We—"

"Preaching again, my darling Xavius?"

The melodic voice would have enchanted any of the other Highborne into killing themselves if it would please the speaker, but not so the onyx-eyed Xavius. With a careless gesture, he dismissed the weary spellcasters, then turned to the one person in the palace who did not rightly show him the respect he deserved.

She glittered as she entered, a vision of perfection that his magical orbs amplified. She was the glory of the night elves, their beloved mistress. When she breathed, she made the crowds breathless. When she touched the cheek of a favored warrior, he went out and willingly fought dragons and more, even if it meant his certain destruction.

The queen of the night elves was tall for a female, taller even than many males. Only Xavius truly towered above her. Yet, despite her height, she moved like the wind, silent grace with every step. No cat walked as silently as Azshara and none walked with as much confidence.

Her deep, violet skin was as smooth as the almost sheer silk garment she wore. Her hair, long, thick, lush, and moonlight silver, cascaded down around her shoulders and artfully curved backside. In contrast to her previous visit, when she had matched her garments to her eyes, she now wore a flowing gown the same wondrous color as her luxurious hair.

Even Xavius secretly desired her, but on his own terms. His ambitions drove him far more than her wiles ever could. Still, he found much use in her presence, just as he knew she found the same in his. They shared an ultimate objective, but with differing rewards for each waiting at the end.

When that goal was finally reached, Xavius would show Azshara who truly ruled.

"Light of the Moon," he began, expression obedient. "I preach only of your purity, your flawlessness! These others I simply remind of their duty—nay, of their *love*—for you. They should not therefore wish to fail . . ."

"For they would be failing you, as well, my darling counselor." Behind the stunning queen, two handmaidens carried the train of her long, translucent gown. They shifted the train to the side as Azshara seated herself on the special chair she had made the Highborne erect so that she could watch their efforts in comfort. "And I think they fear that more than they love me."

"Hardly, my mistress!"

The queen positioned herself to gaze upon the struggling spellcasters, her gown shifting to best display her perfect form.

Xavius remained unmoved by her maneuver. He would have her and whatever else he desired after they had succeeded in their great mission.

A sudden flash of blazing light drew the eyes of both to the work of the sorcerers. Hovering in the center of the circle created by the Highborne, a furious ball of energy continually remade itself. Its myriad displays had a hypnotic effect, in great part because they often seemed to be opening up a doorway into *elsewhere*. Xavius especially spent long hours staring into the night elves' creation, seeing with his artificial eyes what none of the others could.

Watching now, the counselor wrinkled his brow. He squinted, studying the endless depths within. For just the briefest of moments, he could have sworn that he had seen—

"I believe you are not listening to me, darling Xavius! Is that at all possible?"

He managed to recover. "As possible as living without breathing, Daughter of the Moon . . . but I admit I was distracted enough that I may not have understood clearly. You said again something about—"

A brief, throaty chuckle escaped Queen Azshara, but she did not contradict him. "What is there to understand? I simply restated that surely we must soon triumph! Soon we shall have the power and ability to cleanse our land of its imperfections, create of it the perfect paradise . . ."

"So it shall be, my queen. So it shall be. We are but a short time from the creation of a grand golden age. The realm—*your* realm—will be purified. The world will know everlasting glory!" Xavius allowed himself a slight smile. "And the blighted, impure races that in the past have prevented such a perfect age from issuing forth will *cease* to be."

Azshara rewarded his good words with a pleased smile of her own, then said, "I am glad to hear you say that it will be soon. I have had more suppliants today, lord counselor. They came in fear of the violence in and around the great Well. They asked me for guidance as to its cause and danger. Naturally, I referred their requests to you."

"As you rightly should have, mistress. I will assuage their fears long enough for our precious task to come to fruition. After that, it will be your pleasure to announce what has been done for the good of your people . . ."

"And they shall love me the more for it," Azshara murmured, her eyes narrowed as if imagining the grateful crowds.

"If they could possibly love you any more than they do already, my glorious queen."

Azshara accepted his compliment with a momentary lowering of her slitted eyes, then, with a smooth grace of which only she was capable, rose from the chair. Her attendants quickly manipulated the train of her gown so that it would not in the slightest hamper her movements. "I will make the wondrous announcement soon, Lord Xavius," she declared, turning away from the counselor. "See to it that all is ready when I do."

"It will consume my waking hours," he replied, bowing to her retreating form. "And be the dreams of my slumber."

But the moment she and her attendants had departed, a deep frown crossed the counselor's cold visage. He signaled to one of the stone-faced guards ever standing duty at the entrance to the chamber.

"If I am not alerted before the next time her majesty decides to join us, it will be your head. Is that understood?"

"Yes, my lord," the guard returned, expression never wavering.

"I also expect to be notified of Captain Varo'then's arrival before her majesty. His task is nothing with which to sully her hands. Make certain that the captain—and whatever he brings with him—is led directly to me."

"Yes, my lord."

Dismissing the guard, Xavius returned to the task of overseeing the Highborne's spellwork.

A lattice of dancing magical energy now enshrouded the fiery sphere, which continued to remake itself. As Xavius watched, the sphere folded within, almost as if it attempted to devour itself.

"Fascinating . . ." he whispered. This close, the lord counselor could feel the intense emanations, the barely bound forces summoned up from the source of all the night elves' magical might. It had been Xavius who had first suspected that his kind had only so far skimmed the surface of the dark water's potential. The Well of Eternity was aptly named, for the more he studied it, the more he realized that its bounty was endless. The physical dimensions of the Well were only a trick of the limited mind . . . the true Well existed in a thousand dimensions, a thousand places, simultaneously.

And from every aspect of it, every variation of it, the Highborne would learn to draw whatever they pleased.

The potential staggered even him.

Energies and colors unseen even by the others danced and fought before Xavius's magical eyes. They drew him in, their elemental power seductive. The lord counselor drank in the fantastic sight before him—

But from within, from deep beyond the physical world . . . he suddenly felt something stare back.

This time, the night elf knew he was not mistaken. Xavius sensed a presence, a distant presence. Yet, despite that incredible distance, the might he also sensed was staggering.

He tried to pull back, but it was already too late. Deep, so very deep within the captured energies of the Well, the mind of the counselor was suddenly dragged beyond the edge of reality, beyond eternity . . . until . . .

I have searched long for you . . . came the voice. It was life, death, creation, destruction . . . and power infinite.

Had he even desired to do so, Xavius would have been unable to wrench his eyes away from the abyss within. Other eyes now snared his tightly . . . the eyes of the lord counselor's new *god.*

And now you have come to me . . .

The waters bubbled as if boiling. Great waves rose and crashed down time and time again. Lightning flashed from both the heavens and the dark Well.

Then came the whispers.

The first of the night elves to hear them thought the sounds only the wild wind. They soon ignored them completely, more concerned with the possible devastation of their elegant homes.

A few more astute, more attuned to the Well's unearthly energies, heard them for what they were. Voices from the Well itself. But what the voices said, even the majority of those could not say.

It was the one or two who heard clearly who truly feared . . . and yet did not speak of their fear to others, lest they be branded mad and cast out from their society. Thus, they failed to heed the only warning they would truly get.

The voices spoke of nothing but hunger. They hungered for everything. Life, energy, souls . . . they wanted through to the world, through to the night elves' pristine realm.

And once there, they would devour it . . .

SEVEN

Their captors had grown very apprehensive . . . and to Rhonin, that made them even more of a threat.

It had much to do with the new stretch of forest that they had just entered. This area felt different to Rhonin compared to the dark stretches they had so far crossed. Here their captors seemed not so much the lords of the land as they did undesired intruders.

Dawn fast approached. He and Krasus, who appeared to still be unconscious, had been bound and unceremoniously tossed onto the back of one of the animals. Each jostle by the huge panther threatened to crack the wizard's ribs, but he forced himself not to make any sound or movement that would reveal to the night elves that he was awake.

Yet, what did it matter if they knew? He had already tried several times to cast a spell, but for his attempts had gained only a skull-splitting headache. Around his throat had been placed a small emerald amulet, a simple-looking thing that was the source of his frustration. Whenever he tried to concentrate too hard on his spells, his thoughts grew all muddled and his temples throbbed. He could not even shake the amulet free. The night elves had secured it well. Krasus wore one also, but from him it seemed their captors had nothing to fear. Rhonin also noted what had happened each time his former mentor had tried to aid in the struggle. Krasus had even less mastery over his power than Rhonin, a disturbing notion.

"This isn't the path we took," snarled the scarred leader, whom the human had heard referred to as Varo'then. "This isn't the way it should be . . ."

"But we've followed it back exactly as we should've, my captain," replied one of the others. "There was no deviation—"

"Does that look like the spires of Zin-Azshari on the horizon?" Varo'then snapped. "I see nothing but more damned trees, Koltharius . . . and there's something I don't like about them, either! Somehow, even with our eyes keen and our path understood, we've headed elsewhere!"

"Should we turn back? Retrace our route?"

Rhonin could not see the captain's face, but he could imagine the frustrated expression. "No . . . no . . . not yet . . ."

Yet, while Varo'then was not yet ready to give up on the trail, the wizard was becoming concerned about it himself. With each step deeper into the thick, towering forest, he sensed some growing presence, a presence the likes of which Rhonin had never experienced before. In some ways, it reminded him of how he sensed Krasus whenever the dragon mage contacted him, but this was more . . . much more.

But what?

"The sun's nearly upon us," muttered another of the soldiers.

From what Rhonin had so far ascertained, while his captors could function in daylight, they did not like it. In some ways, it weakened them. They were creatures of magic—even if individually they might not wield much of it—but their magic had to do with the night. If he could just rid himself of the amulet once the sun had risen, Rhonin believed the odds would swing back in his favor.

Making certain that no one watched, he surreptitiously shook his head. The amulet swung back and forth, but would not slip off. Rhonin finally tried thrusting his head up, hoping that might dislodge the piece. He risked being noticed by his captors, but that was a chance he had to take.

In the gloom of predawn, a face stared out at him from the nearby foliage.

No . . . the face was *part* of the foliage. The leaves and twigs formed the features, even creating a lush beard. The eyes were berries and a gap between the greenery represented what looked like a mischievous mouth.

It vanished among the bushes as swiftly as it had appeared, making Rhonin wonder if he had simply imagined it. A trick of the coming light? Impossible! Not with so much detail.

And yet . . .

The scrape of a weapon being drawn from its sheath caught his attention. One by one the night elves readied themselves for some battle that they did not understand, but knew was coming. Even the fierce cats sensed trouble, for not only did they pick up their already swift pace, but their backs arched and they bared their savage teeth.

Varo'then suddenly pointed to his right. "That way! That way! Quickly!"

At that moment, the forest erupted with life.

Huge, foliage-thick branches swung down, obscuring the faces of the riders. Bushes leapt up, becoming short, nimble figures with silent, smiling faces of green. The forest floor seemed to snag the claws of every panther, sending more than one rider tumbling. The night elves shouted recklessly at one another, trying to organize themselves, instead only adding to the chaos.

A low moan echoed through the vicinity. Rhonin caught only a glance, but felt certain that he had seen a massive tree bend over and sweep away two of the night elves and their mounts with its thick, leafy crown.

Curses filled the forest as Varo'then tried to regain command of his party.

Those elves who remained mounted sat in a jumble, attempting not only to cut at the things swarming around them, but also to keep their excited panthers under control. For all their size, the huge cats clearly did not like what they faced, often pulling back even when their riders insisted that they move forward.

Varo'then cried out something and suddenly harsh, violet tentacles of radiant energy darted out at various points in the forest. One struck an approaching bush sprite, instantly turning the creature into an inferno. Yet, despite its apparent horrible demise, the creature continued forward without pause, leaving a burning trail in its wake.

Almost immediately, the wind, which had been nearly nonexistent prior to this, howled and roared as if angered by the assault. It blew with such fury that dirt, broken tree limbs, and loose leaves flew up in vast numbers, filling the air and further obscuring the night elves' view. The flames snuffed out, their would-be victim as oblivious to this phenomenal rescue as it had been to its previous peril. A huge, flying branch struck down the night elf next to Varo'then.

"Regroup!" the scarred captain shouted. "Regroup and retreat! Hurry, blast you!"

A leafy hand covered Rhonin's mouth. He looked again into the same startling face. Behind him, he felt other hands grasping his legs.

With a rather unceremonious push, they sent the mage sliding forward.

The panther took notice of this and roared. More of the small shrublike figures swarmed around the beast, harassing it. As the world rocked around him, Rhonin caught sight of Varo'then twisting back to see what was happening. The scowling elf swore as it registered that his prisoners were being stolen, but before he could raise a hand to stop them, more branches came down, both entangling the captain's arms and face and blinding him.

The bush creatures caught Rhonin well before he would have been in danger of striking the ground headfirst. Silently and efficiently, they carried him like a battering ram into the thick forest. Rhonin could only hope that Krasus, too, had been rescued, for he could see nothing but the leafy figures before him. Despite their sizes, his companions were obviously strong.

Then, to his dismay, a lone night elf atop a snarling panther cut off their path. The wizard recognized him as the one called Koltharius. He had a desperate look in his eyes, as if Rhonin's escape would mean the worst for him. From what little Rhonin had learned of the captain, he did not doubt that.

Wasting no words, the night elf urged his beast forward. The elves Rhonin knew, especially his own beloved Vereesa, were beings with the utmost respect for nature. Koltharius's kind, however, seemed not to care a whit for it; he slashed at the tree limbs and shrubbery slowing him with unbridled fury. Nothing would keep him from his prey.

Or so he might have thought. Huge, black birds abruptly dropped from the foliage above, surrounding and harassing the night elf mercilessly. Koltharius swung madly about, but severed not even a pinfeather from his avian attackers.

So engrossed was the night elf by this latest assault that he did not notice another danger rising up from the earth. The trees through which he needed to pass rose by more than two feet, as if stretching their roots.

Koltharius's mount, driven nearly to madness by the birds, did not pay enough attention to its course.

The typically nimble feline first stumbled, then tripped badly as its paws became more and more entangled. A mournful yowl escaped it as it flew sideways. Its rider tried to hold on, but that only served to worsen his situation.

The huge panther twisted, putting Koltharius between it and two massive tree trunks. Trapped, the night elf was crushed between them, his armor crumpling like paper under the tremendous force. His cat suffered little better, a terrible snapping sound at its neck accompanying the crash.

Rhonin's leafy companions moved on as if nothing had happened. For a few more minutes, the wizard continued to hear the struggles of his former captors, but then the sounds suddenly shifted away, as if Varo'then had finally led his bedraggled hunters to escape.

On and on the tiny creatures carried him. He saw a movement to his right and made out what looked to be the dragon mage's still form being brought along in like fashion. For the first time, though, Rhonin started to fear what his rescuers intended to do with the pair. Had they been taken from the night elves in order to face some more horrific fate?

The forest sprites slowed, finally halting at the edge of an open area. Despite the impossibility of the angle, the first hints of daylight already lit up the opening. Small, delicate songbirds twittered merrily. Myriad flowers of a hundred colors bloomed full and tall grass within waved gently, almost beckoningly, to the newcomers.

Again a leafy face filled his gaze. The open-gap smile widened and to his surprise Rhonin saw that a small, utterly white flower bloomed within.

A tiny puff of pollen shot forth, splattering the human's nose and mouth.

Rhonin coughed. His head swam. He felt the creatures move again, carrying him into the sunlight.

But before one ray could touch his face . . . the wizard passed out.

Despite Rhonin's belief otherwise, Krasus had not been unconscious most of the time. Weak, yes, almost willing to let the darkness take him, true, but the dragon mage had fought both his physical and mental debilitation and, if not a victor, he had at least suffered no defeat.

Krasus, too, had noticed watchers in the woods, but he immediately recognized them as servants of the forest. With senses still more attuned than those of his human companion, Krasus understood that the night elves had been *drawn* to this place purposely. Some force desired something of the armored figures and it took no leap of logic to assume that he and Rhonin were the prizes in question.

And so the dragon mage had kept perfectly still throughout the chaos. He had forced himself to do nothing when the party was attacked and the creatures of the forest stole him and Rhonin from under the elves' very eyes. Krasus sensed no malice in their rescuers, but that did not mean the pair might not come to harm later. He had remained secretly vigilant throughout the forest journey, hoping he would be of more aid than the last time.

But when they had reached the sunlit opening, he had miscalculated. The face had appeared too swiftly, breathed too unexpectedly upon him. Like Rhonin, Krasus had passed out.

Unlike Rhonin, he had slept only minutes.

He awakened to, of all things, a small red bird perched atop his robed knee. The gentle sight so startled the dragon mage that he gasped, sending the tiny avian fleeing to the branches above.

With great caution, Krasus surveyed his surroundings. To all apparent evidence, he and Rhonin lay in the midst of a mystical glade, an area of immense magic at least as ancient as the dragons. That the sun shone here so brilliantly, that the grass, flowers, and birds radiated such peace, was no accident. Here was the chosen sanctum of some being whom Krasus should have known—but could not in the least recall.

And that was a problem of which he had not spoken truthfully to his companion. Krasus's memories were riddled with gaps. He had recognized the night elves for what they were, but other things, many of them mundane, had completely vanished. When he tried to focus on them, the dragon mage found nothing but emptiness. He was as weak in his mind as he was in his body.

But why? Why had he suffered so much more than Rhonin? While a human mage of impressive abilities, Rhonin was still a fragile mortal. If anyone should have been battered and beaten by their madcap flight through time and space, it should have rightly been the lesser of the two travelers.

The moment he thought it, Krasus felt guilty. Whatever the reason for Rhonin surviving more, Krasus only shamed himself by wishing for a reversal of their fortunes. Rhonin had nearly sacrificed himself for his former mentor several times.

Despite his tremendous weakness and lingering pain, he pushed himself to his feet. Of the creatures who had brought them here, Krasus saw no sign.

Likely they had returned to being a literal part of the forest, tending to its needs until next summoned to action by their lord. That these had been the simplest of the forest's guardians Krasus was well aware. The night elves were a relatively paltry threat.

But what did the power that ruled here want of two wayward wanderers?

Rhonin still slumbered deep and, judging by his own reaction to the pollen, Krasus expected him to do so for quite some time. With no evident threat in sight, he dared leave the human sleeping, choosing now to investigate the boundaries of their freedom.

The thick field of flowers surrounded the soft, open grass like a fence, with what appeared an equal number pointed outward and inward. Krasus approached the closest section, watching the flowers warily.

As he came within a foot of them, they turned to face him, opening fully.

Instantly the dragon mage stepped back . . . and watched as the plants resumed their normal appearance. A simple, soft wall of effective guardians. He and Rhonin were safe from any danger outside while at the same time they were kept from causing trouble for the forest.

In his present condition, Krasus did not even consider leaping over the flowers. Besides, he suspected that doing so would only unleash some other hidden sentry, possibly one not as gentle.

There remained only one recourse. To better conserve his strength, he sat down and folded his legs. Then, taking a deep breath, Krasus studied the surrounding glade one last time . . . and spoke to the air.

"I would talk with you."

The wind picked up his words and carried them into the forest, where they echoed again and again. The birds grew silent. The grass ceased waving.

Then came the wind again . . . and with it the reply.

"And so we shall talk . . ."

Krasus waited. In the distance, he heard the slight clatter of hooves, as if some animal had chanced by at this important moment. He frowned as the clatter grew nearer, then noticed a shadowy form coming through the woods. A horned rider atop some monstrous steed?

But then, as it drew up to the flowery guardians and the sun, ever shining, caught it full, the dragon in mortal form could only gape like a mere human child at the imposing sight.

"I know you . . ." began Krasus. "I know of you . . ."

But the name, like so many other memories, would not come to him. He could not even say with any certainty whether he had faced this mythic being before and surely that said something for the scope of the holes in his mind.

"And I know something of you," said the towering figure with a torso akin to a night elf and a lower half like that of a stag. "But not nearly as much as I would like . . ."

On four strong legs, the master of the forest strode through the barrier of flowers, which gave way as loyal hounds would to their handler. Some of the flowers and grass even caressed the legs gently, lovingly.

"I am Cenarius . . ." he uttered to the slight figure sitting before him. "This is my realm."

Cenarius . . . Cenarius . . . legendary connotations fluttered through Krasus's tattered mind, a few taking root but most simply fading back to nothing. Cenarius. Spoken of by the elves and other forest dwellers. Not a god, but . . . almost. A demigod, then. As powerful in his own way as the great Aspects.

But there was more, so much more. Yet, strive as he might, the dragon mage could not summon any of it.

His efforts must have shown on his face, for Cenarius's stern visage grew more kindly. "You are not well, traveler. Perhaps you should rest more."

"No." Krasus forced himself up, standing tall and straight before the demigod. "No . . . I would speak now."

"As you like." The antlered deity tilted his bearded head to one side, studying his guest. "You are more than what you seem, traveler. I see hints of night elven but also sense far, far more. Almost you remind me of—but that's not likely." The huge figure indicated Rhonin. "And he is unlike any creature to be found within or without my domain."

"We've come a long distance and are, frankly, lost, great one. We know not where we are."

To the mage's surprise, this brought thundering laughter from the demigod. Cenarius's laughter made more flowers bloom, brought songbirds to the branches around the trio, and set into motion a soft spring breeze that touched Krasus's cheek like a lover.

"Then you *are* from far off! Where *else* could you be, my friend? Where else could you be but *Kalimdor!*"

Kalimdor. That, at least, made sense, for where else would one find night elves in numbers? Yet knowing where he and Rhonin had been deposited answered few other questions. "So I suspected, my lord, but—"

"I sensed an unsettling change in the world," Cenarius interrupted. "An imbalance, a shifting. I sought out its origin and location in secret . . . and while I did not find all I searched for . . . I was led to you two." He stepped past Krasus to once more study the slumbering Rhonin. "Two wanderers from nowhere. Two lost souls from nothing. You are both enigmas to me. I would rather you had not been in the first place."

"Yet you saved us from captivity—"

The forest lord gave a snort worthy of the most powerful stag. "The night elves grow more arrogant. They take what does not belong to them and trespass where they are not wanted. It is their assumption that everything falls under their domination. Although they did not quite intrude upon my realm, I chose to make them do so in order to teach them a lesson in humility and manners." He smiled grimly. "That . . . and they made it simpler for me by bringing what I desired directly here."

Krasus felt his legs buckling. The effort to keep on his feet was proving monumental. With determination, he stood his ground. "They, too, seemed to be aware of our sudden arrival."

"Zin-Azshari is not without its own abilities. It does, after all, overlook the Well itself."

The dragon mage rocked, but this time not because of weakness. In his last statement, Cenarius had said two words that set fear into Krasus's heart.

"Zin . . . Zin-Azshari?"

"Aye, mortal! The capital of the night elves' domain! Situated at the very shores of the Well of Eternity! You know not even that?"

Disregarding the weakness he revealed to the demigod, Krasus dropped to the ground, sitting in the grass and trying to drink in the staggering reality of the situation.

Zin-Azshari.

The Well of Eternity.

He knew them both, even as perforated as his memory had become. Some things were of such epic legend that it would have taken the complete eradicating of his mind for Krasus to have forgotten them.

Zin-Azshari and the Well of Eternity. The first, the center of an empire of magic, an empire ruled by the night elves. How foolish of him not to have realized that during their capture. Zin-Azshari had been the focal point of the world for a period of centuries.

The second, the Well, was the place of magic itself, the endlessly deep reservoir of power spoken of in awed whispers by mages and sorcerers throughout the ages. It had served as the core of the night elves' sorcerous powers, letting them cast spells of which even dragons had learned respect.

But both were things of the past . . . the *far* past. Neither Zin-Azshari nor even the wondrous and sinister Well existed. They had long, long ago vanished in a catastrophe that—that—

And there Krasus's mind faltered again. Something horrible had happened that had destroyed the two, had ripped the very world asunder . . . and for the life of him he could not recall *what.*

"You are no: yet recovered," Cenarius said with concern. "I should have left you to rest."

Still fighting to remember, the mage responded, "I will be . . . I will be all right by the time my friend awakens. We—we will leave as soon as we can and trouble you no longer."

The deity frowned. "Little one, you misunderstand. You are both puzzle and guest to me . . . and so long as you remain the former, you will also remain the latter." Cenarius turned from him, heading toward the guarding flowers. "I believe that you need sustenance. It shall be provided shortly. Rest well until then."

Cenarius did not wait for any protest nor did Krasus bother with one. When a being such as the forest lord insisted that they stay, Krasus understood that it would be *impossible* to argue otherwise. He and Rhonin were guests for as long as Cenarius desired . . . which with a demigod might be the rest of their lives.

Still, that did not worry Krasus so much as the thought that those lives could be very short indeed.

Both Zin-Azshari and the Well had been destroyed in some monstrous catastrophe . . . and the more the dragon mage pondered it, the more he believed the time of that catastrophe was rapidly approaching.

"I warn you, my darling counselor, I adore surprises, but this one I expect to be quite, quite delicious."

Xavius but smiled as he led the queen by the hand into the chamber where the Highborne worked. He had come to her with as much graciousness as he could command, politely pleading with her to join him and see what his sorcerers had accomplished. The counselor knew that Azshara expected something quite miraculous and she would not be disappointed . . . even if it was *not* what the ruler of the night elves had in mind.

The guards knelt as they entered. Although their expressions were the same as always, like Xavius, they, too, had been touched. Everyone now in the chamber understood, save for Azshara.

For her, it would be only a moment more before the revelation.

She eyed the swirling maelstrom within the pattern, her tone dripping with disappointment. "It looks no different."

"You must see it up close, Light of a Thousand Moons. Then you'll understand what we have achieved . . ."

Azshara frowned. She had come without her attendants at his request and perhaps she now regretted that. Nevertheless, Azshara was queen and it behooved her to show that, even alone, she was in command of any situation.

With graceful strides, Azshara stepped up to the very edge of the pattern. She first eyed the work of the Highborne currently casting, then deigned to set her gaze upon the inferno within.

"It still strikes me as unchanged, dear Xavius. I expected more from—"

She let out a gasp and although the counselor could not see her expression completely, he made out enough to know that Azshara now understood.

And the voice he had heard before, the voice of his god, said for all to hear . . .

I am coming . . .

EIGHT

The Ritual of the High Moon had been completed and now Tyrande had time for herself. Elune expected dedication from her priestesses, but she did not demand that they give to her every waking moment. The Mother Moon was a kind, loving mistress, which had been what first drew the young night elf to her temple. In joining, Tyrande found some peace to her apprehension, to her inner conflicts.

But one conflict would not leave her heart. Times had altered matters between her, Malfurion, and Illidan. They were no longer youthful companions. The simplicities of their childhoods had given way to the complexities of adult relationships.

Her feelings for both of them had changed and she knew that they, too, felt differently about her. The competition between the brothers had always been a friendly one, but of late it had intensified in a manner Tyrande did not appreciate. Now it seemed that they battled each other, as if vying for some prize.

Tyrande understood—even if they did not—that *she* was the prize.

While the novice priestess felt flattered, she did not want either of them hurt. Yet, Tyrande would be the one who would hurt at least one brother, for she knew in her heart that when it came time to choose her life mate, it would be either Illidan or Malfurion.

Dressed in the silver, hooded gown of a novice priestess, Tyrande hurried silently through the high, marble halls of the temple. Above her, a magical fresco illustrated the heavens. A casual visitor might have even thought that no roof stood here, so perfect was the illusion. But only the grand chamber, where the rituals took place, was truly open to the sky. There, Elune visited in the form of moonbeams, gloriously touching her faithful as a mother did her beloved children.

Past the looming, sculpted images of the goddess's earthly incarnations—those who had served in the past as high priestess—Tyrande finally strode across the vast marble floor of the foyer. Here, in intricate mosaic work, the formation of the world by Elune and the other gods was depicted, the Mother Moon of course illustrated most dominantly. With few exceptions, the gods were vague forms with shadowed faces, no mere flesh creature worthy of envisioning their true images. Only the demigods, children and assistants to their superiors, had definite visages. One of those, of course, was Cenarius, said by many to be perhaps the child of the Moon and the Sun. Cenarius, of course, said nothing one way or another, but Tyrande liked to think that story the truth.

Outside, the cool night air soothed her some. Tyrande descended the white alabaster steps and joined the throngs. Many bowed their heads in deference to her position while others politely made a path for her. There were advantages to being even an initiate of Elune, but at the moment Tyrande wished that she could have simply been herself to the world.

Suramar was not so glorious as Zin-Azshari, but it had a presence all its own. Bright, flashy colors filled her gaze as she entered the main square, where merchants of all status plied their wares on the population. Dignitaries in rich, diamond-sequined robes of sun red and fiery orange, their noses upward and their eyes only on the path ahead, walked alongside low-caste elves in more plain garments of green, yellow, blue, or some mix of the colors. In the market, everyone made an appearance in order to show themselves off as best they could.

Even the buildings acted as displays for their inhabitants, every color of the rainbow represented in the view Tyrande had. Some businesses had been painted in as many as seven shades and most had dramatic images splashed across every side. Torchlight illuminated most, the dancing flames considered a lively accent.

The few non-night elves whom the novice priestess had met during her short life seemed to find her people garish, even daring to say that Tyrande's race must be color-blind. While her own tastes tended to be more conservative, albeit not so much as Malfurion's, Tyrande felt that night elves simply appreciated better the variety of patterns and shades that existed in the world.

Near the center of the square, she noted a crowd gathered. Most gestured and pointed, some making comments either of disgust or mockery. Curious, Tyrande went to see what could be of such interest.

At first, the onlookers did not even notice her presence, certainly a sign that whatever they watched must be a rare marvel. She politely touched the nearest figure, who upon recognition immediately stepped aside for her. By this method, she managed to wend her way deep into the throng.

A cage just slightly shorter than her stood in the midst of it all. Made of good strong iron bars, it evidently held a beast of some strength, for it rattled harshly and now and then an animalistic growl set the audience to renewed murmurs.

Those directly in front of her would not move, not even when they discovered who had tapped them on the shoulder. Frustrated and curious, the slim night elf shifted position, attempting to see between one pair.

What she beheld made her gasp.

"What is it?" Tyrande blurted.

"No one knows, sister," replied what turned out to be a sentry standing duty. He wore the breast plate and robes of one of Suramar's Watch. "The Moon Guard had to spellcast it at least three times to bring it down."

Tyrande instinctively glanced around for one of the hooded, green-robed wizards, but saw none. Likely they had ensorcelled the cage, then left the secured creature in the hands of the Watch while they went to discuss what to do with it.

But *what* had they left?

It was no dwarf, although in some ways its build reminded her of one. Had it stood straight, it would have been about a foot shorter than a night elf, but at least twice as broad. Clearly the beast was a creature of brute strength, for never had she seen such musculature. It amazed Tyrande that even with spells cast upon the cage the prisoner had not simply bent the bars aside and escaped.

A high-caste onlooker suddenly prodded the stooped figure with his golden staff . . . which caused renewed fury within. The night elf barely pulled his stick out of reach of the thick, meaty paws. The creature's squat, round-jawed face contorted as it snarled its anger. It likely would have managed to snag the staff if not for the thick chains around its wrists, ankles, and neck. The heavy chains were not only the reason it stayed stooped, but also why it could never deal with the bars, even supposing it had the strength and resolve.

From horror and disgust, Tyrande's emotions shifted to pity. Both the temple and Cenarius had taught her respect for life, even that which seemed at first only monstrous. The green-hided creature wore primitive garments, which meant that it—or *he*, in most probability—had some semblance of intelligence. It was not right, then, that he be set up for show like some animal.

Two empty brown bowls indicated that the prisoner had at least been given some sustenance, but from his massive frame, the novice priestess suspected it was not nearly enough. She turned to the sentry. "He needs more food and water."

"I've been given no orders for such, sister," the sentry respectfully replied, his eyes ever on the crowd.

"That shouldn't require orders."

Tyrande was rewarded with a slight shrug. "The elders haven't decided what to do with it yet. Maybe they don't think it'll need any more food or drink, sister."

His suggestion repulsed her. Night elf justice could be very draconian. "If I bring some sustenance for him, will you attempt to stop me?"

Now the soldier looked uncomfortable. "You really shouldn't, sister. That beast's just as liable to tear your arm off and gnaw on that instead of whatever fare you bring. You would be wise to leave it alone."

"I shall take my chances."

"Sister—"

But before he could try to talk her out of it, Tyrande had already turned away. She headed directly for the nearest food merchant, seeking a jug of water and a bowl of soup. The creature in the cage looked fairly carnivorous, so she also decided upon a bit of fresh meat. The proprietor refused to charge her, a benefit of her calling, so she gave him the blessing she knew he wanted, then thanked him and returned to the square.

Apparently already bored, much of the crowd had dissipated by the time Tyrande reached the center. That, at least, made it easier for her to confront the prisoner. He glanced up as the novice priestess approached, at first clearly marking her as just one more jaded gawker. Only when he saw what Tyrande held did he take more interest.

He sat up as best he could considering his chains, deep-set eyes warily watching her under the thick, bushy brow. Tyrande judged him to be toward the latter half of his life, for his hair had grayed and his brutish visage bore the many marks and scars of a harsh existence.

Just beyond what she calculated to be his reach, the young night elf hesitated. Out of the corner of her eye, Tyrande noted the sentry taking cautious interest in her actions. She understood that he would use his spear to gut the creature if it made any attempt to harm her. Tyrande hoped it would not come to that. It would be the most terrible of ironies if her intent to aid a suffering being led to its death.

With grace and care, she knelt before the bars. "Do you understand me?"

He grunted, then finally nodded.

"I've brought you something." She held out the bowl of soup first.

The wary eyes, so different from her own, fixed upon the bowl. She could read the calculation in them. Once they flickered ever so briefly in the direction of the nearest guard. The right hand closed, then opened again.

Slowly, ever so slowly, he stretched forth the hand. As it neared her own, Tyrande saw how huge and thick it really was, massive enough to envelop both of hers without difficulty. She pictured the strength inherent in it and almost pulled the offering back.

Then with a gentleness that surprised her, the prisoner took the bowl from her grasp, placing it securely in front of him and eyeing her expectantly.

His acceptance made her smile, but he did not respond in kind. Slightly more at ease, Tyrande handed him next the meat, then, lastly, the jug of water.

When he had all three safely tucked near, the green-skinned behemoth began to eat. He swallowed the contents of the bowl in one huge gulp, some of the brownish liquid spilling over his jaw. The piece of meat followed, thick, jagged, yellow teeth ripping away at the raw flesh without hesitation. Tyrande swallowed, but did not otherwise show her discomfort at the prisoner's monstrous manners. Under such conditions, she might have acted little better than he.

A few onlookers watched this activity as they might have a minstrel act, but Tyrande ignored them. She waited patiently as he continued to devour his meal. Away went every bit of meat on the bone, which the creature then broke in two and sucked on the marrow with such gusto that the remainder of the crowd—their fine sensibilities disturbed by the animalistic sight—finally left.

As the last of them departed, he suddenly dropped the bone fragments and, with a startling deep chuckle, reached for the jug. Not once had his eyes strayed from the novice priestess for more than a second.

When the water was gone, he wiped his wide mouth with his arm and grunted, "Good."

To hear an actual word startled Tyrande even though she had assumed earlier that if he understood, then he could also speak. It made her smile again and even risk leaning against the bars, an act that at first brought anxiety to the sentries.

"Sister!" cried one of the guards. "You shouldn't be so near! He'll tear—"

"He'll do nothing," she quickly assured them. Glancing at the creature, she added, "Will you?"

He shook his head and drew his hands close to his chest as a sign. The sentries backed away, but remained watchful.

Ignoring them once more, Tyrande asked, "Do you want anything else? More food?"

"No."

She paused, then said, "My name is Tyrande. I am a priestess of Elune, the Mother Moon."

The figure in the cage seemed disinclined to continue the conversation, but when he saw that she was determined to wait him out, he finally responded, "Brox . . . Broxigar. Sworn servant to the Warchief Thrall, ruler of the orcs."

Tyrande tried to make sense of what he had said. That he was a warrior was obvious by his appearance. He served some leader, this Thrall. A name in some ways more curious than his own, for she understood its meaning and therefore understood the contrary nature of a ruler so titled.

And this Thrall was lord of the orcs, which Tyrande assumed must be what Brox was. The teachings of the temple were thorough, but never had she heard there or anywhere else of a race called the orcs. Certainly, if they were all like Brox, they would have been well remembered by the night elves.

She decided to delve deeper. "Where are you from, Brox? How did you get here?"

Immediately Tyrande realized that she had erred. The orc's eyes narrowed and he clamped his mouth shut. How foolish of her not to think that the Moon Guard had already questioned him . . . and without the courtesy that she had shown so far. Now he must have thought that she had been sent to learn by kindness what they had failed to gain by force and magic.

Clearly desiring an end to their meeting, Brox picked up the bowl and held it toward her, his expression dark and untrusting.

Without warning, a flash of energy coursed into the cage from behind the novice, striking the orc's hand.

With a savage snarl, Brox seized his burnt fingers, holding them tight. He glared at Tyrande with such a murderous gaze that she could not help but rise and step back. The sentries immediately focused on the cage, their spears keeping Brox pinned to the back bars.

Strong hands seized her by the shoulders and a voice she knew well anxiously whispered, "Are you safe, Tyrande? That foul beast didn't hurt you, did he?"

"He had no plans to do me any harm!" she blurted, turning to face her supposed rescuer. "Illidan! How could you?"

The handsome night elf frowned, his arresting golden eyes losing some of their light. "I was only fearful for you! That beast is capable of—"

Tyrande cut him off. "In there, he is capable of very little . . . and he is no beast!"

"No?" Illidan leaned down to inspect Brox. The orc bared his teeth but did nothing that might otherwise antagonize the night elf. Malfurion's brother snorted in disdain. "Looks like no civilized creature to me . . ."

"He was merely trying to hand back the bowl. And if there had been any trouble, the guards were already standing by."

Illidan frowned. "I'm sorry, Tyrande. Maybe I overreacted. You must admit, though, that few others, even among your calling, would have taken the terrible risk you did! You might not know this, but they say that when he woke up, he almost throttled one of the Moon Guard!"

The novice priestess glanced at the stone-faced sentry, who reluctantly nodded. He had forgotten to mention that little tidbit to her. Still, Tyrande doubted it would have made a difference. Brox had been mistreated and she had felt the need to come to his aid.

"I appreciate your concern, Illidan, but again I tell you that I wasn't in any danger." Her gaze narrowed as she took in the orc's injury. The fingers were blackened and the pain in Brox's eyes was obvious, yet the orc did not cry out nor did he ask for any healing.

Abandoning Illidan, Tyrande knelt again by the cage. Without hesitation, she reached through the bars.

Illidan reached for her. "Tyrande!"

"Stay back! All of you!" Meeting the orc's baleful gaze, she whispered, "I know you didn't mean me any harm. I can mend that for you. Please. Just let me."

Brox growled, but in a manner that made her think he was not angry but simply weighing his options. Illidan still stood next to Tyrande, who realized that he would strike the orc again at the slightest hint of something gone awry.

"Illidan . . . I'm going to have to ask you to turn away for a moment."

"What? Tyrande—"

"For me, Illidan."

She could sense his pent-up fury. Nevertheless, he obeyed her request, spinning around and facing one of the buildings surrounding the square.

Tyrande eyed Brox again. His gaze had shifted to Illidan and for the briefest moment she read the satisfaction in them. Then the orc focused on her and gingerly offered up the maimed hand.

Taking it in her own, she studied the wound in shock. The flesh had been burned away in places on two fingers and a third was red and festering.

"What did you do to him?" she asked Illidan.

"Something I learned recently," was all he would say.

It had certainly not been something he had learned in the forest of Cenarius. This was an example of high night elven sorcery, a spell he had cast with scant concentration. It revealed how skilled Malfurion's brother could be when the subject excited him. He clearly enjoyed the manipulation of sorcery over that of the more slow-paced druidism.

Tyrande was not so certain she liked his choice.

"Mother Moon, hear my entreaties . . ." Ignoring the aghast expressions of the guards, she took the orc's fingers and kissed each ever so gently. Tyrande then whispered to Elune, asking the goddess to grant her the ability to ease Brox's burden, to render whole what Illidan had, in his rashness, ruined.

"Stretch your hand out as far as you can," she ordered the prisoner.

Watching the sentries, Brox moved forward, straining to thrust his brutish hand beyond the bars. Tyrande expected some sort of magical resistance, but nothing happened. She supposed that since the orc had done nothing to escape, the cage's spellwork had not reacted.

The novice priestess looked up into the sky, where the moon hovered just above. "Mother Moon . . . fill me with your purity, your grace, your love . . . grant me the power to heal this . . ."

As Tyrande repeated her plea, she heard a gasp from one of the guards. Illidan started to turn, but then evidently thought better than to possibly upset Tyrande further.

A stream of silver light . . . Elune's light . . . encompassed the young priestess. Tyrande radiated as if she were the Moon herself. She felt the glory of the goddess become a part of her.

Brox almost pulled away, startled by the wondrous display. To his credit, though, he placed his trust in her, letting her draw his hand as best she could into the glow.

And as the moonlight touched his fingers, the burnt flesh healed, the gaps where bone showed through regrew, and the horrific injury that Illidan had caused utterly *vanished*.

It took but a few scant seconds to complete the task. The orc remained still, eyes as wide as a child's.

"Thank you, Mother Moon," Tyrande whispered, releasing Brox's hand.

The sentries each fell to one knee, bowing their heads to the acolyte. The orc drew his hand close, staring at each finger and waggling them in astonishment. He touched the skin, first tenderly, then with immense satisfaction when no pain jarred him. A grunt of pleasure escaped the brutish figure.

Brox suddenly began contorting his body in the cage. Tyrande feared that he had suffered some other injury only now revealed, but then the orc finished moving.

"I honor you, shaman," he uttered, now prostrating himself as best as his bonds allowed. "I am in your debt."

So deep was Brox's gratitude that Tyrande felt her cheeks darken in embarrassment. She rose and took a step back.

Illidan immediately turned and held her arm as if to steady her. "Are you all right?"

"I am . . . it . . ." How to explain what she felt when touched by Elune? "It is done," she finished, unable to respond properly.

The guards finally rose, their respect for her magnified. The foremost one reverently approached her. "Sister, might I have your blessing?"

"Of course!" The blessings of Elune were given freely, for the teachings of Mother Moon said that the more who were touched by her, the more who would understand the love and unity she represented and spread that understanding to others.

With her open palm, Tyrande touched each sentry on the heart, then the forehead, indicating the symbolic unity of thought and spirit. Each thanked her profusely.

Illidan took her arm again. "You need some recuperation, Tyrande. Come! I know a place—"

From the cage came Brox's gruff voice. "Shaman, may this lowly one, too, have your blessing?"

The guards started, but said nothing. If even a beast so politely requested a blessing by one of Elune's chosen, how could they argue?

They could not, but Illidan could. "You've done enough for that creature. You're practically wavering! Come—"

But she would not deny the orc. Pulling free from Illidan's grasp, Tyrande knelt again before Brox. She reached in without hesitation, touching the coarse, hairy hide and hard, deep-browed head.

"May Elune watch over you and yours . . ." the novice priestess whispered.

"May your ax arm be strong," he returned.

His peculiar response made her frown, but then she recalled what sort of life he must have lived. His wish for her was, in its own odd way, a wish for life and health.

"Thank you," she responded, smiling.

As Tyrande rose, Illidan once more interjected himself into the situation. "Now can we—"

All at once she felt weary. It was a good weariness, though, as if Tyrande had worked long and hard for her mistress and accomplished much in her name. She recalled suddenly how long it had been since she had slept. More than a day. Certainly the wisdom of Mother Moon dictated that she return to the temple and go to her bed.

"Please forgive me, Illidan," Tyrande murmured. "I find myself tired. I would like to return to my sisters. You understand, don't you?"

His eyes narrowed momentarily, then calmed. "Yes, that would probably be best. Shall I escort you back?"

"There's no need. I'd like to walk alone, anyway."

Illidan said nothing, only bowing slightly in deference to her decision.

She gave Brox one last smile. The orc nodded. Tyrande departed, feeling oddly refreshed in her mind despite her physical exhaustion. When it was possible, she would speak with the high priestess about Brox. Surely the temple would be able to do something for the outcast.

Moonlight shone on the novice priestess as she walked. More and more Tyrande felt as if she had experienced something this night that would forever change her. Surely her interaction with the orc had been the design of Elune.

She could hardly wait to talk to the high priestess . . .

Illidan watched Tyrande walk away without so much as a second glance at him. He knew her mind well enough to understand that she still dwelled in the moment of her service for her goddess. That drowned out any other influence, including him.

"Tyrande . . ." He had hoped to speak with her of his feelings, but that chance had been ruined. Illidan had waited for hours, watching the temple surreptitiously for her appearance. Knowing that it would not look good for him if he joined her the moment she stepped out, he had waited in the background, intent on pretending to just happen by.

Then she had discovered the creature the Moon Guard had captured and all his well-thought plans went awry. Now, not only had he lost his opportunity, but he had embarrassed himself in front of her, been made to look the villain . . . and all because of a *thing* like that!

Before he could stop himself, words tumbled silently out of his mouth and his right hand flexed tightly.

There was a shout from the direction of the cage. He quickly glanced toward it.

The cage flared brightly, but not with the silver light of the moon. Instead, a furious red aura surrounded the cell, as if trying to devour it . . . and its occupant.

The foul creature inside roared in obvious pain. The guards, meanwhile, moved about in clear confusion.

Illidan quickly muttered the counter words.

The aura faded away. The prisoner ceased his cries.

With no one watching him, the young night elf swiftly vanished from the scene. He had let his anger get the best of him and lashed out at the most obvious target. Illidan was grateful that the guards had not realized the truth, and that Tyrande had already left the square, missing his moment of rage.

He was also thankful for those of the Moon Guard who had cast the magical barriers surrounding the cage . . . for it was only those protective spells that had prevented the creature inside from being *slain*.

NINE

They were dying all around him.

Everywhere he looked, Brox saw his comrades dying. Garno, with whom he had grown up, who was practically a brother, fell next, his body hacked to pieces by the screaming blade of a towering, fiery form with a hellish, horned face full of jagged teeth. The demon itself was slain moments later by Brox, who leapt upon it and, with a cry that made even the fearsome creature hesitate, cleaved Garno's killer in two despite its blazing armor.

But the Legion kept coming and the orcs grew fewer. Barely a handful of defenders remained, yet every minute another perished in the onslaught.

Thrall had commanded that the way be blocked, that the Legion would not break through. Help was being gathered, but the Horde needed time. They needed Brox and his fellows.

But there were fewer and fewer. Duun suddenly dropped, his head bouncing along the blood-soaked ground several seconds before his torso collapsed in a heap. Fezhar already lay dead, his remains all but unrecognizable. He had been enveloped in a wave of unnatural green flame belched by one of the demons, flame that had not so much burnt his body, but *dissolved* it.

Again and again, Brox's sturdy ax laid waste to his horrific foes, never seemingly the same kind of creature twice. Yet, whenever he wiped the sweat from his brow and stared ahead, all he saw were more.

And more, and more . . .

Now, only he stood against them. Stood against a shrieking, hungry sea of monsters hell-bent on the destruction of everything.

And as they fell upon the lone survivor—*Brox awoke.*

The orc shivered in his cage, but not from cold. After more than a thousand repetitions, he would have thought himself immune to the terrors his subconscious resurrected. Yet, each time the nightmares came, they did so with new intensity, new pain.

New guilt.

Brox should have died then. He should have died with his comrades. They had given the ultimate sacrifice for the Horde, but he had survived, had lived on. It was not right.

I am a coward . . . he thought once more. *If I had fought harder, I'd be with them.*

But even though he had told this to Thrall, the Warchief had shook his head and said, "No one fought harder, my old friend. The scars are there, the scouts saw you battle as they approached. You did your comrades, your people, as good a service as those who perished . . ."

Brox had accepted Thrall's gratitude, but never the Horde leader's words.

Now here he was, penned up like a pig waiting to be slaughtered for these arrogant creatures. They stared at him as if he had grown two heads and marveled at his ugliness. Only the young female, the shaman, had shown him respect and care.

In her he sensed the power that his own people talked about, the old way of magic. She had healed the fiery wound that her friend had caused him with but a prayer to the moon. Truly she was gifted and Brox felt honored that he had been given her blessing.

Not that it would matter in the long run. The orc had no doubt that his captors would soon decide how to execute him. What they had learned from him so far would avail them nothing. He had refused to give them any definitive information concerning his people, especially their location. True, he did not quite know himself how to reach his home, but it was better to assume that anything said concerning that might be hint enough for the night elves. Unlike those night elves who had allied themselves with the orcs, these had only contempt for outsiders . . . and thus were a threat to the Horde.

Brox rolled over as best as his bonds allowed. Another night and he would likely be dead, but not in the manner of his choosing. There would be no glorious battle, no epic song by which to remember him . . .

"Great spirits," he muttered. "Hear this unworthy one. Grant me one last struggle, one last cause. Let me be worthy . . ."

Brox stared at the sky, continuing to pray silently. But unlike the young priestess, he doubted that whatever powers watched over the world would listen to a lowly creature such as him.

His fate was in the night elves' hands.

What brought Malfurion into Suramar, he could not quite say. For three nights he had sat alone in his home, meditating on all Cenarius had told him, on all he himself had witnessed in the Emerald Dream. Three nights and no answers to his growing concerns. He had no doubts that the spell-work continued in Zin-Azshari and that the situation would only grow more desperate the longer no one acted.

But no one else even seemed to *notice* any problem.

Perhaps, Malfurion finally decided, he had journeyed to Suramar simply to find some other voice, some other mind, with which to discuss his inner dilemma. For that he had chosen to seek out Tyrande, though, not his twin. She gave more care to her thoughts, whereas Illidan had a tendency to leap into action regardless of whether or not he had hatched any plan.

Yes, Tyrande would be good to talk with . . . and just to see.

Yet, as he headed in the direction of the temple of Elune, a large contingent of riders suddenly bore down from the other direction. Edging to the side of the street, Malfurion watched as several soldiers in gray-green armor rushed by on their sleek, well-groomed panthers. Held high near the front of the party was a square banner of rich purple with a black avian form at the center.

The banner of Lord Kur'talos Ravencrest.

The elven commander rode at the forefront, his mount larger, sleeker, and clearly the dominant female of the pack. Ravencrest himself was tall, lanky, and quite regal. He rode as if nothing would deter him from his duty, whatever that might be. A billowing cloak of gold trailed behind him and his high, red-crested helm was marked by the very symbol of his name.

Avian also best described his features, long, narrow, his nose a downward beak. His tufted beard and stern eyes gave him an appearance of both wisdom and might. Outside of the Highborne, Ravencrest was considered one of those with the most influence with the queen, who in the past had often taken his counsel.

Malfurion cursed himself for not having thought of Ravencrest before, but now was not a good opportunity to speak with the noble. Ravencrest and his elite guard rode along as if on some mission of tremendous urgency, which made Malfurion immediately wonder if his fears about Zin-Azshari had already materialized. Yet, if that had been the case, he doubted that the rest of the city would have remained so calm; the forces at play near the capital surely presaged a disaster of monumental proportions, quickly affecting even Suramar.

As the riders vanished, Malfurion moved on. So many people clustered into one area made the young night elf feel a bit claustrophobic after his lengthy period in the forest. Still, Malfurion fought down the sensation, knowing that soon he would see Tyrande. As anxious as she made him feel of late, she also calmed his spirit more than anything else could, even his meditations.

He knew he would have to see his brother, too, but the idea did not appeal to him so much this night. It was Tyrande he wanted to see, with whom he wanted to spend some time. Illidan would still be there for him later.

Vaguely Malfurion noted a number of people crowded around something in the square, but his desire to see Tyrande made him quickly ignore the scene. He hoped that she would be readily available and that he would not have to go asking one acolyte after another. While the initiates of Elune were not bothered by friends and relatives desiring to speak with one of them, for some reason Malfurion felt more anxious about it than usual. It had little to do with his concerns about Zin-Azshari, either, and more to do with the odd discomfort he now felt whenever he was near his childhood friend.

As he entered the temple, a pair of guards surveyed him. Instead of robes, they wore gleaming, silver breast plates and kilts, the former marked by a crescent moon design at the center. Like all of Elune's initiates, they were females and well versed in the arts of defense and battle. Tyrande herself was a better archer than either Malfurion or Illidan. The peaceful teachings of the Mother Moon did not preclude her most loyal children learning to protect themselves.

"May we help you, brother?" the foremost guard asked politely. She and the other stood at attention, their spears ready to turn on him at a moment's warning.

"I come seeking the novice priestess, Tyrande. She and I are good friends. My name is—"

"Malfurion Stormrage," finished the second, nearer to his age. She smiled. "Tyrande shares novice chambers with myself and two others. I have seen you with her on occasion."

"Is it possible to speak with her?"

"If she is finished with her meditation, then she should be free this hour. I will have someone ask. You may wait in the Chamber of the Moon."

The Chamber of the Moon was the official title of the roofless center of the temple, where many of the great rituals took place. When not in use by the high priestess, the temple encouraged everyone to make use of its tranquil environment.

Malfurion felt the touch of the Mother Moon the moment he entered the rectangular chamber. A garden of night-blooming flowers bordered the room and in the center stood a small dais where the high priestess spoke. The circular stone path leading to the dais was a mosaic pattern outlining the yearly cycles of the moon. Malfurion had noted from his past few visits that no matter where the moon floated in the heavens, its soft light completely illuminated the chamber.

He strode to the center and sat on one of the stone benches used by initiates and faithful. Although eased much by his surroundings, Malfurion's patience quickly deteriorated as he waited for Tyrande. He also worried that she might be displeased by his sudden appearance. In the past, they had always met only after making prior arrangements. This was the first time that he had been so bold as to intrude without warning into her world.

"Malfurion . . ."

For a moment, all his concerns vanished as he looked up and saw Tyrande step into the moonlight. Her silver robes took on a mystical glow and in his eyes the Mother Moon could have looked no more glorious a sight. Tyrande's hair hung loose, draping her exquisite face and ending just above her decolletage. The nighttime illumination emphasized her eyes and when the novice priestess smiled, she herself seemed to light up the Chamber of the Moon.

As Tyrande walked toward him, Malfurion belatedly rose to meet her. He was certain that his cheeks flushed, but there was nothing he could do about it save hope that Tyrande did not notice.

"Is all well with you?" the novice asked with sudden concern. "Has something happened?"

"I'm fine. I hope I haven't intruded."

Her smile returned, more arresting than ever. "You could never intrude upon me, Malfurion. In fact, I'm very glad you've come. I wanted to see you, too."

If she had not noticed his darkening cheeks before, she certainly had to now. Nevertheless, Malfurion pressed on. "Tyrande, can we take a walk outside the temple?"

"If that makes you more comfortable, yes."

As they departed the chamber, he began, "You know how I said I've had some reoccurring dreams . . ."

"I remember."

"I spoke with Cenarius about them after you and Illidan departed and we took measures to try to understand why they keep repeating."

Her tone grew concerned. "And did you discover anything?"

Malfurion nodded but held his tongue as they passed the two sentries and exited the temple. Not until the pair had started down the outer steps did he continue.

"I've progressed, Tyrande. Progressed far more than either you or Illidan realized. Cenarius showed me a path into the world of the mind itself . . . the Emerald Dream, he called it. But it was more than that. Through it . . . through it I was able to see the real world as I never had before . . ."

Tyrande's gaze shifted to the small crowd near the center of the square. "And what did you see?"

He turned Tyrande to face him, needing her to understand utterly what he had discovered. "I saw Zin-Azshari . . . and the Well over which it looks."

Leaving nothing out, Malfurion described the scene and the unsettling sensations he had experienced. He described his attempts to understand the truth and how his dream self had been repulsed after attempting to see exactly what had transpired with the Highborne and the queen.

Tyrande stared wordlessly at him, clearly as stunned as he had been by his ominous discovery. Finding her voice, she asked, "The queen? Azshara? Can you be certain?"

"Not entirely. I never actually saw much inside, but I can't imagine how such madness could go on without her knowledge. True, Lord Xavius has great influence over her, but even she would never stand by blindly. I have to think that she knows the risks they take . . . but I don't think any of them understand how terrible those risks are! The Well . . . if you could have felt what I had when I walked the Emerald Dream, Tyrande, you would've feared as much as I did."

She put a hand on his arm in an attempt to comfort him. "I don't question you, Malfurion, but we need to know more! To claim that Azshara would put her subjects in danger . . . you have to tread lightly on this."

"I thought to approach Lord Ravencrest on the subject. He, too, has influence with her."

"That might be wise . . ." Again her eyes moved to the center of the square.

Malfurion almost said something, but instead followed her gaze, wondering what could constantly drag her attention from his revelations. Most of those who had gathered had wandered away, finally revealing to him what he had paid no mind to earlier.

A guarded cage . . . and in it some creature not at all like a night elf.

"What is that?" he asked with a growing frown.

"What I wanted to talk with *you* about, Malfurion. His name is Broxigar . . . and he's unlike any being I've ever heard or seen. I know your tale is important, but I want you to meet him now, as a favor for me."

As Tyrande led him over, Malfurion noticed the guards become alert. To his surprise, after a moment of staring at his companion, they suddenly fell to one knee in homage.

"Welcome again, sister," uttered one. "You honor us with your presence."

Tyrande was clearly embarrassed by such respect. "Please! Please rise!" When they had obeyed, she asked, "What news on him?"

"Lord Ravencrest has assumed control of the situation," answered another guard. "Even now he is out inspecting the location of the capture in search of more evidence and possible incursions, but when he returns, it's said that he intends to interrogate the prisoner personally. That means that by tomorrow, it's likely the creature will be transported to the cells of Black Rook Hold." Black Rook Hold was the walled domain of Lord Ravencrest, a veritable fortress.

That the guard was so free with his information surprised Malfurion until he realized how awed the soldier was by Tyrande. True, she was an initiate of

Elune, but something must have happened that made her of particular importance to these soldiers.

Tyrande looked perturbed by the revelation. "This interrogation . . . what will it entail?"

The guard could no longer look at her directly. "It entails whatever satisfies Lord Ravencrest, sister."

The priestess did not press further. Her hand, which had lightly rested on Malfurion's arm, momentarily squeezed tight.

"May we speak with him?"

"For only a moment, sister, but I must ask you to speak so that we can hear you. You understand."

"I do." Tyrande led Malfurion to the cell, where they both knelt.

Malfurion bit back a gasp of astonishment. Up close, the hulking figure inside truly amazed him. He had learned of many strange and unusual creatures during his time with Cenarius, but never had he been taught of such a being as this.

"Shaman . . ." it—*he*—muttered in a deep, rumbling . . . and *pained* voice.

Tyrande leaned closer, obviously concerned. "Broxigar . . . are you ill?"

"No, shaman . . . just remembering." He did not explain further.

"Broxigar, I've brought a friend with me. I'd like you to meet him. His name is Malfurion."

"If he's your friend, shaman, I'm honored."

Shifting nearer, Malfurion forced a smile. "Hello, Broxigar."

"Broxigar is an orc, Malfurion."

He nodded. "I've never heard of an orc before."

The chained figure snorted. "I know of night elves. You fought beside us against the Legion . . . but alliances fade in peace, it seems."

His words made no sense, yet they stirred within Malfurion a new anxiety. "How—how did you come to be here, Broxigar?"

"The shaman may call me Broxigar. To you . . . only Brox." He exhaled, then stared intently at Tyrande. "Shaman . . . you asked about me the last time and I wouldn't tell. I owe you, though. Now I tell you what I told these . . ." Brox made a derogatory gesture toward the nearby guards. ". . . and their masters, but you'll believe me no more than they did . . ."

The orc's tale began fantastic and grew even more so with each breath. He was careful not to speak of his people or where they lived, only that at the command of his Warchief, he and another had journeyed to the mountains to investigate an unsettling rumor. There they had found what the orc could only describe as a *hole* in the world . . . a hole that swallowed all matter as it moved relentlessly along.

It had swallowed Brox . . . and ripped his companion apart.

And Malfurion, listening, began to relive his own sense of dread. Each new revelation by the orc fueled that dread and more than once the night elf found himself thinking of the Well of Eternity and the power drawn from it by the Highborne. Certainly the magic of the Well could create such a horrific vortex . . .

But it could not be! Malfurion insisted to himself. *Surely, this could have nothing to do with Zin-Azshari! They aren't that mad!*

Are *they*?

But as Brox continued, as he spoke of the vortex and the things he had seen and heard as he tumbled through it, it became harder and harder for Malfurion to deny the possibility of *some* link. Worse, without knowing how it struck the night elf, the orc's expression mirrored what Malfurion had felt when his astral self had floated above the palace and the Well.

"A wrongness," the orc said. "A thing that should not be," he added at another stage. These and other descriptions struck Malfurion like well-honed daggers . . .

He did not even realize when Brox's tale ended, his mind swept up by the truth of it all. Tyrande had to squeeze his arm to regain his attention.

"Are you all right, Malfurion? You look as if chilled . . ."

"I—I'm fine." To Brox, he asked, "You told this—this story—to Lord Ravencrest?"

The orc looked uncertain, but the guard responded, "Aye, that's what he told, almost word for word!" The soldier gave a harsh bark of a laugh. "And Lord Ravencrest believed it as little as you now! Come the morrow, he'll pull the truth from this beast . . . and if he has friends nearby, they'll find us not so tempting a target, eh?"

So an invasion by orcs was all that Ravencrest suspected. Malfurion felt disappointed. He doubted that the elven commander would see the possible link between his encounter and Brox's tale. In fact, the more he thought of it, the more Malfurion doubted Ravencrest would believe him at all. Here Malfurion was, ready to tell the noble that their beloved queen might be involved in reckless spellwork with the potential to bring disaster upon her people. The young night elf barely believed it himself.

If only he had more proof.

The guard began shifting anxiously. "Sister . . . I'm afraid I must ask you and your companion to depart now. Our captain will be coming shortly. I really shouldn't have—"

"Quite all right. I understand."

As they started to rise, Brox moved to the front of the cell, one hand reaching toward Tyrande. "Shaman . . . one last blessing, if you could grant it."

"Of course . . ."

As she knelt again, Malfurion desperately pondered what he should do. Properly, any suspicions should have been reported to Lord Ravencrest, but somehow that seemed a futile act.

If only he could consult with Cenarius, but by then the orc might be— *Cenarius . . .*

Malfurion glanced at Tyrande and Brox, a fateful decision coming to mind.

Bidding the orc farewell, Tyrande rose again. Malfurion took her by the arm and the two thanked the guard for their time. The young priestess's expression grew perturbed as they left, but Malfurion said nothing, his own thoughts still racing.

"There must be something that can be done," she finally whispered.

"What do you mean?"

"Tomorrow they will take him to Black Rook Hold. Once in there, he—" Tyrande faltered. "I've every respect for Lord Ravencrest, but . . ."

Malfurion only nodded.

"I spoke with Mother Dejahna, the high priestess, but she says there is nothing we can do but pray for his spirit. She commended me for my sympathy, but suggested I let matters take their course."

"Let them take their course . . ." Malfurion muttered, staring ahead. He gritted his teeth. It had to be done now. There could be no turning back, not if his fears had any merit. "Turn here," he suddenly commanded, steering her down a side avenue. "We need to see Illidan."

"Illidan? But why?"

Taking a deep breath and thinking of the orc and the Well, Malfurion simply replied, "Because we're going to let matters take their own course . . . with our guidance, that is."

Xavius stood before the fiery sphere, staring into the gaping hole in its midst in rapt attention. Deep, deep within, the eyes of his god stared back and the two communed.

I have heard your pleas . . . he said to the counselor. *And know your dreams . . . a world cleansed of the impure, the imperfect. I would grant your desire, you the first among my faithful . . .*

His gaze never wavering, Xavius knelt. The other Highborne continued working their sorcery, trying to expand upon what they had created.

"You will come to us, then?" the night elf responded, artificial eyes flaring in anticipation. "You will come to our world and make it so?"

The way is not yet open . . . it must be strengthened . . . for it must be able to withstand my glorious entrance . . .

The counselor nodded his understanding. So magnificent, so powerful a force as the god would be too much for the night elves' feeble portal to accept. The god's sheer presence would rip it asunder. It had to be made larger, stronger, and more permanent.

That his supposed deity could not perform this task himself, Xavius did not question. He was too caught up in the wonder of his new master.

"What can be done?" he pleaded. Try as they might, the Highborne sorcerers had reached the limits of their knowledge and skills, Xavius included.

I will send one of my lesser host to guide you . . . he may pass through to your world . . . with effort . . . but you must prepare yourselves for his coming . . .

Almost leaping to his feet, the night elven lord commanded, "Let no one stumble in his efforts! We are to be blessed with the presence of one of his favored!"

The Highborne redoubled their efforts, the chamber crackling with raw, fearsome energy drawn directly from the Well. Outside, the skies roared furiously and anyone looking upon the great black lake itself would have turned their gaze away in fear.

The fireball within the pattern swelled, the gap in the center opening like a wide, savage mouth. What sounded like a million voices wailing filled the chamber, music to Xavius's ears.

But then one of the Highborne faltered. Fearing the worst, Xavius pushed himself into the circle, adding his own might and skill to the effort. He would not fail his god! He would not!

Yet, at first it seemed he and the rest would. The portal strained but did not grow. Xavius concentrated the full force of his determination upon it, finally forcing the gap wider.

And then . . . a wondrous, blinding light forced the assembled Highborne *back*. Despite their astonishment, though, they somehow kept up their efforts.

From deep within, an odd-looking form coalesced. At first it stood no more than a few inches tall, but as it swiftly moved toward them, it grew . . . and grew . . . and *grew* . . .

The strain took its toll on more of the spellcasters. Two collapsed, one barely breathing. The others teetered, yet, once again, under Xavius's manic control, they regained power over the portal.

Suddenly, the eerie cries of hounds shook them all. Only the counselor, with his eyes unnatural, saw what first emerged from the gateway.

The beasts were the size of horses and had low-set horns that curled down and forward. Their scaly hides were colored a deathly crimson accented by savage splatterings of black and on their backs fluttered a crest of wild, shaggy brown fur. They were lean but muscular hunters, each three-toed paw ending in sharp claws more than half a foot long. Each creature had back legs slightly shorter than the front, but Xavius had no doubt as to the beasts' speed and agility. Even their slightest movements suggested hunters well skilled in bringing down their prey.

Atop their backs thrust two long, whiplike, leathery tentacles that ended in tiny sucker mouths. The tentacles swayed back and forth, seeming to focus with eagerness on the assembled sorcerers.

The face most resembled some peculiar cross between a wolf and a reptile. From the long, savage jaws jutted scores of tall, sharp teeth. The eyes were narrow and completely white, but filled with a sinister cunning that implied these were no mere animals.

Then, from behind them stepped the towering figure of their master.

He wore body armor of molten steel and in his huge, gauntleted hand he wielded a whip that flashed lightning whenever used. His chest and shoulders, so much wider than the rest of his torso, dwarfed those of even the mightiest warrior. Wherever the armor did not hide his form, pure flame radiated from his scaled, fleshless, and *unearthly* body.

Set deep in the broad shoulders, the flaming visage peered down at the night elves. That it most resembled a brooding skull with huge, curled horns did nothing to dissuade the Highborne that here was a heavenly messenger sent to aid them in their dream of a perfect paradise.

"Know that I am the servant of your god . . ." he hissed, the flames that were his eyes flashing hot whenever he spoke. "Come to help you open the way for his host and his most *glorious* self!"

One of the beasts howled, but a snap of the whip sent lightning crackling over the creature, instantly silencing it.

"I am the Houndmaster . . ." the massive, skeletal knight continued, fiery gaze fixing most upon the kneeling counselor. "I am *Hakkar* . . ."

TEN

At last, Rhonin awoke.

He did so with reluctance, for throughout his magical slumber, his mind had been filled with dreams. Most of those dreams had revolved around Vereesa and the coming twins, but, unlike the sinister keep, these were happy visions of a life he once thought to have.

Waking up only served to remind him that he might not live to see his family.

Rhonin opened his eyes to one familiar, if not so welcome, sight. Krasus leaned over him, mild concern in his expression. That only aggravated the human, for, in his mind, it was the dragon mage's fault that he was here.

At first, Rhonin wondered why his eyesight seemed a bit dim, but then he realized that he looked at Krasus not in the light of the sun, but rather by a very full moon. The moon illuminated the glade with an intensity that was not at all natural.

Curiosity growing, he started to rise . . . only to have his body scream from stiffness.

"Slowly, Rhonin. You have slept more than a day. Your body needs a minute or two to join you in waking."

"Where—?" The young wizard peered around. "I remember this glade . . . being carried toward it . . ."

"We have been the guests of its master since our arrival. We are not in any danger, Rhonin, but I must tell you immediately that we are also unable to depart."

Sitting up, Rhonin gazed at the area. He sensed some presence around them, but nothing that hinted they were trapped here. Still, he had never known Krasus to invent stories.

"What happens if we try to leave?"

His companion pointed at the rows of flowers. "They will stop us."

"They? The plants?"

"You may trust me on this, Rhonin."

While a part of him was tempted to see exactly what the flowers would do, Rhonin chose not to take any chances. Krasus said that they were not in any danger so long as they stayed where they were. However, now that both of them were conscious, perhaps they could devise some manner of escape.

His stomach rumbled. Rhonin recalled that he had slept a day and more without eating.

Before he could comment, Krasus handed him a bowl of fruit and a jug of water. The human devoured the fruit quickly and, although it did not satiate his hunger completely, at least his stomach no longer disturbed him.

"Our host has not delivered any sustenance since early in the day. I expect him shortly . . . especially as he likely already knows that you are awake."

"He does?" Not something Rhonin liked hearing. Their captor sounded too much in control. "Who is he?"

Krasus suddenly looked uncomfortable. "His name is Cenarius. Do you recall it?"

Cenarius . . . it struck a chord, albeit barely. Cenarius. Something from his studies, but not directly tied to magic. The name made him think of stories, myths, of a—

A woodland *god?*

Rhonin's gaze narrowed. "We're the guests of a forest deity?"

"A demigod, to be exact . . . which still makes him a force that even my kind respect."

"Cenarius . . ."

"You speak of me and I am here!" chortled a voice from everywhere. "I bid you welcome, one called Rhonin!"

Coalescing from the moonlight itself, a huge, inhuman figure half elf, half stag stepped forward. He towered even over the tall, lanky Krasus. Rhonin stared openly in awe at the antlers, the bearded visage, and the unsettling body.

"You slept long, young one, so I doubt that the food brought earlier was sufficient for your hunger." He gestured behind them. "There is more for the two of you now."

Rhonin glanced over his shoulder. Where the emptied bowl of fruit had sat there now stood another, this one filled high. In addition, a thick piece of meat, cooked just to the wizard's liking if the aroma indicated anything, lay on a wooden platter next to the bowl. Rhonin had no doubt that the jug had also been refilled.

"I thank you," he began, trying not to be distracted by the nearby meal. "But what I really wanted to do was ask—"

"The time for questions will be coming. For now, I'd be remiss if you did not eat."

Krasus took Rhonin by the arm. With a nod of his head, the wizard joined his former mentor and the pair ate their fill. Rhonin hesitated at first when it came to the meat, not because he did not want it, but because it surprised him that a forest dweller such as Cenarius would sacrifice a creature under his care for two strangers.

The demigod read his curiosity. "Each animal, each being, serves many purposes. They are all part of the cycle of the forest. That includes the necessity of food. You are like the bear or wolf, both of whom hunt freely in my domain. Nothing is wasted here. Everything returns to feed new growth. The deer upon which you now feed will be reborn to serve its role again, its sacrifice forgotten to it."

Rhonin frowned, not quite following Cenarius's explanation, but knowing better than to ask him to clarify it. The demigod saw both intruders as predators and had fed them accordingly. That was that.

When they were finished, the wizard felt much improved. He opened his mouth with the intention of pressing on the matter of their captivity, but Cenarius spoke first.

"You should not be here."

Neither Rhonin nor Krasus knew how to answer.

Cenarius paced the glade. "I've conversed with the others, discussed you at length, learned what they know . . . and we all agree that you are not meant to be here. You are out of place, but in what way, we've yet to determine."

"Perhaps I can explain," Krasus interjected. He still looked weak to Rhonin, but not so much as when they had first materialized in this time.

"Perhaps you can," agreed the young wizard.

The dragon mage glanced at his companion. Rhonin saw no reason to hold back the truth. Cenarius appeared to be the first being that they had come across who might be of assistance to them.

But the story that Krasus passed on to their host was not the one the human expected.

"We come from a land across the sea . . . far across, but that is unimportant. What is of significance is the reason why we ended here . . ."

In Krasus's revised tale, it was he, not Nozdormu, who had uncovered the rift. The dragon mage described it not as a tear in time, but as an anomaly that had upset the fabric of reality, potentially creating greater and greater catastrophe. He had summoned the one other spellcaster he trusted—Rhonin—and the pair had traveled to where Krasus had sensed the trouble.

"We journeyed to a chain of stark peaks in the bitter north of our land, there being where I sensed it strongest. We came across it and the monstrous things it spewed out at random. The wrongness of it struck us both hard, but when we sought to investigate closer . . . it moved, enveloping us. We were cast out of our land—"

"And into the domain of the night elves," the demigod completed.

"Yes," Krasus said with a nod. Rhonin added nothing and hoped his expression did not betray his companion. In addition to Krasus's omissions concerning their true origins, the wizard's former mentor left out one other item of possible interest to Cenarius.

He had made no mention of being a dragon.

Backing up a step, the woodland deity eyed both figures. Rhonin could not read his expression. Did he believe Krasus's altered story or did he suspect that his "guest" had not been completely forthcoming with him?

"This bears immediate discussion with the others," Cenarius finally declared, staring off into the distance. His gaze shifted back down to Rhonin and Krasus. "Your needs will be dealt with during my absence . . . and then we shall speak again."

Before either could say anything, the lord of the forest melted into moonlight, leaving them once more alone.

"That was futile," Rhonin growled.

"Perhaps. But I would like to know who these others are."

"More demigods like himself? Seems the most likely. Why didn't you tell him about your—"

The dragon mage gave him such a sharp glare that Rhonin faltered. In a much quieter tone, Krasus replied, "I am a dragon without strength, my young friend. You have no idea what that feels like. No matter who Cenarius is, I wish that to remain secret until I understand why I cannot recover."

"And the . . . rest of the story?"

Krasus looked away. "Rhonin . . . I mentioned to you that we might be in the past."

"I understand that."

"My memories are . . . are as scattered as my strength is depleted. I do not know why. However, one thing I have been able to recall based on what was told me during your induced slumber. I know now *when* we are."

Spirits rising, Rhonin blurted, "But that's good! It gives us an anchor of sorts! Now we can determine who best—"

"Please let me finish." Krasus's dour expression did not bode well. "There is a very good reason why I altered our story as much as I could. I suspected that Cenarius knew some of what was going on, especially about the anomaly. What I could not tell him are my suspicions as to what it might *presage*."

The quieter and darker the elder mage's voice dropped, the more Rhonin grew concerned. "What?"

"I fear we have arrived just prior to the first coming of the *Burning Legion*."

He could have said nothing more horrifying to Rhonin. Having lived—and nearly died more than once—battling the demonic horde and its allies, the young wizard still suffered monstrous nightmares. Only Vereesa understood the extent of those nightmares, she having fought through more than a few herself. It had taken both their growing love and the coming children to heal their hearts and souls and that after several months.

And now Rhonin had been thrust back into the nightmares.

Jumping to his feet, he said, "Then we've got to tell Cenarius, tell everyone we can! They'll—"

"They must not know . . . I fear it may already be too late to preserve matters as they once were." Also rising, Krasus stared down his long nose at his former pupil. "Rhonin . . . as it originally happened, the Legion was defeated after a terrible, bloody war, the precursor of things to come in our own time."

"Yes, of course, but—"

Evidently forgetting his own concerns about the possibility of Cenarius listening in, Krasus seized Rhonin by the shoulders. Despite the elder mage's weakness, his long fingers dug painfully into the human's flesh. "You still do not understand! Rhonin, by coming here, by simply being here . . . we may have altered that history! We may now be responsible for the Burning Legion this time becoming the *victor* in this first struggle . . . and that would mean not only the death of many innocents here, but the erasing of our own *time*."

It had taken some convincing to make Illidan a part of Malfurion's sudden and very rash plan. Malfurion had little doubt that the deciding factor was not anything he had said . . . but rather Tyrande's own impassioned plea. Under her gaze, even Illidan had melted, readily agreeing to assist even though he clearly did not care for the prisoner one bit. Malfurion knew that something had happened between his brother and the orc, something that Tyrande had also been involved in, and she used that shared experience to bring Illidan to their side.

Now they had to succeed.

The four guards stood alert, each facing a different point on the compass. The sun was only minutes from rising and the square was empty of all save the soldiers and their charge. With most of the other night elves asleep, it was the perfect time to strike.

"I'll deal with the sentries," Illidan suggested, his left hand already balled into a fist.

Malfurion quickly took over. He did not question his brother's abilities, but he also wished no harm to come to the guards, who were only performing their duties. "No. I said I would take care of them. Give me a moment."

Shutting his eyes, he relaxed himself as Cenarius had shown him. Malfurion receded from the world, but at the same time, he saw it more clearly, more sharply. He knew exactly what he had to do.

At his suggestion to them, the necessary elements of nature joined to assist his needs. A cool, tender wind caressed the face of each guard with the gentleness of a loved one. With the wind came the tranquil scents of the flowers surrounding Suramar and the soothing call of a nearby night bird. The calmingly seductive combination enveloped each sentry, drawing them without their noticing into a peaceful, pleasant, and very deep lethargy that left them oblivious to the waking world.

Satisfied that all four were under his spell, Malfurion blinked, then whispered, "Come . . ."

Illidan hesitated, only following when Tyrande stepped out into the open after his brother. The three of them slowly made their way toward the cage and the soldiers. Despite the certainty that his spell held, Malfurion still half expected the four sentries to look their way at any moment. Yet even when he and his companions stood only a few yards away, the soldiers remained ignorant of their presence.

"It worked . . ." murmured Tyrande in wonder.

Stopping in front of the foremost guard, Illidan waved his hand before the watchful eyes—all to no effect. "A nice trick, brother, but for how long?"

"I don't know. That's why we must hurry."

Tyrande knelt down by the cage, peering inside. "I think Broxigar is also caught by your spell, Malfurion."

Sure enough, the huge orc lay slumped against the back of his prison, his disinterested gaze looking past Tyrande. He made no move even when she quietly called out his name.

After a moment's consideration, Malfurion suggested, "Touch him softly on the arm and try his name again. Make certain that he sees you immediately so that you can signal for silence."

Illidan frowned. "He's sure to yell."

"The spell will hold, Illidan, but you must be ready to do your part when the time comes."

"*I'm* not the one who'll risk us," Malfurion's brother said with a sniff.

"Be still, both of you . . ." Reaching in, Tyrande cautiously touched the orc on his upper arm, at the same time calling out his name again.

Brox started. His eyes widened and his mouth opened in what would certainly be a very deafening cry.

But just as quickly he clamped his mouth shut, the only sound managing to escape being a slight grunt. The orc blinked several times, as if uncertain that the sight before him could possibly be real. Tyrande touched his hand, then, with a nod to the orc, looked into Brox's eyes again.

Looking to his brother, Malfurion muttered, "Now! Hurry!"

Illidan reached down, at the same time whispering under his breath. As he grasped the bars, his hands flared a bright yellow and the cage itself suddenly became framed in red energy. A slight hum arose.

Malfurion glanced anxiously at the sentries, but even this wondrous display passed unnoticed by them. He exhaled in relief, then watched as Illidan worked.

There were advantages to night elven sorcery and his brother had learned well how to wield it. The astonishing yellow glow surrounding his hands spread to the cage, rapidly enveloping the red. Sweat dripped from Illidan's forehead as he pressed his spell, but he did not falter in the least.

At last, Illidan released his hold and fell back. Malfurion caught his brother before the latter could stumble into one of the sentries. Illidan's hand continued to glow for a few seconds more. "You can open the cell now, Tyrande . . ."

Releasing Brox, she touched the door of the cage—which then immediately swung open almost of its own accord.

"The chains," Malfurion reminded Illidan.

"Of course, brother. I've not forgotten."

Squatting, Illidan reached for the orc's manacles. Brox, however, did not respond at first, eyes narrowing warily at the sight of the male night elf. Tyrande had to take his hands and guide them to her companion.

With more muttered words, Malfurion's brother touched each of the bonds at the lock. The manacles snapped open like small mouths eagerly waiting to be fed.

"No trouble whatsoever," Illidan remarked with an extremely pleased smile.

The orc emerged slowly, his body stiff due to the cramped conditions of his cell. He curtly nodded his gratitude to Illidan, but looked to Tyrande for guidance.

"Broxigar, listen carefully. I want you to go with Malfurion. He'll take you to a safe place. I'll see you there later."

This had been some cause of argument between Tyrande and Malfurion, the former wanting to see the orc to safety herself. Malfurion—with Illidan's more-than-willing assistance—had finally convinced her that there would be trouble enough when Brox was discovered missing without Tyrande, who had been seen caring for him, also vanishing. It would not be hard for the Moon Guard to add the facts together.

"They'll make the connection quickly," Malfurion had insisted. "You were the only one to give him aid. That's why you need to stay here. They're less likely to think of me and even if they do, it's doubtful that they'll blame you, then. You are an initiate of Elune. That you know me is no crime with which they can label you."

Although Tyrande had given in, she still did not like Malfurion taking on all the responsibility himself. True, he had been the one who had come up with this startling course of action, but it was she who had instigated everything in the first place simply by introducing Malfurion to the imprisoned orc.

Now the young priestess also asked the orc to have faith in one he did not know well. Brox studied Malfurion, then glared again at Illidan. "That one be with?"

Illidan curled his lip. "I just saved your hide, beast—"

"Enough, Illidan! He's grateful!" To Brox, Tyrande answered, "Only Malfurion. He'll take you to a place where no one will be able to find you! Please! You can trust me!"

Taking her hand in his huge fists, the brutish figure fell to one knee. "I trust in you, shaman."

At that moment, Malfurion noticed one of the guards beginning to fidget.

"It's starting to wear away!" he hissed. "Illidan! Take Tyrande and leave! Brox! Come!"

With astonishing speed and grace, the massive orc leapt to his feet and followed after the night elf. Malfurion did not look behind him, praying that his druidic spell would hold long enough. For Tyrande and his brother he had little fear. Their destination was Illidan's quarters, only a short distance away. No one would suspect either of any duplicity.

For Malfurion and Brox, however, the matter was different. No one would mistake the orc for anything but what he was. The two had to escape the city as fast as possible.

But as they left the square and entered the winding streets of Suramar, the sound that Malfurion had feared most arose.

One of the guards had finally awakened. His shouts were quickly multiplied by those of his companions and, mere seconds later, the blare of a horn filled the air.

"This way!" he urged the orc. "I've mounts awaiting us!"

In truth, Malfurion need not have said anything, for the orc, despite his sturdy build, ran with at least as much swiftness as his rescuer. Had they been out in the wilderness, the night elf suspected Brox would have even outrun him.

Everywhere, horns sounded and voices cried out. Suramar had sprung to life . . . much too soon for Malfurion's taste.

At last, the night elf spotted the corner for which he had been waiting. "Here! They're just around here!"

But as they turned into the side street, Brox suddenly stumbled to a halt, the fearsome orc staring wide-eyed at the mounts Malfurion had secured.

The huge panthers were black, sinewy shadows. They snarled and hissed upon first sighting the newcomers, then calmed as Malfurion approached them. He patted each on the flank.

Brox shook his head. "We ride *these*?"

"Of course! Now hurry!"

The orc hesitated, but then nearby shouts urged him forward. Brox took the reins given to him and watched as Malfurion showed how to mount up.

It took the former captive three tries to climb atop the huge cat, then another minute to learn how to sit. Malfurion kept glancing behind them, fearful that at any moment the soldiers—or, worse, the Moon Guard—would arrive. He had not given any consideration to the fact that Brox might not know how to ride a night saber. What other beast could the orc have expected?

Adjusting his position one last time, Brox reluctantly nodded. Taking a deep breath, Malfurion urged his mount onward, Brox following as best he could.

In the space of but a few minutes, the night elf had forever changed his future. Such an audacious act might only serve to condemn him to Black Rook

Hold, but Malfurion knew that he could not let this chance slip away. Somehow, Brox was linked to the disturbing work of the Highborne . . . and come what may, Malfurion had to find out how.

He had the horrible feeling that the fate of all Kalimdor hinged upon it.

Varo'then had little desire to face Lord Xavius, but that choice was not his. He had been commanded to appear before the counselor the moment his party arrived and commands given by Lord Xavius were to be obeyed with as much urgency as if they had been made by Queen Azshara herself . . . perhaps even more so.

The counselor would not like the captain's report. How to explain that they had somehow been led astray, then attacked by a forest? Varo'then hoped to use the late, unlamented Koltharius as a scapegoat, but doubted that his lord would accept such a pathetic offering. Varo'then had been in charge and to Lord Xavius that would be all that mattered.

He did not have to ask where the counselor could be found, for when was his master anywhere but the chamber where the spellwork took place? In truth, Captain Varo'then preferred blades to sorcery and the chamber was not his favorite place. True, he also wielded a bit of power himself, but what Lord Xavius and the queen had in mind overwhelmed even him.

The guards came to attention as he approached, but although they reacted with the respect he was due, something in their manner seemed different . . . almost unsettling.

Almost as if they knew exactly what awaited him better than he did.

The door swung open before him. Eyes down in respect, Captain Varo'then entered the Highborne sanctum—and a nightmarish beast filled his view.

"By Elune!" Acting instinctively, he drew his curved blade. The hellish creature howled, two menacing tentacles above its muscled form groping eagerly toward him. The captain doubted his chances against such a monstrosity, but he would fight it as best he could.

But then a hissing voice that chilled Varo'then's bones to the marrow uttered something in a language unknown. A fearsome whip snapped at the beast's hunched back.

Cringing, the demonic hound retreated, leaving Varo'then to gape at the one who had summoned it away.

"His name is Hakkar," Lord Xavius remarked pleasantly, appearing from the side. "The felbeasts are entirely under his control. The great one has sent him to help open the way . . . ."

" 'G-great one,' my lord?"

To the captain's dismay, the counselor placed an almost fatherly arm around his shoulder, guiding Varo'then to the fiery sphere over the pattern. Something about the sphere looked different, giving the night elf the horrible sensation that if he stood close enough, it would devour him body and soul.

"It's all right, my good captain. Nothing to fear . . ."

He was going to be punished for his failure. If so, at least Varo'then would make a declaration of his mistakes beforehand, so that he would not lose more face. "My Lord Xavius, the captives were lost! The forest turned against us—"

But the counselor only smiled. "You will be given the opportunity to redeem yourself in good time, captain. First, you must understand the glorious truth . . ."

"My lord, I don't—"

He got no further, his eyes snared.

"You understand now," Xavius remarked, his false eyes narrowed in satisfaction.

Varo'then sensed the god, sensed how the wondrous presence peeled away every layer that was the captain. The god within the fiery sphere looked into the deepest depths of Varo'then . . . and radiated a pleasure with what he found there.

You, too, will serve me well . . .

And Varo'then fell to one knee, honoring the one who honored him so.

"He will be coming to us soon, captain," Lord Xavius explained as the soldier rose. "But so magnificent is he that the way must be strengthened in order to accept his overwhelming presence! He has sent this noble guardian to open the path for others of his host, others who will in turn guide our efforts in strengthening the vortex . . . and bringing about the fruition of all of our dreams!"

Varo'then nodded, feeling both pleased and ashamed. "My lord, my failure to capture those strangers I found near the site of the disruption—"

He was interrupted by the hissing voice of Hakkar "Your failure isss moot. They will be taken . . . the great one isss mossst interested in what Lord Xavius hasss told him about this—*disssruption*—and their posssible connection to it!"

"But how will you find them? That forest is the realm of the demigod, Cenarius! I'm sure it was him!"

"Cenarius is only a woodland deity," the counselor reminded him. "We have behind us now much, much more than that."

Turning from the night elves, Hakkar snapped his whip at an open area before him. As the sinewy weapon cracked, a greenish flash of lightning struck the stone floor.

In the lightning's wake, the area hit glowed brightly. The emerald flare increased rapidly in size and as it did, it began to coalesce.

The two felbeasts howled, their fearsome tentacles straining, but Hakkar kept them back.

A four-legged shape formed, growing larger and wider. It quickly took on an aspect already familiar to Captain Varo'then, which it verified with a bloodcurdling howl of its own.

The new hound shook itself once, then joined the others. As the mesmerized night elves watched, Hakkar repeated the step with his whip, summoning a fourth monstrous beast that lined up with the rest.

He then spun the lash around and around, creating a circular pattern that flared brighter and brighter until it created a *hole* in the air before him, a hole as tall as the fearsome figure and twice as wide.

Hakkar barked out a command in some dark tongue.

The hellish felbeasts leapt through the hole, vanishing. As the last disappeared, the hole itself dissipated.

"They know what they ssseek," Hakkar informed his stunned companions. "And they will find what they ssseek . . ." The fiery being wound up the whip, his dark gaze turning to the night elves' spellwork. "And now we shall begin our own tasssk . . ."

ELEVEN

It had taken Krasus an entire day to realize that he and Rhonin were being observed.

It had taken him a half day more to come to the conclusion that the observer had nothing to do with Cenarius.

Who it was with the ability to keep their presence hidden from the powerful demigod, the dragon mage could not say. One of Cenarius's counterparts? Not likely. The lord of the forest would surely be too familiar with their tricks or any of the servants they might send. The night elves? Krasus dismissed that possibility immediately, as he did the chance that any other mortal race could be responsible for the secretive watcher.

That left him with only one logical conclusion . . . that the one who spied upon Cenarius and his two "guests" was of Krasus's own people.

In his own time, the dragons sent out observers to keep track of those with the potential to change the world, either for good or ill. Humans, orcs—*every* race—had its spies. The dragons considered it a necessary evil; left to their own devices, the younger races had a tendency to create disaster. Even in this period of the past, there would be spies of some sort. He had no doubt that some kept a wary eye on Zin-Azshari . . . but, as was typical of Krasus's kind, they would do nothing until absolutely certain that catastrophe was imminent.

In this case, by then it would be too late.

From Cenarius he had kept his secrets secure, but from one of his own, even those of the past, Krasus decided he needed to tell what he knew. If anyone could avert the potential ruin his and Rhonin's presence might have already caused, it was the dragons . . . but only if they would listen.

He waited until the human had gone to sleep and the chances of Cenarius returning became remote. The needs of Krasus and Rhonin were attended to by silent, invisible spirits of the forest. Food materialized at appointed times and the refuse vanished once the pair were finished eating. Other matters of nature were handled in similar fashion. This allowed Cenarius to continue his mysterious discussions with his counterparts—which, with deities, could take days, weeks, months, or even longer—without worrying that the two would starve to death in his absence.

No matter what the cycle of the moon, the glade remained almost as lit as day. Once satisfied that Rhonin slept deeply enough, Krasus quietly rose and headed toward the barrier of flowers.

Even at night, they immediately fixed on him. Moving as close as he could without stirring them, the dragon mage peered out at the forest beyond, studying the dark trees. He knew better than any the secrets of stealth used by his kind, knew them better than even a demigod could. What Cenarius might have missed, Krasus would find.

At first, the trees all looked the same. He studied each in turn, then did so a second time, still with no results. His body cried out for rest, but Krasus refused to let his unnatural weakness take control. If he gave in once, he feared he would never recover.

His gaze suddenly stopped on a towering oak with a particularly thick trunk.

Eyeing it sharply, the weary spellcaster mentally shielded his thoughts, then focused on the tree.

I know you . . . I know what you are, watcher . . .

Nothing happened. No reply came. Briefly Krasus wondered if he had erred, but centuries of experience insisted otherwise.

He tried again. *I know you . . . cloaked as part of the tree, you watch us and the lord of the forest. You wonder who we are, why we are here.*

Krasus felt a presence stir, however slightly. The observer was uncomfortable with this sudden intrusion in his thoughts, and not yet willing to declare himself.

There is much that I can tell you that I could not tell the lord of the forest . . . but I would speak with more than the trunk of a tree . . .

You risk us both, a somewhat arrogant mind finally responded. *The demigod could be watching us in turn . . .*

The dragon mage hid his pleasure at garnering an answer. *You know as well as I that he is not here . . . and you can cloak us from the knowledge of any other onlookers . . .*

For a moment, nothing happened. Krasus wondered if he had pushed too far . . .

Part of the trunk suddenly tore away, assuming as it separated a humanoid figure of ridged bark. As the tall shape approached, the bark faded away, transforming to long, flowing garments and a slim face shadowed to obscurity by a spell with which Krasus himself was long familiar.

In robes the color of the tree, the all-but-faceless figure paused on the outer perimeter of the magical glade. Hidden eyes surveyed Krasus from head to foot and although the imprisoned mage could not read any expression, he was certain of the other's frustration.

"Who are you?" the watcher quietly asked.

"A kindred spirit, you might say."

This was met with some disbelief. "You do not know at all what you suggest . . ."

"I know exactly what I suggest," Krasus returned strongly. "I know it as well as I do that she who is called Alexstrasza is the Queen of Life, he who is called Nozdormu is Time itself, Ysera is She of the Dreaming, and Malygos is Magic incarnate . . ."

The figure digested the names, then, almost as an afterthought, commented, "You did not mention one."

Biting back a gasp, Krasus nodded. "And Neltharion is the earth and rock itself, the Warder of the land."

"Such names are known by few outside my kind, but they *are* known by a few. By what name might I know you, that I should think you kindred?"

"I am known as . . . Korialstrasz."

The other leaned back. "I could not fail to know that name, not when it belongs to a consort of the Queen of Life, but something is amiss. I have observed everything since your capture and you act like none of my kind. Cenarius is powerful, very much so, but he should not so readily hold you as his hostage, not the one called Korialstrasz . . ."

"I have been injured badly." Krasus waved that away. "Time is of the essence! I must reach Alexstrasza and tell her what I know! Can you take me to her?"

"Just like that? You do have the arrogance of a dragon! Why should I risk for all dragons the umbrage of the woodland deity on your questionable identity alone? He will know from now on that he is observed and will act accordingly."

"Because the potential threat to the world—our world—is more important than an insult to the dignity of a demigod." Taking a deep breath, the dragon mage added, "And if you only will permit, I will reveal to you what I mean . . ."

"I do not know if I trust you," the darkened watcher said, cocking his head to one side. "But in your condition, I do not think I have much to fear from you, either. If you know how . . . then show me what colors your words with such anxiety."

Krasus refrained from any retort, despite his growing dislike for this other dragon. "If you are ready . . ."

"Do it."

Their minds touched . . . and Krasus unveiled the truth.

Under the rush of intense images, the other dragon stumbled back. The shadow spell around his face momentarily lost cohesion, revealing a peculiar reptilian and elven combination locked in an expression of total disbelief.

But the shadows returned as quickly as they had dissipated. Still obviously digesting what he had been shown, the watcher nonetheless recovered some of his composure. "This is all impossible . . ."

"Probable, I would say."

"These are pure figments of your creation!"

"Would that they were," Krasus remarked sadly. "You see now why I must speak with our queen?"

His counterpart shook his head. "What you are asking is—"

The two dragons froze, both sensing simultaneously the nearing presence of an overwhelming force.

Cenarius. The demigod had made an unexpected return.

Immediately the watcher began to retreat. Krasus, fearful that his one chance might be lost, reached out. "No. You cannot afford to ignore this! I must see Alexstrasza!"

His arm passed over the flowers. The blossoms reacted, immediately opening wide and spraying him with their magical dust.

Krasus's world swam. He teetered forward, falling into their midst.

Strong arms suddenly caught him. He heard a quiet hiss of anxiety and knew that the other dragon had taken hold of him.

"I am a fool for doing thisss!" the other gasped.

Krasus gave silent thanks for the watcher's decision, until a sudden realization struck the collapsing mage. He tried to say something, but his mouth would not work.

And as he blacked out, his last thoughts were no longer of gratitude to the other dragon for finally taking him with him . . . but rather fury with himself for not having had the chance to make certain that *Rhonin* would be included in the escape.

The panthers darted through the thick forest, Brox's racing with such ferocity that it was all the hapless orc could do to keep seated. Although he was used to riding the huge wolves raised by his own people, the cat's movements differed in subtle ways that constantly left the orc anxious.

Just within sight ahead, the shadowed form of Malfurion bent low over his own beast, urging it this direction or that. Brox was glad that his rescuer had a path in mind, but he hoped that the arduous journey would not take too much longer.

Soon it would be sunrise. The orc had thought this a bad thing, for then they would be visible from a greater distance, but Malfurion had indicated that the coming of day was to their benefit. If the Moon Guard pursued them, the night elven sorcerers' powers would be weaker once the darkness faded.

Of course, there would still be soldiers with which to deal.

Behind him, Brox heard the growing sounds of pursuit. Horns, distant shouts, the occasional snarl of another panther. He had assumed that Malfurion had more of a plan than simply hoping to outpace the other riders, but apparently that was not the case. His rescuer was no warrior, simply a soul who had sought to do the right thing.

The black of night began to give way to gray, but a murky, foggy gray—a morning mist. The orc welcomed the unexpected mist, however temporary it would be, but hoped that his mount would not lose Malfurion's in it.

Vague shapes appeared and disappeared around him. Now and then, Brox thought he made out movement. His hand ached for his trusted ax, still in the custody of the night elves. Malfurion had provided him with no weapon, perhaps a wary precaution on the former's part.

The horns sounded again, this time much closer. The veteran warrior snarled.

Malfurion vanished into the fog. Brox straightened, trying to make out his companion and fearing that his own animal would now run off in an entirely different direction.

The panther suddenly twisted as it adjusted its path to avoid a massive rock. The orc, caught unaware, lost his balance.

With a grunt of dismay, Brox slipped off the fleet cat, tumbling onto the hard, uneven ground and rolling headlong into a thick bush.

Trained reflexes took command. Brox shifted into a crouch, coming up ready to remount. Unfortunately, his cat, oblivious to his misfortune, continued on, disappearing into the mist.

And the sounds of pursuit grew louder yet.

Immediately Brox sought out something, *anything,* that he could use as a weapon. He picked up a fallen branch, only to have it crumble in his beefy hands. The only rocks were either too small to be of use or so huge as to be unmanageable.

Something large rustled the shrubbery to his left.

The orc braced himself. If a soldier, he had a fair chance. If one of the Moon Guard, the odds were distinctly stacked against Brox, but he would go down fighting.

A huge, panting, four-legged form burst from the fogenshrouded forest.

Shock nearly did Brox in, for what leapt at him was no panther. It howled something like a wolf or dog, but only vaguely resembled either. At the shoulder, it stood about as tall as him and from its back stretched two foul, leathery tentacles. The mouth was filled with row upon row of savage fangs. Thick, greenish saliva dripped from its huge, hungry maw.

Monstrous memories filled his thoughts. He had seen such horrors, even if he himself had never fought one. They had run ahead of the other demons, pack upon pack of slavering, sinister monsters.

Felbeasts . . . the forerunners of the *Burning Legion.*

Brox awoke from his renewed nightmares just before the felbeast had him. He threw himself forward, under the huge creature. The felbeast tried to snag him with its claws, but momentum worked against it. The massive beast stumbled to a quick halt and looked back at its elusive prey.

The orc struck it on the nose with his fist.

For most races, such an assault would likely result in nothing save possibly the loss of the hand, but Brox was not only an orc, he was a swift and power-ful one. Not only did he strike before the felbeast could react, but he did so with the full fury and might of the strongest of his kind.

The blow broke the demonic hound's nose. The beast stumbled and a bloodcurdling whine escaped it. Thick, dark green fluid dripped from its wound.

His hand pounding with pain, Brox kept his gaze on his adversary's own. One did not let any animal, especially one so hellish as this, see any sign of retreat or fear. Only by facing it did the orc have any chance, however minute, of survival.

Then, from out of the fog in which it had disappeared, Brox's mount came charging. The cat's cry made the felbeast turn, all interest in the orc for-gotten. The two behemoths collided in a fury of claws and teeth.

Knowing that he could do nothing for the panther, Brox started to back away. However, he had managed only a few steps when the low, steady sound of heavy breathing from behind him filled his ears. With slow, very cautious movements, the orc glanced over his shoulder.

A short distance away, a second felbeast poised itself to leap on Brox.

With no other option, the frustrated warrior finally ran.

The second demon gave chase, howling as it threw itself toward its quarry. The two combatants ignored it, caught up in their own struggle. Already the panther had suffered two savage wounds on its torso. Brox gave silent thanks to the creature for even this momentary rescue, then concerned himself with trying to elude his other pursuer in the enshrouded forest.

Wherever the path narrowed most, the orc pushed himself through. The much larger felbeast had to go around the natural obstacles or, if it could, crash through them, allowing Brox to remain just out of reach. He despised the fact that he had to keep running, but without a weapon Brox knew his chances of defeating the monster were nonexistent.

A short distance away, the mournful call of a dying animal informed Brox that the panther had lost the battle and soon there would be *two* felbeasts out for the orc's blood.

Distracted by the cat's death cry, Brox did not watch his footing well enough. Suddenly a tree root seemed to rise just enough to catch his foot. He managed to keep from falling, but his lack of true balance sent him spinning wildly to the side. He grasped at a slim, leafless tree only a head taller than himself, but the entire trunk broke away in his grip, sending him colliding with a much larger, sturdier one.

Head aching, Brox could barely focus on the oncoming behemoth. The small tree still in his hand, he swung it around and jabbed with it like a lance.

The demon hound swatted at the makeshift weapon, tearing away the top third and leaving jagged splinters on the end. Eyes still blurry, the orc held tight to what remained, then charged the monster.

The damage done by the felbeast gave the makeshift lance a deadliness it had not had prior. Shoving with all his might, Brox buried the sharp, fragmented end deep into the gaping jaws.

With a muffled howl of agony, the demon tried to fall back, but Brox advanced, his entire body straining as he pushed the lance deeper yet.

One of the tentacles reached for him. The orc released one hand, snagged the oncoming threat, and pulled as hard as he could.

With a moist, tearing sound, the tentacle came free.

Now much splattered with its own foul fluids, the felbeast's front legs collapsed. Brox did not relinquish his hold on the tree, adjusting his position to match his adversary's increasingly desperate movements.

The rear legs crumpled. Tail twitching frantically, the fearsome beast pawed at the obstruction in its gullet. It finally managed to snap Brox's weapon in two, but the front portion remained lodged.

Aware that the felbeast might still recover, the orc searched frantically for something to replace his lost lance.

Instead, he found himself facing his first foe again.

The other felbeast had scars across its body and, in addition to the nose wound Brox had given it earlier, a chunk of flesh had been torn from the right shoulder. Still, despite its worsened condition, the beast looked more than healthy enough to finish off the exhausted orc.

Seizing a thick, broken branch, Brox brandished it like a sword. But he knew that his luck had come to an end. The limb was hardly strong enough to ward away the huge monstrosity.

Crouching, the felbeast tensed—

But as it jumped, the forest itself came alive in defense of Brox. The wild grass and weeds under the demonic creature sprouted madly, shooting up with such astonishing swiftness that they caught the felbeast just after it left the earth.

Limbs hopelessly entangled, the horrific creature snarled and snapped at the grass. Its twin tentacles stretched down, trying to touch the animated plant life that held it from its prey.

"Brox!"

Malfurion rode toward the orc, looking as weary as Brox felt. The night elf pulled up next to him and reached a hand down.

"I owe you again," rumbled the veteran warrior.

"You owe me nothing." Malfurion glanced at the trapped felbeast. "Especially since it looks as if that won't hold him for very long!"

True enough, wherever the macabre tentacles touched the grass and weeds, the plants withered. One front paw had already been freed and even as the felbeast worked on liberating the rest, it strained to reach Brox and the night elf.

"Magic . . ." muttered Brox, recalling similar sights. "It's devouring the magic . . ."

Face grim, Malfurion helped his companion aboard. The panther grunted, but did not otherwise protest the added weight. "Then, we'd better leave quickly."

A horn sounded, this time so near that Brox almost expected to see the trumpeter. The pursuit from Suramar had almost caught up.

Suddenly, Malfurion hesitated. "They'll ride right into that beast! If any of them are Moon Guard—"

"Magic can still slay a felbeast if there's enough of it, night elf . . . but if you wish to stay and fight the creature with them, I will stand at your side."

That doing so would mean either his death or recapture, Brox did not add. He would not abandon Malfurion, who had already rescued him twice.

The morning fog had already begun to dissipate and vague figures could already be seen in the distance. Grip tightening on the reins, Malfurion abruptly turned the panther *away* from the felbeasts and the approaching riders. He said nothing to Brox, instead simply urging his mount to as quick a pace as it could set and leaving both threats behind.

Behind them, the demon freed another limb, its attention already seized by growing sounds heralding new prey . . .

Something stirred Rhonin from his slumber, something that made him very uneasy.

He made no immediate motion, instead his eyelids opening just enough to let him see a bit of the surrounding area. Glimpses of daylight enabled the wizard to make out the surrounding trees, the ominous line of flower sentinels, and the grass upon which he lay.

What Rhonin could not make out was any sign of Krasus.

He sat up, searching for the dragon mage. Surely Krasus had to be somewhere in the glade.

But after a thorough survey of the region, Krasus's disappearance could no longer be denied.

Wary, the wizard rose and went to the edge of the glade. The flowers turned to face him, each bloom opening wide. Rhonin was tempted to see how powerful they were, but suspected that a demigod would hardly place them here if they could not readily deal with a mere mortal.

Eyeing the woods, Rhonin quietly called, "Krasus?"

Nothing.

Staring at the trees just beyond his prison, the wizard frowned. Something did not look the same, but he could not say exactly what.

He stepped back, trying to think . . . and suddenly noticed that he was in shadow.

"Where is the other one?" Cenarius demanded, no hint of kindliness in his tone. Although clear, the sky suddenly rumbled and a harsh wind came out of nowhere to swat the human. "Where is your friend?"

Facing the towering demigod, Rhonin kept his expression neutral. "I don't know. I just woke up and he was gone."

The antlered figure's golden orbs flared and his frown sent chills down Rhonin's spine. "There are troubling signs in the world. Some of the others have only just now sensed intruders, creatures not of any natural origin, sniffing around, seeking something—or *someone*." He studied the wizard very closely. "And they come so soon after you and your friend drop from nowhere . . ."

What these unnamed creatures might be, Rhonin could only suspect. If so, he and Krasus had even less time than they had imagined.

Seeing that his "guest" had nothing yet to say, Cenarius added, "Your friend could not have escaped without assistance, but he leaves you behind. Why is that?"

"I—"

"There were those among the others who insisted that I should have given you to them immediately, that they would have found out through more thorough means than I prefer the reasons for your being here and what it is about you that so interests the night elves. I had, up until now, convinced them otherwise in this matter."

Rhonin's highly attuned senses suddenly detected the presence of another powerful force, one which, in its own way, matched Cenarius.

"Now I see I must acquiesce to the majority," the lord of the forest finished reluctantly.

"We heard your call . . ." growled a deep, ponderous voice. "You admit you were wrong . . ."

The wizard tried to turn and see who now spoke, but his legs—his entire body—would not obey his commands.

Something more immense than the demigod moved up behind Rhonin.

Cenarius did not seem at all pleased by the other's comments. "I admit only that other steps must be taken."

"The truth will be known . . ." A heavy, *furred* hand with thick claws enveloped Rhonin's shoulder, gripping it painfully. ". . . and known *soon* . . ."

TWELVE

You should stay in the temple!" Illidan insisted. "Malfurion thought that best and so do I!"

But Tyrande would not be swayed. "I have to know what's happening! You saw how many rode in pursuit! If they captured them—"

"They won't." He squinted, the blinding sun not at all to his liking. He could feel his powers waning, feel the rush of magic fading. Illidan did not like such sensations. He savored magic in all its forms. That had been one reason he had even tried to follow the druidic path—that, and the fact that what Cenarius supposedly taught would not be affected by night or day.

They stood dangerously near the square, a place Tyrande had insisted upon returning to once matters had quieted down. The Moon Guard and the soldiers had ridden off after Malfurion, leaving only a pair of the former to inspect the cage for clues. That they had done, finding nothing to trace the culprits, just as Illidan had expected. In truth, he considered himself at least as proficient as any of the honored sorcerers, if not more.

"I should ride after—"

Would she never give in? "You do that and you'll risk everyone! You want them to take that pet creature of yours to Black Rook Hold and Lord Ravencrest? For that matter, they might take us there as w—"

Illidan suddenly clamped his mouth shut. From the opposite end of the square now entered several armored riders . . . and in their lead, Lord Kur'talos Ravencrest himself.

It was too late to hide. As the night elven commander rode past, his dour gaze shifted first to Tyrande, then her companion.

At sight of Illidan, Ravencrest called a sudden halt.

"I know you, lad . . . Illidan Stormrage, isn't it?"

"Yes, my lord. We met once."

"And this?"

Tyrande bowed. "Tyrande Whisperwind, novice priestess of the temple of Elune . . ."

The mounted night elves respectfully made the sign of the moon. Ravencrest graciously acknowledged Tyrande, then turned his gaze once more to Illidan. "I recall our encounter. You were studying the arts, then." He rubbed his chin. "You are not yet a member of the Moon Guard, are you?"

That Ravencrest would ask the question in such a way indicated that he already knew the answer. Clearly after their initial meeting he had kept an eye on Illidan, something that made the younger night elf both proud and extremely uneasy. He had done nothing he knew of to warrant bringing himself to the commander's attention. "No, my lord."

"Then you are free of some of their restrictions, aren't you?" The restrictions to which the commander referred had to do with the oaths each sorcerer swore upon entering the fabled order. The Moon Guard was an entity unto its own and owed no loyalty to anyone save the queen . . . which meant that they were not at the beck and call of those such as Lord Ravencrest.

"I suppose I am."

"Good. Very good. I want you to ride with us, then."

Now both Tyrande and Illidan looked confused. Likely fearing for Illidan's safety, the young priestess said, "My Lord Ravencrest, we would be honored—"

She got no farther. The night elven lord raised a polite hand to silence her. "Not you, sister, although the blessing of the Mother Moon is always welcome. No, 'tis the lad alone with whom I speak now."

Trying not to show his increasing anxiety, Illidan asked, "But what would you have need of me for, my lord?"

"For the moment, investigation into the escape of the creature we had penned here! News came to me just moments ago of his escape. Assuming that he's not been captured already, I've some notions as to how to find him. I might need the aid of a bit of sorcery, though, and while the Moon Guard are capable, I prefer someone who listens to orders."

To refuse a request by a night elf as highly ranked as Ravencrest would have been suspicious, but joining him risked Malfurion. Tyrande glanced surreptitiously at Illidan, trying to read his thoughts. He, on the other hand, wished that she could tell him the best path to take.

In truth, there was only one choice. "I'd be honored to join you, my lord."

"Excellent! Rol'tharak! A mount for our young sorcerer friend here!"

The officer in question brought forth a spare night saber, almost as if Ravencrest had expected Illidan all the time. The animal crouched low so that its new rider could mount up.

"The sun is well upon us, my lord," Rol'tharak commented to Ravencrest as he handed down the reins of the beast to Malfurion's brother.

"We will make do . . . as will you, eh, sorcerer?"

Illidan understood very well the veiled message. His powers would be weaker in daylight, but the commander was still confident that he would be of use. The confidence which Ravencrest had in him made Illidan's head swell.

"I will not fail you, my lord."

"Splendid, lad!"

As he slipped atop the panther, Illidan gave Tyrande a quick glance, indicating that she should not worry about Malfurion and the orc. He would ride with Ravencrest and aid in whatever way he could so long as the pair would still make good their escape.

Tyrande's brief but grateful smile was all the reward he could have desired. Feeling quite good about himself, Illidan nodded to the commander that he was ready.

With a wave and a shout, Lord Ravencrest led the armed force on. Illidan leaned forward, determined to keep pace with the noble. Somehow he would please Ravencrest while at the same time keeping his altruistic brother from being sent to Black Rook Hold. Malfurion knew the forest lands well, which meant that he would likely stay ahead of the soldiers and Moon Guard, but in the awful chance that pursuit had caught up with Illidan's twin and Tyrande's creature, Illidan had to at least consider sacrificing Brox to save his brother. Tyrande would come to understand that. He would do what he could to avoid it, but blood came first . . .

As often happened, a morning fog draped over the landscape. The thick mist would break up soon, but it meant more hope for Malfurion. Illidan kept his gaze on the path ahead, wondering if it was the same one his brother had used. It might be that the Moon Guard had not even chosen the right direction, which meant that he and Lord Ravencrest now pursued a futile course of action.

But as they raced deeper and deeper into the wooded lands, the fog quickly gave way. The morning sun seemed as eager to drain Illidan of his power as it did to eat away the mist, but he gritted his teeth and tried not to think of what that might mean. If it came to some sort of show of sorcery, he had no intention of disappointing the noble. The hunt for the orc had become as much Illidan's excuse to make new connections within the hierarchy of the night elf world as it had anything to do with the escape of Brox.

But just as they reached the top of a ridge, something farther down made Illidan frown and Lord Ravencrest curse. The commander immediately slowed his mount, the rest following suit. Ahead appeared to be a number of peculiar mounds scattered along the trail. The night elves cautiously descended the other side of the ridge, Ravencrest and the soldiers keeping their weapons ready. Illidan suddenly prayed that he had not overestimated his daytime skills.

"By the Blessed Azshara's eyes!" muttered Ravencrest.

Illidan could say nothing. He could only gape at the carnage revealed as they drew near.

At least half a dozen night elves, including two of the Moon Guard, lay dead before the newcomers, their bodies torn to shreds and, in the case of the two sorcerers, seemingly *sucked dry* by some vampiric force. The two Moon Guard resembled nothing more than shriveled fruit left in the sun too long. Their emaciated forms were stretched in positions of the utmost agony and clearly they had struggled throughout their horrible ordeals.

Five night sabers also lay dead, some with their throats torn out, the others disemboweled. Of the remaining panthers, there was no sign.

"I was right!" Ravencrest snapped. "That green-hided creature was not alone! There must've been two dozen and more to do this . . . and with the Moon Guard along yet!"

Illidan paid him no mind, concerned more with what might have befallen Malfurion. This could not be the work of either his brother or one orc. Did Lord Ravencrest have the right of it? Had Brox betrayed Malfurion, leading him to his savage comrades?

I should've slain the beast when I had the opportunity! His fist tightened and he felt his rage fuel his powers. Given a target, Illidan would have more than proved his sorcerous might to the noble.

Then one of the soldiers noticed something to the right of the carnage. "My lord! Come look! I've seen nothing like it!"

Steering their animals around, Illidan and Ravencrest stared wide-eyed at the beast the other night elf had found.

It was a creature out of nightmare, in some ways lupine in form, but monstrously distorted, as if some insane god had created it out of the depths of his madness. Even in death it lost no bit of its inherent horror.

"What do you make of it, sorcerer?"

For a moment, Illidan forgot that *he* was the fount of magical wisdom here. Shaking his head, he responded with all honesty, "I have no idea, Lord Ravencrest . . . no idea."

However terrifying the monster was, someone had dealt hard with it, jamming a makeshift spear down its gullet and likely choking it to death.

Again Illidan's thoughts turned to his brother, last known by him to be heading into this forest. Had Malfurion done this? It seemed unlikely. Did his twin instead lie nearby, torn apart as readily as the two Moon Guard?

"Very curious," Ravencrest muttered. He suddenly straightened, looking around. "Where are the rest of the first party?" he demanded to no one in particular. "There should be twice as many as we found!"

As if to answer that, a mournful horn blast arose from the south, where the forest dropped abruptly, becoming more treacherous to traverse.

The commander pointed his blade in the direction of the horn blast. "That way . . . but be wary . . . there may be more of those monsters about!"

The party worked their way down, each member, Illidan included, watching the thickening forest with trepidation. The horn did not sound again, not at all a good sign.

Several yards down, they came across another night saber, its entire side opened up by savage claws, its back also broken by the two huge oaks into which it had crashed. Only a short distance away, another of the Moon Guard lay pressed against a massive rock, his emaciated body and his horrified expression chilling even the hardened soldiers of Lord Ravencrest.

"Steady . . ." the noble quietly ordered. "Keep order . . ."

Once more, the horn sounded feebly, this time much closer and directly ahead.

The newcomers wended their way toward it. Illidan had the horrible feeling that something watched him in particular, but whenever he looked around, he saw only the trees.

"Another one, my lord!" the night elf called Rol'tharak blurted, pointing just ahead.

Sure enough, a second hellish beast lay dead, its body sprawled as if even in dying it had sought another victim. In addition to a crushed nose and a shoulder torn apart, it had several strange, ropelike marks on its legs. What had slain it, however, were a number of well-aimed thrusts to its throat by night elven blades. One still remained embedded in the beast.

They found two more soldiers nearby, the highly trained warriors of the realm tossed about like rag dolls. Illidan's brow furrowed in puzzlement. If the night elves had managed to slay both monsters, then where were the survivors?

Moments later, they found what remained.

One soldier sat propped against a tree, his left arm torn free. A poor attempt had been made to bandage the immense wound. He stared without seeing at the new arrivals, the horn still in his one remaining hand. Blood covered his torso.

Next to him lay the other to survive—if to survive meant to have half of one's face ripped apart and one leg twisted under at an impossible angle. His breathing was ragged, his chest barely rising each time.

"You there!" Ravencrest bellowed to the one with the horn. "Look at me!"

The survivor blinked slowly, then forced his gaze to that of the noble.

"Is this it? Are there any more?"

The mauled fighter opened his mouth, but no sound escaped it.

"Rol'tharak! Look to his wounds! Give him water if he needs it!"

"Aye, my lord!"

"The rest of you fan out! Now!"

Illidan remained with Ravencrest, watching warily as the others established what they hoped would be a safe perimeter. That so many of their fellows, including three spellcasters, had been so easily massacred did nothing for morale.

"Speak up!" Ravencrest roared. "I command you! Who was responsible for this? The escaped prisoner?"

At this, the bloody soldier let out a wild laugh, startling Rol'tharak so much that he stepped back.

"N-never saw that one, m-my lord!" the maimed figure responded. "Probably all eaten up h-himself!"

"So it was those monsters, then? Those hounds?"

The stricken night elf nodded.

"What happened to the Moon Guard? Why didn't they stop the things? Surely even in the daytime—"

And again the wounded soldier laughed. "M-my lord! The sorcerers were the easiest of the p-prey . . ."

Through effort, the story came out. The soldiers and the Moon Guard had pursued the escaped creature and another, unidentified figure through the forest, following their tracks even through fog and the coming sun. They had not actually seen the pair, but had been certain that it would only be a matter of time before they caught up.

Then, unexpectedly, they had come across the first beast.

No one had ever seen anything like it. Even dead it had unnerved the night elves. Hargo'then, the lead sorcerer, had sensed something magical about it. He had commanded the rest to wait a few paces behind him while he rode up to investigate the corpse. No one had argued.

"An unnatural thing," Hargo'then had proclaimed as he had begun to dismount. "Tyr'kyn . . ." he had called to one of the other Moon Guard. "I want you to—"

That was when the second beast had fallen upon him.

"It came from out behind the nearest trees, m-my lord . . . and went directly for . . . for Hargo'then! S-slew his mount with one swipe of the c-claws and th-then . . ."

The sorcerer had no chance. Before the startled night elves could react, two horrific tentacles on the creature's back had thrust out, adhering themselves like leeches to Hargo'then's chest and forehead. The Moon Guard leader screamed as no night elf had ever heard one of their own scream and before their eyes he had suddenly shriveled into a dry, limp husk quickly discarded by the slavering, four-legged monstrosity.

Finally recovering from their shock, the other night elves belatedly charged the beast, seeking at least to avenge Hargo'then's death.

Too late they realized that they were also being hunted from behind by a third beast. The attackers had become the attacked, caught between twin demonic forces.

The resulting carnage had been clear for the newcomers to see. The Moon Guard had perished swiftly, their weakened magical abilities actually making them much more attractive prey. The soldiers had fared little better, but at least their blades had some effect on the demons.

As the survivor finished his tale, he grew less coherent. By the time he reached the conclusion, where he and three others had banded together at this spot, it was all Lord Ravencrest and Illidan could do to understand his ramblings.

Rol'tharak looked up. "He's passed out again, my lord. I fear he may not be waking up again."

"See what you can do for him to ease his pain. Check that other one, too." The noble frowned. "I want another look at that first carcass. Sorcerer, attend me."

Illidan followed Ravencrest back along the trail. Two guards broke off from their duties to follow the pair. The other soldiers continued to survey the area, trying unsuccessfully to find any more survivors.

"What do you make of the story?" the veteran commander asked of Illidan. "Have you heard of such things?"

"Never, my lord . . . but I am not part of the Moon Guard and so not privy to all their arcane knowledge."

"For all the good their knowledge did them! Hargo'then was always too confident! Most of the Moon Guard are!"

Illidan gave a noncommittal noise.

"Here it is . . ."

The macabre beast looked as if it still sought to remove the wedge from its throat. Despite the open wounds it bore, the creature was bereft of any eager scavengers, even flies. Even the forest life seemed repelled by the dead intruder.

To the two soldiers, Ravencrest commanded, "Check the path we took. See if the trail the first party and ours followed continues on. I still want that green-skinned brute . . . more than ever now!"

As the other two rode on, both Illidan and the noble dismounted, the latter also unsheathing his blade. The night sabers were not at all keen on remaining so near the carcass, so their riders led them to a thick tree a short distance away and tied the reins to it.

Once back at the corpse, Lord Ravencrest knelt down. "Simply horrid! In all my years, I've never faced such a thing so well designed for carnage . . ." He lifted a leathery tentacle. "Curious appendage. So this is what the other used to suck Hargo'then dry! What do you make of it?"

Trying not to back away from the foul limb thrust in his face, Illidan managed, "V-vampiric in nature, my lord. Some animals drink blood, but this one seeks magical energy." He looked around. "The other's been torn off."

"Yes, so it has. Likely by an animal . . ."

While the noble continued his gruesome examination, Illidan considered the monstrosity's death. The soldier reported that this first one had been dead already. To the young night elf's quick mind, that meant the only ones who could have slain it were Malfurion and Brox . . . and judging by the physical struggle that had taken place, Illidan would have placed his bet more on the powerful orc.

Off to the side, the cats grew increasingly virulent in their protests at being so near the creature. Illidan tried to shut out the sounds of their hissing, still concerned about his brother. They had sighted no other corpses save those of the first party and the second of the three beasts mentioned, but—

Head snapping up straight, Illidan said, "My Lord Ravencrest! We never found any sign of the—"

The snarls of the night sabers reached a new crescendo.

Illidan sensed something behind him.

He threw himself to the side, accidentally colliding with the unsuspecting noble. Both fell flat to the ground, the younger night elf sprawled haphazardly over the commander. Ravencrest's sword flew wildly, landing far beyond either's reach.

The huge, clawed form that had just leapt at Illidan went sailing over the carcass of its twin.

"What in the name of—" Ravencrest managed. The night sabers struggled to attack, but their reins held, keeping the cats from being any aid.

Recovering first, Illidan looked up to see the hellish creature turning to attempt a second strike. He had thought the dead one terrifying enough, but to see one alive and bearing down on him nearly made Illidan flee in utter panic.

But instead of leaping again, the canine horror suddenly lashed at Illidan with the two tentacles atop its back. Memories of the husks that had once been powerful members of the Moon Guard filled the night elf's mind.

Yet, as the gaping appendages sought his magic, sought his very body, self-preservation took over. Recalling how one tentacle on the dead beast had been ripped free, Illidan quickly devised a plan of attack.

He did not try to strike the monster directly, knowing how little that would probably help. It would simply suck up Illidan's spell and perhaps continue draining him directly. Instead, Illidan chose to cast his spell on Lord Ravencrest's lost blade, which lay out of his hellish foe's sight.

The animated sword rose swiftly in the air and began to spin, whirling faster and faster. Illidan directed it at the creature's back, aiming for the parasitic appendages.

With pinpoint accuracy, the whirling blade shot across the shoulders of the toothy behemoth, severing both tentacles as simply as it could have shaved a blade of grass.

With a maddened howl, the houndlike beast shook, thick, greenish fluids spilling over its shoulders and down its backside. It snarled, its unsettling gaze narrowing on the one who had hurt it so.

Emboldened by his success and less fearful now that the danger to his sorcery had been eliminated, Illidan directed Ravencrest's sword back again. As the monster leapt at him, the young night elf smiled darkly at it.

With a force magnified by his intense will, he buried the weapon in the creature's hard skull.

The monster's leap faltered. It stumbled awkwardly. A glazed look filled the horrific orbs. The massive beast took two hesitant steps toward Illidan . . . then crumpled in a limp heap.

An incredible exhaustion overcame the young night elf, but one mixed with a sense of extreme satisfaction and triumph. He had done with little hesitation what three of the Moon Guard had failed to do. That he had learned from their mistakes, Illidan did not care. He only knew that by himself he had taken on a demon and won handily.

"Well done!" A heavy slap on his back nearly sent him stumbling into his monstrous foe. As Illidan fought to maintain his balance, Lord Ravencrest stepped past him to admire his companion's work. "A splendid counterattack! Remove the greatest danger, then strike the death blow while the enemy tries to recoup! Splendid!"

The noble put one boot on a forelimb of the demon and struggled to remove his blade. From the trail rode the two guards and farther behind Illidan, others shouted as realization of the threat finally sank in among the rest of the party.

"My lord!" shouted one of the two guards. "We heard—"

Rol'tharak rushed up. "Lord Ravencrest! You slew one of the beasts! Are you injured?"

Illidan expected Ravencrest to take credit—after all, the noble's weapon still pierced the monster's head—but instead the elder night elf stretched forth his hand and indicated Malfurion's brother. "Nay! Here stands the one who, after risking himself to throw me from the creature's path, readily disposed of the danger with scarcely a concern for his own life! I saw right about you from the first, Illidan Stormrage! More capable than a dozen Moon Guard you are!"

Cheeks darkening, the young night elf accepted the accolades of the powerful commander. Years of hearing how he was expected to be a hero, a champion of his people, had set a heavy load on his shoulders. Yet, now, Illidan felt as if his destiny had finally revealed itself . . . and it had done so with the innate sorcery he had almost rejected for the slower, more subtle druidic spells Cenarius had been teaching.

I was a fool to reject my heritage, Illidan realized. *Malfurion's path was never meant to be mine. Even in daytime, night elven sorcery is mine to command . . .*

It heartened him, actually, for he had felt strange taking up the ways of his brother. What hero of legend had been recorded following the footsteps of another? Illidan had been meant to *lead*.

The soldiers—Lord Ravencrest's capable, veteran soldiers—eyed him with a new and healthy respect.

"Rol'tharak!" the noble called. "I feel luck is with me this day! I want you to lead half the warriors on after the trail! We may still find the prisoner and whoever released him! Go now!"

"Aye, my lord!" Rol'tharak summoned several soldiers, then, after all had mounted, led them in the direction Malfurion and Brox had likely gone.

Illidan scarcely thought of his brother, already assuming that the delay here had given Malfurion all the time he needed to lose his pursuers. He did think of Tyrande, however, who would not only be quite pleased by what she would see as his having delayed the hunters but also would be rightly impressed by the high praise Lord Ravencrest had bestowed upon him.

And it seemed that the noble had more to bestow upon the one he thought had saved his life. Striding up to Illidan, Ravencrest put one gauntleted hand on the other night elf's shoulder, then declared, "Illidan Stormrage, the Moon Guard may be ignorant of your prowess, but I am not. You are hereby marked as one of Black Rook Hold's own . . . and my personal sorcerer! As such, you'll be of a rank outside of the Moon Guard, equal to any of their own and unable to be commanded by any of their order! You will answer only to me and to your queen, the Light of Lights, Azshara!"

The rest of the night elves put their left hands to their chests and dipped their heads in homage at the mention of the queen.

"I am—honored—my lord . . ."

"Come! We ride back immediately! I want to gather a larger force to bring these carcasses to Black Rook Hold! This must be investigated thoroughly! If we're to be invaded by some hellish horde, we must learn everything we can, then alert her majesty!"

Caught up in his euphoria, Illidan paid scant attention to any mention of Azshara. Had he done so, he might have had at least some slight concern, for it was because of her that Malfurion had dared the wrath of his brother's new patron. She it was who Malfurion insisted was involved in madness that might prove catastrophic to the entire night elf race.

But for the moment, all Illidan could think was, *I have found my destiny at last . . .*

THIRTEEN

H*e's strong of mind, strong of soul, strong of body . . .* said a powerful, aggressive voice in Rhonin's head.

An admirable quality . . . at other times . . . replied a second, calmer voice otherwise identical to the first.

The truth will be known, the first insisted. *I've never failed to make it so . . .*

Rhonin seemed to float outside his body, but where he floated, the wizard could not say. He felt as if he hung between life and death, sleep and waking, darkness and light . . . nothing seemed quite right or absolutely wrong.

No more! interjected a third voice somehow familiar to him. *He has been through enough! Return him to me . . . for now . . .*

And suddenly Rhonin awoke in the glade of Cenarius.

The sun hung high overhead, although whether that meant it was noon or merely a trick of the enchanted area, the human could not say. Rhonin tried to rise, but, as before, his body would not obey him.

He heard movement and suddenly the sky filled with the antlered aspect of the forest lord.

"You're resilient, Rhonin wizard," Cenarius rumbled. "You surprised one who is usually little surprised . . . and, more to the point, you held your secrets, however foolish that may be in the long run."

"Th-there's nothing . . . I can . . . tell you." It amazed Rhonin that his mouth even worked.

"That remains to be seen. We will know what happened to your companion and why you—who should not be here—are." The demigod's visage softened. "But for now, I would have you rest. That much you deserve."

He waved his hand over Rhonin's face . . . and the wizard slept.

Krasus himself would have liked to know the answer of exactly where he was. The cavern in which he now awakened stirred no memories. He could not sense the presence of any other creature, especially not one of his own kind, and that worried him. Had the watcher simply brought him here to be rid of him? Did he expect Krasus to die here?

The last was a very real danger. Pain and exhaustion continued to wrack the dragon mage's lanky frame. Krasus felt as if someone had ripped half of him away. His memory continued to fail him and he feared that all his maladies would only grow worse with time . . . time he did not have.

No! I will not give in to despair! Not me! Forcing himself to his feet, he peered around. For a human or orc, the cavern would have been all but black, yet Krasus could make out its interior almost as well as if the light of the sun shone within. He could see the huge, toothy stalactites and stalagmites, identify each crack and fissure along the walls, and note even the tiny, blind lizards darting in and around the smallest crevices.

Unfortunately, he could not make out any exit.

"I do not have time for these games!" he snapped at the empty air. His words echoed, seeming to grow more self-mocking with each repetition.

He was missing something. Surely he had been put in this place for a reason . . . but what?

Then Krasus recalled the ways of his kind, ways that could, for those not dragons, be very cruel, indeed. A grim smile played across his face.

Straightening, the cowled mage slowly turned in a circle, eyes never blinking once. At the same time, he began reciting a ritual greeting, speaking in a language older than the world. He repeated the greeting three times, emphasizing the nuances of it as only one who had learned it from the very source of that language could.

If this did not garner the attention of his captors, nothing would.

"It speaks the tongue of those who set the heavens and earth in place . . ." thundered someone. "Those who brought us into being."

"It must be one of us," said another. "For it can surely not be one of them . . ."

"More must be known."

And suddenly from the empty air they materialized around the tiny figure . . . four gargantuan red dragons seated around Krasus, their world-spanning wings folded in dignified fashion behind them. They eyed the mage as if he were a small but tasty morsel of food.

If they thought to shock his supposedly primitive senses, then once again they had failed.

"Definitely one of us," murmured a heavier male, so noted by his larger crest. He snorted, sending puffs of smoke Krasus's way.

"And that isss why I brought him," a smaller male bitterly remarked. "That . . . and hisss incessant whining . . ."

Perfectly at ease surrounded by the smoke, Krasus turned to the second male. "If you had the sense the creators gave you, you would have known me for what I am and the urgency of my warning immediately! We could have been spared the chaotic retreat from the realm of the forest lord."

"I am ssstill not certain that I did not make a missstake in bringing you here!"

"And where is here?"

All four dragons leaned their heads back in slight astonishment. One of the two females now spoke. "If you are one of us, little dragon, then you should know it as well as you know your nest . . ."

Krasus cursed his addled memory. This could be only one location. "Then I am in the home caverns? I am in the realm of beloved Alexstrasza, Queen of Life?"

"You did want to come here," reminded the smaller male.

"The question remains," interjected the second female, younger, sleeker than the rest. "Do you come any farther?"

"He comes as far as he desires," intruded a new voice. "If he can but answer me a simple question."

The four leviathans and Krasus turned to where a fifth and obviously much more mature dragon suddenly sat. In contrast to the two other males, this one had an impressive crest running from the top of his head to down past his shoulders. He outweighed the second-largest dragon by several tons and his claws alone were longer than the tiny figure standing in the midst of the behemoths.

But despite his immense form and clear dominance, his eyes were sharp and full of wisdom. He more than any of the others would decide the success of Krasus's journey.

"If you are one of us despite that guise you wear, you must know who I am," the dragon rumbled.

The mage struggled with his tattered memories. Of course he knew who this *was,* but the name would not come to him. His body tensed and his blood boiled as he fought the fog in his mind. Krasus knew that if he did not speak to this giant by name, he would forever be rejected, forever be unable to warn his kind of the possible danger his presence in this time represented.

And then, with titanic effort, the name he should have known almost as well as his own sprang from his lips. "You are *Tyranastrasz* . . . Tyran the Scholarly One . . . *consort* to Alexstrasza!"

His pride at recalling both the name and title of the crimson giant must have been noticeable, for Tyranastrasz let out a loud, almost human chuckle.

"You are indeed one of us, although I cannot place you yet! I have been given a name for you by the one who brought you, but clearly it is wrong, as, among us, a name is granted to one and one alone."

"There is no mistake," the dragon mage insisted. "And I can explain why."

Alexstrasza's consort shook his mighty head. A hint of smoke escaped his nostrils. "The explanation you have given, little one, has been relayed to us . . . and still it is found too astonishing to be true! What you say falls into

the realm of the Timeless One, Nozdormu, but even he would not be so careless as to do as you have shown!"

"He is addled, plain and simple," said the watcher from the forest. "One of
our own, I will grant, but injured by accident or device."

"Perhaps . . ." Tyranastrasz startled the other dragons then, lowering his
head to the ground just before Krasus. "But by knowing me you have
answered my question! You are of the flight and thus have the right and privilege to enter the innermost recesses of this lair! Come! I will take you to the
one who will settle this matter for us all, the one who knows all her flight as
she knows all her children! *She* will recognize you and, therefore, recognize
the truth . . ."

"You will take me to Alexstrasza?"

"None other. Climb atop my neck, if you are able."

Even with his physical debilitation, Krasus readily managed to climb up.
Not only did the thought of at last finding help spur him on . . . but so did the
simple opportunity to see his beloved once more, even if it turned out she did
not recognize him after all.

The huge dragon carried Krasus through long-worn tunnels and chambers that should have been easily recognizable but were not. Now and then,
some hint of memory stirred, but never enough to satisfy the mage. Even
when they came across other dragons, none looked at all familiar to Krasus,
who once had known all those of the red flight.

He wished that he had been awake when the watcher had flown him here.
The landscape surrounding the red flight's domain might have sparked his
memories. Besides, what more glorious sight could exist than to see the dragons at the peak of their rule? To witness once more the tall, towering mountains, the hundreds of great gaps in every cliff side, each of the latter an
entrance into Alexstrasza's realm. It had been countless centuries since that
time and Krasus had always mourned its passing, mourned the passing of the
Age of Dragons.

Perhaps once I have convinced her . . . she will let me see the land of dragons from
without one last time . . . before she decides what to do with me.

Tyranastrasz's huge form moved effortlessly through the high, smooth
tunnels. Krasus felt a twinge of jealousy, for here he was, about to speak with
his beloved, and forced to do so in this meager, mortal body. He greatly loved
the lesser races, enjoyed his time among them, but now, when he might be
putting his very existence on the line, Krasus would have preferred his true
shape.

A bright yet comforting glow suddenly appeared ahead of them. The red-
dish glow warmed Krasus inside and out as they neared and made him think
of childhood, of learning to grow up in the sky as well as the earth. Fleeting

memories of his life danced in his head and for the first time since his arrival in this time period, the dragon mage almost felt himself.

They came to the source of the magnificent glow, the mouth of a vast cave. Kneeling at the entrance, Tyranastrasz lowered his head and rumbled, "With your permission, my love, my life."

"Always," returned a voice both delicate and all-powerful. "Always for you."

Again Krasus felt a twinge of jealousy, but he knew that the one who spoke had loved him as much as she loved the leviathan on which he rode. The Queen of Life had so much love not only for her consorts, but for all her flight. In truth, she loved all creatures of the world, although that love would not stop her from destroying those that in some way threatened the rest.

And that was one thing he had purposely failed to mention to Rhonin. It had occurred early on to Krasus that one way to avoid any further damage to the timeline might be to remove those objects that were not where they were supposed to be.

To save history from going further awry, Alexstrasza might have to slay both him and the human wizard.

As he and Tyranastrasz entered, all thought of what might happen to him vanished as Krasus beheld the one who would forever command his heart and soul.

The wondrous glow which permeated every corner and crevice of the huge chamber radiated from the shimmering red dragon herself. Alexstrasza was the most monumental of her kind, twice the size of the titan upon which Krasus rode. Yet, despite that, an inherent gentleness could be sensed within the massive frame, and even as the mage watched, the Queen of Life delicately moved a fragile egg from the warmth of her body to a smoking vent, where she secured it safely.

She was surrounded by eggs, eggs and more. The eggs were her latest clutch, a bountiful one. Each stood only a foot in height—large by most standards, tiny when compared to the one who had laid them. Krasus counted three dozen. Only about half would hatch and only half of those would survive to adulthood, but that was the way of dragons—a harsh beginning heralding a life of glory and wonder.

Framing the image was an array of flowering plants that should not have been able to exist under such conditions and especially underground. There were wall-crawling creepers and sprawling carpets of purple phlox. Golden daylilies decorated the area of the nest and roses and orchids lined the area where Alexstrasza herself rested. Every plant bloomed strong, all fed by the glorious presence of the Queen of Life.

A crystal-clear stream flowed through the cavern, passing within reach of the female dragon's maw should she desire a sip at any time. The calm gurgle of the underground added to the tranquillity of the scene.

Krasus's mount lowered his head so that his tiny rider could dismount. Eyes never leaving Alexstrasza, the dragon mage stepped to the cavern floor, then went down on one knee.

"My queen . . ."

But she looked instead to the huge male who had brought Krasus here. "Tyranastrasz . . . would you leave us alone for a time?"

Wordlessly the other behemoth backed out of the chamber. The Queen of Life shifted her gaze to Krasus, but said nothing. He knelt there before her, waiting for some sign of recognition yet receiving none.

Unable to hold his silence any longer, Krasus gasped, "My queen, my world, can it be that you of all beings do not know me?"

She studied him through slitted lids before answering, "I know what I sense, and I know what I feel, and because of both I have taken the story you have told the others under serious consideration. I have already decided what must be done, but first, there is another who must be involved in this situation, for his august opinion is as dear to me as my own—ahh! He comes now!"

From another passage emerged an adult male only slightly smaller than Tyranastrasz. The newcomer moved ponderously, as if each step was a heavy labor. Long, with faded crimson scales and weary eyes, he at first appeared much older than Alexstrasza's consort—until the mage realized that it was not age that afflicted this dragon, but some unknown malady.

"You . . . summoned me, my Alexstrasza?"

And as Krasus heard the weakened giant speak, his world turned upside down again. He stumbled to his feet, backing away from the male in open dismay.

The Queen of Life was quick to notice his reaction even though her gaze for the most part remained on the newcomer. "I asked your presence here, yes. Forgive me if the effort strains you too much."

"There is . . . nothing I would not do for you, my love, my world."

She indicated the mage, who still stood as if struck by lightning. "This is— what do you call yourself?"

"Kor—Krasus, my queen. Krasus . . ."

"Krasus? Krasus it is, then . . ." Her tone hinted of amusement at his sudden choice of names at this moment. She turned again to the ill leviathan. "And this, Krasus, is one of my most beloved subjects, my most recent consort, and one to whom I already greatly look for guidance. Being one of us, you may have heard of him. His name is *Korialstrasz* . . ."

Along the winding forest path they rode, Malfurion finally coming to believe that they had lost any possible pursuit. He had chosen a route that led over rocks and other areas where the night saber's paws would leave few tracks, hoping that anyone following would soon ride off in the wrong direction. It meant taking more time than usual to reach the point where he always met Cenarius, but Malfurion had decided he needed to take that chance. He still did not know what the forest lord might think when he heard what his pupil had done.

As they neared the meeting place, Malfurion slowed his cat.

"We stopping?" grunted the orc, looking around and seeing nothing but more trees. "Here?"

"Almost. Only a few minutes more. The oak should soon be in sight."

Despite being so near his goal, the night elf actually grew more tense. One time he thought he felt eyes watching them, but when he looked, he saw only the calm forest. The realization that his life had forever changed continued to shake him. If the Moon Guard identified him, he risked being shunned, the most dire punishment that could be inflicted upon a night elf other than death. His people would turn from him, forever marking him as dead even though he still breathed. No one would interact with him or even meet his gaze.

Not even Tyrande or Illidan.

He had only compounded his crimes by leaving the hunters to face the demonic creature, something Brox had called a "felbeast." If the felbeast had hurt or slain any of the pursuit party, it would leave Malfurion with no hope of ever mending his situation . . . and, to make matters worse, he would be responsible for the loss of innocent lives. Yet, what else could he have done? The only other choice would have involved turning Brox over to the Moon Guard . . . and eventually to Black Rook Hold.

The oak he sought suddenly appeared ahead, giving Malfurion the opportunity to dwell no more, for the time being, on his growing troubles. To anyone else, the tree would have simply been a tree, but to Malfurion, it was an ancient sentinel, one of those who had served Cenarius longer than most. This tree, tall, thick of trunk, and so very wrinkled of bark, had seen the rest of the forest grow over and over. It had outlasted countless others of its kind and witnessed thousands of generations of fleeting animal lives.

It knew Malfurion as he approached, the leaves of the wide crown audibly shaking despite a lack of wind. This was the ancient speech of all trees and the night elf felt honored that Cenarius had taught him early on how to understand some of it.

"Brox . . . I must ask a favor of you."

"I owe you much. Ask it."

Pointing at the oak, Malfurion said, "Dismount and go to that tree. Touch the palm of your hand to the trunk where you see that gnarled area of bark."

The orc clearly had no idea why this would be required of him, but as it had been Malfurion who had requested it, he immediately obeyed. Handing the reins to the night elf, Brox trudged over to the sentinel. The huge warrior peered closely at the trunk, then planted one meaty hand where Malfurion had indicated.

Twisting his head so as to look back at his companion, the orc rumbled, "What do I do n—"

He let out a snarl of surprise as his hand sank into the bark as if the latter had become mud. Brox almost pulled the appendage free, but Malfurion quickly ordered him to remain still.

"Do nothing at all! Simply stand there! It's learning of you! Your hand will tingle, but that's all!"

What he did not go on to explain was that the tingling meant that tiny root tendrils from within the guardian now penetrated the orc's flesh. The oak was learning of Brox by becoming, however briefly, a part of him. Plant and animal meshed together. The oak would forever recall Brox, no matter how many centuries might pass.

The vein in the orc's neck throbbed madly, a sign of his growing anxiety. To his credit, Brox stood as still as the oak, his eyes ever fixed on where his hand had vanished.

Suddenly he fell back a step, the appendage released as abruptly as it had been taken. Brox quickly flexed the hand, testing the fingers and possibly even counting them.

"The way is open to us now," Malfurion proclaimed.

With Brox mounted once more, the night elf led the way past the oak. As he rode by the sentinel, Malfurion sensed a subtle change in the air. Had they not been given permission, he and Brox could have ridden on forever and never found the glade. Only those Cenarius permitted to come to him would find the path beyond the sentinels.

The differences in their surroundings became more noticeable as the pair journeyed on. A refreshing breeze cooled both. Birds hopped about and sang from the trees surrounding them. The trees themselves shook merrily, greeting the night elf—who could understand them—especially. A feeling of comfort embraced both to the point that Malfurion even caught a hint of a smile on the orc's rough visage.

A barrier of dense woods abruptly barred their way. Brox looked to Malfurion, who indicated that they should now dismount. After both had done so, Malfurion guided the orc along a narrow foot trail not at first visible between the trees. This they followed for several minutes before stepping out into a richly lit open area filled with tall, soft grass and high, brightly petaled flowers.

The glade of the forest lord.

But the figure encircled by a ring of flowers in the midst of the glade could never have been mistaken for Cenarius. Seated in the ring's center, he leapt up at sight of the pair, his odd eyes especially lingering on Brox—as if he knew exactly what the orc was.

"You . . ." the stranger muttered at the green-skinned warrior. "You shouldn't be here . . ."

Brox mistook the thrust of his remark. "I come with him, wizard . . . and need no permission of yours."

But the fire-haired figure—to what race he belonged, Malfurion could not yet say—shook his head and started toward the orc, only to hesitate at the edge of the ring. With a curious glance at the flowers—which in turn looked as if they now studied him—the hooded stranger blurted, "This isn't your time! You shouldn't exist here at all!"

He raised his hand in what seemed a menacing posture to the night elf. Recalling Brox's use of the word "wizard," Malfurion quickly prepared a spell of his own, suspecting that Cenarius's druidic teachings would avail him better in this sacred place than the stranger's own magic.

Suddenly the sky thundered and the ever-present light breeze became an intense gale. Brox and Malfurion were pushed back a few feet and the wizard was almost thrust into the air, so hard was he forced away from the edge of the ring.

"There will be none of this in my sanctum!" declared the voice of Cenarius.

A short distance to the side of the flower barrier, the harsh wind picked up leaves, dirt, and other loose bits of the forest, throwing them around and creating a whirlwind. The small twister grew swiftly in size and intensity while the leaves and other pieces solidified into a towering figure.

And as the air quieted again, Cenarius stepped forward to survey Malfurion and the others.

"Of you I expect better," he quietly remarked to the night elf. "But these *are* strange times." He eyed Brox. "And growing stranger with each passing hour, it seems."

The orc growled defiantly at Cenarius. Malfurion quickly silenced him. "This is the lord of the forest, the demigod Cenarius . . . the one to whom I said I would bring you, Brox."

Brox eased somewhat, then pointed at the hooded wizard. "And that one? Is he another demigod?"

"He's part of a puzzle," Cenarius replied. "and you look to be another piece of the same one." To the figure in the ring, he added, "You recognized this newcomer, friend Rhonin."

The robed spellcaster said nothing.

The demigod shook his head in clear disappointment. "I mean you no harm, Rhonin, but too much has come about that I and the others find disturbing and out of place. You and your missing companion and now this one—"

"His name is Brox," Malfurion offered.

"This one called Brox," Cenarius amended. "Another being the likes of which even I have never seen. And how does Brox come to be here, my student? I suspect that there is a tale to tell, a disturbing one."

With a nod, the night elf immediately went into the story of his rescue of the orc, in the process laying any possible blame at his feet alone. Of Tyrande and Illidan, he scarcely even spoke.

But Cenarius, far older and wiser than his pupil, read much of the truth. "I said that the destinies of your brother and you would take different roads. I believe that fork has now come, whether you know it or not."

"I don't understand—"

"It is a talk for another time." The demigod suddenly stepped past Malfurion and Brox, staring into the forest. Around the glade, the crowns of the trees suddenly shook with great agitation. "And time is not something we have at the moment. You had better prepare yourselves . . . you included, friend Rhonin."

"Me?" blurted the wizard.

"What is it, shan'do?" Malfurion could sense the trees' fury.

The sunlit sky filled with thunder and the wind picked up again. A shadow fell over Cenarius's majestic countenance, a dark shadow that made even Malfurion wary of his teacher.

The forest lord stretched forth his arms, almost as if to embrace something that no one else could see. "We are about to be attacked . . . and I fear even I may not be able to protect all of you."

The lone felbeast had followed the trail as no other animal or rider could, smelling not the scent of its quarry, but rather the magic the latter commanded. As much as blood and flesh, the energy that was magic and sorcery was its sustenance . . . and like any of its kind, the felbeast was always ravenous.

Mortal creatures would not have noticed the magic of the oak sentinel, but the demon did. It seized upon this unmoving prey with eagerness, the dire tentacles quickly thrusting out and striking the thick trunk.

The oak did its best to combat this unexpected foe. Roots sought to entangle the paws, but the felbeast dodged them. Loose branches dropped from high above, battering the monster's thick hide futilely.

When that did not work, from the oak came a peculiar keening sound, one that picked up in intensity. It soon reached a level inaudible to most creatures.

But for the felbeast, the sound then became agony. The demon whined and tried to bury its head, but at the same time it refused to release its hold on the guardian. The two wills struggled . . .

In the end, the felbeast proved the stronger. Increasingly drained of its inherent magic, the oak withered more and more, finally dying as the Moon Guard had, slain in its duty after thousands of years of successfully protecting the way.

The felbeast shook its head, then sniffed the air before it. The tentacles eagerly stretched forth, but the demon kept its position. It had grown as it devoured the oak's ancient magic and now stood almost twice as tall as before.

Then, metamorphosis took place. A deep, black radiance surrounded the felbeast, completely enveloping the demon. Within it, the felbeast twisted in various directions, as if trying to escape from itself.

And the more it tried, the more it succeeded. One head, two heads, three, four . . . then five. Each head strained harder, pulling and pulling. The heads were followed by thick necks, brawny shoulders, then muscular torsos and legs.

Fueled by the rich magic of the ancient guardian, the one felbeast became a pack. The great effort momentarily weakened each of the demons, but within seconds they recouped. The knowledge that ahead lay more sustenance, more power, urged them on.

As one, the felbeasts charged toward the glade.

FOURTEEN

*Y*ou *are a true servant,* the great one told Lord Xavius. *Your rewards will be endless . . . all you desire I will grant you . . . anything . . . anyone . . .*

Artificial eyes unblinking, the night elf knelt on one knee before the fiery portal, drinking in the god's many glorious promises. He was the most favored of the great one's new minions, one to whom miraculous powers would be granted once the way had been opened.

And the more the Highborne failed to accomplish the last, the longer the god's arrival was delayed, the more the counselor's frustration grew.

His frustration was shared by two others. One of those was Queen

Azshara, who longed as much as he for the day when all the imperfect would be eradicated from the world, leaving only the night elves—and only the best of that race—to rule the paradise that would follow. She did not know, of course, that, in his wisdom, the great one would make her Xavius's consort, but the counselor expected any protests to fade once their wondrous god informed her.

The other frustrated with the utter lack of success was the towering Hakkar. Ever flanked by two felbeasts, the Houndmaster marched around the Highborne sorcerers, pointing out the flaws in their casting and adding his own might whenever possible.

Yet even with the addition of his arcane knowledge, only now had they at last achieved some minor triumph. Now at last Hakkar and his pets no longer stood alone among the night elves. Now there were three others, horned giants with crimson visages that some found horrific but that Lord Xavius could only admire. At least nine feet tall, they loomed over the Highborne, who themselves were more than seven feet in height.

These were anointed champions of the god, celestial warriors whose only purpose was to do his bidding regardless of the cost to them. Each was roughly nine feet in height and although built oddly thin, the bronze-armored figures had no difficulty wielding the massive, oblong shields and flaming maces. They obeyed to the letter any command given them and treated the counselor with as much respect as they did Hakkar.

And soon there would be more. Even as Xavius stepped back, he saw the portal flash. It bloomed, growing to fill the pattern over which it hovered, swelling until—

Through it came another of the Fel Guard, as Hakkar called these worthy fighters. The moment he entered the mortal plane, the newcomer bowed his fearsome head toward the Houndmaster, then toward Xavius.

Hakkar signaled for the warrior to join his predecessors. Turning to Xavius, the Houndmaster indicated the four. "The great one fulfills his first promise to you, lord night elf! Command them! They are yoursss to do as you pleassse!"

Xavius knew exactly what to do with them. "As they have been a gift to me, so they will best serve as a gift for the queen! I shall make them honored bodyguards for Azshara!"

The Houndmaster nodded approvingly. They both knew the value of pleasing the queen of the night elves, just as both knew the counselor's secret desire. "You'd do bessst to bring sssuch a present to her yourssself, lord night elf! The work will continue while you are gone, I will sssee to that!"

The notion of making the presentation himself greatly appealed to Xavius. With a bow to Hakkar, the counselor snapped his fingers and led the four gigantic warriors out of the tower chamber. He knew exactly where he would find Azshara at this time.

And as he departed, the Houndmaster, stony eyes flaring brightly, watched the night elf intently.

Although her lord counselor slept very little—almost not at all of late—as queen of the realm, Azshara had the right and privilege to rest as she pleased. After all, she had to be perfect in every way, especially where her beauty was concerned. Therefore, the ruler of the night elves generally slept through the entire day, avoiding completely the harsh, burning sunlight.

Thus, Azshara did not take well at first to the meek entrance of one of her attendants. The latter fell quickly onto both knees before the rounded edge of the queen's room-spanning, down bed, the young female almost hiding behind the gossamer curtains that encircled it.

With a languid hand, the Light of Lights indicated that her servant could speak.

"Mistress, forgive this humble one, but the lord counselor requests an audience with yourself, stating he has brought something of interest to you."

There was nothing which Azshara could imagine desiring at the moment that would make her leave her bed, not even for the counselor. Silver hair draping her pillows, she pursed her lips as she pondered whether or not to send Xavius on his way.

"Make him wait five minutes," she finally purred, already artfully positioning herself. Well aware of Xavius's tastes, the queen knew best how to use them to her advantage. The counselor might think himself superior to his monarch, but as a female, she was superior to any male. "Then grant him entrance."

The attendant did not question her mistress's decision. Azshara watched her depart through slitted eyes, then stretched gracefully, already planning her encounter with her chief advisor.

The young servant nervously returned . . . but only after Xavius had already been waiting for several minutes. Keeping her head low—and thus her expression all but hidden—she ushered the counselor through the thick, skillfully carved oak doors leading into the queen's personal chambers.

Only a handful of times had he dared see her in this, her most private sanctum. Xavius knew something of what to expect; Azshara would appear flawless and seductive, all without seeming to notice this herself. It was the game she played and played well, but he was prepared. He was her superior.

Sure enough, the queen of the night elves lay in repose, one arm behind her head, two silken-clad attendants kneeling nearby. A silver stand with an emerald flask of wine stood within reach of the queen and one half-filled goblet gave evidence to her having already sampled its rich bounty.

"My darling lord counselor," she breathed. "You must have something dreadfully important to say to me to request an audience at such an hour." The thin, glistening sheet framed her exquisite shape. "I've therefore tried to accommodate you as best I can."

Fist to his heart, he went down on one knee. Gazing at the white, marble floor, Lord Xavius replied, "Light of Lights, Cherished Heart of the People, I am grateful for this time given me. I apologize for disturbing you now, but I have brought with me a most interesting gift, a gift truly worthy of the queen of the night elves, the queen of the world. If I may summon it?"

He glanced up and saw that he had her attention. Her veiled eyes failed to hide both her growing curiosity and anticipation. Azshara shifted on her bed, the sheet ever clinging just so to her torso.

"You pique my interest, my dear Xavius. I grant you the honor of presenting me with your gift."

Rising again, the tall counselor turned to the doors and snapped his fingers.

There was a gasp from the outer room and two more attendants rushed inside, fleeing to the comfort and protection of their mistress. Frowning, Azshara sat up, almost but not quite letting the sheet slip.

The four fearsome warriors marched two abreast into the queen's sanctum, so tall that they had to duck through the doorway to avoid scraping the top with their horns. They spread out as they entered, shields before their armored bodies and maces held high in salute.

Azshara leaned forward, utterly fascinated. "What are they?"

"They are *yours*, my queen! The protection of your life is their duty, their only reason to exist! Behold, your majesty, your new bodyguards!"

He saw that he had pleased her well. There would be more and more celestial warriors sent through by the great one, but these were the very first and they were to be *hers*. That made all the difference.

"How wonderful," she murmured, stretching one arm out to a servant. The young maiden immediately reached for Azshara's gown. The other attendants created a wall, obscuring all but the queen's head from the view of Xavius and the Fel Guard. "How very fitting. Your gift is acceptable."

"I am pleased that *you* are pleased."

The servants stepped back. Now clad in a translucent, frost-colored gown, Queen Azshara rose from her bed. With calculated steps, she walked up to the towering figures and inspected each, her gown trailing along over the marble floor. For their part, the Fel Guard stood so motionless that they might have been mistaken for statuary.

"Are there more?"

"There will be, eventually."

She frowned. "So few after so long? How will the great one himself come through if we cannot manage more than a few of his host at a time?"

"We draw from the Well as best we can, oh glorious queen. There are contradictory currents, outside reactions, the influence of other spellcasters elsewhere—"

Like a child reaching out to touch a new toy, Azshara let her fingers just graze the blazing armor of one of her new bodyguards. There was a slight hiss. The queen pulled back her fingers, an oddly pleased expression crossing her perfect features. "Then why haven't you cut off the Well from such outside interference? It would make your task then much simpler."

Lord Xavius opened his mouth to explain why the intricacies of the Highborne spellwork would not permit such—then realized that he had no good answer. Theoretically, Azshara's suggestion had tremendous merit.

"Truly you are the queen," he finally commented.

Her golden eyes seized his own. "Of course I am, my darling counselor. There has only ever been, only ever will be . . . *one* Azshara."

He nodded wordlessly.

She strode back to the bed, seating herself delicately on the edge. "If there is nothing else?"

"Nothing . . . for now, my queen."

"Then, I think you must have more work to do now."

Dismissed, Lord Xavius bowed low to his monarch, then backed out of her chambers. He did not take any umbrage at her regal tone or attitude, did not even grow more than slightly annoyed at her mastery of the situation.

Cut off the Well from interference . . .

It could be done. If not by the Highborne alone, then with Hakkar's good guidance. Surely the Houndmaster would know best how to do it. With use of the Well limited only to those of the palace, the power the Highborne drew from it would be more easily manipulated, more easily transformed . . .

Small matter what havoc cutting off the Well would wreak upon the *rest* of their people.

"He is definitely one of us . . . somehow I know this as well as I know myself."

The words were perhaps the most ironic ever spoken in history, or so Krasus believed at that moment. They had, after all, been uttered by the dragon Korialstrasz, the newest of Alexstrasza's consorts.

And also Krasus's younger self.

Korialstrasz did not recognize himself, at least, not consciously. However, the fact that Alexstrasza had not informed him of the newcomer's true identity raised many questions.

One question possibly related to the others had to do with the male dragon's present condition. While it was true that Krasus's memory was full of holes, he doubted that he could have forgotten such an illness as his earlier incarnation seemed to be suffering at this moment. Korialstrasz looked far older, far more feeble than his age. He looked older than Tyran, who was centuries Korialstrasz's senior.

"What else do you say about him?" Alexstrasza asked her mate.

The other dragon squinted at Krasus. "He is older, very old, in fact." Korialstrasz tilted his head. "Something in his eyes . . . his eyes . . ."

"What about them?"

The huge male drew back. "Forgive me! My head is addled! I am not worthy of being in your presence at this time! I should withdraw . . ."

But she would not yet let him go. "Look at him, my mate. I ask you this one last thing; with what little you know, would you trust the word of this one?"

"I . . . yes, my Alexstrasza . . . I . . . would."

Suddenly, a curious thing happened to Krasus. As the dragons continued conversing about him, he began to feel stronger, stronger than he had ever felt since first arriving in the past. Not quite as strong as he should have been, but at least much closer to normal.

And it was not him alone. He also noted that, despite words to the contrary, his younger self also started looking more fit. A bit of color had returned to the scales and Korialstrasz moved with somewhat better ease than earlier. His words did not come out in gasps anymore.

Alexstrasza nodded in response to her consort's answer, then said, "So I wanted to hear. It tells me much that you feel so."

"Is there more that you wish of me? My strength is better; being with you, being of assistance to you, has clearly heartened me."

The smile that Krasus knew so well graced the dragon queen's reptilian countenance. "Always the poetic one, my loving Korialstrasz! Yes . . . I wish much more of you. I know it will be difficult, but I must request your presence when I bring this one before the other Aspects."

She succeeded in stunning both versions of Krasus. The young incarnation spoke first, echoing the older's surprise. "You would convene a gathering of the Five? Over this one? But why?"

"Because he has told a story that they must hear, a story I tell you now . . . and you may choose again afterward to answer whether you trust him or not."

So at last his earlier self would know the truth. Krasus readied himself for the other's shock.

But as he had startled Rhonin by relating a tale that left out not only part of the truth but also his very identity, so now did the dragon queen tell much the same. She spoke of the disruption and all else Krasus had told the watcher, but of the mage's true identity, Alexstrasza said nothing. To her consort, Krasus was merely another of the red flight, one whose mind had been torn asunder by the powerful forces that had assailed it.

Krasus himself made no attempt to reveal himself. This was Alexstrasza—his life, his love. Advisor to her he might be, but she still wielded the wisdom of an Aspect. If she felt that his younger self should remain ignorant . . . then who was he to disagree?

"An astonishing tale," Korialstrasz murmured, looking and sounding even better. "I would have trouble believing it from any mouth but your own, my queen . . ."

"So your trust of him has faded?"

The eyes of the younger self met the eyes of the older. Even if Korialstrasz did not recognize himself, he must have recognized still the kindred spirit. "No . . . no, my trust has not faded. If you think he should be brought before the others . . . I must acquiesce."

"Will you then fly with me?"

"But I am not one of the Five . . . I am merely me."

The Queen of Life laughed lightly, a musical sound coming as it did from a dragon. "And thus you are as worthy as any of us."

Korialstrasz was clearly flattered. "If I am as strong as I now feel, I will gladly fly at your side and stand before the other Aspects."

"Thank you . . . that is all I ask." She leaned forward and briefly nuzzled heads with him.

Krasus felt a peculiar jealousy. Here he was, watching himself be intimate with his mate, yet it was not him. He wished that for just one moment he could have changed places with Korialstrasz, that for just this one particular moment, he could be his true self again.

With a last lingering glance, the male turned and left the chamber. As the tip of Korialstrasz's tail vanished into the passage, the mage suddenly felt light-headed. The weakness returned in a rush, causing him to teeter.

He would have fallen, but suddenly a massive, scaled appendage wrapped softly around him—Alexstrasza's own tail come to his rescue.

"The two parts made whole . . . at least for a time."

"I don't—" His head swam.

"You felt much better in his presence, did you not?"

"Y-yes."

"Would I were Nozdormu at this moment. He would understand this more. I think . . . I think that in the earthly realm, no creature can coexist with himself. I believe you and he, being one, draw off the same life force. When you are far from each other, you are halved, but when you are so very near, as just before, the draining is not so terrible. You help each other."

Nestled safely, Krasus recovered enough to think over her words. "So that is why you requested him to come with."

"Your story must be told and it will be told better if he is near. As to your unspoken question—why I did not reveal to him the truth—that is because of what may have to be done to salvage matters."

Her tone grew grim as she said the last, verifying for Krasus his own suspicions. "You think it may come to the point where one of us must be removed from this period . . . even if that means *death.*"

The leviathan nodded reluctantly. "I am afraid so, my love."

"I accept the choice. I knew it from the beginning."

"Then there is only one more matter to discuss before I reach out to the others . . . and that is what must be done with this other who came with you."

Although inside he asked Rhonin to forgive him, Krasus did not hesitate to reply. "If it must be done, he will share my fate. He, too, has those he cares about. He would give his life for them."

The Queen of Life nodded. "As I trusted your counsel when it came to you, so I trust your counsel when it comes to him. Should the other decide so, he will also be removed." The dragon's expression softened. "Know that I will be saddened by this forever."

"Take no blame unto yourself, my queen, my heart."

"I must contact the others. It would be best for you if you waited for me here. In this place you will find yourself not so weary."

"I am honored, my queen."

"Honored? You are my *consort.* I could do no less."

With her tail she guided him to an area of the nest near the stream. Krasus settled into a natural depression that acted for him like a huge chair.

As the dragon queen moved to the passage, she paused and, with a trace of remorse, added, "I hope you will be comfortable among the eggs."

"I will be careful not to touch any." Krasus understood the value of any egg.

"I am certain you will, my love . . . especially knowing that they are yours."

She left him wordless. As the crimson giant disappeared, Krasus glanced from one egg to another. As consort, he had, of course, bred with his mate. Many of his children had grown to adulthood, bringing pride to the flight.

He slammed his fist against the rock, ignoring the pain the foolish act sent through him. For all he had revealed to his beloved Alexstrasza, he had kept from her several important facts. Most immediate was the coming of the Burning Legion. Krasus feared that even his queen, wise as she was, would be tempted to play with history . . . and that might create a more horrifying disaster.

Yet, even worse than that, Krasus had been unable to tell her about the future of their own kind, a future in which only a few would survive . . . a future in which most of the hatchlings of this and successive clutches would perish before they ever had the opportunity to reach full maturity.

A future in which the Queen of Life herself would become a slave, her children the war dogs of a conquering race.

FIFTEEN

The felbeasts charged through the enchanted forest, their snouts raised high as the scent of magic increased. Their hunger and their mission urged them on, the huge hounds snarling their impatience. But as one leapt over a fallen trunk, limbs from another tree nearby bent down and entangled its legs. A second felbeast racing along a path found its paws sinking into suddenly muddy earth. A third collided with a sprouting bush filled with razor-sharp brambles that pricked even the demon's hard flesh and brought it immense agony.

The forest came alive, defending itself and its master. The charge of the five monsters faltered . . . but did not fail. Huge claws tore at the tangling branches, ripping them from trunks. Another felbeast aided the one trapped in the mire, dragging its comrade to solid ground before moving on. Hunger and fury enabled the one caught in the sharp brambles to burrow through even though it meant bleeding cuts everywhere.

The hunters would not be denied their prey . . .

"Shan'do! What is it?"

The demigod glanced down at his pupil, no recriminations in his fiery gaze. "The hounds of which you spoke . . . they have followed you here."

"Followed? Impossible! There was only one left and it—"

Brox interrupted, his rumbling voice offering no comfort. "The felbeasts . . . they are dark magic. Where there was one . . . there can be more if they're able to feed well . . . this I saw . . ."

"A good friend and able guardian fell to one," Cenarius commented, attention once more on the thick woods ahead of them. "He bore within him magic most ancient, most powerful. It only served to make him more susceptible to their evil."

The orc nodded. "Then the one is now many." Brox instinctively reached behind his back, but his beloved war ax did not await him there. "I've nothing to fight with."

"You will be armed. Quickly find a fallen limb the length of your favored weapon. Malfurion, attend me."

Brox swiftly did as commanded. He brought to the demigod and the night elf a massive branch, which Cenarius then had him place before Malfurion.

"Kneel before it, my student. You, too, warrior. Malfurion, place your hands upon the branch, then let him place his palms atop your hands." When they had done this, the forest lord commanded, "Now, warrior, clear your mind of all but the weapon. Think *only* of it! Time is of the essence. Malfurion, you must open your mind and let his thoughts flow to yours. I will guide you more when that is done."

The night elf did as he was told. He cleared his thoughts as his shan'do had early on taught him, then reached out to link himself to the orc.

Instantly a primal force bullied its way into his mind. Malfurion almost rejected it, but then calmed. He accepted Brox's thoughts and let the image of what the warrior wanted take shape.

You see the weapon, my student? came Cenarius's voice. *You sense the feel of it, the lines of its forming?*

Malfurion did. He also felt the orc's relationship to the weapon, how it was more than simply a tool, but also a true extension of the warrior.

Guide your hands over the wood, ever keeping the image in your head. Follow the natural grain and turn it to the shape desired . . .

With Brox's hands atop his own, the night elf began running his fingers along the branch. As he did, he felt it soften at his touch, then shift in form.

And under his guidance materialized a thick-bladed ax composed entirely of oak. Malfurion watched it shape, felt the satisfaction of creating a good solid weapon like the one he had lost when captured by the night elves—

He tensed. Those were the *orc's* emotions, not his. Quickly thrusting them back, Malfurion concentrated on the final bits—curvature of the handle, the sharpness of the blade.

The task is done, interjected Cenarius. *Return to me . . .*

The night elf and the orc pulled away. For a brief moment, they stared into each other's eyes. Malfurion wondered if Brox had experienced some of his own thoughts, but the green-skinned creature gave no hint of such a thing happening.

Between them lay a smoothly polished re-creation of that which Brox desired, though even the night elf wondered how the weapon could last more than one or two strikes.

In answer, the forest lord extended his hands—and suddenly the ax lay across them. Cenarius studied the weapon with his golden eyes.

"Let it always swing true, always protect its master. Let it be wielded well for the cause of life and justice. Let it add to the strength of its master and, in turn, let him strengthen it."

And as he spoke, a blue radiance surrounded the ax. The light sank into the wood, adding a sheen to Malfurion's creation.

The demigod offered the ax to the orc. "It is yours. It will serve you well."

Eyes wide, the graying orc took the gift, then swung it back and forth, testing the quality. "The balance . . . perfect! The feel . . . like a part of my arm! But it will crack—"

"No," interjected the forest lord. "In addition to Malfurion's work, it now has my blessing. You'll find it stronger than any mortal-forged ax. You may trust me on that."

As for the night elf, he did not reach for a weapon nor did he desire one such as Brox now carried. Despite knowing that the demonic beasts fed off of magic and sorcery, he still understood that his chances were better with spells than with some weapon with which he had only moderate skill. He already had some ideas as to how to use his talent without it becoming the cause of his defeat.

And so the three faced the coming foe.

The nightmares of Rhonin's recent past had come back to haunt him, but now they did so in the flesh. Felbeasts, the harbingers of the Burning Legion, were already here in the mortal plane. Could the endless ranks of horned, fiery demon warriors be far behind?

Krasus had put into the red-haired wizard's mind the fear of what would happen if either interacted more with the past. What might seem a victory could spell the end of the future as they knew it. To best preserve the lives of those he loved, it behooved Rhonin to do nothing at all.

But as the first felbeast leapt into the glade, such noble notions instantly vanished from his thoughts.

Thunder crashed around the demigod as he stepped up to meet the felbeasts. His stomping hooves shook the ground and even caused the earth to crack open slightly. He swung his hands together and lightning flashed as they met.

And from those hands, Cenarius unleashed what seemed a miniature sun at

the foremost demon. Perhaps the demigod only tested his adversary or somehow underestimated the resilience of it, for the felbeast thrust forth both tentacles and, instead of the sunburst striking dead its target . . . the demon's hungry
appendages *absorbed* Cenarius's spell with ease.

The felbeast hesitated, shimmered . . . and suddenly, where there had been
one, there were now two.

They leapt upon the stag lord, clawing at him and trying to drain him of his
great magic. With one hand Cenarius held the first at bay, the demon wriggling
madly and snapping at the arm that kept him high in the air. But the other
clamped itself onto his shoulder, the tentacles seeking the demigod's flesh. The
three combatants fell back in a frenzy of movement.

They never did that! Rhonin himself had not faced felbeasts, but he had studied their corpses and read all the information gathered about them. He had
heard the few rare tales of the hounds multiplying themselves, but only after
gorging on magic and even then the process had been said to be slow, difficult.
*It must be the ancient magic that the demigod and the forest itself wield . . . it's so rich
and powerful that the creatures are made even more terrible by it . . .*

He shivered, knowing that magic had always been his best tool. He could
fight by hand, yes, but he had no weapon and doubted that Cenarius could
give him one now. Besides, against these creatures, his skill with a sword
would be more than lacking. Rhonin needed his magic.

When Cenarius had first brought Krasus and him to the ring, Rhonin had
found himself unable to cast any spell. The forest lord had placed an enchantment on his mind, keeping the might of both his "guests" in check. However,
Rhonin had felt that enchantment removed from him the second that Cenarius had realized the danger to them all. The demigod meant no true harm to
the wizard; he had acted only out of concern for his forest and his world.

But even if he disobeyed Krasus's recommendation, Rhonin wondered
just how much good having his powers back would do him. Surely the
demons would be most eager for his magic, just as they had hungered for the
magic of so many wizards sucked dry in the future war against the legion.

The felbeasts pressed their foes, in the process drawing nearer and nearer
to Rhonin. His hands curled into fists and words of power stood ready on his
tongue.

And yet . . . still he did nothing.

As Cenarius and the twin felbeasts met, two more charged at Brox. The huge
warrior met the creatures head on with a war cry that made one demon falter
slightly. The orc used that hesitation to his advantage, swinging hard at his
adversary.

The enchanted ax buried itself deep in the forepaw of the felbeast, severing three clawed toes as easily as if the orc had cut through air. The foul greenish fluid that passed for blood in many of the demons spilled over the grass, burning the blades like acid.

The injured felbeast let out a yelp and stumbled to the side, but its comrade continued its charge, throwing itself upon the orc. Brox, trying to recover from his swing, barely saved himself by using the bottom end of the ax shaft. He drove the end into the chest of the leaping behemoth.

A monstrous gasp escaped the felbeast, but did little to slow its momentum. It fell upon Brox, nearly crushing him under its massive form.

As for the night elf, the monster he faced eagerly reached for him with its vampiric tentacles. Malfurion concentrated, trying to think as Cenarius would think, drawing upon what he had learned from the demigod about seeing nature as both his weapon and his comrade.

Recalling the demigod's own arrival, Malfurion created from the ever-present wind a roaring twister that immediately surrounded the monstrous felbeast. The sinewy, gaping tentacles swung wildly about, seeking the magic, but Malfurion's spell had accented only the inherent forces of the wind and so the demon found little upon which to drain.

With a wave of his right hand, the night elf then asked of the surrounding trees the gift of whatever spare leaves they had to offer. He sought the strongest only, but he needed them in great numbers and quickly.

And from the crowns of the towering guardians descended hundreds, whatever each could give. Malfurion immediately used another breeze to guide the leaves toward the whirlwind.

Within it, the felbeast pushed forward, relentlessly closing on its intended prey. The twister matched each determined step, ever keeping the demon at its center.

The leaves poured into the whirlwind, spinning around faster and faster and increasing in number rapidly. At first the felbeast paid them no mind, for what were a few bits of refuse in the wind to a powerful fiend, but then the first sharp edge of a leaf sliced across its muzzle, drawing blood.

The enraged demon batted at the offending leaf, only to have several more cut it successively on its paw, its legs, and its torso. The wind now a hundred times more intense, the sharp edges of each soaring leaf became like well-honed blades, cutting and slashing wherever they touched the felbeast. Greenish ooze spilled over the demon's body, drenching its hide and even obscuring its vision.

Cenarius and the beasts who had attacked him now fought far from the rest. The cries of the demons were well matched by the majestic roar of the forest lord. He seized the foreleg of the felbeast that had attached itself to him and with a single twist snapped the bone. The demon howled and its tentacles released their hold, flailing about in response to its pain.

Momentarily rid of one menace, Cenarius focused on the other. His countenance took on a dark wonder and his eyes blazed in fury. Suddenly, there burst from them a spark of light that enveloped the demon held at bay. The slavering creature's tentacles greedily sought that light, drinking it in eagerly and wanting even more.

But this was not a wizard or sorcerer from which it sought to siphon magic. Now surrounded by a fearsome blue aura, Cenarius pressed with his attack, feeding his foe and giving it what it desired . . . but much too quickly and in abundance so great that even the demon could not take it all in.

The felbeast swelled, blowing up like a quickly filled water sack. Briefly it seemed as if about to divide . . . but the forces already ingested by it were more than it could handle.

The monstrous hound *exploded*, gobbets of stench-ridden flesh raining down upon the glade.

Thus far, Rhonin had been fortunate. No felbeast had come for him. He remained at the center of the ring, hoping that its power would keep him from having to decide whether or not to use his own abilities.

Rhonin watched Brox fend off the creature that had nearly crushed the orc. The veteran warrior appeared to have his struggle well in hand despite two foes. But as he continued to observe Brox, a terrible notion filled the human mage. If he and Krasus could not be returned to their time, Rhonin had understood that it might be best if both were slain quickly, the sooner to prevent whatever further alterations they might make to history. What neither had counted on, however, was a single orc warrior also being thrown into this era.

And as he stared at Brox's back, Rhonin began to contemplate a different sort of spell. In the midst of the struggle, it might go unnoticed by the others and would eliminate another danger to the timeline. Krasus would have told him he was making the right decision, that, more than even the demons, Brox was a danger to the very existence of the world.

But his hand faltered, the spell forming in his mind pushed back into the darkest recesses. Rhonin felt ashamed. Brox's people had become valuable allies and this orc now fought to save not only himself but others, *including* the wizard.

Everything Krasus had said urged Rhonin to deal quickly with Brox and worry about the consequences later, but the more he watched the orc battle beside the night elf—another allied race in the future—the more Rhonin regretted his moment of insanity. What he had contemplated seemed to him as horrible as the atrocities perpetrated in his time by the Burning Legion.

But Rhonin could no longer stand and do nothing . . .

"I'm sorry, Krasus," he muttered, calling up a new spell. "I'm truly sorry."

Taking a deep breath, the hooded mage stared from under his brow at one of the felbeasts in combat with the orc. He recalled the incantations that had helped him against the Scourge and other inhuman servants of the Legion. It would have to be done in such a way that the felbeasts would have no time to draw away the power of his spell.

Far, far to his right, Cenarius had finally managed to peel off his remaining foe. With one forelimb dangling, the demon could not maintain its hold. Muscles straining, the demigod bent back, held the beast over his head, and, with a roar of triumph, threw it high over the tops of the trees and deep into the waiting forest.

Rhonin cast his spell.

He had hoped to send a withering blast at the felbeast in focus, at least wounding it enough for Brox to finish the task. What Rhonin achieved instead, however, was far beyond his hopes.

An invisible, thundering wall of power that caused the very air to ripple madly materialized before him, then raced like the wind toward his objective. It spread as it moved, covering in the blink of an eye the entire expanse of the glade.

Through Brox and the night elf it passed without even the slightest hint of acknowledgment, but for the three savage demons in its path the fury that Rhonin had unleashed gave no quarter. The felbeasts had no time to react, no time to bring their hungry tentacles into play. They were as gnats in a raging fire.

As the wall of force passed through them, the demons burned to ash. The spell ate away at them from nose on back, a cloud of dust particles scattering from each decimated felbeast as it crumbled. One managed to unleash a short-lived howl, but then the only sound after was the rush of the wind as it sent to the heavens what had once been the rampaging monsters.

Silence filled the glade.

Brox dropped his ax, his wide, tusked mouth open in sheer disbelief. Malfurion stared at his own hands, as if somehow they had been responsible, then turned in the direction of Cenarius, thinking the answer lay with the demigod.

Rhonin had to blink several times to convince himself that what he witnessed had not only been real, but of his own creation. Belatedly the wizard recalled the brief struggle against the armored night elves, a struggle in which Krasus had proven disturbingly weak and Rhonin had excelled in a manner he could never have thought possible of him.

But any pleasure at his astonishing victory vanished immediately as agony tore into him from his back. He felt himself being ripped apart from inside, as if his very soul was being drained away—

Drained away? Even despite his horrific ordeal, Rhonin understood all too well what had just happened. Another felbeast had come around unnoticed from the rear and, as was its way, sought a source of magic to attack.

Rhonin recalled what had happened to spellcasters caught by the demons. He recalled the terrifying husks that had been brought back to Dalaran for investigation.

And he was about to become yet another . . .

But although now down on one knee, Rhonin rebelled. With all the power at his command, surely he could escape this parasitic beast!

Escape . . . it became the driving thought in his pain-wracked mind. Escape . . . all Rhonin sought was to flee the agony, to go somewhere where he would be safe.

Through the haze of his distress, he vaguely heard the voices of the orc and the night elf. His fear for himself overlapped them. With what it had sucked from him, the felbeast would be more than a match for either.

Escape . . . that was all Rhonin sought. *Anywhere* . . .

Then the pain vanished, replaced by a heavy but comforting numbness that spread throughout his body like fire. Rhonin gratefully accepted the startling change, letting the numbness take hold and envelop him completely . . .

Swallow him whole.

Not for the first time, Tyrande slipped through the silent corridors of the huge temple—past the countless chambers of sleeping acolytes, the meditation rooms, and places of public worship—and headed to a window near the main entrance. The bright sun nearly blinded her, but she forced herself to search the empty square beyond, seeking what she would likely still miss.

No sooner had she peered out than a clank of metal warned her of an approaching guard. The stern visage of the other night elf softened a touch upon recognition.

"You again! Sister Tyrande . . . you should really stay in your quarters and get some sleep. You've hardly had any rest for days and now you put yourself at risk. Your friend will be all right. I'm certain of it."

The guard meant Illidan, for whom Tyrande also worried, but what the novice priestess really feared was that when Illidan did return, it would be with his brother and the hapless orc in tow. She did not think that Malfurion's twin would ever betray him, but if Lord Ravencrest captured the pair, what could Illidan do but go along with matters?

"I cannot help it. I'm just so restless, sister. Please forgive me."

The sentry smiled sympathetically. "I hope he realizes how much you care for him. The time for your choosing is fast approaching, isn't it?"

The other's words bothered Tyrande more than she revealed. Her thoughts and reactions since the three had freed Broxigar had more than hinted to her of her preference, but she could not yet come to believe it herself. No, her concern was just that of one childhood friend for another.

It had to be . . .

There came the harsh clank of metal upon metal and the hiss of night sabers. Tyrande immediately darted past the bemused guard, heading to the outer steps of Elune's temple.

Somewhat dust-laden, Lord Ravencrest's party rode into the square. The cloaked noble himself seemed quite at ease, even very pleased about something, but many of his soldiers wore darker expressions and constantly looked at one another as if sharing some terrible secret.

Of either Malfurion or Broxigar, there was no sign.

All but hidden on the far side of Lord Ravencrest, Illidan rode tall and proud. He appeared the most satisfied of the group and if that pleasure had to do with keeping his twin from capture, then Tyrande could certainly not blame him.

Without realizing what she did, the young priestess stepped down to the street. Her presence caught the attention of Lord Ravencrest, who smiled graciously and pointed her out to Illidan. The bearded commander whispered something to Malfurion's brother, then raised his hand.

The soldiers came to a halt. Illidan and Ravencrest steered their mounts toward her. ·

"Well, if it isn't the most lovely of the Mother Moon's dedicated servants!" the commander declared. "How interesting to find you awaiting our return despite the late hour!" He glanced at Illidan, whose expression bordered on embarrassment. "Very interesting, don't you think?"

"Yes, my lord."

"We must make for Black Rook Hold, sister, but I think I can spare a precious moment for you two, eh?"

Tyrande felt her cheeks darken slightly as Ravencrest guided his panther back to the rest of the party. Illidan dismounted quickly, stepping up to her and taking her hands in his own.

"They're safe, Tyrande . . . and Lord Ravencrest has taken me under his wing! We fought a fearsome beast and I kept it from harming him! Destroyed it with my own power!"

"Malfurion escaped? You're certain of it?"

"Of course, of course," he returned excitedly, waving away any further questions about his brother. "I've found my destiny at last, don't you understand? The Moon Guard's all but ignored me, but I slew a monster that killed three of theirs, including one of their senior sorcerers!"

She wanted to hear what he knew about Malfurion and the orc, but it was clear that Illidan was caught up in his own good fortune. Tyrande could appreciate that, having watched him work hard and fruitlessly to achieve the glorious future so many had predicted for him. "I'm so glad for you. I feared that you were frustrated some with the pace of Cenarius's teaching, but if you were able to protect Lord Ravencrest with it where his own soldiers could not, then—"

"You don't understand! I didn't use those slow, cumbersome spells that Malfurion's adored shan'do tried to show us time and again! I used good, traditional night elf sorcery . . . and in the daytime, yet! It was exhilarating!"

His quick renunciation of the druidic ways did not entirely surprise Tyrande. On the one hand, she was grateful that he had successfully come into his own at such a drastic moment. On the other, it was yet another sign of the growing differences between the twins.

And another consideration for her already-overwrought mind.

Behind Illidan, Lord Ravencrest politely cleared his throat.

Malfurion's brother grew more animated. "I have to go, Tyrande! I'm to be shown my place at the Hold and then help organize a larger party to retrieve the dead beasts and all the bodies!"

"Bodies?" It had registered on her that some of the Moon Guard had perished because of a monster, but now she realized that *only* Ravencrest's band would be returning. The one that preceded them out after Malfurion had been completely slaughtered.

The horror of it all made Tyrande shiver . . . especially the fact that Malfurion had also been out there.

"The other creatures wiped out the pursuit almost to a soldier, Tyrande, didn't you understand?" Illidan's voice grew almost gleeful. He paid no mind to the increasing dismay on her face. "The sorcerers perished immediately, no help at all to the rest. It took the fighters all but two lives to stop them and *I* killed one creature with just two quick spells!" His chest swelled. "And these were monsters that devoured magic, too!"

Again, the noble coughed. Illidan quickly pulled her hands to his lips, kissing them ever so lightly. Releasing Tyrande, he leapt back atop the night saber.

"I wanted to be worthy of you," Illidan suddenly murmured. "And soon, I will be."

That said, he turned the cat about and headed to the waiting commander. Ravencrest gave Illidan a companionable slap on the back, then looked over his shoulder at Tyrande. The noble nodded his head toward Malfurion's twin and winked.

As Tyrande watched, still dazed by all she had heard, the armed party rode off in the direction of Black Rook Hold. Illidan peered back one last time before he vanished from the square, his golden eyes intent upon his childhood friend. Tyrande had no trouble reading in them his desires.

Drawing her robe around her, she rushed back up into the temple. The same sentry who had spoken to her earlier met her just within.

"Forgive me, sister! I couldn't help hearing much of what was said. I grieve for the lives lost on the futile hunt, but I also wish to give my congratulations on the fine future for your friend! Lord Ravencrest surely must have the highest respect for him to so readily take him under his guidance! Truly it would be hard to find a better match, eh?"

"No . . . no, I suppose not." When she realized how she sounded, Tyrande quickly added, "Forgive me, sister, I believe my exhaustion is catching up with me. I think I should return to bed."

"Understandable, sister. At least you know that you'll be in store for some pleasant dreams . . ."

But as Tyrande hurried to her room, she suspected that her dreams would be anything but pleasant. True, she was happy with the news that Malfurion and Broxigar had made good their escape and that no one apparently had linked Malfurion to the matter. Tyrande was also glad that Illidan had finally found himself, something she had begun to fear would never come about. What bothered her now, though, was that Illidan appeared to have made a decision regarding the two of them while Tyrande herself had not yet done so. There was still Malfurion to consider in the equation, and still his emotions to define.

Of course, that all depended upon whether or not Malfurion continued to evade the wary eye of the Moon Guard and Lord Ravencrest. If either discovered the truth, it would very likely mean Black Rook Hold for him.

And from there, not even Illidan would be able to save his brother.

The trees, the foliage, nothing had stopped the felbeast's plummet earthward. Cast into the sky by the demigod, the demonic hound could not save itself.

But the capricious nature of chance did what nothing else could. Cenarius had tossed his evil foe as far as he could, assuming logically that the fall would finish his task. Had the felbeast landed on rock or earth or hard against the trunk of one of the mightier oaks, it would have been killed in an instant.

Where the forest lord had thrown it, however, proved to be a body of water, so deep that even at the velocity with which the felbeast dropped, it did not strike the bottom.

The journey to the surface almost did what the fall failed to do, but still the demon managed to haul itself ashore. One foreleg hanging useless, the felbeast moved to a shaded depression where it paused for several minutes to recover.

Once it had recuperated as best as its wounds would allow, the demon sniffed the air, searching for a particular scent. The moment the felbeast located what it sought, it grew alert. Pulling itself forward, the injured horror slowly but steadily began to wend its way toward the source. Even from this distance, it could smell the power emanating from the Well of Eternity. There it would find the magic it needed to heal, the magic with which it could even restore the limb that had been ruined.

The felbeasts were not exactly the simple creatures that even Brox and Rhonin, who knew of them from their own war, assumed them to be. No creature that served the lord of the Burning Legion was without some wit, save perhaps the rampaging goliaths called Infernals. The demon hounds were a part of their handler and what they learned, Hakkar learned.

And from this lone survivor, the Houndmaster would learn much about those who might stand in the way of the Legion's coming . . .

SIXTEEN

I t is time."

Both Alexstrasza's return and her declaration caught Krasus by surprise. The dragon mage had sunk so deep into his thoughts that the passage of minutes and hours had become meaningless. He truly had no idea whether or not he had waited long for her return.

"I am ready."

She bent down and took him up onto her neck. Moving gracefully through the ancient passages carved out over generations by the red dragon flight, Alexstrasza and Krasus soon arrived at a wind-tossed opening overlooking a vast cloud-enshrouded region. Here was the realm of the red dragons, a breathtaking vista of proud mountain peaks capped with permanent snow and wrapped in endless stretches of mist. Krasus understood full well how high his clan's mountain home had to be for most of the clouds to be *below it*. Vaguely his splintered memory now recalled the majesty of the land, the great valleys carved out by ice and time, the jagged, individual faces of each peak.

He suddenly teetered, the rarefied air not quite sufficient for his battered body. Alexstrasza used her wings to keep him from falling off.

"Perhaps this might not be the best thing for you," she suggested, her voice filled with concern.

But as abruptly as he had almost collapsed, Krasus now felt renewed strength course through him.

"I trust . . . I am not late."

Korialstrasz lumbered toward his mate, initially looking much the way the mage had felt moments before. Yet the male dragon, too, now moved as if given an unexpected boost of energy. His somewhat haggard expression vanished as he neared.

"You are not. Do you feel up to the journey?"

"Until this very moment, I thought perhaps I could not . . . but it seems that I am feeling better again." His gaze flickered from Alexstrasza to Krasus and back again, as if he suspected the reason for his startling recuperation but could not accept it.

The dragon queen transferred Krasus to her consort. As Krasus touched his younger self, he felt his own body recover even more. Direct contact with Korialstrasz almost made him feel whole again.

Almost.

"Are you settled?" the male dragon asked of him.

"I am."

Stepping forward, Alexstrasza spread her huge wings and dove out of the passage. She dipped low, then vanished into the clouds. Korialstrasz stepped to the edge of the precipice, giving his tiny passenger an even more astounding view of the vast, mountainous terrain, then leapt out into the sky.

At first they dropped several yards—entering the clouds in the process—but then Korialstrasz caught the wind and the pair soared up. Through the mists, Krasus saw that Alexstrasza already flew far ahead. However, her pace was slow enough that her consort quickly caught up with her.

"All is well?" she roared, her question posed to *both* companions.

Krasus nodded and Korialstrasz replied in the affirmative. The dragon queen focused ahead and said no more.

The sensations of flying, even on the back of another, exhilarated the mage. Having been born to this, it made his present circumstances that much harder to accept. He was a *dragon*! One of the masters of the sky! He should not be condemned to such a paltry existence . . .

They flew past mountain after mountain, through thick cloud cover and above many other startling peaks. Krasus's mortal body grew chilled, but he scarcely noticed, so fascinated was he.

With the utmost elegance the two massive dragons skirted a savage-looking peak, then dipped down into a wide valley in the midst of the chain. Krasus strained to see anything other than the landscape, but failed. Yet, somehow he felt that they were very close to their goal.

"Keep your grip tight!" Korialstrasz called out.

Before Krasus could ask why, the level to which the dragons descended *rippled*. The air itself twisted and wriggled like the surface of pond after a stone had been tossed into it. At first Krasus feared that the anomaly which had brought him to this time had materialized again, but then he noted the eagerness with which his mount headed for the unsettling display.

Ahead, Alexstrasza calmly entered the titanic ripple—and vanished.

Ancient memories grudgingly arose from the black abyss of Krasus's mind, memories of other times when he, as a dragon, had willingly tossed himself into this very sight. Krasus braced himself, recalling sensations that would assail him when Korialstrasz followed the queen.

They entered.

A static charge covered every inch of the mage's body. His nerves tingled. Krasus felt as if he had become a part of the heavens themselves, a child of lightning and thunder. The urge to fly on his own became demanding. It was all he could do to keep himself from letting go of his mount and joining the clouds and the wind.

The sensation passed, evaporating so unexpectedly that Krasus had to grip Korialstrasz tighter just to maintain his balance. He blinked, feeling very earthbound, very mortal. The shift in perspective overwhelmed him so much that at first Krasus did not realize his surroundings had completely changed.

They hovered within a vast, monumental cavern, so expansive that even Alexstrasza appeared as little more than a gnat in comparison. Entire kingdoms could fit inside, kingdoms with rolling landscapes and farmed fields. Even then, there would have been space for much, much more.

But this was not simply a cavern of tremendous size, for there were other features—or rather lack thereof—that marked it as a place most distinct from all others. The walls were smooth yet curved, rubbed so perfectly that if one put a hand to the rock and ran it across or down, there would be no friction, no resistance. That continued all the way down to the bottom, where the floor itself was an immense, flat circle that, had it been measured, would have been geometrically flawless.

The floor was indeed the only flattened area, for as the walls rose high, they continued to curve inward, sloping toward one another and creating overall a sphere-shaped chamber whose appearance was further accented by the utter lack of any mineral growth. No stalactites hung menacingly above; no stalagmites thrust up from the ground below. There were no fissures, not even one tiny crack. There were no flaws whatsoever in what Krasus finally recalled as the *Chamber of the Aspects*.

A chamber that had been ancient before even *they* had existed.

It was said that here the creators had shaped the world, molded it and grown it in this sacred place until it had been ready to be set into the cosmos. Even the great dragons could not completely argue the validity of that tale, for with no exit other than the magical one they had discovered by accident centuries earlier, they could not even say for certain that they met in a location situated on the mortal plane. All attempts to penetrate the walls had met with complete failure and the Aspects had long ago given up even trying.

To further add to the mystery of the astonishing cavern, a bright, golden illumination filled the Chamber of the Aspects, a comforting glow with no source. Krasus recalled that experimentation by his kind had never been able to prove whether that glow vanished when the chamber was empty or whether it was perpetual, but all who entered felt welcomed by it, as if it acted as a sentinel.

As Korialstrasz descended, it suddenly occurred to Krasus that, despite his splintered memories, he remembered this sacred place very distinctly. It said something about the Chamber of the Aspects—here were recollections he could never misplace, never let fade.

The two red leviathans alighted on the rock floor, peering around. Despite the great expanse, it became obvious that none of the others had arrived yet.

"You spoke to each?" asked Korialstrasz.

The Queen of Life shook her majestic head. "Only Ysera. She said she would contact the others."

"And I did what I could," responded an almost dreamy but certainly feminine voice.

Some distance beyond them, a faint emerald form coalesced from thin air. It never truly solidified, but Krasus noted enough details to identify it as a slim, ethereal dragon almost as tall as Alexstrasza. A permanent haze surrounded the half-seen figure, but still she was visible enough to mark the fact that her eyes remained closed at all times, even when she spoke.

The other dragons dipped their heads in honored greeting, Alexstrasza adding, "I am pleased that you came so swiftly, good Ysera."

She of the Dreaming, as Krasus also knew her, gave greetings in turn. Her face turned to the two who had come with her counterpart and although the lids did not open, Krasus felt her penetrating gaze. "I come because you are my sister, my friend. I come because you would not request a gathering if you did not have good reason."

"And the others?"

"Nozdormu is the only one I could not reach directly. You know his ways.

I was forced to contact one who serves him, who said he would do what he could to let his master know . . . that is the best I could accomplish there."

Alexstrasza nodded gratefully, but was unable to hide her disappointment with this last news. "Then, even if the others attend, we cannot come to a final decision."

"The Timeless One may still join us."

Still perched atop his younger self's neck, Krasus took as ill news the lack of any contact with Nozdormu. He understood the complexities of the Timeless One's nature, how Nozdormu was past, present, future . . . all history. Of all the others, it had been Nozdormu whom Krasus had secretly hoped to see here, for he offered the hope that there might still be a chance to send the two wayward travelers back to their own period, ending the matter peacefully.

And without that hope, Krasus once again had to look to the one other option . . . that to preserve the timeline, the Aspects might have to eliminate Rhonin and him.

Suddenly from above there came a brilliant flash of red bolts, an electrical storm that descended with swift fury to the ground. Once there, it exploded in a display of awe-inspiring colors before spreading out and forming a huge shape.

And as the last bits burned away, in place of the brief but startling storm stood a tall, glistening dragon who seemed part crystal, part ice. For a dragon, his expression was one quite merry, as if he had enjoyed the spectacle he created even more than any who witnessed it.

"Welcome, Malygos," Alexstrasza said politely.

"Such a pleasure to see you, Queen of Life!" The gleaming behemoth laughed heartily. "And you, too, my fair dream!"

Ysera nodded silently, a hint of humor touching her own expression.

"How fares your realm?" the red queen asked.

"As wondrous as I would wish it! Filled with brightness, filled with colors, and filled with young!"

"Perhaps the creators should have made you Father of Life instead of Guardian of Magic, Malygos!"

"An interesting thought! Perhaps a matter to discuss some other day!" He laughed again.

"Are you not well?" Korialstrasz asked Krasus, who, upon seeing the newcomer, had stiffened in horror.

"I am fine. I was simply adjusting my seating." The tiny figure was thankful that Korialstrasz had not been able to see his expression. The more Krasus watched and listened to Malygos, the more he regretted his need to keep from even the Aspects the full truth concerning the future.

What would you say, Guardian of Magic, if you knew the fate awaiting you? Betrayal, madness, a realm frozen and empty of all save yourself . . .

Krasus could not recall all he knew of Malygos's future, but he recalled enough from the bits and pieces to understand and regret the tragedy—and yet once more he could not bring himself to warn the glittering leviathan.

"And is that the one to whom we owe this gathering?" asked Malygos, his gleaming gaze now upon Krasus.

"It is," Alexstrasza replied.

The Guardian of Magic sniffed the air. "He has the scent of us upon him, although that may also be due to his proximity to your consort. I cannot say for certain. I also detect old magic surrounding him. Is he bespelled?"

"We shall let him tell his own story," Alexstrasza replied, sparing Krasus from any interrogation. "Once the others have arrived."

"One is coming even now," Ysera sagely announced.

The ceiling above rippled, then shimmered. A huge, winged form materialized, then swooped down grandly, circling the vast cavern twice in the process. The other Aspects grew respectfully silent, each watching the massive figure draw near.

In size he rivaled the largest of them, a winged behemoth as black as night with a bearing as noble as any depiction ever made of a dragon. Narrow veins of actual silver and gold streaking from front to back accented his spine and sides, while gleaming flashes between the scales hinted at diamonds and other precious stones embedded naturally in his hide. The newcomer radiated a sense of primal power, the power of the world itself in all its most basic forms.

He landed just beyond the rest, his huge, webbed wings folding masterfully behind him. In a voice deep and full, the black dragon said, "You have called and I have come. It is always good to see my friend Alexstrasza . . ."

"And I welcome your presence, dear Neltharion."

Before, it had been all Krasus could do to keep from reacting to Malygos's presence. Now he fought to keep himself from shaking, from showing the slightest sign at all of how he felt about this latest arrival. Yet, while his earlier reaction came from his knowledge concerning the doomed future of the Guardian of Magic, now Krasus worried more for the future of *all* dragons . . . and the world itself, should it survive the Burning Legion.

Before him stood Neltharion.

Neltharion. The Earth Warder. Most respected of the Aspects and, in addition, the close friend of Krasus's beloved queen. Had Neltharion been of her own flight, he surely would have long been chosen as one of her mates. Outside of her consorts, the Earth Warder was the one whom Alexstrasza most often sought for consultation, for the brooding black had a sharp mind that saw all angles. Neltharion did nothing without considering the consequences and, as a young dragon, Krasus had in some ways emulated him.

But in the future to which the mage belonged, any thought of emulating

Neltharion would have gone beyond the point of madness. Neltharion had rejected his role, rejected the protection the Aspects gave the mortal realm. He had instead turned to the belief that the lesser races were the root of all that was wrong with the world, that they should be removed . . . and those who would aid them should be removed as well.

Neltharion had come to envision a world where only dragons—specifically his own flight—ruled all. That growing obsession had led him to countless acts of an increasingly dark design, acts so horrible that eventually Neltharion became as terrible a danger to the world as the demons of the Burning Legion. The other Aspects had finally banded together against him, but not before he had spilled much blood and caused wholesale destruction.

And in rejecting all he had once been, Neltharion had also rejected his own name. From his former counterparts had come the name by which he was known to *all* creatures, one that had become synonymous with evil itself.

Deathwing . . .

There before Krasus loomed Deathwing, the Destroyer, the Black Scourge. Yet, the dragon mage could do nothing to warn the others. In fact, although he knew the danger that Neltharion would eventually become, Krasus could not recall when and where the tragedy had begun. To foment distrust among the Aspects at this critical juncture risked even more of a disaster than what the Earth Warder's future held.

And yet . . .

"I was surprised when Ysera, not you, contacted me," the black rumbled. "You are well, Alexstrasza?"

"I am, Neltharion."

He eyed her companions. "And you, young Korialstrasz? You are not at your best, I think."

"An illness passing," the red male answered respectfully. "It is an honor to see you again, Earth Warder."

They conversed like friendly acquaintances and yet Krasus managed to recall that as Deathwing, Neltharion would barely recognize him. By the time of the orc wars, the black behemoth would have dwelled so long in his madness that past friendships would be forgotten. All that would matter would be whatever advanced his dark cause.

But here still was Neltharion the comrade. He peered over Korialstrasz's neck, noting the tiny, cowled figure. "And you are the one. You have a name?"

"Krasus!" the mage snapped. "Krasus!"

"A defiant little one!" Neltharion said with amusement. "I believe that he is definitely a dragon, as Ysera hinted."

"A dragon with a tale to tell," Alexstrasza added. She gazed up at the ceiling, specifically the spot from which she and the others had entered. "But I would prefer to give Nozdormu more time before we begin."

"Give the Timeless One more time?" Malygos laughed. "How droll! I will not let dour Nozdormu leave without pressing him on *that* jest!"

"Yes and you will press him *time* and *time* again with it, will you not?" returned Neltharion, a vast, toothy smile spreading across his reptilian countenance.

Malygos laughed further. He and Neltharion shuffled to one side, already deep in some conversation.

"Brothers they may not be in blood," commented Ysera, her closed eyes following the pair. "But they are truly brothers in nature."

Alexstrasza agreed. "It is good that Neltharion has Malygos to turn to. He has been quiet with me of late."

"I, too, sense a distance. He does not take the actions by these night elves with pleasure. He stated once that they have grandiose visions of becoming like the creators without the knowledge and wisdom of the latter."

"There may be something to what he has said," the Queen of Life returned, her eyes sweeping briefly over Krasus.

The mage grew increasingly uncomfortable under her study of him. Of them all, Alexstrasza deserved this other warning. It would be Deathwing's doing that she would be turned into a slave of the orcs, whose warhounds readily sacrificed her children to their brutal cause. Deathwing would then use the chaos of the last days of the orc wars to seek what he truly desired . . . the eggs of the Queen of Life to re-create his own decimated flight, all but slain because of his past mad plots.

What limit do I set? Krasus demanded of himself. *When must the line finally be crossed? I can say nothing about the orcs, nothing about the Earth Warder's betrayals, nothing about the Burning Legion . . . all I can do is state enough facts to possibly exterminate myself and Rhonin!*

In frustration, he glared at one of the causes of his dilemma. Neltharion spoke merrily with Malygos, the latter's back turned to the other waiting dragons. The huge black stretched his wings and nodded at some remark by his gleaming counterpart. Had they been humans, dwarves, or some other mortal race, the pair would have looked quite at home drinking ale in a tavern. The lesser races saw the dragons as either monstrous beasts or dignified founts of wisdom, when in truth their characters were in some ways as earthy as the tiny creatures over which they watched.

Neltharion's eyes flickered past Malygos, meeting, however briefly, Krasus's.

And in that moment of contact, Krasus realized that all he and the others had seen so far of the black at this gathering had been a charade.

The darkness had already descended upon the Earth Warder.

Not possible, not possible! Krasus insisted, barely able to keep his expression neutral. *Not now!* It was too soon, too delicate a point in time for the transformation of Neltharion to Deathwing to begin. The Aspects needed to be united, not only to join against the coming invasion, but to deal with the disruptions of time caused by Krasus and his former student. Surely he had been mistaken about the black leviathan. Surely Neltharion was still one of the fabled protectors of the mortal plane.

Krasus cursed his feeble memory. When *had* Neltharion turned to betrayal? When *had* he forever become the bane of all other living creatures? Was it meant to be now or had Neltharion worked with his comrades even though darkness had already claimed him?

The cowled mage could not help but stare at the Earth Warder. Despite his own oath, Krasus began to think that perhaps here he had to bend the rules. How could it do anything but good to unveil the villain in the Aspects' midst? How—

Once more Neltharion glanced his way . . . but this time the eyes did not leave Krasus's own.

And only then did Krasus discover that Neltharion in turn saw the recognition in him, only then did he realize that the black dragon understood that here was one who could reveal his terrible secret.

Krasus tried to look away, but his eyes were held fast. Too late he realized the cause of that. The Earth Warder, having seen that he had been found out, had acted quickly and decisively. He now held Krasus with his power as easily as he breathed.

I will not fall to him! Yet, despite his determination to escape, his will did not prove strong enough. Had he been better prepared, Krasus could have battled Neltharion's mind, but the unexpected discovery had left him wide open . . . and the black one had seized the opportunity.

You know me . . . but I do not know you.

The chilling voice filled his head. Krasus prayed that someone would notice what passed between the pair, but to all appearances, everything passed as normal. It astounded him that not even his beloved Alexstrasza recognized the terrible truth.

You would speak against me . . . make the others see me as you do . . . you would have them distrust their comrade of old . . . their brother . . .

The Earth Warder's words gave clear indication of how deep his madness had already become. Krasus sensed within Neltharion a raging paranoia and an adamant belief that no one but the black dragon understood what was good for the world. Anyone who seemed at all the slightest threat to him was, in Neltharion's eyes, the true evil.

You will not be allowed to spread any of your malicious falsehoods . . .

Krasus expected to be struck down there and then, but, to his surprise, all Neltharion did was turn his gaze away and resume his conversation with Malygos.

What games does he play? the dragon mage wondered. *First he threatens me, then seems to forget my presence!*

He watched the black leviathan carefully, but Neltharion seemed entirely oblivious to him.

"He is not coming," Ysera finally said.

"He may still appear," suggested Alexstrasza.

Glancing at them, Krasus realized that they referred to Nozdormu.

"No, I have been contacted by the one with whom I spoke. He cannot locate his master. The Timeless One is somewhere beyond the mortal plane."

Ysera's news boded further ill. Knowing what he did of Nozdormu, Krasus suspected that the reason that even the Timeless One's servants could not contact him was because of the anomaly. If, as Krasus believed, Nozdormu held Time together all by himself, he would have needed to summon every instant of his existence. Multiple Nozdormus would be battling Time . . . leaving no moment for this gathering.

Krasus's hopes dwindled further. Nozdormu lost and Neltharion mad . . .

"I agree, then," Alexstrasza said, responding to Ysera's assessment. "We shall go on without the full Five. There is no rule that we cannot at least discuss the matter after the story is told, even if a course of action cannot yet be taken."

Lowering his head, Korialstrasz allowed his rider to dismount. Keeping his expression guarded, Krasus stepped out among the gathered giants, trying not to look at the Earth Warder. Alexstrasza's eyes encouraged him, enough so that the dragon mage knew what he had to do.

"I am one of you," he announced in a voice as booming as any of the leviathans surrounding him. My true name is known to the Queen of Life, but for now I am simply Krasus!"

"He bellows well, this hatchling," Malygos jested.

Krasus faced him. "This is not a time for humor, especially for you, Guardian of Magic! This is a time when a balance is nigh upset! A terrible mistake, a distortion of reality, threatens everything . . . absolutely everything!"

"How dramatic," Neltharion commented almost absently.

It took everything in Krasus's power not to blurt out the truth about the Earth Warder. *Not yet . . .*

"You will hear my story," insisted Krasus. "You will hear it and understand . . . for there is a worse danger on the horizon, one which touches us as well. You see—"

But as the first words of his tale ushered forth from his mouth, Krasus's tongue seemed to catch everywhere. Instead of a coherent telling, babbled words of whimsy escaped him.

Most of the gathered dragons pulled their heads back, startled by his peculiar behavior. Krasus looked quickly to Alexstrasza, seeking her help, but her expression indicated an astonishment as strong as any.

The mage's head spun. Vertigo worse than any he had suffered so far seized him, made him unable to keep his balance. Nonsense words continued to spew from his lips, but even Krasus no longer knew what he tried to convey.

And as his legs buckled and the vertigo took full hold of him, Krasus heard within his head the deathly calm voice of Neltharion.

I did warn you . . .

SEVENTEEN

Darkness came and the world of the night elves awoke. Merchants opened their businesses while the faithful went to their prayers. The general populace lived their lives, feeling no different then on any other eve. The world was theirs to do with as they chose, whatever other, lesser races might believe.

But for some, tiny annoyances crept into their lives, minor deviations from their routines, their notions.

A senior master of the Moon Guard, his long silver hair bound behind him, absently raised one long, nailed finger toward a flask of wine at the opposite end of the room as he perused the star charts in preparation for a major casting by the order. Although he was among the eldest of the sorcerers, his skills had remained undiminished, a reason for his continued high position. Spellcasting was to him as much a part of his existence as breathing, a matter simply and naturally done, almost without thought.

The crash that jarred him from his plush chair and made him crumple the parchment nearly to shreds proved to be caused by the flask's swift and fatal descent to the floor. Wine and glass spilled over the rich emerald and orange carpet the sorcerer had only recently purchased.

With a hiss of fury, the spellcaster snapped his fingers at the disastrous spill. Bits of glass suddenly rose into the air as the wine itself puddled together and formed into the shape of the container that had held it. The glass then began to mold together over the wine . . .

But a second later . . . everything again spilled all over the carpet, creating a worse mess than before.

The aged sorcerer stared. With a grim expression, he snapped his fingers again.

This time, the glass and the wine performed as he desired, even the slightest hint of stain removed. Yet, they did so with some sluggishness, taking far longer than the Moon Guard master would have expected.

The aged night elf returned to his parchment and tried once more to concentrate on the coming event, but his gaze constantly shifted back to the bottle and its contents. He pointed a finger at the flask again—then, with a frown, pulled the finger back and purposely turned his chair *away* from the cause of his annoyance.

At the edges of every major settlement, armed sentinels patrolled and guarded the night elves from any possible foe. Lord Ravencrest and those like him ever watched the areas beyond the main boundaries of the realm, their belief that the dwarves and other races constantly coveted the night elves' rich world. They did not look inward—for who of their own people would ever threaten them?—but permitted every settlement to maintain its own security simply in order to comfort the general citizenry.

In Galhara, a great city some distance on the opposing side of the Well from Zin-Azshari, sorcerers began the nightly ritual of realigning the emerald crystals that lined its boundaries. In conjunction with each other, the crystals acted, among other things, as defense against general magical attack. They had not, to anyone's recollection, ever been utilized, but the people took great comfort in their presence.

Despite there being hundreds, it was no troublesome feat to set the crystal arrays. All drew their power directly from the Well of Eternity and the sorcerers merely had to use the stars to adjust the lines of force that ran from one to another. In truth, this mostly required a simple twist of the crystal on the tall, obsidian pole upon which each had been placed. Thus, the local spellcasters were able to do several in the space of only a few minutes.

But with more than half already realigned, the crystals began to dim, even darkened completely. The sorcerers of Galhara, while not as proficient as the Moon Guard, knew their tasks well enough to understand that what happened now should *not* be happening. They immediately began checking and rechecking the arrays, but found nothing wrong.

"They are not drawing properly from the Well," one younger spellcaster finally decided. "Something has tried to cut them off from its might!"

But no sooner had he said that than the crystals renewed their normal activities. His elder associates looked at him in bemusement, trying to recall if, when as new to their roles as he was, they had made such outrageous statements.

And life among the night elves went on . . .

"It hasss *failed!*" Hakkar roared. He nearly whipped the closest of the Highborne, but pulled his savage lash back at the last moment. Eyes deathly dark, he looked to Lord Xavius. *"We* have failed . . ."

The felbeasts at the Houndmaster's flanks echoed their handler's fury with sinister snarls.

Xavius was no less displeased. He eyed the work that both the Highborne and Hakkar had wrought and saw in it hours of futility . . . and yet both he and the Houndmaster had seen the merits of the queen's suggestion.

They simply did not have the knowledge or power needed to make it happen.

That the efforts of the Highborne had still enabled more than a score of Fel Guard to join those already on the mortal plane did nothing to assuage them. Such numbers were only a slow dribble and did nothing to pave the way for the great one's coming.

"What can we do?" asked the night elf.

For the first time, he read uncertainty in the Houndmaster's haunting visage. The huge warrior turned his baleful gaze toward the portal, where others of the Highborne ever continued to try to make it stronger and larger. "We mussst asssk *him.*"

The counselor swallowed, but before his monstrous counterpart could take the step, Lord Xavius pushed himself forward, falling down on one knee before the portal. He would not shirk from his failures, not to his god.

Yet, even before his knee touched the stone, Xavius heard the voice in his head.

Is the portal strengthened?

"Nay, great one . . . the work in that regard has not progressed as we hoped."

For just the hint of a moment, what almost seemed an insane fury threatened to overwhelm the night elf . . . but then the sensation passed. Certain that he had imagined it, Xavius awaited the god's next words.

You seek something . . . speak.

Lord Xavius explained the notion of sealing off the Well's power from all but the palace and the failure to make that come to pass. He kept his head low, humble before the power that made the combined might of all night elves look no more terrible than that of an insect.

I have already considered this . . . the god finally answered. *The one I sent first has failed in his duty . . .*

Behind Xavius, the Houndmaster let out a brief sound bordering on dismay.

Another will be sent to you . . . you must make certain that the portal is made ready for him . . .

"Another, my lord?"

I now send you one of my . . . one of the commanders of my host. He will see to it that what is needed will come to pass . . . and quickly.

The voice departed Xavius's head. He swayed for a moment, the departure as stunning to him as if someone had just cut off one of his arms. Another of the Highborne helped him to his feet.

Xavius looked at Hakkar, who did not seem at all happy despite what the counselor saw as the most wonderful of news. "He sends us one of his *commanders!* Do you know which one?"

The Houndmaster anxiously rolled up his whip. Beside him, the two fel-beasts cringed. "Aye . . . I know which one, lord night elf."

"We must make ready! He will be coming immediately!"

Despite whatever disturbed him, Hakkar joined Xavius as the latter inserted himself among the casting Highborne. The pair added their knowledge and skill, amplifying as best they could the framework of energy that kept the portal ever open.

The burning sphere swelled, sparks of multicolored forces constantly shooting out from it. It pulsated, almost breathing. The portal stretched, a savage, roaring sound accompanying the physical change.

Sweat already poured down Xavius's face and body, but he did not care. The glory of what he sought gave him strength. Even more than the Houndmaster, he threw himself into making the spell not only hold, but expand to what was needed.

And as it grew to touch the ceiling, the portal suddenly disgorged a huge, dark figure at once so wonderful and terrible that it was all Xavius could do to keep from crying out in gratitude to the great one. Here now stood one of the celestial commanders, a figure before whom Hakkar seemed as unworthy as Xavius had felt before the Houndmaster.

"Elune save us!" one of the other sorcerers gasped. He pulled free, all but destroying the precious portal. Xavius barely seized control and, straining mightily, held it in place until the others could recover.

A huge, four-digited hand large enough to encompass the counselor's head stretched forth, pointing a taloned finger toward the careless spellcaster.

A voice that was both the roar of a crashing wave and the ominous rumble of an erupting volcano uttered a single, unrecognizable word.

The night elf who had stumbled away screamed as his body twisted like a piece of wet cloth being drained of water. A grotesque procession of cracking sounds matched the faltering scream. Most of the other Highborne immediately looked away and Hakkar's felbeasts whined.

Black flames erupted all over the macabre sight, enveloping what was left of the unfortunate sorcerer. The flames ate away at him like a pack of starved wolves, swiftly devouring the victim until but seconds later only a slight pile of ash on the floor remained to mark his passing.

"There will be no more failure," the thundering voice stated.

If the Houndmaster and the Fel Guard had not amazed Lord Xavius enough, surely only the god himself could have awed the counselor more than this new arrival. The fearsome figure moved forward on four thick, muscular limbs reminiscent of a dragon, save that these ended in blocky feet with three massive, clawed toes. A magnificent, scaled tail swept the floor over and over, the movement very likely a sign of the celestial one's impatience. From the top of his head down his back to the very tip of his tail ran a wild mane of pure green flame. Huge leathery wings also stretched from his back but even despite their span, Xavius wondered if they could lift so gigantic and powerful a form.

His hide, where black armor did not cover it, was a dark gray-green. He stood twice as wide as Hakkar and at least sixteen feet high, if the counselor was any judge. The massive tusks sprouting from the sides of his upper jaw nearly scraped the ceiling and the other, daggerlike teeth measured as long as the night elf's hand.

Under a thick brow ridge that almost completely obscured his burning orbs, the chosen of the great one stared down at the lord counselor . . . and the Houndmaster, especially.

"You have disappointed him . . ." was all the winged commander declared.

"I—" Hakkar paused in his protest, hanging his head. "I have no excussse, Mannoroth."

Mannoroth tilted his head slightly, looking at the Houndmaster as if studying an unpleasant bit of refuse found on his dinner plate. "No . . . you do not."

The felbeast on Hakkar's right suddenly whined loudly. Black flames akin to those that had removed the negligent sorcerer enveloped the frightened hound. It rolled desperately on the floor, trying to douse flames that would not be doused. The fire spread over it, consuming it . . .

And when only a wisp of smoke marked where the felbeast had stood, Mannoroth said again to the Houndmaster. "There will be no more failure."

Fear filled Xavius, but a wondrous, glorious fear. Here was power incarnate, a being that sat at the right hand of the great one. Here was one who would know how to turn their defeat into victory.

The dark gaze turned on him. Mannoroth gave a short sniff with his blunt nose . . . then nodded. "The great one approves of your efforts, lord night elf."

He had been blessed! Xavius lowered himself further. "I give thanks!"

"The plan will be followed. We will cut off the place of power from the rest of this realm. Then the arrival of the host can begin in earnest."

"And the great one? He will come then?"

Mannoroth gave him a wide smile, one with which he could have swallowed the counselor whole. "Oh, yes, lord night elf! *Sargeras* himself will want to be here when the world is cleansed . . . he will want to be here very, very much . . ."

Grass filled Rhonin's mouth and nose.

At least, he assumed it was grass. It tasted like grass, although he had not had much experience in such dining. The smell reminded him of wild fields and more peaceful times . . . times with Vereesa.

With effort, he pushed himself up. Night had fallen and while the moon shone fairly brightly, it revealed little beyond the fact that he lay in a lightly wooded area. Rhonin listened, but heard no sound of civilization.

The sudden fear that he had been catapulted into yet another era briefly overwhelmed him, but then the wizard recalled just what had happened. His own spell had sent him here, his desperate attempt to escape the demon draining him of his magic—and in the process, his life.

But if in the same time, then *where* had he landed? His surroundings gave no hint. He could be a few miles away or on the other side of the world.

And if the latter . . . could he return to Kalimdor? He hoped Krasus still lived somewhere, and only with his former mentor's aid did the wizard think that they might yet return home.

Staggering to his feet, Rhonin tried to decide which direction to go. Somehow he had to at least discover his whereabouts.

A noise in the woods behind him made the human whirl about. His hand came up in preparation for a spell.

A hulking figure emerged.

"No quarrel, wizard! Only Brox before you!"

Rhonin cautiously lowered his hand. The huge orc trudged forward, still clutching the ax Malfurion and the demigod had fashioned for him.

At the thought of the night elf, Rhonin looked around. "Are you alone?"

"Was until I saw you. You make a lot of noise, human. You move like a drunken infant."

Ignoring the jibe, the wizard looked past the orc. "I was thinking of Malfurion. He was also nearby when I cast the spell. If you were drawn into it, he might've been."

"Sound." Brox scratched his ugly head. "Saw no night elf. Saw no felbeast, either."

The human shivered. He certainly hoped that he had not included the demon in his escape. "Any idea where we might be?"

"Woods . . . forest."

Rhonin almost snapped at him for the useless answer, but realized that he could do no better. "I was planning to go that way," he said, pointing toward what he believed was east. "You have any better ideas?"

"Could wait until sunrise. Better able to see and night elves, they don't like sun."

While that made much sense, Rhonin did not feel comfortable waiting for daylight and told his companion so. Brox surprised him by nodding in agreement.

"Better to scout, wizard." He shrugged. "Your direction as good as any."

As they started off, a question occurred to Rhonin that he simply had to ask. "Brox . . . how did you get here? Not this exact location—I know that, of course—but how did you come to this realm?"

At first the orc only clamped his mouth shut, but then he finally told the wizard. Rhonin listened to the tale, careful to hide his emotions. The veteran and his ill-fated partner had been right behind Krasus and him and, like the others, had been caught by the anomaly.

"Do you understand what swallowed us?"

Brox shrugged. "Wizard's spell. Bad one. Sent us far from our home."

"Farther than you might know." Deciding that Brox had a right to the truth regardless of what Krasus might think, Rhonin told him what had happened.

To the wizard's surprise, Brox accepted his story quite readily. Only when Rhonin thought about the history of the orc's people did he realize why. The orcs had already journeyed through time and space from another world. A spell that would cast one into the past was hardly that much different.

"Can we return, human?"

"I don't know."

"You saw. The demons are here. The Legion is here."

"This is the first time they tried to invade our world. Most beyond Dalaran don't know that history anymore."

Brox gripped his ax tighter. "We'll fight them . . ."

"No . . . we can't." Rhonin explained Krasus's reasoning.

But while Brox had quickly accepted all else, he drew the line when it came to leaving the past alone. The matter was simple for the orc; here was a dangerous, foul enemy who would slaughter all in their path. Only cowards and fools let such horror happen and Brox said so more than once.

"We might change history by interfering," the wizard insisted, in his heart wanting to agree with the orc.

Brox snorted. "You fought."

His simple statement completely repudiated Rhonin's only argument. The wizard *had* fought already and by doing so had made a choice.

But was it the right one? Already the past had been altered, but to what degree?

They moved on in silence, Rhonin in battle with his inner demons and Brox keeping a wary eye out for physical ones. Nowhere did they see any hint of where they might have ended up. At one point Rhonin considered concentrating on the glade and trying to send them both back there. Then he remembered the felbeast and what it had almost done to him.

The woods thickened, eventually becoming a full forest. Rhonin silently cursed, his choice of directions now seeming a poor one. Brox gave no indication of his own opinion, simply chopping away with his enchanted ax whenever the path grew impossible. The ax sliced through everything with such ease that the wizard hoped that his companion would never accidentally cut him with it. Not even bone gave the blade any pause.

The moon vanished, the thick foliage of the surrounding trees completely obscuring the heavens. The path became impossible. After a few more minutes of fruitlessly fighting their way along, the pair decided to turn back. Again, the orc said nothing about Rhonin's choice.

But when they turned around, it was to find that the way they came had completely *vanished*.

Huge trees stood where once the path had been and dense undergrowth around the trunks gave further evidence that this surely was not the right direction. Yet, both orc and human eyed the trees with distrust.

"We came from through there. I know we did."

"Agreed." Raising the ax, Brox moved in on the mysterious trees. "And we go back that way, too."

But as he swung, huge, branchlike hands seized the weapon by the sides of the blade and pulled it up.

Unwilling to relinquish the ax, Brox hung by the handle, the orc's legs dangling as he sought to use his weight to wrest the weapon free.

Rhonin ran up. He tugged on the orc's feet with no success. Staring at the long, inhuman fingers, he began to mutter a spell.

Something struck him from behind. The wizard stumbled forward and would have soundly hit the tree before him if not for the fact that it *moved* aside at the last moment.

Momentum sent Rhonin flailing to the earth. However, instead of striking either harsh ground or one of the many gnarled roots around him, he landed atop something softer.

A body.

Rhonin gasped, assuming that he had come across a previous victim of the sinister trees. But as he pushed himself up, a brief glimmer of moonlight that somehow had penetrated the vast crowns above allowed him to see the face.

Malfurion . . .

The night elf suddenly moaned. His eyes flickered open and he saw the wizard.

"You—"

Farther back, Brox shouted something. Both human and night elf quickly looked that way. Rhonin raised a hand in preparation for attack, but Malfurion surprised him by seizing his wrist.

"No!" The dark-skinned figure sat up, quickly scanning the trees. He nodded to himself, then shouted, "Brox! Do not fight them! They mean no harm!"

"No harm?" growled the orc. "They want my ax!"

"You must do as I say! They are protectors!"

From the warrior came a reluctant groan. Rhonin looked at Malfurion for explanation, but received none. Instead, the night elf released the wizard's wrist, then pushed himself to his feet. With Rhonin trailing behind, Malfurion walked calmly toward the area where Brox battled.

They found the orc surrounded by ominous-looking trees. A cluster of branches hung above and in them was tangled Brox's ax. The orc panted from effort, his body still tense. He looked from his companions to his weapon and back again, as if still not certain he should not try to climb after it.

"Knew your voice," he grunted. "You better be right."

"I am."

As the wizard and the warrior watched, Malfurion stepped up to the tallest of the trees and said, "I give thanks to the brothers of the forest, the keepers of the wild. I know you watched over me until my friends could find me. They mean no harm; they just did not understand."

The leaves of the trees began to rustle even though Rhonin could feel no wind.

Nodding, the night elf continued, "We will trouble you no longer."

More rustling . . . then the branches entangling Brox's ax separated and the weapon slipped earthward.

They could have let the ax fall harmlessly to the ground, but the orc suddenly stepped forward. He reached up with one powerful hand and caught the ax handle perfectly. Yet, instead of waving the weapon at the trees, he knelt before them, the blade turned downward.

"I ask forgiveness."

Again, the crowns of the towering trees shook. Malfurion put a hand on the orc's broad shoulder. "They accept."

"You can really speak with them?" Rhonin finally asked.

"To a point."

"Then ask them where we are."

"I already have. Not at all that far from where we were, but far enough away. Actually, we're both fortunate and unfortunate."

"How so?"

The night elf smiled ruefully. "We're only a short distance from my home."

This was excellent news to the wizard, but not such good news to the night elf, he gathered. Nor did it seem good news to Brox, who cursed in his native tongue.

"What is it? What do the two of you know?"

"I was captured close to here, wizard," growled the brawny warrior. "Very close."

Recalling his own capture, Rhonin could see why Brox might be upset. "I'll take us from here, then. This time I know what to expect—"

Malfurion held up a hand in protest. "We were fortunate once, but here, you risk being sensed immediately by the Moon Guard. They have the skill to usurp your spell . . . in fact, they may have, at the very least, already sensed the first one."

"What do you suggest?"

"As we are near my home, we should make use of it. There are others who could be of assistance to us. My brother and Tyrande."

Brox embraced his suggestion. "The shaman . . . she will help." His tone darkened. "Your twin . . . yes."

Rhonin still worried about Krasus, but with no notion as to how to find his former mentor, the night elf's decision made the most sense. With Malfurion in the lead, the trio headed off. The path through the forest now proved startlingly easy, considering the trek through which the human and the orc had earlier suffered. The landscape seemed to go out of its way to make Malfurion's journey a comfortable one. Rhonin knew something of druids and for the first time marked Malfurion as of that calling.

"The demigod—Cenarius—he taught you to speak with the trees, to cast such spells?"

"Yes. I seem to be the first to truly understand them. Even my brother prefers the power of the Well to the ways of the forest."

At mention of the Well, a feeling of anticipation and hunger suddenly touched Rhonin. He fought the emotions down. The Well that his companion had mentioned could only be the Well of Eternity, the fabled fount of power. Were they that near? Was that why his own spellwork had become magnified?

To wield such power . . . and so readily . . .

"We're not much farther," Malfurion said a short while later. "I recognize that gnarled elder."

The "elder" he referred to was a twisted old tree that, to Rhonin at least, looked like little more than a dark shape. Something else, however, attracted the wizard's attention.

"Do I hear rushing water?"

The night elf sounded more cheerful. "It flows very near my home! Only a few more minutes and—"

But before he could finish, the forest filled with armored figures. Brox snarled and made ready with his ax. Rhonin readied a spell, certain that these were the same foul attackers who had first seized Krasus and him.

As for Malfurion, the night elf looked entirely perplexed at the sudden appearance of the attackers. He started to raise a hand toward them, then hesitated.

Malfurion's hesitation caused Rhonin in turn to pause. That proved a mistake, for in the next instant a red shroud of energy fell upon each. Rhonin felt his muscles freeze and his strength fade. He could not move, could not do anything but watch.

"An excellent piece of work, lad," proclaimed a commanding voice. " 'Tis the beastman we sought—and no doubt those who aided in his escape!"

Someone replied, but too low for Rhonin to make out the words. A band of riders, two bearing glowing emerald staffs, entered the circle of soldiers. At their head was a bearded night elf who had to be the one in charge. Next to him—

Rhonin's eyes widened, the only response left to him in his present condition. It hardly signified his astonishment upon recognizing the figure next to the commander.

The garments were different and the hair was bound back, but there was no mistaking that the dour face was an exact duplicate of Malfurion's.

EIGHTEEN

Mannoroth was pleased . . . and that pleased Lord Xavius. "It is good, then?" the night elf asked the celestial commander. So much hinged on everything going as planned.

Mannoroth nodded his heavy, tusked head. His wings stretched and folded in satisfaction. "Yes . . . very good. Sargeras will be pleased."

Sargeras. Again the celestial commander had uttered the true name of the great one. Xavius's magical eyes burned bright as he savored it. *Sargeras.*

"We will work the portal the moment that the spell is set in place. First will come the host, then, when all is made ready, my lord himself . . ."

Hakkar approached, the much subdued Houndmaster falling on one knee before Mannoroth. "Forgive thisss interruption, but one of my huntersss hasss returned."

"Only *one?*"

"Ssso it sssseems."

"And what have you learned from it?" Mannoroth loomed over his counterpart, making the Houndmaster seem smaller and smaller.

"They found two with the sssscent of othernessss that the lord night elf ssspoke of, plusss one of hisss *own* kind with them! But in the hunt they alsso fell afoul of a being of power . . . great power."

For the first time, Mannoroth displayed a slight hint of uncertainty. Xavius noted carefully the reaction, wondering what could disturb so wondrous a being. "Not—"

Hakkar quickly shook his head. "I think not. Perhapsss with a touch of their power. Perhapsss a guardian left behind."

The pair spoke of something significant, but what, the counselor could not say. Taking a risk, he interrupted. "Is there a description of this last creature?"

"Aye." Hakkar held out one hand, palm up.

Above his palm there suddenly burst to life a tiny image. It moved violently and often lost focus, but revealed by bits and pieces an almost full view of the one in question.

"Ssseen through the eyesss of the felbeasssst. An antlered entity asss tall asss one of the Fel Guard."

Lord Xavius frowned. "The legend is true, then . . . the forest lord is real . . ."

"You know this creature?" Mannoroth demanded.

"Ancient myth speaks of the forest lord, the demigod Cenarius. He is said to be the child of the Mother Moon . . ."

"Nothing more, then." The tusked mouth twisted into a grim smile. "He will be dealt with." To Hakkar, he commanded, "Show the others."

The Houndmaster quickly obeyed, revealing a green-skinned brute of warrior, a young night elf, and an odd, fire-haired figure clad in hooded garments.

"A curious trio," Xavius remarked.

Mannoroth nodded. "The warrior shows much promise . . . I would see more of his kind, learn their potential . . ."

"Such a beast? Surely not! He's more grotesque than a dwarf!"

The winged figure did not argue, instead recalling the last of the threesome. "A spindly creature but with wary eyes. A creature of magic, I think. Almost like a night elf—" He cut off Xavius's new protest. "—but not." Dismissing Hakkar's images, the huge, reptilian limbs maneuvered through the chamber as Mannoroth contemplated what he had learned.

"More felbeastsss could be sssent to find them," suggested the Houndmaster.

"But with Fel Guard behind. This time, the objective will be capture."

"Capture?" echoed both the counselor and the Houndmaster.

The deepset eyes narrowed more. "They must be studied, their weaknesses and strengths assessed in case there are others . . ."

"Can the Fel Guard be ssspared?"

"There will soon be many, many more. Lord night elf, are your Highborne prepared?"

Studying the sorcerers, Xavius bowed his head. "They are ready to do what they must to see the glorious fulfillment of our dream, the cleansing of the world of all that is—"

"The world will be cleansed, lord night elf, you may trust to that." Mannoroth glanced at Hakkar. "I leave the hunt to you, Houndmaster. Do not fail again."

Keeping low, Hakkar backed away.

"And now, lord night elf . . ." the towering being continued, gaze turning to the place of casting. "Let us begin the molding of your people's future . . ." Mannoroth's wings flexed as they always seemed to do when he contemplated something agreeable to him. "A future I promise you that they cannot possibly even imagine . . ."

Deathwing soared over the landscape, breathing fire everywhere. Screams came from every direction around Krasus, but he could not find any of those who pleaded for his aid. Trapped in his tiny mortal form, he scampered over the burning earth like a field rat, trying to keep from being engulfed while in vain he sought to help the dying.

Suddenly a dark shadow covered the area over which he ran and a thundering voice mocked, "Well, well! And what little morsel is this?"

Huge claws twice the size of the dragon mage encircled Krasus, trapping him. With no effort whatsoever, they dragged him into the sky . . . and turned him to face the malevolent visage of Deathwing.

"Why, it's only a bit of old dragon meat! Korialstrasz! You've been around the lesser races much too long! Their weakness has rubbed off on you!"

Krasus tried to cast a spell, but from his mouth emerged not words but tiny bats. Deathwing inhaled, drawing the bats mercilessly into the hot, gaping maw.

The black behemoth swallowed. "Not much of a treat! I doubt you'll be any better, but you're already going to waste so I might as well finish you off!" He raised the flailing figure above his gullet. "Besides, you're of no use to anyone, anyway!"

The claws released Krasus, but as he plummeted into Deathwing's mouth, things changed. Deathwing and the burning landscape vanished. Krasus suddenly floated in the midst of a horrendous sandstorm, spun around and around by its ever more turbulent forces.

A dragon's head formed in the midst of the storm. At first Krasus thought that the black beast had followed him, determined not to let his snack escape. Then another head identical to the first appeared, followed by another and another until an endless horde filled Krasus's view.

"Korialstraaaasz . . ." they moaned simultaneously over and over. "Korialstraaasz . . ."

It occurred to Krasus then that the heads had a different shape to them from Deathwing's and that each had formed from the sandstorm itself.

Nozdormu?

"We . . . are ssstretched through all!" the Timeless One managed. "We . . . ssseee alll . . ."

Krasus waited, knowing that Nozdormu spoke as his efforts permitted him.

"All endsss lead to nothing! All endsss . . ."

Nothing? What did he mean? Did he indicate that all the mage had feared had come to pass, that the future had been eradicated?

"... but one ..."

One! Krasus seized hold of the tiny ray of hope. "Tell me! What path? What do I do?"

In answer, the dragon heads changed. The snouts shrank and the heads elongated, becoming more human—no! Not human—elven ...

A night elf?

Was this someone he should fear or someone he should seek? He tried to ask Nozdormu, but then the storm grew wild, mad. The winds tore apart the faces, scattering the grains of sand everywhere. Krasus tried to protect his body as sand ripped at his flesh even through his garments.

He screamed.

And sat up a moment later, his mouth still open in a silent scream.

"My queen, he is with us again."

Gradually Krasus's mind returned to reality. The nightmare involving Deathwing and the subsequent vision of Nozdormu still wreaked havoc with his thoughts, but he was at last able to focus enough to realize that he lay in the egg chamber where he and Alexstrasza had first spoken. The Queen of Life herself looked down in grave concern at him. To his right, his younger self also watched with worry.

"Your spell has passed?" Alexstrasza quietly inquired.

This time, he was determined that she would know regardless of the consequences. Nozdormu's frightening words indicated that the path to the future already had all but shut. What more trouble, then, would it be if he told her of Neltharion's madness and the horror the black dragon would cause?

But once more, when Krasus tried to speak of the fiend, the vertigo nearly did him in. It was all he could do to keep conscious.

"Too soon," cautioned Alexstrasza. "You need more rest."

He needed much more than that. He needed the sinister and subtle spell which the Earth Warder had evidently cast upon him removed, but clearly none of the Aspects had even recognized his condition as one caused by sorcery. In all his incarnations, Deathwing had always been the most cunning of evils.

Unable to do anything about the black dragon, Krasus's mind drifted to the night elf whose features Nozdormu had attempted to show him. He recalled the ones who had attacked Rhonin and him, but none had looked at all like this new figure.

"How far are we from the land of the night elves?" Krasus asked ... then touched his mouth in surprise when he realized that the words had come out with no trouble. Apparently Neltharion's handiwork only involved the dragon himself, not any other matter of importance.

"We can take you there soon enough," his mate replied. "But what of the matter of which you spoke?"

"This . . . this still concerns that matter, but my course has changed. I believe . . . I believe I have just been contacted by the Timeless One, who tried to tell me something."

His younger self found this too much. "You had nightmares, delusions! We heard you moan several times. It is doubtful that the Aspect of Time would reach out to you. Alexstrasza, perhaps, but not you."

"No," corrected the red queen. "I believe he may have the truth of it, Korialstrasz. If he says that Nozdormu touched his thoughts, I suspect he states fact."

"I bow to your wisdom, my love."

"I must go to the night elves," Krasus insisted. With Korialstrasz nearby and no intention of mentioning Neltharion's duplicity, his condition had improved much. "There is one I seek. I hope I am not already too late."

The female leviathan tilted her head to the side, her eyes seeking within Krasus's own. "Is all you told me before still truth? All of it?"

"It is . . . but I fear there is much more. The dragons—all dragons—will be needed for a struggle."

"But with Nozdormu absent, a consensus cannot be reached. The others will not agree to anything!"

"You must convince them to go against tradition!" He forced himself to his feet. "They could very well be all that stands between the world and oblivion!"

And with that, he told both all he could recall of the horror of the Burning Legion.

They listened to his tales of blood, of decimation, of soulless evil. Even the two dragons shook as he regaled them with the atrocities. By the time he had finished, Krasus had told more than enough for them to see his fear.

But even then, Alexstrasza said, "They may still not decide. We have watched the world, but we leave its progress in the hands of the younger races. Even Neltharion, who is warder of the earth itself, prefers to leave it that way."

He so much desired to tell her of Neltharion, but even thinking that made his head swim. With a reluctant nod, Krasus said, "I know you will do what you must."

"And you must do what you will. Go to the night elves and seek your answer if you think it will help this situation." She looked up at her consort. After a moment's consideration, the queen added, "I ask that you go with him, Korialstrasz. Will you do it?"

The male lowered his head in respect. "If you ask, I am only too glad to oblige."

"I also ask that you follow his lead, my consort. Trust me when I say that he has wisdom which will be of value to you."

It was not entirely clear from his reptilian visage whether or not Korialstrasz believed the last, but he nodded to that, too.

"Night has fallen," Alexstrasza informed Krasus. "Will you wait until light?"

The dragon mage shook his head. "I have already waited far too long as it is."

The first to bear the clan designation of Ravencrest had looked upon the huge, granite formation atop the high and treacherous mount. He had remarked to his companion how its stocky formation resembled a piece from a chessboard, a rook colored black. That huge, dark birds constantly circled about the formation and even nested atop it was taken as a sign that this was a special place, a place of power.

For more than a generation—and the generations of night elves were longer than those of most races—servants of the Ravencrest line had continually carved out the clan stronghold, gradually building from solid rock a fortress like none seen among their kind. Black Rook Hold, as it quickly became known, was an ominous, uncolored place which spread its influence over much of the night elf realm, becoming second only to the palace. When conflict arose between the night elves and the dwarves, it was the power of Black Rook Hold that tipped the balance. Those of the clan of Ravencrest became the honored of the throne and the blood of both sides intermingled. If the Highborne who served Azshara were jealous of any others of their race, it had to be those of the ebony fortress.

Windows had been carved out on the top floors of the hold, but the only way to enter was by the twin iron gates located not at the base of the structure, but at the very bottom of the hill. The solid gates were sealed shut and well guarded. Only fools would have thought to enter there without permission.

But for the present Lord Ravencrest, those gates had opened readily. They had also opened for his three prisoners, one of whom knew the stories of Black Rook Hold and grew worried.

Malfurion had never thought that he would enter the dark hold, especially under such dire conditions. Worse, he could never have imagined his twin being the main reason for his having to do so. In the course of their journey he had learned that it was Illidan, somehow suddenly associated with Lord Ravencrest, who had detected Rhonin's spell. With Malfurion's brother to aid him, the night elven commander had ridden out with a full force, determined this time to capture any invaders.

He had been most pleased to see Brox . . . and quite puzzled to see Illidan's twin.

In a chamber lit by glittering emerald crystals positioned high in each of the five corners, Lord Ravencrest inspected his catch. The commander sat upon a chair carved from the same stone as his hold. The chair stood upon a dais, also stone, giving Ravencrest the ability to look down on the trio even while seated.

Armed soldiers lined the walls of the chamber while others surrounded Malfurion and his comrades. Ravencrest himself was flanked by his senior officers, each of whom stood with his helm in the crook of one arm. At the noble's immediate right waited Illidan.

Present also were two high-ranking members of the Moon Guard. They were a late addition to the proceedings, having arrived at Black Rook Hold just as the commander had brought his prisoners to the gates. The Moon Guard, too, had detected Rhonin's spell, but their spies had informed them of Ravencrest's party before there had been any chance to send out searchers of their own. The sorcerers were not at all pleased by the noble's actions nor were they pleased with Illidan's presence, he being an unsanctioned spellcaster in their eyes.

"Once again, my Lord Ravencrest," began the thinner, elder of the two Moon Guard, an officious figure by the name of Latosius. "I must request that these outsiders be turned over to us for proper questioning."

"You've already had the beastman and lost him. He was to come to me, anyway. This simply shortens the procedure." The noble eyed the three again. "There's more here than what we see on the surface. Illidan, I would hear from you."

Malfurion's brother looked slightly ill at ease, but he answered strongly, "Yes, my lord, he is my brother."

"That much is as obvious as night and day." He studied the captive twin. "I know something of you, lad, just as I know something of your brother. Your name is Malfurion, yes?"

"Yes, my lord."

"You rescued this creature?"

"I did."

The commander leaned forward. "And you've an excellent reason why? One that would excuse this heinous act?"

"I doubt you would believe me, my lord."

"Oh, I can come to believe many things, young one," Lord Ravencrest replied calmly, tugging lightly on his beard. "If they're spoken in honesty. Can you do that?"

"I—" What other choice did Malfurion have? Sooner or later, through one method or another, they would pluck the truth from him. "I'll try."

And so he told them of his studies under Cenarius, which immediately raised doubtful brows. He explained his reoccurring dreams and how the demigod had taught him to walk in the world of the subconscious. Most of all, Malfurion described the disconcerting forces that had drawn him to, of all places, Zin-Azshari, and the palace of the night elves' beloved queen.

They listened as he told of the Well itself and the turbulence that the sorcerers within the palace had stirred up. He painted for Ravencrest, the Moon Guard, and the others the vision of the tower and what he sensed went on inside.

The one thing he did not mention, assuming that from his story it would be obvious, was his fear that Queen Azshara sanctioned everything.

Ravencrest did not comment on his story, instead looking to the Moon Guard. "Has your order noticed any such trouble?"

The elder sorcerer answered. "The Well is more turbulent than usual and that could be from misuse. We have not monitored any such activity from Zin-Azshari, but then, such an incredible fiction as this—"

"Yes, it is incredible." The bearded commander glanced up at Illidan. "What say you concerning your brother?"

"He's never been one for delusions, my lord." Illidan would not look at Malfurion. "As to whether it's the truth . . ."

"Indeed. Still, I wouldn't put it past Lord Xavius and the Highborne to instigate some devilment without her knowledge. They act as if the queen is their prized possession and no one else has a right to her."

Even by the Moon Guard, this was greeted with nods. The arrogance of the lord counselor and those surrounding Azshara in the palace was well known.

"If I may," Latosius interjected. "Once we've settled matters here, I will pass on word to the heads of our order. They will put into motion surveillance of the Highborne and their activities."

"I should be most interested in that. Young Malfurion, your story—on the assumption that it is for the most part truth—explains some of your actions, but how does that fit into the freeing of a prisoner of your people, a most serious crime?"

"I can perhaps answer that better," Rhonin suddenly said.

Malfurion was not so sure it was a good thing that the other outsider spoke. Night elves were not so tolerant of other races and although Rhonin had some vague resemblance to his kind, he still might as well have been a troll for all the good it would do him.

But Ravencrest appeared willing to listen, if nothing else. He waved a negligent hand toward the hooded wizard.

"In my land . . . a land not far from where he's from," explained Rhonin, nodding toward Brox. "A strange magical anomaly opened up. My people sent me and Brox's sent him. We both discovered it separately . . . and were drawn unwilling through it. He ended one place, I another."

"And how does this pertain to young Malfurion?"

"He believes . . . as I do . . . that this anomaly was caused by the spellwork mentioned."

"That would be some cause for alarm," commented the senior Moon Guard dubiously. "The green-skinned creature hardly seems what one would send to study a creation of sorcery or magic."

"My Warchief commanded I go," retorted Brox with a defiant snarl. "I went."

"I cannot speak for the orcs," Rhonin answered. "But I am certainly adept at such a study." His eyes, so different from those of the night elves, dared the Moon Guard to deny him.

After a pause, both sorcerers nodded their agreement. Malfurion realized that they did not know what exactly Rhonin was, but they recognized one versed in the arts. Indeed, it was likely for that reason that the wizard had been allowed to speak at all.

"Perhaps I'm growing old, but I'm inclined to believe much of all this." This admission from Lord Ravencrest drew some looks from his officers and sent a wave of relief through Malfurion. If the commander took their story to heart—

"We remain undecided," Latosius declared. "Such information cannot be taken on faith alone. There must still be an inner interrogation."

The noble's brow rose. "Did I say otherwise?"

He snapped his fingers and the guards seized Malfurion tightly by the arms, dragging him toward the dais.

"Now I would like to test the faith I've placed in my new sorcerer. Illidan, we must ascertain the absolute truth, however distasteful that might seem to you. I trust I can rely on you to prove to us that *all* your brother says is true?"

The pony-tailed night elf swallowed, then looked beyond Malfurion. "My brother's word I trust, but I can't say the same for the robed creature, my lord."

Illidan was trying to keep from having to use his powers on his brother by instead focusing on an outsider. While Malfurion appreciated that concern, he did not like the idea of Rhonin or Brox suffering in his place.

"Lord commander, this is absurd!" The senior sorcerer marched up to the dais, eyeing Illidan with contempt. "An unsanctioned spellcaster who is the brother of one of the prisoners? Any questioning will be suspect!" He turned on Malfurion, silver eyes narrowed menacingly at the younger night elf. "In accordance with the laws set down at the very dawn of our civilization, in matters magical it is the responsibility and right of the Moon Guard to oversee all such interrogations!"

He advanced, coming within arm's reach of the prisoner. Malfurion tried not to show his anxiety. Against the physical threats of Black Rook Hold, he hoped his druidic training would allow him to survive, but the delving of a sorcerer into his mind threatened him much more. Such a questioning could leave his body whole, but his brain so shattered that he might never recover.

Illidan leapt down from the dais. "My lord, I'll interrogate my brother."

Whatever his twin would do to him, Malfurion suspected that Illidan would be much more careful in his approach than the Moon Guard, who only wanted answers. Malfurion looked at Lord Ravencrest, hoping that the noble would accept Illidan's offer.

But the master of Black Rook Hold only leaned back against his chair, stating, "The laws shall be followed. He is yours, Moon Guard . . . but only if you do the questioning here and now."

"That is agreed."

"Consider, in your work, that he may be telling the truth."

It was the closest Malfurion guessed Ravencrest would come to trying to preserve Illidan's twin from harm. First and foremost the bearded commander was protector of the realm. If that cost the life or mind of one night elf, then the sacrifice had to be made.

"The truth will be known," was all the sorcerer would answer. To the guards, he commanded, "Hold his head straight."

One of the armored figures positioned Malfurion for the Moon Guard. The robed figure reached up and touched the struggling prisoner's temples with his index fingers.

A shock ran through Malfurion and he was certain that he screamed. His thoughts swirled around, old memories rising to the surface unbidden. Yet, each one was swiftly thrust back down as what felt like a clawed hand dug into his mind, seeking ever deeper . . .

Struggle not! commanded a harsh voice that had to be that of Latosius. *Release your secrets and it will go the better for you!*

Malfurion wanted to, but did not know how. He thought of what he had already told the gathering and tried to project that forward. Of Azshara's possible duplicity, Malfurion still resisted revealing. It would lessen his chances of ever being believed if that suspicion leaked free—

Then, just as suddenly as the intrusive probe had burrowed into his thoughts . . . it ceased. It did not withdraw, did not gradually fade away. It simply ceased.

Malfurion's legs buckled. He would have fallen if not for the guards holding him.

Gradually he became aware of shouts, some in disbelief, others in consternation. One of the voices most strident sounded like that of the elder Moon Guard.

"It's outrageous!" someone else cried out. "Surely not the queen!"

"Never!"

He had let slip his ultimate fear. Malfurion cursed his feeble mind. Barely had the questioning begun and he had already failed himself, failed Cenarius's teaching . . .

" 'Tis the Highborne! It has to be! This is Xavius's doing!" another voice insisted

"He has committed evil against his own kind!" agreed the First.

What were they talking about? Although Malfurion's head refused to clear, he still felt certain that something was not right about the shouted conversation. The speakers were too excited, reacting too adamantly to his beliefs. He was only one night elf and not even of high rank. Why would his vague suspicions throw them into growing panic?

"Let me see to him," a voice said. Malfurion felt the guards hand him over to a single person, who lowered him gently to the floor.

Hands touched the sides of his face, lifting it up. Through bleary eyes, Malfurion met the gaze of his brother.

"Why didn't you give in immediately?" Illidan muttered. "Two hours! Do you still have a mind left?"

"Two—hours?"

Noting the response, Illidan breathed easier. "Praise Elune! After you spouted that nonsense about the queen, that old fool was determined to rip everything out of your head regardless of the cost! If not for his spell failing suddenly, he probably would have left you an empty husk! They haven't forgiven the loss of their brethren and blame you for it!"

"H-his spell failed?" That hardly made sense. Malfurion's interrogator had been a most senior sorcerer.

"*All* of their spells have failed!" Illidan persisted. "After he lost control of the first, he tried another and when that didn't work, his companion attempted a third . . . with no success!"

Malfurion still did not understand. What his twin hinted at sounded as if both of the Moon Guard had lost their powers. "They can't cast?"

"No . . . and my own powers feel muted . . ." He leaned next to Malfurion's ear. "I think I have some control . . . but barely. It's as if we've been cut off from the Well!"

The commotion continued to grow. He heard Lord Ravencrest demand if the Moon Guard still maintained contact with their brethren, to which one of the sorcerers admitted that the ever-present link had been severed. The noble then asked of his own followers if any still retained their own skills, however slight.

No one answered in the affirmative.

"It's begun . . ." Malfurion whispered without thinking.

"Hmm?" His twin frowned. "What's that? What has?"

He looked past Illidan, recalling the violent forces carelessly summoned by those in the tower. He saw again the lack of regard for what such spell-work might do to those beyond the palace walls.

"I don't know . . ." Malfurion finally told his brother. "I wish by the Mother Moon I did . . . but I just don't." Beyond Illidan he saw the concerned countenances of Brox and Rhonin. Whether or not they understood as he did, both looked as if they shared his growing fear. "I only know that, whatever it may be . . . it's *begun.*"

All over the realm of the night elves, all over the continent of Kalimdor, thousands of others sensed the loss. The Well had been cut off from them. The power that they had so blithely wielded . . . was all but gone. A sense of alarm swiftly grew, for it was as if someone had reached up and just stolen the moon.

Those living nearest to the palace naturally turned to their queen, calling upon Azshara for guidance. They waited before the bolted gates, gathering in greater and greater numbers. Above, the sentries watched blank-faced, neither moving to open the gates nor calling down to calm the growing crowd.

Only after more than half the night had passed and most of the city had emptied out into the areas before the palace did the gates finally open. The people poured forward, relieved. They were certain that Azshara had finally come out in response to their pleas.

But what emerged from within the palace walls was not the queen, nor was it anything ever imagined in the night elf world.

And so fell the first victims of the Burning Legion.

NINETEEN

A wave of vertigo struck Krasus, the attack so unexpected that it nearly cost him his life. Only moments before, he had felt much his old self, that due in great part to his immediate proximity to Korialstrasz. The dragon now carried him swiftly toward the general direction of Cenarius's glade, although not near enough that the demigod might notice. A determination to find this one night elf Nozdormu had revealed to him had further fueled the mage—and that was why the sudden vertigo had caught him so off guard that he had nearly fallen from the dragon's neck.

Korialstrasz adjusted for him at the last moment, but Krasus's younger self also seemed oddly disoriented.

"Do you fare better?" the dragon roared to him.

"I am . . . recouping." Krasus peered into the night sky, trying to make sense of what had just happened. He searched his ragged memories, finally coming up with a possible answer. "My friend, do you know of the night elves' capital city?"

"Zin-Azshari? I am vaguely familiar with it."

"Veer toward there."

"But your quest—"

Krasus was adamant. "Do it now. I believe it is of the utmost importance that we go there."

His younger self grumbled something, but arced toward the direction of Zin-Azshari. Leaning forward, Krasus peered ahead, awaiting the first signs of the legendary city. If memory served him—and he could not be certain that it did—Zin-Azshari had been the culmination of the night elf civilization, a grand, sprawling metropolis the likes of which would never be seen again. However, the opulence of the ancient city was not what interested him. What concerned Krasus was his recollection of Zin-Azshari's nearness to the fabled Well of Eternity.

And it was the Well that now drew him. Although the origins of the Burning Legion's first entrance into the world was lost to him, Krasus still retained a sharp enough mind to make some fairly accurate assumptions. In this time period, the Well *was* power, and power was not only what the demons sought, but also what enabled them to reach the very realms that they destroyed.

Where more likely to find the portal through which the Burning Legion would *have* to arrive than in the immediate proximity of the greatest fount of sorcerous energy ever known?

They soared across the night sky, Korialstrasz flying mile after mile in the space of only minutes. Even still, hours passed, precious hours that Krasus suspected the world could not afford.

At last, the dragon called, "We will soon be in sight of Zin-Azshari! What do you hope to see?"

It was more what he hoped not to see, but Krasus could not explain that to his companion. "I do not know."

Ahead appeared lights, countless lights. He frowned. Of course the night elves would have illumination for some of their activities, but there seemed too many for a realm of nocturnal beings. Even a city as great in size as Zin-Azshari would not be so bright.

But as the duo neared, they saw that the illumination came not from torchlight or crystals—but from raging fires coursing throughout the night elven capital.

"The city is ablaze!" roared Korialstrasz. "What could have started such an inferno?"

"We need to descend," was all Krasus replied.

The red dragon dipped, dropping hundreds of feet. Now details became visible. Elaborate, colorful buildings burned, some of them already collapsing. Sculptured gardens and massive tree homes had become pyres.

And scattered throughout the streets lay the bodies of the dead.

They had been brutally slaughtered, with no compassion given for the elderly, the infirm, or the young. Many had died in clusters while others had clearly been hunted down one by one. In addition to the populace of Zin-Azshari, a variety of animals, especially the great night sabers, lay dead as well, their demises no less foul.

"There has been war here!" snarled the winged leviathan. "No—not war! This is genocide!"

"This is the work of the Burning Legion," Krasus muttered to himself.

Korialstrasz veered toward the city center. Curiously, the damage lessened as they neared what looked to be the palace. In fact, certain walled sections of the center appeared completely untouched.

"What do you know of these sections?" Krasus asked his mount.

"Little, but I believe that those linked by walls to the queen's palace belong to what are referred to as the 'Highborne.' They are considered the most esteemed of the night elves, all somehow involved directly in service to her majesty, Azshara."

"Circle once around them."

Korialstrasz did. Studying the vicinity, Krasus had his suspicions verified.

None of the quarter that housed the regal Highborne had been touched in the slightest by the monstrous disaster.

"There is movement to the northwest, Krasus!"

"Fly there! Quickly!"

He need not have encouraged his companion, for Korialstrasz clearly sought the answers as much as he. Not at all surprising, considering that they were one and the same.

Krasus now saw what the dragon's superior vision had already noted. A wave of movement, almost like locusts, pouring through the city. Korialstrasz descended further, enabling the pair to identify individuals.

And for Krasus, it was the return of evil.

The Burning Legion marched relentlessly through Zin-Azshari, leaving nothing untouched in their wake. Buildings fell before their might. There were the tall, brutal Fel Guard with their maces and shields. Mindless Infernals battering their way through stone walls or any other physical opposition. Near them hovered huge, winged figures with blazing green swords, molten armor, and cloven feet . . . the Doomguard.

As the dragon moved toward the front of the horde, Krasus identified the houndlike felbeasts, ever the precursors of the Legion. They seemed especially active; not only were their noses raised high to smell the air, but the sinister tentacles with which they absorbed magic darted forward eagerly.

And then the mage saw what the Legion hunted.

Refugees swarmed from the city's center, families and individuals creating a desperate flow through the narrow avenues. At their rear, trying to keep the demons at bay, were a small contingent of armored soldiers and a few robed figures that Krasus believed to be the legendary Moon Guard.

Even as the two neared, one of the Moon Guard in the forefront attempted to cast a spell. But by placing himself in the open, he only served to add to the list of victims. One of the felbeasts leapt forward, landing just before the sorcerer. Its tentacles shot forth with astonishing speed.

They adhered to the spellcaster's chest, physically lifting him into the air. Before anyone—even Krasus and Korialstrasz—could come to his aid, the thrashing Moon Guard sorcerer was drained of his magical forces . . . leaving a dead, dry husk in his place.

The red dragon roared. Had he even wanted to, Krasus could not have stopped his younger self from taking reprisals. In truth, his own memories of such horror kept the mage quiet. Too many had perished because of the Legion and even though by Krasus's interference Korialstrasz had come here, the former no longer cared. He had tried to keep from wreaking any more havoc on the time line, but enough was enough.

It was time for retribution.

As Korialstrasz swept past the front ranks of the demonic host, he let loose with a great blast of flame. The stream of fire engulfed not only the fel-beast that had slain the sorcerer, but many of the pack following. Whining, the few survivors retreated, some singed badly.

Korialstrasz did not pause. He turned now to face the main horde, a second wave of fire enveloping the foremost demons.

Most perished instantly. A few of the more hardy Fel Guard struggled through the flames, only to collapse shortly after from their fiery wounds. One blazing Infernal sought to bat out the dragonfire and, when that did not work, ran headlong into a building, possibly in some vague hope that doing so would smother the flames. Seconds later, it, too, collapsed.

Even the Burning Legion could not stand the pure might of a dragon, but that did not make them defenseless. Up from their ranks suddenly flew a score of Doomguard. Krasus noticed them first and, though well aware of the risk, cast a quick spell.

Winds buffeted the foremost demons, throwing them back into the rest. The Doomguard became entangled with one another.

Korialstrasz let loose another breath.

Five of the winged terrors plummeted to the ground, fiery missiles that further inflicted damage on the horde below.

The rest of the Doomguard regrouped. Others shot up into the sky, doubling the numbers.

Korialstrasz clearly desired to face them, but Krasus abruptly felt the telltale warning signs of weakness. As Alexstrasza had said, together the two were nearly complete—but not quite. The added use of their strength depleted both quicker than normal. Already the dragon flew more slowly, less smoothly, even if he did not recognize that fact.

"We must leave!" Krasus insisted.

"Abandon the fight? Never!"

"The refugees have made good their escape thanks to us!" The delay had been just enough for the night elves to scatter into the lands beyond. Krasus had every confidence that they could keep ahead of the Legion at this point. "We must get word to those who can do more! We must continue on our original path!"

It pained Krasus to speak so, for in his heart he would have wanted to burn to ash every demon in sight, but even now, more and more flew up to deal with the lone dragon.

With a roar of frustration, Korialstrasz unleashed one final blast that destroyed three of the Doomguard and sent the others fluttering back. The red behemoth then turned and flew off, easily outpacing the Legion despite his growing exhaustion.

As they soared past the palace again, Krasus saw with horror that more demons poured from its gates. Most disconcerting, however, were the night elven sentries that still stood guard on the battlements, warriors who seemed to have no regard at all for the desperate straits in which their fellow citizens found themselves.

Krasus had seen such blatant disregard in the face of horror before. There had been those during the second war who had acted in the same horrifyingly indifferent manner. *They are mesmerized by the demons' growing influence! If the lords of the Legion have not set foot on the mortal plane already, it cannot be long at all before they do!*

And when that happened, he feared that there would be no future for the world . . . nor, in this case, even a past.

There were dreadful noises disturbing her relaxation. Azshara had ordered music played for her in the hopes that it would drown out the objectionable noises, but the lyres and flutes had failed miserably. Finally, she rose and, with her new bodyguards surrounding her, gracefully wended her way through the palace.

It was not Lord Xavius but rather Captain Varo'then whom first she met. The captain fell down on one knee and clasped a fist against his heart.

"Your wondrous majesty . . ."

"My darling captain, what is the cause of such awful clamor?"

The scarred night elf looked up at her with a veiled expression. "Perhaps it'd be easier to show it to you."

"Very well."

He led her to a balcony overlooking the main area of the city. Azshara rarely came to this balcony save for public displays, much preferring the view of her extravagant gardens from her chambers or the glimpses of the Well of Eternity that her visits to the tower offered her.

But the sight before the queen was not the one to which she had grown so accustomed. Azshara's golden eyes drank in the images of her city, the ruined structures, the endless fires, and the bodies littering the streets. She glanced to her right, where the walled quarter of the Highborne still stood peacefully.

"Explain this to me, Captain Varo'then."

"It's been told to me by the counselor that these have proven unworthy. To fully prepare for a world of perfection, all the imperfect must be swept away."

"And those below were considered lacking in the judgment of Lord Xavius?"

"With the recommendation of the great one's most trusted servant, the celestial commander, Mannoroth."

Azshara had briefly met the imposing Mannoroth and, as with her counselor, she had been overwhelmed by the great one's high servant.

The queen nodded. "If Mannoroth says it must be so, it must be so. Sacrifices are always required in the name of glorious pursuits, I always think."

Varo'then bowed his head. "Your wisdom is boundless."

The queen accepted his compliment with the regal aplomb with which she took the *many* compliments she received on a daily basis. Still gazing at the carnage below, Azshara asked, "Will it be long, then? Will the great one soon come, too?"

"He will, my queen . . . and it's said that Mannoroth has called him *Sargeras.*"

"Sargeras . . ." Queen Azshara tasted the name, ran it across her lips. "Sargeras . . . truly a fit name for a god!" She put a hand to her breast. "I trust I will be given advance warning when he makes his entrance. I would be deeply disappointed if I could not be there to greet him myself."

"I shall see to it personally that all is done to give you fair warning," Varo'then said, then bowed. "Forgive me, my queen, duty demands my attention now."

She waved a negligent hand, still fascinated by both the scene below and the true name of the god. The captain left her alone with her bodyguards.

In her mind, Azshara began picturing the world that would replace what had been decimated. A more magnificent city, a true monument to her glory. It would no longer be called Zin-Azshari, as gracious as the people had been to name it that. No, next time it would simply be called *Azshara.* How much more appropriate a title that was for the home of the queen. *Azshara.* She said it twice, admiring the way it sounded. She should have requested the change long ago, but that did not matter now.

Then another, more intriguing thought entered her mind. True, she was the most perfect of her race, the icon of her people, but there was one who was even more glorious, more magnificent . . . and soon he would come.

His name was Sargeras.

"Sargeras . . ." she whispered. "Sargeras the god . . ." An almost childlike smile crossed her face. ". . . and his consort, Azshara . . ."

Messengers arrived at Black Rook Hold at the rate of one every few minutes. All demanded to see the master of the hold immediately, for each had news of import.

And every missive to Lord Ravencrest boiled down to the same dire news.

Sorcery had been all but stolen from the night elves. Even the most skilled could do little. In addition, other spells that constantly relied on drawing from the Well to keep them maintained had failed, in one or two places with catastrophic results. Everywhere, panic ensued and it was all officials could do to keep chaos from erupting.

From the most important place itself, from those regions near Zin-Azshari . . . there had been no word.

Until now.

The messenger brought in by the sentries could barely stand. His armor had been in part ripped from his body and bloody scars covered his flesh. He staggered before Lord Ravencrest, falling to one knee.

"Has he been given food and water?" the noble asked. When no one could answer, he growled out an order to one of the soldiers standing near the entrance. Within seconds, sustenance was brought for the newcomer.

Among those waiting impatiently were Rhonin and the others. They had gone from being prisoners to some undefinable status. Not allies, but not outsiders. The wizard had chosen to remain silent and in the back of the throng, the better to ensure that his status did not slip back to prisoner.

"Can you speak now?" Ravencrest rumbled to the messenger once the latter had eaten some fruit and drunken almost half a sack of water.

"Aye . . . forgive me, my lord . . . for not being able to do so earlier."

"Judging by your condition, I find it hard to believe you actually even made it here . . ."

The night elf kneeling before him looked around at the others assembled. Rhonin noted how hollow his eyes had become. "I find it hard to believe I'm here myself . . . my lord." He coughed several times. "My lord . . . I come to tell you . . . that I believe it . . . it is the end of our world."

The flat tone with which he said the last only served to add to its horrific impact. Dead silence filled the chamber. Rhonin recalled what Malfurion had said before. *It's begun.* Even Malfurion had not understood what he meant, only that he knew that something terrible was taking place.

"What do you mean?" persisted Ravencrest, leaning close. "Did you receive some terrible message from Zin-Azshari? Did they bid you to relay this monstrous announcement?"

"My lord . . . I come *from* Zin-Azshari."

"Impossible!" interjected Latosius. "By the best physical means it would take three to five nights and sorcery is not available—"

"I *know* what was available better than you!" snapped the soldier, disregarding the Moon Guard's high rank. To Lord Ravencrest, he said, "I was sent to plead for help! Those who *could* funneled what little power they could gather to send me here! They may be dead . . ." He swallowed. "I may be the only one to survive . . ."

"The city, lad! What of the city?"

"My lord . . . Zin-Azshari is in ruins, overrun by bloodthirsty fiends, creatures out of nightmare!"

The story flowed from the messenger like a wound beyond sealing. Like all other night elves, those of the capital had been stunned by the abrupt and inexplicable loss of nearly all their power. Many had gone to the palace to seek reassurances. The crowds had swelled to hundreds.

And then from the palace had poured out an endless multitude of monstrous warriors, some horned, some winged, all armed and eager to slaughter those in their midst. In seconds, people had died by the scores, no quarter given. Fear followed and others were trampled by those who sought to escape.

"We ran, my lord, all of us. I can only speak for those who fled in my direction, but even the most hardened warriors did not long stand."

But the demonic horde followed, catching those who could not keep up the pace. Scattered groups managed to flee out of the city, but even there the fiends hunted them.

No one interrupted his tale. No one argued that he suffered delusions. They all read the truth in his eyes and voice.

The messenger then described how he came to be here. A group of Moon Guard and officers had put their heads together, trying to come up with some defense or course of action. It had been determined that Black Rook Hold had to be informed and by lot that duty had fallen to the soldier present.

"They warned that the spell might not work as planned, that I could instead be sent to the bottom of the Well or even back to the c-city . . ." He shrugged. "I saw little choice . . ."

With tremendous strain, the spellcasters had begun their work. He had stood in the middle as they gathered up what little energy they could. The world had begun to fade around him—

And just as he had vanished, he had seen the monstrous hounds leaping upon the party.

"I landed some distance north of here, my lord, battered but alive. It took some time to reach an outpost where I could obtain a night saber . . . and then I headed to y-you as best I could."

A much subdued Ravencrest slumped back. "And the palace? The palace, too, is in ruins? All slaughtered there?"

The messenger hesitated, then said, "My lord, there were sentries atop the walls. They watched the people before the gates opened . . . and then they watched the monsters come out and butcher all of us!"

"The queen would never allow that!" spouted one of the noble's officers. Others nodded agreement, but many kept their opinions hidden.

Their commander had his own notion as to what such news meant. His expression already grim, he muttered, "It's as we believed, then. This must be the work of the Highborne."

"Surely even they would not be so insane!" Latosius argued. "True, their sorcerers think themselves superior even to the Moon Guard, but they are night elves just like us!"

"So we would believe, but their arrogance knows no bounds!" Ravencrest slammed his fist on the arm of his stone chair. "And let us not forget that the Highborne obey the dictates of the lord counselor . . . Xavius!"

Rhonin had heard the name mentioned prior, but now the venom with which it was repeated stunned him. He leaned by Malfurion, asking, "Who is this Xavius?"

Malfurion had much recovered, thanks in great part to his twin's aid. With some slight help from Brox, he now stood next to the others. "He who whispers in the queen's ear. Her most trusted advisor and a rival of Lord Ravencrest. I don't doubt myself that Xavius is involved, but he couldn't do this without Azshara's compliance! Even the Highborne worship her!"

"They'll never believe that," Illidan remarked. "Forget that for now! Let them think it's the counselor! Their choices will still be the same in the end!"

Although he did not exactly trust Illidan, Rhonin had to agree with the other night elf in this regard.

And it seemed that the choice of villains had already been made. Ravencrest stood, shouting to the others in attendance. His officers jammed their helmets on as if ready to go and ride out toward the capital immediately.

"All Moon Guard, all spellcasters of any reasonable ability, should be gathered as quickly as possible! Garo'thal! Send out messengers to every military post and commander! Resistance must be organized! This foul situation must be contained!"

Latosius confronted the noble. "Something must be done to regain the use of the Well! Force of arms alone will not stand against those monsters! You heard the messenger!"

The bearded noble thrust his face into that of the Moon Guard. "I hope to have some sorcery at hand, especially from your vaunted order, but, otherwise, force of arms is all we really have at the moment, isn't it?"

Illidan suddenly abandoned his brother and the rest. "My lord, I feel I may be of some aid! I still have some ability for casting spells!"

"Splendid! We'll need it! Zin-Azshari must be avenged, and the queen freed from the Highborne!"

Rhonin could not stand still. He had seen what the Burning Legion could do and, even though this was all in his past, he could not stand by as Krasus hoped. Within him he still sensed the ability to summon magic, use it as he willed. "My Lord Ravencrest!"

The noble looked him over, clearly not yet certain what to make of him. "What do you want?"

"You need someone who can cast spells. I offer myself."

Ravencrest looked doubtful.

In response, the wizard summoned a ball of blue light over his left palm. It took him more effort than usual, but not enough that he showed that effort.

The commander's expression of doubt melted away. "Aye, you're welcome to our ranks—" Out of the corner of his eye, he must have noticed Latosius about to object. "Especially since little else has been offered to us."

"If whatever spell cuts us off from the Well's strength can be but removed—"

"Which would require sorcery of some magnitude in the first place . . . and if you could do that, Moon Guard, we wouldn't have a problem at all!"

As he listened to them argue, Malfurion's heart sank deeper. Such bickering served no good cause. Action was what was called for, but with little in the way of any sort of magic to back up Lord Ravencrest's intended military force, the future looked dark, indeed. If only—

His eyes widened. Perhaps he could do something.

As his brother and Rhonin had done before him, Malfurion stepped up to the noble. Ravencrest eyed him with some disbelief.

"And now you? You plan to offer sorcery such as Illidan here claims to still wield? I would welcome it if you have it, regardless of your past crimes."

"I offer not sorcery, Lord Ravencrest, but a magic of a different sort. I offer what has been taught to me by my shan'do, Cenarius."

Latosius laughed mockingly. "This is the worst jest yet! The teachings of a mythical demigod?"

But Ravencrest did not dismiss Malfurion out of hand. "You truly believe you can be of some aid?"

The younger night elf hesitated, then said, "Yes, but not from here. I need to go somewhere . . . quieter."

The noble's brow furrowed. "Quieter?"

Malfurion nodded. "I must go to the temple of Elune."

"The temple of the Mother Moon? I hadn't even thought of them. Their support is definitely needed in this time of crisis—but what do you hope to achieve there?"

Trying to keep his uncertainty hidden, Malfurion Stormrage answered, "The removal of the spell that keeps the Well of Eternity's power from our sorcerers, of course."

TWENTY

All was well in the world . . . for Lord Xavius, anyway.

His dreams, his goals, were well within reach. Better yet, the great one was quite pleased with him. The shield spell that he and Mannoroth had set into motion had not only succeeded in sealing the Well's might from all but the Highborne, it had also enabled them to widen and solidify the portal. In the space of only a few scant hours, hundreds of the celestial host had poured through.

Mannoroth had immediately taken control of them, sending them out to purge the unfit. Once, Xavius might have found that idea horrific, but he now fully embraced the ways and methods of Sargeras. The god knew best how to achieve the perfect paradise the counselor sought. Had not the quarter reserved for the homes of the Highborne been completely spared? From those who served the palace would arise the new Golden Age of the night elf race, an era eclipsing any existing prior to it.

Lord Xavius had been granted the further honor of monitoring the work that made all this possible. He kept in delicate balance the spell that constantly regenerated the shield. The labor required had been more than even Mannoroth had planned and if the spell failed now, it would be near impossible to repeat without effectively sealing the portal first and using the combined might of all the Highborne sorcerers.

But Xavius had no intention of letting any disaster befall the precious shield. Not that he expected any trouble. What could happen here in the heart of the palace?

A brooding figure stalked into the chamber, peering around impatiently.

"Where isss Mannoroth?" hissed the Houndmaster.

"He commands the host, of course," responded the night elf. "He goes to clear Zin-Azshari of the unfit."

Something in Hakkar's expression momentarily disturbed Xavius. Almost it seemed that the counselor had said something that the Houndmaster found amusing. What that could be, though, the night elf could not possibly say.

Through the portal materialized four more of the Fel Guard. One of the even more menacing Doomguard stood nearby. He barked something in an unknown tongue to the newcomers, who immediately marched out of the chamber.

The celestial host moved with remarkable military precision, instantly obedient to orders and constantly aware of their duties. Even Captain Varo'then's elite Guard paled in comparison, at least in Lord Xavius's mind.

"How fare preparations for the hunt?" the counselor asked Hakkar.

The hint of mockery left the hulking figure's expression. "It goesss well, lord night elf. My houndsss and the Fel Guard who run with them have their explicit ordersss. Thossse that Mannoroth desssiresss captured will be."

He turned and stalked out of the room, leaving in his wake an oddly satisfied Lord Xavius. While he much respected the status of the Houndmaster, the night elf now saw himself closer in rank to the great one's commander.

The counselor looked once again at the spell of which he had been an integral part. Only a few yards from the portal, the cluster of blue, flashing nodules over the diagram Mannoroth had drawn were the only physical signs of the shield spell. With his magical eyes, however, Xavius could make out other swirling patterns in orange, yellow, green, and more. A powerful cornucopia of magical forces of which he was now in control.

Just as he was now in control of the destiny of not only his own people . . . but the rest of the world as well.

The temple of Elune did not need to be warned of the catastrophe that had befallen the realm of the night elves. They had not personally been touched by the Well's loss, but they could still sense the sudden emptiness. When throngs came to the various temples to ask for guidance, the priestesses throughout the realm conversed with one another through methods utilized since the Mother Moon had first touched the heart of her initial convert, discussing what could be done. They chose to invite the people in for mass prayer, let Elune give them comfort. They also searched with their skills in the direction of the Well . . . but like the Moon Guard, they could not divine just what had happened.

Yet, even though they still retained the gifts granted them by their goddess, that did not mean the priestesses were safe from the horror unleashed soon afterward. When the Legion overran the temples in the capital, even those as far away as Suramar felt the deaths of their sisters there, felt their agonies as the horde slaughtered them without mercy.

"Sister," one of the other priestesses called to Tyrande, who had been pouring water for the faithful. "There is one at the front entrance who requests to see you."

"Thank you, sister." Tyrande handed the jug to another priestess, then hurried off. She could only assume that Illidan had come to see her again. Tyrande dreaded speaking with him, unsure what she would say if he brought up a possible match between them.

Yet, it was not Illidan, but rather another she had not thought to see for a very, very long time.

"Malfurion!" Without realizing what she did, Tyrande threw her arms around him, hugging Malfurion tightly.

His cheeks darkening, he whispered, "It's good to see you, Tyrande."

She released him. "How did you come to be here?" A sudden fear arose within her. "Broxigar? What have they done with—"

"He's with me." Malfurion pointed behind himself, where Tyrande saw that the orc waited in a dark corner near the entrance. The monstrous warrior looked quite uncomfortable as he eyed the many night elves.

She glanced around but saw no guards other than those of the temple. "Malfurion! What madness brings you here? Did the two of you sneak back into the city just to see me?"

"No . . . we were captured."

"But if—"

He gently put a finger to her lips, silencing her. "That story must wait. You know of the terror in Zin-Azshari?"

"Only some . . . and even that's too much! Malfurion, the *terror* we felt in the minds and souls of our sisters there! Something dreadful—"

"Listen to me! It spreads beyond the capital even as we speak. What's worse, now the Moon Guard are helpless against it! Some spell all but cuts off the Well's power from them!"

She nodded. "So we have surmised . . . but what does that have to do with your coming here?"

"Is the Chamber of the Moon in use now?"

She thought. "It was earlier, but so many have come for guidance that the high priestess had the main worship chamber opened instead. The Chamber of the Moon may be empty now."

"Good. We need to go there." He signaled Brox, who hurried over. To Tyrande's astonishment, the orc even carried an ax.

"You were captured . . ." she reminded Malfurion.

"Lord Ravencrest saw no more reason to detain us, providing Brox stayed with me."

"I owe you both," reminded the broad-shouldered warrior. "I owe my life."

"You owe us nothing," Illidan's brother returned. To Tyrande he said, "Please take us to the chamber."

With her in the lead, they headed into the temple. Despite Brox's attempt to stay as close to his companions as possible, he could not hide his appearance from those night elves gathered inside. Many looked in horror at him and some even screamed, pointing at the orc as if he was the one responsible for their turmoil.

Guards caught up to them just as they neared the Chamber of the Moon. The foremost was the one who had spoken with Tyrande about Illidan.

"Sister . . . it is the custom to allow any entry into the Mother Moon's temple, but that creature—"

"Elune says that he does not have the same right as any other believer?"

The sentries looked uncertainly at one another, the first finally replying, "It does not say exactly anything about other races in that regard, but—"

"But are not all the children of Elune? Does he not have the right to come to her for guidance, make use of all facets of the temple?"

There was no answer to this. Finally, the lead guard waved them by. "Just please keep him from sight as much as possible. There is already enough panic out there."

Tyrande nodded gratefully. "I understand."

As they entered, they found only two other acolytes in attendance. Tyrande immediately walked up to the pair and explained the need for privacy, pointing specifically at Brox. In truth, the orc's presence was all that was needed to encourage the other sisters to quickly retreat.

Returning to Malfurion, she asked, "What do you hope to do?"

"I intend to walk the Emerald Dream again, Tyrande."

She did not like the sound of that at all. "You plan to journey to Zin-Azshari!"

"Yes. There I hope to learn the truth about what has been done to the Well."

Tyrande knew him better. "You don't hope to simply learn the truth, Malfurion; I think you intend to *do* something about it . . ."

Instead of replying, he studied the center of the chamber. "That seems the most tranquil location."

"Malfurion—"

"I've got to hurry, Tyrande. Forgive me."

With Brox in tow, he walked to the place he had chosen, then seated himself on the ground. Legs folded in, Malfurion looked up into the moonlit sky.

The orc seated himself across from the night elf, but made room when Tyrande joined. Malfurion glanced questioningly at her. "You needn't stay."

"If in any way the Mother Moon can help me guide you, protect you from harm, I intend to do so."

Malfurion gave her a grateful smile, then grew grim again. "I must begin now."

For reasons beyond her, Tyrande suddenly seized his hand. He did not look at her, his eyes now shut, but briefly the smile returned.

And suddenly Tyrande felt him leaving her.

It had been a quickly devised, desperate plan, one from which Malfurion understood Lord Ravencrest actually expected little result. Yet, with the Moon Guard virtually powerless, he had seen no reason why the upstart young night elf could not at least try.

Now Malfurion only had to hope that he had not made empty promises.

Tyrande's hand on his own proved invaluable to wending his way into the sleeplike trance. Her touch had comforted Malfurion, eased the incredible tension the horrific events of the past few days had created.

Soothed, he reached out to the world around him, to the trees, river, stones, and more as he had with Cenarius.

Yet, this time he was met not by the tranquil elements of nature—but rather *turmoil*.

The world was no longer in balance. The forest knew it, the hills knew it, even the heavens felt the wrongness. Everywhere he focused, Malfurion sensed only disharmony. It struck with such force that for a moment the night elf nearly drowned in it.

Instead, he fixed again on Tyrande's light touch, drawing peaceful strength from her nearby presence. The discord faded, still there but unable to overwhelm him.

Once more steady, Malfurion reached out to the spirits of nature, touching each and letting them feel his own calm. He understood their turmoil and promised that he would act in their name. The night elf asked in turn that they be there if he needed their assistance, reminding the spirits that both he and they desired a return to the balance.

The sense of discord dwindled more. It would not go away so long as the Highborne meddled with the Well, but Malfurion had at least created some semblance of harmony again.

And with that done, he was able once again to enter the dreamscape safely.

Free from earthly confinement, he paused to gaze down at his friends, especially Tyrande. It was easier this time to summon the images, transpose the reality over the idyllic landscape. Both Brox and Tyrande immediately materialized . . . as did his own body, of course.

To his surprise, he noted a tear drifting down one of Tyrande's cheeks. Instinctively, Malfurion reached to wipe it away, only to have his finger pass through it. Yet, as if feeling his nearness, the young priestess reached up with her free hand and not only wiped away the tear, but also touched the area.

Forcing himself to turn away, Malfurion looked to the sky again. He focused on the direction of Zin-Azshari, then stepped up.

The familiar greenish tint permeated everything. Malfurion concentrated, again overlapping the shadow world with elements of reality. With what seemed a combination of half walking, half flying, he drifted over the now-covered dreamscape, sensing the myriad aspects of both the true and sub-conscious worlds.

But as he journeyed, an unexpected presence caught his attention. At first he doubted his senses, but a quick search verified his first suspicions.

Shan'do? he called.

Malfurion felt his mentor touch his thoughts, but only in an indistinct manner. However, the touch was enough to convey that Cenarius was well. The last of the felbeasts had been dealt with, but some other matter urgently demanded the demigod's attention. Malfurion realized that the forest lord had felt the presence of his student in the Emerald Dream and had quickly reached out to let the night elf know that all was not yet lost.

Comforted by Cenarius's unspoken message, Malfurion moved on. The green haze thinned further and soon he saw the world below almost as he would had he been truly able to fly like a bird. Hills and rivers passed swiftly by as he focused more on his destination.

And as he neared the capital, for the first time Malfurion beheld the horror.

As terrifying as the messenger's descriptions had been, they had not fully conveyed the monstrous cataclysm that had befallen the fabled city. Much of Zin-Azshari had been razed to the ground as if a great boulder had rolled over it time and again. No building on the outskirts had been left standing. Fire ruled everywhere, but not simply the crimson flames with which Malfurion was familiar. The capital was also awash in foul green or pitch black fire clearly of an otherworldly nature. As Malfurion passed over them, he could feel their evil heat despite being in the dream realm.

Then he caught his first glimpse of the demons.

The felbeasts had been monstrous enough, but the creatures following them sent new chills through him, the more so because they were clearly intelligent. Despite the huge horns, devilish faces, and horrific forms, they moved in concert, with terrible purpose. This was not some mindless horde, but an army dedicated to evil.

And more and more poured out of the gates of the palace even as he approached.

He was not surprised to see that the vast, beautiful structure was not touched in the slightest. As the messenger had said, sentries still lined the walls. Malfurion passed near a few and saw in their eyes a terrible pleasure at the horrific panorama below. Their silver orbs were tinted with red and some looked as if they desired to join the demons.

Revulsed, Malfurion quickly pulled away from them. He looked to the side of the palace and noted that the homes of the Highborne had also been left whole. Some of the queen's servants even journeyed from one building to another as if nothing of consequence was taking place around them.

His revulsion growing, the night elf pushed on toward the tower. As before, Malfurion sensed the incredible forces being drawn up haphazardly from the dark Well. If anything, the Highborne had more than doubled their efforts. Savage storms raged over the Well, touching even within the embattled city.

Last time, he had tried to enter the tower at the point where he had sensed the spellwork. For this attempt, however, Malfurion dove lower, finding a balcony near the bottom. Moving much the way he would have if he had been entering by physical means, the night elf hovered just above the balcony, then moved through the open entrance there.

To his surprise, his attempt worked. He almost laughed. None had thought to protect this interior entrance from such as him. The hubris of the Highborne had enabled him to penetrate the palace with ease.

Slowly Malfurion floated along the corridor, seeking the path up. Near the rear, he found the main stairway—and with it, more than a dozen of the huge, horned warriors he had seen outside.

Malfurion's first instinct was to pull back in the hopes that they would not see him. Unfortunately, there was nowhere to hide. He braced for their attack . . . then cursed himself for his stupidity when the first of the demonic band lumbered past him.

They could not see his dream form. He breathed a sigh of relief, watching as the last vanished down the hall. When it became clear that no more followed, Malfurion steeled himself and ascended the stairway.

He passed several chambers on the way up but did not pause for any of them. What Malfurion sought lay at the very top of the looming tower and the sooner he reached it, the sooner he could devise some plan.

Just what he intended, the night elf did not know. Despite having turned to druidism, Malfurion was almost as adept at sorcery as his brother and even in his present condition he believed that he could cast some sort of spell.

Some distance up, Malfurion suddenly encountered a barrier. He reached out, feeling the air. An invisible force blocked his way, perhaps the same force that had prevented him from entering on his previous attempt. Perhaps the Highborne had not been so negligent after all.

Still determined, the night elf thrust himself forward with all his might. He felt the barrier squeeze against him, almost as if Malfurion attempted to walk through a true wall. Yet, the more he pushed, the more it seemed the wall softened some, almost as if about to—

Malfurion fell through.

His entrance was so abrupt that he floated there, unsure that he had actually succeeded. Turning, he tried to touch the barrier, but felt only a vague, very weak force. Either his presence had disrupted the barrier or it had been designed only to prevent intrusion, not departure.

A short distance up, he found himself confronting two guards and a thick door that had to lead to where the Highborne worked. Once satisfied that the guards did not see him, Malfurion put a hand to the door, testing it.

His fingers slipped through the door as if it were nothing. Bracing himself, the young night elf entered.

His first sensation was one of absolute disorientation, for the chamber where the Highborne performed their foul work was far more massive than the outside implied. Malfurion's own home was dwarfed by the vast room.

And the Highborne needed all that space, for what they did not fill themselves swarmed with ranks of grotesque warriors, all heading toward the very door through which Malfurion had passed. Up close their monstrous faces shook him more. There was no compassion, no mercy . . .

Forcing away such thoughts, he drifted toward where the Highborne worked, watching their efforts with a combination of fascination and disgust. The Highborne appeared driven beyond sanity. Most had a hungry look to them. Their once-elaborate garments hung from their bony bodies and a few strained to stand, but all stared intently, eagerly, at the product of their toil, a fierce, pulsating gap in reality.

Malfurion started to gaze into the center of that gap, but suddenly had to look away. His brief study had been enough to let him sense the monstrous evil deep within. It amazed him that the Highborne could not see what it was with which they dealt.

Trying to forget the fear that had almost now gripped him, Malfurion turned—and came face-to-face with who could only be the queen's counselor, Lord Xavius.

Malfurion floated only inches from the elder night elf's unsettling eyes. He had heard of the advisor's artificial orbs, the magical eyes with which Xavius had purposely replaced his own. Streaks of ruby darted across the ebony lenses, lenses almost as black as the dark force Malfurion had sensed in the magical gap.

The counselor stood there with such an intense expression on his harsh visage that at first the younger night elf thought that he had been seen, but that, of course, was only his own fanciful notion. After a moment, Xavius stepped forward, walking through Malfurion and heading to where the High-borne relentlessly continued their efforts.

It took Malfurion a moment more to recover from the unexpected encounter. Lord Xavius more than anyone else was the one the Moon Guard and Ravencrest had blamed for the horror outside. Seeing him now, Malfurion could believe it. He still felt that the queen also knew what happened, but that was a fact that could be verified later.

With determination, Malfurion headed toward what had to be the array that controlled the shield. Three Highborne sorcerers stood around it, but they seemed to be monitoring its actions, not actively shaping it. He drifted past them, moving up to study the details.

It was a masterfully crafted display, some of it on a level far beyond that which Malfurion himself could cast. Still, it did not take him long to see how he could affect it, even cancel it.

Of course, that assumed that Malfurion could do *anything* in his dream form.

To test the possibility, he whispered to the air, asking of it a simple jest. Even as the request left his lips, a breeze tousled ever so slightly the hairs on the back of one sorcerer's head.

His success thrilled Malfurion. If he could do this much, he could do enough to disrupt the shield spell. That would be all the Moon Guard would need.

He stared at the heart of the magical matrix, focusing on its weakest link—

"A foolish, foolish thing to attempt," commented a cold voice.

Malfurion instinctively glanced over his shoulder.

Lord Xavius stared back at him.

At him.

The counselor held up a narrow white crystal. His eyes—eyes with which he could evidently see even a dream form—flared.

A tremendous force sucked Malfurion toward the crystal. He tried to pull back, but his efforts went for naught. The crystal filled his view . . . then became his world.

From within the tiny, impossible prison, he looked out at the huge, mocking visage of the elder night elf.

"An interesting thought occurs to me," Lord Xavius commented almost clinically. "How long do you think it will take your body to die without your spirit within?" When Malfurion did not answer, the counselor simply shrugged. "We shall just have to see, shall we?"

And with that, he pocketed the crystal and plunged Malfurion into darkness.

They had reached the outskirts of the area where Krasus hoped to find the elf in question. He did not comprehend how he knew that the one he sought lived near here, but suspected that Nozdormu had left that information in the back of his mind during the vision. Krasus silently thanked the Aspect for considering the difficulty of such a search. It also gave him hope that soon this catastrophe would be corrected, and that he and Rhonin would return home.

That assumed, of course, that he could *find* Rhonin.

His guilt at not immediately hunting for his former pupil was only partially assuaged by the fact that the one he pursued now had been identified by one of the five elemental powers as essential to both the past and the future. The moment he located this mysterious night elf, the dragon mage intended to look for Rhonin, to whom he owed much more than the human knew.

Korialstrasz suddenly slowed, dipping down toward the trees in the process. "I can bring you no nearer."

"I understand." Any closer to the night elven settlement and the inhabitants would notice the leviathan.

The red dragon alighted, then lowered his head to the ground so that Krasus could dismount. That done, Korialstrasz inspected the vicinity.

"We are not far. No more than an hour or two."

Krasus did not mention how much of a struggle those two hours would be once he left the company of his younger self. "You have done more than I could ask."

"I do not intend to abandon you now." Korialstrasz replied, folding his wings together. "Despite the form you wear, you may have forgotten that our kind can shift shape. I will transform into something more akin to those among whom we must mingle."

The dragon's huge frame suddenly shimmered. Korialstrasz started to shrink and his form took on a more humanoid appearance.

But a second later, he reverted to his natural shape, his eyes momentarily glassy and his breath ragged.

"What is it?" Krasus eyed his younger self helplessly.

"I—I cannot transform! To even attempt it fills me with agony!"

The mage recalled his own reaction when he had first attempted to resume his dragon form after arriving in this time. It did not surprise him that Korialstrasz suffered a similar difficulty. "Do not try again. I will have to go on my own."

"Are you certain? I note that when we are together, we both suffer less from whatever maladies afflict us . . ."

A mixture of anxiety and pride touched Krasus. Trust the younger version of himself to see the truth. Did Korialstrasz know *why*, though?

If he did, the dragon did not say so. Instead, Korialstrasz added, "No . . . I know you must go on."

"Will you remain here?"

"So long as I can. It does not appear that the night elves journey much to this region and the trees are tall and will hide me well. If you need me, though, I will come at your call."

"I know you will," responded Krasus because he knew himself well.

The mage bid the dragon farewell and started the arduous journey toward the night elven settlement. However, just before he would have been out of sight of Korialstrasz, the latter called quietly to him.

"Do you think you can find the one for which you search?"

"I can only hope . . ." He did not add that if he failed, then *everyone* would suffer because of it.

Korialstrasz nodded.

The closer he journeyed to the city—and the farther he moved from the dragon—the more ill and weary Krasus felt. Yet, despite his growing infirmity, the lanky figure continued on. Somewhere in there was the night elf in question. What he would do when he found him, Krasus did not yet know. He only hoped that Nozdormu had perhaps left that information locked away in his subconscious, to be released only when needed.

If not, it would be up to Krasus's own judgment.

It seemed to take forever, but at last he noticed the first signs of civilization. The distant torches likely marked a surrounding wall or even an entrance to the city itself.

Now would come the most difficult part. Although in this form he somewhat resembled a night elf, they would still recognize him as other than that. Perhaps if he pulled his cowl over his head and leaned forward—

Krasus suddenly realized that he was no longer alone in the forest.

They came from all sides, night elves clad in much the same armor as those who had captured him prior. Weapons resembling lances and swords pointed menacingly at the intruder.

A young, serious officer dismounted from a night saber, then approached him. "I am Captain Jarod Shadowsong! You are a prisoner of the Guard of Suramar! Surrender and you will be treated fairly."

With no other option, Krasus held out his hands so that they could be bound. Yet, deep inside, he felt some satisfaction about his capture. Now he had his way into the city.

And once there, all he had to do was try to escape . . .

TWENTY-ONE

The night saber hissed as Rhonin tried to mount it. He held the reins tightly, hoping that the beast would understand he was supposed to be where he was.

"Are you settled?" Illidan asked him.

Malfurion's brother had become the wizard's unofficial warder, a task which Illidan seemed not to mind at all. He constantly watched Rhonin as if trying to learn from his every movement. Whenever the human did anything at all remotely magical, the night elf paid the utmost intention.

It had not taken Rhonin long to understand why. Of all those present, he represented the most potent source of magic available. For all their arrogance, the night elves apparently had limited understanding of the forces they wielded. True, Rhonin found it more difficult to draw the power for his spells, but not so much that he was helpless as most of them were. Only young Illidan came anywhere near having Rhonin's ability.

I can help him, the wizard decided. *If he wants to learn, I'll help him learn.* Whatever his personal opinion of Malfurion's twin, Rhonin saw in Illidan much potential.

He only hoped that some of that potential would be available by the time they confronted the Burning Legion.

They rode out of Suramar, heading at the swiftest pace the panthers could set for Zin-Azshari. Rhonin felt some trepidation at leaving, for now he put more distance between himself and Krasus. More and more the wizard was certain that he was destined never to return to his own future. He could only hope that, whatever time had in store for Vereesa and their children, it would be a life worthy of them.

That assumed, of course, that there would be any future at all.

Lord Ravencrest kept his force riding for the rest of the night and into the day. Only when it was clear that many of the animals could go no farther did he reluctantly call for a stop.

Their ranks had grown, others joining them along the way thanks to advance riders sent out. They now numbered more than a thousand strong, with more arriving constantly. Lord Ravencrest wanted as huge an army as possible before they encountered the enemy, a desire matched by Rhonin, who knew well the terrible might of the demons.

Having settled on his own course of action, the wizard finally approached Lord Ravencrest, offering whatever information he could recall of their potential foes. As a way of explanation, he indicated that the Burning Legion had once invaded his "far-away land," ravaging everything—the last, at least, certainly the truth. Rhonin also described to the noble the course of the terrible war and how much devastation had been caused before the defenders were able to beat the demons back.

While it was not clear how much Lord Ravencrest believed, he at least took Rhonin's descriptions of the demons to heart, ordering his soldiers to adjust their tactics as necessary based on what he saw as their weaknesses. Latosius and the Moon Guard looked askance at the prospect of confronting the felbeasts in particular, but Ravencrest assured them that a contingent of his finest would surround them at all times. He also made certain that the fighters in question would know to strike first at the tentacles if they could, removing further the danger to the spellcasters.

The night elven commander obviously recognized that Rhonin had left much out, but did not press the latter further because of the valuable knowledge already gleaned. He also rightly assumed that Rhonin held his own life in enough regard to do what he could to see that defeat was out of the question.

Despite the massive growth of their force, they never slowed. One night became two, then three. Casting a minor spell that enabled him to see in the dark as well as his companions, Rhonin quickly adjusted to the nocturnal activity. However, he remained well aware that the demons cared not in the least whether the sun or the moon shone down and impressed this upon the noble. The monstrous warriors of the Burning Legion would fight until they could fight no more. The defenders had to be ready to face them even during the day.

As the night elves neared Zin-Azshari, they noticed an eerie green light illuminating the area ahead, a light that seemed to emanate not from the murky heavens, but from the city itself.

"By Elune!" muttered one soldier.

"Steady," commanded Lord Ravencrest. He stretched up, peering ahead. "Something is coming . . . and fast."

Rhonin did not have to ask what. "It's them. They already knew we were coming and plan to meet us as quickly as possible. They never waste time. The Legion lives only to fight."

The commander nodded. "I would've preferred a chance to scout the area and make judgments on the enemy. But if they wish to fight immediately, then by all means, we shall not disappoint them. Sound the call!"

Horns blared and the lines of the night elves spread out, moving into battle formation. Now an army of several thousand, the armored riders and foot soldiers were a tremendous sight to behold. Rhonin recalled the might of the Alliance and how it had similarly awed him the first time he had seen it prepare to battle the demon's allies, the Scourge.

He also recalled how the lines that day had been shattered by the monstrous fury of the invaders.

It won't happen again! He looked to Illidan, who seemed far less confident now that he faced reality.

"Don't lose yourself in fear," the wizard remarked, having seen where it could lead. "You have a gift, Illidan. I've taught you some on how better to draw power. The Well may be cut off from us, but its essence permeates the land, the sky, and everything else. If you know how to sense it, you can do anything you did before the shield appeared."

"I follow your wisdom, shan'do," returned the young night elf somberly.

Rhonin had heard the word before, especially when Malfurion had referred to his teacher, the demigod, Cenarius. He wondered where the forest lord was now. Such an elemental being was needed at a time like this.

Then the first horrific figures marched into sight and Rhonin's thoughts turned only to survival.

Survival . . . and Vereesa.

The Burning Legion had laid waste to everything up to this point and yet they hungered for more destruction, more mayhem. The felbeasts bayed and the demon troops behind them roared in pleasure and anticipation upon seeing the row upon row of figures before them. Here were more lambs to the slaughter, more blood to be spilled.

With a single horrific battle cry, they charged.

Lord Ravencrest nodded.

"Archers stand ready!" shouted an officer.

More than a thousand curved bows aimed skyward.

The noble held his hand high, watching. The demon horde drew nearer . . . nearer . . .

He dropped his hand.

Like a flight of screaming banshees, the rain of arrows flew toward the enemy. Even knowing that death fell toward them, the Burning Legion did not slow. All they saw were those who must die.

The shafts descended.

Demons they might be, but they were demons with flesh. The first rank fell almost to the warrior, some with so many arrows in them that they could

not lie flat on the ground. Felbeasts collapsed everywhere. One or two
Doomguard dropped from the sky.

But the Burning Legion trampled over their own as if not even seeing
them. Felbeasts ignored their dead brethren, howling and slavering as they
neared the night elves' lines.

"Damn!" muttered Ravencrest. "One more volley! Quickly!"

With smooth precision, the archers readied. The bearded noble lost no
time in signaling them to fire.

Again death rained down upon the horde, but this time with far less effect.
Now the Legion raised shields, formed better ranks.

"These are not mere beasts," uttered an officer near Rhonin. "They learn
too fast!"

Lord Ravencrest ignored him. "All archers to the rear! Position and be
ready to fire on the inner ranks! Lancers! Prepare to charge!"

"My lord!" Rhonin called. "May I?"

"At this point, wizard, anything you wish to do is granted! Just do it!"

Rhonin stared at the area before the front ranks of the oncoming demons.
He concentrated, drawing in the power. It took more effort than usual, but
not enough to keep him from success.

His eyes narrowed.

The ground erupted before the Burning Legion, an explosion of dirt and
rock that assaulted the monstrous warriors like a line of heavy catapults.
Many Fel Guard flew in the air while others were buried under tons of earth.
A huge boulder landed atop one felbeast, cracking its spine in two like a twig.
The rushing mass halted, many colliding.

The archers took advantage, sending another volley into the packed
horde. Scores more fell, adding to the chaos.

Cheers rose among the soldiers. The Moon Guard, on the other hand,
looked somewhat jealously at Rhonin. Latosius snarled at his fellow sorcerers,
urging them to action.

The efforts of the night elven spellcasters proved to be far less spectacular
than Rhonin's. Rings of energy that fell upon warriors of the Burning Legion
often faded without any effect. A handful of demons dropped, but even some
of those recovered.

"They're useless!" Illidan snapped.

"They're trying," the wizard corrected.

Instead of arguing, the young night elf suddenly pointed at the horde,
muttering.

Serpentine tentacles of black energy snaked around the throats of several
dozen of those in the Legion's forefront. The demons dropped their weapons
and shields and tried to tear the tentacles free, but before they could do that,

the tentacles burned through their necks, going through flesh and bone with little trouble . . . and eventually decapitating every one of Illidan's targets.

It was all Rhonin could do to hide his distaste. Something about the night elf's choice of attack did not sit well with him, but when Illidan looked for approval, the wizard still managed to nod. He could not discourage the only other person who had any ability. If they survived, Rhonin would teach Illidan other, better ways to deal with a foe.

And if they did not survive . . .

Once again, the Burning Legion surged on. Under their feet they crushed the corpses of their comrades. They roared as they approached, their maces and other horrific weapons held high and ready.

"We have to close with them now," Ravencrest decided. "You two stay in the back and continue doing whatever you can! You're our best weapons for now . . . possibly forever!"

Illidan bowed his head to the noble. "Thank you, my lord."

" 'Tis the truth, young one . . . the terrible truth."

With that, the night elven commander urged his mount ahead of them, joining his warriors. Lord Ravencrest drew his weapon, raising it high.

The lancers tensed. Behind them, the foot soldiers stood poised to follow. At the rear, the archers prepared for another shot.

Ravencrest slashed downward with his sword.

Horns blared. The archers fired.

The night elven force charged to meet the enemy, their night sabers snarling challenge to the demons.

Just as the lancers neared, the arrows struck. Distracted by the charge, those demons in front were whittled down by the bolts. Disarray momentarily took hold of the foremost line, exactly as Lord Ravencrest had intended.

The swiftness of the night sabers enabled the lances to drive in deep. Despite their immense size, several Fel Guard were thrust into the air as the night elves' spears penetrated not only the armor but everything within.

The sheer force of the charge actually pushed back the Burning Legion for a moment. Night sabers did more damage, biting and tearing at those packed tight before them. Foot soldiers joined in from behind, filling in gaps and thrusting at anything that was not one of them.

Their lances all but useless now, the riders drew their own weapons and did battle. Far back, the archers continued to unleash volleys at the ranks beyond the fighting.

Another row of riders, Lord Ravencrest among them, still waited. The noble's gaze flicked back and forth, studying each individual struggle, seeking the weak areas.

Rhonin and Illidan were not idle, either. The wizard cast a spell that solidified air above one section of the horde, literally dropping the sky on them. Illidan, in the meantime, repeated his serpentine spell, throttling and beheading several demons at a time.

The Moon Guard did what they could, their efforts slight but still of some aid. They could not, despite their best efforts, overcome the lack of direct contact with the Well of Eternity and it showed in their increasingly frustrated expressions.

Then, one of the night elven sorcerers screamed and pitched backward, his skin sloughing off like water. By the time he hit the ground, he was little more than a skeleton in a pool of what had once been his flesh. The other Moon Guard stared at the corpse in consternation, only Latosius's berating voice driving them back to their task.

Rhonin quickly surveyed the Legion, seeking the spell's source. It did not take him long to spot the culprit, a sinister figure farther back in the lines. The spellcaster resembled one of the Fel Guard, but with a long, reptilian tail and far more ornate armor. It also wore a black and bloodred robe over the armor and the eyes that watched over the battlefield revealed an intelligence far superior to those on the front line.

He had never faced one himself, but the wizard recognized from descriptions an Eredar warlock. Not only were they the sorcerers of the Burning Legion, but they also acted as its officers and strategists.

But the warlock had made the mistake in assuming that the Moon Guard were the ones responsible for the most devastating spells. That gave Rhonin the opportunity he needed.

He watched the warlock cast again, but as the latter let loose with his dark spell, Rhonin usurped it, turned it back on its creator.

The demon gaped as his skin slipped free of his body. His fanged mouth stretched in an inhuman cry and his gaze turned toward the wizard.

It was the last act by the warlock. The demon's mouth continued to stretch, but only because nothing now held the jaw bone tight. For the briefest of moments, the fleshless figure stood there . . . then the skeletal remains collapsed in a pile that disappeared beneath the endless wave of Fel Guard.

With no one to command them, that part of the Legion grew disoriented. The night elves pressed forward. The front ranks of the demons buckled . . .

"We are defeating them!" one young officer near Ravencrest proclaimed.

But as quickly as the demons had wavered, they now moved forward again with even more determination. In the back came Doomguard who drove them forward with whips. More felbeasts struggled to get through the defenders and reach the sorcerers.

Night elves screamed as two Infernals barreled their way into the riders, tossing animals and soldiers alike. A hole opened up and demons poured through.

"Advance!" Ravencrest shouted to those with him. "Don't let them cut up the lines!"

He and the other riders charged the monstrous warriors who had broken through. Ravencrest himself slashed off the tentacles of a felbeast, then drove his blade into its head. A night saber fell upon one of the demon soldiers, ripping apart the latter with its claws and long fangs.

The gap dwindled . . . then vanished. The night elven lines reformed.

But although they now had a solid front again, the defenders were still pushed back. For all the armored horrors that the night elves had slain, it seemed twice as many came to reinforce the swarm.

Rhonin swore as he cast yet another spell that inflicted the Burning Legion with a series of deadly lightning bolt attacks. As magnified as his power still was, he knew he could have done even more with the Well open to him. More important, he and Illidan still provided the vast bulk of magical support for the night elves, but neither could be everywhere. Illidan, for all his eagerness to use whatever spell he could to slaughter the demons, was tiring quickly and Rhonin felt little better. With the Well's power free to their use, both could have cast fewer times yet with much more satisfactory results.

More screams arose as the night elves continued to be pushed back. Fel Guard smashed in heads, caved in armored chests. Their hellish hounds ripped apart foot soldiers. Doomguard leapt above the fray, then dove into the elven throngs, swinging away with their weapons. Infernals began popping up everywhere, raining down upon the defenders much the way the night elves' arrows had done to them earlier.

Another of the Moon Guard cried out, but this time because a felbeast had slipped through. Four soldiers managed to sever its tentacles, then thrust their blades through its chest, but by then it was too late for the sorcerer.

Another volley went up from the archers . . . and then immediately arced around and flew back at them. Although many had the good sense to run, several stood transfixed by the astonishing reversal.

Those died swiftly as their own bolts pierced their throats and their chests.

Rhonin searched, but could not see the Eredar warlocks responsible. He cursed again that he could not be in more than one place and that the actions he took were not what he had hoped.

We're losing! For all their dedication, against the demons the soldiers needed the Moon Guard . . . and the Moon Guard needed the Well. Back at Black Rook Hold, Malfurion had said that he hoped to deal with the shield the Highborne had placed, but that had been days ago. Rhonin could only

assume that the young night elf's spell had failed . . . either that, or Malfurion
had died in the attempt.

"The line's buckling again!" someone called.

Rhonin forgot all about Malfurion. There existed now only the
battle . . . the battle and Vereesa. With what perhaps might have been a last
silent farewell to her, he focused once more on the endless ranks of demons,
trying to devise yet another devastating spell and already knowing that, by
itself, it would not be nearly enough.

But was there anything *anyone* could do that would be enough?

"Shaman, has there been any change?"

Tyrande shook her head. "Nothing. The body breathes but the spirit is
absent."

The orc frowned. "Will he die?"

"I don't know." Would it be better if he did? She had no idea. For more
than three nights, Tyrande had watched over Malfurion's body, first in the
Chamber of the Moon, then in an untenanted room farther inside the temple. The senior priestesses had been quite sympathetic, but they had clearly
believed that nothing could be done for her friend.

"He may sleep forever," one had told her. "Or the body may wither and
die from lack of sustenance."

Tyrande had tried to feed Malfurion, but the body was limp, unrespon-
sive. She dared not trickle water down his throat for fear that he would choke
to death.

Last night, Brox had cautiously made the suggestion that perhaps, if they
knew there was no hope, it would be better to quickly end Malfurion's suffering. He had even offered himself as the one to do it. As horrifying as it had
been to hear, the novice priestess understood that the orc had offered what he
would have given a good comrade. He cared for Malfurion.

They had no notion what had happened to his dream form. For all they
knew, it floated around them, unable for some reason to enter the body.
Tyrande doubted that, however, and suspected that something had happened
to him when he had tried to destroy the shield spell. Perhaps his spirit had
been eradicated in the attempt.

The thought of losing Malfurion stressed Tyrande more than she could
have ever thought possible. Even Illidan's precarious mission did not bother
her as much. True, she worried about the latter twin, too, but not quite in the
same way that she did the one whose body lay before her.

Putting a hand to his cheek, the priestess of the moon thought not for the
first time, *Malfurion . . . come back to me.*

But once again, he did not.

Thick, green fingers gently touched her arm. Tyrande looked into the worried eyes of the orc. He seemed not at all ugly to her at this moment, simply a fellow soul in this hour of grief.

"Shaman, you've not slept, not been out of this room. Not good. Step out. Breathe the night air."

"I can't leave him—"

He would not hear her protest. "What'll you do? Nothing. He lies there. He'll be safe. He'd want you to do this."

The others saw the orc as a barbaric creature, but more and more Tyrande realized that the brutish figure was simply a being who had been born into a more basic society. He understood the needs of a living being and understood the dangers of losing track of those needs.

She could not help Malfurion if she herself grew weak or ill. As difficult as it was for her, Tyrande had to step away.

"All right . . . but only for a few minutes."

Brox helped her to her feet. The young priestess discovered then that her legs were stiff and almost insufficient to keep her standing. Her companion had been correct; she needed to refresh herself if she hoped to go on for Malfurion.

With the orc beside her, Tyrande journeyed through the temple to the entrance. As before, the outer halls were filled with frightened and confused citizens, all trying to gain reassurance from the servants of the Mother Moon.

She feared that they would have to fight their way outside, but the crowds moved quickly to avoid Brox. He took their continual repulsion of him in stride, but Tyrande felt embarrassed. Elune had always preached respect of all creatures, but few night elves cared for other races.

The two stepped into the square. A cool breeze touched her, reminding Tyrande of times as a child. She had always loved the wind and, had it not looked unseemly, would have stretched out her arms and tried to embrace it as she had when little.

For several minutes, Tyrande and Brox simply stood there. Then, guilt once more caught hold of the priestess, for her childhood memories began to include times with Malfurion. She finally apologized to the orc and insisted that they return inside. Brox merely nodded his understanding and followed.

Yet, they had not quite reached the steps of the temple when one of the Suramar Guard called out to her. Tyrande hesitated, uncertain if the soldier sought to bother her because of Brox.

But the officer apparently had another mission in mind. "Sister, forgive me. I am Captain Jarod Shadowsong."

She knew his face if not his name. He was only slightly older than she and with somewhat round features for a night elf. His eyes were slanted slightly more than average, too, giving him a probing expression even when he tried to be friendly and courteous, such as now.

"You wish something of me, captain?"

"A bit of your time, if I might be so bold. I have a prisoner who has need of aid."

At first Tyrande wanted to decline, her urge to return to Malfurion foremost in her thoughts, but her duties took priority. How could she turn from some unfortunate in need of her healing skills? "Very well."

As the orc started to follow, Captain Shadowsong looked askance. "Is *that* coming with us?"

"Would you rather he stand out in the square by himself, especially during these troublesome times?"

The officer reluctantly shook his head, ending the matter. He turned and quickly led the pair on.

Suramar had only a small facility for prisoners, most of any import ending up in Black Rook Hold. The structure that Captain Shadowsong led them to had been created out of the base of a long dead tree. The roots formed the skeleton of the building and workers had created the rest from stone. There was no more solid a building than this save Lord Ravencrest's hold and the Suramar Guard were proud of that.

Tyrande eyed the rather bland building with some trepidation, imagining from its monotone exterior that it could only house the worst of villains. However, she steeled herself and did not reveal any misgivings as the captain bid her to enter.

The outer chamber was devoid of any furnishings save a simple wooden desk where the officer on duty no doubt worked. With most of the armed might of Suramar gone, the rest of Captain Shadowsong's comrades were no doubt out trying in vain to keep the peace.

"We found him in the woods the very evening Lord Ravencrest and the expeditionary force departed. Many of our detection spells have failed, sister, but some do contain their own power. One of those alerted us to the intruder. With some escapes in the recent past—" He looked momentarily at the orc. Captain Shadowsong clearly knew of Brox's present status, else he would have immediately tried to arrest him. "—we took no chances and immediately went to investigate."

"And how does that pertain to me?"

"The—prisoner—we found was quite weary. After deciding it was not a ruse, we brought him back. He grows no better since then. Because of his *peculiar* nature, I want him alive if and when Lord Ravencrest returns. That's why I finally came to you."

"Then, by all means, please lead the way."

There were only a dozen cells in the chamber behind, although the officer was willing to tell Tyrande that he had more down below. She nodded politely, now a bit curious as to what sort of being lay inside the one. After Brox, she almost expected it to be another orc, but Captain Shadowsong's reaction to Brox made that assumption inaccurate.

"Here he is."

The priestess had expected something huge and warlike, but the figure within was no taller than the average night elf. He was also thinner than most. Underneath the hood of his rather plain robes she noted a gaunt face very much akin to one of her own, but pale, almost ghostly, and with eyes less pronounced. Judging by the shape of his hood, his ears were also smaller.

"He looks like one of us . . . but not," she remarked.

"Like a *ghost* of one of us," the captain corrected.

But Brox moved forward, almost seeming hypnotized by the unsettling figure. "Elf?"

"Perhaps . . ." remarked the prisoner in a voice much more deep and commanding than his appearance let on. He seemed equally interested in Brox. "And what is an orc doing here?"

He knew what her companion *was.* Tyrande found that extremely interesting, especially with so many strange visitors of late.

Then the prisoner coughed badly and her concern took over. She insisted that Captain Shadowsong open the door for her.

As she neared the mat on which he lay, the young priestess could not help but look into that face again. There was more to it than appearance alone indicated. She sensed a depth of wisdom and experience that literally shook her to the core. Somehow, Tyrande recognized that here was a very, very ancient being whose condition had nothing to do with his age.

"You are gifted," he whispered. "I had hoped for that."

"Wh-what ails you?"

He gave her a fatherly smile. "Nothing even your abilities can cure. I convinced the captain to find one such as you because time is running scarce."

"You never told me to do any such thing!" Jarod Shadowsong protested. "I went by my own choice."

"As you say . . ." but the prisoner's eyes said otherwise to Tyrande. He then looked again at Brox. "Now *you* are something I did not calculate on, and that worries me. You should not be here."

The orc grunted. "Other said so, too."

"Other? What other?"

"The one with flame for hair, the one who said . . ." Here Brox paused and, after a surreptitious glance at the Guard captain, murmured, "The one who spoke of this as past."

To Tyrande's astonishment, the prisoner sat up. Captain Shadowsong started forward, his weapon already drawn, but the priestess waved him back.

"You saw Rhonin?"

"You know him?" asked Tyrande.

"We came here together . . . I thought him trapped . . . elsewhere."

"In the glade of Cenarius," she added.

He actually laughed. "Either chance, fate, or Nozdormu moves this matter forward, praise be! Yes, that place . . . but how do you know of it?"

"I've been there . . . with friends of mine."

"Have you?" The gaunt face moved closer. "With friends?"

Tyrande was uncertain now what to make of him. He knew many things that most ordinary night elves did not, of that she was certain. "Before we go on . . . I would have a name from you."

"Forgive my manners! You may call me . . . Krasus."

Now Brox reacted. "Krasus! Rhonin spoke of you!" The orc actually went down on one knee. "Elder . . . I am Broxigar . . . this is the shaman, Tyrande."

Krasus frowned. "Perhaps Rhonin spoke too much . . . and likely has inferred more."

Her companion's reaction settled one matter for the novice priestess. Rising she turned to the captain. "I would like to take him with me to the temple. I believe he could be better cared for there."

"Out of the question! If he escapes—"

"You have my promise that he will not. Besides, you yourself said that it was essential he be well. After all, if he must face Lord Ravencrest—"

The Guard officer frowned. Tyrande smiled at him.

"Very well . . . but I'll have to escort you there myself."

"Of course."

She turned to help Krasus rise, Brox coming from the prisoner's other side. As Tyrande held him close, she noticed Krasus hide a satisfied smile.

"Something pleases you?"

"For the first time since my inopportune arrival, yes. There is hope, after all."

He did not clarify and she did not ask him to do so. With their aid, he left the Guard headquarters. Tyrande realized that Krasus played no game in one regard; he was seriously weak. Even still, she sensed the authority within him.

With Jarod Shadowsong behind them, they returned to the temple. Once again, it took only the appearance of the orc to create a path for them.

Tyrande feared that the guards and senior priestesses would be another problem, but, like her, they seemed to innately sense Krasus's prominence. The elder priestesses actually bowed toward him, although she suspected that they did not quite understand why.

"Elune has chosen well," Krasus remarked as they neared the living quarters. "But then, I knew that when I saw you."

His comment made her face darken, but not because of any attraction. Rather, Tyrande felt as if she had been given a compliment by one at least as significant as the high priestess herself.

She intended to bring him to a separate chamber, but without thinking instead walked into the one where she had been keeping Malfurion. At the last moment, Tyrande tried to halt.

"Is there trouble?" asked Krasus.

"No . . . only that this room is being used for a stricken friend of mine—"

But before she could get any further, the cowled figure struggled away from her, pushing toward Malfurion's prone form.

"Chance, fate, or Nozdormu, indeed!" he spat. "What ails him? Quickly!"

"I—" How to explain?

"He walked the Emerald Dream," Brox responded. "He's not come back, elder."

"Not come back . . . where did he seek to go?"

The orc told him. Tyrande had thought Krasus's face pale enough, but now it literally whitened. "Of all the places . . . but it makes bitter sense. If I had only known before I left there!"

"You were in Zin-Azshari?" Tyrande gasped.

"I was in what *remained* of the city, but I came here in search of your very friend." He studied the still body. "And if, as you say, he has been like this for the past few nights, I may be much, much too late . . . for *all* of us."

TWENTY-TWO

A night elf cried out, his breast plate and chest cut open by a demon blade. Another near him had no chance to utter a sound, a Fel Guard mace crushing in his skull.

Everywhere, the defenders were dying and nothing Rhonin had done so far had been sufficient to alter that horrific fact. Despite Lord Ravencrest's determined figure at the forefront, the night elves were slowly being slaughtered. The Burning Legion gave them no respite, constantly pummeling the lines.

But even knowing he and the rest would die, the wizard fought on.

He had no other recourse.

The news of the defending army's arrival had taken Lord Xavius by some surprise, but it had not made him any less confident of the final outcome. He saw how many of the great one's celestial host flooded through the portal and felt certain that no army arrayed against them could possibly stand long. Soon, the unfit would be cleansed from his world.

Mannoroth led the Legion against the fools and Hakkar was on the hunt, leaving all in the counselor's skilled hands. He peered briefly in the direction of a small alcove near the entrance, wherein he had stored his most recent prize. After news arrived that the defending forces had been decimated, Xavius would take the time to see to his "guest." At the moment, he had far more important things to do.

He returned his attention to the portal, where yet another group of Fel Guard had materialized. They received their instructions from the towering Doomguard left by Mannoroth, then marched to join their bloodthirsty brethren. The scene had repeated itself some dozen times in just the past few minutes, the only difference being that each successive batch of arrivals was larger in number than the last. Now they almost took up the entire chamber.

As the latest troop of Fel Guard passed, Lord Xavius heard Sargeras's glorious voice in his head. *The pace increases . . . I am pleased.*

The night elf knelt. "I am honored."

There is resistance already.

"Merely some of the unfit delaying the inevitable."

The portal must be protected . . . it must not only remain open, but be strengthened more. Soon . . . very soon . . . I will come through . . .

The counselor's heart leapt. The momentous event neared!

Rising, he said, "I shall see that everything is done to prepare the way for you! I swear it!"

He felt a wave of satisfaction . . . then Sargeras departed his thoughts.

Lord Xavius immediately turned to the array that kept the shield spell functioning. He had inspected it after the intruder's attempt to destroy it and found it intact, but one could never take chances.

Yes, it was still in perfect order. Thinking of his "guest," Xavius mulled over some of the things he would do when Sargeras finally stepped forth from the portal. Surely the queen would have to be there and, of course, an honor guard had to be arranged. Captain Varo'then would deal with the last

matter. The counselor himself intended to be the first to greet the celestial
one. As a proper gift, Xavius decided that he would hand over the crystal and
its contents to Sargeras. After all, this was one of the three that Mannoroth
had felt significant enough to send the Houndmaster after again. How foolish
Hakkar would look when he came back to discover that the advisor had so
easily captured one already.

Lord Xavius could hardly wait to present his prisoner to the great Sargeras. It would be especially interesting to see just what the god did with the
young fool . . .

His nightmare continued.

Malfurion drifted within the crystal, staring out at what little he could
see of the chamber. He had been placed in a small nook in the alcove, the
crystal set on an angle. The alcove gave him a glimpse of the area near the
doorway, which meant that the captive watched a constant stream of
demonic warriors lumbering by, death clearly on their minds. That, in turn,
twisted his heart further, for he knew that they went out to slay every night
elf they could find . . . and all because Malfurion had failed to destroy the
shield.

Although his surroundings did not give any indication of the passage of
time, Malfurion felt certain that at least two nights had gone by since his capture. In his dream form, he did not sleep, and that made those two or more
nights even longer.

How stupid he had been! Malfurion had heard the tales of Lord Xavius's
eyes, how people said they could even see the shadows of shadows, but he
had taken those for fanciful stories. Little had he suspected that the same lenses
that enabled the counselor to observe the natural forces of sorcery also let
him take note of a spirit in his sanctum. How Lord Xavius had laughed!

Malfurion had tested his crystalline cage several times early on and found
it too strong. Perhaps with more teaching the young night elf might have discovered some flaw, but that hardly mattered now. He had *failed*. He had failed
himself, his friends, his race . . . his world.

Now, nothing but Lord Ravencrest's defenders likely stood in the way of
the demons.

He had to do *something*.

Steeling himself, Malfurion once again tried to use what Cenarius had
taught him. The crystal was a part of nature. It was susceptible to his spells.
He ran his hands over the edges, seeking a weakness in the matrix that held it
together. It was not quite a druidic spell he utilized, but close.

But still he found nothing.

Malfurion screamed out of frustration. Thousands would die because of his failure. Illidan would perish. Brox would perish. Tyrande—

Tyrande would perish.

He could picture her face, visualize it better than any other. Malfurion imagined her concern for him. He knew that she likely sat near his body, trying to summon him back. The imprisoned night elf could almost hear her calling to him.

Malfurion . . .

The night elf shook. Surely, he had begun to lose his mind. It astounded Malfurion that the process had started so quickly, but then, his situation was a most terrible one.

Malfurion . . . can you hear me?

Again it felt as if Tyrande's voice echoed in his thoughts. He peered out of his prison, trying to see if perhaps Lord Xavius had begun some sort of mental torture, but of the counselor Malfurion could see no sign.

With some trepidation, he finally thought, *Tyrande?*

Malfurion! I'd scarcely hoped!

He could hardly believe it himself. True, she was a priestess of Elune, but still, such an act should have been beyond her. *Tyrande . . . how did you reach me?*

Thanks to another . . . he's been searching for you, he says.

The only ones that Malfurion could think of were Brox and Rhonin. Tyrande had met the orc, though, and while a courageous warrior, Brox lacked any magical skills. Could it be Rhonin? Even that made little sense, the wizard having supposedly ridden off with Lord Ravencrest.

Who? he finally asked. *Who?*

My name is Krasus.

The sudden switch unsettled Malfurion. The voice was like none he had ever felt, although in some ways it hinted of Cenarius's. Whoever this Krasus was, he was not simply some night elf, but much, much more.

Do you sense us still? asked the new voice.

I do . . . Krasus.

I have shown Tyrande how we can work through her bond to you to reach out to your dream self. The trick is difficult, but we hope to do it only long enough to free you.

Free me? Glancing again at his prison, Malfurion doubted that it would be possible.

A cunning trap, yes, Krasus went on, surprising the night elf. Apparently the link enabled them to see just where Lord Xavius had imprisoned him. *But I have dealt with its like before.*

Now Malfurion's spirits rose further. *What must be done?*

Now that we have moved your body—

You've done what? Moved his body? The risk to it—

I am quite familiar with the risks. When Malfurion protested no more, Krasus continued, *It was necessary to bring it . . . closer to one of our party. Now you must listen, for we must do this quickly.*

The night elf waited tensely. If they could release him from the crystal, he would do anything they said.

I must see the crystal, see every facet of its nature. You are a druid. This you can show me.

Acknowledging his understanding, Malfurion surveyed the entire interior of his magical cell. He looked at every corner, every facet, showing the crystal's strengths and its possible weaknesses. Nothing he saw gave him any encouragement, but he suspected that Krasus knew far better than he what to look for.

There! The disembodied voice made him pause before one edge. Malfurion had studied it earlier, noticing a slight fault to it, but had not been able to make any use of the spot.

It is the key to your escape. Touch it with your mind. See how the flaw works?

For the first time, he did. The fault was minute, but still distinct. How had he failed to see that earlier?

With experience comes wisdom, they say, Krasus suddenly replied. *However, I am still working to prove that adage.*

He ordered Malfurion to use the skills the forest lord had taught him to feel the entire width and breadth of the flaw, to understand its ultimate nature. To know it as well as he knew himself.

You should be able to note its most vulnerable place, its key, so to speak.

I don't— Yes! He did! Malfurion sensed the location. He pressed against it, eager to be free . . . but it would not give way.

You are strong, but not yet fully trained. Open your thoughts further to us. Let us in, no matter how many of us there are. We shall be your added strength and knowledge.

Clearing his mind as much as he could, Malfurion left himself open to Tyrande and the mysterious Krasus. He immediately felt the distinction between the two of them. Tyrande's thoughts were caring but firm, Krasus's wise but frustrated. Curiously, the frustration had nothing to do with Malfurion's situation.

Now . . . try again.

The imprisoned night elf pictured his dream form as a physical one. He literally pushed against the flaw as he would have any weak barrier. Surely, it would give if he pushed hard enough . . .

It suddenly felt as if the other two pushed with him. Malfurion could almost envision Tyrande and the other at his side, straining.

The flaw began to give. A minute crack developed . . .

A tiny, tiny gap appeared as the fault opened ever so slightly.

It is your doorway! urged Krasus. *Go through it!*

And Malfurion's dream form *poured* through the slim opening.

He grew as he left the counselor's cell, expanding until he stood his normal height. The change was simply a change in his own perspective, but he much preferred it to the insectlike position in which he had been while imprisoned.

Now . . . before you are noticed . . . return to us!

But here Malfurion disagreed. He had come this far to do what needed to be done to save his people, his world. The shield spell *had* to fall.

Malfurion! Tyrande pleaded. *No!*

Ignoring both, he floated around the corner . . . and stopped. Lord Xavius stood at the other end of the chamber, attention riveted on the dark portal through which the demons constantly arrived. Almost it seemed the counselor communed with whatever lurked deep within. Malfurion shuddered, recalling the inherent evil of that entity.

Still, the present situation worked in his favor. If Xavius would just keep staring into the vortex a few moments more, Malfurion could accomplish his task and be away.

He drifted toward the array, already aware of how to destroy it. A few simple alterations and it would be no more.

Both Tyrande and Krasus had ceased speaking, which either meant that they intended to let him see this through or . . . or the link with him had been somehow severed. Whichever the case, he could not turn back now.

With one last glance at the lord counselor, Malfurion reached in with his power. He first altered one of the interior components of the spell, guaranteeing its eventual instability regardless of what he did next.

It was the strength of the world, of nature, that Malfurion summoned now. He used it to force the array into a new combination, a new form that would negate its purpose and ultimately cause it to dissipate.

The shield spell faltered . . .

Lord Xavius instantly sensed the wrongness. Something terrible was happening to the shield spell.

Within the portal, Sargeras, too, sensed something amiss.

Seek! he commanded his pawn.

The counselor spun about. His dark, magical eyes fixed on the precious array—and the ghostly intruder whom he had captured before.

The imbecile was meddling with the spell!

"Stop him!" roared Lord Xavius.

The shout nearly upset everything Malfurion had set into motion. He managed to regain his control, then looked to where Xavius pointed furiously at him, screaming for the Highborne or the demons to seize him. However, neither seemed able to obey that command, for, unlike the counselor, they could not see Malfurion's dream form, much less touch it.

Lord Xavius, on the other hand, could do both.

When it became clear that the others were of no use to him, the queen's advisor threw himself toward Malfurion. His artificial eyes radiated dark energy and Malfurion sensed an attack of some sort coming. Instinctively he raised his hand, asking aid of the wind and air.

Bolts of crimson lightning darted toward him and, had they actually reached the younger night elf, would surely have obliterated him. However, mere inches from Malfurion, the bolts not only struck some invisible barrier—solid air, perhaps—but were diverted back by the wind that the ghostly figure had summoned.

With deadly accuracy, the bolts struck the huge warriors near the portal.

The demons were tossed about like leaves in a storm. Several crashed against the walls while two collided with the sorcerers who kept working on the portal. That, in turn, threw the latter's efforts into near chaos. The portal heaved as if breathing raggedly, opening and closing in mad fashion.

The Highborne sorcerers struggled to keep the portal under control. Several demons about to step through suddenly vanished back into the darkness within.

One of the larger, winged figures standing near the opening charged in the direction of Malfurion. The huge demon obviously could not see the night elf, but swung about with its weapon in the clear hope of striking something. Malfurion tried to avoid the weapon as best he could, not at all certain that he was immune to it.

Lord Xavius had ducked away from his reversed spell, but now the counselor returned to the fray. From a pouch at his side, he removed yet another crystal.

"From this one, you shall not escape . . ."

The magical eyes flared.

Moving quickly, Malfurion set the demon between himself and the counselor. Instead of his intended victim, the advisor drew in the startled demon. The brutish figure roared its rage at such trickery and grasped in vain in the general direction of Malfurion before being sucked into the crystal.

Xavius swore and tossed the crystal aside, caring little for the fate of its contents. All his attention remained focused on the ghostly form that only he could see.

"My lord!" cried one of the sorcerers. "Shall we—"

"Do nothing! Keep at the task at hand! The portal must remain open and the shield must keep intact! I *will* deal with our invisible intruder!"

That said, Xavius prepared to cast again. Malfurion, however, had no intention of waiting for him. He turned and darted from the chamber, passing through the outer door without so much as a glance from the wary sentries.

The furious counselor immediately rushed after him. "Open the door!"

The guards obeyed. Xavius rushed out of the chamber and down the steps in pursuit of his adversary.

But Malfurion had not fled downstairs, instead floating within an inner wall of the tower. There, unseen by the lord counselor, he waited until he was certain the trouble had passed.

Returning to the chamber, Malfurion immediately drifted to the array. He had to destroy it quickly, before the Highborne had the chance to reinforce it.

However, as he reached for it, a familiar dread returned to him. Malfurion shivered and, despite himself, looked toward the portal.

You will not touch the shield . . . the terrible presence within uttered in his mind. *You do not wish to. You wish only to serve me . . . to worship me . . .*

Malfurion fought the urge to give in to that voice. He knew what would happen to everyone if the one who spoke had the chance to enter the world. All the evil unleashed by the demons so far paled in comparison to what commanded them.

I . . . will . . . not be one of your pawns! Almost screaming from effort, Malfurion tore his gaze from the vortex.

He could feel the dread figure's fury as he sought to recover. The evil within could not affect him directly other than to play with his thoughts. Malfurion had to ignore him, think only of those he cared about and what failure meant to them.

Just a few seconds more—

His dream form twisted, suddenly wracked by incredible pain. He spun around, falling to his knees.

"No more games . . ." muttered Lord Xavius, standing at the doorway. Near him, several perplexed guards searched in vain for the enemy with whom he spoke. "No more near disasters! I will rend your spirit form to shreds, scatter your essence over the world . . . and only then will I give you to the great one to do with as he pleases . . ."

He pointed at Malfurion.

More and more the Burning Legion crushed the lines of the night elves. Lord Ravencrest kept his followers from being ripped apart, but they continued to give ground.

A fierce battering ram created by Rhonin plowed into the demons, tossing several back and digging deep into the horde. It slowed them in that one place, but everywhere else the Legion continued to advance.

From somewhere, Rhonin heard Lord Ravencrest shouting orders. "Strengthen that right flank! Archers! Take out those winged furies! Latosius, get your Moon Guard back!"

It was hard to say if the senior sorcerer heard the noble's command, but, either way, the Moon Guard remained where they were. Latosius stood at the forefront, ordering this spellcaster or that to deal with various situations. Rhonin grimaced. The elder night elf had no concept of tactics. He wasted what little might his group had on several minuscule attacks rather than on one concerted effort.

Illidan saw this, too. "The damned old idiot's making no use of them at all! I could lead them better!"

"Forget them and concentrate on your own spells—"

But even as the wizard said this, Latosius suddenly reeled. He grabbed at his throat and slumped over, blood pouring from his mouth. His skin blackened and he collapsed, clearly dead already.

"No!" Rhonin surveyed the Legion, found the warlock, and pointed.

Using the trick unleashed earlier by perhaps this same demon, Rhonin seized several arrows in flight and sent them hurtling down upon the warlock. The robed figure glanced up, saw the bolts, and simply laughed. He gestured in a manner Rhonin assumed created a defensive shield around him.

The Eredar ceased laughing when each bolt not only penetrated his shield, but went *through* his torso.

"Not as strong as you think, are you?" muttered the wizard in grim satisfaction.

Rhonin turned again to Illidan—only to find the latter gone. He looked around, found the determined young night elf riding madly toward the Moon Guard, who seemed in complete disarray without their leader.

"What does he—?" But Rhonin had no time to worry about his would-be protégé, for incredible heat suddenly surrounded him. He felt as if his skin were about to melt.

The Eredar warlocks had finally identified him as a major threat. More than one certainly had to be attacking him. He managed to summon enough strength to momentarily ease the incredible heat, but no more. Slowly, they were cooking him alive.

So this was it. Here he would die, never knowing if his part in this battle would keep history more or less intact or destroy it utterly.

Then . . . the intense pressure on him all but ceased. Rhonin reacted instinctively, using his magic to completely counter the remaining danger. His eyes cleared and he finally managed a fix on the key spellcaster.

"You like fire? I'd like it a little cooler."

The wizard reversed the spell cast upon him, sending at its user an intense wave of cold.

Rhonin sensed the bitter chill overwhelm the warlock. The Eredar stiffened, turning a pale white. His expression contorted, freezing in mid-agony.

One of the Fel Guard bumped the warlock. The frozen figure toppled, striking the hard ground with a harsh crash and scattering bits of iced demon over the battlefield.

Trying to catch his breath, Rhonin looked to the Moon Guard, the direction from which he had felt aid come. His eyes widened as he saw Illidan at their head.

The young night elf smiled his way, then turned back to the struggle. He directed the veteran sorcerers as if born to it. Illidan had them aligning in arrays that magnified what little strength they had through *him*. He, in turn, drew forth their power, thereby increasing the intensity of his own spells.

An eruption in the midst of the Burning Legion destroyed scores of demons there. Illidan let out a triumphant cheer, unaware of the strain now on the faces of the other sorcerers. He had used their power to good effect, but if he repeated such steps too often, the Moon Guard would burn out one by one.

But there was nothing Rhonin could do to let Illidan know that and, in truth, he was not all that certain he should try. If the defenders fell here, who else was there?

If only Malfurion had not failed . . .

Mannoroth looked upon the battlefield and was pleased. His host swept across the land—not just where they encountered no resistance, but even where the puny inhabitants of this world had quickly decided to meet the Legion in battle.

He appreciated their effort to bring this struggle to a close so soon. It meant paving the way sooner for his master, Sargeras. Sargeras would be pleased with all that had been accomplished in his name. He would reward Mannoroth well, for the demon had managed this feat without having had to ask for the aid of Archimonde.

Yes, Mannoroth would be rewarded well, receiving more favor, more power, among the Legion.

As for the night elves who had so far aided the demons in their endeavor to take this world, they would receive the only reward Sargeras ever gave to such . . .

Utter annihilation.

TWENTY-THREE

Malfurion thought he had outfoxed Lord Xavius, but once again, it was the young night elf who had played the fool. What had made him think that the counselor would continue to hunt for him through the stairways and corridors when clearly Malfurion would want to return to the tower and complete his mission?

It would be his final mistake. Lord Xavius was a gifted sorcerer with the power of the Well upon which to draw. Malfurion had learned much from his shan'do, but not enough, it seemed, to stand up to such a deadly foe.

And Lord Xavius was aware of that as well.

Yet, in Malfurion's head suddenly came a voice . . . not the voice from within the portal, but rather that of the mysterious Krasus, who Malfurion had long thought had abandoned him.

Malfurion . . . our strength is your strength . . . as you did in the crystal, draw upon the love and friendship of those who know you . . . and draw from the determination of those like myself, who stand with them for you.

Not all of what he said made perfect sense to the night elf, but the essence of it was clear. He sensed not only Tyrande and Krasus, but also Brox now. The three opened up their minds, their souls to Malfurion, giving to him whatever strength he needed.

You are a druid, Malfurion, perhaps the first of your kind. You draw from the world, from nature . . . and are not we all a part of both? Draw from us as well . . .

Malfurion obeyed . . . and just barely in time.

Lord Xavius cast his spell.

It should have left little trace of Malfurion's dream self. The younger night elf raised his hand to ward off the evil attack, but he did not expect his powers to be sufficient even now. The counselor's previous assault had weakened him badly.

But the spell never struck. The attack was dismissed as easily as if Malfurion had brushed away a gnat from his face.

Rise up! Krasus urged. *Rise up and do what must be done!*

He did not mean that Malfurion should do battle with the counselor. That would be a dangerous waste of time. Instead, the night elf had to finish what he had started.

Malfurion struck at the shield spell.

The array shifted out of sequence. Two of the Highborne hurried to adjust it, but the floor beneath their feet suddenly gave way as the stones there acted on Malfurion's silent request to cease their natural tendency to be strong and hold things together. With a scream, the pair dropped from sight.

Lord Xavius struck angrily at Malfurion, enshrouding him in a vapor that clung to the latter's dream form and tried to eat away at it. Malfurion struggled at first, but the combined strength of Tyrande, Brox, and Krasus steeled him again. He quickly summoned a wind that assailed the vapor, scattering it.

But while Malfurion dealt with the vapor, Xavius took the opportunity to restore the shield spell to some order. He then turned toward his adversary, his next intent obvious.

Malfurion grew frustrated. This could not go on indefinitely. Eventually, he would either lose or be forced to flee. Something had to change . . . and quickly.

He spun, but not toward either the array or Lord Xavius.

Instead, Malfurion now faced the portal.

Again he called upon the wind, this time asking it to prove it was strong enough to push about more than simple vapor. Malfurion eyed the Highborne in particular, daring the wind to show what it could do.

And within their sanctum, the sorcerers suddenly found themselves assaulted by a gale. Three of their number were quickly thrown across the chamber, where they struck the opposing wall hard. As they fell, another stumbled away from the pattern, then tumbled over one of the still forms.

The rest bent low, seeking to keep from the wind's full wrath. Yet, despite no more falling prey, it was clear that the losses already suffered had put a strain on the survivors, for the portal shimmered and twisted dangerously. The sense of evil that Malfurion had felt lessened.

Fiery hands suddenly seized him by the the back of the neck, throttling Malfurion. They burned into Malfurion's dream form as if into his own flesh, causing him to unleash a scream that, despite its intensity, only his attacker could hear.

"The power of the great one is with me!" roared the queen's advisor with much satisfaction. "You are no match for us both!"

Indeed, Malfurion felt the evil reaching out again from the shifting portal.

While still not as potent as when it had sought to turn him to the Highborne's side, it added much to the counselor's already fearsome might. Against it, even the strength Malfurion received from the three proved insufficient.

Tyrande . . . He did not try to summon the priestess, only feared in his mind that he might never see her again, never be near her.

The voice of Krasus suddenly filled his head again. *Courage, druid . . . there is another of us who has been waiting for just this moment.*

A fourth presence intruded, immediately adding itself to those strengthening Malfurion. Like Krasus, it was a being far superior to a mere night elf. He sensed a weakness in it, but compared to any of Malfurion's own kind, such weakness was minute, laughable. Oddly, it almost felt as if the new presence was the twin of Krasus, for they were so much alike in feel that at first he had some trouble differentiating between the pair.

Even the new voice in his head reminded him much of Krasus. *I am Korialstrasz . . . and I freely give what I have.*

Their gifts were those with which life, nature, had endowed them. The added presence of Korialstrasz multiplied Malfurion's will a hundredfold, giving him hope such as he had never had.

You are a druid . . . Krasus reminded him yet again. *The world is your strength.*

Malfurion felt invigorated. Now he sensed not only his distant companions, but the stones, the wind, the clouds, the earth, the trees . . . *everything.* Malfurion was nearly overwhelmed by the fury the world radiated now. The evil thus far perpetrated by the Highborne and the demons offended the elements as nothing ever had before.

I promised I would do what I could, he said to them. *Grant me your strength as well and it will be done!*

To Malfurion, this took place over what felt like an eternity, but when he at last glanced at Lord Xavius, he saw that only a second at most had perhaps passed. The counselor stood almost as if frozen, his expression sluggishly altering as he prepared, with the power of his master behind him, to finally destroy his ghostly adversary.

Malfurion smiled at the other night elf's folly. He raised his hands to the hidden sky and called upon its might.

Outside, thunder roared. The Highborne around the portal and the array faltered again, aware that this was not a part of their work. Even Lord Xavius frowned.

And suddenly the palace tower shook—then *exploded.*

Captain Varo'then knelt before Azshara, his helmet carried in the crook of his arm. "You summoned me, my glorious queen?"

Two of Azshara's servants brushed her luxurious hair, something she had them do several times a day to keep it fluffed and perfect. While they performed this task, she amused herself with sampling the exotic scents brought to her recently by traders.

"Yes, captain. I wondered what that noise was coming from above. It sounded as if it originated from the tower. Is there some trouble of which I have not been informed?"

The male night elf shrugged. "None that I am aware of, Light of a Thousand Moons. Perhaps it is the prelude to the great Sargeras's entrance."

"You think so?" Her eyes lit up. "How wonderful!" She waved him off. "In that case, I should be prepared! Surely we are in for a wonderful event!"

"As you say, Glory of Our People. As you say." The captain rose, replacing his helmet on his head. He hesitated. "Would you like me to investigate, just to be certain?"

"No, I am certain you are correct! By all means do *not* bother Lord Xavius!" Azshara sniffed another vial. The scent made her blood race in ways she enjoyed. Perhaps she would wear *this* one when she met the god. "After all, I am certain the good counselor has everything in hand."

The top half of the tower chamber had been sheared off, the lightning bolts sent by the heavens ripping it away and sending the roof and more hurtling into the black Well below.

Several large chunks of stone had collapsed into the room, killing two of the Highborne and scattering most of the rest. The shield array and the portal still stood . . . but both had been badly weakened.

Shrieking winds tore at those within. One sorcerer thrown near the edge by the blasts made the mistake of rising. The winds caught his robed form, carrying him backward.

With a pathetic shriek, he followed the top of the tower down into the Well.

An intense downpour battered at the survivors. Still struggling to keep their spells intact, the Highborne fell to their knees. This did little to preserve them, though, so severe was the storm.

Only two figures remained untouched by the elements. One was Malfurion, his dream form allowing the wind and rain to pass through harmlessly. The other was Lord Xavius, protected not only by the power he drew from the Well, but by the evil still managing to leak through from the dark vortex.

"Impressive!" shouted the counselor. "If, in the end, futile, my young friend! You have but the power of the Well upon which to draw . . . while I also have the might of a god!"

His remarks made Malfurion smile. The lord counselor did not yet realize what he now fought. He assumed that he still simply faced another adept sorcerer.

"No, my lord," the younger night elf called back. "You have it turned around! For you, there's only the Well and the supposed might of a demon that *claims* godhood! For me . . . there's the power of the world itself as my ally!"

Xavius sneered. "I've no more use for your babbling . . ."

Malfurion felt him summon from the Well such power as surely none before ever had. It jarred the druid for a moment, but then the strength that served Malfurion reassured him.

"You must be stopped," he declared to the counselor. "You and the thing you serve must be stopped."

Whatever spell Lord Xavius intended to cast, Malfurion would never know. Before the counselor could complete it, the elements themselves assailed him. Lightning struck again and again at Xavius, burning him from within and without. His skin blackened and peeled, yet he did not fall.

The rain became a torrent that poured all its might down on Malfurion's foe. Xavius seemed to melt before the younger night elf's eyes, flesh and muscle sloughing off—and yet the counselor still strained to reach him.

Then, thunder cracked, thunder so loud that what remained of the tower shook, sending another of the Highborne into the dark waters of the Well. Thunder so loud it shook Malfurion himself to his very being.

Thunder so loud that Lord Xavius, counselor to the queen and highest of the Highborne—*shattered.*

He howled like one of the hellish felbeasts as he exploded, a howl that continued even as the pieces scattered in the air. The cloud of dust that had once been the advisor spun around and around, tossed about by an angry, fearsome wind.

The remaining Highborne finally abandoned their posts, fleeing from the wrath of the one who had bested their feared leader. Malfurion let them depart, knowing that he had depleted himself beyond measure but still needing to deal with one final matter.

With Lord Xavius no longer there to protect it, the shield array collapsed easily. A simple gesture from the young druid finally dismissed the evil spell, removing at last the possible impediment to his people's survival. He only prayed that it was not already too late.

At last, he returned his attention to the portal.

It was but a faint shadow of itself, a mere hole in reality. Malfurion glared at it, knowing that he could not permanently seal off his world from the evil within . . . but he could at least give it some respite.

You delay the inevitable . . . came the voice he dreaded. *I will devour your world* . . . *just as I have so many others* . . .

"You'll find us a sour treat," Malfurion retorted.

Once again he unleashed the elements.

The rain washed away the precious pattern over which the portal floated. Bolt after bolt of lightning struck the very center of the hole, forcing that within to retreat further. The wind swirled around the weakened spell, tearing away at it with the intensity of a fierce twister.

And the earth . . . the earth shook, finally succeeding in breaking up the last bits of foundation left to the high tower.

With no corporeal form, Malfurion had nothing to fear from the collapsing structure. Despite his growing weariness, he watched it all happen, determined to see for himself that there would be no last reprieve.

The floor tipped. Instruments of dark sorcery and pieces of what remained of the walls clattered toward the lower end. A tremendous groan accompanied the collapse.

The tower fell.

As it did, the portal closed in on itself, rapidly shrinking.

A sudden suction caught Malfurion off guard. He felt his dream form pulled by a powerful force toward the vanishing hole.

I will still have you . . . came the faint yet baleful voice.

The night elf struggled, urging his dream form away from the gap. Dust flowed through him and into the shrinking portal. Other refuse followed.

The strain became unbearable. He was dragged closer and closer . . .

Malfurion! Tyrande called. *Malfurion!*

He clung to her call, trying to use it as a tether. Below him, the last of the tower joined the rest in the dark abyss of the Well of Eternity. Only Malfurion and the tiny but malevolent hole remained.

Tyrande! he silently called. He shut his eyes, trying to picture her, trying to come to her.

I have you . . . said a voice he could not identify.

The world turned upside down.

Mannoroth felt the loss. Mannoroth felt the emptiness even before it happened.

The huge, bestial commander paused in the rear of the horde, turning his ugly, tusked head in the direction of the tower.

The tower that was no longer there.

"Noooooooo!" he roared.

Rhonin felt it. He felt the sudden surge of power, the surge of strength. He suddenly imagined himself able to build worlds, take the stars from the heavens and rearrange them to his desire. He was invincible, omnipotent.

The spell sealing off the Well of Eternity had been destroyed.

Immediately he looked to Illidan, to see if the young night elf had sensed the same. Rhonin need not have feared, though, for Illidan clearly had experienced the same rush of strength as he had. In fact, not only did the Moon Guard all look strong and ready, but so did the *rest* of the defenders as well.

The Well and the night elves are one, the wizard realized. Even those who could not cast spells were still tied to it to some extent. Its loss had stripped them in ways that they could never realize. Now, though, Rhonin saw in every figure, from Lord Ravencrest down to the lowliest soldier, a renewed confidence and determination. Truly they now thought themselves unbeatable by any force.

Even the Burning Legion.

Horns blared. The night elves gave a collective roar well matching anything emitted prior by the demons. The front lines of the Legion faltered, not at all certain what this abrupt change meant.

"Have at them!" shouted Ravencrest.

The defenders surged forward. Demons suddenly found themselves harried as never before. Felbeasts were slaughtered before they could make their way back to the horde. Tusked warriors dropped one after another as each time the night elves' blades sank true. The encroaching Legion was stopped dead in its tracks.

Illidan led the Moon Guard against the invaders, continuing to guide their efforts through his own spells. The land itself rippled beneath the Burning Legion's feet, tossing demons about as if they were nothing. Several of the winged Doomguard burst into flames as they darted overhead, becoming instead fiery missiles that added further mayhem to their own ranks.

Rhonin did not stay out of the battle, either. With the memories of all those who had died this day and all those who would perish in the future war in mind, he struck again and again at the ones responsible. An Eredar warlock who foolishly sought to match him was enveloped by his own robes, which twisted tightly until they snapped the demon in twain. From the wizard then came a punishing series of blue lightning bolts that methodically hunted down other spellcasters among the Legion, leaving behind only slight piles of ash to mark the former foes.

For the first time, true pandemonium broke out among the fearsome warriors. This was not the battle expected, the bloodshed desired. There was nothing here now save their own deaths, a prospect even the demons found daunting.

Their lines buckled. The night elves pushed forward.

"We have them now!" shouted Lord Ravencrest. "Give them no quarter!"

The defenders rallied further around his cry. Despite the imposing size of the invaders, the night elves advanced undaunted.

And Rhonin and Illidan continued to pave the way to victory. The wizard looked up, spying several of the savage Infernals plummeting toward the defenders. As ever, the fiery demons were rolled up into balls, dropping like boulders to create the most disastrous results.

For once, Rhonin made some use of Illidan's tactics. With the Well from which to draw, he created a huge golden barrier in the sky, one which the Infernals could not avoid. The barrier was not simply a wall, however, for Rhonin had another purpose in mind. He shaped it according to those desires, curving it and forcing those demons who crashed into it to bounce instead in the direction he chose.

The very midst of their own army.

Even the bolts he had cast down upon the demons earlier could not have done as much devastation as the fearsome behemoths did now. More than two dozen Infernals struck the Legion's center at various points, decimating the ranks and creating huge, smoking craters. The bodies of the enemy flew everywhere, crashing down upon others and multiplying the damage tenfold.

From far to his side, the wizard heard triumphant laughter. Illidan clapped his hands in honor of the human's successful effort, then pointed at the harried enemy.

A part of the Burning Legion's left flank suddenly floundered, many immediately sinking to their knees. The solid earth below them had become as soup and the heavy, armored forms of the demons could do nothing but plunge beneath its surface like stones. A few struggled, but, in the end, any who had the misfortune of being where Illidan had cast vanished.

With a wave of his hand, the young night elf resolidified the earth, erasing all trace of his victims. He then turned back to Rhonin and, with a grand flourish, bowed to the wizard.

Rhonin kept his expression set, only nodding again. If nothing else, Illidan surely kept the demons at bay.

At last, under such brutal assault, the Burning Legion did the only thing it could do—retreat en masse.

There was no horn, no call. The demons simply began to back away. They kept a semblance of order, but clearly it was all their commanders could do to maintain that much. Even still, they did not move fast enough to suit the defenders, who took full advantage of the victory.

The Moon Guard in particular savored the turn of events. They hunted the felbeasts especially, turning some into gnarled bits of wood, others into rodents. Several simply burst into flames as they ran—their tails between their legs—for the questionable safety of the Legion ranks.

Here and there, pockets of resistance remained, but those were quickly whittled down by the eager soldiers. Fel Guard lay everywhere. Rhonin had no doubt that each night elf thought about the countless dead the Burning Legion had already left in its wake. There had to have been many friends and loved ones among Zin-Azshari's victims.

However, one cause for which the night elves continued to fight concerned the wizard. Even now, Ravencrest shouted her name, using it to further rally the troops.

"For Azshara! For the queen! We ride to her rescue!"

Rhonin had heard Malfurion's suggestion that the queen was likely as complicit in the slaughter as most believed her counselor and the Highborne were and he suspected that to be the truth. The wizard could only keep telling himself that the truth would come out if and when they reached the palace.

Back and back the Burning Legion went, edging into the very borders of the ruined capital. They died in droves, they died by weapon or wizardry, but they *died*. The battle raged unceasingly through the darkness, the ground buried under the corpses of the fiendish invaders.

Perhaps it would have gone on, perhaps they could have taken the fight into Zin-Azshari itself and even reached the palace, but as day forced its will upon night, the defenders at last flagged. They had given their all in an effort well worth praise, but even Lord Ravencrest saw that to go on would put the night elves at more risk than they could afford. His expression reluctant, he nonetheless signaled the horns to sound the halt.

As the horns called, Illidan's expression grew cross. He tried to make the Moon Guard follow him forward, but while some seemed eager enough, all clearly had spent themselves of their physical energy.

Rhonin, too, was exhausted. True, he could still cast spells of great destruction, but his body was covered in sweat and he felt faintness in his head if he moved too quickly. His concentration slipped more and more . . .

Illidan aside, the rest of the night elves knew that they could go no further—not in the daylight—but that did not take away from what they had accomplished. True, the threat had not been removed, but they now saw that the demons were limited. They could be slain. They could be driven back.

The commander quickly sought volunteers to ride out through the various parts of the night elf realm, their mission of two purposes. They were to rally those they found in order to create yet a vaster force, a multipronged defense with which to meet the next assault of the Burning Legion—for surely there would be one—and also to see the extent of the devastation elsewhere.

In addition to that effort, the noble also immediately set his personal sorcerer—Illidan—in charge of the Moon Guard already with them. There was some mild protest from those most senior among the survivors, but a simple show of power in the form of one last harsh explosion among the retreating demons quickly silenced the young spellcaster's critics.

Pleased with his new status, Illidan sought out Rhonin to tell him. The wizard nodded politely, on the one hand wondering if he had ever been so enthusiastic when younger, and on the other worried about how Illidan's new status would affect his personality. Illidan had greater potential yet than what had so far been revealed, but his recklessness was a trap that could create of him a danger in its own way as deadly as the Burning Legion. Rhonin vowed to keep an eye on his counterpart.

Left alone again, the one human among the night elves slowly surveyed the force that had been arrayed against the demons. Sunlight made their armor glitter, giving the host an epic appearance. They looked and acted as if they could defeat any enemy. Despite that, however, Rhonin remained aware that they needed a far greater force if they hoped to win the final struggle. History said that victory was ensured, but too many factors—himself included—now muddied the outcome. Worse, the Burning Legion was well aware of the magical might against them; they would be seeking the wizard and Illidan more now.

Rhonin had been the target of the demons and their allies in his own time. He did not look forward to repeating that situation.

And what of the one most responsible for this night's success? Not Rhonin. Not Illidan. Not all the Moon Guard or Lord Ravencrest and his legions. None of them was the real reason for victory.

What, the weary wizard thought as he gazed out at dark Zin-Azshari and the disorganized horde, *what has happened to Malfurion?*

TWENTY-FOUR

He lay as still as death, that image made all the worse by the fact that none of them could sense any trace of the link they had once had with him. Tyrande nestled Malfurion's head in her lap, the soft grass underneath acting as the rest of his bed.

"Is he lost to us?" asked a perplexed Jarod Shadowsong. The captain had accompanied the group out to this location far in the woods, ostensibly to keep an eye on his prisoner, Krasus. He had not played a role in their spell-work, but had instead ended up acting as guard when the situation had changed. He had grown from reluctant addition to concerned companion even though he still understood little of what had taken place.

"No!" Tyrande snapped. In a more apologetic tone, she added, "He can't be . . ."

"He does not smell dead," rumbled Korialstrasz.

Jarod Shadowsong looked askance each time Korialstrasz spoke. He had yet to grow used to the presence of the red dragon. It might have amused Tyrande at one time, but not under the present circumstances. She herself had quickly come to accept the behemoth, especially since she sensed some hidden relationship between Korialstrasz and Krasus. They seemed almost like brothers or twins.

Thinking of twins made her gaze down at Malfurion again.

Krasus paced the area. He seemed much healthier now and the young priestess had noted that the effect had magnified when he had come within sight of the dragon. Unfortunately, that health did not help the pale figure now, for he appeared as worried as she did about Malfurion—even though Krasus had clearly never met him before seeing the night elf in the temple.

Brox knelt across from Tyrande, his ax placed next to his stricken friend. The orc's head was buried in his chest and she could hear him muttering what sounded like a prayer.

"The area was charged with powerful magical forces," murmured Krasus to himself. "It could have dispersed parts of his dream self to every corner of the world. He might be able to regather himself . . . but the odds of that . . ."

Captain Shadowsong looked around at the others. "Forgive this imperti-nent question, but did he at least accomplish what he hoped to?"

The cowled figure turned to him, expression flat. "He did do that at least. I pray it is enough."

"Stop talking like that . . ." Tyrande insisted. She wiped a tear from her eye, then gazed up at the sunlit sky. Despite the brightness, Tyrande refused to look away. "Elune, Mother Moon, forgive this servant for disturbing your rest! I do not dare ask for him to be returned . . . but at least give us an answer as to his fate!"

But no glorious light shone down on Malfurion. The moon did not sud-denly appear and speak to them.

"Perhaps it would be better if we brought him back to the temple," sug-gested the Guard captain. "Maybe she can hear him better there . . ."

Tyrande did not bother to answer him.

Krasus paused in his pacing. He stared to the south, where the woods thickened. His eyes narrowed and he pursed his lips in frustration. "I know you are there."

"And I now know what you are," returned a booming voice.

The nearest trees suddenly melded together, forming a figure with a lower torso akin to that of a huge stag and a chest, arms, and face more like those of Tyrande and Jarod Shadowsong.

Fists tight, Cenarius moved slowly toward the band. He and Krasus matched gazes for a time, then both nodded in respect.

The forest lord walked over to where Tyrande held Malfurion. Brox respectfully stepped out of the way while the Guard captain stared open-mouthed from where he stood.

"Daughter of my dear Elune, your tears touch the heaven and the earth."

"I cry for him, my lord . . . one you also loved."

Cenarius nodded. His forelegs bent in a kneeling motion and he touched Malfurion's forehead ever so gently. "He is a son to me . . . and so I am pleased that he has one like you who also holds him so near . . ."

"I—we've been friends since childhood."

The forest lord chuckled, a sound that brought songbirds near and made a cool, refreshing breeze caress the cheeks of each in the party. "Yes, I heard your pleas to dear Elune, both the spoken and unspoken ones."

Tyrande did not hide her embarrassment. "But all my entreaties have been for nothing."

His expression turned to one of honest puzzlement. "Did you think that? Why would I come, then?"

The others froze. The novice priestess shook her head. "I don't understand!"

"Because you are young still. Wait until you reach my age . . ." With that, Cenarius opened his left hand.

An emerald light rose from his open palm. It floated a few inches above as if orienting itself.

Rising, the demigod stepped back to observe his student. "I walked the Emerald Dream, seeking answers to our many terrible questions. I hunted through there looking for what could be done about these followers of death . . ." A gentle smile crossed his bearded visage. ". . . and imagine my surprise when I found one I knew drifting in the Emerald Dream . . . but in a very dazed and much confused state. Why, he didn't even know himself, much less me!"

And as Cenarius finished, the light drifted over to Malfurion, sinking harmlessly into his head.

The night elf's eyes opened.

"Malfurion!"

Tyrande's voice was the first thing that registered with Malfurion and he quickly seized upon it, using it as a tether, a lifeline. He pulled himself from the abyss of unconsciousness toward a bright but comforting light.

And when he opened his eyes, it was to see Tyrande under the morning sun. Surprisingly, the daylight did not bother him and he even thought that it revealed to him a Tyrande so beautiful he could not at first believe it.

He almost told her, but then the presence of the others made him shut his feelings inside again. He settled for touching her hand, then acknowledging the others.

"The—the shield—" His voice sounded like that of a frog. "Is it—"

"Gone," replied a figure who was and was not a night elf. To Malfurion, surely this had to be Krasus. "For now, the Burning Legion has been held in check . . . at least in one place."

Malfurion nodded. He knew that the war was not over, that his people still faced annihilation. Yet, that did not take away from the night's triumph. If nothing else, there was still hope.

"We will fight them," Tyrande promised. "We will save our world."

"They can be beaten," agreed Brox, brandishing proudly the weapon that the young druid had helped create. "This I know."

Krasus remained pragmatic. "They can . . . but we will need more help. We will need the dragons."

"You'll need more than the dragons!" Cenarius bellowed. "And I go now to see to that!" He stepped from the others, but gave Malfurion one last smile. "You've made me proud, my *thero'shan* . . . my honored student."

"Thank you, shan'do." He watched as the demigod melted back into the trees.

"Do we return to Suramar now?" asked a figure in a Guard officer's uniform. Malfurion could not place him, but assumed the others had a reason for him being here.

"Yes," said Krasus. "We return to Suramar."

With Tyrande's help, Malfurion rose. "But only for a short time. The portal through which the demons flowed was destroyed, but, unlike the shield, the Highborne can remake it easily. More will come, I'm afraid."

Despite his wish otherwise, no one disagreed. Malfurion looked to the direction of Zin-Azshari. A terrible evil had come to his land, one that had to be stopped before it could raze all in its path. Malfurion had helped in great part to stop the Burning Legion's initial advance and, for reasons he could not himself explain, he did not doubt that it would somehow fall to him again to assist in keeping the invading demons from destroying his beloved Kalimdor.

Malfurion only prayed that when that time came he would be found ready to face them . . . or else not only Kalimdor but the *entire* world risked obliteration.

The Demon Soul

For Thomas "Sonny" Garrett,
Accomplished Writer and Friend

ONE

The voices whispered in his head as he moved through the huge cavern. Where once they were but an occasional occurrence, now they never ceased. Even in his sleep, he could not escape their presence . . . not that he wanted to do so anymore. The huge black dragon had heard them for so long that they were now a part of him, indistinguishable from his own twisted thoughts.

The night elves will destroy the world . . .

The Well is out of control . . .

No one can be trusted . . . they want your secrets, your power . . .

Malygos would take what is yours . . .

Alexstrasza seeks dominion over you . . .

They are no better than the demons . . .

They must be dealt with like the demons . . .

Over and over, the voices repeated such dire things, warning him of duplicity, betrayal. He could trust no one but himself. The others were tainted by the lesser races. They would see his decision as a danger, not the only hope for the world.

The dragon unleashed a puff of noxious smoke as he snorted at such treachery from those who had once been his comrades. Though he had the power to save everything, he had to be careful; if they discovered the truth too soon, it would mean calamity.

They must not know its secret until it is beyond their altering, he decided. *It cannot be presented until the spell must be cast. I will not let them destroy my work!*

Huge claws scraped fresh the rock floor of the cavern as the scaly behemoth entered his sanctum. As massive as the dragon was, the rounded cavern dwarfed him. A molten river flowed through the center. Massive crystal formations glittered in the walls. Huge stalactites hung like swords of doom from above, while stalagmites grew from the ground so sharp that they looked as if they waited for someone to be impaled upon them.

And, in fact, such was the case with one.

Teeth bared, the great black dragon peered down at the puny figure struggling to free himself despite the stony spike thrusting up through his heaving chest. The remains of a tattered, black and bloodred robe and fragments of ornate, golden armor hung around his oddly-shaped torso. High, goatlike horns thrust from his skull and the crimson visage resembled most to the dragon a long skull with a wide, fanged maw. The eyes were pits of darkness that immediately tried to suck the behemoth in, but they were no match for the will of the creature's captor.

In addition to being impaled, the horned figure was bound by thick, iron chains to the cavern floor. The chains had been set especially tight, pinning the demon to the stalagmite and keeping his limbs spread downward.

Constantly the captive's mouth moved as if he furiously shouted something, yet no sound emerged. That did not keep him from trying, however, especially when he saw the dark leviathan approach.

The dragon mulled over his prisoner for a moment, then blinked.

Immediately the cavern chamber filled with the venom-laced, rasping voice of the creature. "—is Sargeras! Your blood will flow! Your skin he will wear for a cloak! Your flesh will feed his hounds! Your soul he will keep in a vial, ever to torment at his pleasure! He—"

Blinking again, the dragon silenced once more his captive. Even still, the demonic figure continued mouthing threats and obscenities until, finally, the dark behemoth opened his huge jaws and exhaled, enveloping the prisoner in a searing plume of steam that left the latter shaking in renewed agony.

"You will learn respect. You are in the presence of my glorious self, I, Neltharion," the dragon rumbled. "I am the Earth Warder. You will treat me with the reverence which I deserve."

The demon's long, reptilian tail slapped at the rocks below. The mouth opened in what was obviously more silent blasphemies.

Neltharion shook his crested head. He had expected better from the Eredar. The warlocks were supposed to be among the commanders of the Burning Legion, demons not only skilled at casting spells but well-versed in battle tactics. The dragon had assumed that he would hear far more intelligent conversation from such a creature, but the Eredar might as well have been one of the brutish Infernals, the flaming, skull-headed behemoths who acted like fearsome battering rams or airborne missiles. The one he had tested before capturing the Eredar had only the wit of a rock, if even that much.

But then, Neltharion had not sent his flight out to pluck the demons from their rampaging horde for conversation. No, the captives had another purpose, a grand one that they, unfortunately, could never come to appreciate.

And the Eredar was the last, the most significant. His innate magical abilities made him the key to fulfilling the first part of the Earth Warder's quest.

It is time . . . the voices whispered. *It is time . . .*

"Yes . . ." Neltharion answered absently. "Time . . ."

The dragon raised one huge paw palm up and concentrated. Immediately a golden aura flared to life in his palm, growing so brilliant that even the captive demon paused in his tirades to stare at what Neltharion had summoned to him.

The tiny disk was as golden as the aura that had presaged its coming, but otherwise it was an astoundingly simple-looking piece. It would not have even quite filled the hand of a much smaller creature—say a night elf, for instance. The disk resembled a large, featureless gold coin with rounded edges and a gleaming, untarnished shell. Its very unassuming appearance was all by Neltharion's design. If the talisman was to perform its task properly, it had to seem entirely innocent, harmless.

He held it toward the warlock, letting the Eredar see what awaited him. The demon, however, appeared quite unimpressed. He stared from the disk to the dragon, mockery filling his eyes.

Neltharion noted the reaction. It pleased him that the Eredar did not recognize the strength of the disk. That meant that others would also fail to realize the truth . . . until it was too late.

At the Earth Warder's silent command, the object rose gently from his palm. It floated above the paw for a moment, then drifted over to the captive.

For the first time, a hint of uncertainty colored the warlock's monstrous visage. As the disk descended, he renewed his futile struggles.

The golden talisman alighted on the demon's forehead. A brief flash of crimson light bathed the Eredar's face—and then the disk sealed itself to his flesh.

Speak them . . . urged the voices as one. *Say the words . . . seal the act . . .*

From the savage, lipless maw of the dragon erupted words from a language whose origins lay not in the mortal world. Each one was tinged with an evil that made even the demon quiver. To the Earth Warder, though, they were the most wondrous sounds he had ever heard, perfect musical notes . . . the language of gods.

As Neltharion spoke them, the disk began to glow again. Its radiance filled the vast chamber, growing brighter and brighter with each syllable.

The light suddenly flared.

The Eredar warlock stretched his mouth as wide as it would go in a noiseless cry. His horrific eyes rained tears of blood and his tail slashed madly against the rocks. He tore at his bonds with such fervor that he scraped away the flesh from his wrists and ankles. But still the demon could not escape.

Then the Eredar's skin started to decay. It crumbled from his still-twisting body, his still-shrieking countenance. The demon's flesh became as if a thousand years dead, dropping from him in dry, ashy bits.

The eyes sank in. The tail shriveled. The warlock swiftly reduced to a cage of bone surrounding rapidly-putrefying entrails. Yet throughout the macabre ordeal, he continued to scream, for Neltharion and the disk had not so far permitted him the comfort of death.

But at last, even the bone gave way, collapsing inward and fragmenting. The jaw fell loose and the ribs rolled away with a clatter. With terrible efficiency, the power unleashed by the disk absorbed the demon's remains from the bottom up. The trail of dry dust spread fast from the feet to the legs to the torso until only the skull was left.

And only then did the Eredar grow still.

The sinister light ceased. The chains once holding the demon dangled empty.

Like a doting father reaching for a cherished offspring, the black dragon used two claws to gently lift the talisman from the skull. As Neltharion did this, the skull, too, turned to ash. The gray powder scattered over the ground.

He stared with admiration at what he had wrought. Neltharion could not even sense the extraordinary forces now residing in the disk, but he knew that they were there—and when the time came, they would be his to command.

No sooner had he thought this than another presence touched his mind. The voices subsided abruptly, as if they feared discovery by this intruder. The Earth Warder himself immediately smothered his own desires.

Neltharion knew the touch well. Once he had believed it to come from a friend. Now the dark leviathan understood that he could trust her no more than he could the rest.

Neltharion . . . I must speak with you . . .

What is your wish, dear Alexstrasza? The Earth Warder could imagine her. A sleek, fire-colored dragon even slightly more imposing than himself. As he was the physical Aspect of the world's innate strength, so was she the Aspect of the Life that flourished in, on, and above it.

There are dangerous forces again playing around the palace of the night elves' queen . . . we must come to some decision and soon . . .

Fear not, Neltharion replied soothingly. *What must be done will be done . . .*

I pray it will be so . . . how soon can you make the journey to the Chamber?

The Earth Warder imagined that other place in his mind, a mammoth cavern that made his own seem but the burrowing of a single worm. The Chamber of the Aspects, as the lesser dragons respectfully called it, was also perfectly round and smooth, as if at some point in the past—before even the coming of the dragons—someone had set some great sphere into motion, completely shaving away the ripples and outgrowths found normally in caves. Nozdormu, to whom all things involving history were fascinating, believed that the creators of the world had made it, but even he could not prove so with any certainty. Hidden by a field of magic that kept it from the mortal world, the Chamber was the most trusted and secure of places anywhere.

Thinking that, the black dragon hissed low in anticipation. His crimson gaze shifted to the disk. Perhaps he should go there now. The others would all be there. It could be done . . .

No . . . not yet, said the voices just barely audible in the back of his subconscious. *The timing must be right or they will steal what is yours . . .*

Neltharion could not let that happen, not when he was so near to triumph. *Not now,* he finally told the red dragon, *but soon . . . I promise it will be soon . . .*

It must be, Alexstrasza replied. *I fear it must be.*

She left his thoughts as quickly as she had entered them. Neltharion hesitated, trying to determine whether or not he had left to her some hint of what was going on. The voices, however, assured him that he had not, that he had done very, very well.

The black dragon held high the disk, then, with a satisfied look in his blazing eyes, conjured it back to where he kept it hidden from all others, even his own blood.

"Soon . . . " he whispered as it vanished, a toothy grin stretching across his monstrous visage. "Very soon . . . after all, I *did* promise . . ."

The mighty palace stood on the edge of a mountainous precipice overlooking a vast, turbulent lake whose waters were so dark as to be utterly black. Trees augmented magically by solid rock created tall, spiral towers that jutted up like fearsome warriors. Walls made of volcanic stone that had been bound by monstrous vines and tree roots surrounded the huge edifice. A hundred gargantuan trees had been drawn together by the power of the builders to create the framework of the main building, then the rounded structure had been covered with stone and vine.

Once, to any who gazed upon it, the palace and its surroundings had been one of the wonders of the world . . . but that had changed, especially in recent times. Now the foremost tower stood shorn of its upper half. The blackened stone fragments and dangling bits of vine spoke of the intensity of the explosion that had destroyed it. That alone had not turned the palace into a place of nightmare, though. Rather, it was what now surrounded the once-proud edifice on all sides, save where the foreboding lake demanded dominion.

It had been a magnificent city, the culmination of night elf rule. Spread out over the landscape and very much a part of it, the high tree homes and sprawling habitations built into the earth itself had created a wondrous setting for the palace. Here had been built Zin-Azshari—"The Glory of Azshara" in the old tongue, and the capital of the night elves' realm. Here had stood a teeming metropolis whose citizens had risen every eve to give homage to their beloved queen.

And here, save for a few select, walled regions flanking the palace, had been a slaughter of innocents such as the world had never seen.

Zin-Azshari lay in ruins, the blood of its victims still staining the broken and burnt shells of their homes. The towering tree homes had been ripped to the ground and those built into the earth had been plowed under. A thick, greenish mist drifted over the nightmarish landscape. The stench of death yet prevailed—the corpses of hundreds of victims lay untouched and slowly rotting, a process made all the slower and more grotesque by the absolute absence of any carrion creatures. No crows, no rats, not even insects nibbled at the chopped and torn bodies, for they, too, had either fled with the few survivors or fallen to the onslaught that had claimed the city.

But although such carnage surrounded them, the remaining inhabitants of Zin-Azshari seemed not to notice it one bit. The tall, lanky night elves remaining in the city went about their tasks in and around the palace as if nothing had changed. With their dark, purple skin and extravagant, multicolored robes, they looked as if they attended some grand festival. Even the grim guards in forest-green armor standing watch at the parapets and walls appeared out of place, for they stared out at wholesale death without so much as batting an eye. Not one narrow, pointed visage reflected the slightest dismay.

Not one registered fear or horror at the grotesque giants moving in and among the debris in search of any possible survivor or spy.

Hundreds of armored, demonic warriors of the Burning Legion scoured Zin-Azshari while hundreds more marched out of the palace's high gates to supplement those moving beyond the capital. At their hand had this fair realm fallen and, given the chance, they would scour over the rest of the world, slaying all in their path.

Most were nine feet high and more, towering over even the seven-foot-tall night elves. A furious green flame perpetually surrounded each, but did not harm them. Their lower bodies were oddly thin, then expanded greatly at the chest. Their monstrous countenances resembled fanged skulls with huge horns atop and all had eyes of red blood that peered hungrily over the landscape. Most carried massive, pointed shields and glowing maces or swords. These were the Fel Guard, the bulk of the Legion.

Above them, with wings of fire, the Doomguard kept watch on the horizon. Similar otherwise to their brethren below save for a slight difference in height and a look of deeper intelligence, they darted back and forth over Zin-Azshari like prospecting vultures. Now and then, one would direct the efforts of the Fel Guard below, sending them wherever someone or something might be hiding.

Hunting alongside the Fel Guard were other fiendish creatures of the Legion, most of all huge, horrendous, four-legged monstrosities with a vague resemblance to either hounds or wolves. The scaled abominations, coarse fur atop their backs, sniffed the ruined ground not only with their massive muzzles, but also with two sinewy tentacles with suckers on the end. The felbeasts raced along through the carnage with extreme eagerness, occasionally halting to sniff over a ravaged corpse before moving on.

But while all this continued beyond the palace grounds, a quieter, yet no less horrific, scenario played out in the southernmost tower. Within, a circle of the Highborne—as those who served the queen of all night elves were called—bent over a hexagonal pattern etched into the floor. The hoods of their elegantly-embroidered, turquoise robes hung low, all but obscuring their silver, pupilless eyes . . . eyes now tinged with an unsettling red glow.

The night elves loomed over the pattern, muttering repeatedly the great words of their spell. A foul, green aura surrounded them, permeating their very souls. Their bodies were wracked with the continual strain of their efforts, but they did not falter. Those who had shown such weakness in the past had already been eliminated. Now, only the hardiest weaved the dark magic summoned from the lake beyond.

"Faster," rasped a nightmarish figure just beyond the glowing circle. "It must be done this time . . ."

He moved about on four titanic legs, a gargantuan, tusked demon with broad, clawed hands and huge, leathery wings now folded. A reptilian tail as thick as a tree trunk beat impatiently on the floor, leaving cracks in the sturdy stone. His toadlike head nearly scraped the ceiling as he moved among the much tinier Fel Guard—who wisely scattered from his path— for a better view. The green, fiery mane running from the top of his head to the tip of each of his squat hooves flickered wildly with every earthshaking step.

Under a heavy, hairless brow, sinister orbs of the same baleful green gazed unblinking at the dark tableau. He who commanded the night elves in their unsettling task was one used to *spreading* fear, not feeling it. Yet, on this tempestuous night, the demon called Mannoroth was afflicted with the disturbing emotion. He had been given a command by his master, and he had failed. Never before had this happened. He was Mannoroth, one of the commanders of the Great One's chosen . . .

"Well?" the winged demon growled to the night elves. "Must I rip the head off another of you pathetic vermin?"

A scarred night elf wearing the forest-green armor of the palace guard dared to speak. "She won't approve of you doing that again, my lord."

Mannoroth turned on the upstart. Fetid breath washed over the pinched face of the helmed soldier. "Would she complain as much if I chose to give her *your* head, Captain Varo'then?"

"Very likely," returned the night elf without any sign of emotion flickering over his own face.

The demon thrust out one meaty fist more than large enough to engulf Captain Varo'then's skull, helmet and all. The clawed fingers encircled the elf—then withdrew. Mannoroth's master had decreed early on to him that the queen of the night elves and those important to her were to be left untouched. They were valuable to the lord of the Burning Legion.

At least for now.

Varo'then was one whom Mannoroth could especially not touch. With the death of the queen's advisor, Lord Xavius, the captain had become her liaison. Whenever the glorious Azshara opted not to gift those working in the chamber with her magnificent presence, the guard captain took her place. Everything he saw or heard, Varo'then reported succinctly to his mistress . . . and in the short time that Mannoroth had observed the queen, he had determined that she was not so empty a vessel as some might have imagined. There was a cunning to her that her oft-languid displays hid well, but not well enough. The demon was curious what his master intended for her when he finally stepped into this world.

If he finally stepped into this world.

The portal to that other place, that realm between worlds and dimensions where the Burning Legion roamed between their rampages, had collapsed under a magical assault. That same force had also ripped apart the original tower, where the Highborne and demons had worked. Mannoroth still did not know what exactly had happened, but several survivors of the destruction had hinted of an invisible foe in their midst, one who had also slain the counselor. Mannoroth had his suspicions as to who that invisible intruder was and had already dispatched hunters to seek him out. Now he concentrated only on restoring the precious portal—if it could be done.

No, he thought. *It* will *be done.*

Yet so far the fiery ball of energy floating just above the pattern had done nothing but burn. When the tusked behemoth looked into it, he did not sense eternity, did not sense the overwhelming presence of his master. Mannoroth only sensed *nothing.*

Nothing was failure and, in the Burning Legion, failure meant death.

"They're weakening," Captain Varo'then remarked blandly. "They'll lose control of it again."

Mannoroth saw that the soldier spoke the truth. Snarling, the monstrous demon reached out with his mind and thrust himself into the spellwork. His intrusion shook the Highborne sorcerers, nearly upsetting everything, but Mannoroth seized control of the group and refocused their efforts.

It will be done this time. It will be . . .

Under his guidance, the sorcerers pressed as never before. Mannoroth's determination whipped them into a manic state. Their crimson-edged eyes widened to their fullest, and their bodies shook from both physical and magical stress.

Mannoroth glared grimly at the recalcitrant ball of energy. It refused to change, refused to open access to his master. Yellow drops of sweat poured down over the demon. Foam formed on his broad, froglike mouth. Even though failure meant being cut off from the great one, Mannoroth felt certain that somehow he would be punished.

No one escaped the wrath of Sargeras.

With that in mind, he pushed even more furiously, tearing from the night elves whatever power he could. Moans arose from the circle . . .

And suddenly, a point of utter blackness formed in the center of the fiery sphere. From far within it, a voice filled Mannoroth's mind, a voice as familiar to him as his own.

Mannoroth . . . it is you . . .

But not that of Sargeras.

Yes, he reluctantly replied. *The way is open again.*

We have waited too long . . . it said in a cold, analytical tone that made even the huge demon shrink into himself. *He is disappointed in you . . .*

I did all that was possible! Mannoroth protested before common sense warned him of the foolishness of doing so.

The way must be made completely open for him. I will see to it that it is finally done. Be ready for me, Mannoroth . . . I come to you even now.

And with that, the blackness spread, becoming a huge emptiness above the pattern. The portal was not quite as it had been when first the night elves created it, but that was because the one who spoke from the other realm now also strengthened it. This time, it would not collapse.

"To your knees!" Mannoroth roared. Still under his sway, the sorcerers had no choice but to immediately obey. The Fel Guard and night elven soldiers in attendance followed suit a moment later. Even Captain Varo'then quickly knelt.

The demon was the last to kneel, but he did so with the most deference. Almost as much as he feared Sargeras, he feared this one.

We are ready, he informed the other. Mannoroth kept his gaze now on the floor. Any single act, however minute, that could be construed as defiance might mean his painful demise. *We, the unworthy, await your presence . . . Archimonde . . .*

TWO

The world he had known, the world they all had known, was no more. The central region of the continent of Kalimdor was a ravaged plain. Spreading out in every direction, the demons had wreaked carnage on the complacent, jaded night elf civilization. Hundreds, possibly thousands, lay dead and still the Burning Legion pressed on relentlessly.

But not everywhere, Malfurion Stormrage had to remind himself. *We've stopped them here, even pushed them back.*

The west had become the place of greatest resistance to the monstrous invasion. Much of that credit went to Malfurion himself, for he had been the principal agent in the destruction of the Highborne spell that sealed off the Well of Eternity's power from those outside Queen Azshara's palace. He had faced Lord Xavius, the queen's counselor, and destroyed him in epic combat.

Yet, although Lord Kur'talos Ravencrest, master of Black Rook Hold and the commander of the night elf forces, had acknowledged his part before the gathered leaders, Malfurion did not feel like any hero. He had been tricked more than once by Xavius during the encounter, and only the intervention of his companions had enabled him to overcome the sinister counselor and the demons Xavius served.

His loose, shoulder-length hair a startling dark green, Malfurion Stormrage stuck out among the night elves. Only his twin brother, Illidan—who shared his narrow, almost lupine features—garnered more notice. Malfurion had eyes completely silver, as was most common among his people, but Illidan had gleaming orbs of amber, said to be the portent of great things to come. Of course, Illidan tended to dress more with the flamboyance most accepted of his kind, while Malfurion wore simple garments—a cloth tunic, a plain leather jerkin and pants, and knee-high boots. As one who had turned to the nature-oriented path of druidism, Malfurion would have felt like a clown had he sought to commune with the trees, fauna, and earth of the forest while clad like a pretentious courtier about to attend a grand ball.

Frowning, he tried for the thousandth time to put an end to such superfluous thoughts. The young night elf had come to this lonely spot in the hitherto untouched forest of Ga'han to calm and focus his mind for the days ahead. The huge force massed under Lord Ravencrest would be on the march soon—to where, no one knew just yet. The Burning Legion advanced in so many places that the noble's army could travel hither and yon for countless years, facing battle after battle without ever making any true progress. Ravencrest had summoned the top strategists to discuss the best way to gain a decisive victory, and quick. Each day of hesitation cost more and more innocent lives.

Malfurion's brow furrowed as he struggled harder to find his inner peace. Slowly, his mind relaxed enough to sense the rustling of leaves. That was the talk of the trees. With effort, he could speak with them, but for now the night elf satisfied himself with listening to their almost-musical conversations. The forest had a different sense of time, and the trees especially reflected that difference. They knew of the war, but spoke of it in an abstract manner. Although aware and concerned that other forests had been ravaged by the demons, the woodland deities who watched over them had so far given the trees here no reason to be truly worried. If the danger neared, they would surely know soon enough.

Their complacency jarred Malfurion again. The threat of the Burning Legion to *all* life, not just the night elves, was obvious. He understood why the forest might not fully comprehend that yet, but surely by now its protectors should.

But where *were* Cenarius and the rest?

When he had first sought to learn the way of the druid, a life which none of his kind before him had ever chosen, Malfurion had journeyed deep into this forest outside the city of Suramar in search of the mythic demigod. Whatever made him think he could find such a creature when no one else had, he could not say, but find Cenarius the night elf had. That in itself had been astonishing enough, but when the forest lord had offered to indeed teach him, Malfurion could not believe it.

And so, for months, Cenarius had been his shan'do, his honored instructor. From him, Malfurion learned how to walk the Emerald Dream, that place between the mortal plane and sleep, and how to summon the forces of nature to create his spells. Those very same teachings had been a tremendous part of the reason for not only Malfurion's survival, but that of the other defenders as well.

So why had Cenarius and the other woodland deities not added their own prodigious strength to the desperate defenders?

"Ha! I thought you'd be here."

The voice so similar to his own immediately identified the newcomer for Malfurion. Giving up on his quest for balance, he rose and solemnly greeted the other. "Illidan? Why do you search for me?"

"Why else?" As ever, his twin kept his midnight blue hair bound tight in a tail. In contrast to the past, he now wore leather pants and an open jerkin, both of a black identical to that of his high, flaring boots. Attached to the jerkin and hanging just over his heart was a small badge, upon which had been etched an ebony bird's head surrounded by a ring of crimson.

The garments were new, a uniform of sorts. The mark on the badge was the sign of the house of Kur'talos Ravencrest . . . Illidan's new patron.

"Lord Ravencrest will be making an announcement come dusk, brother. I had to get up early just so I could find you and bring you back in time to hear it."

Like most night elves, Illidan was still used to sleeping during much of the day. Malfurion, on the other hand, had learned to do just the opposite in order to best tap into the latent forces permeating the natural world. True, he could have studied druidism at night, too, but daylight was the time when his people's link to the Well of Eternity was at its weakest. That meant less chance of falling back on sorcery when casting a spell for the first time, something especially necessary during Malfurion's earliest days as a student. Now, he felt more comfortable in the light than in the dark.

"I was just about to head back, anyway," Malfurion said, going toward his twin.

"It would've looked bad if you hadn't been there. Lord Ravencrest doesn't like disorder or delay of any kind, especially from those integral to his plans. You know that very well, Malfurion."

Although their paths in the study of magic had gone in opposing directions, both brothers were adept at what they had chosen. After having been saved from a demon by Illidan, the lord of Black Rook Hold had appointed him personal sorcerer, a position of rank generally given to a senior member of the Moon Guard, the master mages of the night elves. Illidan, too, had played a pivotal role in the crushing of the demon advance in the west. He had seized control of the Moon Guard after the death of their leader, and guided their power effectively against the invaders.

"I had to leave Suramar," Malfurion protested. "I felt closed in. I couldn't sense the forest."

"Half the buildings in Suramar were formed from living trees. What's the difference?"

How could he explain to Illidan the sensations more and more assailing his mind each day? The deeper Malfurion delved into his craft, the more sensitive he became to every component of the true world. Out in the forest he felt the general tranquillity of the trees, the rocks, the birds . . . everything.

In the city, he felt only the stunted, almost insane emanations from what his own people had wrought. The trees that were now houses, the earth and rock that had been shifted and carved to make the area habitable for night elves . . . they were no longer as they had been in nature. Their thoughts were confused, turned inward. They did not even understand themselves, so transformed had they been by the builders. Whenever Malfurion walked the city, he sensed its wrongness, yet he also knew that his people—and, in fact, the dwarves and other races, too—had the right to create their civilizations. They committed no crime by building homes or making the land usable for them. After all, animals did the same thing . . .

And yet the discomfort he felt worsened each time.

"Shall we return to our mounts?" Malfurion asked, pointedly forgoing any reply to his brother's question.

Illidan smirked, then nodded. The twins walked side-by-side in silence up the wooded rise. Often of late they had little to say to each other, save when matters concerned the struggle. Two who had previously acted as one now had less in common with each other than they sometimes did with strangers.

"The dragon intends to leave us, likely by the time the sun sets," Illidan abruptly remarked.

Malfurion had not heard that. He paused to gape at his brother. "When did he say that?"

Among the night elves' few powerful allies was the huge red dragon, Korialstrasz. The young but mighty leviathan, said to be a mate of the Dragon Queen, Alexstrasza, had come to them along with one of a pair of mysterious travelers, the silver-haired mage known as Krasus. Korialstrasz and Krasus were somehow linked deeply to each other, but Malfurion had not yet discovered in what way. He only knew that wherever the gaunt, pale figure in gray went, the winged behemoth could be found. Together, they proved an unstoppable force that sent demons running in panic and paved the way for the defenders' advances.

Separated, however, they both seemed at death's door . . .

Malfurion had decided not to pry into either's affairs, in part due to their choice to aid the night elves, but also because he respected and liked both. Now, though, Korialstrasz intended to leave, and such a loss would be disaster for the night elves.

"Is Master Krasus going with him?"

"No, he's staying with Master Rhonin." Illidan spoke the last name with as much respect as his brother did Krasus. Flame-haired Rhonin had come with the elder mage from the same unnamed land, a place they sometimes briefly spoke of when relating facts about their own experiences against the Burning Legion. Like Krasus, Rhonin was a wizard of high learning, although much younger in appearance. The bearded spellcaster wore dour blue travel clothes almost as conservative as Malfurion's, but that alone was not what offset him from those around. Krasus could pass for a night elf—albeit a very sickly, pasty one—but Rhonin, equally pale, was of a race no one recognized. He called himself a *human,* but some of the Moon Guard had divulged that their studies indicated he was some variation of a dwarf who had simply grown much taller than his fellows.

Whatever his background, Rhonin had become as invaluable as Krasus and the dragon. He wielded the Well's magic with an intensity and skill even the Moon Guard could not match. More important, he had taken Illidan under his wing, teaching him much. Illidan believed it was because Rhonin saw his potential, but Malfurion understood that the cloaked stranger had also done it to rein in his twin's impetuousness. Left to his own devices, Illidan had a tendency to risk not only his own life, but those of his comrades.

"This isn't good, Illidan."

"Obviously not," retorted his amber-eyed twin, "but we'll make due." He raised his hand for Malfurion to see; a red aura surrounded it. "We're not without strength of our own." Illidan caused the aura to cease. "Even if you seem a little reluctant to make full use of what Cenarius taught you."

By full use, Malfurion's sibling meant unleashing spells that wreaked havoc not only on the enemy, but the landscape and anything else caught in the path. Illidan still did not understand that druidism required working *with* the peaceful balance of nature, not against it.

"I do what I can in the way I must. If you—"

But Malfurion got no further, for, at that moment, a figure out of nightmare dropped down before them.

The Fel Guard opened his grisly maw and roared at the pair. His flaming armor did not make Malfurion in the least hot, but rather chilled the night elf to the very core of his soul. Sword raised, the horned demon swung at the nearest foe—Illidan.

"No!" Malfurion shoved his brother aside, at the same time calling upon the forest and heavens to come to his aid.

A sudden, intense wind slammed into the demon, flinging him like a leaf several yards back. He fell against a tree—cracking the trunk—then slid to the ground.

As if the tentacles of some huge squid, the roots of every tree within reach squirmed over the stunned attacker. The demon tried to rise, but his arms, legs, torso, and head were suddenly pinned to the earth. He struggled, but only succeeded in losing what remained of his grip on his weapon.

Their victim secure, the roots then immediately sank back into the ground—and, in the process, *through* the demon.

A hissing gasp was all that escaped the monstrous assassin before the roots severed his head from his body. Green ichor poured out of the horrific wounds. Like a puzzle someone had just spilled, the parts of the demon tumbled back toward his would-be targets.

Yet, even as Malfurion dealt with the first, two more Fel Guard dropped from the trees. Cursing, Illidan rose to his knees and pointed at the nearest.

A demon in the midst of lunging at him abruptly turned his mace on his comrade, caving in the unsuspecting victim's skull with one terrible blow.

Malfurion suddenly detected something amiss. The hair on his neck rising, he started to look over his shoulder.

A humongous, four-legged beast leapt upon him. Two wriggling tentacles with toothy suckers at the end drove into his chest. Row upon row of yellowed, fanged teeth filled his gaze. A stench like rotting flesh assailed him.

Somewhere beyond his own ghastly predicament, he heard Illidan cry out, the shout cut off by a sound vaguely reminiscent of a hound's howl.

They had been deceived, put purposely off-guard by the frontal attack so that an even worse foe could come at them from behind. The felbeasts had been set to spring the moment the opportunity arose.

Malfurion screamed as the vampiric suckers literally tore the magic from his body much as the teeth would soon tear his flesh. To any spellcaster, felbeasts were an especially insidious foe, for they hunted those with the gift for magic and drank from them until nothing but husks remained. Worse, given enough energy to devour, the demonic hounds could multiply themselves several times over, creating an epidemic of evil.

He tried to tear the tentacles free, but they had clamped tight. The night elf felt his strength waning . . .

. . . And then what sounded like the patter of rain filled his ears.

The felbeast shook. The tentacles released their hold and flailed about until, with a ponderous groan, the demon fell to the side, almost collapsing on Malfurion's arm.

Blinking away his tears, the night elf discovered more than a dozen sharp bolts sticking out of the felbeast's thick hide. Each shaft had been expertly aimed to strike the most vulnerable areas. The demon had been dead before it had even dropped.

From the forest above came more than twoscore riders clad in gray-green armor and sitting atop huge, black saber-toothed panthers called night sabers. The massive cats darted between the trees with an agility and swiftness unmatchable by almost any other creature.

"Spread out!" called a young officer whose voice sounded familiar to Malfurion. "Make certain there are no more!"

The soldiers moved out quickly, but with caution. Malfurion could appreciate their care, for he knew that, this being daylight, they were not at their best. Still, the druid could not deny that their skills were admirable, not after they had saved his life.

Riding up to Malfurion, the officer reined the hissing cat to a halt. The night sabers, too, did not like this switch from dark to light, but they were gradually growing to tolerate it.

"Is this to be my fate, then?" asked the somewhat round-featured night elf. He seemed to be studying Malfurion very intently, though the latter knew part of that was simply due to the sharper slant of the officer's silver eyes. "Trying to keep from getting yourselves slaughtered? I should've begged his lordship to let me keep my posting in the Suramar Guard."

"But then this might've turned out different, Captain Shadowsong," Malfurion replied.

The soldier exhaled in frustration. "No . . . it wouldn't have, because Lord Ravencrest would've never let me go back to the Guard! He seems to think I was anointed by the Mother Moon herself to protect the backs of his special servants!"

"You came back to Suramar in the company of myself, a novice priestess of Elune, a mysterious wizard . . . and a dragon, captain. I'm afraid we marked you in the eyes of Lord Ravencrest and the other commanders. They'll never see you as a simple Guard officer again."

Shadowsong grimaced. "I'm no hero, Master Malfurion. You and the others slay demons with barely the wave of a hand. I just try to preserve your heads so that you can continue to do it."

Jarod Shadowsong had had the misfortune to capture Krasus while the latter had tried to enter Suramar. The mage had used the captain to gain aid for himself, which in turn had resulted in bringing Malfurion and the others, including Korialstrasz, together at last. Unfortunately for the good officer, his dedication to duty meant that he had accompanied his prisoner through the entire incident; that, most of all, had stuck in Lord Ravencrest's mind when he determined that his spellcasters needed someone to watch over them. Jarod Shadowsong soon found himself "volunteered" to command a contingent of hardened soldiers, most of whom had far more military experience than himself.

"There was no need for all this charging about," Illidan snapped as he joined his brother. "I had this situation in hand."

"My orders, Master Illidan. As it is, I barely caught sight of you leaving on your own, against his lordship's commands." Shadowsong swung his gaze back to Malfurion. "And when I discovered how long *you* had been missing . . ."

"Hmmph," was all Illidan responded. For one of the few times in recent days, the twins were in agreement—neither cared for Lord Ravencrest's demand that they be constantly watched. Doing so only made them more eager to escape. In Malfurion's case, it was due to the nature of his calling; in Illidan's it was because he had no patience for the endless councils. Illidan did not care for battle plans; he just wanted to go out and destroy demons.

Only . . . this time it had almost been the demons who destroyed him. Neither he nor Malfurion had sensed their nearness, a new and frightening aspect. The Burning Legion had learned how to better cloak its assassins. Even the forest had been blithefuly ignorant of the taint in its midst. That did not bode well for the future of the struggle.

One of the other soldiers rode up to Shadowsong. Saluting, he said, "The area's clear, captain. Not a sign of any more—"

A bone-shivering cry echoed through the forest.

Malfurion and Illidan turned and ran in the direction of the source. Jarod Shadowsong opened his mouth to call them back, then clamped it shut and urged his mount after.

They did not have far to go. A short distance farther into the woods, the gathered party paused before a gruesome sight. One of the night sabers lay sprawled across the ground, its torso ripped open and its entrails spilled out. The huge cat's glassy eyes stared sightlessly skyward. The animal had been dead no more than a minute or two, if that long.

But it was not the beast that had been the source of the blood-chilling cry. That had been the soldier who now hung skewered on his own sword against a mighty oak. The night elf's legs dangled several feet above the earth. Like the cat, his chest had been methodically torn open—that despite his armor. Below his feet lay most of what had fallen free. His mouth hung open and his eyes were a perfect copy of the panther's own empty orbs.

Illidan eagerly looked around, but Malfurion put a sturdy hand on his brother's shoulder and shook his head. "We do as the captain said. We go back. Now."

"Get his body down," ordered Shadowsong, his face losing some of its violet pigment. He pointed at the twins. "I want an escort around them this instant!" Leaning down to the pair, the captain added with some impatience, "If you don't *mind*, of course."

Malfurion prevented his brother from making any remark back. The pair dutifully marched up the rise toward their mounts, the bulk of the escort constantly circling them like a pack of wolves surrounding prey. It was ironic to Malfurion that he and his brother wielded more power than all the soldiers put together and yet they would likely have died if not for Jarod Shadowsong's intervention.

We've much to learn still, the young druid thought as he neared his night saber. *I have much to learn still.*

But it seemed that the demons were not going to allow anyone the precious time needed for that learning.

Krasus had lived longer than any of those around him. His lanky, silver-haired form gave some indication of the wisdom he had gathered over that time, but only by gazing deep into his eyes did one garner any hint of the true depths of the mage's knowledge and experience.

The night elves thought him a variant of their own race, some sort of albino or mutation. He resembled them enough, even though his eyes were more like a dwarf's in that they had pupils. His hosts accepted his "deformities" by marking them as evidence of his powerful links to magic. Krasus wielded the arcane arts better than all the vaunted Moon Guard combined, and with good reason.

He was neither a night elf nor even merely an elf . . . Krasus was a dragon.

And not any dragon, but the elder version of the very leviathan with whom he spent much of his time, *Korialstrasz*.

The cowled mage had not, as he had indicated to others, come with red-haired Rhonin from a distant land. In fact, both he and the human wizard had come from far, far in the future, from a time after a second and decisive battle against the Burning Legion. They had not, however, come by choice. The two had been investigating a curious and unsettling anomaly in the mountains when that anomaly had swallowed them, tossing both through time and space into ancient Kalimdor.

They were not the only ones, either. An orc—the veteran warrior, Broxigar—had also been swallowed. Brox's people had also fought the demons that second time and his Warchief had sent him and another to investigate a troubled shaman's nightmare. Caught on the edge of the anomaly, Brox's companion had been ripped apart, leaving the older orc to fend for himself when he arrived in the past.

Circumstance had gradually thrown the dragon, the orc, and the human—all former enemies—together. But circumstance had *not* given them a way back to the future and that, most of all, worried Krasus.

"You are brooding again," rumbled the dragon.

"Merely concerned about your coming departure," Krasus told his younger self.

The red dragon nodded his huge head. The pair stood at the wide, solid battlements of Black Rook Hold, the imposing citadel from which Lord Ravencrest commanded his forces. Contrary to the lively, extravagant homes of his contemporaries, Ravencrest kept a very martial residence. Black Rook Hold had been carved from thick, ebony rock, as solid a structure as any ever made. All the chambers above and below ground had been chiseled out. To many, Black Rook was a fortress impenetrable.

To Krasus, who knew the monstrous fury of the Burning Legion, it was one more house of cards.

"I do not wish to depart," spoke the red dragon, "but there is a silence among our kind. I cannot even sense my beloved Alexstrasza. You of all should understand my need to discover the truth."

Korialstrasz knew that his companion was a dragon like himself, but he had not made the connection between past and future. Only his queen and mate, the Mother of Life, understood the truth and she had not told her new consort. That had been a favor to him—or rather, to his *older* self.

Krasus, too, felt the emptiness and so he accepted that his younger version would have to fly off to discover the reason why, even if it meant risk for both of them. Together they were an astonishing force, one most valued by Lord Ravencrest. While Korialstrasz sent showers of flame down on the demons, Krasus could expand that flame into a full firestorm, slaying a hundred and more of the foe in a single breath. But when they were divided, illness struck them, rendering both nigh impotent.

The last vestiges of sunlight disappeared on the horizon. Already the area around the edifice bristled with activity. The night elves dared not grow complacent at any time, day or evening. Too many had perished early on because of habit. Still, the darkness was always welcome, for as much as they were tied to the Well of Eternity, the night elves were also strengthened by the moon and stars.

"I have been thinking," said Krasus, letting the wind caress his narrow features. Because of his immense size, Korialstrasz could not enter Black Rook Hold. However, the solid rock structure of the keep enabled him to stay perched atop it. As such, Krasus chose to sleep there, too, using only a thin woven blanket for comfort. He also ate his meals and spent nearly all his waking moments on the battlements, descending only when duty called. For other matters, he turned to Rhonin, the only one here besides himself who truly understood his situation.

"There may be a way by which we can still journey alongside one another," he continued. ". . . So to speak."

"I am eager to hear it."

"There is on you at least one loose scale, yes?"

The dragon spread his wings and shook like a huge dog. His scales clattered in rhythmic fashion. The behemoth's great brow furrowed as he ceased and listened, then twisted his serpentine neck to investigate an area near his rear right leg. "Here is one, I think."

Dragons generally lost scales in much the way other creatures lost fur.

The areas exposed generally hardened, eventually becoming new scales. At times when more than one broke free, a dragon had to take care, for the soft flesh was, for a time, susceptible to weapons and poison.

"I would like to have it . . . with your permission."

For anyone else, Korialstrasz might have refused, but he had come to trust Krasus as he did himself. Someday, Krasus hoped to tell him the truth, providing that they lived that long.

"It is yours," the crimson giant replied readily. With his back paw, Korialstrasz scratched at the spot. Moments later, the loose scale fell to the floor.

Quickly retrieving it, Krasus inspected the scale and found it to his liking. He looked up at his companion. "And now, I must give you something in return."

"That is hardly necessary—"

But the dragon mage knew better; it would bode him ill if anything happened to his younger self because of Krasus's interference with the past. "Yes, it *is*."

Putting aside the head-sized scale, he stared at his left hand and concentrated.

The slim, elegant fingers suddenly gnarled, becoming reptilian. Scale spread across the flesh, first from the fingertips, then racing down the hand until just past the wrist. Sharp, curved claws grew from what had once been flat nails . . .

As the transformation took place, a sharp agony coursed through Krasus. He doubled over and nearly collapsed. Korialstrasz instinctively reached for the tiny figure, but the mage waved him back. "I will survive it!"

Gasping for breath, still doubled over, Krasus seized the hand he had altered and tore at the tiny scales. They resisted his efforts. He finally gritted his teeth and tugged on two as hard as he could.

They tore free, leaving a trail of blood pooling on the back of his monstrous appendage. Swallowing hard, the gaunt figure immediately let the hand revert, and, as it did, the pain receded.

Ignoring his self-inflicted wound, Krasus inspected his prizes. Eyes sharper than any night elf's looked for the slightest imperfection.

"You know that what afflicts us both does not allow you to transform to your natural shape any more than it lets me change into other than a dragon," Korialstrasz chided. "You risk yourself terribly when you attempt such an act."

"It was necessary," Krasus replied. He turned the bits over, frowning. "This one is cracked," he muttered, letting the scale in question fly away in the wind, "but the other is perfect."

"What do you intend to do with it?"

"You must trust me."

The dragon blinked. "Have I ever done otherwise?"

Taking the tiny scale, the mage went to where Korialstrasz had scratched free his own. The area was still red and soft and large enough for any good archer to hit.

Whispering words older than dragons, Krasus pressed the scale directly on the center of the open region.

The scale flared a bright yellow as it touched. Korialstrasz let out a gasp, but did not otherwise react. The dragon's eyes gazed intently on what his companion did.

Krasus chanted the elder words over and over, each time increasing the speed with which he spoke them. The scale pulsated and with each pulsation seemed to grow a little larger. Within seconds, it had become almost identical to those surrounding it.

"It will adhere to your flesh in a matter of seconds," Krasus informed the leviathan. "There will be no chance of losing it."

A moment later, he stepped back and inspected his handiwork. The dragon's head came around to do the same.

"It feels . . . normal," the leviathan commented.

"I hope it does more for you. As I now carry a part of you with me, so you, in turn, carry a part of me with you. I pray the synergistic magics involved will give us some of the benefit we receive when actually with each other."

Korialstrasz spread his wings. "There is only one way to find out."

Krasus agreed; to discover whether the spell had worked, they would have to separate. "I bid you farewell, then, good Korialstrasz."

The huge beast dipped his head low. "And I, you."

"Alexstrasza—"

"I will tell her of you and your wishes, Krasus." The dragon eyed the tiny figure carefully. "I have suspicions about our links, but I respect the need you have to keep your secrets from me. One thing I discovered quickly, though, is that you love her as much as I. *Exactly* as I."

Krasus said nothing.

"As soon as I can, I will tell you how she fares." Moving to the edge of the battlements. the dragon looked to the sky. "Until we meet again, my blood . . . "

And with that, the crimson titan leapt into the air.

My blood . . . Krasus frowned at the choice of words. To dragons, such a term meant close ties. Not mere comrade or clan, but closer yet, such as brothers from the same clutch of eggs or offspring and parent . . .

Or . . . the same being in two bodies . . .

Krasus knew himself better than anyone. He had no doubt as to his younger self's intelligence. Korialstrasz almost had the truth in his grasp and the mage had no idea what that might mean for both of them.

Weakness suddenly overtook him. Through quickly watering eyes, Krasus sought out Korialstrasz's scale. The moment he seized it, some of the pain and weariness left him. But touching it was not enough; he had to keep it closer to him for the effect to be worthwhile.

Exposing his chest to the cool night wind, the dragon mage planted the large scale against his flesh. Again he muttered the ancient words, stirring up forces no night elf could understand, much less wield.

The same golden aura flared around the scale. Krasus shook, fighting to keep his balance.

As quickly as it had appeared, the aura faded. He stared down at his chest, now covered in the center by his younger self's parting gift.

A slight hint of weariness still pervaded his being, though both it and the tinge of pain also present were nothing Krasus could not readily suffer. Now at last he could walk among the others and not feel their pity. Now he could stand beside them against the demons. The mage wondered why he had not thought of this plan much earlier—then recalled that he had, but only bothered to put it into action once Korialstrasz had declared his intention to seek out the other dragons.

It is hard to part with one's self, apparently. How Rhonin would have laughed at his conceit. The irony made even Krasus chuckle. How Alexstrasza would have enjoyed the jest as well. She had more than once suggested that his continuous intrusion into the matters of the lesser races had a touch of vanity involved, but this act now more than topped that in every—

A sudden wave of vertigo struck him.

It was all he could do to keep himself from slipping over the battlements. The attack ended swiftly, but the repercussions kept Krasus leaning against the stone wall and breathing heavily for more than a minute.

When he could at last stand straight, the dragon mage immediately looked far beyond Black Rook Hold, far beyond Suramar.

To distant, dark Zin-Azshari.

Krasus continually had many secretive spells in play, several designed to keep track of what other sorcerers might be casting. He was, without conceit, perhaps more attuned to the shifts in the intensity of the world's magical forces than anyone—but even he had not been prepared for a change of such magnitude.

"They have done it . . ." he breathed, staring at the unseen city. "The portal is again open to the Burning Legion."

THREE

The pain of his death had been unbearable. He had been destroyed in more than a dozen horrific manners simultaneously, each one sending through him such torture that he had embraced oblivion as a long-yearned-for lover.

But the agony of his death could not even compare to that which followed.

He had no body, no substance, whatsoever. Even *spirit* was not the right word for what was left of him. He knew that he existed by the sufferance of another, and understood that the anguish he constantly felt was that other's punishment for him. He had failed the other and failure was the ultimate sin.

His prison was a nothingness without end. He heard nothing, saw nothing, felt nothing other than the pain. How long had it been—days, weeks, months, years, centuries . . . or only a few horrible minutes? If the last, then his torture was truly monstrous, indeed.

Then, without warning—the pain ceased. Had he a mouth, he would have shouted his relief, his joy. Never had he felt so grateful.

But then he began to wonder if this respite only signaled some new, more horrendous terror.

I have decided to redeem you . . .

The voice of his god filled him with both hope and fear. He wanted to bow, to grovel, but lacked the form with which to do either . . . or anything else, for that matter.

I have decided that there is a place for you. I have looked into the darkness within you and found that which once pleased me. I make it the core of what you are to become and in doing so make you a far superior servant than you were . . .

His gratitude for this greatest of gifts was boundless, but again he could do nothing.

You must be reshaped, but so that others will mark in you the glory I give and the punishment I mete out, I return that by which they will know you best . . .

A crackle of energy shook him. Tiny specks of matter suddenly flew into the center of the energy storm, gathering and condensing, creating of him substance once again. Many had been bits of him when he had been destroyed and, like his soul, had been taken by his god at the moment of death.

Slowly, vaguely, a body formed around him. He could not move, could not breathe. Darkness covered him, and he realized that the darkness was actually his vision returning to him.

And as he truly began to see for the first time since dying, he noted that he had arms and legs different from those which he had formerly worn. The legs bent back at the knee and ended in cloven hooves. Like the legs, his arms and hands were covered in a thick fur, and his fingers were long and clawed.

He felt his face mold differently and sensed the bent horns sprouting from his forehead. Nothing about him reminded him at all of his previous incarnation and he wondered how he could still be known to others.

Then, with hesitation, he reached up and touched his eyes . . . and knew that they were the mark. He felt the innate forces within them growing more powerful, more precise with each passing second. He could now make out the very strands of magical energy recreating him, and saw how the invisible hand of his god restructured his body to make him far greater than that which he had once been.

He watched as his god's work continued, marveling and admiring the perfection of it. He watched as he became the first of a new kind of servant, one which even the others who attended the master would envy.

And he watched with artificial eyes of black crystal, across the center of which ruby streaks coursed.

The mark by which those who had once known him would recall his name—and know new fear.

Lord Kur'talos Ravencrest stood in front of the high, stone chair where he usually held court and faced the assembled commanders. A tall figure even among the seven-foot-high night elves, he had a long, narrow visage much akin to that of the black bird whose name he bore, even to the downward turn of his nose. His tufted beard and stern eyes gave him an appearance of both wisdom and might. He wore the gray-green armor of his troops, but also marked his superior rank with a billowing cloak of gold and a mighty, red-crested helm from which the stylized head of a raven peered down.

Behind the chair hung the twin banners of his house, square flags of rich purple with the ebony silhouette of the avian in the middle. The banner of House Ravencrest had become the de facto symbol of the defenders, and there were those who spoke of the noble in terms once reserved only for the queen.

But Lord Ravencrest himself was not among those and as Malfurion listened, his anxieties concerning the direction in which the counterattack was headed increased.

"It is clear," stressed the bearded night elf, "that the point of focus *must* be Zin-Azshari! There is where these abominations originated and there is where we must strike!"

Rumbles of approval swept over the night elves gathered to listen to him. Cut off the foe at his most critical point. Without Zin-Azshari to strengthen them, the demons already on the field would surely fall to defeat.

Ravencrest leaned toward his audience. "But it is not merely monsters from beyond we face! In Zin-Azshari, we confront a most duplicitous foe— our own kind!"

"Death to the Highborne!" someone shouted.

"Yes! The Highborne! It is *they,* led by the queen's advisor, Lord Xavius, who have brought this calamity upon us! It is *they* who now must face our swords and lances and pay for their crimes!" The noble's countenance grew even more grim. "And it is *they* who hold our dear Azshara prisoner!"

Now roars of anger burst forth. Several cried, "Blessed is our Azshara, the Light of Lights!"

Someone next to Malfurion muttered, "They remain blind even now."

He turned to see the red-haired mage, Rhonin. Although a foot shorter, the odd-looking figure was broader of build and looked as much a fighter as a master wizard. The only human among them—the only human *anywhere* as far as Malfurion knew—Rhonin caused comment merely by existing. The night elves, haughty and prejudiced when it came to other races, treated him with deference because of his power, but few would have invited him into their homes.

And even less likely to receive such an invitation was the grotesque, brutish figure next to him, one almost as tall as Malfurion but built like a bear. Slung on his back was a huge, twin-edged battle ax that appeared made of wood, yet somehow gleamed like steel.

"Those who do not see the truth in battle march willingly to defeat," grunted the tusked, green-skinned warrior, his philosophical words belying his savage form.

Broxigar—or Brox, as he preferred to be called—shook his head at the night elves' unwavering devotion to their queen. Rhonin's cynical smirk in response to the orc's words only added to Malfurion's discomfort at how his people appeared to the outsiders. They could readily see what few of his kind other than himself could—that Azshara *had* to know what happened in the palace.

"If you knew what she has been to us," the night elf muttered, "you would understand why it is so difficult for them to accept her betrayal."

"It doesn't matter *what* they think," Illidan interjected from in front of him. "They'll attack Zin-Azshari either way and the end result will be the same. No more demons."

"And what if Azshara comes out and tells them that she's seized control of the demons from the Highborne, and that everyone's now safe?" Rhonin countered pointedly. "What if she tells her people to lay down their arms, that the battle's over? And then what if the Burning Legion falls on Ravencrest and the rest while the queen laughs at their folly?"

Illidan had nothing to say to that, but Brox did. He gripped the hilt of his dagger and muttered under his breath, "We know her betrayal. We know. We make sure this queen plays no tricks . . ."

Rhonin tilted his hooded head to the side in consideration of this suggestion, while Illidan's face masked whatever opinion he had on the dread subject. Malfurion frowned, caught between the remnants of his own devotion to Azshara and his realization that eventually someone would *have* to put an end to the queen if the world hoped to survive this monstrous invasion.

"If and when the time comes, we do what we have to," he finally replied.

"And that time approaches swiftly."

Krasus slipped into the back of the chamber to join them, an arrival that left all of them silent. The pale, enigmatic wizard moved with more assurance, more health, yet obviously the dragon from whom he seemed to draw strength could not be out in the hall.

Rhonin immediately went to him. "Krasus, how is this possible?"

"I have done what I have done," the latter said, absently touching the three small scars on his face. "You should know that Korialstrasz has departed."

While the news was unexpected, it still struck them hard. Without the dragon, the night elves would have to depend upon their small band even more.

At the other end of the room, Lord Ravencrest continued his speech. "Once there, the secondary force, under Lord Desdel Stareye, will then pull in from the south, squeezing them in from the two sides . . ."

Next to the dais, a very slim night elf—clad in the same armor as Ravencrest but wearing a cloak of intertwining green, orange, and purple lines—nodded to the speaker. Stareye's helm had a long, shimmering crest of night saber fur. The helm itself was decorated with a multitude of tiny, gem-encrusted stars. In the center of each had been set a golden orb—an overall gaudy display to the outsiders, no doubt, but well-appreciated by Stareye's compatriots. The night elf himself seemed to be constantly staring down his long, pointed nose at anyone he looked at—anyone other than his host, that is. Desdel Stareye knew the importance of attaching himself to the House of Ravencrest.

"We must move swiftly, surely, yes," Stareye added uselessly. "Strike at the heart, yes. The demons will cower at our blades, grovel for our mercy, which we shall not give." Reaching into a pouch on his belt, he took a white powder and sniffed it.

"May the heavens help us if that popinjay ever becomes leader," murmured Rhonin. "His armor gleams as if newly-forged. Has he ever fought a war?"

Malfurion grimaced. "Few of our kind have. Most prefer that 'distasteful' duty to Lord Ravencrest, the Moon Guard, or the local forces. Unfortunately, bloodline dictates who is granted a high rank in troubled times."

"Not unlike humans," Krasus said before Rhonin could respond.

"Strike at the heart and quickly," Lord Ravencrest agreed. "And we must do so before the Highborne succeed in reopening the way for more of the monsters—"

To the surprise of Malfurion and the others, Krasus stepped forward and dared interrupt. "I fear it is already too late for that, my lord."

Several of the night elves took affront at this interruption by one not of their own kind. Ignoring them, Krasus strode toward the dais. Malfurion noted that the mage still showed subtle signs of strain. Whatever he had done to enable him to walk free of the dragon had not completely rid him of his mysterious malady.

"What's that? What do you mean, wizard?"

Krasus stood before Ravencrest. "I mean that the portal is already open."

His words reverberated through the assembly. Several night elves lost a shade or two of their purple color. Malfurion could not blame them. This was hardly welcome news. He wondered how they would react when they discovered that they had also lost the one dragon who had been aiding them.

Desdel Stareye looked down at the outsider. "And you know this *how*?"

"I felt the emanations. I know what they mean. The portal is open."

The haughty noble sniffed, his way of indicating his distrust of such questionable evidence. Lord Ravencrest, on the other hand, accepted Krasus's dire pronouncement with grave faith. "How long?"

"But a few minutes before I entered here. I verified it twice before I dared come."

The master of Black Rook Hold sat back in his chair, brooding. "Ill tidings, indeed! Still, you said it was but a short time ago . . ."

"There is some hope yet," the mage said, nodding. "It is weak. I can sense that. They will not be able to bring through too many at once. More important, their master will be unable to physically enter yet. Should he attempt to do so, he will destroy the portal . . ."

"What does it matter if he stays where he is and simply directs them?" asked Stareye with another sniff.

"The Burning Legion is but a shadow of his terrible darkness. Trust in me when I say that we have hope even if every demon who serves him comes through, but *no* hope if we destroy all only to have him step into the world."

His words left silence in their wake. Malfurion glanced at Rhonin and Brox; their expressions verified Krasus's warning.

"This changes nothing," Ravencrest abruptly declared. He faced the audience again, expression resolute. "Zin-Azshari remains the focus, now more than ever! Both the portal and our beloved Azshara await us there, so there is where we march!"

The night elves rallied almost immediately, so trusted was the elder commander when it came to war. Few night elves had the reputation that Lord Ravencrest held. He could draw people to his banner almost as well as the queen could to hers.

"The warriors are already set to march! They have but been awaiting our decision! I give you all leave to depart after this gathering and prepare each of your commands! By the fall of day tomorrow, we push on toward the capital!" Ravencrest raised his mailed fist high. "For Azshara! For Azshara!"

"For Azshara!" shouted the other night elves, Illidan included. Malfurion knew that his brother added his voice because of his position as Black Rook Hold's sorcerer. Whatever Illidan believed concerning Queen Azshara, he would not jeopardize his recently-gained status.

The night elven officers nearly stormed out of the chamber in their eagerness to return to their soldiers. As they poured into the hall, Malfurion thought to himself how mercurial his people could be. A moment before, they had been lamenting the news of the portal's resurrection. Now they acted as if they had never even heard the terrible report.

But if they had forgotten it, Rhonin and Brox had not. They shook their heads and the red-haired wizard muttered, "This bodes ill. Your people don't realize what they're marching into."

"What other choice do they have?"

"You must reconsider sending messengers as I suggested," Krasus suddenly insisted.

The wizard still stood before Lord Ravencrest, who now was accompanied only by a pair of dour guards and Desdel Stareye. Krasus had one foot on the dais and his expression was as animated as Malfurion had ever seen it.

"Send out messengers?" scoffed Stareye. "You jest!"

"I accept your anxiety," their host replied, "but we've hardly sunk so low. Fear not, Master Krasus, we *will* take Zin-Azshari and cut off the portal! I promise you that!" He adjusted his helmet. "Now, I think we both have plans to make before the march, eh?"

With Lord Stareye and the guards in tow, the noble marched out of the room as if already the victor. Illidan joined his patron just before the party vanished. Krasus watched Ravencrest depart, his countenance anything but pleasant to behold.

"What was that you tried to convince him of?" asked Rhonin. "Messengers to whom?"

"I have been trying—in vain, it appears—to persuade him to ask for assistance from the dwarves and other races—"

"Ask the *other* races?" blurted Malfurion. Had Krasus asked him beforehand the odds of success, the young night elf would have immediately tried to dissuade him from even suggesting such to the master of Black Rook Hold. Even with Kalimdor under siege and hundreds or more already dead, no lord would ever demean himself by even thinking of contacting outsiders. To most night elves, dwarves and such were barely one step above vermin.

"Yes . . . and I see from your expression that attempting to speak later with him about it will be just as futile."

"You know how hard it was to convince the dwarves, orcs, elves, and humans to work together in our—where we came from," Rhonin remarked. "Not to mention the complexity of getting each of the factions and kingdoms within those groups to trust one another."

Krasus nodded wearily. "Even my own kind have their prejudices . . ."

It was as close as he had ever come to identifying what he truly was, but Malfurion did not press. His curiosity concerning his ally's identity was a slight thing compared to the potential holocaust they all faced.

"You didn't tell them about the dragon leaving," he said to Krasus.

"Lord Ravencrest knows of it. I sent word of it to him as soon as Korialstrasz declared his decision."

Rhonin frowned. "You shouldn't have let Korialstrasz go."

"He shares a concern with me about the dragons. As should you." Some wordless communication passed between the two wizards, and Rhonin finally nodded.

"What do we do?" asked Brox. "We fight with the night elves?"

"We have no choice," Rhonin answered before Krasus could. "We're trapped here. Things've become too tangled *not* to take an active part." He stared deep into the elder mage's eyes. "We can't just stand by."

"No, we cannot. It has gone beyond that. Besides, I find I will not abide waiting for assassins to come targeting me. I *will* defend myself."

Rhonin nodded. "So it's settled."

Malfurion did not understand all that they said, but he recognized the end of what had been a long, stressful argument. Evidently, despite all he had done for the night elves, Krasus still had reservations about aiding them. An irony, so the druid saw it, after how much effort Krasus had spent pushing for Lord Ravencrest to approach the dwarves and tauren.

It occurred to him then that they had all decided to join the host marching on Zin-Azshari. With those last doubts erased, Malfurion realized there was one other person with whom he needed to speak before that happened. He could not leave Suramar without seeing her.

"I must go," he informed them. "There—there is something I need to do."

His cheeks must have flushed, for Krasus kindly nodded, adding, "Please give her my greetings, will you?"

"I—of course."

But as he started past the elder mage, Krasus took hold of his forearm. "Do not steel yourself against your emotions too much, young one. They are a part of your calling, your destiny. You will need them greatly in the days ahead, especially as *he* is no doubt here now."

"Here?" Rhonin's brow furrowed. "Who? What else haven't you told us?"

"I am only using logic, Rhonin. You saw the beast Mannoroth guiding the Legion when it first swept out from the city. You know that, despite him, we were able to not only cut off the portal, but also inflict serious damage to the demon army."

"We beat Mannoroth. I know. We did it in the—back home, too."

Krasus's eyes had a veiled look to them that stirred Malfurion's anxiety anew. "Then you should also recall what happened *after* his defeat."

The night elf saw Rhonin blanch. Brox, too, seemed disturbed, but his reaction was more like Malfurion's. The orc understood that something dire was about to be revealed, but did not know just what.

"Archimonde." The human whispered the name so quietly that he almost appeared worried that its bearer might hear it even in Ravencrest's sanctum.

"Archimonde," repeated Brox, now understanding. He gripped the hilt of his dagger and his eyes darted back and forth.

"Who—who is this Archimonde?" asked Malfurion. Even saying the name brought a distaste to his mouth.

It was Rhonin who answered him, Rhonin with his eyes unblinking and his mouth set in utter hatred. "He who sits at the right hand of the lord of the Burning Legion . . ."

Captain Varo'then brought the news to his queen as he always did. With Lord Xavius dead, he had become her favored . . . in more ways than one. His new uniform—a resplendent, glittering emerald green with golden sunbursts across the chest—was the latest gift bestowed upon him by Azshara. His title remained that of captain, but in truth, he commanded more than some generals, especially as even demons followed his orders.

Varo'then swept aside his glittering golden cape as he entered the queen's sanctum. Her attendants immediately curtsied, then stepped away.

Azshara herself lay draped across a silver couch, her head resting perfectly on a small cushion. Her hair, more silver than the couch, cascaded gracefully down her back and shoulders. The queen had long, almond-shaped eyes of pure gold and features of perfection. The gown she wore—a wondrous, translucent blue and green—displayed her curved form magnificently.

In her hand, Azshara held a view globe, a magical artpiece that displayed for its user a thousand different exotic images of night elven creation. The image that faded away as the soldier knelt appeared to be that of Azshara herself, but Varo'then could not be certain.

"Yes, my dear captain?"

Varo'then forced his cheeks not to flush from desire. "Radiance of the Moon, Flower of Life, I bring important tidings. The Great One, Sargeras—"

She immediately sat up. Eyes wide, full lips parted, the queen asked, "He is here?"

A pang of jealousy struck the officer. "Nay, Light of Lights, it is not yet possible for the portal to hold the magnificence of the Great One . . . but he has sent his most trusted to finally make the way ready."

"Then I must greet him!" Azshara declared, rising. Attendants immediately darted out of hiding to take her train. The long, silken gown trailed for some distance. The skirt was cut so that the queen's long, smooth legs briefly revealed themselves as she walked. Everything about Azshara spoke of seduction and although he knew that she toyed with him as she did others, Varo'then did not care.

The instant that she started forward, several new figures lurched out of the shadows. Despite their huge forms, the Fel Guard who acted as her personal bodyguard had remained unseen until now. Two stepped in front of the pair while the rest lined up behind. The demons waited patiently, emotionlessly, for the queen to move again.

He raised his armored forearm so that she might place her perfect, tapering fingers upon it. The captain led her through the gaily-painted marble halls of the palace to the tower where the surviving Highborne sorcerers had restarted their efforts. Sentries both night elf and demon stood at attention as they passed. Varo'then had studied the Legion enough to understand that while Mannoroth and Hakkar seemed astoundingly oblivious to the queen's beauty, the lesser demons appeared not so immune. Her bodyguard had become especially protective of her, even keeping a wary eye on their own brethren at times.

It did not do for even demon lords to underestimate the ruler of the night elves.

A pair of felbeasts guarded the outside door. The tentacles on each hound-like demon twitched toward the pair.

Immediately the Fel Guard created a protective wall between Azshara and the hounds. Felbeasts drained magic the way some insects drank blood, and Azshara had, contrary to appearances, a great aptitude for sorcery. To the creatures, she would seem a feast.

Varo'then had his own weapon out and ready, but Azshara touched his cheek gently and said, "No, dear captain."

With a wave of her hand, she parted the Fel Guard, then walked up to the fel-beasts. Ignoring the menace of the tentacles, the queen knelt before the pair and smiled.

One monster immediately planted his fearsome head under her out-stretched hand. The other opened a mouthful of rows of jagged teeth and let his thick, brutish tongue loll out the side. Both acted as Varo'then had seen three-day-old night saber kits do around Azshara.

After petting both on their coarse heads, the queen urged the monsters aside. The felbeasts readily obeyed, sitting down near the wall and looking as if hoping for some tiny treat.

The captain sheathed his weapon. No, it would not be good for *anyone* to underestimate his beloved monarch.

The way opened for Azshara as she stepped past the felbeasts. Following close behind, Varo'then saw immense Mannoroth look over his shoulder at the new arrivals. As much as he could read the demon's expression, the captain noted some distress. Mannoroth, at least, was not so pleased with the coming of the Great One's second.

And as the night elves entered, they could not help but notice that Archi-monde had already arrived.

For the first time, Azshara momentarily lost a bit of her cool composure. The brief, open-mouthed gasp vanished swiftly, but it still startled Varo'then . . . almost as much as the demon himself did.

Archimonde stood as tall as Mannoroth, but that was where the likenesses ended. By any standard, he was far more handsome and in some ways resem-bled the night elves over whom he towered. His skin was a black-blue, and it took Varo'then a moment to realize that Archimonde surely had to be related to the Eredar warlocks. His build was similar and he even sported a fearsome tail like theirs. No hair covered any part of his body. His skull was huge and his ears wide and pointed. From under a narrow brow ridge, orbs of deep green stared out. He wore armor plating on his shoulders, shins, forearms and waist, but little else. An arresting display of lines and circles tattooed over his body radiated high magic.

"You are Queen Azshara," he said in smooth, articulate words, a vast contrast to Mannoroth's more guttural speech or Hakkar's hiss. "Sargeras is pleased by your loyalty."

The female night elf actually flushed.

His steady, unblinking gaze turned to Captain Varo'then. "And the Great One always approves of the capable warrior."

Varo'then went down on one knee. "I am honored."

As if no longer acknowledging the pair as anything of interest, Archimonde turned to where the sorcerers worked. A black gap hung in the midst of the pattern they had created, a gap that, despite its tremendous size, had surely disgorged the huge demon with difficulty.

"Hold the way steady. He will be coming through now."

"Who?" Azshara blurted. "Sargeras is coming?"

With utter indifference, Archimonde shook his head. "No. Another."

Varo'then chanced a glance Mannoroth's way and saw that the tusked demon, too, was puzzled.

The edges of the black gap suddenly shimmered. The Highborne maintaining the portal immediately shook as their efforts demanded more than ever from them. Several gasped, but wisely did not falter.

And then . . . a shape coalesced in the portal. Though smaller than the demons, it somehow radiated a forceful presence nearly on par with Archimonde or Mannoroth even before it put one foot out onto the mortal plane.

Or rather . . . one hoof.

On two legs like those of a shaggy goat, the figure stepped toward the demon commanders and night elves. The lower half of his body was pure animal in design. The unclad torso, however, while so deep a purple that it was nearly black, was otherwise identical to that of a night elf, save far more muscled. A long mane of black-blue hair hung loose around the narrow visage. The huge, curled horns contrasted sharply with the elegant, pointed ears. The only clothes the newcomer wore was a wide loincloth.

But if any thought because of the lower half and horns that this was only a beast sent by the lord of the Legion, they had only to look into its eyes and sense the deep, cunning intelligence within. Here was a mind sharper and quicker than most, devious and adaptive where it needed to be.

Only then did the eyes themselves register on the soldier. There could be no mistaking the black, crystalline orbs—clearly artificial—and the streaks of crimson running across the centers.

Only one being he had ever known had possessed such fantastic eyes.

Captain Varo'then stood, but it was not from his mouth that the identity of the other was uttered. That came instead from Queen Azshara, who leaned forward, studied with pursed lips the leering visage that was and was not the face both she and the officer had known, and said, *"Lord Xavius?"*

FOUR

The night elven host assembled by Lord Ravencrest was truly impressive to behold, but Malfurion found no comfort in their great numbers as he waited for the noble's signal to begin the march. The young night elf looked to his right, where his brother and companions also awaited astride their mounts. Rhonin and Krasus constantly discussed some matter between themselves, while Brox stared ahead at the horizon with the clear patience of a seasoned warrior. Perhaps of all of them, the orc understood the overwhelming task they faced. Brox held the ax Malfurion and Cenarius had created for him as if already seeing the endless tide of enemy.

Despite Brox's clear knowledge of combat, Ravencrest and the rest of those in command of the host had not once turned to the orc for his experience and knowledge. Here was a creature who had fought hand-to-hand with the demons, yet no one asked him of their weaknesses, their strengths, or anything else that might give those on the front line a further edge. True, Krasus and Rhonin had provided some such insight, but theirs was tempered by a more familiar use of magic. Brox . . . Malfurion suspected that Brox could have taught everyone far more when it came to true fighting.

We are a people whose downfall may yet come because of our own arrogance . . . Malfurion frowned at his own pessimism, then lost the frown as the only sight that could cheer his heart came riding up to him.

"Malfurion!" Tyrande called, her expression pensive and worried. "I thought never to find you in all this!"

Her face was as he always remembered it, for he had long ago burned it into his memory. Once a childhood friend, Tyrande had now become for him a desire. Her skin was a smooth, violet shade and her dusky blue hair was tinged with silver. She had a fuller face than many of their kind, which added to her beauty. Her features were somehow delicate yet determined, and she had veiled silver eyes that ever pulled Malfurion inside. Her lips were soft and often wore a hint of a smile.

In contrast to the previous times that they had met, the novice priestess of Elune—the Mother Moon—wore an outfit more befitting the way of war than the peace of the temple. Gone was her flowing, white robe. In its place was a form-fitting suit of armor with layered plates that allowed much mobility. The armor covered Tyrande from neck to foot, and over it, almost as an inconsistency, was a shimmering, gossamer cloak the color of moonlight. In the crook of her arm, the young priestess held a winged helmet that would protect the upper portion of her face as well.

To Malfurion, she looked more like the priestess of a war god and evidently Tyrande could read such in his expression. With a bit of defensiveness, she admonished him, "You may excel at your new calling, Malfurion, but you seem to have forgotten the elements of Mother Moon! Do you not recall her aspect as the Night Warrior, she who takes the courageous dead from the field and sets them riding across the evening sky as stars for their reward?"

"I meant no disrespect to Elune, Tyrande. It was more that I've never seen you dressed so. It makes me greater fear that this war will forever change us all . . . providing we survive it."

Her expression softened again. "I'm sorry. Perhaps my own uneasiness makes my temper short. That, and the fact the high priestess has declared that I myself shall lead a group of novices into this conflict."

"What do you mean?"

"We are not going to ride with the host simply to offer our healing powers. The high priestess has had a vision in which the sisterhood *must* actively fight alongside the soldiers and the Moon Guard. She says that *all* must be willing to take upon themselves new roles if we're to keep the demons from victory."

"That may be easier said than done," Malfurion responded with a grimace. "I was just thinking how hard it is for our people to adjust to change of any kind. You should have been there when Krasus suggested that they call upon the dwarves, tauren, and other races to work with them."

Her eyes widened. "It's a wonder they work with him and Rhonin, much less tauren. Doesn't he realize that?"

"Yes, but he's as stubborn as one of us, possibly more."

He quieted as his brother suddenly joined them. Illidan gave him a cursory glance, then focused his attention completely on Tyrande.

"You look like a warrior queen," he told her. "Azshara herself could appear no finer."

Tyrande flushed and Malfurion wished that he had made some compliment—*any* compliment—for which the priestess might remember him before the host set off.

"You are the Night Warrior herself, in fact," Illidan continued smoothly. "I hear you've been put in charge of a band of your sisters."

"The high priestess says that my skills have much increased of late. She says that in all her years of guidance, I'm one of the swiftest to attain such levels."

"Not a surprise."

Before Malfurion could say anything similar, a horn suddenly blared. It was followed by another, then another, and so on as each segment of the mighty army signaled its readiness for departure.

"I have to return to the sisters," Tyrande told them. To Malfurion, she added, "I came to wish you well." Instinctively, the priestess turned to Illidan. "And you, of course."

"With your blessing, we're certain to ride to victory," Malfurion's sibling returned.

Again Tyrande flushed. Another horn sounded, and she quickly donned the helmet, turned her panther around, and rode off.

"She looks more suited for battle than either of us," Malfurion commented.

"Yes. What a mate she'll make for someone, eh?"

Malfurion looked at his brother, but Illidan had already urged his night saber toward Lord Ravencrest. As the noble's personal sorcerer, Illidan had to ride near the elder night elf. Malfurion and the others had been ordered to remain within shouting distance, but otherwise they did not have to stay with Ravencrest. The master of Black Rook Hold did not want all of his strongest weapons clustered together. The Eredar already knew to focus on the druid and the wizards whenever possible.

Jarod Shadowsong and three soldiers rode to him. "It's time to go! I must ask you to come with us!"

Nodding, Malfurion followed the captain back to the rest. Rhonin and Krasus wore almost identical dour expressions. Brox's had changed not one bit, but under his breath the orc appeared to be chanting.

"A march at night," commented Krasus, turning to watch the last vestige of day vanish. "How very predictable. Archimonde will note it. Despite their best to adapt, your people are still inclined to fall back to comfortable tendencies."

"With such numbers, we'll still be able to push the demons back," Captain Shadowsong insisted. "Lord Ravencrest will sweep the monsters from our fair land."

"So we can only hope."

A final horn sounded and the night elven host moved as one in the direction of Zin-Azshari. Regardless of his misgivings, Malfurion swelled as he watched the armed force cover the landscape. The banners of three dozen major clans highlighted a collection of alliances spanning the width and breadth of most of the realm. Foot soldiers marched in perfect unison like a swarm of dedicated ants heading to a feast. Night sabers leapt along in great prides a hundred strong and more, their helmed riders staring wearily ahead.

The bulk of the soldiers wielded swords, lances, and bows. Behind them came siege machines—ballistae, catapults, and the like—drawn by teams of the dark panthers. Most of those operating the machines were of Lord Raven-crest's clan, for in general night elves did not work with such devices. Only Ravencrest seemed to have the foresight necessary to lead his people to victory. That he had not sought the aid of the dwarves and others was bothersome to the druid, but in the end it would not matter. Despite his misconception that Azshara was innocent, the noble would still see to it that the Burning Legion fell to bloody defeat.

After all, there was really no other choice.

Urged on by Ravencrest and their own belief in certain victory, the night elves made good distance that first eve. Their commander finally gave the order to halt two hours into daylight. Immediately the host set up camp, a long line of sentries marking the front to ensure the demons would not catch them by surprise.

Here the land had not yet been touched by the horror of the Burning Legion. To the south, forest still stood. To the north, high, green hills dotted the landscape. The elder night elf sent out patrols to investigate each direction, but no foes were found.

Malfurion was immediately drawn to the woods, almost as if they called his name. When chance came, he separated from his companions and turned his mount toward them.

Jarod Shadowsong immediately noted his act. The captain rode after him, calling out as he approached, "I must ask you to turn back! You cannot go out there by yourself! Remember what happened—"

"I'll be all right, Jarod," Malfurion replied quietly. In truth, he felt that this particular patch of wilderness was shielded even from the demonic assassins who had so often preyed on him and his companions. How this could be, Malfurion could not say, but he knew it with the utmost certainty.

"You cannot go alone—"

"I'm not. You're with me."

The soldier gritted his teeth, then, with a look of resignation, followed the druid into the forest. "Please . . . just not so long."

Promising nothing, Malfurion continued on into the deeper part of the forest. A feeling of trust, of faith, overwhelmed him. The trees welcomed him, even seemed to recognize him—

And then he understood why he felt so at home in this place.

"Welcome back, my *thero'shan* . . . my honored student."

Captain Shadowsong looked around for the source of the stirring voice, a voice reminiscent of both the wind and thunder. Malfurion, on the other hand, waited patiently, knowing that the speaker would reveal himself in his own fashion.

The wind abruptly picked up around the duo. The officer held tight to his helmet while the druid bent his head back to better feel the breeze. Loose leaves began rising up in the wind, which grew stronger, fiercer. Yet, only the captain appeared dismayed by this; even the night sabers raised their snouts up to inhale the fresh wind.

A miniature whirlwind arose before the riders. Leaves, brush, bits of stone and earth . . . more and more they gathered within, compacting together to form something solid.

"I have been waiting for you, Malfurion."

"By the Mother Moon!" Jarod gasped.

The giant moved on four strong legs akin to those of a stag; the bottom half of his torso was indeed the body of one. Above that, a barrel-chested form similar in coloring and shape to a night elf peered down at the two intruders with orbs of pure golden sunlight. A hint of forest green tinged the otherwise violet flesh and the fingers ended in gnarled but deadly talons of aged wood.

The newcomer shook his head, sending his thick, moss-green mane fluttering. Leaves and twigs appeared to be growing naturally within both the mane and the wide, matching beard, but they were not as astonishing as the huge, multilayered set of antlers rising high over the giant's head.

Malfurion bowed his head in reverence. "My *shan'do*. My most honored teacher." He looked up. "I am happy to see you, Cenarius."

Although both night elves stood a good seven feet tall, Cenarius towered over them and their mounts. At least ten feet in height himself, his antlers gave him at least another four feet. He was so impressive, in fact, that the captain, who had conversed face-to-face with a dragon, could only gape.

With a slight chuckle that seemed to make all the nearby birds decide to sing, Cenarius declared, "You are welcome here, Jarod Shadowsong! Your grandsire was a true friend of the forest!"

Jarod shut his mouth, opened it again, shut it once more, then merely nodded. Like all night elves, he had grown up hearing the tales of the demigod, but like most of his people, he had assumed that they were simply that—tales.

The forest lord gazed down at his pupil. "Your thoughts are in crisis. I felt it even in the Emerald Dream."

The Emerald Dream. It had been some time since Malfurion had walked it. In the Emerald Dream, one saw the world as it might have been in its earliest creation—no animals, no people, no civilization. There was a tranquillity to it; a dangerous one, in fact. One could become so caught up in it that one forgot how to return to the mortal plane. The walker might instead wander forever while his body finally perished.

Taught to travel it by Cenarius, Malfurion had used the dreamscape to enter the palace prior to his struggle with Lord Xavius. Since that event, however, the young druid had been afraid to return, the vague memories of the aftermath still haunting him. He would have drifted through the Emerald Dream for eternity if not for his teacher just barely noticing him.

Cenarius saw his anxiety. "You must not be afraid to walk it again, my son, but now is not the time. However, there are other parts of your training that have lagged and that is why I chose this pause to come to you."

" 'This pause'? What do you mean?"

"The others are still divided as to what to do about the demons. We will fight them, yes, but we are creatures of individual spheres of power. It is difficult for us to work in harmony, for we all feel we know what is best to do."

The news did nothing to temper Malfurion's uncertainties. First the dragons had failed to show any inclination to battle the Burning Legion, and now even the demigods, the guardians of the natural world, could not agree on the proper course of action. Truly, it was all up to the night elves . . . likely Malfurion and his comrades, in particular.

"Our time together will not be long. There are some things that I must quickly try to teach you. We will need use of the entire day—"

"Out of the question!" blurted Captain Shadowsong, surprising himself. "My orders are—"

With a benevolent smile, the woodland deity trotted toward the soldier. Jarod's face paled as Cenarius loomed over him.

"He will be protected while he is with me and will be back when he is needed by your commander, Jarod Shadowsong. You will not be shirking your responsibility."

The officer shut his mouth, already clearly dumbfounded that he had dared interrupt Cenarius in the first place.

"Return to your other charges. I will see to it that Malfurion comes back safe and sound."

The druid felt as if the pair discussed a child, but the demigod's words were evidently what Jarod had wanted precisely to hear. He nodded to Cenarius, turning the nod into a bow at the last moment. "As you say, my lord."

"I am not your lord, night elf. I am Cenarius only! Go with my blessing!"

With one last awed glance at Malfurion and his teacher, the captain turned his night saber and rode off toward the night elven host.

Cenarius turned back to his student. "Now, my *thero'shan*, we must begin in earnest." All congeniality vanished from the deity's expression. "For I fear we will need all the knowledge we have if we are to save our world from the demons . . ."

At that moment, another who feared they would need all that they could gather to defeat the Burning Legion flew over the realm of the dragons, seeking the lofty mountain peak where his kind made their homes.

Korialstrasz had spent his long flight considering many things. The silence of his brethren was one. Dragons were reclusive, but never had he encountered such utter quiet. No one responded to his summons, not even his beloved mate, Alexstrasza.

This caused him to think of the demons. He could not believe that they could have attacked and destroyed the dragons, but the lack of communication left that fear alive. He almost wished that Krasus had accompanied him, for at least then there would have been one other red dragon with whom to discuss the dire thoughts.

But Krasus himself was a subject on par with all else. More and more, Korialstrasz had begun eliminating the possible theories concerning this enigmatic dragon to whose words even Alexstrasza paid close attention. She did so as if Krasus were the equal to her consorts, even perhaps *was* one. Yet, this could not be . . . unless . . .

No . . . that is not possible, the soaring behemoth thought. *It is too extraordinary . . .*

Still, it would explain so very much.

He would confront Alexstrasza with his thoughts once he found her. Korialstrasz banked, turning toward the familiar, mist-enshrouded mountain. Unlike all times past, there were no sentinels keeping watch, yet another ominous sign.

The great red dragon descended toward the high cavern mouth used as one of the main entrances to the sanctum. As he alighted, he turned his massive head back and forth, seeking some sign of his fellows. The area was deathly silent.

But as he folded his wings and moved forward, he collided with a sudden, distinct force invisible to all his other senses. It felt as if the air had taken on a thickness akin to honey. With great determination, Korialstrasz threw himself forward, barreling into the unseen wall as he would against a rival dragon.

Slowly it gave way. He felt it press around his body as he advanced, almost enveloping him. The dragon had difficulty breathing, and his view became as if he saw the world from under water. Yet still Korialstrasz did not falter.

And suddenly, without warning, he was through.

Sounds instantly filled his ears. Bereft of any barrier, the leviathan fell forward. He would have landed headfirst, but huge paws caught him.

"It is good that you are back," a deep voice rumbled. "We feared for you, young one."

Tyranastrasz lifted him up, the reptilian countenance of Alexstrasza's senior consort filled with concern. Behind him, other dragons moved about through the system of tunnels . . . and what surprised Korialstrasz most about the activity was the fact that there were dragons of *other* colors. He saw blue, green, bronze, and, of course, red. The dragons intermingled constantly, all seeming on some task and all obviously quite anxious.

"Alexstrasza! Is she—"

"She is well, Korialstrasz. She gave word that she would speak with you the moment that you returned . . ." The larger male glanced at the younger's shoulder, seeking something. ". . . and Krasus, too, but I see that he is not with you."

"He would not leave the others."

"But your condition—"

Flexing his wings, Korialstrasz replied, "He has devised a manner by which we are both *nearly* whole. It is not perfect, but it is the best we could do."

"Most interesting . . ."

"Tyran . . . what happens here? Why are the other flights among our own?"

The elder consort's expression grew veiled. "She has commanded that she be the one to tell you all and I will not disobey her."

"Of course not."

With Tyranastrasz in the lead, the pair wended their way into the lair of the red flight. Korialstrasz could not help but eye the other dragons as they passed among them. The greens were mere flitting shadows, gone before one realized they were even there, and made more disconcerting by the fact that they ever kept their eyes closed, as if sleepwalking. The bronze figures of Nozdormu's flight seemed not to move at all, but somehow were elsewhere whenever he blinked. As for the blues, they appeared here, there, everywhere in almost random fashion, darting about through the use of magic as much as physical movement. The more Korialstrasz saw of them, the more he welcomed the stable, solid presence of his own kind. When they moved, they moved. When they rushed to one destination, he could follow their every step, see their every breath.

Of course, in all fairness, he suspected that the newcomers felt the same way about their respective flights.

So many different dragons, and yet we all fit in here, he suddenly thought. *Are we so few as all that, then?* Had they tried to crowd the night elves or dwarves in this mountain, either lesser race would have filled it to overflowing, yet the dragons ever found room to maneuver.

Thinking of the endless horde that was the Burning Legion, Korialstrasz wondered if even the dragons had the strength to stop them.

But as he entered the next chamber, his fears melted away. She stood there as if waiting for him in particular. Her simple presence filled the male with calm, with peace. When she looked his way, Korialstrasz felt confidence. All would be well. The Queen of Life would see that it was so.

"Korialstrasz . . . my beloved." Only her eyes gave indication of how much force that simple sentence had. The lesser creatures might often see dragons only as savage beasts, but even the best of them could not possibly match the intensity of emotions Korialstrasz's kind wielded.

"My queen, my existence." He bent his head low in homage.

"It is good that you are back. We feared for you."

"As I feared in return. No one answered my summons, or explained the sudden silence."

"It was necessary," the huge female responded. Despite the sleekness of her form, Alexstrasza outweighed her consorts by half again as much. Like all of the great Aspects, she commanded forces that dwarfed those of even her mates. "The demand for secrecy is paramount."

"Secrecy? For what?"

She studied him. "Krasus is not with you?"

He noted her tremendous concern. She worried about Krasus as she would have Korialstrasz. "He chose to stay behind. He managed a trick that enables us to spend our time apart from each other without suffering . . . much."

A brief smile spread across her scaled visage. "Of course *he* would."

Before Korialstrasz could pursue the line of conversation to what he desired to know about Krasus, another entered the high chamber from the right. Korialstrasz looked at the new arrival, and his eyes widened.

"It is necessary that *all* dragons take part in this ritual," the black giant rumbled, his voice like a smoldering volcano. "Mine have already done so. The other flights must now do the same."

Neltharion filled the other end of the chamber, the only one who could possibly match Alexstrasza in size and power. The Earth Warder radiated an intensity that made Korialstrasz a bit uncomfortable.

"My final consort is here," Alexstrasza returned. "The bronze flight has come and although Nozdormu is not with them, they have brought that which is part of his essence so that he, too, will be joined with us in this struggle. That leaves only Krasus, a single entity. Is that so terrible a thing?"

The ebony dragon tilted his head. Never had Korialstrasz seen so many teeth. "One dragon only . . . no . . . I think not."

"What is this about?" the younger male dared ask.

"The demons have reopened the way to our world," Alexstrasza explained. "Once more, they flow through like water, doubling their strength with each passing day."

Korialstrasz imagined the monstrous army and what its numbers had already accomplished. "Then we *must* act!"

"We are. Neltharion has devised a plan, possibly the only hope for our world's survival."

"What is it?"

"Neltharion must show you."

The ebony behemoth nodded, then closed his eyes. The air shimmered before him. A sense of astounding power touched Korialstrasz's magical senses. He felt as if the chamber had filled with a thousand dragons.

But instead, a tiny, almost insignificant little golden disk materialized in the air, hovering just below eye level for the gathered leviathans. Korialstrasz sensed nothing within it, yet somehow knew that very fact meant the disk was much, much more than it seemed.

The Earth Warder opened his eyes, an expression of exaltation spreading over his reptilian features. To Korialstrasz, it was as if Neltharion worshipped his creation.

"Behold that which will exorcise the demons from our world!" the black leviathan thundered. "Behold that which will cleanse the lands of all taint!"

The tiny disk flared bright, suddenly no longer insignificant to the eye. Now, the young red male felt the full extent of the powers within . . . and understood why even Alexstrasza believed it to be their best recourse.

"Behold," Neltharion roared proudly. *"The Dragon Soul."*

FIVE

Captain Varo'then was not one to be made ill at ease by shadows and noises. He confronted all such things with the same dour earthiness with which he did everything else in his life. The scarred soldier had been born to the role of warrior and, despite his inherent cunning, never saw himself in any other role. He had no desire to be king or consort save that it would then place him even closer to Azshara. He commanded his forces in her name and was satisfied with that. The political machinations he had always left to Lord Xavius, who understood and savored them far more than Varo'then ever could.

But of late, his mind had been forced to turn to paths other than those of battle. That had to do with the return of one he had assumed quite dead . . . Xavius himself. Now the queen's advisor, brought back from the afterlife by the astounding power of the great Sargeras, again guided the will of the Highborne. That should have not bothered Varo'then, but Xavius had changed in ways even the queen did not see. The captain was certain that the advisor—or this thing that had once been the advisor—concerned himself not with the glory of Azshara, but with other matters. Varo'then, whatever his loyalty to the lord of the Legion, was ever first and foremost his queen's servant.

"The ever-efficient captain. Of course I find you stalking the halls even when not on duty."

The officer jumped, then silently cursed himself for reacting so.

As if pouring out of the shadows themselves, Xavius stepped out in front of the night elf. His hooves clattered on the marble floor and he breathed in snorts as he moved. Archimonde had called Xavius a satyr, one of Sargeras's blessed servants. The unnatural eyes that the noble had himself put in place of his own stared out from under the deep brow ridge. They snared the captain's own, drawing him inexorably into some unsettling place.

"Sargeras sees much promise in you, Captain Varo'then. He sees one whose status could be great among those who serve him. He sees you as a commander of his host, set up there along with Mannoroth—nay—*Archimonde,* even!"

Varo'then saw himself at the head of a horde of demons, his sword thrust out before him as they poured over their foes. He felt the pride and love of Sargeras as he rode down those who would defy the Great One.

"I am honored to serve," the soldier murmured.

Xavius smiled. "As are we all . . . and we would serve in any way we could, if it would make the dream come true sooner, is that not so?"

"Of course."

The hooved figure leaned close, his face nearly touching the soldier's own. The eyes continued to pull Varo'then in, both tantalizing and unnerving him at the same time. "You could serve in a manner better suited for you, in a role that will lead you sooner to the command you desire . . ."

Excitement coursed through the officer. He again pictured himself leading armies in the name of his queen and Sargeras. He imagined his conquest of their enemies, the blood of the foe flowing so much it created rivers.

But when Captain Varo'then tried to imagine himself doing all this, he could not see his own form distinctly. He tried to draw forth an image of himself as a warrior, an armored and armed commander such as in the old epics . . . but another shape persistently pushed itself on him.

A shape much like that worn by Lord Xavius.

That, at last, enabled him to pull free of the advisor's gaze. "Forgive me, my lord, but I must be about my duties."

The artificial eyes flared briefly. Then Xavius nodded ever so politely and with a sweep of his hand bid the soldier to move on. "But of course, Captain Varo'then, but of course."

At a quicker pace than he would have preferred to display before the horned figure, Varo'then marched away. He did not look back. His hand clutched the hilt of his sword as if about to draw it. The night elf did not slow until he was certain that Lord Xavius had been left far behind.

But even then he could still hear the beguiling words of the satyr . . . and Varo'then knew that where he had managed to deny them, others would not.

As night fell upon Lord Ravencrest's forces, the Sisters of Elune spread out among the night elves to give their blessings. Even clad like warrior maidens, the priestesses brought peace and comfort to the soldiers. Elune offered the night elves strength and confidence, for she was always there in the heavens, watching down on her favored children.

Although her expression did not reveal it, Tyrande Whisperwind felt none of the peace or strength she passed on to her people. The high priestess seemed to think that she especially had been touched by the Mother Moon, but Tyrande sensed no great presence within herself. If the Mother Moon had chosen her for something, she had failed to inform Tyrande.

The last bit of daylight fled beneath the horizon. Tyrande hurried, knowing that soon the horns would sound and the host would move on toward Zin-Azshari. She touched the heart of one more soldier, then strode to her waiting panther.

But before she reached it, another night elf confronted her. Out of reflex, Tyrande put a hand to his chest—only to have him take her hand by the wrist.

The priestess looked up and her own heart at first leapt with joy. Then she noted the dark uniform and the hair bound back in a tail.

Most of all, Tyrande noticed the amber eyes.

"Illidan . . ."

"I'm grateful for your blessing, of course," he responded with a wry grin. "But I'm comforted more by your near presence."

Her cheeks flushed, though not for the reason he thought. Still gently holding her wrist, Malfurion's twin leaned close.

"Surely this is fate, Tyrande! I've been looking for you. We're entering fast-moving times. Decisions must be made without hesitation."

With sudden anxiety, she understood what he intended to ask—nay, *tell* her. Without meaning to, Tyrande pulled back her hand.

Illidan's face immediately grew stony. He had missed neither her reaction nor the meaning behind it.

"It's too soon," she managed, trying to assuage his feelings.

"Or too late?" The wry grin returned, but to her it now appeared to be slightly hollow, more of a mask. After a moment, though, Illidan's face relaxed. "I've been too impetuous. This isn't the right time. You've been trying to comfort too many. I'll speak with you again, when the moment is more appropriate."

Without another word, he headed toward where a mounted guard in the garb of Ravencrest's clan awaited with the sorcerer's own night saber. Illidan did not look back as he and his escort rode off.

More troubled than ever, Tyrande sought her own panther. Yet, even as she mounted, another came to interrupt her thoughts. This time, however, it proved to be a more welcome soul.

"Shaman, forgive this intrusion."

With a gentle smile, she greeted the orc. "You are always welcome, Broxigar."

Only she was allowed to call him by his full name. To all others, even Lord Ravencrest, he was merely Brox. The massive orc stood a good head shorter than her, but made up for it with a girth three times her own and nearly all of that muscle. She had seen him wade into enemies with the ferocity of one of the huge cats, but around her he acted with more respect than many of those who asked for her blessing.

Thinking that a blessing was what the orc had come for, Tyrande reached down to touch his chest. Brox looked startled, then welcomed the touch.

"May the Mother Moon guide your spirit, may she grant you her silent strength . . ." She continued on for a few seconds more, giving the orc a full blessing. Most of the other priestesses found him as abhorrent as the rest of the night elves did, but in Tyrande's eyes, he was no less one of Elune's creatures than herself.

When she had finished, Brox dipped his head in gratitude, then muttered, "I am not worthy of this blessing, shaman, for that is not why I've come to you."

"It isn't?"

The tusked, squat face twisted into what Tyrande recognized as remorse. "Shaman . . . there is something that burdens my heart. Something that I must confess."

"Go on."

"Shaman, I have tried to find my death."

Her lips pursed as she struggled to understand. "Are you telling me that you tried to kill yourself?"

Brox pulled himself up to his full height, his expression darkening. "I am an orc warrior! I've not guided my dagger to my own chest!" As abruptly as his fury had arisen, it now vanished completely, replaced only by shame. "But I've tried to guide the weapons of others to it, true."

And the story came flowing out. Brox told her of his last war against the demons, and how he and his comrades had held the way while they awaited reinforcements. Tyrande heard how, one by one, all the other orcs had perished, leaving only the veteran. The actions of Brox and the others had helped save the battle, but that had in no manner made him feel any less guilty about surviving where others had not.

The war had ended soon after, leaving Brox with no proper method by which to atone for what he saw as a tremendous failing on his part. When the Warchief Thrall had requested that he hunt down the anomaly, he had seen it as a sign that the spirits had finally granted him an end to his misery.

But the only one to die in that search had been his young comrade, which added to Brox's already heavy burden. Then, when it became clear that the Burning Legion would invade Kalimdor, the orc had once more hoped for redemption. He had thrown himself into the struggle and fought as hard as any warrior could be expected. He had always been at the forefront, daring any foe to take him on. Unfortunately, Brox had fought too well, for even after slaying a score of the demons, he had survived with barely a scratch.

And as the gathered host had set out from Suramar, the graying orc had finally started to think that he had committed a different sin. He realized that the shame that he had felt in surviving his former comrades had been a false one. Now Brox felt a new shame; everyone around him fought for life while he sought to *escape* it. They went to battle the Burning Legion for reasons opposite his own.

"I accept that I might die in battle—a glorious fate for an orc, shaman— but I am filled with dishonor for seeking it at the possible cost of those who fight against evil for their lives and those of others."

Tyrande stared into the eyes of the orc. Beast he was to the rest, but once more he had spoken words of eloquence, of meaning. She touched his rough cheek, smiling slightly. How arrogant her people were to see only the image, not the heart and mind.

"You need not confess to me, Broxigar. You've already confessed to your heart and soul, which means that the spirits and Elune have heard your remorse. They understand that you have realized the truth of things and regret your earlier thoughts."

He grunted, then, to her surprise, kissed her palm. "I give thanks to you even still, shaman."

At that moment, the horns sounded. Tyrande quickly touched the orc on the forehead, adding a slight prayer. "Whatever fate battle holds for you now, Broxigar, the Mother Moon will watch over your own spirit."

"I thank you for saying so, shaman. I will trouble you no more now."

Brox raised his ax in respect, then trotted off. Tyrande watched the orc vanish among the other fighters, then turned as a signal she recognized as coming from the sisterhood alerted her to her own need for haste. She had to be ready to lead her own group forward as soon as the host began to move. She had to be ready to meet the fate that Elune had planned for *her*.

And that, she understood, included matters other than the coming battle.

"They added soldiers from two more settlements in the northwest," Rhonin commented as he and Krasus rode. "I heard as many as five hundred."

"The Burning Legion can bring forth such a number in but a few scant hours, perhaps even less."

The red-haired wizard gave his former tutor a sour expression. "If none of this helps, then why bother? Why not just sit on the grass and wait for the demons to slit our gullets?" He took on a mock look of surprise. "Oh, wait! That's not what happened! The night elves *did* fight—and they won!"

"Quiet!" hissed Krasus, giving Rhonin as sharp a glare as the human had given him. "I do not downplay the additions, only point out the facts. Another fact to be recalled is that our presence here and the existence of the anomaly through all time means that what *has* happened in the past may not be what *will* happen this time. There is a very, *very* good chance that the Burning Legion *will* triumph now . . . and all we know will never have been."

"I won't let that happen! I *can't!*"

"To eternity, the fates of your mate Vereesa and your unborn twins are nothing, Rhonin . . . but I will fight for their sakes as much as I fight for my own flight's future, however monstrous that may still be even with victory."

Rhonin quieted. He knew as well as the dragon mage what fate would eventually befall the red flight. Even if the Burning Legion was defeated in this period, the dragons would still suffer terribly. Deathwing the Destroyer would see to it that the orcs gained control of them, especially Krasus's own red flight, and used them as beasts of war. Many, many dragons would die for no good reason.

"But there was just beginning to be hope for us again," Krasus added, his stare drifting momentarily. "And *that,* more than anything else, gives me another reason to see that history does not change."

"I only know what happened from the histories preserved by the wizards of Dalaran, Krasus. You know them from living this time—"

The gaunt, almost elven figure hissed again. "Your recollections based on the writings are likely more accurate than my own riddled mind. I have come to the conclusion that Nozdormu's intrusion into my thoughts, while helpful in setting us on this mission, also were too much for me to absorb completely without the loss of other memories." Nozdormu, the Aspect of Time, had been the one to call upon Krasus and warn him of the crisis. The huge, sand-colored dragon now could not be contacted even in this period, and Krasus feared that he was, in all his incarnations, trapped in the anomaly. "I fear that I will never entirely recall this time period—and what is missing is enough to fuel my uncertainties as to the outcome."

"So we fight and hope for the best."

"As has been done by everyone in battle throughout history, yes."

The bearded human nodded grimly. "Suits me just fine."

On and on the night elven forces traveled, advancing miles without pause or delay. Most of the soldiers marched with high spirits, for it seemed that the enemy was not at all eager to match blades with them. With ears sharper than any of the creatures around him, Krasus heard soldiers pointing out that much of the destruction and death caused by the demons had been on unsuspecting and ill-prepared innocents. Once they had faced an organized resistance, the demons themselves had been slaughtered. Some even speculated that if the night elves had pursued the Burning Legion back to Zin-Azshari after that first battle instead of withdrawing to gather more strength, then the war would have already been over.

Such comments bothered Krasus; it was one thing to go into battle with confidence, another to believe the foe so easily defeated. The night elves had to understand that the Burning Legion was death incarnate.

His gaze turned to the one night elf who seemed to realize some of this. Krasus recalled that Malfurion would be a key to winning this struggle, but he could not remember exactly how. That he was the first of the druids was a significant point, though not the only one. The dragon mage had already determined that everything must be done to protect him.

With nearly most of the night spent, scouts suddenly returned from the southeast. Ravencrest had organized a steady stream of outriders to ensure the most up-to-date information possible.

The three night elves looked quite bedraggled. Clearly, they had ridden their heavily-panting night sabers at a swift pace for some time. Sweat covered their faces and grime colored their garments. Pausing only to sip water, they reported their findings.

"A small column of the fiends is moving methodically through the region of Dy-Jaru, my lord," said the senior scout. "We've seen smoke and fire and sighted refugees heading away."

"Estimate of the enemy's numbers?"

"Difficult to say for certain, but far less than this host, definitely."

Ravencrest tugged on his beard, considering. "Where are the refugees heading?"

"It looks to be Halumar, my lord, but they'll not make it. The demons are on their heels."

"Can we come between them?"

"Aye, if we hurry. There's just enough of a gap."

The noble reached out a hand to one of his aides. "Chart."

Immediately the proper map was handed to Ravencrest. He unrolled it, then had the scouts point out the locations of the refugees and the Burning Legion. When he saw them, he nodded. "We must move up the pace and prepare to meet them in daylight, but it can be done. We will still be on the path to Zin-Azshari. We can afford this minor detour."

"Especially as it might save a few innocent lives," Rhonin muttered under his breath to Brox.

Krasus leaned forward. "Did you mark the demons? What kind did you see?"

"Mostly those called the Fel Guard."

One of the other scouts added, "I saw a couple of the hounds and one of the winged demons, the Doomguard."

The dragon mage frowned. "A meager assortment."

"They no doubt ran far ahead of the rest in their zeal," Lord Ravencrest announced. "We shall teach them the benefits of restraint . . . not that they'll live long enough to appreciate the lesson." To his officers, he commanded, "Give the order! We head to meet them!"

The army shifted almost instantly. The night elves moved with eagerness, ready not only to save their kin, but to taste the first victory in their grand march to the capital.

Illidan and the Moon Guard shifted position, taking up areas along the width of the host. The Sisters of Elune did likewise, their groups poised to aid in whatever way necessary, be it healing or war. As the only outsiders, Rhonin, Krasus, and Brox remained together, although the two wizards had already agreed that Rhonin would watch Illidan once the battle began. Neither still trusted him to be cautious.

Malfurion stayed with them, in great part because Ravencrest was still uncertain over how best to use his unusual abilities. With Captain Shadowsong's unit guarding the four, the noble felt satisfied that the druid would be protected well enough for him to decide on his own what attacks would work against the demons.

Between having studied with Cenarius all day and riding most of the night with the prospect of battle imminent, Malfurion felt his exhaustion growing. The demigod had taught him how to better draw strength from the natural world and Malfurion hoped that he would be given the opportunity to do so before the night elves met the Burning Legion.

The sun rose over the horizon, vanishing quickly into a thick, low cloud cover that actually benefited the host. The spells that Krasus and Rhonin had used on both them and Brox enabled their vision to immediately adjust to the changing light, but the soldiers for the most part had let their eyes grow accustomed in the normal fashion. The cloud cover gave the nocturnal race some relief, further stirring their enthusiasm for the coming conflict.

The scouts continued to ride in and out gathering information. The demons had not yet caught up to the fleeing night elves, but they were close. Encouraged, Ravencrest urged his warriors on. Sending forth a large contingent of night saber riders, he planned to come at the Burning Legion from two sides.

When word came that the host had begun to cut between the refugees and their pursuers, the noble had the horns sounded. The signal set the soldiers into battle readiness.

And at last, as they flowed over a series of low hills, the night elves came upon the foe.

The fiery demons had laid waste to every inch of the land, leaving all scorched. No life existed behind them. The dead lands that Krasus witnessed while astride Korialstrasz spread to the horizon and the horror of it steeled the defenders more.

"It's as the scouts have reported," the master of Black Rook Hold muttered, drawing his sword. "All the better. Now we show them the folly of ravaging our fair land."

Krasus studied the horde. Still a great enemy, but nothing the night elves could not destroy readily. "My lord, caution is still suggested . . ."

But Ravencrest did not hear him. The elder night elf twice waved his sword back and forth, and every horn in the host blared at once.

With a single shout, the night elves descended upon the demons.

The Burning Legion did not falter at the sight of the superior force. Rather, the armored demons roared lustily, eager to add to the carnage that they had already wreaked upon Kalimdor. The refugees forgotten, they surged toward the night elves.

A set of two high notes was followed almost instantly by a wave of arrows that filled the sky. Like shrieking banshees, the bolts dropped among the monstrous warriors, piercing throats, limbs, and heads. Dead and wounded demons toppled over everywhere, forcing others to slow to clamber over them.

A bolt of golden lightning struck the center of the horde, tossing Fel Guard left and right. Gobbets of flesh and the ooze that was the demons' blood rained down upon the survivors. Krasus looked to his left and saw Illidan laughing at the successful results of his first attack. The young sorcerer immediately directed several of the Moon Guard into a pattern akin to the one used during their first battle against the Burning Legion. Illidan planned to draw from his comrades and amplify their power through him.

The dragon mage frowned. Such tactics tended to drain those providing the power more than the one who cast the spell. Should he not pay attention to the condition of his companions, Illidan threatened to weaken them to the point where they could not defend themselves if personally attacked by the Eredar.

But concern for what Malfurion's brother might cause because of his negligence gave way to concentrating on the enemy alone. For the first time, Krasus cast a spell without the aid of Korialstrasz's presence. He did not know what to expect, but when he felt the power build up inside him, the elder conjurer smiled.

A fearsome wind swept over the center of the demons' front ranks. It threw the horned warriors together, even directed their weapons against one another. Mayhem arose among the enemy there.

The chaos gave the night elves a perfect opportunity. As the first of the soldiers reached the demons, they quickly slaughtered those they faced. The Legion's front lines could not maintain any organization. Fel Guard dropped by the scores as they sought in vain to regroup.

Another flight of arrows decimated the ranks farther back. Within minutes, a good quarter of the horde lay either dead or dying. Krasus should have felt more confident, but he still found the battle moving much too easily. The Burning Legion had never fallen with so little trouble.

Not that he could discuss his uncertainty with the others. Brox had slipped in among the fighters and somehow gotten all the way to the front. Astride his night saber, he swung the huge ax around and around. Wherever the weapon's blades cut, the orc left death. The head of a demon flew over Brox as the green-skinned warrior shouted his challenge to the enemy.

As for Rhonin, he cast spells whose intensity made Krasus envious. Touching upon the green flames that were an inherent part of the demons, the red-haired wizard made them truly fiery and, in a sense, caused the demons to consume themselves. One after another they fell, quickly reducing to ash and a few bits of armor. Rhonin's expression was among the grimmest that Krasus had seen among the defenders; the dragon mage had no doubt that his former pupil thought constantly of his wife and unborn children, whose future literally hung on victory in this war.

Where was Malfurion? At first the lanky wizard could not spot the druid, but then he saw the young night elf at the rear of the host. Malfurion sat quietly atop his mount, his eyes closed in concentration. Krasus felt nothing at first, but then he noted a pressure in the earth, a pressure that moved toward the Burning Legion. With his magical senses, he followed its path, curious as to what would happen.

And suddenly, beneath the first few rows of the horde, roots sprouted up. Tree roots, grass roots . . . any and every sort of root that one could imagine. Krasus realized that Malfurion had caused them to not only stretch forth from the untainted ground, but to grow as most could never possibly do under natural conditions.

A horned warrior stumbled, then, with a startled roar, fell forward into the waiting blade of a night elf. A felbeast growled and snapped as its massive paws became entangled. Everywhere demons tripped, twisted, and battled just to keep standing. They made for easy prey and scores more perished because of the roots. However, none of the night elves, Krasus saw, had even the slightest difficulty with the tendrils. In fact, several times the roots cleared paths for the soldiers, further aiding their cause.

With less than half of the demons still fighting, victory was surely at hand . . . and yet Krasus did not trust in the host's success. He surveyed the entire scene, finding nothing to add credence to his concerns.

Nothing, that is, save one lone winged demon flying up into the cloud cover. Krasus watched him ascend, then quickly tried to cast a spell.

He caught the demon just before the creature would have vanished into the clouds. The mist itself wrapped around the Doomguard warrior like a shroud, sealing his wings to his tall, armored form. The demon struggled, but could do nothing. A moment later, he dropped like a deadly missile toward his own comrades.

Krasus did not congratulate himself for his quick action. Urging his mount toward Lord Ravencrest, he sought the noble's attention. Unfortunately, Ravencrest moved away from him as he, in turn, attempted to give commands to some of his soldiers.

The dragon mage peered up at the clouds. There was still a chance. If the night elves were warned quickly enough, disaster could yet be averted.

Then a tingling coursed through his body. Krasus lost control of his limbs. He slumped over the shoulders of his panther, and would have fallen off if not for the girth of the beast. Too late did Krasus realize that his fears for the host had left him momentarily open to the attack of an Eredar warlock.

And as he struggled to overcome the spell, Krasus's gaze twisted skyward. The clouds had thickened, darkened. They seemed to sag from their immense weight . . .

No . . . all that he saw was illusion, and he knew it. Fighting both the warlock's attack and the vision above, Krasus finally pierced the facade the demons had cast on the stormy sky. The swelling bottoms of the clouds vanished, revealing the truth.

From out of the heavens, the Burning Legion rained down upon the defenders.

SIX

Malfurion sensed something amiss even as his spell took full effect. The plants had been all too pleased to be a part of his desire, for they found the demons an abhorrence. With silent coaxing, he made them expand to lengths far greater than normal, then manipulated them so that they were more like the squirming, seeking tentacles of a kraken than simply roots. By doing so, he had enabled the soldiers to slay many of the demons.

But from another point far from the battle, his heightened senses detected a wrongness which he realized had to be a protective spell. Without opening his eyes, Malfurion reached out and discovered that the source lay not anywhere on the ground, but rather high above.

In the clouds.

Still seeing with the powers taught him by Cenarius, the druid delved into the cloud cover and sought what attempted to be hidden.

And in his mind Malfurion saw hundreds of airborne demons.

They were Doomguard for the most, so many that Malfurion could only assume that they had been gathered from other parts of the horde just for this. With their savage weapons and horrific faces, they were terrible to behold. Alone, they would be a terrible enough foe to confront.

Even more unnerving, however, were those that flew among them. There were Eredar warlocks, scores of them. They had no wings, but kept aloft through spells. Watching them, Malfurion knew that some kept the illusion consistent while others already sought out weaknesses in the night elven forces.

But as terrible as all this was, what soared toward the battle, from behind the Doomguard and Eredar, shook Malfurion the most. As if launched by a thousand catapults, huge, fiery rocks descended with terrible precision through the clouds. The druid pressed harder, avoiding the warlocks' senses as best he could, and saw the missiles for what they truly were.

Infernals.

Eyes snapping open, Malfurion shouted to any who could hear, "Beware the skies! They attack us from the skies!"

He caught Lord Stareye's attention briefly, but the noble simply sniffed his direction, then focused again on the demons' decimated ranks. Malfurion pushed his mount forward and seized one of the sentinels.

"Sound the warning! The demons attack us through the clouds!"

But the soldier only looked at him in befuddlement, not understanding. The illusion above still held, and any who looked upward surely thought the druid mad.

Finally, Malfurion saw another who seemed to understand. Krasus crossed his field of vision, the mysterious and pale mage seeming frantic about something. As their gazes met, both realized that the other understood. Krasus pointed, not at Ravencrest but rather at Illidan. Malfurion nodded, catching his meaning immediately; the druid had to warn one of the few who could quickly react to the threat above.

"Illidan!" Malfurion shouted, standing in the saddle in the hopes that his twin would see him. Illidan, though, was far too caught up in his spells to notice anything.

Concentrating, Malfurion asked the wind to aid him. When it agreed, he had it concentrate its efforts. Guiding it with his finger, the druid rubbed his own cheek twice.

His brother abruptly touched his cheek in turn, the wind having imitated Malfurion's touch. Illidan glanced over his shoulder and saw his twin.

Pointing skyward, Malfurion made a warning expression. Illidan almost turned away, but Malfurion grew angry and glared. His brother finally looked up.

At that moment, the first of the demons dropped through the illusion.

The Eredar struck the moment that they were visible, casting spells in unison that swept over the night elves' lines. Heavy droplets fell upon the soldiers, causing no major concern until the first began burning through armor and flesh. Cries arose from those struck as the shower became a monstrous downpour. Night elves fell writhing as their faces were seared away.

Malfurion spoke with the wind again, asking it to blow the torrent away from his people. As he did, he sensed Illidan and the Moon Guard casting their own spells.

One of the warlocks exploded with a shriek, one of the Doomguard nearby also perishing. However, when the night elven sorcerers sought to slay others, their attacks were met by an invisible shield.

The strong wind summoned by the druid pushed away the horrendous downpour, but the damage had already been done. The defenders' lines faltered.

Then, the Infernals began dropping.

The initial wave did not reach the earth. Two exploded and several more suddenly bounced against empty air, soaring in random directions away from the night elves. A bolt of blue lightning cut through one, two, three demons in rapid succession.

But despite the efforts of the sorcerers, the wizards, and the druid, too many of the Infernals descended. One struck the center of the already-ravaged line with catastrophic results. A dozen catapults filled with explosive powders could have done only a fraction of the havoc the single demon did. Like leaves in the wind, the night elves were tossed about. The shock of the strike sent others tumbling to the ground, where the Fel Guard quickly and viciously dispatched them.

More Infernals struck in rapid succession. All order fled the defenders' front. Worse, each massive demon who landed then rose from the steaming craters that they had created and began barreling through the night elves.

The powerful roots that Malfurion had summoned proved ineffectual against the skull-faced Infernals, who ripped through them as if they were nothing. By the scores the fiery behemoths pounded the night elves, wreaking mayhem wherever they moved.

Then a lance lost by a fallen soldier rose into the air just before one Infernal. Blazing blue, it suddenly shot toward the demon at a speed that made even the Infernal appear sluggish. As it flew with unerring accuracy at the demon, the lance grew, its head transforming into a sharp, almost needlelike point.

It skewered the one Infernal with such ease that the demon did not at first realize he was dead. The behemoth gaped, then twitched madly. His forward momentum ceased as the lance, propelled by magic, continued to drive ahead.

As if no heavier than an infant, the huge Infernal was dragged backward. The lance continued to speed up, catching another Infernal just as he emerged from the crater. The demon had time only to stare wide-eyed before it, too, was impaled.

Its swiftness not in the least decreasing, the magical spear caught a third Infernal unaware. Only then did its momentum cease and the missile and its victims dropped among the dead.

From Malfurion's side, Rhonin, his brow furrowed, nodded his satisfaction. But just when it appeared that the defenders might turn the battle again, horns sounded from the north.

"The Legion!" Krasus shouted. "They come from the other side!"

The full, awful truth now lay revealed. As if rising from the earth itself, an immense horde emerged from the north and fell upon the soldiers there. Like those above, they had been hidden by a spell. Now they swarmed like ants. The night elves fought valiantly, but their already-damaged lines buckled under the new onslaught.

The demons had planned their trap well, relying much on the arrogance of the night elves. What Ravencrest had seen as a minor skirmish, an easy victory with which to stoke the courage of his troops, had been instead a costly, sinister trick.

"We've got to retreat!" Rhonin said. "It's the only way at this point!"

At first, it appeared that Lord Ravencrest would not do what needed to be done. No signal to retreat came even though the demons pressed hard. Infernals continued to drop upon the night elves and the Eredar, some protecting the others, cast one vile spell after another. Malfurion and his companions could no longer attack; they had to do everything they could simply to deflect most of the warlocks' assaults. Even the Moon Guard could do little but shield the battered host.

Finally, the horns called out for retreat. The Burning Legion gave no quarter, though, and each step back was bought with more blood.

"This attrition is too great!" Krasus hissed, joining the druid. "We must create a gap between us and them!"

"But how?" asked Malfurion.

The slim mage's expression grew darker yet. "We must cease trying to fight the Eredar and concentrate only on keeping the main force of the demons from us!"

"But the warlocks will strike hard while we do that! They'll slay countless soldiers—"

"And *more* will perish if we move at this snail's pace!"

Krasus spoke the truth, however much the druid did not wish to hear it. The Fel Guard whittled away at the night elves left and right, constantly cutting at whatever foe lay within reach. The Eredar, on the other hand, needed time to cast their spells, and while those also did terrible damage, overall they now did less than the blades of their comrades.

"You must tell your brother to do as we do," the mage instructed.

"He won't listen to me. Not for that." It had been trouble enough to make Illidan look up. To convince him to do as Krasus desired would take far too long, if it was even possible.

"*I'll* do it," Rhonin offered. "He may listen to me better."

In truth, Illidan looked up to the human. Rhonin knew how to cast spells even Malfurion's twin could not yet handle. Illidan almost saw him as a *shan'do*.

"Do what you can, then," Krasus said to Rhonin.

As the fire-tressed wizard rode off, Malfurion asked, "What do we do?"

"Anything that separates them from us."

The druid had hoped for more, but he understood that Krasus did not wish to overly guide him. They would work best if each did what they felt was most comfortable. The ways of the elder mage were not necessarily those of Malfurion.

Without waiting to see what the night elf would attempt, Krasus gestured toward the battle. At first Malfurion could not tell what he did, but then he noticed the foremost demons seem to shrink a foot or two. Only after a moment more did he see that they struggled with a sudden bog that had opened up beneath their feet. Those behind them clustered together, trying to battle through to the other side.

Rather than trying to attack again, the night elves wisely continued their retreat. But Krasus had only managed to aid *one* area of the battle; in others, Malfurion saw that the demons continued to cut down the defenders. He immediately reached down and spoke to the plants again, asking that they give of themselves their roots once more. They knew the dire developments and were aware that once the night elves left, they and all other life would be purged by the Legion. Nevertheless, they freely offered what they could.

Tears rolling down his eyes at this sacrifice, Malfurion carefully crafted his spell. The roots came up in even greater clusters than previously, becoming a veritable forest in reverse. The demons hacked away at the strong tendrils. Even the Infernals were finally slowed. The druid felt each cut into the roots, but his spell had the effect that he had intended. More and more, the night elves pulled away from their devious foe.

An unexpected reprieve came in the south in the form of night saber riders. Malfurion had forgotten about the force sent earlier by Ravencrest. Their numbers were smaller than he recalled, though they fought with no less fury. Several of the panthers had wounds already and more than one rider looked battered, but still they cut into the Burning Legion, buying precious seconds for those comrades on foot.

"The north!" Krasus shouted. "Focus on the north!"

Although they could not physically see the struggle in the north, both Malfurion and the mage had other methods by which to observe it. Reaching out, the druid sought birds or winged insects. He found none of the former, but still a few of the latter. Even the smallest fauna understood that to stay near the demons was to invite death. Yet the beetles he came across, already in the process of fleeing, agreed to be his eyes.

Through their peculiar field of vision, the druid soon viewed the other end of the struggle. What he saw made his heart sink. In even more vast numbers than he had ever seen them, the Burning Legion poured over the soldiers. The dead lay scattered everywhere. Faces too much like his own stared sightlessly in horror at what had slain them. Felbeasts tossed the dead around while other demons eagerly sought to add to the piles.

Malfurion looked for some creature or plant that he could use, but only the beetles seemed present. A breeze blew one of the insects about, finally giving the druid an idea. Speaking with the wind through the beetle, he first told it how much he admired its forceful gale, then convinced it to show him more.

The wind responded obligingly, creating a dust devil. With more urging by Malfurion, the dust devil grew larger and larger, soon dwarfing the huge demons. As it swelled in size, its intensity also increased a hundredfold.

When it had grown powerful enough, the druid directed its force against the demons in the forefront.

The Burning Legion ignored the fierce wind at first . . . that is, until it engulfed the first few and threw them to their deaths. Those nearest then scattered, but now they were pursued by a full-fledged tornado. Malfurion felt no pity for the demons, and hoped that they would soon be joined by many of their comrades.

"Do not grow overconfident," came Krasus's voice. "Our tactics have bought the army time, but nothing more."

The druid did not have to be told that, but he said nothing. The night elves were in no state to turn events around. All that Malfurion and the other spellcasters had done simply enabled the soldiers to survive.

Not satisfied that he had done enough, Malfurion sought through the beetles' eyes anything else that might be of use against the demons. The insects fluttered bravely over the Burning Legion, giving him five views simultaneously. Surely there had to be *something* that—

The druid screamed as something seized one of the beetles and crushed the life from it. Two of the survivors immediately fluttered away, but the remaining pair turned, giving the shaking night elf a glimpse at what had killed the hapless insect.

In the midst of the demons stood a dark-skinned figure who towered over the rest of the Burning Legion. He strode like a giant among his children, calmly directing the fearsome warriors in their monstrous efforts. Vaguely he reminded Malfurion of the Eredar, but was as much above them as they were above the Infernals. He wore elaborate shoulder armor and surveyed the violent battlefield with analytical indifference. From his right hand, the massive demon dropped the bits of shell that were all that remained of the beetle . . . then stared directly at one of those still being used by Malfurion.

And into the druid's mind.

So . . . you are the one.

An intense pressure filled Malfurion's head. He felt as if his brain was expanding, pressing against his skull.

Malfurion tried to call out for help, but his mouth would not work. In desperation, he sought the aid of anything near the demon, something that would distract the druid's attacker before it was too late.

Deep within the earth, something stirred. The rocks themselves, the eldest and hardiest of living forms, woke from their eternal slumber. They touched Malfurion with anger at first, for few things mattered to them more than their sleep. But the druid quickly focused their attention on what lay in the wake of the Burning Legion's rampage, pointing especially to the landscape itself.

Few there were who understood that rock lived, much less had any sense of the world. Now those he had awakened discovered the awful truth about the demons—that even the earth itself could not escape death at their hands. The foul magic that was an inherent part of the demons killed *everything*. Nothing, no matter how deeply buried, ever escaped.

And that fate included even the rocks. Those that lay buried behind the Burning Legion lacked any sentience whatsoever. Their life essences had been destroyed as readily as the blades of the Fel Guard killed night elves.

Malfurion fell to one knee as the demon's attack squeezed his skull tight. It became impossible to think. The druid started to black out . . .

The ground rumbled. Malfurion dropped to both knees. Oddly, the pressure in his head now decreased.

Through the eyes of the beetles, he watched with astonishment as crevices opened up all around the monstrous figure who had attacked him. A smaller demon nearby tumbled into one fissure, which promptly shut on him. Other demons scattered from the area, leaving their gigantic leader to his own defenses.

The indifferent look never left the face of Malfurion's foe, but it was clearly all he could do to keep from falling into one of the many increasingly-vast chasms surrounding him. The sinister colossus reached out toward one of the beetles, but Malfurion immediately ordered both remaining creatures away.

As they retreated, the druid saw the demon draw a circle around himself. An immense green sphere formed, protecting its occupant from the savage quake. It hovered above the chaos even as other, lesser demons spilled into the new ravines.

The deep, monstrous orbs watched in turn the retreating forms.

I will know you, insect . . .

He did not refer to the beetles, but rather Malfurion. As his foe dwindled from sight, the druid realized that he, too, would recognize the demon when next they met. Already Malfurion suspected he knew by what name to call him, for surely this could only be one of the horrific commanders of the monstrous horde.

Surely this could only be *Archimonde*.

Hands seized him by the shoulder, breaking his link to the beetles. Instinctively, Malfurion expected to be torn apart by some other demon, but the hands were gentle, and the voice soft and caring.

"I have you, Malfurion," Tyrande whispered in his ears.

He could only nod. Vaguely noticing that he was no longer seated atop his night saber, Malfurion wondered what had become of the animal. Tyrande gently drew him up onto her own mount. Showing surprising strength, she hefted him in front of her, then urged the massive feline on.

Heart still pounding, Malfurion caught bits and pieces of the catastrophe as the priestess of Elune carried him off. Hundreds of soldiers trudged quickly over the rolling landscape as, far in the background, demons pursued them. In several places, flames rose between the forces, and here and there an explosion caused by some spell was punctuated by screams—whether night elf or demon, he could not say. Once, Malfurion witnessed the personal banner of Lord Ravencrest flutter by, but he saw no sign of the noble himself.

Faces passed across his vision as the night saber brought Tyrande and him to safety. Gone from the soldiers was the look of expectant triumph. In its place a terrible truth could now be witnessed; it was very possible that the night elves might *lose* this struggle.

He must have moaned upon seeing this, for Tyrande leaned close to his ear, whispering, "Never fear, Malfurion . . . I'll attend to your wounds the moment we can pause."

The druid managed to twist around and see her face. Much of it was hidden behind the war helmet of the sisterhood. The rest was covered in grime—and blood. From the determination with which Tyrande moved, Malfurion gathered the blood was not hers. It startled him to think that she had likely gotten closer to the heart of the battle than he had. He had always thought her calling a more gentle one, even with the armor.

"T-tyrande," the druid finally managed. "The others?"

"I've seen Broxigar, the wizards, and your brother all. Even the erstwhile Captain Shadowsong, who guides them like a protective herder." She said the last with an all-too-brief smile.

"Ravencrest?"

"He is still master of Black Rook Hold."

So, even after many losses, the core strength behind the host remained intact. Still, neither Ravencrest nor his many spellcasters had been able to prevent the disaster.

"Tyrande—"

"Hush, Malfurion. It amazes me that you can still speak, considering all that has happened to you."

He understood the intensity of the mental assault Archimonde had thrust at him, but did not know how she could have sensed it.

The priestess suddenly held him close. While Malfurion welcomed her touch gladly, he did not like the anxiousness he felt.

"Elune must have truly watched over you! So many ripped apart around you, even your own mount stripped bare, a horrific tangle of flesh and bone—and you barely marked."

Ripped apart . . . his own night saber torn to pieces . . . what had happened around him? Why had he not noticed the butchery? How had he survived all that in addition to the mental attack? The very notion of the terrible spectacle that had taken place unnoticed around him made him shiver.

Malfurion had no answers to his questions, but he did understand one thing. He had survived what had been thrown at him by one of the archdemons. On the one hand, he could be grateful for the miracle; on the other, he was aware that he had now been marked by Archimonde. They would meet again, that was almost assured.

And when they did, Malfurion knew the demon lord would do his best to make certain that next time, there would be no escape.

SEVEN

Peroth'arn struggled wearily into his personal chamber, finally free to recuperate a little of the strength that his constant work on the portal had drained from him. Before leaving to take personal command of the demonic horde, Archimonde had laid in place a concise plan by which the portal would gradually be adapted to withstand the entrance of the great Sargeras. Unlike Mannoroth, who flung the Highborne sorcerers into their work with no regard for their flagging power, Archimonde recognized that the night elves would not survive long enough to fulfill their duty if they did not have a chance to sleep or eat. He worked them hard, yes, but the respites he gave them actually had enabled the work to advance as never before, even under the guidance of Lord Xavius.

Thinking of his former master, Peroth'arn could not help but look over his shoulder. The room—a small chamber with but a wooden bed, a table, and a brass oil lamp—was filled with shadows, each of them reminding the sorcerer of the thing that had emerged after the glorious Archimonde. That the beast who walked on two legs had once been Xavius unnerved most of the Highborne. They had all lived in fear of the queen's advisor when he had been one of them, but now he radiated an unsettling presence that of late even haunted Peroth'arn's dreams.

Trying to shake off such concerns, the night elf distastefully inspected the bed. He was as dedicated to the work as they all were, but as one of the Highborne he was used to far better accommodations. He longed for his villa and his mate, neither of whom he had seen in days. Mannoroth had permitted no one to leave the palace, and in that, he and Archimonde were in full agreement. Therefore, the sorcerers had to sleep wherever they could—in this case, chambers once used by the officers of the guard. Captain Varo'then had willingly offered them up to the spellcasters, but Peroth'arn could have sworn that the scarred soldier had done so with a slight wry smile. Varo'then and his underlings were used to a more spartan existence and Peroth'arn suspected that they enjoyed the discomfort the sorcerers now had to endure for the sake of the cause.

But all would be worth it when the lord of the Legion made his entrance. The world would be expunged of the unclean, the undeserving. Only the Highborne, the most perfect of Azshara's subjects, would survive. Peroth'arn and others like him would populate a fresh, remade land, creating a paradise as none had ever before dreamed.

There would be much work after, of course. As had been explained to them by the queen, the Burning Legion had to raze what already existed out of necessity. The world would have to begin from scratch. Much would be expected from the Highborne, but boundless were the rewards their efforts would reap.

With a martyr's sigh, Peroth'arn sat down on the hard bed. Once paradise was created, a softer, more lush place to sleep would be among his first requests.

He had barely put his head to the gray lump that acted as his pillow when a voice whispered in his ear.

"So much sacrifice . . . so much hardship undeserved . . ."

Peroth'arn bolted to a sitting position. Again he peered around the chamber, but saw nothing save the horribly-unadorned walls and meager, undecorated furniture.

"Forced to take such squalor . . . you are to be admired, dear Peroth'arn . . ."

A sharp intake of breath was the Highborne's only response as a piece of shadow detached itself from a corner. Onyx eyes with streaks of ruby coursing across them fixed upon the startled sorcerer.

"Xavius . . ."

The satyr's hooves clattered ever so slightly as he moved closer to Peroth'arn. "I lived that name once," he murmured. "It doesn't mean as much to me as it did then."

"What are you doing here?"

Xavius chuckled, a sound much like the bleat of the creature he resembled. "I know your ambition, Peroth'arn. I know your dreams and how hard you've struggled for them."

Despite his distrust of the horned figure, the night elf felt a sense of appreciation. No one else seemed to understand all that he contributed. Not even the queen or Archimonde.

"I pushed you hard, you know, because I expected much from you, my friend."

Peroth'arn had not known and hearing it now from his former master made his chest swell with pride. Lord Xavius had been the bar by which the other Highborne had measured their skills. He had been the unparalleled master of his craft. Who else would willingly forfeit their own eyes to better understand the powers that they wielded? There was no sacrifice asked of the others that the advisor himself had not first suffered.

"I . . . I am honored."

Tilting his head, the horned satyr grinned. For some reason, Peroth'arn did not find that grin as frightening as he had earlier.

"No . . . 'tis *I* who am honored, good Peroth'arn . . . and I come now in the hope that I may be honored even more."

"I don't understand, my—I don't understand."

"A little wine?" The hooved figure produced a flask from the air and offered it to the night elf. Peroth'arn opened the flask and sniffed. The heady bouquet thrilled his senses. Surely this was rainbow flower wine, his personal favorite.

Xavius leaned near. "From her own cellar . . ." he said, leering. "But we can keep that secret between us, eh?"

The thought of so bold a transgression against Azshara initially stunned the sorcerer, but then thrilled him. Xavius had performed this act of betrayal against the queen just for Peroth'arn's sake. Azshara had executed loyal subjects for far less.

"Captain Varo'then would be aghast," Peroth'arn suggested.

"He is not one of us . . . and therefore not a concern."

"True." To the rest of the Highborne, the captain and his soldiers were a necessary evil. They were servants of the queen, to be certain, but they lacked the noble blood and flamboyant airs of the others. Most of the Highborne considered them no better than those who had once lived beyond the walls of the palace, but never let such notions show in their expressions. Captain Varo'then had ways of quietly dealing with those who showed him contempt.

"Drink," Xavius urged, pushing the flask up.

With the mouth of the bottle already near his lips, Peroth'arn saw no reason to hesitate anymore. He let the gentle liquid flow over his tongue and down his throat. His entire body tingled as he swallowed the rare vintage.

"A long-overdue reward," Xavius said. "One of many."

"Delicious."

His hooved companion nodded. The more he sat with the satyr, the less Peroth'arn feared Xavius. The former advisor gave him the respect he so richly deserved. That was truly an honor for the night elf, for was not Xavius now a much respected servant of the great Sargeras? Was he not now more to the lord of the Legion than all the Highborne combined?

"He watches you, too," the satyr commented quietly, as if passing a secret to a trusted comrade.

" 'He'? You mean—"

"*All* are under his wise gaze, even from so far away." A tapering finger thrust at the sorcerer. "But some are observed more than others . . . in the hopes that they may be groomed for further greatness."

Peroth'arn was speechless. *Sargeras* had marked him so? He quickly downed another huge gulp of wine, his eyes wide and calculating. How the others would have envied him.

"To his enemies, Sargeras is death incarnate, but to those who serve him well, he is benevolence unbridled." Xavius guided the flask to Peroth'arn's lips again. "He took me from beyond. He drew me back and granted me not only life again, but a special place at his side."

Stretching to his full length, the satyr displayed his form for Peroth'arn. Seeing it now as a precious gift of the great god, the night elf admired it. In truth, Xavius was now much more than he had been in his previous life. His features were broader, more imposing. Xavius looked stronger, more agile despite the hooves. It was also evident that he had an even greater mastery of the arts. Peroth'arn could sense the power radiating from his former master and suddenly felt pangs of jealousy. This was power such as he, too, deserved.

Perhaps the wine had made Peroth'arn not so cautious in guarding his emotions, for suddenly Xavius pulled away from him as if struck. The satyr nearly melted back into the shadows. Peroth'arn clutched the flask tightly, fearing that he had offended one blessed by the god.

But as quickly as he had retreated, Xavius returned to him. The satyr loomed over the seated night elf, staring deep into Peroth'arn's eyes. The sorcerer could not look away.

"No . . ." whispered Xavius half to himself. "It is too soon . . . but . . . he said that I must find those worthy . . . perhaps I could . . . yes . . . but to take on such a mantle, one would need the strength and resolve . . . dare I hope that *you* have such resolve, friend Peroth'arn?"

Leaping from the bed, Peroth'arn gasped, "I have whatever strength and resolve you need! I would do anything to be more worthy of my queen and Sargeras! Grant me the chance to be one of the worthy, I beg you!"

"It is a fearsome path you would take, dear Peroth'arn . . . but you would rise above the other Highborne! You would be under my guidance! All who beheld you would know you for one blessed by the lord of the Legion! Your power would grow tenfold and more! You would be the envy of all others, the first to join me!"

"Yes!" roared the night elf. "I will do whatever I must, Lord Xavius! Do not forsake me! I am worthy, I swear! Grant me this gift!"

The horned figure grinned, a sight that now filled his companion not with anxiousness, but rather with hope. "Yes, my dear Peroth'arn . . . I believe you. I believe that you are indeed worthy to take on the aspect of one of his most trusted, just as I have."

"I am."

"Your world will never be the same . . . it will be far better."

Peroth'arn set the flask on the bed, then went down on one knee. "If I can be accepted here and now, I ask that it be so. Please say it is possible!"

The grin grew wider. "Oh, it can be done now."

"Then I plead with you, Xavius—make me as you are! Give me the blessing of the god so that I may be a more perfect servant! I am worthy!"

"As you wish." Taking a step back, Xavius seemed to grow. He filled Peroth'arn's view completely. The ruby streaks in the satyr's eyes flared wildly.

"It may cause you some pain at first," he murmured to his convert, "but you will have no choice other than to endure it."

Xavius raised his clawed hands high . . .

But as the spell struck him, Peroth'arn shrieked. He felt as if his body were being stripped to the bone bit by bit. The agony was like none he could have ever imagined. Tears filled his eyes and, unable to articulate words, he pleaded by moans for the pain to end. This was not what he wanted.

"No," responded the satyr, ignoring his pleas. "We must finish now."

And the screams rose to new, horrific levels. That which had once been

Peroth'arn would hardly have been recognizable to his fellow Highborne. His body constantly mutated, pushed slowly and deliberately by Xavius's power to what he desired. The screams became sobs, but even they did not disturb the satyr's dark work, no matter how loud they, too, eventually became.

"Yes . . ." Xavius said with a gleam in his unholy orbs. "Unleash the pain. Unleash the fury. No one beyond this chamber will hear. You may scream as much as you like . . . just as *I* did." His grin grew savage, animalistic. "It is little enough to suffer for the glory of Sargeras . . ."

The night elves had thought that the demons would pause somewhere along the way. They had expected that when they returned to Suramar they would at least be able to regroup and hold the enemy. And they had been certain that, if all else failed, Black Rook Hold would become their sanctuary.

They were wrong on all counts. Rhonin and Krasus understood why before Lord Ravencrest or any of the other night elves did. They had seen foremost the work of Archimonde, the sinister giant who, for a very good reason, commanded the Legion with the foul blessing of his master.

"He will give us no respite," the dragon mage said, putting to voice what both had long thought. He absently touched his chest where he had adhered the scale, recalling Archimonde's unholy relentlessness.

"He'll run the demons into the ground before he lets that happen," Rhonin agreed. "But we'll all collapse long before they ever do."

The night elves tried in vain to stop the rout at Suramar, if only so that the Hold could be readied for their entrance. It was hardly large enough to contain the population of the area, much less the huge force Ravencrest had gathered, but the noble had hoped that securing it would steel the hearts of his followers again. That, however, was not to be. There was not even time to enter the edifice. The soldiers held long enough for the civilians to flee behind them, but that was it. There was no chance to make Black Rook Hold ready and, to his credit, Ravencrest did not seek shelter there while the Burning Legion crushed all else.

"Never would I have thought the Hold so useless!" he snarled at Illidan. "But our host is too great despite our losses and if we sit here, the demons will chop away at those left outside, then starve those within."

"Surely we can survive a siege!" Malfurion's twin insisted.

"Against others, aye, but these will not tire and leave! They will destroy all around us, then wait for the inevitable!" The bearded night elf shook his head. "I will not let our end be so ignoble!"

After less than a day, they abandoned Suramar to the enemy, aware that nothing would be left to rebuild should the Burning Legion eventually be defeated. Wherever the demons marched, nothing remained but ruin. Even before the last glimpse of the city dwindled in the distance, the defenders could see the massive trees toppling, the walls collapsing under the relentless onslaught.

But even though so much of the Burning Legion had to be taking part in Suramar's demise, those stalking the army continued after as if undrained of even a single warrior. So far there had been only one slim benefit to the lengthy retreat and that being the fading airborne threats. The Eredar still cast what spells they could to harass the night elves, but their demanding efforts had clearly exhausted them. The Infernals' attacks had also lessened, at least from above. However, they still barreled ahead of the other demons, striking the defenders' lines whenever the opportunity arose.

Day faded into night, then night into day, and still Ravencrest's force was pushed back. More than one night saber rider lay asleep atop their mounts, and many a foot soldier eyed them with envy. Those who were stronger aided the ones beginning to falter. Worse, the population of refugees ahead of the soldiers grew with each hour, and they lacked the coordination and stamina of the fighters. Generations of peace had left them unprepared for such a catastrophe, and soon the army found itself merging unwillingly with the weary civilians.

"Get along there!" shouted Jarod Shadowsong to a number of slow-moving figures in front of him and his charges. "You can't stop in the middle of this! Keep going!"

Krasus frowned. "This will only worsen. Ravencrest will be unable to maintain order even over his soldiers if they and the refugees become too entangled. This is exactly what Archimonde desires."

"But what can we do?" Rhonin's eyes had deep shadows. Like the others, he had not truly rested since before the trap had been sprung. Of all of them, only Brox looked at all fit. Having grown up in wartime, the orc had been forced many times to survive days without sleep. Still, even he appeared ready to nap if given the chance.

In fact, it was Brox who answered Rhonin's question, but not in words. With their own party becoming as trapped by the flow of refugees as the rest of the armed force, the orc began taking action. Pushing ahead of Jarod and the bodyguard, Brox roared at the nearest of the mob and swung his ax around his head. He was such a sight to behold that the night elves fearfully started to open the way for him.

"No!" he rumbled. "Ahead! No going that way! Ahead only! Help others!"

And as his companions watched, the grotesque figure began herding the refugees as if he had been doing the same with cattle or sheep all his life. None of the night elves sought his fury and they obeyed his commands to the letter.

Jarod quickly took up his example, spreading the guard unit wide and using them to sweep forward the civilians before his party. Order was soon re-established there and as more officers became aware of what was happening, a true line started to form. With careful deliberation, the armed host herded their charges on. The night elves' pace as a whole picked up.

Yet still the Burning Legion drove them on. Krasus noticed a mountain in the distance, one that struck a vague recollection. He looked to Jarod and asked, "Captain Shadowsong, is there a name to that dire peak?"

"Aye, Master Krasus. It's Mount Hyjal."

"Mount Hyjal . . ." The mage pursed his lips. "Are we driven back so far as that?"

Rhonin noted his expression. Speaking only for Krasus's ears, he asked, "You recall that name?"

"Yes . . . and it means that the night elves' situation is most dire."

The human snorted. "Something we already knew."

Krasus's eyes took on a darker cast. "We cannot permit this retreat to go on much farther. The host must make a stand, Rhonin. If we fall back beyond Mount Hyjal, then surely all is lost."

"Memories stirring?"

"Or simply common sense. Whichever the case, I remain resolved that we can go no farther than the mountain. Despite what history says, I cannot see the night elves triumphing if we fail to make a halt."

"But Lord Ravencrest is already doing all he can and we've worn ourselves out just buying time."

"Then we must do more." The dragon mage raised himself up as much as riding a night saber would permit. "Would that I could find Malfurion. His skill would be one needed now."

"I last saw him with the priestess, Tyrande. He looked as pale as one of his kind could get. He battled something out there that nearly destroyed him."

"Yes, I think it was Archimonde."

"Then Malfurion would be dead."

Krasus shook his head. "No . . . and that is why I wish he were here. Nonetheless, with or without him, we must begin our assault anew."

"Begin *what* anew?"

Rhonin's former mentor turned back toward the direction of the demons. "Yes, we must take the offensive again."

The greatest of the dragons gathered in the Chamber of the Aspects, led there by Alexstrasza and Neltharion. The four Aspects present guided the pro-ceedings, attended only by their consorts and those of the absent Nozdormu.

All other dragons had given of themselves already; but for those of such power as now awaited their turn, the process required more delicacy.

The Earth Warder's three mates remained all but hidden behind him. They were larger than Korialstrasz, but were still dwarfed by the black male. As he studied them, Alexstrasza's youngest consort noted that they seemed but shadows of the Earth Warder, their every movement based upon what Neltharion did or said. The red dragon found this disturbing, but no one else seemed to notice.

The emerald males attending Ysera were slim, almost ghosts in comparison to the other great leviathans. More unsettling, they, like their mistress, moved about with their eyes constantly closed. Yet, beneath those lids, one could see the eyes shift back and forth. The greens constantly existed in two planes, more often than not in the Emerald Dream. They were silent and still, but Korialstrasz felt their magical senses monitoring the situation closely.

Malygos and his mates were a distinct contrast. They were constantly in motion, nudging one another and looking here and there and everywhere. Their blue-white scales glittered in merry little displays of magic and occasionally small details concerning one or the other would alter as the whim struck. Korialstrasz found them more refreshing than the blacks and greens.

Almost as solemn as Ysera and her mates were the four consorts of Nozdormu. They had the same sandy bronze texture as the Aspect, but were more solid than the almost-fluid monarch of Time. Korialstrasz wondered exactly where Nozdormu had gone that he would miss such events. From what little he had gleaned from his queen, it seemed that even the Aspect's mates did not know with certainty what had happened.

Yet, the Timeless One was still here in essence and that was a vital point. In the paws of the eldest of the females stood an hourglass made of what appeared to be pure golden sunlight. Within it, glittering bronze sands flowed not down but up. When the top filled, they then descended, only to begin their upward march once more.

The sands were a part of Nozdormu, set separate by him for urgent need by his flight. All the Aspects supposedly had some part of their essence put aside, for they were more than huge, reptilian beasts. They represented the most powerful forces of the world, the very fabric of its being, created by those who had molded the world itself. True, they were bound by its earthly laws, but they were as much above the other dragons as dragons were the younger races.

The various flights had alternated their offerings, one at a time. Now only two remained, the last, ironically, being Korialstrasz.

For some reason, he did not feel very much honored.

But before Korialstrasz presented himself, the essence of the Timeless

One had to be brought forth. Saridormi, the Aspect's prime mate, carried the hourglass gently in her left forepaw as she stepped up to the Dragon Soul.

Neltharion's creation floated in the very midst of the chamber, its simplistic form radiating a fearsome yet majestic glow. All were bathed in a rainbow of colors that, not coincidentally, matched the shadings of the dragons.

"I come bearing representation of He Who Is Without End, He Who Sees Past, Present, and Future!" Saridormi intoned. She raised the glittering timepiece above the shimmering disk. "In his name I add his strength, his power, his *self*, to this weapon that we will use against the fiends attacking our realm!"

With a single squeeze of her powerful paw, the gargantuan dragon broke the hourglass.

The sand that was the essence of Nozdormu did not fall in a heap, as Korialstrasz had expected. Instead, it swirled out—as if itself a live, sentient thing—and began to spin above the Dragon Soul. As it spun, a light sprinkle of bronze rained down upon the disk. Each particle struck with a brilliant flash, then vanished within.

A bright radiance filled the chamber as the last grain sank inside, a luminous sunburst that momentarily blinded Korialstrasz. He turned his eyes away and did not look again until the light had faded. The red leviathan saw that the rest, even the greens, had been forced to shield their view. Only Neltharion appeared to have watched it all, his wide, avid gaze drinking in everything.

"My love," came Alexstrasza's whisper.

Still ill at ease for reasons he could not explain, Korialstrasz strode forward. By himself, he would have chosen to deny the Dragon Soul his essence, but his queen had asked this boon of him as she had all the others; how could *he* be the only one to say no? Nevertheless, he stared at the talisman as if seeing not the salvation of the world, but something that tainted it.

That was foolish, though, he thought. *For what reason would the Earth Warder do such a heinous thing?*

Then, the Dragon Soul loomed before him. So close, Korialstrasz found nothing insignificant about it. Here was power such as many in the past had dreamt of, and others would do so again for centuries on. Here was the joined essences of all the dragons, the most powerful of the world's children.

"It is waiting for you."

The red dragon looked up into the huge visage of the black. Neltharion never blinked. His breathing came in rapid gasps, as if he grew more and more frenzied with each second that Korialstrasz hesitated.

There is something not right in this . . . Alexstrasza's mate thought. But then he recalled how willingly she, Malygos, and Ysera had given of themselves. Malygos, in fact, had been determined to be the first among them to sacrifice a bit of himself, his way of championing his friend's cause. If the Master of

Magic trusted the work of Neltharion, who was mere Korialstrasz to say otherwise?

And with that thought still hanging over him, the red opened himself up to the Dragon Soul.

The disk flared, bathing him in its daunting illumination. Korialstrasz bared his chest to it and willed away all the natural magical defenses dragons kept about themselves. He felt the Dragon Soul reach into him as he had seen it do to the others, reach in as if his armored hide were nothing but illusion . . .

Seconds later, the unsettling force reemerged from his chest—but with it the Dragon Soul drew something else. It was an intangible, squirming thing—not exactly light, not exactly substance. A faint crimson aura surrounded it, and as the last bit separated from Korialstrasz, he felt a loss that saddened him.

Steeling himself, the red watched as the illumination of the Dragon Soul pulled the offering toward it. Slowly, the light sank back into the disk.

As that which the Dragon Soul had taken from him followed suit, Korialstrasz gasped. He wanted to reach out and take back what was his, but to do so would destroy the effort and, worse, shame him before his beloved Alexstrasza.

And so Korialstrasz watched helplessly as the Dragon Soul absorbed his essence, added it to the others. He watched helplessly as Neltharion snatched the disk almost covetously and held it before the other leviathans.

"It is done . . ." the Earth Warder declared. "All have given that which must be given. I now seal the Dragon Soul forever so that what has been attained will never be lost."

Neltharion shut his eyes. His body took on a black, ominous aura, one that flowed from him to the tiny but mighty talisman in his forepaw.

The other great dragons started. For a moment, a very brief but telling moment, the Dragon Soul burned as black as its creator.

"Should that be?" asked Ysera quietly.

"For it to be as it must, yes," Neltharion replied almost defiantly.

"It is a weapon like no other. It must be like no other," added the knowledgeable Malygos.

The Earth Warder nodded his appreciation for the blue dragon's words. Neltharion gazed around the chamber, seeing if anyone had further questions. A few came to Korialstrasz's mind, but he felt unworthy to ask them in the face of his queen's satisfaction with events.

"The final casting will take time," the black leviathan informed the others. "It has to be taken from here to a place of silence and privacy, where the most delicate castings will be made."

"How long?" asked Alexstrasza. "It must not be too late."

"It will be ready when it needs be ready." And with that, Neltharion spread his wings and rose into the air. His mates followed suit almost perfectly, like puppets whose strings were attached to the Earth Warder.

The other dragons watched as he vanished through what seemed the solid wall of the chamber, then also began taking off. Alexstrasza remained where she was, and so Korialstrasz did likewise.

But as his gaze followed the departing behemoths, his thoughts continued to reflect upon what they had wrought this day. He could never deny the incredible power of the tiny, golden disk. Truly, Neltharion had crafted a weapon the likes of which even the endless hordes of the demons could not stand against.

Nor, for that matter, he realized belatedly, even *dragons*.

EIGHT

Malfurion dreamed. He dreamed that he and Tyrande lived in a beautiful tree home in the midst of grand Suramar. It was the high time of the year and all was in bloom. Lush plant life covered the region like a beautiful carpet. The immense tree cooled them with its thick, shading foliage, and flowers of all colors and patterns surrounded the trunk's base.

Tyrande, clad in a glorious gown of yellow, green, and orange, played a silver lyre while their children, a boy and a girl, darted around the tree, giggling and laughing as they ran. Malfurion sat near the window of his proud abode, breathing in the fresh air and savoring the life he had attained. The world was at peace, and his family knew nothing but happiness . . .

Then, a violent tremor shook the tree. Malfurion clutched the window and saw with horror the homes and towers of Suramar quickly tumble over. Other structures collapsed. People screamed, and massive fires burst to life in every direction.

He looked for his children, but they were nowhere to be found. As for his mate, Tyrande continued to sit on one of the thick branches just outside, her fingers strumming a tune on the lyre.

Daring to lean out, Malfurion shouted, "Tyrande! Come inside! Quickly!"

But she ignored him, blithely caught up in her music despite the growing catastrophe and her own precarious position.

The tree house abruptly tipped. Malfurion tried using his druidic powers to keep it from collapsing, but nothing happened. The tree—all the flora—felt dead to his senses.

The house's fall finally awoke Tyrande. Dropping the lyre, she screamed and reached for Malfurion, but the distance was too great. Malfurion's mate lost her balance and slipped off the branch—

But a figure in black swiftly rose into the air, readily catching her. Illidan smiled magnanimously at Tyrande, then nodded congenially to his brother. However, instead of coming to Malfurion's aid, the other twin began to fly off with his catch.

"Illidan!" Malfurion shouted, trying to maintain his hold. "Come back!"

His sibling paused in midair. Still holding Tyrande tight, he turned and laughed at Malfurion.

And as he laughed, Illidan transformed, growing larger, more horrific. His garments tore as armor hidden underneath burst through. His skin color darkened and a savage, jagged tail sprouted from behind him. A clawed hand held out the druid's mate over the ruined city, shaking her like a rag doll.

And Malfurion stared in horror as Archimonde dangled Tyrande before him—

"Nooo!"

He bolted upright, then nearly tumbled off the night saber upon which he had been half-sitting. Strong but slim fingers kept him from losing what remained of his balance and pulled him tight against an armored torso. Recalling Archimonde, the druid instinctively sought to pull away from that armor.

"Hush, Malfurion! Be careful!"

Tyrande's voice brought him completely back to consciousness. He gazed up into her concerned face. She had the helmet back so that he could fully see her features, a most welcome sight.

"I dreamt—" he began, then stopped. There were parts of his dream that were too personal to tell one who was not promised to him. "I . . . dreamt," Malfurion concluded apologetically.

"I know. I heard you speak. I thought I heard my name, and Illidan's."

"Yes." He dared not say more.

The priestess touched his cheek. "It must've been a terrible dream, Malfurion . . . but at least you finally slept."

Suddenly aware of his close proximity to her, the druid straightened. He looked around, noting for the first time the sea of figures surrounding them. Most were civilians, many of whom looked confused and completely out of their element. Few night elves had ever suffered much. This displacement surely had to have pushed many to the brink.

"Where are we?"

"Near Mount Hyjal."

He gaped at the peak. "So far? This can't be!"

"I'm afraid it is."

Malfurion hung his head. So, after all their efforts, his people were still doomed. If the demons had already driven the defenders this far back, how could the night elves possibly hope to recover?

"Elune watches over us," Tyrande whispered, reading his expression. "I pray to her for guidance. She'll give us some reprieve, I'm certain."

"I hope so. Where are the others?"

"Your brother is with the Moon Guard, over there." She pointed north. "I've not seen Krasus or the others."

It was not Illidan to whom Malfurion desired to speak. After his confrontation with Archimonde, the druid wanted desperately to find the wizards. They had to be warned that the powerful demon led the forces pursuing them.

That assumed, of course, that Krasus and the rest still lived. Had Archimonde hunted them down after dealing with Malfurion?

"Tyrande, I've got to find the outsiders. I believe they are still the key to our survival."

"You'll never make it on foot. You're still weak. Take my night saber."

He felt ashamed that she would sacrifice her own mount for his possibly-futile search. "Tyrande, I—"

But she gave him a look that he had never seen before, a steadfast, determined expression such as Malfurion had noticed only on the most senior, most dedicated priestesses of Elune. "It is important, Malfurion. I know that."

She slipped off the huge cat before he could argue again. Taking only her pack and her weapons, Tyrande looked up at the druid and insisted, "Go."

Unable to do anything but nod his thanks, Malfurion shifted his position, then urged the night saber through the throng. He was determined that he would not fail Tyrande's trust; if the others lived, Malfurion would find them.

The cat battled its way through soldiers and civilians, snarling but never striking despite its obvious discomfort of being surrounded by so many bodies. The druid was pleased to see that the soldiers had kept order for the most part. The majority of the civilians were being politely but firmly herded on, their pace consistent. The demons had no doubt counted on the chaos caused by mixing the two diverse groups together. At least that danger had so far been avoided.

But with so many more bodies added to the host, finding even three such unique figures as the orc, the human, and Krasus proved daunting. Only after letting his gaze sweep over the crowds for the dozenth time did Malfurion finally think to make use of his arts.

He refused to enter the Emerald Dream just yet, as there were other means by which he believed he might sense them. Reining the night saber to a halt, the druid shut his eyes and reached out around him. Throughout the region, he touched the minds of the other night sabers that he could see, speaking to them as he had the beasts of the forest during his lessons. Malfurion even touched the mind of Tyrande's mount so as not to miss the slightest chance of a sighting. The cats, well-familiar with their masters, surely would notice the differing scents of the three strangers.

But the first animals did not recognize those the druid sought. Bracing himself, Malfurion stretched his senses farther, reaching to creatures far beyond his sight. Some of the refugees carried with them pets, and even those Malfurion asked. The more minds he contacted, the better his odds.

At last, one of the dark panthers responded. The answer came not in words, but rather smells and images. It took the druid a moment to digest them, but in the end he realized that this creature had recently seen the orc. Brox was the most distinctive of the trio, and so it was small wonder that the night saber would recall him best. To the cat, the warrior was a mix of heady, thick smells reminiscent of the deeply-buried wild side of the mount. In Brox, the night saber sensed a kindred spirit. In fact, the animal's image of the tusked warrior made the orc resemble a night saber on its hind legs, one arm ending in a huge pair of claws that had to be Brox's ax.

Finding out exactly when and where the cat had seen Brox proved a bit trickier. Animals did not measure time and distance as night elves did. Yet, with some effort, the druid finally determined that the panther had seen Brox only an hour or two earlier, near the center part of the great exodus.

Veering his own mount in that direction, Malfurion continued to ask other night sabers of any sightings. More and more, he came upon those who recalled not only Brox, but also Rhonin and Krasus. Something about the elder mage now took prominence in the creatures' minds; they looked to him with a respect that such able predators reserved only for far superior ones. However, they did not fear Krasus as they might have another beast, almost as if they understood that he was something much, much more. In truth, Malfurion soon discovered that the night sabers would have been more likely to obey a command by Krasus than they would the handlers who had raised them.

Marking this as yet another of the many mysteries surrounding the not-quite-night-elven mage, Malfurion spurred his cat to greater speed. The going was difficult, for they rode against the living tide, but with the druid's guidance, the night saber made headway without injuring any of those in its path.

The general situation worsened as he approached where the outsiders had to be. The sounds of battle rose in the distance and unsettling flashes of crimson and dank green light rose from the horizon. Here the soldiers were more wary and exhausted. These were clearly those who had been most recently up on the front line holding the demons back. The scars and terrible wounds Malfurion passed gave testament to the unabated fury of the Burning Legion.

"What are you doing here?" demanded an officer with blood and ichor on his once-immaculate armor. His eyes teared. "All noncombatants to the head of the flow! Begone with you!"

Before the druid could explain, someone behind Malfurion called, "He's *supposed* to be up here, captain! That should be plain with just a look at his face!"

"Illidan?" Glancing over his shoulder, Malfurion saw his brother, virtually unscathed, riding up. Illidan wore the first grin that his twin had seen in his journey; it looked so out of place in the situation that Malfurion feared his sibling had gone mad.

"I had thought you lost!" the sorcerer said, slapping Malfurion hard on the shoulder. Failing to notice his brother wince, Illidan turned to the officer. "Any more questions?"

"No, Master Illidan!" The soldier saluted quickly and moved on.

"What happened to you, brother?" the black-clad twin asked. "Someone said that they saw you struck down, your mount torn to pieces . . ."

"I was saved . . . Tyrande brought me to safety." The instant he mentioned her name, Malfurion regretted it.

The grin remained, but the good humor behind it fled. "*Did* she? I'm glad that she was so close to you."

"Illidan—"

"It's good that you're here at this time," the druid's sibling went on, cutting off any further discussion of the priestess. "The old wizard's been trying to organize something and he seems to think *you're* important."

"Krasus? Where is he?"

The sorcerer's grin grew almost macabre. "Why, just where you're heading, brother. Up at the very edge of the fight . . ."

The wind howled. An oppressive heat tore at the night elves who had been chosen to be the defending line. Now and then, a cry would come from somewhere in the ranks, and the triumphant roars of a demon would immediately follow.

"Where is Illidan?" Krasus asked, even his tremendous patience wearing thin. "The Moon Guard refuses to act without him save to shield themselves!"

"He said he was coming," Rhonin interjected. "He needed to speak with Ravencrest first."

"He will receive credit enough if we succeed, and no one will blame him if we fail, for we'll all be dead . . ."

Rhonin could not argue with his former mentor. Illidan wanted nothing more than to please his patron. Malfurion's brother was the opposite of the druid—ambitious, wild, and oblivious of the risks to others. The two wizards had already discovered that three of the Moon Guard they had hoped in part to rely on were no longer available. The demons had not slain them; they were simply crippled with exhaustion from feeding Illidan their power.

Yet, despite his reckless use of the other night elves, they appeared to have bound themselves to him. When it came to casting spells of any substance, Illidan could do what they could not. He also had the political backing of Lord Ravencrest, and night elves were nothing if not status-conscious, even in the face of annihilation.

Rhonin suddenly straightened. "Beware!"

What resembled most a floating mushroom made of mist descended upon the line. Before the spellcasters could act, the edges touched where the soldiers stood.

Several of the fighters screamed as their faces suddenly swelled with dozens of red, burning pustules. One after another, the pustules burst, regrew, and burst again, spreading rapidly over any unprotected part of the victim's body.

"*Jekar iryn!*" Krasus hissed, gesturing at the cloud.

A blast of rich, blue light ate away at the foul mushroom with such swiftness that scores more were saved from the horrendous plague. Unfortunately, there was no saving those already affected. They dropped one after another, their ravaged flesh reminiscent of a field of erupting volcanoes.

Rhonin stared in disgust. "Horrible! Damn them!"

"Would that we could! We can wait no longer! If the Moon Guard will not follow our lead, then we must hope we can do something by ourselves!"

But as the wizards prepared to do just that, Rhonin spotted a pair of riders approaching. "Illidan comes—and he's got Malfurion with him!"

"Praise the Aspects!" Krasus turned to meet the duo. As they rode up, he set himself before Malfurion's brother. "You are late! Gather the Moon Guard! You must be ready to follow my lead!"

From most others, Illidan likely would have not taken such a brusque command, but he had a healthy respect for both wizards, especially Rhonin. Peering over Krasus and seeing Rhonin's dark expression, the sorcerer nodded, then hurried to obey.

"What do you hope to do?" asked Malfurion, dismounting.

"The demons must be stopped here," Krasus answered. "It is vital that we not be pushed back beyond Mount Hyjal and that we turn this rout into an aggressive attack on our part!"

The druid nodded, then said, "Archimonde is out there. I barely escaped him."

"I had suspected that he was." Krasus considered the night elf. "And the fact that you lived through a confrontation with him says I was correct in desiring your presence at this moment."

"But—what can *I* do?"

"What you have been trained to do, naturally."

With that, Krasus turned back to Rhonin, who had already set himself to face the distant demons. The elder mage stood next to his former pupil, with Malfurion imitating him a moment later.

Krasus glanced at the human. "Rhonin, in matters of magic, Illidan looks to you more than anyone. I leave it to you to establish a link with him."

"As you wish." The fiery-tressed figure blinked once. "It's done."

The mage returned his attention to the druid. "Malfurion, imagine the most powerful spell you think you can cast. But by all means, do *not* tell me what it is! Use whatever method, whatever contact with the powers of the world you require, but do not complete your casting until I say so. We must be relentless against our foes."

"I . . . I understand."

"Good! Then, we begin. Follow my lead. Rhonin?"

"I'm ready," the younger wizard replied. "I know just what I want to do."

Krasus's eyes widened. "Ah! One other detail, Malfurion; be prepared to randomly shift the focus of your attack. Move your spell to wherever it seems there is a gap in our effort. Do you understand?"

"I believe so."

"May the powers of light be with us, then."

That said, Krasus abruptly froze. His eyes stared unblinking across the gap separating the night elves from the demons.

Rhonin quickly leaned toward Malfurion. "Use everything. Leave no defenses. This is all or nothing."

"They are approaching the point." Krasus informed his companions. "Would that Archimonde be among the first ranks."

They could all sense the approaching horde. The evil permeated the very air, sending a foul radiation their way. Even Krasus shuddered, but from disgust, not fear.

"Rhonin, I have Jarod Shadowsong prepared. Are the Moon Guard ready?"

"Yes."

"Almost . . . " The pale visage tightened. Krasus's eyelids flickered. "Now."

They had no knowledge of one another's attack, exactly how Krasus intended it. He desired true random effort, the better to foul up whatever defense Archimonde and the others might devise. His plan had as much potential for disaster—if not *more* even—than success, but that very fact was what the dragon mage counted on.

From the clouds suddenly dropped glittering spears of ice that fixed on the enemy horde. To the north, the ground shook, and demons suddenly scattered as the earth swelled. Elsewhere, huge, black birds appeared from nowhere, heading toward the airborne elements of the Legion.

All along the front, one spell after another assaulted the enemy. Some were concentrated in specific areas while others seemed to act everywhere. No two were alike and although a few appeared to be in conflict with one another, they did far worse damage to the oncoming horde.

Demons died pierced by ice, burned by crimson flame, or buried by molten earth. Those in the sky fell beaten and torn by hundreds of claws or tumbled to their deaths after winds tossed them against one another.

The Eredar attempted to counter, but Krasus suddenly commanded, "Shift your focus!"

Immediately, Malfurion, Rhonin, and—to the north—the Moon Guard and Illidan altered the direction in which they focused their spells. Krasus sensed the warlocks grow confused, uncertain as to where to first apply their counter-assaults. On the ground, the Fel Guard and other demon warriors tried in vain to defend against something that their weapons could not cut in two or impale.

The relentless advance finally came to a halt.

"They are stalled!" shouted Krasus. "Shift focus again and push harder! We must begin to retake ground!"

Again they adjusted the locations of their attacks. A few areas quieted, but just as the Burning Legion sought to take advantage of those lulls, someone among the spellcasters filled the gaps. Nowhere could the demons now stand their positions, much less press forward.

"They're giving way!" Malfurion called.

"Do not let up!" Krasus gritted his teeth. "Rhonin, I am alerting the captain!"

The druid dared to look at the human for a moment. "What does he mean?"

"It took some convincing, but Shadowsong rode to Ravencrest! He's been waiting for our signal!"

"For what?"

In answer, the battle horns sounded. A sudden electricity filled the night elves. Gone was the dying hope, the resignation. Once more the soldiers responded to the horns' cries with vigor, and the host advanced.

The spellcasters adjusted as they, too, slowly moved forward on foot. Their trained cats following close behind, they marched with the soldiers toward the enemy.

And finally the Burning Legion began to retreat full.

First the night elves crossed the ruined gap that the Moon Guard and wizards had earlier wrought to buy them time. Then they started to climb their way over the first of the demon dead. They also passed many of their own, lost hours earlier, but more and more, it was the demons who lay as corpses before the soldiers. The Burning Legion, softened by the unpredictable attacks of the spellcasters, fell away easily as the night elves cut into them.

Another set of horns blew. A lengthy, well-savored roar of anticipation unexpectedly erupted throughout the host. The night elves surged forward, more than doubling their pace.

"Ravencrest must follow the plan!" Krasus snapped. "They cannot chase the Legion too far or too fast!"

A flight of arrows fell upon the demons, slaying scores more. Panther riders charged the remaining fragments of the opposing line, the great cats eagerly tearing into their prey.

Malfurion's heart beat swifter. "We're doing it!"

"Do not let up!" stressed the mage.

They did not. Fueled by their success, the druid and the others continued adding to the support of the troops. Exhausted though they might be, they understood well that this was a most critical juncture. Mount Hyjal still loomed behind them, but now it receded slightly.

Then, another welcome surprise—chanting came from the center of the advance. The Sisterhood of Elune, resplendent in their battle armor, strengthened the fighters further. Day might have held precedence at the moment, but the priestesses' rhythmic singing literally fed the nocturnal warriors. It was as if the moon herself suddenly hung over the host.

Yard by yard they struggled, demons falling with each step. Krasus looked to the shrouded sky and said, "Now! Strike the Eredar at will!"

Every spellcaster focused his efforts on the airborne warlocks. Thunder ravaged the sky. Lightning flashed in a jarring display of colors. Winds howled.

They could not see the results of their attacks, but they could sense them in other ways. The Eredar tried to regroup, but they had to also protect their bearers. That left them strained, weaker. Whenever a spell slew one of the demon mages, the defenders felt a sudden lessening of the evil forces arrayed against them. And the more that happened, the harder Krasus's group attacked the survivors.

At last, the warlocks pulled completely back. Their retreat left the monstrous warriors on the ground bereft of any shield against the wizards and the Moon Guard.

"They're fleeing!" Malfurion whispered, awed by the success of his party.

"They are too valuable. Archimonde will need them again," Krasus replied more dourly. "And he *will* need them again. The war is not won, but the battle is saved."

"Should we not keep after them until we push them through the portal and back into their hellish domain?"

Krasus chuckled, so unusual a sound from him that even Rhonin started. "You sound more like your brother than you, Malfurion. Let not the euphoria of the moment take you too far. This host will never survive a pitched battle all the way back to Zin-Azshari. They are running on will alone right now."

"Then . . . what is the point?"

"Look around you, young night elf. Your people *survive*. That is more than they thought they could do only an hour before."

"Will Ravencrest follow your instructions, though?" asked Rhonin, peering back to look for the noble's banner.

"I believe he will. Look there, to the north."

The advance had slowed there and now the soldiers seemed more interested in securing the ground that they had gained rather than taking more. Mounted officers went about waving other soldiers back to the main group. Some seemed a bit disappointed, but others looked more than happy to rest, even if they still had to stand to do it.

Within minutes, the entire front line had completely halted. Night elves soon began clearing the carnage and creating a strong front line, with solemn but determined warriors positioning themselves to repel anyone who might seek to undo the miracle that they had accomplished.

And only then did Krasus exhale. "He listened. Praise the Aspects. He listened."

Ahead of them they could see only the vague shapes of the horde. The Burning Legion had moved far beyond the range of the arrows, even beyond the efforts of the weary spellcasters at the moment.

"We've done it," Rhonin uttered, his voice almost a croak. "We kept them from pushing us back beyond Mount Hyjal."

"Yes," murmured Krasus, eyes not on the demons, but rather the haggard defenders. "Yes, we did. Now the most difficult part begins."

NINE

Mannoroth bent before the black portal, his stocky front legs in a kneeling position and his wide, leathery wings folded tight behind him. The tusked demon tried to make himself as small as possible, for he now communed with Sargeras, who seemed not at all in a pleasant mood.

The way is not yet open to me . . . I had expected better . . .

"We struggle," Mannoroth admitted, "but the task . . . it's almost as if the world itself seeks to prevent your coming, Great One."

I will not be denied . . .

"N-no, Great One."

There was silence for a time, then the voice in Mannoroth's head said, *There is a disruption, a wrongness . . . there are those who should not be but are, and those who seek to awake what should not be awoken.*

The massive demon did not pretend to understand, but he still replied, "Yes, Sargeras."

They are the key. They must be hunted.

"Archimonde is in the field and the Houndmaster is long on the trail. The transgressors will be brought to ground."

The sinister-looking gap fluctuated, squirming as if alive. Mannoroth could feel the lord of the Legion's desire to make his way into this rich world. The frustration Sargeras radiated chilled even his hardened lieutenant.

One must be brought whole . . . so that I may have the pleasure of tearing him asunder slowly and delicately.

An image materialized full-blown in Mannoroth's mind. An insignificant creature of the same race as the Highborne. He was younger, though, and wore, in comparison to his fellows, rather drab garments of green and brown. The vision the demon had of him showed the night elf in the palace itself. Mannoroth recognized the chamber where the original portal had been created . . . a place now only a windswept ruin.

Mark him well.

"I have already, Great One. Archimonde, Hakkar, and I all watch for his presence. One of us will snare him."

Alive, commanded the presence from beyond, now beginning to recede from Mannoroth's head. *Alive . . . so that I might have my pleasure with his torture . . .*

And as Sargeras vanished, Mannoroth shuddered, knowing full well what fate this Malfurion would face once the Great One had him in his grasp.

The monumental task of reorganizing the host was made more so by the countless refugees accompanying them, but to his credit, Lord Ravencrest did as best as possible. He took an accounting of all supplies, especially food and water, and distributed accordingly. Some of the high-ranking among the refugees protested at not receiving what they thought their rightful—and more *bountiful*—shares, but one black glare from the bearded commander silenced all.

Tyrande and the sisters also did what they could for the soldiers and civilians. Her helmet pushed back, the priestess of Elune led along a night saber she had borrowed earlier as she stopped to speak with one person after another. All, whether old or young, of high caste or low, welcomed her presence. Perhaps it was just the moment, but they appeared to her especially comforted after she was through. Tyrande did not mark this as the result of any special gift she had, merely assuming that her gentle demeanor was an extreme relief in contrast to all else the others had faced of late.

A small figure crouched by herself seized the priestess's attention. A young female, two or three years away from being able to enter into the service of Elune, sat in miserable silence, staring at nothing.

Kneeling at her side, Tyrande touched her shoulder. The girl started, turning to glare at her like a wild beast.

"Be at peace . . ." Tyrande said soothingly, handing her a water sack. She waited until the girl had finished, then added, "I am from the temple. What's your name?"

After a moment's hesitation, the child answered, "Sh-Shandris Feather-moon."

"Where is your family?"

"I-I don't know."

"Are you from Suramar?" The priestess could not recall her, but that did not mean that Shandris was not from the same city.

"No . . . Ara-Hinam."

Tyrande tried to hide her concern. Shandris was one of the refugees that the demons had been pursuing when they had set their trap. Based on what the priestess had gathered from other survivors, many people had perished before the Burning Legion had allowed the rest to escape. The child's family might still live . . . but then again might not.

"When did you last see them?"

Shandris's eyes grew huge. "I was with a friend . . . when the monsters came. I tried to run home, but someone grabbed me . . . told me I had to run the other way. I did." She put her hands to her face, the tears spilling over them. "I should have gone home! I should have gone home!"

The tragic tale was not what Tyrande had wanted to hear. The priestess would make inquiries wherever she could, but she was near-certain that no one in Shandris's immediate family had survived and that the girl was now all by herself in the world.

"Has anyone taken care of you since your flight?"

"No."

The refugees from Ara-Hinam, a smaller settlement, had been on the run for two days prior to meeting up with the host. It was remarkable to think that Shandris had survived on her own even for that period. Many older night elves had fallen to the side; the priestess's people were not, in general, up to such strife. Night elves, while hardly weak, were very ill-prepared for life outside their cushioned world—a failing only now becoming evident. Tyrande gave thanks to Elune that she, Malfurion, and Illidan had been raised differently, but they were in the minority.

There were so many in the same situation Shandris suffered, but something about the child especially touched the priestess. Perhaps it was that she somewhat resembled Tyrande in face and form at that age. Whatever the case, the sister bade the child to rise.

"I want you to climb atop the night saber. You're going to come with me." It went against her orders, but the priestess did not care. Though she could not save everyone, she would do what she could for Shandris.

Her face drawn but her eyes for the first time clear, Shandris mounted the cat. Tyrande made certain that she was secure, then led the night saber on.

"Where are we going?" the child asked.

"I've more work to do. You'll find some dried fruit in the pouch hanging on the left side."

Shandris eagerly twisted to the pouch, rummaging through it until she discovered the simple fare. Tyrande made no mention of the fact that the girl was also devouring her ration. The sisterhood trained its members to learn to survive at times with minimal sustenance. There were even four periods of ritual fasting each year, done in general as a sign of dedication to the goddess. Now, it paid off in time of war.

Moving on to the next refugees, Tyrande continued her ministrations.

Most were simply exhausted beyond belief, but some had injuries. The latter she always tried to help as much as possible, praying to the Mother Moon for the strength and guidance necessary. To her joy, the goddess saw fit this day to grant success in all her efforts.

But then she came upon one infected injury that shocked her. Whether an intentional wound or an accident, it was at first difficult to say. Tyrande studied the unsettling greenish pus around it and wondered at the peculiar cuts. The victim, an older male, lay pale and unconscious, his breath coming in rapid gasps. His mate, her hair bound back with what remained of a ruby- and emerald-encrusted broach, cradled his head.

"How did he do this?" asked Tyrande, not certain if she could even slow the course of the infection. There was something disquieting about it.

"He did not. It was done to him."

"I don't understand."

The elder female's expression tightened as she fought to maintain her calm long enough to explain. "This thing . . . he said it looked like . . . like a wolf or hound . . . but twisted, as if out of a horrible dream . . ."

Tyrande shivered. She knew that the other female spoke of a felbeast. The four-legged demons had nearly slain Malfurion more than once. They especially desired those who wielded any sort of magic, draining it from the bodies and leaving only a dry husk.

"And he made it all the way from Ara-Hinam like this?" The priestess marveled that anyone could survive so long with so hideous a wound.

"No . . . from there we escaped whole." Bitterness tinged her words. "This he got but two days ago, while sneaking off to find us food."

Two days? That would have put them with the mass of bodies flowing toward Mount Hyjal. But none of the demons had managed to break ahead of the horde, of that Tyrande was certain.

"You swear that it was only two days? It happened near here?"

"Back in the wooded lands now again to our south, I swear it."

The priestess bit her lip; woods that were behind the night elven lines.

Leaning over the wound, Tyrande said, "Let me see what can be done."

She forced herself to touch it, hoping that she could at least prevent it from spreading. From behind her she heard Shandris gasp. The girl feared for her, and rightly so. One never knew what a demon-caused wound might do. The Burning Legion would not be averse to spreading plague.

The moon was not present in the sky, but that did not concern Tyrande. While the priestesses were strongest when it was visible, they were fully aware that it was never far away. Their link to Elune was powerful no matter what time of day or night or even cycle.

"Mother Moon, hear my entreaties," she whispered. "Grant this humble one the cool, soothing powers of your touch. Guide my hands to the source of this abomination, and let me remove the taint so that this innocent might recover . . ."

Tyrande began humming under her breath, a way of focusing her will into her work. The injuries that she had healed for Broxigar paled in comparison to what she attempted now. It took all her control just to keep from feeling that she would fail.

Without warning, a pale, silvery light shone around her fingers. The victim's mate stared wide-eyed, and again Shandris gasped. Tyrande's hopes rose; once again, Elune was responding to her. Truly the goddess was with her this day!

The healer traced her fingers around the wound, taking special care where the foulness was worst. Tyrande could not help but grimace as she touched the pus-ridden areas. What sort of evil were the demons that their very bite or scratch left such horror in its wake?

As her fingertips went past the ravaged areas, the injury grew less horrific in appearance. The pustules shriveled, finally disappearing. The bloody crevice narrowed at each end, as if slowly sealing itself.

Encouraged, Tyrande continued praying to Elune. The infection shrank to a small, oval patch, while the wound itself became a scar, first fresh, then nearly gone.

The male suddenly groaned, as if awaking from a deep sleep, but Tyrande did not stop. She could not presume that the disappearance of outer signs meant that the wound had completely healed *inside*. There would be poisons from the infection in the victim's blood.

Several tense seconds later, when the male's chest finally rose and sank at a more sedate rate and his eyes fluttered open, the priestess knew that she had defeated the demon's work. With a long exhalation, Tyrande leaned back and gave thanks to Elune. The goddess had granted her a miracle.

The female reached forward and took one of Tyrande's hands. "Thank you, sister! Thank you!"

"I am merely the vessel for the work of the Mother Moon. If there is one to thank, it is Elune."

Nevertheless, both the stricken male—Karius—and his mate continued to express their gratitude for what they saw as the priestess's heroic effort. Tyrande nearly had to fend them off, so thankful were they.

"You can repay me by telling me in more detail what occurred," she finally told the former victim.

Nodding, Karius related the story as much as he could recall. In the midst of their troubles, the two had realized that they needed food. However, the chaos at the time prevented them from finding anyone among the refugees who had enough to share. Most had fled with only as much as they could carry in their arms.

Spotting an area of forest he thought might contain berries and fresh water, Karius had left his mate with the promise that he would return shortly. Desperation made him attempt the foolhardy hunt at all, for surely others had stripped the forest of anything edible long before.

Karius had been forced to go deeper into the woods than he had intended. He began to worry that he might never find his mate again, although she had told him that she would stay behind if he was gone too long. When at last he discovered a bush with ripe, purple berries, Karius had quickly tried to fill the pouch on his belt, allowing himself an occasional berry to eat immediately so as to preserve his strength.

But just as he had filled the pouch, he heard something huge rummaging through the forest. His first thought was that it might be a tauren or bear. He had started back, his gaze constantly over his shoulder so that whatever emerged would not catch him by surprise.

And so it was that he was looking in the wrong direction when the beast charged him from the front.

Having once served Black Rook Hold, Karius still had some swiftness left to him despite the debilitating journey. He twisted around just as the monster— some sort of demonic hound with two horrific tentacles sprouting from its upper back—had tried to fall upon him. The beast did not seize his throat as it had intended, but instead clamped down on the leg.

Somehow, Karius had managed not to scream, although every fiber of his being had demanded it. Instead, the night elf grabbed for something, any- thing, with which to defend himself. His groping hand found a thick, pointed rock, and he swung it with all his might against the creature's nose.

He had heard something crack. A harsh whine filled his ears and the beast released his leg. Even then, Karius doubted that he would have escaped the demon, but from somewhere in the distance, a sharp sound had suddenly echoed.

The hideous hound's reaction to it had been both instantaneous and astonishing. It cringed first, then immediately leapt toward the source of the noise. Self-preservation urged Karius to immediately drag himself in the opposite direction. He had not even paused to bind the wound, which at that time had only been bloody. The mauled night elf had struggled all the way back to his waiting mate, each harsh step of the journey expecting the crea- ture to return to finish him.

Tyrande digested his tale with a great sense of foreboding. Karius had indeed been very fortunate to survive an encounter with a felbeast. What that abomination had been doing behind the lines, however, worried her. Of course, one such beast, while dangerous, could be readily dealt with by Malfurion or the wizards. But what if there were more?

That in mind, she asked, "You mentioned a sound that drew it away. What sort of sound?"

Karius thought for a moment before responding, "It was a sharp, cracking sound."

"Like thunder?"

"Nay . . . it reminded me of . . . of the crack of a whip, I'd say."

The priestess rose to her feet. "I thank you for your patience. If you'll forgive me, I must be on my way."

"Nay!" protested the female. " 'Tis *we* who thank you again, sister! I thought to lose him!"

Tyrande did not have time to argue any more. She gave both the blessing of the temple, then quickly went to where Shandris watched her with eyes as wide as plates.

"You healed him completely! I-I thought he would be dead before you could start!"

"As did I," Tyrande returned, mounting behind the child. "The Mother Moon was generous to me."

"I've never seen a priestess heal a wound so horrible . . . and that monster that made it—"

"Hush, Shandris. I must think." The priestess took command of the night saber, turning the cat toward where last she recalled seeing the spellcasters. In her role as cleric, Tyrande often obtained information that even Lord Ravencrest's strategists never picked up. Now, once again, she had heard something that Malfurion and Krasus needed to know.

The Legion's assassins were closing in on them.

The black dragons returned under cover of night to their vast lair. Neltharion had been eager to come home, for there was much to be done. His plan was so near to fruition that he could taste it.

A smaller male atop a peak resembling an upraised talon dipped his head in homage. The Earth Warder paid him no mind, his thoughts too caught up in the moment. He landed in the mouth of the flight's main cavern and immediately turned to his consorts, who dropped behind him. Deeper within the cavern, the roars of other dragons could be heard.

"I go below. I must not be disturbed."

The females nodded, having heard this command from him oft before.

They did not ask what the Aspect did down there. Like all in the black flight, they existed to obey. Every creature in the mountain was touched to some degree by the same madness that affected Neltharion most of all.

The huge black maneuvered through tunnels that barely allowed his immense form passage. As he descended deeper, the sounds of dragon life vanished and a new, odd noise echoed over and over. To any who listened, it most resembled what one might note in a blacksmith's shop, for there could be heard repeated hammering on metal. The hammering went on without end, and as it increased in tempo, Neltharion's savage smile grew wider, more satisfied. Yes, everything was coming to pass.

But the dragon did not head to the source of the hammering. Instead he turned at a side passage and continued his descent. After a time, the hammering faded away, leaving only Neltharion's heavy breathing to echo in the dark corridors. No one but he was allowed to walk these lower chambers.

At last, the Earth Warder reached the vast chamber where he had cast his spell upon the Eredar. Yet, as he entered, the dragon's head picked up, for he sensed that, despite appearances, he was not alone.

And the voices in his mind, the voices that had remained but steady murmurs while he had been among the other dragons, suddenly rose in a frenzy of excitement.

Soon . . .

Soon . . .

The world will be set to right . . .

All those who have betrayed you will know their place . . .

Order will be restored . . .

You will take your rightful rule . . .

This and more they repeated over and over to the Earth Warder. His chest swelled with pride and his eyes glittered with anticipation. Soon his world would be as *he* desired it!

"They have all given of themselves," he told the empty air. "Even absent Nozdormu."

The voices did not reply, but the dragon seemed to accept that they were pleased. He nodded to himself, then closed his eyes and concentrated.

And at his summoning, the Dragon Soul materialized.

"Behold its beauty," he rumbled as it floated level with his admiring gaze. "Behold its perfection, its power."

The golden aura surrounded his creation, glowing with an intensity never before achieved. As Neltharion fixed his will upon it, the Dragon Soul began to quietly vibrate. Throughout the chamber, the stalactites and stalagmites began to shake as if stirring to life.

The disk's vibration increased with each eager breath by the Earth

Warder. The entire chamber now trembled. Fragments of rock broke free from the ceiling, and several huge stalactites quivered ominously.

"Yes . . ." the dragon hissed eagerly. Neltharion's eyes burned with anticipation. "Yes . . ."

Now the very mountain rumbled as if some huge volcanic eruption or great tremor took place. The ceiling began to break in earnest. Huge stones dropped everywhere, striking the floor with ear-shattering booms. Many bounded off the massive dragon's hard hide, but he cared not at all.

Then, from the Dragon Soul ethereal shapes arose. They were shadows of light, vague images that darted around. Most had wings and their outlines were akin to that of Neltharion. Some were black, some bronze, others blue or red. They began to swarm above the disk, rapidly growing in number.

There were other shapes as well, smaller but more grotesque ones. They glowed a sickly green and many had horns and deep pits for eyes. Their numbers were far smaller, but there was an intensity, an evil, that made them as arresting as the intermingling ghosts above them.

They were the essences of all those who had contributed to the Dragon Soul's creation, willingly or not. Tied to the disk, they represented, together, power that dwarfed even that of an Aspect such as Neltharion. Their simple appearance was enough to cause cracks and fissures in the solid mountain as the entire region now shook with vehemence.

A gargantuan stalactite suddenly broke free. Caught up in his reverie, the Earth Warder did not notice it until it was too late.

Only a formation of this magnitude could have injured the black dragon. It struck Neltharion on the left side of his jaw, ripping away even the hard, scaled flesh. One piece of bloody scale went flying, its hard edge hitting the Dragon Soul at the center.

Neltharion roared with horror, not for himself but rather at what had happened to his precious creation. The scale gouged the disk deep, ruining its perfection. The shapes above and below spun in an uncontrolled frenzy.

The dragon acted quickly, ending the spell. The ghostly figures sank back into the disk, but slower, more hesitantly than he desired. As they vanished, the tremor ceased, leaving only drifting dust to mark its brief but terrible passage.

When it was safe to do so, Neltharion seized the Dragon Soul and held it close. The gouge was not as deep as he had thought, but that it existed at all nearly threw him into a new fit. He had not expected anything, much less *himself*, to be a danger to the disk.

"You will be healed," he whispered, cradling the tiny piece in his paw as a mother might cradle her child in her arms. "You will be my perfection again . . ."

Clutching the disk tightly, he departed the chamber as quickly as he could on three limbs, heading back up in a swift, half-hopping motion. Neltharion radiated a pensiveness that would have unnerved even his consorts. The Earth Warder's breathing turned ragged, as if he feared that all he had wrought would now be for nothing.

Rather than return to where his own kind dwelled, however, the dragon veered to another series of tunnels. The hammering echoed louder as Neltharion moved his tremendous bulk through the narrow corridors, soon becoming distinct sounds of hard work. Peculiar voices chittered away, but their exact words were drowned out by the hammers.

Neltharion thrust himself into the new chamber. The fiery illumination forced him to let his eyes adjust for a moment. When they had, they revealed scores of tiny, limber goblins busy in various stages of metalwork. There were huge ovens everywhere, all fueled by the raging, molten earth far below. Half a dozen of the green-skinned creatures struggled to remove from one huge casing what seemed an oval shield fit for a giant. The metal inside blazed a bright orange. The goblins quickly turned the casing over, letting its contents drop into a vat of water. Steam rose in a tremendous burst, nearly boiling one slow worker.

Other goblins hammered away at various pieces. A few wearing smocks wandered among the rest, making certain that everyone did his task properly.

Not finding what he searched for around the chamber, Neltharion roared, "Meklo! Meklo, attend me!"

The leviathan's cry overwhelmed all other sounds. Startled, the goblins halted in their work. Two almost poured molten iron on a comrade.

"To work, to work!" snapped a high-pitched, irritated voice. "Want to ruin all?"

The laborers immediately obeyed. From a walkway above, a spindly goblin of elder years, with a tuft of gray fur atop his otherwise bald head, scampered down to the impatient dragon. The chief goblin muttered to himself all the way, but his words held no anger against his master. Instead, he appeared to be constantly calculating things.

"Density of eight inches with a surface area of a hundred twenty square feet, which means approximately adding forty-two more pounds to the mix and—" His foot bounced against the center toe of the remaining forepaw. The goblin glanced up, acting almost surprised to see the leviathan. "My Lord Neltharion?"

"Meklo! See this!"

The Earth Warder brought his huge paw close so that the goblin could study the disk. Meklo squinted, making a *tsk*ing sound.

"Such craftwork, and now marred! The design was flawless!"

"A scale of mine fell upon it, goblin! Explain why that should damage the invulnerable!"

"Blood, too, I see." Meklo looked up, surveying Neltharion's injury for a moment before tsking again. "Of course, this makes perfect sense! My Lord Neltharion, you were integral in the formation of the disk itself, yes?"

"You were there, goblin. You know."

"Yes. You created the matrix of its construction." The head goblin thought a moment more, than asked, "The others, they've given their essences? They're tied into the disk's matrix?"

"Of course."

"Aaah, but *you* are not. You created the Dragon Soul matrix, formed it with your power and blood, but you are the only dragon not directly bound to it." The goblin grinned, showing pointed yellow teeth. "That makes you its *only* weakness, my lord. The scale, your blood . . . any part of you has the capability of destroying the Dragon Soul. You could crush the disk with ease, I imagine." Meklo made a squashing gesture with his index finger and thumb.

The Earth Warder's eyes grew monstrous to behold, even for the goblin. "I would never do such a thing!"

"Of course not, of course not!" babbled Meklo, groveling for Neltharion. "Which means that *nothing* can ever destroy it, eh?"

The fury smoldering within the dragon lessened. Neltharion's lip stretched back, revealing teeth larger than the goblin. "Yes, *nothing*. So, my Dragon Soul is . . . is invulnerable!"

"So long as you take no part in its destruction," the spindly figure dared remind him.

"Which shall never happen!" Neltharion gazed down at the damage wrought on the Dragon Soul. "But this must be repaired! The disk must be perfect again!"

"It'll require what it did last time."

The dragon scoffed. "You will have all of my blood that you need! It will be whole!"

"Naturally, naturally." Meklo peered back at the other goblins. "It will slow completion of your other plans. We need your blood and magic for those, as well."

"All else can wait! The disk cannot!"

"Then we shall begin now, my lord. Permit me a moment to shut down work. I will return with the necessary assistance, then."

As the goblin retreated, Neltharion breathed easier. His precious creation would be healed. Like him, it would be perfect once more.

And together, they would rule all . . .

TEN

This is insufferable!" Lord Stareye said, removing a pinch of powder from his pouch and sniffing into one nostril. "A perfect opportunity wasted, Kur'talos!"

"Perhaps, Desdel. Perhaps not. Still, it's done and must be looked past now."

The two nobles stood in Lord Ravencrest's tent with several other aristo-cratic officers, discussing a plan of action now that the rout had been stopped. Desdel Stareye, however, was convinced that Krasus had been premature in deciding that the host had to come to a halt just when they had their enemy on the run. Stareye felt certain that the night elves could have advanced all the way to Suramar unhindered if they had just listened to him—an opinion he had voiced more than once since Krasus and the others had joined the group.

"The soldiers have fought valiantly," the mage replied politely, "but they are of flesh and blood and are flagging. They must have this rest."

"Food, too," grunted Brox, who had accompanied the spellcasters. The night elves had clearly not desired the orc's company, but as Ravencrest had not commanded him to be put out, no one, not even Stareye, would make an objection to his presence.

"Yes, there is that," the master of Black Rook Hold agreed. "The soldiers and refugees are eating and bedding down and that's the end of it. Now, then, we move on to what must happen next."

"Zin-Azshari, certainly!" piped up Lord Stareye. "Queen Azshara must be saved!"

The other nobles echoed his sentiments. Krasus frowned, but said noth-ing. He and the others had discussed the matter before their arrival, and all had agreed that the night elves would cling to the belief that their monarch was a prisoner of the demons. Since Zin-Azshari was also the access point by which the Burning Legion entered Kalimdor, it seemed futile to argue for any other course of action. For one reason or another, the capital had to be taken.

Krasus did not think, however, that Malfurion's people could do it alone.

Ignoring protocol, he stepped up and demanded, "My Lord Ravencrest! I must speak again on a subject I know you wish not to hear, but that cannot be avoided!"

Ravencrest accepted a goblet of wine poured by Lord Stareye. Even in the midst of crisis, the hierarchy of the night elves insisted on some benefits. "You'd be referring to communications with dwarves and such."

Next to him, Stareye scoffed. Similar expressions graced the features of most of the other nobles.

Despite that it was clear that this would be a repeat of all his previous defeats, the mage persisted. "At this moment, the dwarves, tauren, and other races are surely fighting their own struggles against the Burning Legion. Separately, there is some small chance that you will survive, but a concerted effort by all *could* see Zin-Azshari taken with a loss of far fewer lives!"

"Tauren in Zin-Azshari?" blurted one noble. "How barbaric!"

"They'd rather have the *demons* there?" muttered Rhonin to Malfurion.

"You wouldn't understand," the druid replied morosely.

"No, I wouldn't."

The bearded commander downed his wine, then handed the goblet back to Lord Stareye. He eyed the mage as one would a respected, albeit misguided, elder. "Master Krasus, your contributions to our strategy have been well appreciated. Your knowledge of your craft exceeds that of any of our sorcerers. In the guidance of the arts, I heartily turn to you for suggestions." Ravencrest's frown deepened. "However, when it comes to *other* matters, I must remind you that you aren't one of us. You don't understand basic truths. Even if I did something as mad as summon the dwarves and tauren to our aid, do you think honestly they would come? They distrust us as much as we do them! For that matter, even if they would join us, do you expect our soldiers to fight alongside?"

"The dwarves are more likely to turn on us," interjected Stareye. "Their avarice is well-documented. They would rob us and then scurry back to their holes."

Another officer added, "And the tauren would spend as much time fighting with one another. They are beasts more than intelligent creatures! Their chaos would spill over into *our* fighters, cause such disarray that we would be easily wiped out by the demons!"

Lord Ravencrest agreed. "You see, Master Krasus? We would be inviting not only bedlam into our midst, but certain destruction."

"We may yet face that by going on alone."

"This particular discussion is at an end, good wizard, and I must respectfully order that you do not bring it up again."

The two stared at each other for several seconds . . . and it was Ravencrest who glanced away first. Despite that small victory, though, Krasus acquiesced.

"Forgive me for overstepping my bounds," he said.

"We are about to discuss supplies and logistics, Master Krasus. There really is no need for the presence of any spellcaster during this session, save Illidan, who serves me directly. I would suggest that you and the others get some much needed rest yourselves. Your skills will be welcome when we advance again."

Krasus bowed politely, saying nothing more. With the others following, he calmly glided out of the tent.

But once out of earshot of those within, the pale mage commented bitterly, "Their shortsightedness will put a tragic end to this struggle. Alliance with the other races is the key to victory . . ."

"They won't accept them," Malfurion insisted. "My people will never fight alongside such."

"They accepted Korialstrasz readily enough," countered Rhonin.

"There are few who can deny a dragon, Master Rhonin."

"Too true," muttered Krasus, looking thoughtful. "Rhonin, I must go find them."

"Find who?"

"My—the dragons, of course."

Brox snorted and Malfurion looked startled. The druid knew that Krasus had a link with Korialstrasz, but even now he did not understand the full truth.

"The dragons, Master Krasus? But they're a force unto themselves! How can you possibly think to do so?"

"I have my methods . . . but to accomplish the fact also requires swift transportation. The night sabers will never do for that. I need something that can fly."

"Like a dragon?" Rhonin asked wryly.

"Something smaller will suffice, my friend."

To the surprise of the others, it was Malfurion who suddenly came up with a suggestion. "There are woods not far from here. Perhaps . . . perhaps I can contact Cenarius. He may have a solution."

From Krasus's expression, this was not entirely satisfying, but no one could come up with anything better. He finally nodded, saying, "We shall have to depart as soon as possible, then. Captain Shadowsong will otherwise either seek to detain us or, even worse, follow with his troops behind us. I fear that will draw both the Burning Legion and the night elves to our mission."

Jarod and the rest of the bodyguard had been given time to recuperate. No one thought the wizards in physical danger amidst the host, and the soldiers could hardly defend against any magical assault better than their charges. Come the march, the bodyguard would immediately resume its duties, of course.

But by then, Krasus hoped to be on his way.

"Do you really think this necessary?" asked the red-tressed wizard.

"I go for two reasons, Rhonin. The first is that of which we speak. The dragons can turn the tide. As for the second reason, that is more personal. I go to see why I sense only silence from them. That should not be so, as you understand. I need to discover the truth."

He received no more objections. Lord Ravencrest intended for the night elves to march at first dark, and Krasus had to be far from here before he was discovered missing.

Rhonin nodded. "What about Brox and me?"

"If our druid friend here can gain me transportation as he says, he will be able to return well before nightfall. In the meantime, you and Brox must try to stay from the sight of Lord Ravencrest. He may ask about us. He will be furious enough when he discovers I have left."

"Maybe, maybe not. At least no one will be questioning his decisions out loud."

Ignoring the human's jest, Krasus turned to Malfurion. "We must go. If we take a pair of night sabers toward the area of the refugees, the soldiers will not bother with us much. We can then come around and head toward the woods." He let out a slight hiss. "And then we must pray that your patron will come to our aid."

They quickly left the others, following the elder mage's suggestion as to their course. Soldiers eyed them with some suspicion and curiosity, but as the pair were not heading toward the front, the looks did not last long.

Malfurion was still uncomfortable with Krasus's mission, but did not question the conjurer. He respected the latter's wisdom and knew that Krasus understood the dragons better than anyone he had ever met. Often, he even seemed almost one of them. Surely somewhere in his past, Krasus had enjoyed the unique experience of having dwelled among the ancient creatures for some period of time. What other explanation could there be for his link to the leviathans?

It took nearly three hours, but they finally entered the woods. The comfort Malfurion felt the last time he had entered such a place did not touch him now. This forest had experienced the taint of the Legion and the marks remained. If not for the sudden turnaround by the defenders, it very well would have been reduced to ruin already.

Despite the imminent threat, life still abounded here. Birds sang, and the druid could sense the trees sending ahead word of the new intruders. The rustling grew particularly fierce whenever Krasus neared, almost as if the forest, too, could sense his differences. They did, of course, also welcome the night elf, clearly noting his aura and the obvious blessing of Cenarius.

But of the demigod, the druid sensed nothing. Cenarius had many tasks at hand, foremost trying to stir his counterparts to an active and organized defense of their world. How, then, could Malfurion hope that the woodland deity would have time to respond to his call?

"This land has suffered much already," his companion uttered. "I can taste the evil that has been here."

"So do I. Krasus, I don't know if Cenarius will hear me here after all."

"I can but ask you to attempt to reach him, Malfurion. If you fail, I will not hold it against you. I will then have to make do with the night saber, although that will slow my journey greatly."

They reached a spot deep in the woods where the druid sensed a bit more tranquillity. He informed Krasus of this and the pair dismounted.

"Shall I leave you alone?" asked the mage.

"If Cenarius chooses to come, he will do so even if you are with me, Master Krasus."

Malfurion found a seat among the soft, wild grass. Krasus stepped respectfully to one side so as not to disturb the druid.

Closing his eyes, Malfurion focused. He reached out first to the trees, the plants, and other life, seeking from them any hint of the demigod's recent presence. If Cenarius had been here, he would soon know.

But the forest offered no hints of the deity. Frustrated, the druid considered his other options. Unfortunately, only the Emerald Dream truly offered him a certain way of immediately contacting his *shan'do*.

It was as he had feared. Exhaling, Malfurion concentrated on the ethereal realm. He did not have to enter it completely, only touch upon its edges. Then he could send out his thoughts to Cenarius. Even interacting that much with it bothered Malfurion, but it had to be done.

He felt himself beginning to separate from his mortal shell. However, instead of allowing the transition to complete, the druid held himself midway. Doing so proved more of a strain than he had thought, but Malfurion did not plan to stay in such a state long. He imagined Cenarius as he knew him, using that to help create a link . . .

His concentration was suddenly jarred by a voice in his ear.

"Malfurion! We are not alone!"

The rapid retreat back into his body shook the druid. Momentarily stunned, he could do nothing else save open his eyes . . . in time to see a felbeast charging toward him.

Someone muttered words of power, and the hideous hound shriveled within itself. The beast curled and twisted, swiftly becoming a grotesque, mangled pile of bone and sinew.

Krasus grabbed Malfurion by the arms, lifting him with startling strength. The elder mage asked, "Can you defend yourself yet?"

The druid had no time to respond, for suddenly the woods came alive with not only the demonic hounds, but horned, bestial Fel Guard. The two spellcasters were outnumbered at least ten to one. Their mounts, bound to one tree, snarled and pulled at their tethers, but could not free themselves. The demons, however, ignored the panthers, their targets clearly being the mage and the druid.

Drawing an invisible line around them, Krasus uttered another short spell. Crystalline spikes thrust up from the ground, growing to the height of a night elf.

Three Fel Guard became impaled on the spikes. A felbeast howled as another spike tore off part of its muzzle.

Krasus's swift action gave Malfurion time to think. He looked to the trees nearest the oncoming demons and asked of them their aid.

Thick, foliage-covered branches stretched down and snagged four of the monstrous warriors. They pulled the demons high, dragging them from sight. Malfurion could not see what happened to the victims, but he noted well that they did not reappear.

Other trees merely stuck their branches out, timing their appearance to the Legion's charge. One felbeast tumbled helplessly as it fell over a branch; another was even less fortunate, its neck cracking when it collided with the unexpected obstruction.

Yet still the demons swarmed them, especially the hounds. They seemed to leer as they approached, the notion of two trapped spellcasters no doubt stirring their hunger.

Despite the effectiveness of Malfurion's attack, the demons seemed to fear Krasus more, and with good reason. Possessing knowledge of his craft far greater than the night elf's of his own, the mage cast with both speed and extreme ruthlessness. It was a far cry from the sickly figure he had been when first they had met. True, Krasus appeared under immense strain even now, but he in no way faltered because of it.

A crack like thunder echoed throughout the forest. Krasus grasped at his throat, where a thin, blazing tentacle now wrapped around it, tightening like a noose. The mage was pulled back off his feet and dragged toward the very spikes he had created.

Daring a glance over his shoulder, the night elf beheld a sight nearly as frightening as Archimonde—a huge, skeletal knight, his head a horned skull with flames for eyes, using a fearsome whip to drag Krasus to his doom. The newcomer stood taller than the other demons, and from the way they parted for him, Malfurion guessed that this was the leader.

Seizing a few blades of grass, the druid tossed them toward the sinister lash. The grass blades spun swiftly as they flew, then sliced away at the whip like well-honed knives until at last one cut completely through.

Krasus gasped as the end of the lash separated. He fell to his knees, trying to unbind what remained. The demon stumbled a few steps back but managed to sustain his balance. He drew back the whip and prepared to use its still-formidable length against the druid.

Surrounded by demons, his companion incapacitated, Malfurion did not hold much hope for his chances of survival. He and Krasus had not only left themselves open to the demonic assassins ever trailing them, but this time their leader had come to ensure there would be no escape. No Jarod would come to their aid. Only Rhonin and Brox knew of their departure, and both assumed that the pair would be all right. How misguided they had all been.

To his surprise, though, the demon did not immediately strike again. Instead, he hissed to Malfurion, "Sssurrender, creature, and you will be ssspared! I promissse thisss in the name of my mossst honored massster, Sssargerasss! It isss your only hope of sssurvival . . ."

Krasus coughed, trying to clear his throat. "S-surrendering to the Burning Legion i-is a fate far worse than the most terrible death! We must fight even if we are destined to lose, Malfurion!"

Grim memories of his brief encounter with Archimonde made the night elf think the very same thing. He could just imagine what the demons would do with prisoners, especially those who had been instrumental in foiling their plans so far. "We'll never surrender!"

His fiery orbs flickered angrily, and the demon snapped his whip four times. Lightning flashed as the lash struck the earth. Huge shapes suddenly formed before the demon. With each snap, a fiendish hound materialized.

"Then my petsss will feed well upon you, ssspellcastersss!"

Krasus steadied himself, then turned to gaze at the lead demon. His eyes narrowed dangerously.

But the skeletal knight was prepared for his attack. He swung the whip around and around, creating a haze. The haze sparkled suddenly, as if something exploded against it.

The night elf bit back an epithet. Their adversary had easily dealt with what should have been a powerful spell.

"It is as I feared," Krasus muttered. "It is the Houndmaster. *Hakkar!*"

Malfurion would have liked to ask him what he knew of the demon, but at that moment the other monsters resumed their charge. The spikes provided some defense, but the demons now began tearing, clawing, and chopping them apart. In the background, their leader laughed, a sound like a hundred angry serpents.

Yet, just as the first of the Fel Guard tore through and started for the pair, warriors astride night sabers charged into the battle from all sides, their beasts mauling some of the demons before the latter realized they were under assault. As the newcomers attacked, they sang.

Malfurion gaped at them, only belatedly realizing that they were not the soldiers of Jarod Shadowsong. Their armor was more silver and—he looked twice—shaped for more feminine figures. The song he heard was in praise of the Night Warrior, the fearsome battle incarnation of the Mother Moon.

The Sisterhood of Elune had come to their rescue.

For the first time, Malfurion saw the quiet, gentle priestesses in their wartime roles. Many carried long, curved swords, while others wielded short lances with points on both ends. A few even had bows no longer than their forearms, from which they swiftly shot dart after dart.

The effect on the demons was immediate. Felbeasts dropped, riddled. A priestess swung her blade with the ease of a soldier, decapitating a horned warrior. Two night sabers dropped upon another hound, slashing it repeatedly from both sides until all that remained was a bloody carcass.

And among the fearsome figures now wreaking havoc on the Burning Legion, he saw Tyrande.

Before he could call to her, a demon thrust at him. The towering Fel Guard would have cut through the druid if not for his swift reflexes. The night elf rolled out of range, then cast a spell.

The ground beneath his adversary's feet turned into a wet, sandy mixture. The Fel Guard sank in up to his waist, but managed to keep from dropping any farther. He clawed at the edge with his free hand, trying to pull himself free.

Malfurion gave him no such opportunity. He kicked the blade out of the demon's hand, then ran after it. The monstrous warrior twisted about, trying to snare his legs. Malfurion slipped, one foot caught by his foe. He seized the hilt of the sword just as the demon dragged him to the quicksand.

Swinging with all his might, the druid buried the blade in the Fel Guard's head.

As the demon sank slowly into the mire, Malfurion saw that not all was going well. The sisterhood had the upper hand, but more than one of them faced imminent threat. Even as he straightened, one priestess was torn from the saddle by a felbeast, who bit through her neck as easily as through silk. Another sister tumbled to the ground as a demon drove his weapon through the open jaws of a night saber, the other end of the blade bursting out between the cat's shoulder blades. A second warrior dispatched the priestess a moment later.

But what terrified Malfurion most was when his gaze fixed upon Tyrande once more. Locked in combat with one of the Fel Guard, she failed to notice the Houndmaster and his whip.

The lash should have wrapped around her throat, but a chance shift by her mount instead had it bind her arms to the sides. The skeletal knight tugged hard, pulling Tyrande off her panther as if her armored form weighed nothing.

"No!" cried Malfurion, starting after her.

Krasus, in the midst of casting a spell, tried to grab his arm. "Druid, you are safer here—"

But the night elf cared only about Tyrande. His training all but forgotten, he angled his way through the battle. When he got near enough, he leapt— but not for his childhood friend.

The immense form of the Houndmaster resisted Malfurion's weight as he struck the demon, but it did cause the hideous figure to lose his concentration. The whip loosened its grip on the priestess, letting her land softly on the earth.

"Fool!" spat the Houndmaster, grabbing the druid by his shoulder. "I am Hakkar . . . and you are nothing."

He did not see the dagger that Malfurion pulled from his belt. The small blade sank into the demon's arm at the place where the elbow joint offered some vulnerability.

With a howl, Hakkar dropped his quarry. He pulled the dagger free, the sharp blade covered in the thick ooze that was the demon's blood. However, instead of using the dagger on Malfurion, the Houndmaster tossed it aside and retrieved his fallen whip. He stalked toward the rising druid, arm already raised.

"Hisss ordersss are to keep you alive if posssible . . . I think it will *not* be posssible, though . . ."

Hakkar struck. Malfurion clamored in pain as lightning flared all over his body. He felt as if he were being burned alive.

However, a part of him remained calm throughout his agony. It drew upon Cenarius's teachings, pulling Malfurion away from his pain. The anguish of the whip faded into nothing. The Houndmaster struck him a second and third time, but it might as well have been a slight breeze for all the druid felt it.

Malfurion understood that the punishment would eventually ravage his body regardless of the lack of pain. His *shan'do*'s teachings but gave him the chance to do what he could to defend himself . . . if at all possible.

"I will keep you jussst barely alive, perhapsss," mocked Hakkar, hitting him again. "All he ssseeksss isss enough life to torture! There will be jussst that . . . "

The fearsome giant raised his whip again.

Malfurion's gaze twisted up to the heavens. The cloud cover offered him his best hope, and the Houndmaster, ironically, had aided in that choice.

The wind assisted him first, stirring the clouds to motion. They disliked being so disturbed and in their anger quickly grew black. Although it went against his nature, Malfurion fed their rage, then played on their vanity. There was one here who commanded lightning of his own and flaunted it.

Hakkar took his stillness for surrender. Eyes blazing, the Houndmaster pulled his arm back. "One more ssstroke, I think! One more ssstroke . . ."

The clouds rumbled, shook.

Lightning shot down, not one but *two* bolts that hit the huge demon dead on.

Hakkar let out a roar of pain that made every bone in Malfurion's body shiver. The Houndmaster stood bathed in brilliant light, his arms outstretched as if he sought to embrace that which destroyed him. The whip, already burnt black, fell from his trembling grasp.

All around the scene of the battle, the felbeasts abruptly paused in their struggles and howled mournfully.

At last, the heavenly illumination faded away . . . and the ashy corpse of the demon lord dropped limply to the grass.

The monstrous hounds howled once more, then their bodies glowed as they had when first summoned. As one, the felbeasts *vanished*, their cries still resounding.

Bereft of both Hakkar and his pets, the few remaining demons put up little resistance against the priestesses and Krasus. As the last fell slain, Malfurion staggered over to Tyrande.

She sat on the ground, still half-stunned. When she saw him, however, Tyrande's face broke out into a wonderful smile that made Malfurion forget his own pain.

"Tyrande! This miracle is yours . . ."

"No miracle, Malfurion. One who I healed told me of a felbeast behind our lines. He also described hearing what I believed was the demon commanding them." She gazed briefly at what remained of Hakkar. "I went to warn you and the others, only to find that Krasus and you had departed for here. Perhaps it was Elune speaking to me, but I felt certain that you were at risk."

"So you turned to the sisterhood. I've seen few soldiers who fight better."

She gave him another smile, this one tired but pleased. "There is much about the temple that outsiders do not understand." Her expression grew more serious. "Are you all right?"

"I am . . . but I fear that Krasus and I came here for no good reason. I'd hoped to contact Cenarius so that the wizard might be able to gain some sort of mount that could carry him to the land of the dragons."

"Rhonin and Brox hinted as much, but I could scarcely believe—does he truly dream that he can meet with them?"

The druid glanced over at Krasus, who had been aided in rising by two of the sisters. Like so many others, they treated him with reverence even though they were not quite certain why. The mage strode toward where the Hound-master lay, his expression perturbed. "You see him. You sense something within him, Tyrande. I think he can do it, if somehow he reaches their realm."

"But unless a dragon itself carries him there, how else can he make the journey in good time?"

"I don't know. I—" A sudden shadow covered the pair. Malfurion looked up, and his hopeless expression changed to one of wonder.

They circled the party thrice before finally ascending in an area away from the nearest night saber. The cats hissed, but did not otherwise attempt to attack the new arrivals, perhaps because they themselves were not sure what to make of them.

With their vast, feathered wings and ravenlike heads, they resembled jet-black gryphons at first sight. Even the forelimbs were scaled and taloned like those of the aforementioned creature. Beyond that, however, they were entirely different animals. Instead of leonine torsos and hindquarters, these two had equine forms, even down to the thick tails.

"*Hippogriffs,*" declared the knowledgeable Krasus, his disturbed expression shifting to one of intense satisfaction. "Swift and certain fliers. He could not have chosen better, your Cenarius."

Tyrande did not look so thrilled. "But there are *two* of them."

The mage and Malfurion studied each other, both recognizing why Cenarius would send more than one mount.

"I'm to go with Krasus, it seems," answered the druid.

Seizing him by the arm, Tyrande snapped, "No, Malfurion! Not there!"

"I see the sense of the forest lord's decision," Krasus interjected. "The druid will be better able to guide the hippogriffs, and his link to Cenarius will give him good standing with the queen of the reds, Alexstrasza . . . She Who Is Life."

The priestess's eyes pleaded with him, but Malfurion had to agree. "He's right. I have to go with him. Forgive me, Tyrande." On impulse, the druid hugged her. Tyrande hesitated, then returned the brief hug. Malfurion gazed down at her and added, "I fear you might have to help Rhonin and Brox explain our absence. Will you do that for me?"

She finally surrendered to the inevitable. "Of course I will. You should know me that well."

The hippogriffs squawked, as if impatient to be on their way. Krasus obliged them by quickly mounting. Malfurion climbed aboard the second one, eyes still on Tyrande.

Seizing his wrist, she suddenly started whispering. It took a moment for the two riders to realize that Tyrande was giving Malfurion a blessing from Elune.

"Go safely," she finished quietly. "And return the same way . . . for me."

The druid swallowed, unable to say anything. Krasus ended the awkwardness of the situation by gently prodding his hippogriff in the ribs with his heels. The beast squawked again, then turned in preparation for flight. Malfurion's mount instinctively followed suit.

"Farewell and thank you, Tyrande," he called. "I'll be back soon enough."

"I will hold you to that, Mal."

He smiled at her use of his childhood nickname, then had to cling on tight as the hippogriff charged into the air after its mate.

"The journey will be long," shouted Krasus, "but not nearly so long, thanks to the demigod's gift!"

Malfurion nodded, not entirely paying attention. His gaze remained on the shrinking figure below. He watched her watch him in turn, until finally he could no longer see her at all.

And even then he watched more, at that instant knowing in his heart that Tyrande did exactly the same.

ELEVEN

The demons did not regroup and attack, which the night elves took as a promising sign even if Rhonin and Brox felt otherwise. Ravencrest dared use another evening to let his troops rest more and although both outsiders agreed with the need for that, they also knew that the Burning Legion would be in no way idle during that period. Archimonde would be plotting, planning, each second his adversaries delayed.

The discovery of the disappearance of Krasus and Malfurion did not sit well with the night elves. Jarod looked as if he were heading to the gallows, and not without good reason. It had been his responsibility to see that nothing happened to the desperately-needed spellcasters, and now some of them had abandoned the host under his very nose.

"Lord Ravencrest will have my hide for this!" the former Guard officer uttered more than once as he and the others headed to the noble's tent. That Tyrande, who had just returned after seeing Malfurion and Krasus off, had insisted on coming to help explain matters did not comfort Jarod in the least. He was certain that he would receive the most terrible punishment for having let such valuable members of the host simply leave.

And, indeed, it initially appeared that the bearded elder might do as he said. Upon hearing the news, Lord Ravencrest let out a furious roar and struck aside the small table that he had been using for his various charts and notes.

"I gave no permission for such foolish activities!" yelled the master of Black Rook Hold. "By perpetrating this outrage, they threaten the stability of our forces! If word should leak out that two of our spellcasters have abandoned us at this integral moment—"

"They didn't abandon anyone," protested Rhonin. "They went for help."

"From the dragons? Those two might as well walk directly into the jaws of the first one they see, for all the aid we can expect from those creatures! The wizard's pet was good enough assistance under his guidance, but wild dragons . . ."

"The dragons are the oldest, most intelligent race of our world. They know more than we will ever learn."

"And they're likely to *eat* most of us before we even get the chance to!" Ravencrest retorted. He glanced at Tyrande, and his tone grew a bit more respectful. "And what part does a Sister of Elune have in all this?"

"We have met before, my lord."

He peered closer. "Aaah, yes! We have! Your female friend, Illidan!"

The sorcerer, who had been silently standing to the side, nodded. Illidan's expression revealed nothing.

Ravencrest crossed his arms. "I had hopes that *either* of you might have some influence over young Malfurion at least. I know that no one can command Master Krasus, no one, indeed."

"Malfurion meant to come back," the priestess countered, "but his patron gave indication that he should travel with the wizard."

"Patron? You refer to that nonsense about the demigod, Cenarius?"

Tyrande pursed her lips. "Illidan can attest to the existence of the forest lord."

His mask crumbling, Malfurion's twin muttered, " 'Tis true. Cenarius is real. I've seen him."

"Hmmph! Dragons and now demigods! All this might and magic abounding around us, yet we are *losing* strength, not gaining! I suppose this Cenarius also has reasons for not siding with us!"

"He and his kind battle the demons in their own manner," she answered.

"And speaking of the demons, did not either of these fools consider that they're constantly at risk from assassins? What if they were attacked before they ever—" Ravencrest paused as he noted the shifting gazes of the party. "*Were* they attacked?"

The priestess bowed her head. "Yes, my lord. I and my sisters were there. We aided them in defeating the demons. Both left uninjured."

Next to her, Jarod grimaced and Illidan shook his head in exasperation. Ravencrest exhaled, then fell back onto the short bench he had been utilizing for a chair. Grasping an open flask of wine, he downed a good portion and rasped, "Tell me about *that*."

Tyrande did, briefly recapping her discovery of assassins nearby, then her horror when she found out that Malfurion and Krasus had already ridden off to the woods. She and her sisters had raced like the proverbial wind after the pair, and had come upon them in the midst of a titanic struggle. The priestesses had charged in fully aware that they risked their own lives and a few had perished, but all had felt that Krasus and the druid were essential to the overall victory. No sacrifice was too great to keep them alive.

At this point, a slight snort escaped Illidan, but Ravencrest appeared most interested. He listened carefully to the details of the battle, and when Tyrande spoke of the demon with the whip, his eyes lit up.

"One of their commanders, surely, the leader of their assassins," he noted.

"It seemed so. He was powerful, but Malfurion summoned the lightning from the heavens and slew him."

"Well struck!" The noble seemed caught between admiration and frustration. "And exactly the reason why at least the druid should've returned to us! We need his power!"

"The Moon Guard and I will make up for his unpermitted absence," Illidan insisted.

"It'll have to, sorcerer. It'll have to." He put the flask aside and stared at the party, especially Rhonin. "Do I have the word of *you*, wizard, that you'll not follow the path of your compatriot?"

"I want to see the Burning Legion defeated, Lord Ravencrest."

"Hmmph! Not at all a satisfactory answer, but one I expected from one of your ilk. Captain Shadowsong . . ."

Swallowing, the younger night elf stepped forward and saluted. "Yes, my lord!"

"I at first considered having you punished severely for your failure to keep this band under control. However, the more I know of them, the less I can imagine *anyone* managing to do that. That you've kept them alive and intact this long speaks of your merits. Continue your task—so long as you still have anyone to watch, that is."

It took a few seconds for the words to register with Jarod. When he realized that the noble had actually *complimented* him for surviving his time with the spellcasters, the officer quickly saluted again. "Yes, my lord! My thanks, my lord!"

"No . . . *my* sympathies to you." Ravencrest leaned forward, reaching for one of the charts. "You are dismissed, all of you. You, too, Illidan." He shook his head as he eyed the sheet and muttered, "Mother Moon, spare me from all spellcasters . . ."

Malfurion's brother took his expulsion as if his patron had struck him full across the face with his gauntlet. Dipping his head in an aborted bow, the sorcerer followed the rest out of the commander's tent.

Brox and Rhonin strode side by side, both silent. Tyrande walked with the captain, who still looked awed that he had departed with his head attached to his neck.

A hand touched the priestess's shoulder. "Tyrande . . ."

The others moved on while she turned to face Illidan. Gone was his brief anger at being dismissed by his lord. Now he wore an intense expression akin to the last time that the pair had talked.

"Illidan? What—"

"I can't stay quiet any longer! Malfurion's terrible naïveté brings this on! This is the final straw! He's grown reckless, undeserving of you!"

She tried to politely step away. "Illidan, it's been a long, difficult—"

"Hear me out! I accepted his desire to learn this 'druidism' because I understood his hopes to be different! *I*, of all people, understood my brother's ambitions!"

"Malfurion is not—"

But again he would not let her finish. Amber eyes almost glowing, the sorcerer added, "This path he follows is erratic, dangerous! It is no saving grace! I know! He should've followed my path! The Well is the answer! See what I've accomplished in such a short time! The Moon Guard are mine to command and through them I've sent many a demon to death! Malfurion's path leads only to his own destruction—and possibly yours, as well!"

"What could you mean by that?"

"I know you care for both of us, Tyrande, and we, in turn, feel much for you. One of us will be your intended, we all know that, but where once I was willing to stand aside and let you choose without influence, I can't anymore!" He clutched her arm tightly. "I've got to protect you from Malfurion's insanity!

I say again that the Well of Eternity is the only true source of power that can save us! Even the priestesses of Elune cannot cast the spells that I do! Be mine, and I can protect you properly! Better yet, I can *teach* you as your temple never could, make you understand the might the Well can offer you! Together, we could be a force more formidable than all the Moon Guard combined, for we'd be one in spirit and body! We'd—"

"Illidan!" she suddenly snapped. "Recall yourself!"

He immediately released her, looking as if stabbed in the heart. "Tyrande—"

"You shame yourself with your words concerning your brother, Illidan, and make assumptions with no basis in fact! Malfurion has done everything he could to save all our lives and the path he's chosen is a valued one! He may be the true survival of our kind, Illidan! The Well's becoming tainted! The demons draw from it in just the same manner as you. What does that say?"

"Don't be ridiculous! You compare the demons with my work?"

"Malfurion would—"

"Malfurion!" he shouted, his countenance increasingly grim. "I see it now! What a bungler, what a buffoon I must seem to you!" He clenched his fist and raw energy flashed around it. "You've already chosen, Tyrande, even if you haven't said so."

"I've done nothing of the sort!"

"Malfurion . . ." Illidan repeated, teeth clenched tightly. "May the two of you be very happy . . . if we survive."

He spun around and headed to where the Moon Guard had stationed themselves. Tyrande watched him stride away. A tear fell unbidden from her eye.

"Shaman?" came a voice from behind.

The priestess jumped. "Broxigar?"

The orc nodded solemnly. "He's hurt you, shaman?"

"N-no . . . just a misunderstanding."

Brox eyed Illidan's receding backside. A low growl escaped the bestial warrior. "That one misunderstands much . . . and underestimates more."

"I'm all right. Did you wish something?"

Shrugging, the orc answered, "Nothing."

"You came back because I was with Illidan, didn't you?"

"This unworthy one owes you much, shaman . . . and owes that one something more."

The priestess's brow furrowed. "I don't understand."

Brox flexed his fingers, the same fingers that had been burned once by Illidan. "Is nothing, shaman. Is nothing."

"Thank you for coming to my aid, Broxigar. I'll be all right . . . and so will Malfurion. I know it."

The orc grunted. "This humble one hopes so."

But his eyes continued to watch Illidan closely.

Rhonin paused, watching the orc and the priestess talk. He understood perfectly why Brox had suddenly turned back to speak with Tyrande. Illidan's affections for her had begun to border on obsession. The sorcerer had not seemed all that fearful for his brother's life, and—from what the wizard could see—had been attempting to use Malfurion's absence to further his own cause with Tyrande.

But the triangle among the three night elves was the least of Rhonin's concerns. He was more preoccupied with what he had learned of the attack in the forest. While Rhonin was relieved that both Krasus and the druid had survived, their victory had, without meaning to, unnerved the human more than anything else since his arrival here.

They had battled Hakkar, the Houndmaster. Rhonin recalled that name with dread, for with his whip the foul demon could summon an endless pack of felbeasts, the scourge of any spellcaster. How many wizards from Dalaran had perished horribly because of the demon's pets during the Legion's second coming?

Yes, Rhonin had good reason to despair even hearing the Houndmaster's name, but he feared something else even more.

He feared Hakkar's death, here in the past.

The Houndmaster had perished in the *future*. The demon had survived the war against the night elves.

But not this time. This time, Hakkar had been slain . . . which now meant the future was certain to be different.

Which now meant that this first war, despite the slaying of a most powerful demon, could definitely be lost.

The hippogriffs soared over the landscape, cutting away the miles with each heavy beat of their vast wings. Though they could not fly as swiftly as a dragon, few other creatures could match them. The animals lived for flying, and Krasus felt their excitement as they raced each other over hills, rivers, and forest.

Born to the sky, the dragon mage lifted his face to the wind, savoring the sensation now forbidden him because of his transformation. He smiled as an unbidden memory of his first flight with Alexstrasza returned to him. That day, he had only just become her consort, and the pair had finally begun the ritual before their initial mating.

During that ritual, Krasus—or Korialstrasz in his true form—had circled the much larger female over and over, displaying for her his strength and agility. She, in turn, flew in a vast circle around the realm of dragons. The female had kept her speed constant, neither too fast nor too slow. Her new mate was supposed to show his prowess in all things, but he also had to have the energy needed afterward to breed with her.

Korialstrasz had performed all manner of aerial maneuvers to impress his mate. He flew on his back. He darted between tightly-packed peaks. He even let himself drop toward one of the most jagged ones, missing impalement by a few bare yards. Reckless he had been at times, but that was part of the game, part of the ritual.

"My Alexstrasza . . ." Krasus whispered to the wind as the memory faded away. It may have been that a tear briefly graced one eye or perhaps it was only a drop of moisture in the sky. Either way, the wind quickly carried it off and he concentrated again on the journey ahead.

The landscape had just begun to turn more rocky and hilly. They had almost reached the midway point. Krasus was pleased but still impatient. Something was amiss and he had a fairly good idea as to the cause.

Neltharion.

The Earth Warder.

Known in Krasus's true time period as the monster *Deathwing*.

Although he had lost much of his memory during his fall through history, there was no way by which Krasus could ever forget the black beast. In the future, Deathwing was evil itself, ever working to bring the world to ruin so that he might have dominion over the wreckage. Already Neltharion had crossed the threshold of madness, and Krasus had suffered for it. When last he had traveled to his home—brought there by his younger self—Krasus had run afoul of the Earth Warder's paranoia. Fearing that the dragon mage would warn the others of his coming treachery—a reasonable assumption, in fact—the black leviathan had crafted a subtle spell that prevented his foe from speaking out about him. Most of the other dragons now thought Krasus half-mad himself because of that spell.

The silence noted first by young Korialstrasz and now detected by his elder self as well could only mean that Neltharion had pressed on with his intentions. What exactly they were, Krasus could not yet recall and it pained him that of all things this should be lost. If there was one thing the mage would change in the past without fear of repercussions in the future, it would be the Earth Warder's betrayal. That, more than anything, had been the final spiral down for the dragon race.

Krasus suddenly realized that Malfurion was calling his name. Shaking his head, he looked to the druid.

"Krasus! Are you ill?"

"In a manner in which I can never be cured!" returned the elder spellcaster. He frowned at his own carelessness. Centuries of learning to keep his emotions masked had all vanished with his return to this turbulent time. Now Krasus had little more self-control than Rhonin or even the orc.

Nodding even though he did not understand, the druid looked away. Krasus continued to silently berate himself. He had to maintain control. It was essential if he hoped to keep everything from collapsing into chaos.

Malfurion did not understand what the death of Hakkar meant, but how could he? He did not know that the Houndmaster had been among the demons who perished in the future. Rhonin would understand when he heard. The implications were staggering. Now Krasus had no idea what the future held.

If there still *was* a future.

On and on their journey continued. The hippogriffs descended once to satisfy their thirst at a river, and the duo took the opportunity to do the same. After sharing some rations, they mounted their beasts and took to the air again. The next time they landed, Krasus hoped it would be in the domain of his kind.

The landscape grew more mountainous. Huge peaks jutted up to the heavens. In the distance, a pair of large black birds flew toward them from the opposite direction. The dragon mage became tense. Soon, very soon, he would be home.

Krasus only prayed that he would find everything intact.

Malfurion's hippogriff squawked. The mage belatedly noticed that the two birds continued to fly toward them . . . and that they were much larger than he had first calculated.

Too large, in fact, to be birds at all.

He leaned forward, squinting.

Dragons . . . *black* dragons.

Krasus prodded his mount on one side, at the same time shouting to Malfurion, "To the southern edge of the mountain chain! Hurry!"

The druid, too, now recognized the threat and obeyed. As the two hippogriffs veered away, the dragons did not adjust. Despite their keen eyesight, the behemoths had not yet noticed the smaller creatures.

Aware that at any moment that might change, Krasus urged his beast to as swift a pace as it could set. Perhaps it was simply coincidence that these two giants were out here, but the mage suspected otherwise. Understanding Neltharion's growing paranoia, Krasus believed it more likely that the Earth

Warder had sent these two guardians out to watch for any intruders entering the dragon lands. Ironic that his madness would now prove him correct.

The hippogriffs descended at a breathtaking rate, soaring toward the lower mountains. Once there, Krasus could relax; the blacks would surely fly right past them.

Yet, one of the dragons glanced their way just when it seemed that they would evade notice. He roared, and his comrade twisted his sinewy neck around to see what had garnered the first's attention. When he noted the two riders, he, too, bellowed his outrage.

With the perfection of creatures born to fly, the dragons banked and raced after their prey.

"What can we do?" called Malfurion.

"Fly lower! We can skirt the mountains better than they! They must follow or risk losing us, and they will not wish to displease their lord!"

It was as much as he could say about Neltharion without the Earth Warder's spell taking hold. He thanked the Aspects that the druid had not tried to ply him with foolish questions such as why they were fleeing from dragons when dragons were what they had come to find. Malfurion clearly recognized Krasus's knowledge in this circumstance and understood that if the mage wanted them to flee, they needed to flee.

The larger of the two beasts—and, therefore, the older—began to push ahead of his companion. He roared again, and a burst of what at first seemed like flame shot from his savage maw.

It came within only a few scant yards of the wizard, causing his mount to squawk loud and heating the air around the fleeing figures several degrees. The "flames" began falling earthward, revealing themselves to have actually been a column of molten lava, a breath spell inherent to the black flight.

Before the dragon could send forth another shot, the hippogriffs darted into the mountain chain. Their pursuers were right behind, dipping to the side to avoid colliding with the hard peaks.

Krasus scowled. He knew how talented his kind was at maneuvering through mountains. Dragons played at such games from the moment they could fly. He had his doubts that even here he and the druid could escape, but they had to do what they could.

Then the mage thought of those games again, and his hopes rose.

He caught Malfurion's attention and made several gestures to try to explain what he wanted, the last a quick jab with his finger toward a peak to the northeast. Fortunately, the druid was quick to read him. From Malfurion's expression, the night elf also had his doubts, but like Krasus, he understood that they had little other hope. Casting a spell sufficient to drive back not one but two dragons would be very difficult even for the most trained mage.

As they dove toward one particular peak, the druid abruptly steered his hippogriff to the right. Krasus did the opposite. The mage quickly glanced over his shoulder and saw the dragons do the same, the larger one pursuing him.

"Alexstrasza guide me . . . this must work . . ." he muttered.

He could see neither Malfurion nor the other dragon, but that was to be expected. Krasus no longer concerned himself with the druid; there were two ways that his plan might succeed, but both depended upon him keeping ahead of his pursuer.

That was proving far from simple. The huge black was a skilled flyer, rolling and banking as the narrow gaps his prey sought necessitated. The hippogriff, too, excelled in flying, but had to beat its wings much, much more just to keep pace with the monster behind it. Even with those efforts, however, the dragon slowly inched closer.

A roar warned Krasus moments before another column of lava flew past where he had just been. Only his knowledge of a black dragon's tactics had saved him that time. Even still, several places on his robe smoked from where tiny splatters had caught him, while his mount squirmed from ash that had landed on one hind leg.

Krasus rode under a massive beaklike projection on the side of one mountain, then soared through a crack that made two peaks out of one. Each time, the dragon managed to avoid crashing despite the incredible speed with which he raced.

The mountain that the dragon mage had pointed out to Malfurion was fast approaching. In spite of the danger to him, Krasus took the time to peer south, where the druid should have been. He neither heard nor saw anything, but continued on as he planned, hoping that somehow matters would work out.

Again the dragon roared. A blast shot past Krasus, who frowned at his pursuer's sudden lack of aim.

Only when the mountainside ahead on his right shattered, spilling toward him, did Krasus know that he had been outmaneuvered.

He had the hippogriff pull up swiftly and away. Even still, both were pelted by a storm of earth and rock. A chunk the size of Krasus's head bounded off the flank of the animal, causing it to squeal and nearly toss its passenger to his doom. Only Krasus's deathlike grip kept him from slipping.

A great stench washed over rider and steed. The black was right behind them. Krasus raised his hand and uttered the quickest spell he could command.

A random series of light bursts exploded in front of the leviathan. They were relatively harmless, but they startled the dragon, even blinded him momentarily. He twisted, roaring his anger. One wing struck a mountain, tearing away tons of stone.

Krasus's quick thinking had bought him a few scant seconds, nothing more. He hoped that the druid had managed to outpace the other dragon, but Krasus knew his kind's tenacity. If Malfurion still lived, he likely held no greater a lead on his hunter than the mage did with his own.

Then, just as the mountain he had chosen for the rendezvous arose before him, Krasus caught a glimpse of the other rider. The hippogriff looked frantic, and Malfurion had his head buried in its neck. Right behind them came the second behemoth.

Krasus guided his own mount toward Malfurion's, trying to keep just a little ahead of where the druid would be when they crossed paths. His animal called out, alerting not only its mate, but the druid, too. Malfurion lifted his head, the only sign that he had noticed his companion.

As they met at the southern face of the mountain, Krasus urged his hippogriff around it. Malfurion cut in the opposite direction. A moment later, the larger black, ignoring the other tiny figure, followed after Krasus. His comrade continued his chase of the druid.

If there was one advantage that Krasus had over the black dragons, it was that they did not know he was one of their kind. Nor, for that matter, did they realize that he had flown this region so often in his long life that he likely knew its myriad paths better than anyone or anything.

Again the giant behind him roared, and this time the blast struck so close that it left a seared edge on the mountain. making Krasus choke. Still the hippogriff raced along, trusting in its swiftness and its rider's guidance. Krasus had it drop slightly, then forced it to slow. The animal fought the second command, but the mage used his considerable will to overcome any resistance.

And just as the hippogriff obeyed, Malfurion materialized around the mountain's edge.

Krasus had his beast rise slightly to compensate for the oncoming druid. He and Malfurion rode nearly level; any closer and they would have collided.

The mage caught sight of the edge of a leathery wing behind his companion.

He forced the hippogriff down again.

Malfurion had the second animal drive up into the sky with such speed and abruptness that the druid almost slid off its back.

Krasus's pursuer had no time to register the change in direction. Nor, for that matter, did the druid's. So caught up in their own hunts, the dragons could not stop their momentum.

With a thundering boom, the two giants collided head on.

The dragons roared in pain and shock. Tangled together, they rolled to the side, crashing into the very peak that Krasus had earlier chosen.

The entire region shook as they battered against it. From his high seat, Krasus thought he heard the crack of bone, but he did not wait around to find out. As the two dragons fell from sight, Krasus waved Malfurion on. By the time the two leviathans recovered, the mage and the druid would be long gone.

Krasus eyed the peaks rising ahead. He was very near his goal now . . . and more than ever, he needed to know just what was happening.

TWELVE

Illidan should have been going over strategy with the Moon Guard, but at that moment he couldn't have cared less about the war. All he could think about was that he had made an abysmal fool out of himself in front of Tyrande. He had bared his soul to her, only to discover that his brother had already staked his territory. Tyrande had chosen Malfurion.

The worst of it was, his twin was probably too caught up in his craft to notice.

Lord Ravencrest's personal sorcerer stalked past a picket. The guard stationed there raised his weapon and, in a slightly anxious voice, declared, "All are to stay within the bounds of the camp, Master Illidan! By order of—"

"I know whose order it is."

"But—"

Illidan's amber eyes stared deep. The soldier swallowed and stepped aside.

The area beyond was still slightly wooded, the Burning Legion having lost the opportunity during their brief hold to destroy everything. While many took heart from this fact, Illidan would not have cared if the entire area had been scorched. He raised one hand slightly and even considered starting the conflagration himself, then dropped the idea.

Even though Malfurion had run afoul of demons in the lands south, his brother had no fear of doing likewise here. In the first place, Illidan walked only a short distance from the camp, stepping barely out of sight. In the second place, any demon who tried to attack him now would have been reduced to ash in the blink of an eye. Illidan's inner rage was such that he dreamed of fighting something, *anything,* in order to drain himself of the jealousy he felt now against Malfurion.

But no felbeast sought to drain him dry, no Infernal attempted to barrel him over. No Eredar, no Doomguard, not even one of the laughable Fel

Guard. The whole of the Burning Legion feared to face Illidan alone, for they knew he was an unbeatable force.

Save where it concerned the love of one person.

Finding a huge rock upon which to sit, Illidan thought over all his wonderful plans. Lord Ravencrest's adoption of him as one of his most trusted servants had been a coup; it had enabled the twin to at last seriously consider what had been formulating in his mind for the previous three seasons. He had long looked past Tyrande as a child, and saw her as the beauteous female that she was. While Malfurion had talked to birds, he had planned on how to ask Tyrande to be his mate.

In his head, everything had fallen into place perfectly. One could not but help admire his position, and he knew that many other females had indicated their desire for him. Over a short period of time, Illidan had gained control of those Moon Guard left alive, and his hand had saved many night elves from destruction. He was powerful, handsome, and a hero. Tyrande should have fallen over herself to be his.

And she *would* have, if not for Malfurion.

With a snarl, the sorcerer gestured at another rock nearby. It transformed instantly into a recreation of his brother's face, so much his own and yet not.

Illidan clenched his fist.

The face shattered, fragments crumbling into a loose pile.

"She should've been mine!"

His words echoed through the woods. Malfurion's sibling snarled at his own voice, each repetition reminding him how much he had lost.

"She would've been mine . . ." he corrected himself, lost in pity. "If not for you, brother Malfurion, she would've been mine."

He is always taking precedence, came the sudden thought into his head, *when clearly it should be you.*

"Me? Because I have these eyes?" Illidan laughed at himself. "My miraculous amber eyes?"

A sign of greatness . . . an omen of legend . . .

"A jest played upon me by the gods!" The sorcerer rose, heading deeper into the woods. Even on the move, however, he could not escape the voice, the thoughts . . . and some part of him did not truly wish to.

Malfurion does not even know she wants him. What if he would never know?

"What am I supposed to do? Keep them apart? I might as well try to keep the moon from rising!"

But if Malfurion would perish in the war before he could ever know the truth, it would be as if her choice never happened! She would surely come to you if there was no more Malfurion . . .

The sorcerer paused. He cupped his hands, and in the palms he created an image of Tyrande dancing. She was slightly younger and wearing a flowing skirt. The image was her as Illidan recalled from a festival a few seasons back. That had been the first time he had considered her more than a play friend.

If there was no more Malfurion . . .

Illidan suddenly clapped his hands shut, dissipating the vision. "No! That'd be barbaric!"

And yet Illidan paused immediately after, perversely fascinated by the thought.

Many things could happen to one in the midst of battle. Not death, perhaps, but the demons must know about Malfurion, especially. He destroyed the first portal, slew the queen's advisor, and now one of the Legion's commanders . . . they would want him alive . . . very much alive . . .

"Turn him over . . . to them? I—"

Battles become confused, some are left behind. No one is ever to blame . . .

"No one is ever to blame . . ." murmured Illidan. He opened his hands, and once again Tyrande's image danced for him. He watched it for a time, considering.

But once more, the sorcerer clapped his palms tight. Then, as if sickened by his dark thoughts, he brushed his hands against his garments and quickly headed back to camp. "Never!" he growled under his breath. "Not my brother! Never!"

The sorcerer continued muttering to himself as he walked. He therefore did not notice when the figure separated itself from the trees, watching him from a distance and chuckling at the night elf's momentary lapse of honor and brotherhood.

"The groundwork is laid," it whispered in amusement, "and you yourself will build upon it, twin of the druid."

With that, it snuck off in the opposite direction . . . moving along on two furred limbs ending in hooves.

Unwilling to wait any longer for the druid and the mage to return, Lord Ravencrest ordered the night elves to move out the next day. It was clear that most of his followers would have preferred to march at night, but the noble would not let the demons see him as too predictable. His fighters were gradually becoming as accustomed to the sun as much as they could, even though it meant that their strength was not at its peak. Ravencrest now relied on the determination of his people, their understanding that, if they failed, this would be their end.

The Burning Legion, in turn, awaited them not all that far away. The night elves marched knowing that bloodshed lurked just beyond the horizon, but they marched nonetheless.

And so, once more the struggle for Kalimdor went on.

While the night elves battled to survive and Illidan sought to come to grips with his foul thoughts, Krasus struggled with an entirely different matter, one that Malfurion suspected he had not planned for.

"It goes on for as far as I can detect," the mage hissed in frustration.

"It" was invisible to the eye, but not to the touch. "It" was a vast, unseen shield that held them but a day—by Krasus's measurement—from their goal.

They had discovered it the hard way. Krasus's hippogriff had collided with *nothing*, the crash so violent that the mage had been thrown from the injured animal's back. Malfurion, aware that his own hippogriff could never reach Krasus in time, sought out the aid of the wind. A powerful mountain blast threw his companion *up* again, close enough for the druid to grasp the mage's arm. They had then landed to study this new obstacle.

And after several hours of study, Krasus appeared no closer to the answer . . . and the sight of him looking so baffled unnerved the druid more than he let on.

At last, Krasus uttered the unthinkable. "I am defeated."

"You find no method by which to pierce it?"

"Worse, druid, I cannot even contact anyone within. Even my thoughts are barred."

Malfurion had come to deeply respect Krasus. The mysterious mage had helped save him when Lord Xavius had captured his spirit. Krasus had also been instrumental in enabling the night elf to vanquish the queen's advisor and destroy the first portal. To see him thus . . .

"So close," continued the mage. "So very close! This is his work to be sure!"

"Whose work?"

His eyes narrowing, Krasus looked just enough like a pale night elf to make his expression that much more unsettling. He appeared to be measuring his companion and Malfurion suddenly found himself hoping to be found worthy.

"Yes . . . you should know. You deserve to know."

The druid held his breath. Whatever Krasus desired to reveal, it surely had to be of monumental importance.

"Look directly into my eyes, Malfurion." When the night elf had obeyed, Krasus said, "There are three of us that you and yours term 'outsiders.' There is Rhonin, who calls himself a human, and there is Brox, the orc. You know not their races, but they are as you see them—a human and an orc."

The elder figure paused. Thinking he had to respond, Malfurion nodded. "A human and an orc."

"Have I ever said what it is *I* am? Have either of the others specified?"

Thinking back, the night elf could not recall anyone giving name to Krasus's race. "You're of night elven blood. You look enough like us to be kin, if—"

"I might look like one of your kind if he were dead a year or more, but that is as close to a resemblance as we can admit, yes? What you see is only a guise; there are no blood ties between your race and mine . . . nor, for that matter, mine with humans, orcs, dwarves, or tauren."

Malfurion looked confused. "Then . . . what are you?"

Krasus's gaze drew him in further. All he could see were those alien eyes. "Look deep, druid. Look deep and think of what you know of me already."

As he stared into his companion's eyes, Malfurion recalled everything he knew, which was not much at all—a spellcaster of remarkable knowledge, and talent. Even at his most ill, Krasus had carried about him an aura of incredible age and ability. The sisterhood had sensed it, although none of them seemed to understand exactly what it meant, as did the Moon Guard. Even the night sabers treated him better than they did the masters who had raised them.

And for a time, the mage had even commanded the friendship of a dragon . . .

. . . A dragon . . .

Without the behemoth near, Krasus had suffered as if on his deathbed. The dragon, too, had shown signs of weariness beyond the ordinary. Together, however, they had been as one, their strength magnified.

But there had been more to it than that. Korialstrasz had spoken with Krasus like none other—as an equal, almost a brother.

Seeing the growing realization on the druid's face, Krasus whispered, "You are at the threshold of understanding. Cross it now."

He opened himself up for Malfurion to see. In the night elf's mind, Krasus transformed. His robes ripped to shreds as his body grew and twisted. His legs bent in reverse and his feet and hands became long, clawed appendages. Wings sprouted from his back, expanding until they were great enough to blot out the moon.

Krasus's face stretched. His nose and mouth became one, growing into a savage maw. His hair solidified, turning into a scaled crest that ran down the length of his back all the way to the tip of the tail that had formed at the same time as the wings.

And as crimson scales covered every inch of the other's body, Malfurion blurted the name by which all knew such huge, fearsome leviathans.

"Dragon!"

Then, as quickly as the incredible image had appeared before him it now vanished. Malfurion shook his head and eyed the figure before him.

"Yes, Malfurion Stormrage, I am a dragon. A red dragon, to be precise. Long have I worn the form of one mortal creature or another, however, for it has been my choice to walk among you, teaching and learning as I strive for peace among all of us."

"A dragon . . ." Malfurion shook his head. It explained so much in retrospect . . . and raised many more questions in turn.

"Among those in the host, only Rhonin fully knows who and what I am, although the orc may understand and the sisterhood likely has its suspicions."

"Are humans allied to dragons?"

"Nay! But in my guise as you see me, Rhonin was my student, an exceptional mage even for one of his versatile race! I trust him in some ways more than I do many of my own people."

As if to emphasize that fact, Krasus—Malfurion could not yet accept terming him a dragon—slapped one hand against the invisible barrier. "And *this* only adds credence to why that is so. This should not be here."

"A dragon . . . but why didn't you transform in order to fly here? Why have me summon the hippogriffs?" More curious incidents occurred to the night elf. "You could've been slain more than once, including when last we fought the demons!"

"Some things must remain hidden, Malfurion, but I tell you this much; I do not transform because I *cannot*. That ability has been stripped from me for the time being."

"I . . . I see."

Krasus turned his gaze back to the concealed wall, again seeking some entrance through it. "You perceive why I felt so certain that I would be able to confront the dragons. They will listen to one of their own. They will also tell one of their own why they are acting so mysteriously." He hissed savagely, startling the night elf. "If I can contact them first."

"Who would do this?"

It almost appeared that Krasus intended to answer, but then he clamped his mouth tight. After several seconds of obvious inner turmoil, he glumly responded, "It does not matter. What does is that I have failed. The one hope I had for ensuring the outcome of the war is beyond my reach."

There was much that the dragon mage had not told Malfurion, and the night elf knew it. However, the druid also respected Krasus enough not to pursue the matter any further. All Malfurion wanted to do now was help, especially with his new understanding of the situation. If Krasus could convince his kind to join with the defenders, then surely that would spell a quick end to the Burning Legion.

But their spells could not open the wall, and neither of the two could simply walk through it like a ghost or—

Swallowing hard, the druid said, "I may know of a way through, at least for me."

"What do you mean?"

"I-I could walk the Emerald Dream."

The mage's visage darkened, then grew thoughtful. Malfurion wanted him to reject the idea out of hand, but instead Krasus nodded. "Yes . . . yes, that may be the one way."

"But will it help? I don't even know whether or not they'll be able to hear or see me . . . and if they do, will they listen?"

"One may be able to do all. You must seek her specifically. Her name is Ysera."

Ysera. Cenarius had spoken her name when offering to teach his student how to walk the dream realm. Ysera was one of the five great Aspects. She ruled the Emerald Dream. Certainly, Ysera would be able to both hear and see the druid's spirit form . . . but would she bother to listen to his words?

Reading the night elf's obvious reluctance, Krasus added, "If you can convince her to bring you to the attention of Alexstrasza, the red dragon, then perhaps she, in turn, can question Korialstrasz, who knows us both. Alexstrasza will listen to him."

From the way the inflection of his voice changed whenever he spoke the other name, Malfurion understood that this other dragon was very, very important to Krasus on a personal level. He knew of Alexstrasza as another of the Aspects and wondered how Krasus could speak of her so easily. His companion was more than simply a dragon who spied on the younger races; he held some status among even his own kind.

The knowledge strengthened Malfurion. "I'll do what I can."

"Should Ysera show reluctance," Krasus further advised, "it would be good to mention Cenarius to her. More than once, if necessary."

Not certain why that should make a difference but trusting to Krasus's wisdom, the night elf nodded, then sat down right where he was. Krasus watched him in silence as he positioned his body. Satisfied with the arrangement, Malfurion shut his eyes and focused.

At first he meditated, calming his body. As he relaxed, the night elf felt the first hints of slumber touch him. He welcomed them, encouraged them. More and more, the mortal world retreated from the druid. Peace draped over Malfurion like a blanket. He knew that Krasus watched over him, so there was no fear of letting go. The mage would protect his defenseless form.

And before he knew it, Malfurion slept. Yet, at the same time, he felt more awake than ever. The night elf concentrated now on departing from the mortal plane. He did as Cenarius had bid him, working to separate his spirit from his body.

It proved so simple to do both that and locate the way into the Emerald Dream that Malfurion felt ashamed about his earlier hesitation. So long as he remained fixed on his quest, surely it would be safe to traverse the other realm.

A hint of green immediately shaded everything. Krasus faded away as Malfurion's surroundings changed. The mountainous region looked surprisingly similar in both dimensions, but the peaks in the Emerald Dream were sharper, less weathered. Here was how they appeared when the creators had first raised them up from the primal soil. Despite the urgency of his mission, Malfurion paused to admire the celestials' handiwork. The sheer majesty of all he saw astounded him.

But nothing would remain in the true world if the Burning Legion was not stopped, and so the druid finally moved on. He reached out to the barrier, expecting resistance, yet nothing slowed his hand. Sure enough, in the Emerald Dream, the spell did not exist. The dragons expected any intruders to be of the more earthly kind and, therefore, subject to the world's natural laws.

Drifting on past where the wall had been, Malfurion headed toward the tallest peaks in the distance. Prior to his collision with the barrier, Krasus had indicated them as where his kind could be found. Since the elder mage had said nothing contrary before the druid had acted, Malfurion took it for granted that he should continue on in that direction.

He flew over the silent land, the huge mountains making him feel most insignificant. The green hue coloring everything, coupled with the lack of any animal life, added to the surreal feel of his surroundings.

As he neared what he believed his destination, Malfurion concentrated. The green coloring faded somewhat, and he began to notice details of weathering. The druid's spirit still "walked" the Emerald Dream, but he now saw into the present-day world as well.

And his first view was that of the overwhelming, ferocious countenance of a crimson dragon.

Startled, Malfurion pulled back. He expected the behemoth's head to dart forward and snap him up, but the sentinel continued to stare through him. It took the druid a few seconds to realize that the dragon could not see him.

The presence of the guardian, who perched atop a high, pointed peak, verified that the night elf had to be near where the dragons gathered. However,

Malfurion did not feel he had the time to go searching one mountain after another for their location. Instead, he thought of what he knew. Ysera was mistress of the Emerald Dream. This near to her, surely she would hear his mental summons.

Whether Ysera would answer, however, was another question.

Knowing he could only try, the druid faded back into the Emerald Dream and imagined the green dragon. He knew that his perception of her was far from fact, but it gave his thoughts something upon which to concentrate.

Ysera, mistress of the dream land, great Aspect, I humbly seek communion with you . . . I bring the word of one who knows She Who Is Life, your sister, Alexstrasza . . .

Malfurion waited. When it became clear that he would not be receiving an answer, he tried again.

Ysera, She of the Dreaming, in the name of Cenarius, Lord of the Wood, I ask this boon of you. I call upon you to—

He broke off as he sensed the sudden presence of another. The druid twisted his head to the right and beheld a thin female of his race, clad in a translucent robe that fluttered even though there was no wind. The hood of the robe covered all but her face, a beautiful yet calm face whose only offsetting feature was the eyes . . . or rather, the closed lids that covered them.

The figure might have looked like a night elf, but in addition to the bright emerald hair she had—more arresting than the green of any true night elf—her skin, garments . . . all were tinted one shade or another of the same color.

There could be no doubt that this was Ysera.

"I have come," she responded, quiet but firm, her eyes never opening, "if only to put an end to your shouting. Your thoughts reverberated through my mind like an unceasing drumbeat."

Malfurion sought to kneel. "My lady—"

She waved a slim hand. "I need not be flattered by such gestures. You have called. I have come. Have your say and begone."

His success still amazed the night elf. Here, in this other form, stood one of the great Aspects. That she had deigned to respond, he could scarcely believe. "Forgive me. I would never seek to disturb you—"

"And yet, here you are."

"I've come with one who knows of you well—a dragon called Krasus."

"His name is known, even if his mind is suspect. What of him?"

"He seeks an audience with Alexstrasza. He can't break through the barrier that surrounds this place."

As he spoke, Malfurion had to focus hard on the Aspect. Ysera constantly shimmered in and out, almost as if she were a figment of his imagination. Her expression did not change, save that beneath the eyelids there was constant movement. That she saw, Malfurion did not doubt, but *how* she did made him most curious.

"The barrier has been set because the planning we do is of the most delicate nature," spoke the Aspect. "No word of what we do must be revealed until the time is ripe . . . so says the Earth Warder."

"But he must enter—"

"And he will not. I have no say over the matter. Is that all?"

Malfurion mulled over Krasus's words. "Then, if he can speak to Alexstrasza through you . . ."

Ysera laughed, such a startling shift that the night elf stood as if stricken. "You are audacious, mortal creature! I am to be your conduit as he interrupts my sister during a most pressing time! Is there anything *else* you would like while you are asking?"

"By my *shan'do,* Cenarius, this is all I seek, and I wouldn't do it if it wasn't necessary."

A peculiar thing happened when he mentioned the demigod by name. Ysera's image grew especially hazy, and the eyes beneath her lids seemed to look down. The reaction, although very brief, was so very noticeable.

"I see no reason to continue this irritation. Return to your companion, night elf, and—"

"Please, mistress of the Emerald Dream! Cenarius will vouch for me. He—"

"There is no reason to bring him up!" she suddenly snapped. For just the briefest of moments, Ysera almost looked ready to open her eyes. Her expression had become one that Malfurion recognized all too well from his childhood. Earlier, he had thought that Cenarius and Ysera had been lovers. But that was not the case, from what he could read in her expression.

Ysera—She of the Dreaming, one of the five great Aspects—had reacted to the demigod's name as might a loving *mother.*

Somewhat ashamed, the druid retreated from her. Ysera, clearly caught up in some memory, paid him no mind. For the first time since he had met Krasus, Malfurion was angry with him. This was ill knowledge and his companion should have known that.

He started to depart the dream realm, but Ysera turned her sightless gaze toward him and suddenly announced, "I will be the bridge you need to reach Alexstrasza."

"My lady . . ."

"You will speak no more about this situation, night elf, or I will cast you out of my domain forever."

Shutting his mouth tight, Malfurion acquiesced. Whatever her relationship with the forest lord, it had been very, very deep and long in term.

"I will guide your spirit to where we now meet, and you will wait until I indicate that your time to converse with my sister has come. Then and only then will I transmit your words to her—your words and *his*."

The acidic tone by which she said the last word spoke of her fury toward Krasus. Praying that his companion's rash suggestion would not get them both killed, the druid voicelessly agreed.

She stretched forth her hand. "Take it."

With the utmost respect, Malfurion obeyed. He had never touched another spirit in the Emerald Dream, and had no idea what to expect. To his surprise, though, Ysera's hand felt like a mortal one. It had no ethereal quality. He might have been holding his mother's hand.

"Remember my warning," the Aspect said.

Before he could respond, they entered the mortal plane. The transition was so immediate, yet so smooth, that the night elf had to adjust to his change in surroundings. Then he had to adjust to Ysera's sudden disappearance.

No, she had not disappeared. She stood but a few yards from where he floated, the mistress of the Emerald Dream now revealed in her full glory. A massive dragon with glittering green scales, she dwarfed Korialstrasz, the only other dragon that the druid had ever met.

And she was not the only one. As his surroundings registered on him, the night elf discovered the two of them were far from alone. Three other gargantuan dragons stood near the center of the huge chamber. The red one surely had to be Alexstrasza, the one Krasus sought. She had a beauty and dignity akin to Ysera, but more animation, more life. Next to her was a male nearly as large whose scales constantly shifted—from silver to blue to a combination of both—seemingly at whim. He had, for one of his kind, an almost bemused expression.

In utter contrast to blue, the huge black beast that Malfurion eyed next sent shivers through even his spirit form. Here was raw power, the strength of the earth . . . but something more. Malfurion had to look away from the ebony giant, for each time he attempted to study him, a sense of unease touched the night elf. It was not simply because two of the same color had pursued the druid and his companion. No, it was something more . . . something dread.

But if he thought to find more peace looking elsewhere, Malfurion had chosen the wrong direction, for now he stared at what so intrigued the giants.

It was tiny, tiny enough to fit into his own palm. In the paw of the huge black, it was almost a speck.

"You see?" rumbled its wielder. "All is in readiness. It is but the moment that we wait for."

"And when will that moment come?" asked Alexstrasza. "Each passing day, the demons ravage the lands. If not for the fact that their commanders have drawn more of their forces to take on the night elves, the other directions would be all but lost by now."

"I understand your concern . . . but the Dragon Soul will be best applied when the heavens are in alignment. It must be that way."

The red Aspect gazed at the golden disk. "Let us pray then that when it is utilized, it is all you say, Neltharion. Let us pray it is the deliverance of our world."

The black only nodded. Malfurion, still awaiting Ysera's signal to talk with Alexstrasza, peered closely at the simple-looking creation, his hopes rising. The dragons were acting. They had come up with a solution, a talisman of some sort that would rid Kalimdor of the Burning Legion.

His curiosity got the better of him. He weakened his end of the link with Ysera so that with all else going on she might not notice what he attempted. With his mind, he probed the shining disk—so insignificant in appearance, and yet, apparently filled with such power that even dragons paid it homage. Truly, the demons would stand no chance against something like this . . .

Not at all to his surprise, a protective spell surrounded the Dragon Soul. The druid studied it and in its elements, he detected a peculiarity. Each of the great dragons had their own distinct auras—as all creatures did—and Malfurion sensed some of those auras now. He felt Ysera's—most known to him—plus those of Alexstrasza and the blue. The black dragon's was also present, but not in the same manner. His seemed entwined around the rest, as if it held them at bay. It almost seemed to the druid that the spell had been designed to keep the others from sensing something within.

More curious than ever, Malfurion used Cenarius's teachings to infiltrate the spell. He slipped through with far more ease than he had expected, perhaps because the disk's creator had never thought one such as he would even make an attempt. The druid pushed deeper, finally touching on the forces within.

What he discovered within made him reel. He pulled out, stunned. Even in his present form, he shivered, unable to come to grips with what he had sensed. Malfurion looked again at the black dragon, astounded by what the leviathan had wrought.

The Dragon Soul . . . that which was to save Kalimdor . . . held within it an evil as great as the Burning Legion itself.

THIRTEEN

The demons had a tendency to slaughter anything and anyone in their path. That made it difficult to gather prisoners for questioning, something Captain Varo'then felt a necessity. He had finally convinced Archimonde to send him a few, but the ones that arrived proved more a tangle of broken body parts than living creatures.

The scarred night elf spent a few minutes on the last of the lot, then did the ruined figure a favor by slicing open his throat. The interrogations had been a debacle, but not through any fault on his part. The Legion's commanders did not seem to understand the basic need for questioning.

Varo'then would have preferred to be out in the field, but he did not want to leave the palace, especially not of late. The thing that had been Lord Xavius had not been seen for days, but in that time several of the Highborne had utterly vanished. Mannoroth took it in stride, and so the captain suspected that he knew the reason. The officer disliked being left out of the information loop in any way.

"Dispose of that rubbish," he ordered the two guards. As they moved to obey, Captain Varo'then cleaned his dagger and replaced it. He gazed around the interrogation chamber, a blocky six-by-six room with only a single blue glow-crystal to illuminate it. Shadows filled the corner. An iron door three inches thick was the only exit.

Centuries of blood stained the floor. The queen never visited the lowest depths of her residence, and Varo'then did not encourage her. Such work was not for one of her acute sensibilities.

The soldiers dragged the unfortunate's corpse out, leaving the captain to his thoughts. There had been no news from the Houndmaster. Mannoroth had not revealed any concern, but the night elf wondered if something had befallen the powerful demon. If so, then it behooved someone to take the lead in hunting down the spellcasters. The demons had failed so far, and Varo'then itched for a chance to redeem himself in that regard after having lost two of them to an enchanted and hostile forest.

But that would mean leaving the palace . . .

He reached down with both hands to adjust the sword at his side—and suddenly brought the blade out, thrusting it into the shadows to his left.

The keen edge came within an inch of a figure unseen in those shadows until now. Rather than be startled, however, the other simply leered at the captain.

"A sharp sword, a sharp wit, Captain Varo'then . . ."

At first the soldier thought that he was dealing with Xavius again, but a closer study showed differences in the face. Varo'then ran through his analytical mind the faces of all the Highborne and matched this hooved creature's visage with one.

"Master Peroth'arn . . . we'd wondered where you'd gone."

The former sorcerer edged out of the shadows as Varo'then sheathed his weapon. "I have been . . . relearning."

With barely-concealed distaste, the night elf eyed the transformation. To him, the satyrs were an abomination. "And have others been 'relearning' also?"

"A select few."

At last the captain had an explanation as to where the missing Highborne had gone. They were still here, merely changed into these grotesque parodies. Xavius's new form had been one of the few decisions by Sargeras that Varo'then questioned. More powerful he supposedly might be, but the former advisor's mind had clearly been altered, too. There was something animalistic about him that went beyond his outer appearance, something animalistic and devious.

And from what little he had seen of Peroth'arn so far, the rest of the missing Highborne were likely as unstable as their leader.

"Where is Xavius?" he asked of the satyr.

"Wherever he must be, good captain," replied the horned figure. "Performing that which will make sooner come true our glorious god's desire . . ."

"He's no longer in the palace?"

Peroth'arn chuckled. "A sharp sword, a sharp wit . . ."

Captain Varo'then felt tempted to draw that sword again and impale the mocking creature, perhaps even mount Peroth'arn's head over a fireplace afterward. The satyr grinned back, as if daring the soldier to react.

Restraining himself, the scarred night elf asked, "And what, then, are you doing down here? You've some interest in the interrogations?"

"Amusement, you might say."

"I've no time to waste on your antics and silly wordplay." Varo'then pushed past Peroth'arn, reaching for the door handle. "Nor, for that matter, those of the one who leads you."

"You served him once. You'll serve him again."

"I serve the great Sargeras and my queen and no other!" retorted the officer. "And if he thinks—"

As he spoke, the captain glanced back to where the satyr had stood. However, when he sought Peroth'arn, he found only shadow.

With a snarl, the night elf barged out of the chamber. The queen would have to be told more about these accursed satyrs. He did not trust them. He certainly did not trust Lord Xavius anymore.

If only he knew where the former advisor had gone . . .

Malfurion could not believe the utter evil he sensed within the Dragon Soul. How could a thing created to be the *savior* of the world radiate such *malevolence*? What had the dragon Neltharion wrought?

Bracing himself, the druid cautiously probed the disk again. So simple, so innocent in appearance. Only by seeking within could anyone understand the awful truth.

It amazed him that Ysera could not sense it. Surely the mistress of the Emerald Dream would have understood. Yet, like the others, the disk was shielded from her in such a subtle fashion that even if she held it, he doubted the Aspect would have noted a thing.

Perhaps . . . perhaps if Malfurion dismantled the protective spell, then the others would realize the truth before it was too late.

Putting aside his disgust, he pushed deeper into the disk. Through his highly-trained senses, he located the spell's nexus. The druid began trying to unravel it—

A jolt like a thousand bolts of lightning instantly ravaged his ethereal form, almost tearing it to insubstantial shreds. Malfurion silently screamed. He looked for aid from Ysera, but to his horror she did not seem to note his agony.

But another did.

He did not look directly at the night elf, but his thoughts practically barreled over the stricken druid. In an instant, the madness of the Dragon Soul's creator became all too clear.

So! Neltharion roared even though on the mortal plane he continued speaking so politely and amiably with the others. *You try to steal my glorious Dragon Soul!*

A monstrous, invisible force compressed Malfurion from all sides. At first he stared in fear as his body contorted. Then he realized that the image he had of himself in his present state was just that—an image. Neltharion could have stretched him into a thin string and it would not have much affected the druid's health. That was not what the Earth Warder intended; he sought to crush Malfurion into a magical prison, preventing the intruder from giving any warning or touching the disk again.

Stirred on by dread memories of his confinement at the hands of Lord

Xavius, Malfurion managed to break free of the spell before it sealed. He immediately turned his focus to Ysera, hoping she would yet sense his danger.

No! They will not interfere! Neltharion's mental presence was staggering. *You will not betray all I have done! None of you will!*

With Ysera still ignorant of his danger, the druid did the only thing he could think of—he abandoned the chamber and the mortal plane, retreating into the solitude of the Emerald Dream.

A calmness immediately surrounded him. He floated over the indistinct vision of the mountains where he had first contacted She of the Dreaming. Relieved, Malfurion tried to collect his thoughts.

With a roar, a huge shadowy form sought to swallow him whole.

Pulling back at the very last moment, the druid could not believe what had now happened; Neltharion had followed him into the dream realm! The dragon was even more terrible to behold here than in the mortal plane. His face was a distorted, diabolical caricature of its true self, every element of the evil with which the black had imbued the Dragon Soul evident in his jagged, disfigured countenance. Neltharion was twice as huge as in true life and his sharp claws spread for miles. His wings alone shadowed the entire mountain chain.

I will not surrender what is mine by right! Only I am fit to rule! You will tell no one!

Neltharion exhaled. Green flames filled the Emerald Dream.

Malfurion screamed as the fire engulfed his form. What the behemoth was doing should have been impossible; not only had he invaded Ysera's domain without her evidently knowing, but now he sought to burn away the druid's intangible essence.

Something that Cenarius had once taught him suddenly came to mind. *Perception is deceptive, my student,* his *shan'do* had told him. *What you think must be is not always the truth. In the world of which you are now part as a druid, perception can become whatever you think it.*

Not certain that he understood, but already nearly consumed, Malfurion denied the flames killing him. They could not exist as such here. They were, like his body and Neltharion's huge form, what he *expected* to be real, yet they were not. They were images, illusions.

And so the fire could not burn so much as one false hair on his imaginary head.

Both the agony and the flames vanished. Neltharion still remained, his face and form more distorted than ever. He eyed the tiny figure with some repugnance, as if he wondered how the druid had dared not to perish.

Not certain how lucky he might be against whatever next the Aspect might throw at him, Malfurion took the only route of escape remaining to him. He concentrated on his body, willing himself to return to it.

The green-tinted mountains suddenly flew away from him. Neltharion, too, dwindled swiftly in the distance. The druid felt the closeness of his own body—

No! came Neltharion's fearsome voice again. *I will* have *you!*

Just as the night elf felt himself re-entering his mortal form, something struck him hard. With a grunt, Malfurion, still half-asleep, fell back, his head hitting the hard, rocky ground. The last vestiges of the Emerald Dream disappeared, and with their going ceased the angry roar of the black dragon.

"Druid!" called another. "Malfurion Stormrage! Can you hear me? Are you whole again?"

He tried to focus on the new speaker. "K-Krasus?"

But when Malfurion first glanced at the mage's visage, he instantly tried to pull away. A dragon's monstrous face filled his view, the jaws opening to swallow him—

"Malfurion!"

The sharp cut of Krasus's voice sliced cleanly through his fear. The night elf's vision cleared, revealing not a dragon but the determined, pale countenance he had come to know well.

Concern colored Krasus's expression. He helped Malfurion to a sitting position, handing him a water sack from which to drink. Only after the druid had satiated his thirst did Krasus ask him what had happened.

"Did you reach She of the Dreaming?"

"Yes, and I had to mention Cenarius more than once . . . as you hinted."

The dragon mage allowed himself a brief one-sided smile. "I had recalled some bit of knowledge Alexstrasza had once passed on to me. I thought that this far in the past, the feelings would be stronger yet."

"So I was right to think that she and my *shan'do*—"

"Does it surprise you? Their spheres of influence cross in many ways. Kindred spirits are often drawn together, regardless of their differing backgrounds."

Malfurion did not press. "She agreed to bring me to where they were meeting."

Krasus's eyes widened. "All five of the Aspects?"

"I saw only four. Ysera, your Alexstrasza, a silver-blue dragon with a mirthful expression—"

"Malygos . . . how that one will change."

"And—and—" Suddenly, the night elf could not speak. The words teetered on the tip of his tongue, but they would not fall. The harder he tried, the more infantile the druid sounded. Sounds that made no sense whatsoever escaped him.

Putting a hand on Malfurion's shoulder, Krasus nodded sadly. "I understand, I think. You cannot say more. There was another there."

"Yes . . . another."

It was all Malfurion could add, but he saw that Krasus did indeed understand. The night elf eyed his comrade in shock, realizing that the mage could no more speak of Neltharion than he could. At some point in the past, Krasus, too, had fallen afoul of the black behemoth.

Which meant that Krasus likely also knew of the Dragon Soul.

They stared into each other's eyes, the silence communicating much of what their mouths could not. Small wonder that the dragon mage had been so adamant about reaching his people and discovering the truth. The ancients themselves had been betrayed by one of their own, and the only two who knew could say nothing about it, not even to each other.

"We must leave," muttered Krasus, helping him to his feet. "You may well imagine why."

Malfurion could. Neltharion would not rest with leaving him alive. The spell had been a last effort before the druid had escaped the Emerald Dream, but the black dragon would not be satisfied. He was too near his goal. Likely only circumstance had saved Krasus earlier, but from what Malfurion had witnessed of the black's madness, neither would be safe long. And although Neltharion would not dare act directly . . .

"The sentinels!" he managed to gasp.

"Aye. We may see them again. It would be good if we returned to the hippogriffs and departed."

So the idiosyncrasies of the spell allowed them that indirect communication. A small and fairly useless gift. They could hint to each other about their doom.

Still weary, he had to rely on Krasus to help him walk. With effort, they made their way to where the animals waited impatiently. One of the hippogriffs squawked when he noticed the pair, causing the other to flap its wings in startlement.

"Will they carry us the entire way back?" the mage asked Malfurion.

"Yes. Cenarius would—"

The ground shook violently. The night elf and Krasus toppled over. Nearby, the hippogriffs fluttered a few feet upward.

From beneath where the mounts had waited, a monstrous worm thrust its sightless head into the air. A wide crack at the tip of its head opened incredibly wide, revealing a round mouth with teeth lining the edges. With a savage rumble, the worm swallowed the slower of the two hippogriffs whole.

"Run!" commanded Krasus.

The duo scurried across the harsh landscape. Despite the meal it had just eaten, the worm turned in their direction. Again it rumbled, then burrowed back into the earth.

"Separate, Malfurion! Separate!"

No sooner had they gone in opposite directions than again the ground exploded and the horrific creature burst up. It snapped at the area around it, seeming frustrated that it found nothing to add to its earlier course.

Although the worm had no visible eyes, it somehow sensed where Malfurion had gone. Its mammoth, segmented body twisted toward him, the rounded mouth opening and closing hungrily.

This could be no coincidence. Neltharion had surely sent this burrowing monstrosity after them. The dragon's paranoia had grown so terrible that now nothing was allowed to risk his dark desires.

The worm darted forward. The smell of decay emanating from within its mouth nearly overwhelmed the druid. Malfurion ran as fast as he could, even knowing that it would not be fast enough.

But just before the worm reached him, something flew in its path. With a savage squawk, the surviving hippogriff ripped at the fleshy head with its talons. Its beak tore into the hide as it likely sought to avenge its mate.

Rumbling ominously, the worm tried to bite its flying adversary. The hippogriff darted out of range, then dropped again in order to cut at the head.

"Kylis Fortua!" shouted Krasus.

Huge chunks of hard earth and rock, dug free by the worm's arrival, rose up into the sky and began battering the creature. The worm swung back and forth, trying to avoid the onslaught. Most of the rocks did little true damage, but Krasus's spell had clearly frustrated the beast.

Taking a breath, the druid tried to aid in his own way. There were few plants in this mountainous region, but one nearby caught his attention. Apologizing to it, Malfurion plucked several barbs from its branches, then threw them at the huge predator.

The wind carried the barbs along for him, thrusting them faster and faster toward their target. Malfurion concentrated, touching upon that which controlled the barbs' growth.

And just before they struck, the thorny pieces swelled. They tripled in size, then tripled again. By the time they hit the worm, many were nearly as large as the druid himself.

More important, they were also harder of hide. Each of the needles facing the worm impacted with the force of a steel lance. Scores of thorns more than a yard long buried themselves in the monster's body.

This time, the creature let out a roar. Green, sizzling pus flowed from its wounds, spilling onto the ground where it continued to burn. The barbs stuck wherever they had hit. The worm shook back and forth, but none would release.

"Well done!" exclaimed Krasus, seizing Malfurion by the arm and pulling him along. "Try to summon the remaining hippogriff!"

Malfurion reached out to the animal, trying to get it to come to them, but the hippogriff's fury overrode his summons. The worm had devoured its mate and it wanted vengeance.

"It won't listen!" yelled the druid, panic creeping into his voice.

"Then we must continue to run!"

Still trying to shake off the savage barbs, the worm followed after them. It did not move quite as fast as before, but still fast enough to force the pair to their limits.

The segmented giant slammed into the ground again, burrowing deep. The earth below vibrated so violently that Malfurion stumbled. Krasus kept on his feet, but made little progress.

"I must attempt something!" he shouted. "I have feared to try it since coming to your land, but without the hippogriff, it seems our only hope!"

"What?"

Krasus did not respond, the dragon mage already casting. Malfurion felt unsettling forces arise near his companion, who drew an arc with his right arm and muttered words in a language the night elf had never before heard. As Krasus's hand cut the air, the latter literally sliced away, creating a gap in reality.

No, not *a gap,* Malfurion mentally corrected himself. A portal.

As the wizard completed the huge circle, the earth quaked. Turning to the druid, Krasus cried, "Through the gate, Malfurion! Through the—"

The worm again broke through to the surface. Krasus tumbled backward. The night elf, just starting to obey, turned back to aid his companion.

"You should have gone on!" snapped Krasus.

Its maw wide open, the monstrous burrower closed on the pair. Malfurion pulled the mage up, then threw both of them toward the portal. He could feel the worm closing on them, smell its deathly odor. Escape seemed so far away—

And as they entered the portal, the worm lunged . . .

FOURTEEN

The demons met them in earnest just west of Suramar. The new advance halted completely and a deadlock began. The night elves could not push the Burning Legion any farther, but neither could their foe regain ground.

The warriors of the Burning Legion fought relentlessly, but there was one thing in the night elves' favor. They were far more familiar with the landscape than the demons. The region around Suramar was one of rolling hills and rivers. Forest, too, had marked much of the region, but now most of that was scorched or torn asunder. Still, many dead trunks and ruined dwellings dotted the area, and they acted not only as additional landmarks, but also protection.

Scouting parties were sent out to discover the exact extent of the demons' lines. One such group consisted of Brox, Rhonin, and several members of Jarod Shadowsong's company, including the captain himself. The orc and the human had volunteered themselves for this mission, well aware that they understood the ways of the Burning Legion better than anyone. However, Ravencrest had made them swear that, like the rest of the scouts, they would return at an appointed hour and no later. Otherwise, he could not promise that they would be safe should he decide it opportune to strike one flank or another quickly, based on whatever the other outriders reported.

Night had fallen, but that by itself did not make the going so slow. Simple darkness alone had no effect on any of the party and, in fact, would have aided their search. However, a thick, foul mist with a dank, greenish tinge covered *everything*. The mist seemed to spread wherever the demons went, and left open the threat that monstrous warriors could be lurking only yards away unnoticed.

Slowly the group, numbering a dozen, crossed the ruined land. Withered and blackened trees cast eerie shapes in the mist. No amount of squinting could much penetrate the haze.

It was perhaps fortunate in one way. So near Suramar, the scouting party crossed through an area where once there had been a settlement. Now and then, the remnants of a treehouse could be spotted sprawled on its side, the entire structure ripped out at the roots, then chopped to pieces. All knew that the inhabitants themselves had likely suffered a similar fate.

"Barbaric . . ." muttered Jarod.

Brox grunted. The night elves had been very quickly forced to harden themselves to the butchery, but they could scarcely learn to accept it the way the orc could. Brox had grown up around brutality. First the end of the war against the Alliance, then the violent march to the reservations, and lastly the struggle against the Burning Legion and the Scourge. He mourned the dead, yes, but there was little he saw that twisted his gut anymore. In the end, death was death.

To the orc's right, Rhonin quietly cursed. The spellcaster clamped his hand tight, then thrust his palm into a pouch attached to his belt. He had tried using a scrying stone to survey the area for any hint of demons, but the mist apparently befouled the sensitive magics involved.

Brox had his own method for seeking out the enemy. Every few yards, he lifted his nose up and sniffed. The smells that mostly assailed his nostrils were pungent and spoke quite succinctly of death. So far, the only demons he noted were foul corpses covered in the ichor that had once flowed through their veins.

There were, of course, many other bodies. The mangled remains of night elves littered the settlement—some of them soldiers from the retreat, others hapless civilians who had moved too slow. No victim had been left whole; arms, legs, even heads had been lopped off. Several corpses appeared to have been cut up *afterward,* which strengthened the expressions of disgust and bitterness worn by the soldiers in the party.

"Stay spread out, but within sight," Jarod commanded, tightening the reins of his own night saber. "And keep your beasts under control."

The last order he had repeated more than once already. The huge panthers seemed particularly distressed about their situation, as if they knew something that their riders did not. It made the scouting party even more tense.

A nightmarish shadow rose up before them . . . the outer edge of Suramar. The Burning Legion had not had sufficient time to ravage the entire city, and so part of its skeleton still stood as a grim reminder of all that had been lost . . . and all that still could be.

"By the Mother Moon . . ." whispered one soldier.

Brox glanced at Jarod. The captain stared at his home with eyes that barely blinked. His hands crumpled the reins. The vein in his neck throbbed.

"Hard to have no home," the orc commented to him, thinking of his own life.

"I *have* a home," Jarod growled. "Suramar is still my home."

The orc said nothing more, understanding the night elf's pain.

Through the fallen gates they entered the city. Utter silence surrounded them. Even their breathing seemed far too raucous a noise for this still place.

Once inside, they paused. Jarod looked to the wizard for a suggestion as to their next move. Ahead of them the path split in three directions. Safety demanded that they all stay together, but the time limit set to them made inspecting Suramar that way impossible.

Rhonin frowned, finally saying, "No one goes wandering off in this. There's a magic in the mist. I don't care if we can't search everything, captain."

"I'm inclined to agree," Jarod returned with some relief. "I never thought to be so distrusting of a place in which I grew up."

"This is no longer Suramar, Shadowsong. You must remember that. Whatever the Burning Legion touches, it taints. Even if the city is empty of demons, it could be very, very dangerous."

Brox nodded. He recalled all too well the things that had come out at him from the mist during his people's fight against the demons. What the night elves had battled so far proved pale by comparison.

Just enough of the city remained intact to give the ruins a semblance of their former self. Now and then, a building would materialize that had not been touched. Jarod had soldiers check these structures out, thinking that anyone who had survived the carnage might have taken refuge inside.

Not once did they find a living soul, though.

In spite of their intention to stay together, the devastation eventually demanded otherwise of them. The path became too confused and debris-filled to allow the scouting party to ride together without vastly slowing the search down. With great reluctance, Jarod had three soldiers on each end head off toward side streets.

"Go around the wreckage and meet up with us as soon as your route allows," he told the six. As the two groups rode off, the captain quickly added, "And keep together!"

With Shadowsong and his remaining three fighters creating an escort for Rhonin—and Brox by association—the main group moved on. The night sabers had to pick their way up and over the rubble. Three huge tree homes had been torn down and in the process collided with one another over the path. One leaned atop the other two, the former residence dangling menacingly over the orc and his companions.

Brox's night saber hissed as it stepped on something. Rhonin leaned over, then informed the orc, "The owner never left."

They found more corpses as the cats reached the highest point. Again they were residents of the city, but these had evidently tried to flee when they were caught by the Burning Legion. Other than the grotesque wounds left by their slayers, the victims were oddly untouched. Neither decay nor carrion eaters had disturbed them.

"They had to have perished in the initial destruction," the wizard noted. "You'd think they'd look even worse."

" 'Tis a foul enough sight for me already," Jarod Shadowsong gasped.

With the panthers moving as gingerly as possible, they finally began descending to the original path. As he held on tight, Brox again raised his nose to the air and sniffed.

For a brief moment, the orc thought he sensed something, but the scent was faint and old. He looked around and discovered the body of a felbeast that some soldier had speared. Brox grunted in satisfaction and resumed clinging on for dear life.

Finally, the six reached level ground. Jarod pointed ahead, saying, "I recall an avenue just out of sight. We should be able to join up with the others, Master Rhonin."

"I'll be glad of that."

Only a short distance later, the captain's chosen avenue materialized. The party paused when it reached the intersection and Jarod looked around.

"We must've gotten ahead of them," he noted.

Brox straightened. Rhonin shifted uneasily in the saddle, his fingers flexing in what the orc knew was a preamble to spellcasting.

"Aah!" Jarod looked relieved. "Here comes one party now!"

From the orc's left rode three of the soldiers. They looked very pleased to see their comrades again. Even the cats moved with much eagerness.

"What did you find?" Shadowsong asked the new arrivals.

"Nothing, captain," responded the most senior in rank. "More ruins, more corpses. As many of our people as those monsters."

"Damn . . ."

"Are several of those you knew not among the refugees with us, Shadowsong?" asked Rhonin.

"Far too many. And the more we find here, the less chance that I've just missed them in the crowds."

It was an old tale to Brox. How many of those with whom he had grown up had died in one battle or another? Small wonder that he had once regretted outlasting his comrades in the war; by then, the orc had already survived most of his blood brothers. He realized that part of his desire to die had also been due to loneliness.

Jarod eyed the opposite direction. "The others should be here at any moment."

But that moment and a hundred others came and went, and still the missing soldiers did not reappear. The riders grew tense. Their darkening mood spread to the night sabers, who hissed and spat more and more as the minutes passed.

Brox could finally wait no longer. Even as Captain Shadowsong began to raise his hand in order to suggest that they move out and look for the vanished soldiers, the orc rode past him, toward where last the trio should have been.

He steered his mount down the other pathway, searching warily for any sign. Far behind him, Rhonin and the night elves hurried to catch up.

Rubble filled the street. Torn cloth and old bloodstains added the only color to the scene. The orc readied his ax and forced his mount to continue on.

Then a peculiarity about his present surroundings struck Brox. He twisted in the saddle, carefully looking around for one hint that his suspicions were correct.

But nowhere did he see any sign of even a single body. No night elves, no demons. Even the likely corpses of the three missing soldiers and their mounts could not be found.

What had happened to them? Brox wondered. How had this street remained unsullied by the deaths of innocents?

The slight sliding of rocks caused the green-skinned warrior to jerk to his right. A figure slowly coalesced in the mist—a soldier, but on foot, with his weapon drawn.

"Where's your mount?" the orc rumbled.

The soldier trod awkwardly toward him. There were splotches on his armor, and his mouth hung open.

As his face came into better view, Brox saw with consternation that part of it had been ripped open. One eye was completely gone, and the jagged gap descended all the way to the center of the throat . . . or what remained of it.

And as he neared the orc, the macabre figure raised his weapon. Behind him, Brox suddenly noted other shapes following the soldier.

Although no coward, the green-skinned fighter pulled hard on the reins, turning the night saber about. As it moved, the cat swung one clawed paw at the oncoming soldier, batting him away like a toy.

The others rode up just as he started back. Jarod glanced beyond him, to where the soldier had fallen. "What did you do to him? You made your beast strike him dead—"

"Already dead before! Hurry! More coming!"

The night elf started to argue, but Rhonin put a hand across his chest. "Look into the mist, Shadowsong! Look!"

Jarod did—and shook his head in horror. The soldier arose, his face and chest now even more terrible to behold. Still wobbling, he gripped his sword and headed toward the party. Behind him, the first of the other shapes grew distinct—night elves, but in even more monstrous shape than the soldier. Several were ripped open from head to toe and others missed limbs. All wore the same empty expressions, and moved with the same deathly determination.

"Ride!" the captain shouted. "Back through the city gates! Follow me!"

With Jarod and the wizard in the lead, the party pulled away just before the first of the ghoulish figures could reach them. They sped up the way that they had just come, but when they reached the intersection, Jarod had everyone turn in the opposite direction.

"Why this way?" shouted Rhonin.

"A shorter and smoother path to our goal . . . I hope!"

But as they rode, other figures began to emerge from the ruins. Brox growled as what had once been an elder female in the blood-encrusted remains of a once-glittering silver, turquoise, and red gown snatched almost hungrily at his leg. He kicked her back, and for good measure severed her head with one mighty swing of the enchanted ax. Even after that, her body grabbed wildly for anything it could reach, but, fortunately, by then the orc had ridden away.

Rhonin suddenly pulled up short. "Watch out!"

His warning came too late for one of the soldiers nearest him. A mass of clawing, tearing hands pulled the night elf off his mount. He slashed one with his sword, but he might as well have been stabbing the air for all the good it did.

Jarod started to come to his aid, but before he could reach his comrade, the hapless victim vanished beneath the shambling corpses. His scream cut off almost immediately.

"It's too late for him!" the wizard insisted despite Jarod's clear intention of still trying to retrieve the soldier. "The rest of you, keep riding! I've some notion what to do here!"

"We can't leave you!" argued the captain.

Brox steered his mount next to Rhonin. "I stay with him!"

"We'll only be a few moments behind, Shadowsong! The way looks clear a little after this! You should be able to get out of the city!"

The night elf did not want to leave, but to stay would risk more lives. Of them all, Rhonin had the best chance for survival.

"This way!" the captain called to the rest of his command.

As they pushed off, the riderless night saber behind, Rhonin turned to face the oncoming mob. "Brox! I need a few seconds!"

Nodding, the orc pushed forward. With a battle cry, he slashed back and forth, his ax sweeping out before his mount with deadly accuracy. Grasping hands, gore-encrusted chests, torn throats . . . all he chopped at with every iota of strength that he could muster.

Just as Brox began to flag, Rhonin called, "Enough! Pull back!"

No sooner had the orc done so than the wizard tossed a small vial at the encroaching horde. As it flew, it somehow managed to arc along the front row, splattering each of the undead.

And the moment the spilling liquid touched its targets, the ghouls burst into blue flame.

An inferno quickly blossomed. The corpses behind the first row walked mindlessly into the flames, igniting themselves. Some of those already ablaze teetered into others, spreading the fire to them.

"Something I once used against the Scourge," the human remarked with grim satisfaction. "Come on! We've got to—"

A fiery figure rushed forward and collapsed into Brox's mount, setting it, too, ablaze. The orc struggled as the night saber abruptly turned and raced madly away from the source of its agony . . . in the process dragging its rider deeper into Suramar.

Rhonin called out after him, but Brox could not stop his animal. Crazed by the smoldering flames, the panther charged wildly through the streets.

The orc tried to smother the fire, but only made his situation worse. His night saber suddenly slowed, then threw itself on the side that burned. Brox barely had time to fling himself to safety lest his leg be crushed under the beast's immense weight.

The night saber rolled over on the affected area, then, seeming unsatisfied with its attempts, ran off before the orc could stop it. Brox whirled around, expecting to be attacked on all sides by the horrific mob. Breath coming out in heavy pants, he swung his ax again and again, only gradually realizing that he was not in any imminent danger.

Of course, he was also without either a mount or the presence of the wizard.

Eyes wary, Brox started back the way from which he thought the night saber had come. Yet, as the brawny fighter proceeded through the ruins, he saw nothing that gave any hint as to whether his path was the right one. The injured cat had run with such manic swiftness that it had clearly dragged its rider farther than first imagined.

The orc smelled the air, but caught no scent of either the human or the night elves. Worse, his usually infallible sense of direction failed him here. The mist had a headiness to it that played with all of his senses.

Growing more confused as to his whereabouts, Brox turned down what seemed a vaguely familiar avenue. Ruined trees, scorched landscape, and the crumbling remains of dwellings appeared out of the haze, but none did he recognize with any certainty.

Then, something momentarily assailed his nose. The hulking orc hesitated, sniffing the air again. His heavy brow crushed together and he ground his yellowed teeth.

With new resolve he headed to his right, every other step smelling the air again. His new path demanded that he climb over the tangling roots of an upturned giant oak and across the crushed shell of a night elven home, but Brox would not be deterred. He climbed cautiously, trying not to make the slightest sound—a difficult task considering that he also refused to free his other hand by putting away his ax.

As he reached the top of the shattered domicile, Brox caught a fresh scent. It made his nostrils wrinkle in disgust, but urged him forward.

And when he peered over, it was to see the demons at work.

There were four of the Fel Guard and one Doomguard soldier, as well. However, they were not so much of a threat in Brox's eyes as the two standing in the forefront. The orc snarled as he recognized from his own time the horrific, winged figures in midnight blue armor. They gestured with fingers that ended in savage, bladelike nails, a pale green aura covering their hands as they worked.

Nathrezim, also called *Dreadlords.*

They stood taller than the other demons, and their aspects were more terrible to behold. Huge, dark, curled horns thrust high from their heads. They had dead, gray skin like a corpse, and no hair whatsoever on their monstrous heads. Two sharp canines jutted down, reminding Brox of the tales he had heard of the Dreadlords' vampiric traits. In point of fact, the Nathrezim were psychic vampires, feeding on the weak-minded and often using their victims as slaves.

The pair stood on thick, powerful legs like those of goats, their feet cloven hooves. While cunning and extremely skilled at magic—even more so than the Eredar—they were also deadly fighters. Yet, it seemed that in this particular incidence, it was their dark spells that the orc and his companion had to fear most.

Brox had found the necromancers.

The two Nathrezim had done the abominable, successfully raising the dead they and their comrades had so brutally slaughtered. The orc recalled what he had heard of the Undead Scourge and their own ghoulish spells. To one of his kind, what these creatures did now was far more monstrous than any death caused by the weapons of the Fel Guard of Doomguard.

In his mind, Brox imagined what he would have felt like if the bloody bodies of his comrades had risen up to join the enemy against the orcs. This was sacrilege, a dishonoring of spirits. His heart pounded, and Brox felt an uncontrollable rage filling him.

He suddenly thought of Rhonin and the night elves. It was possible that they had escaped, but with so many dead under the control of the Nathrezim, it was also possible that they fought dearly for their lives . . . provided they had not already been slain.

And if slain . . . they would likely join those the Dreadlords had raised.

Brox could hold back no longer. He rose from his hiding place and, with a war cry akin to the one he had uttered with his comrades back at the pass, leapt upon the group.

His shout echoed through the stillness. To his immense pleasure, the demons actually jumped at the sound, so unexpected in this place. Their surprise slowed their reflexes, exactly as the warrior had planned.

The ax Malfurion and the demigod had created for him cut smoothly through the armored chest of the first Fel Guard, spilling the demon's foul innards. As his first foe collapsed, Brox brought the ax up, slicing through the forearm of another creature.

The Dreadlords did not cease their work, relying on their comrades to deal with one attacker. However, they had not fought orcs—not yet—and that lack of understanding worked well for Brox. He slammed into the next nearest Fel Guard, bowling over the huge demon with his own considerable mass, then rolled away as the Doomguard soldier attempted to run him through.

Brox traded blows with the winged warrior, then whirled just in time to deflect a strike by another opponent. He cleaved the second demon in half at the waist, then for good measure used the back end of his war ax to crush in the skull of the fighter that he had maimed earlier.

Now one of the spellcasters at last took notice. Leaving his comrade to continue their foul work, he turned and pointed at the orc.

In desperation, Brox threw himself between the spellcaster and the Doomguard. Yet, no sooner had he done that than the winged figure shrieked and twisted. He contorted as if something sought to burrow out of him—and then his chest exploded.

Something struck the orc from behind. Brox fell dazed. The last of the Fel Guard loomed over him, the Nathrezim coming up next to the monstrous warrior. The fiendish spellcaster stared down at their adversary, demonic eyes gleeful.

"You will fight well for us . . ." he hissed. "Kill many of your friends . . ."

The vision of himself shambling toward Tyrande and the others sickened Brox; he had been willing to accept death, but this was a terrible parody of it.

"No!" Brox pushed himself up, knowing full well that he would never beat either the Fel Guard's weapon or the Nathrezim's unholy spell.

Then, the other Nathrezim unexpectedly howled. The agonizing cry barely escaped his mouth before he burst into blue flames.

The two demons turned, giving Brox his chance. He immediately went for the remaining spellcaster, thrusting up the ax. The sharp blade not only cut through the Nathrezim's throat, but also completely severed the head.

A blade came at his side, cutting a streak along the orc's torso. Brox grunted with pain, then turned to face his adversary. His ax met the demon's blade, shattering the other weapon. The Fel Guard tried to retreat, but the orc cut him down.

Breathing heavily, the veteran warrior looked around. From the wreckage of another downed tree, Rhonin led his own night saber forward.

"I thought you might be able to handle the situation if I provided a little diversion." The wizard studied the bodies. "If I needn't have bothered at all, please tell me."

With a snort, Brox replied, "A good warrior welcomes all allies, human. This one thanks you."

"I should thank *you*. You found the ones animating the dead. It was like the horror of the Scourge all over again."

Thinking of the shambling corpses, Brox quickly surveyed the area again, but saw nothing.

"Rest easy, Brox," Rhonin assured him. "When the Nathrezim perished, I sensed their work cease. The dead are at rest again."

"Good."

"You're wounded."

The orc gave a noncommittal grunt. "Had many wounds."

Rhonin grinned. "Well, for now you'll be riding. Jarod and the others should be just outside the gate. I doubt the erstwhile captain will go far without us. He's already lost Krasus and Malfurion. He doesn't want to go back to Ravencrest empty-handed."

Most other times, Brox would have argued about accepting a ride. To show anything but the utmost strength to another was considered shameful in the eyes of his people. Still, he felt weak in the legs and decided that a good warrior also did not unnecessarily risk those who had come to his aid. The orc mounted the night saber and allowed Rhonin to guide it.

"It's beginning . . ." muttered the human. "They're starting to experiment with creating an army of the unliving. This is probably not the only place that they've been attempting this."

The thick mist made their going slow. Brox, peering about, saw the body of a dead night elf, one of the original inhabitants by the look of the garments. That it lay unmoving gave the orc a conflicting feeling of relief and distaste.

"You understand what I'm saying, don't you, Brox?"

The orc did. Anyone who had survived the final war against the Burning Legion and lived through the awful aftermath would have understood. No one in their time period had not at the very least heard the horror stories, the tales of the Plaguelands and the ghoulish hordes wandering it. Too many more had experienced their own loved ones rising up from the dead and trying to add the living to their grisly ranks.

The Scourge now stalked the world, spreading terror as they attempted to make of it one vast Plagueland. Quel'Thalas was all but gone. Most of Lordaeron, too. The undead haunted nearly every realm.

Here, in the far past, Brox and Rhonin had just come across the first inklings of the Scourge's creation . . . and both knew that, despite this small victory, there was nothing that they could do to change *that* terrifying part of the future.

FIFTEEN

The voice was constantly in Illidan's head, whispering what at first were unthinkable things. Yes, he was jealous of his brother, but the sorcerer could never see himself causing Malfurion any harm. That would have been like cutting off his own left arm.

And yet . . . he could not help finding such thoughts also a slightly bit *comforting,* a way in which his misery over losing Tyrande could be somewhat assuaged. Deep down, Illidan still harbored some slight hope that she would see things differently, that the priestess would realize how superior he was to his brother.

The foul mist that had spread all the way from Zin-Azshari did nothing to lighten his mood. As he strode up to Lord Ravencrest, he saw that the bearded noble looked none too pleased, either. Despite their renewed progress, now not only were Malfurion and Krasus gone, but Rhonin had yet to return from the mission upon which he had insisted on going. Illidan was certain that the night elves could survive without the other spellcasters, but he at least would have preferred the human to return. Rhonin was the only one capable of teaching him anything concerning his craft.

Going down on one knee before his master, Illidan bowed his head. "My lord."

"Rise, sorcerer. I summon you to prepare yourself and the others for departure."

"But Master Rhonin—"

"Has but minutes ago returned and reported. What he tells me urges our immediate march. We must crush the demons and take the capital as soon as possible."

That Illidan had not sensed the wizard's return surprised the younger night elf. As he stood, he said, "We shall be ready to ride."

The sorcerer turned to depart, but Ravencrest shook his head. "That isn't the only reason I've summoned you, lad. It's to tell you what the wizard discovered, and it is for your ears only."

Illidan's chest swelled with pride. "I will tell no one, not even the Moon Guard."

"Not until I tell you to do so, yes, lad. Hear what Master Rhonin discovered and digest it well . . . if you can."

Then, the master of Black Rook Hold related the horrific tale of what had happened to Rhonin's party. The sorcerer listened first with disbelief, then astonishment. He did not, however, react with the disgust, the dread, with which Lord Ravencrest did. Instead, for the first time, Illidan found himself *admiring* the audacity of the demons.

"I didn't think such possible!" he said once the noble had finished. "What command they have of their spellwork!"

"Yes," returned Ravencrest, not noting Illidan's morbid fascination. "Too dark and lethal a command. We now face a greater threat than even I believed. How abominable a thing to consider, even by them!"

Illidan did not see the matter in the same light. The demon's spellcasters allowed no limits to their imagination. They worked to create whatever their abilities allowed, the better to gain their ultimate goal. While the goal itself was not to be admired, the efforts of the warlocks surely were.

"I wish that we could capture one of the Eredar," he murmured. The sorcerer imagined conversing with the demon, learning how its manner of spellcasting differed from his own.

"Capture one? Don't be silly, lad! I expect them to be slain on sight, especially now! Every dead warlock means less chance for a repeat of this horror that Master Rhonin and the others confronted!"

Quickly smothering any hint of his esteem for the warlocks, Malfurion's brother quickly nodded. "O-of course, my lord! That remains one of our highest priorities!"

"I should hope so. That's all, sorcerer."

Illidan bowed, then immediately retreated. His mind was awhirl with thoughts concerning what he had just learned. *To raise the dead!* What other fantastic feats could the Eredar perform? Even the two wizards had never hinted of such abilities, or surely they would have seen the good sense in calling up the battlefield casualties of both sides to use against the Burning Legion!

Lord Ravencrest was making a terrible mistake. How better to defeat an enemy than to learn their strengths and add them to your own arsenal? With such skills added to those which he had already picked up, Illidan believed he would be nearly capable of crushing the demons by himself.

Surely *then* Tyrande would see that he was the superior choice.

"If only I could learn from them . . ." he whispered.

Almost as soon as he said it, Illidan glanced around anxiously, certain that there was someone nearby who had heard. However, the sorcerer found his immediate surroundings empty, the nearest soldier many yards away.

More confident again, Illidan marched off to rejoin the Moon Guard. He had much thinking to do. Much thinking.

The shadow moved away from Illidan's retreating back, skirting the tent of Lord Desdel Stareye. Even with his hooves, the figure walked silently across the harsh ground. Guards making their rounds somehow missed seeing him despite being very near at some points. Only those he chose to hear or see him ever did so.

Xavius leered, quite pleased with his efforts. The satyr had not only served his glorious master, but set well into motion his own vengeance. He had marked the druid's brother immediately, and now the process of corruption had begun. The questions, the desires, were there, and Illidan Stormrage himself would now fan the flames. It was only a matter of time.

The satyr slipped out of the camp to where the others awaited him. Even Archimonde did not realize everything Xavius plotted, for the former night elf answered now to Sargeras alone. Neither Archimonde nor Mannoroth had any sway over him.

Yes, Xavius thought, if all went as planned, when Sargeras entered the world, it would be *he* who stood at the right hand of the demon lord . . . and Archimonde and Mannoroth who would be forced to kneel before him.

Pain woke Krasus, pain that wracked every fiber of his being. Even trying to breathe hurt so very much.

"Hush, hush," twittered a feminine voice. "You are not yet fit to rise."

He tried opening his eyes, but that also proved too much of a strain. "Wh-who . . ."

"Sleep, sleep . . ." Her voice was pure music, but had in it something that told the stricken wizard that she was more than a human or a night elf.

Krasus fought against the suggestion, but his strength abandoned him and he drifted off. Dreams of flight filled his slumber. He was a dragon again, but this time he had a proud plumage like a great bird. The mage thought little of this, simply thrilled to be aloft once more.

The dream went on and on, never ceasing to tantalize him. When someone shook Krasus and finally tore him from it, he almost cursed the intruder.

"Krasus! It's Malfurion! Awaken!"

The dragon mage grudgingly returned to consciousness. "I . . . I am with you, druid."

"Praise Elune! I thought you would sleep forever."

Now that he was awake, Krasus realized that the night elf had quite possibly done him a tremendous favor. "I believe I was supposed to sleep . . . at least until our host returned." The slim spellcaster looked around at their surroundings. "And perhaps I am still sleeping."

The room around them, while spacious, was of such odd construction that Krasus had to inspect it. It was formed from many, many branches, vines, and other material packed together with dirt and more. The room was rounded at the ceiling, and the only entrance appeared to be a hole far to his right. He looked down and noticed that his own bedding was of similar material, made soft by a draping of fresh leaves artfully woven together. On a small table made from the stump of a tree, a bowl carved from an impossibly-huge nut held water, which he assumed was for him.

Sipping from it, the dragon mage continued his inspection. His eyes narrowed as he realized that what he had taken for an inner wall was, in point of fact, a passage. The curve of the room and the way the walls had been created made it almost impossible to see the corridor without standing directly in front of it.

"It goes for a very long distance," Malfurion offered. "I found another, much larger chamber, and from that I went on to two more. Then I ran across more corridors and decided I had better return to you."

"A wise thing." Krasus frowned. His sharp ears had picked up a sound from without that he had finally been able to identify. Birds. Not just one type, however; the wizard heard at least a dozen different calls, some of them extraordinarily unique.

"What is outside?"

"I'd rather not say, Master Krasus. You should see it yourself."

His curiosity stirred, the slim figure rose and walked to the opening. As he neared it, the calls grew more intense, more varied. It was as if every type of bird nested outside . . .

Krasus hesitated, surveying the room again. *That* was what his surroundings reminded him of . . . a huge bird's nest.

Already suspecting he knew what he would see, the dragon mage stuck his head through the entrance.

It seemed that every species of bird *did* nest around them. Certainly they had the room. Everywhere Krasus looked, he saw huge, outstretched branches filled with foliage. In each of the branches, some avian had made its home. At a quick glance, he saw doves, robins, cardinals, mockingbirds, and more. There were birds from temperate zones and others from more exotic climes. They intermingled. They sang together. There were berry feeders, fish catchers, and even those who preyed on other birds—although the last seemed quite content with the rabbits and lizards they now brought for their young.

Gazing above, Krasus discovered more nests. The foliage of this incredibly huge tree was filled to the brim with all the birds of the world.

It was also filled with the astounding structure of which his chamber was one of only hundreds.

Like the myriad tunnels of a giant ant colony, the "nest" spread throughout the branches. A quick estimate by the wizard measured it large enough to house the entire night elven army—mounts included—plus the refugees with more than ample room to spare. Despite its outwardly weak appearance, Krasus was also quick to see that the edifice was more durable than it seemed. As the wind rocked the foliage, the "nest" waved and adjusted accordingly. The dragon mage touched one edge of the entrance and realized that it was held together better than the stones of a mighty fortress.

Then . . . he finally looked down.

To imagine that a dragon could suffer from vertigo would once have been impossible for Krasus to even consider. Yet now he teetered at the entrance, unable to come to grips with what he saw.

"Master Krasus!" Malfurion pulled him away from the entrance. "You almost fell! I'm sorry! I should've told you what to expect!"

Krasus exhaled, regaining his senses. "I am all right, my friend. You can release me. I know full what to expect now."

"I had to throw myself back when I first looked," the druid told him. "I was afraid that I'd be blown outside by the wind."

Now better prepared, Krasus returned to the opening. He gripped the sides, then peered down again.

The tree extended down for as far as he could see, branches jutting out everywhere. As elsewhere, birds perched or nested in them. Krasus stared as best he could, but of the base of the tree he could still make out no sign. Clouds drifted past, huge ones that signified just how high up they were.

The night elf came up beside him. "You can't see the ground, either, can you?"

"No, I cannot."

"I've never heard of a tree so vast, so *huge,* that one could not see the ground beneath it!"

"I have," Krasus replied, dredging up ancient memories from his ravaged mind. "It is . . . it is G'hanir. The Mother Tree. It is the place of all winged creatures, separate from but a part of the mortal world in a manner akin to the Emerald Dream. G'hanir is the tallest tree atop the tallest peak. The fruit it bears carries the seeds of all earthly trees." He thought further. "It is the home of our host . . . the demigoddess, Aviana."

"Aviana . . . ?"

"Yes." A fleet, white form flying toward their general direction caught his attention. "And I believe she is on her way to us even now."

The winged figure grew rapidly in size as it approached, finally coalescing into a massive white peregrine falcon larger than either of them. Krasus urged the druid back, leaving the entrance completely open.

The gigantic falcon fluttered through. A transformation then overtook it. The legs grew, thickened. The wings shrank, turning into slim, feathered hands. The body reshaped, becoming more like that of a female night elf or human, and the tail shifted into the trailing end of a gossamer white gown.

A slim, wide-eyed woman almost human in features eyed the pair. Her nose was sharp, but very elegant. She had a pale, beautiful face the color of ivory, and for hair she wore a wondrous mane of downy feathers. Her gown fluttered as she walked—on two delicate but still sharply-taloned feet.

"Awake, awake you are," she said with a slight frown. "You should rest, rest."

Krasus bowed to her. "I am grateful for your hospitality, mistress, but I am well enough to continue on now."

She cocked her head as a bird might, giving the mage a reproving look. "No, no . . . too soon, too soon. Please, sit."

The duo looked around and discovered that two chairs, made in the same fashion as the nest, waited behind them. Malfurion waited for Krasus, who finally nodded and sat.

"You are the Mother of Flight, the Lady of the Birds, are you not?" asked the dragon mage.

"Aviana I am, if that is what you mean." Her wide eyes inspected Krasus. "And you are one of mine, one of mine, I think."

"The thrill of the sky is known to me, yes, mistress. I owe my soul to Alexstrasza . . ."

"Aaah . . ." The demigoddess smiled in a motherly fashion. "Dear, dear Alexstrasza . . . it is long since we spoke. We must do so."

"Yes." Krasus did not push the point that now was hardly the time for visits. He did not doubt that Aviana knew exactly what was going on in the world and that despite her pleasant visage, she conferred with the other demigods and spirits on how to deal with the Burning Legion.

The sky deity looked to the night elf. "You, you, on the other wing, are one of Cenarius's . . ."

"I am Malfurion."

Aviana twittered, a sound like a songbird. "Of course, of course, you are! Cenarius speaks well of you, youngling."

The druid's cheeks darkened.

A question burned in Krasus's mouth, and he finally had to blurt, "Mistress . . . how do we come to be here?"

For the first time, she looked surprised. "Why, you chose to come here, of course, of course!"

The last thing Krasus could recall was the worm closing in on them as they reached the gate. He looked to Malfurion for clarification, but the night elf obviously knew less than him. "You say I chose to send us here?"

Aviana raised one delicately-boned hand. A multicolored songbird with a sweeping tail flew through the entrance and alighted onto the back of the hand. The demigoddess cooed at the small creature, which rubbed its head against hers. "Only those who truly desire to come here do. This one found you and your friend lying among the branches, the branches. There was also much scattered flesh of a very large and tasty worm. The children will feast for some time on it . . ."

Malfurion looked sick. The mage nodded. When he had blacked out, the portal had collapsed, cutting the huge worm in two.

Ignoring his own distaste, Krasus said, "I am afraid that this is the sole time that it was in complete error, mistress. I did not mean for us to come here. I cast a spell that went awry."

Her petite mouth formed another smile. "So you do not wish to fly again, to fly again?"

Krasus grimaced. "I would like nothing more."

"Then that, then that, is in part why you ended up here."

The dragon mage mulled over her words. His continual longing to be what he was had evidently influenced his spellcasting and Aviana had sensed it. "But there's nothing you can do for me."

"So sad, so sad." The demigoddess let the songbird fly out again. "But perhaps I can, perhaps I can . . . if you truly insist on departing."

"I do."

"Very well, very well." From within the inner plumage of her left wing, Aviana plucked one feather. As she held it up, a silver sheen covered it. The sky deity handed the feather to Krasus, who took the gift with reverence and studied it. Certainly Aviana's feather had power, but how would it enable him to fly?

"Place it upon your chest."

After some hesitation, Krasus pulled open the top of his robe, revealing his chest. He heard Malfurion gasp and even Aviana stared at him with wider eyes.

"So, so, you are indeed one of mine."

He had forgotten about the scale. Taken from his younger self, it felt so comforting that he had forgotten it. Briefly he pondered whether he could have used it to somehow penetrate the barrier, but quickly realized that by the time they had reached the area, Neltharion had sealed off the dragons' domain from all but his own sentinels. The Earth Warder had wanted no one disturbing his final spellwork. "Will your plan still work?" he asked.

"But of course, but of course! More so now, more so!"

Placing the feather against a part of his chest that was not covered by the dragon scale, Krasus waited.

The downy piece adhered much as the scale had. The silky tendrils of the feather spread flat, and as Krasus watched, the tendrils suddenly grew. They reached along his torso, snaking over it in every direction.

Malfurion looked distraught, but Krasus shook his head. He understood what Aviana intended and welcomed it. The dragon mage's heart pulsated at twice its normal rate, and he felt the urge to go leaping out of the nest.

"Not yet, not yet," warned the demigoddess. "You will know when its work is done, when its work is done."

A peculiar sensation spread across his upper back, near the shoulder blades. Krasus felt his garments shift and heard slight rips.

"There's something coming out of the back of your robes!" the druid gasped.

Even before they began to stretch, to define themselves, Krasus knew what they would be—huge, expansive white wings identical to the ones that Aviana had worn when transformed into a bird. Thick, white feathers covered them. Krasus instinctively flexed the wings and found them as responsive as his own.

"They are yours for this journey, for this journey."

The dragon mage indicated his companion. "What about him?"

"He is not born to the sky, to the sky. With learning, yes, with learning. Too long, too long, though. You must carry him, carry him."

In his present form, Krasus doubted that he had the strength for such a lengthy trek and said so. His concerns did not seem to bother their host, though.

This time, Aviana plucked a single strand from another feather. She brought it to her lips and gently blew it toward Malfurion. The druid looked uncertain, but stood his ground as the tiny bit of feather drifted over to him.

It touched his shoulder, adhering there. Malfurion shook once, then found great satisfaction with his hands, his legs, his entire body.

"I feel—" He jumped up and nearly struck the ceiling. Landing, Malfurion grinned like a child.

The birdlike deity smiled at both, her gaze returning to Krasus. "You will find him no burden at all, no burden at all."

"I—" Krasus choked up. He had not realized until now how great his distress had been over losing his ability to soar among the clouds. A tear slipped from one eye as he went down on his knee before Aviana and said, "Thank you . . ."

"No need for gratitude, no need." She bid him to rise, then led both toward the entrance. "Away you will fly, you will fly. To that high branch, then the right, the right. Through the clouds, through the clouds and descend. Well on your way you will be, you will be."

"The feather. How will I—"

She put a gentle finger to the mage's lips. "Hush, hush. It will know, it will know." As Malfurion joined Krasus, Aviana grew more solemn and said to the druid, "Your *shan'do* wishes you to know that he is with you, with you. We do not ignore the danger, the danger. Our will, our will, is strong . . ."

"Thank you. That gives me hope."

"Gives all of us hope," added Krasus. "If only we could do something about the dragons."

She agreed. "Yes . . . even we do not understand what goes on there, what goes on there."

Her two visitors eyed each other, Krasus saying, "They have a plan, but there is a threat to—"

Suddenly, his mouth felt as if full of cotton. His tongue seemed to twist. Aviana waited for more, but Krasus could give her nothing.

Seeing his silence as some hesitation of his own, the demigoddess gave him a respectful nod, then bid the dragon mage to step through the hole.

Krasus did so immediately, almost leaping into the sky. The wings instantly reacted, carrying him aloft. Around the area, birds twittered and sang out in recognition of a fellow flying creature.

The heady experience made him momentarily forget Malfurion and his mission. The sensation of having his own wings was so spectacular that Krasus had to fly up among the branches, then dive around them before rational thought returned.

Somewhat chagrined, the mage finally dropped down to where the druid and Aviana awaited him. The night elf had an awestruck expression and the demigoddess smiled like a proud parent. She indicated to Malfurion that he should step out and, after a cautious glance down, the druid obeyed.

Coming up over the night elf, Krasus took him under the shoulders. He felt as if he carried nothing.

"Are you comfortable?" the mage asked his companion.

"Not until my feet touch the ground," Malfurion muttered, "but I'll be good enough until then, Master Krasus."

"Go then, go then," Aviana said to the pair. To Krasus in particular, she added, "And when the end of your days comes, youngling, I will have your nest here ready, your nest here ready."

Krasus blanched. He looked around at the endless number and variety of birds; so many species living together, even though they should not be.

And the reason that they could live together here . . . was that they did not live at all. These were their spirits, brought up here by the demigoddess.

Somewhere there would be larger flying creatures, perhaps the hippogriff that had been slain and . . . and, of course, those dragons who had seen the end of their days.

"Go now, go now," the white figure cooed. "You shall return soon enough, soon enough . . ."

Put off guard as he had never been before, Krasus swallowed. "Yes, mistress . . . thank you again."

She smiled, which in no way eased his mind.

Rising up several yards, Krasus studied the direction in which she had told him to fly. He adjusted his grip on an anxious Malfurion, then started off.

As they flew, the night elf asked, "What did she mean by that? What did she mean that you would return?"

"We must all die someday, Malfurion."

"We—" The druid shivered, the truth finally dawning on him. "You mean . . . all of this—?"

"All of it." Krasus refused to say more, but, his curiosity aroused, he dared look back at the nest. His eyes widened as the mage realized that he had seen only a tiny bit. For the first time Krasus saw the structure in all its immensity. It ran everywhere and at each turn a huge, rounded chamber stood. The dragon mage studied the entire edifice, then the towering tree that dwarfed it. High up, he noticed winged creatures that even he could not identify.

And then, while he was still caught up in the sight . . . they entered the clouds.

SIXTEEN

The night elven host met the demons again just beyond Suramar. The Burning Legion held them there for a short time, then fell back toward Zin-Azshari. Midway through the next evening, the battle intensified, and once more no ground was gained or lost. Night elves and demons perished horribly, either through the blade or the magic arts.

Ravencrest could not stand this repeated stalemate, and so he had summoned Rhonin and Illidan again.

"Magic looks to be the deciding factor in this!" he said to the human in particular. "Can you do anything?"

Rhonin considered. "There is something that may be possible, but I'll need the full cooperation of the Moon Guard to put it into effect. It may backfire, too."

"I doubt it can make anything worse. Well, Illidan?"

"I eagerly await to aid Master Rhonin in whatever spell he crafts, my lord," Malfurion's twin said with a bow to the wizard.

Rhonin kept his expression neutral. He hoped that Illidan would maintain control and not try to build on what the red-haired spellcaster planned. If he did, chaos might ensue.

And chaos meant defeat.

"We're going to draw upon the Well as deeply as we can," Rhonin informed Illidan as they made their way to the Moon Guard. "I want to try something that the wizards of Dal—that the wizards of my homeland discussed doing, but were unable to try before things fell apart."

"Will it be that complicated, Master Rhonin?"

"No. They spent weeks preparing it, but I have in here—" He tapped his head. "—all that they completed. It may take us a few hours, but we should be successful."

Illidan grinned. "I have the utmost faith in you, Master Rhonin!"

Again, the human wondered if the night elf would be able to follow orders without attempting to turn the spell into something of his own rash design. More and more, Illidan appeared unable to *not* be the center of any casting. He lived for his sorcery, and cared not that much of his prowess had to do with the forces fed into him by the Moon Guard.

By the gods! Rhonin thought suddenly. *He almost sounds like a demon that way . . .*

But in so many other ways, the amber-eyed night elf was a potentially more terrible threat. An Illidan who sought to dominate . . . there, indeed, was a path to destruction.

I'll keep him under control. I have to with Krasus gone. He could only hope that his former mentor had succeeded in reaching the dragons. If not, Rhonin did not know what might happen. He had not planned on utilizing such a very dangerous spell, but with the knowledge that the outcome of this war was anything but set, there seemed no other choice.

Not wanting to leave the soldiers defenseless against the warlocks' dark magic, Rhonin had Illidan pick out a dozen of the best from the sorcerers' ranks, and left the rest to see to the battle. He would only need them once he had the spell ready to cast. The Moon Guard would amplify it, spread it where he needed it to go.

But only if Rhonin succeeded with his part.

"Illidan . . . I need you to guide me," the wizard said when everything else was prepared. "I need you to bring me to the Well itself."

"Yes, Master Rhonin!" The night elf eagerly stood next to him as they prepared to reach out with their minds to the source of all night elven magic. Up until this point, Rhonin had been touching peripherally on the power of the Well. Unlike Illidan's people, he had not needed to rely on direct use, which gave him a very distinct advantage. Illidan and a few others had learned from the human how to do this, but not to the same degree. Now, however, Rhonin needed to draw as much as he could so that he could be guaranteed of the results he desired.

Far away, a horn sounded. Lord Ravencrest was setting up everything in preparation for Rhonin's grand spell . . . or grand catastrophe.

Standing side by side, the two spellcasters reached out with their thoughts and linked. Rhonin felt Illidan's wild nature and tried to keep it in check. The night elf's zealousness was a definite threat to the stability of the spell.

Illidan's mind drew the wizard forward. Through his inner eye, Rhonin watched the landscape rip past as he and his companion sought to touch the Well. Endless rows of demons followed by miles of ravaged landscape passed within a single second. Briefly, the ruined city of Zin-Azshari rose up, then filled his gaze. The grand palace of Queen Azshara dominated next . . . and finally the black waters of the Well of Eternity greeted the human.

Its power staggered him. Rhonin had always assumed that he had sensed the Well enough simply by drawing upon that part of it which permeated all Kalimdor. Now he realized he had been mistaken, that the Well itself was such a fount of pure energy that if he could command it all, he felt it would make of him a god.

A god . . .

Everything that Rhonin had dreamed of when first he had taken up the robes of wizardry now seemed so simple. He could raise up entire cities, or tear them down with the blink of an eye. He could call up the power of the earth, then send it crashing down on any who opposed him. He could—

With tremendous effort, Rhonin freed himself of his dark ambitions. A sudden anxiety filled him as he recognized the Well. He had known what it was all along, and yet his mind had denied the evil.

It had the same taint as the demons. Pure magic it might be, but in its way it corrupted as much as Sargeras did.

But it was too late to turn back. Rhonin had to delve into the Well this once, then never touch it in such a manner again. Even drawing upon it as he had in the past now repulsed him, but to give it up completely meant that he would have to give up all magic . . . and Rhonin knew he was too weak of soul to ever do that much.

Sensing Illidan's impatience and curiosity, the wizard quickly took up the power he needed from the dark depths. The temptation to let it all engulf his mind proved daunting, but with effort he retreated from the cursed waters.

Within moments, the minds of the night elf and him had returned to their bodies. The link to the Well remained as strong as ever. Rhonin prepared to cast, knowing that the sooner he did, the sooner he could be rid of the foul sensation in his soul.

It begins now, he told Illidan.

Instantly, he felt Malfurion's twin prepare the Moon Guard for the task. What the wizard fed them they would send out toward the enemy, multiplying its intensity more than a hundredfold.

With ease, Rhonin constructed the spell matrix that his masters in Dalaran had died working on. He briefly thanked their departed souls, regardless of the fact that none of the wizards would be born for centuries to come. Then, when Rhonin was satisfied that the matrix would remain stable—the wizard unleashed the spell.

Illidan and the others mentally shook as it reverberated through their systems. To his credit the young sorcerer kept the much more practiced spellcasters from buckling. The very ambition that Rhonin feared now kept his plans together.

And so, they struck at the demons' lines.

A ripple of ear-shattering sound hit the Burning Legion without even touching the soldiers who frantically battled them. Massive demons shrieked and dropped their weapons as they tried to shut the sound out. The vibrations shattered their insides, tore apart their minds. As the wave raced over their forces, the demons fell as if swept by some giant broom.

All across the front, they perished. The soldiers stood frozen, shaken up by what they witnessed.

"Now, Ravencrest," Rhonin whispered. "Now."

The horns sounded, urging a rapid advance.

The night elves shouted. Panther riders led the way. They charged across the field, seeking the enemy . . . but ahead of them lay only the dead. The sound wave continued to race on, cutting a swath of swift but violent death. No demon caught in its path lived. Hundreds perished.

Rhonin suddenly felt his body give up on him. He wobbled, his head feeling as if it, like the demons', would explode.

The wizard fell.

"I have you, Master Rhonin . . ."

Illidan eased him to the ground, the night elf none the worse for the wear. He was, in fact, the only one. The rest of the Moon Guard involved in the grand spell looked as terrible as the wizard felt. Most of them sat or even fell down, not at all caring that the soldiers now advanced from them.

"Did you see it? Did you see what we did?" demanded Illidan eagerly. "This proves it! There's no power like the Well!" He glanced at something or someone whom Rhonin himself could not see. "The Well is the way, brother! You see? Nothing else compares!"

He continued shouting to an absent Malfurion. Rhonin, still seeking to regain his strength, could only stare. Illidan's avarice, his jealousy, was so apparent that it almost bordered on hatred for the druid.

Rhonin's spell had sent the demons into flight, possibly turned the tide of the war forever . . . but as he watched Illidan's intense expression and thought of his own near seduction by the Well, the wizard wondered if he had just unleashed something more terrible on the night elf race.

Korialstrasz brooded, his patience growing very thin. The dragons had all been ordered to await the word of the Aspects. When that came, every flight would take to the air as if of one mind, one soul. The plan was to descend upon the demons as a terrifying force, the Dragon Soul ripping apart the demon lines before the leviathans themselves struck.

A simple, workable plan. A faultless plan.

A plan that, for reasons he could not express even to himself, Korialstrasz did not trust.

But the male red was loyal to his queen, his mate, and so he did nothing. Alexstrasza trusted in Neltharion's creation. More to the point, she trusted in the Earth Warder himself. Whatever uncertainties Korialstrasz had, they had to remain unspoken.

"Ever the thinker, my love. Ever the worrier."

He raised his head in surprise as the gigantic female entered his lair. "Alexstrasza," he rumbled. "You are to be with the other Aspects . . ."

"I have made excuses for my momentary absence. Neltharion is not pleased, but he will have to control himself."

Korialstrasz lowered his head in homage to her. "How may I be of service to you, my queen?"

A hint of indecision glinted in her eyes. In a voice so very quiet for a dragon, she replied, "I need you to disobey me."

Her consort was perplexed. "My love?"

"All save the sentinels that each of us posted are supposed to remain in this, the vastest of the cavern systems, until the moment of the launch. I wish you to ignore my earlier command and leave."

He was stunned. Clearly the other Aspects were not to know of this departure. "And where am I to go?"

"I don't know precisely, but I hope that you'll be able to sense exactly where once you're beyond the barrier. I want you to find Krasus."

Krasus. The mysterious mage had been much on the mind of Korialstrasz, too. Krasus likely knew things that would have cleared up much that disturbed the consort. "He should still be with the night elves—"

"No . . . he was near us only a short time ago. Ysera told me that a night elf called Malfurion sought to act as his messenger through her. However, she distrusted such an action, and so made the night elf wait until the moment was right."

"And?"

"When Ysera sought for Malfurion again, he had vanished. She told me all this while Neltharion and Malygos discussed the spellwork of the Soul."

"But why would Krasus come here?" The anxieties felt by the male red multiplied. The journey from the lands of the night elves was quite a distance for one who could not fly several miles in the space of a few minutes.

"That is what I want to know."

"I'll do my best to find him, but it may prove harder than you imagine."

The queen snorted. She shut her eyes in thought for a moment, then nodded. "Yes, you must know now."

"Know what?"

"My love, you've felt the closeness between you and Krasus. You would almost describe him as a clutch brother, wouldn't you?"

He had not thought so before, but now that Alexstrasza said it, Korialstrasz realized that, yes, Krasus did hold such an esteemed place in his heart. It had nothing to do with the scales they had shared to overcome their weakness; something about the mysterious figure had made the consort come to trust him as much as he did his glorious mate.

And, at times, even more so.

Alexstrasza read his face. "Know this, my love. The reason you and Krasus are so close is that he and you are one and the same."

The male red blinked. Surely he had heard wrong. Surely Alexstrasza meant something else.

But she shook her massive head, stating, "Krasus is *you*, Korialstrasz. He is you much older, much more learned, much wiser. He is you countless centuries forward."

"That is impossible—" A sudden thought occurred to him. "Is this some trick of Nozdormu? His absence has been very questionable . . ."

"Nozdormu has some part in this, yes, but I can't tell you exactly how. Just understand that Krasus is here because he must be."

"Then, the outcome of the war is assured. The Dragon Soul will help us triumph over the demons. My concerns were for naught."

"Your concerns are valid. We don't know anything about the outcome. Krasus fears that Nozdormu has sent him here because the timeline has shifted. There was a point where I had to consider eliminating him and his companion in order to preserve it, but it soon became evident that matters had gone beyond such."

Korialstrasz gazed at her with wide, wondering orbs. "You would have slain . . . me?"

"At his insistence, my love."

He mulled that over and saw her reasoning. "Forgive me. Yes, my queen, I'll go searching for him."

"I thank you. His memories were much damaged by the journey to our time, perhaps because he already existed here as you. Still, he is sharp of wit in most ways, and if there is something he urgently needed to discuss, then it behooves us to find him."

"I go immediately."

Alexstrasza dipped her head in gratitude. "I must pretend that you do this by your own leave, Korialstrasz."

"Of course. I won't fail you, my queen."

She gave him a most loving look, then departed his lair. The male waited just long enough for her to be nowhere near, then left, too.

To his relief, it proved not at all difficult to leave the mountain itself, for most of the dragons now sat poised, awaiting the command to fly. The few others were like himself or Tyran, consorts with positions of leadership who had to be near if the Aspects needed them.

Evading the sentinels beyond was slightly more troublesome. The first—of his own flight—he managed to evade by being aware of the other's personality traits. Horakastrasz was a young, eagle-eyed male, but he had a tendency to become distracted. As Korialstrasz came upon him, the bored guardian had begun batting large rocks into the air with his tail, then watching them plummet to the ground far below. As he hit the next, Korialstrasz soared over him, flying high enough that the other red would not sense the shift in the air currents.

By one means or another, he passed the rest undiscovered. As he flew toward the barrier, Korialstrasz prepared himself for contact. He struck the invisible wall head-on, feeling as if he pushed through molasses. Wings flapping as hard as possible, the dragon burst through the other side, soaring miles beyond before he managed to regain proper control.

Perching on a squat mountain, Korialstrasz quickly imagined Krasus. For good measure, he touched with one claw the scale that his older self had traded to him. So much made more sense now; he had wondered why the exchange should aid the pair so well. By doing so, the two halves of himself had become more complete. Korialstrasz still suffered some pain and weariness, but nowhere near what he had before that event.

He put all his concentration into finding Krasus, seeking that link that only two who were one could possibly have. The dragon doubted that his other half was still near, for if it had been him—and it was—Korialstrasz would have continued seeking some way to enter. He would not have gone into hiding. Therefore, circumstances had demanded that Krasus flee.

Trying not to think of just what might have forced his elder form to abandon the area of the barrier, the red reached out. Only a dragon's will could encompass the expanse that Korialstrasz's did now. Over countless lands his mind stretched, hunting that which was him.

But his patience soon frayed as nowhere did he sense himself. It should have been a relatively simple task. Had some dire fate befallen Krasus? The very thought sent shivers through Korialstrasz. No creature yearned to discover his ultimate fate.

But then, as if abruptly reborn, the dragon sensed the familiar presence. He could not detect the exact location, but knew which direction he should at least fly.

Korialstrasz immediately launched into the air, flapping as hard as he could. The sooner he retrieved his other self, the sooner he could feel secure once more.

Krasus became his utter focus. His surroundings blurred. With his huge wings, he ate away at the miles, but, even still, he felt it much too slow.

So obsessed, Korialstrasz did not know that he was under attack until the claws tore into his back.

With a startled roar, he rolled in the air, taking his attacker by surprise. The monstrous visage of a black dragon filled his gaze.

"Stop!" the red shouted. "By the glory of the Aspects, I demand that you—"

In response, the other dragon opened his mouth.

Korialstrasz ceased flapping, his huge body immediately dropping like a rock. It was the only thing that saved him from a fearsome burst of molten flame. The searing heat shot just past his head, making his eyes tear.

Pain wracked Korialstrasz where the other's claws had torn through scale. Although slightly larger than the black, Korialstrasz's inherent weakness more than evened the battle.

"Leave me be!" he said, trying again to use reason. "There is no need for confrontation between us!"

"You will not interfere!" the black retorted, eyes wide and surely mad.

Alexstrasza's consort had no idea what his adversary meant by that, but it strengthened the fear that something had happened to Krasus.

The ebony behemoth dropped down on Korialstrasz, forcing him, in turn, to descend farther. Korialstrasz allowed it to happen, intending to spin out from under his foe at the last moment.

But as he neared the mountain tops, he discovered that he had been played for a fool.

Korialstrasz's adversary suddenly released his hold. As he did, another black dragon leapt from behind a nearby peak. It collided with the red, sending both spinning out of control. The jagged earth below rushed up toward the pair.

"You'll slay us both!" shouted Korialstrasz.

"For the glory of my master!"

The rushing wind forced back the black's wings. Only then did Alexstrasza's consort see that one had been broken and torn. This dragon could no longer fly properly; he intended to sacrifice himself in order to send his foe to his death.

Korialstrasz, however, had no intention of perishing so. Beating his wings hard, he did what the other was incapable of doing, using the leathery appendages to direct their fall. Suddenly, instead of the red being on the bottom, the sinister black found himself there.

The injured giant roared and tried to flip them back around. Farther up, an answering cry warned Korialstrasz that his other foe had realized what was happening.

Pulling in all four legs but keeping his grip, the red calculated the seconds remaining. He watched the harsh landscape near, his attention in particular on the short, sharp hills mixed among the mountains.

And as he and the black reached them, Korialstrasz stretched his legs, thrusting his adversary down even as he beat his wings hard to lift his own considerable mass.

With a painful howl that echoed throughout the region, the injured black collided with the ground. His bones shattered, and he briefly flailed like a leaf caught in a breeze. Blood spilled over the immediate area.

A final gasp escaped the stricken leviathan . . . and then his head rolled to the side, his tongue lolling free.

The second attack nearly caught Korialstrasz as he struggled to keep from joining the dead dragon. Again the claws raked the red's back, forcing a cry from him. The strain of the battle began to tell on Korialstrasz. His breathing grew weary, and it took increasing effort to keep aloft. Neither he nor Alexstrasza had expected this betrayal by Neltharion's flight.

"You must die!" roared the black wildly, as if by telling his prey this Korial-strasz would understand.

The red dragon managed to avoid the deadly talons again, but his foe pressed him hard. The other behemoth was not only swift, but driven by a manic desire to please the Earth Warder. Like the second black, he appeared ready to sacrifice himself if it would serve the cause.

But what cause? Why be so furious that one dragon was not among the rest? Why had fear of that very fact caused Neltharion to command these to die for him?

Whatever the reason, Korialstrasz could no longer worry about it. A fierce column of molten fire caught him full in the chest. He spun around madly, unable to focus.

Claws dug into his chest. The fetid breath of the black nearly caused him to gag.

"I have you!" roared the insane creature. The dark giant inhaled for another blast, one certain to slay his opponent at such close range.

Desperate, Korialstrasz thrust his head forward. His huge jaws clamped tight on the black's neck, squeezing so hard that it cut off the air passage.

The other dragon shook violently as the forces it sought to unleash could not find an exit. He clawed frantically at Korialstrasz, leaving scars in the face and body.

The black literally exploded.

Releasing the neck, Korialstrasz roared in agony as burning ichor poured over him from the ruined corpse. It was too much. His strength gone, he and his dead adversary dropped to the earth.

And as he blacked out, the red dragon could only wonder how his death would affect his future self.

SEVENTEEN

Archimonde watched his legions retreat from the spell and the oncoming night elves. He watched as the landscape before him filled with the forest-green armor of the foe. The demon commander could feel their sense of triumph, hear their roars of imminent victory.

How easy these creatures are to deceive, he thought. *They think that they will win now.*

With that, the gigantic demon turned and slowly, confidently, walked after his fleeing minions.

"Unngh!"

Malfurion started at the sound from Krasus. A moment later, he felt the mage struggle with his grip. Looking down, the druid saw that they were much too high up for him to drop safely even with the magical feather.

Clutching onto Krasus's arms as best he could, Malfurion shouted, "What is it?"

"I do not—I feel as if my beating heart has been torn from my chest! I—I must land quickly!"

The night elf quickly scanned the area. There were woods and grassy plains below, more of the latter fortunately. He saw one area that looked softer than the rest and pointed at it. "Can you make it to there?"

"I—will—try!"

But Krasus flew haphazardly, and the spot that Malfurion had chosen began to disappear to the right. Instead, they headed for a copse of trees that might break their fall, but would also likely break their necks and skulls.

Krasus grunted hard, lifting them into the air a bit higher. The trees passed and again open plain welcomed them. They started to descend, slowly at first, then much too fast for the druid's taste.

"I think—I think you must be prepared to save yourself, Malf—"

Suddenly, the mage released him.

Precious seconds passed before Malfurion realized what he could do. He reached out with his thoughts to the grass below . . .

That area of the field rapidly grew taller and thicker. The grass bunched so tight it created a padding of sorts. As the night elf dropped on it, it gave slightly, then reshaped. Every bone in his body shook, but Malfurion survived intact.

He felt his shoulder, only to find the gift from Aviana missing. Still, Malfurion gave thanks that he had acted swiftly and avoided disaster.

Krasus fluttered several yards farther, moving like a hawk fatally shot by an archer. Malfurion could not react quickly enough to aid the dragon mage, who finally crashed into the tall grass beyond.

The instant that he hit, Krasus's wings dissipated like dust in the wind. The limp figure fell forward, vanishing from the druid's sight.

"Master Krasus! Krasus!" Pushing himself to his feet, the night elf struggled through the field toward where he had last seen his companion.

But of his companion, there was no sign. Malfurion gazed at the grass, certain that he had the correct location.

Then, some distance to the south, he heard a brief moan. Shoving aside the grass, Malfurion hunted for the source.

Moments later, the still form of Krasus greeted his fearful eyes.

He knelt by the mage, cautiously looking for any outward injury. Finding none, Malfurion slowly turned him over. As he did, he noticed something slip from his companion's body.

Krasus's feather. It looked withered, brown. Touching it with one finger, the druid gasped as the feather crumbled, vanishing in the dirt and grass.

Another moan escaped Krasus. Adjusting him so that he lay perfectly on his back, Malfurion checked for broken bones. However, despite his much harder fall, Krasus appeared untouched. Apparently, the only thing affecting him had been whatever ailment had stricken him in flight.

The pale figure's eyes flickered open. "I . . . I am tired . . . of waking in s-such a condition . . ."

"Careful, Krasus. You shouldn't move yet."

"I will soon not be moving at all . . . Malfurion, I . . . believe I am dying."

"What do you mean? How? What happened to you?"

"Not me . . . another. I am tied to Korialstrasz . . . and he to me. I think—I think he has been attacked. He is . . . nearly dead, and . . . if he goes, there is no hope for me."

Malfurion looked Krasus over again, trying to find something he could do to help. "Is there no hope?"

"Perhaps if you could—could heal him . . . but he is far from here, and . . . as he is a dragon . . . it would be most d-difficult. I—"

He grew silent. Malfurion thought quickly, but nothing else came to mind. All the skills that Cenarius had taught him could be applied, but not when the true victim lay countless miles away.

Then he saw—half-revealed by the wizard's crumpled robe—the scale. "Krasus. This piece—"

"Wh-what I thought would . . . save us earlier. A bit of him . . . for a b-bit of me. It did—did work for a time."

"This is *his* scale," Malfurion said to himself. "*His* scale."

It was an audacious, impossible plan—and the only one he had. He ran his finger across the scale, marveling at its texture and sensing the power of it. The druid's intention borrowed from differing aspects of his learning, things that Cenarius had never linked together. Still . . . certain basics surely applied . . .

"I may have an idea, Krasus."

But the mage did not answer; his eyes once again had closed. At first the night elf feared that he had already passed away. Only when he leaned close and listened to Krasus's quiet but still steady breathing did Malfurion's tensions ease slightly.

He could not hesitate any longer. Krasus had only minutes remaining.

Placing both hands on the scale, the druid opened his mind back up to his surroundings. Already the grass knew him and it reacted to his call. The wind tousled his hair and the earth stirred to waking, curious about his plea.

But before he could ask of them anything, he also needed to see if he could truly link with the dragon, Korialstrasz. Eyes shut, the druid let himself flow into the scale, seek of it the bond to its original wearer.

At first there was some confusion, Krasus and Korialstrasz so bound together that he almost mistook the former for the latter. Finally realizing his mistake, Malfurion steered his thoughts toward the red dragon, hoping that a tenuous link remained between the scale and Korialstrasz.

To his surprise, that part proved quite easy. Immediately his senses threw him across miles, across lands, to a harsher, mountainous region. Both the landscape and the journey reminded him of his attempt to reach the dragons hidden behind the barrier, only this time he did not travel quite so far, nor had he, thankfully, had to make use of the Emerald Dream.

Then, a horrible sense of loss hit Malfurion. He nearly blacked out. Fearful, however, of accidentally joining Krasus's and Korialstrasz's death experience, the night elf steeled himself. His senses stabilized, and he discovered that he now felt the dragon's dying emotions.

There had been a battle, a terrible battle. Malfurion thought at first that the Burning Legion had attacked, but then he sensed from the red's splintered thoughts that the foe had been other dragons—black ones.

Recalling the sinister pair who had pursued Krasus and him, Malfurion suspected that he knew which beasts had attacked. He gathered that they were dead, which made him marvel that Korialstrasz had even survived to this point. Truly a powerful, magnificent creature this dragon had been . . .

No! He was thinking of Korialstrasz as already dead. That condemned not only the dragon, but Krasus as well. Malfurion had to stop such speculation if he hoped to save them.

One of the first true lessons that Cenarius had taught him had been the health and healing of woodland creatures. In the past, Malfurion had saved the lives of foxes, rabbits, birds, and more. He could apply that work now, just amplifying the effect.

Or so the druid hoped.

Malfurion called to his surroundings. He needed their sacrifice; only life could give life. The earth, the flora, they had the capability of regenerating in a manner no animal could. The night elf still asked much from them, however, for now he sought to save a *dragon*. If his plea was rejected, he could lay no blame.

Trying to relay the importance of saving Korialstrasz—and by doing so,

Krasus—Malfurion reached out to the grass, the trees, anything that would give to him. In the back of his mind, he noted the dragon's life force ebbing. There was barely any time left.

Then, to his relief, Malfurion felt the land give of itself for his efforts. The life force flowed into him, exhilarating the night elf so much that he almost forgot for what purpose he had requested it. Recalling himself, he positioned his fingertips on the scale, then fed the energy through.

Krasus's body shook once, then calmed. Through the link, Malfurion sensed the life force pouring into the dragon. The night elf's heart raced, sweat dripping down his face, as he struggled to maintain the bond.

So much flowed through, and yet, Malfurion felt no change in Korialstrasz. The dragon continued to hang on the edge of death. Gritting his teeth, the druid drew more and more, sending it to the stricken giant as quickly as he could.

At last, he noted a slight change. Korialstrasz's soul pulled back from the abyss. The tenuous link to life solidified.

"Please . . ." the harried night elf gasped. "More . . ."

And more came. The land around him gave as he needed, understanding that the dire situation affected not just the two ill figures, but also so many others.

Slowly, ever so slowly, the tide turned in life's favor. Korialstrasz grew stronger. The druid felt the leviathan's consciousness return and knew that the dragon wondered at this miracle.

Krasus's body again shook. The elder mage moaned. His eyes slowly opened.

At that point, Malfurion finally knew that he had done enough. Pulling his fingertips from the scale, the night elf leaned back and exhaled.

Only then did he see that the grass for yards around him was black.

All life had been drained from the tendrils. Peering around, Malfurion saw that the field for as far as he could see was dry and black. A pair of trees stood leafless in the distance.

Fear at what he had done made the druid shiver until he felt the stirring of life beneath the earth. The roots of the grass still lived and, with the earth's help, they would soon grow new, mighty stalks. The trees had also survived and, if given the opportunity, would create for themselves healthy new leaves.

The night elf sighed in relief. For a few desperate seconds, he had imagined himself no better than the Burning Legion.

"What . . . what have you done?" managed Krasus.

"I had to save you. I did the only thing I could think of."

The mage shook his head as he pushed himself up to a sitting position. "That is not what I meant. Malfurion . . . do you have even the slightest concept of what you have accomplished? Do you understand all that your effort entailed?"

"It was needed," Malfurion explained. "I regret that I had to ask so much of the land, but it was willing to give it."

For the first time, Krasus noted the blackened grass. His eyes narrowed as he surveyed the evidence of the night elf's tremendous work. "Malfurion, this is not possible."

"It was based off of my *shan'do's* teachings. I merely modified it to suit the situation."

"And managed a result that should have been *beyond* you—beyond almost any spellcaster." With some doing, the dragon mage rose. He frowned as he discovered the true extent of the blackened grass. "Astounding."

Still not understanding just what so disturbed Krasus about his spell, Malfurion asked, "Can you sense Korialstrasz? Is he well?"

Krasus concentrated. "The link is fading to what it was before your spell, but I can still sense him for the moment. He is . . . fit . . . but his mind is confused. He recalls the battle some and that he was supposed to find me, but there are gaps." This, for some reason, caused Krasus to let loose with a very uncustomary chuckle. "Now we are more alike than ever, he and I. Truly, the fates mock me."

"Do we wait for him?"

"We do, but not for the reason for which I suspect he wanted to find me. Knowing him as I do, he likely planned to bring me back to Alexstrasza, but there is no more time. I have this terrible feeling that we need to return to the host now. You may call it a hunch or perhaps much too much experience. Whichever, when Korialstrasz reaches us, we head back there."

Malfurion immediately thought of Tyrande . . . and then, belatedly, his brother. "How long will it take him to do that?"

"He is a dragon . . . and now a very healthy one," Krasus remarked with a brief but satisfied smile. "Not too long at all if I know him . . ."

Tyrande had become very unique among the Sisters of Elune. She was the only one of them who had two shadows, the second even named.

It was called Shandris Feathermoon.

Wherever the priestess went, the orphan followed. Shandris watched everything that her savior did with the eyes of one who wanted desperately to learn. When Tyrande prayed over an injured or wounded night elf, the young female repeated those words, trying at the same time to match the former's gestures.

Tyrande felt conflicted about Shandris. With no parents, Shandris had no one to turn to. True, there were others in similar straits, but something about this one orphan still struck her. Her dedication to Tyrande's work marked her as a possible novice, and the temple always welcomed new sisters. How would it look, then, to fling her back among the refugees and forget her? The priestess had to keep her nearby; she could not live with herself otherwise.

Unfortunately, not every situation was one where an untried, unblooded female was safe. The sisterhood continued to take their turn fighting on the front line, each group switching off as the high priestess commanded. Tyrande did not want Shandris wandering up near the demons, who would have no compunction about cutting up an innocent. Shandris, however, had already once almost frightened her to death by sneaking along behind the sisters when they had ridden out to warn Malfurion and Krasus. Only belatedly had the priestess discovered that, when the orphan let slip a comment about the event that could have only been spoken by one who had witnessed it.

"No more!" Tyrande commanded her. "Please stay behind when we go to battle! I can't worry about you and fight!"

Looking crestfallen, Shandris nodded, but Tyrande doubted that this was the end of the discussion. She could only pray to Elune that the young one would see sense.

But as she contemplated her predicament, Tyrande noticed one of the sisters in charge of a neighboring group approach her. The other priestess, taller and senior by several years, wore an expression of deep thought as she joined Tyrande.

"Hail, Sister Marinda! What brings you to this humble one?"

"Hail, Sister Tyrande," Marinda returned dourly. "I come from the high priestess."

"Oh? Has she news for us?"

"She . . . she is dead, sister."

Tyrande felt as if her entire world had just been shattered at its foundations. The venerable mother of the temple—dead? She had grown up watching and listening to the woman, as had nearly all other worshippers. It was because of her that Tyrande had taken up the robes of the novice.

"H-how?"

Tears streaked down Marinda's cheeks. "It was kept secret from us. She insisted that only her attendants would know. During the push back toward Suramar, a demon lanced her in the stomach. She might have survived that, her skills for healing strong, but a felbeast caught her first. She was apparently almost dead when some of the others slew it. They brought her back to her tent, where she's been since . . . until she died but an hour ago."

"Horrible!" Tyrande fell to her knees and started praying to the Mother Moon. Marinda joined her and, without coaxing, Shandris imitated them.

When the two priestesses had finished their farewell to their superior, Marinda rose. "There is more, sister."

"More! What could there be?"

"Before her death, she named a successor."

Tyrande nodded. This was to be expected. The new high priestess had, of course, immediately sent out messengers like Marinda to spread the word of her ascension.

"Who is it?" There were several worthy candidates.

"She named you, Tyrande."

Tyrande could not believe her own ears. "She—Mother Moon! You jest!"

Shandris squealed and clapped. Tyrande turned and gave her a severe look. The orphan quieted, but her eyes gleamed with pride.

Marinda did not appear to be at all jesting, and that put fear into Tyrande. How could she, barely into the role of priestess, take over the *entire* sisterhood—and in time of war yet?

"Forgive me for saying so, Sister Marinda, but she . . . she must have been stressed of mind because of her injuries! How could she with all sincerity choose me?"

"She was of clear mind, sister. And you should understand, she had made mention of you before this. The senior sisters all understood that you were the one . . . and no one among them argued the decision."

"It's . . . it's impossible! How could *I* lead? How could I, with so little experience, take on the mantle? There are so many more who know the temple better!"

"But none so attuned to Elune herself. We've all seen it, all felt it. There are already tales of you spreading among the refugees and soldiers. Miracles. People healed by you when others have failed them utterly—"

This was something that Tyrande had not heard. "What do you mean?"

And Sister Marinda explained. All the priestesses spent part of their rest period doing anything but resting, with so many in need, none of the sisters felt right *not* helping. But desiring to help and actually doing so were two different things. Yes, they succeeded in healing many, but countless others their skills could not touch.

Tyrande, on the other hand, had left behind her an unbroken string of successes. Anyone and everyone she attempted to heal had recovered. Without realizing it, Tyrande had even aided several whom other sisters had failed to heal. If that had not surprised the rest of the priestesses enough, she had then gone on without rest to aid others.

"You shouldn't even be able to stand, yet you fight, too, Sister Tyrande."

It had never occurred to the young priestess that she had done anything other than fulfill her duty. She would pray to Elune and Elune would answer.

Tyrande would feel grateful, then move on in the hopes of healing someone else.

But according to the others, she had done much, much more.

"I—this can't be right."

"It is. You must accept it." Marinda took a deep breath. "You know that, normally, there would be a ceremony, a long entailed one that as many worshippers as possible would be invited to see."

Lost in thought, Tyrande vaguely replied, "Yes . . ."

"We'll do our best to prepare something, obviously. With your permission, I'll pull the other sisters from the battle and have them—"

"What?" In addition to all else, they planned to do *that*—and because of *her*? Drawing herself together, Tyrande declared, "No! I'll not have that!"

"Sister—"

Using her newfound, if undesired authority, she gave Marinda a look that would brook no argument, then added, "It seems that I've no choice in accepting this, but I can't do it if it means setting up a ceremony that distracts us from the danger! I'll become high priestess—at least until this war is over—but I will keep my present garments—"

"But the robes of state—"

"I will *keep* my present garments and there will be *no* ceremony! We can't afford to take such a risk with our people. Let them see us continuing to heal and fight in the name of the Mother Moon. Is that understood?"

"I—" Marinda went down on her knees, bending her head forward. "I obey, mistress."

"Rise up! I want none of that, either! We are all sisters, *equal* in heart! All of us give homage to Elune! I want no one doing so for me."

"As you wish." But the elder sister did not rise and, in fact, seemed to expect something of Tyrande. After a moment's confusion, she finally understood just what.

Forcing her hand not to shake, Tyrande reached out and touched the top of Marinda's head. "In the name of the Mother Moon, great Elune who watches over all, I give the blessing."

She heard the other priestess sigh in relief. Marinda rose, her expression now akin to those that had been worn by the other sisters—Tyrande included—when in the presence of their venerable mistress. "I'll convey your will to the others. If I may be permitted?"

"Yes . . . thank you."

As Marinda departed, Tyrande nearly collapsed. This could not be possible! In some ways, it was almost as terrible a nightmare as facing the Burning Legion. *She* the head of the order! Truly, Kalimdor faced destruction.

"How wonderful!" Shandris exclaimed, clapping again. She ran up to

Tyrande, nearly hugged her, then tried instead to look very serious. As Marinda had done, the orphan knelt before the new high priestess and awaited a blessing.

Defeated, Tyrande gave her one. Shandris's expression changed to awe. "I'll follow you for the rest of my life, my lady!"

"Don't call me that. I'm still Tyrande."

"Yes, my lady."

Unleashing an exasperated sigh, the new head of the temple considered what she had to do next. There were probably endless details and rituals that the high priestess had to perform. Tyrande recalled her predecessor leading this chant and that. The temple also held a blessing each evening for the rising of the moon and the good will of the gods. In addition, the leading nobles always had to have some sort of recognition ceremony for various anniversaries and other events . . .

She stared bleakly at her future, feeling trapped, not honored.

Her contemplations were jarred by a sudden moan from somewhere among the refugees. Tyrande recognized that sound, having heard it so often before. Someone was in terrible agony.

The ceremonies could wait. The rituals could wait. Tyrande had joined the order for one thing most of all—to help others through the gifts of Elune.

Following the sound of the moan, the new high priestess continued her work.

EIGHTEEN

The queen had decided to go riding, and when Azshara set her mind on something, not all the demons in the world could convince her otherwise . . . which meant that Captain Varo'then had no chance whatsoever.

It had been quite some time since she had left the confines of the palace. Surrounded on foot by her hulking bodyguards and an additional unit of the captain's crack troop, Azshara and her retinue of handmaidens rode serenely through the gates and out into Zin-Azshari.

The *ruins* of Zin-Azshari.

It was the first time since its destruction that the ruler of the night elves had seen it up close. Her lidded eyes studied the crushed domiciles, the littered streets, and the occasional corpse still left untouched due to a lack of enough carrion eaters. Azshara's lips pursed, and on occasion she sniffed at something not to her liking.

Varo'then glowered at the outside world. He wanted nothing to disturb his queen. Had he been able to take a sword to the destruction as he would a foe, the officer would have done it.

A felbeast rose from behind a crumpled tower, its savage jaws filled with something. It chewed loudly as the queen's column passed, then darted back into hiding.

They rode for some distance, Azshara not speaking once and so no one else daring to do so. Her Fel Guard kept close despite a lack of threat, the demons now as adamant in their loyalty to her as any of the soldiers. Had she demanded of them to attack their own kind, they likely would have obeyed without hesitation. Of course, Azshara would have never done that, for there was only one other than herself whom she did not wish to displease and that was the lord of the Burning Legion, Sargeras.

"Will it be soon, do you think, my dear captain?" she asked.

The officer was confused. "Light of Lights?"

"His coming, captain. *His* coming."

Varo'then nodded immediately. "Oh, yes, my queen, very soon! Mannoroth claims that each night sees the portal stronger than the previous."

"He must truly be a god among gods for it needing to be so powerful simply to allow him entrance."

"As you say, my queen."

"He must be . . . *glorious*," Azshara uttered in a tone she generally reserved only for herself.

The scarred night elf nodded again, trying to hide his envy. No one could compete with a god.

The same green mist that now covered so much of Kalimdor continued to drape over the city. To Azshara, it added a wonderfully mysterious look to her capital, while at the same time keeping from her eyes many things which might have offended her sensibilities. When the world was rebuilt, she would ask Sargeras to remove the haze; until then, it suited her well.

As they came to what had once been an open square, Azshara looked around. She reined her night saber to a halt, patting its head afterward to keep it calm. Like all else in the palace, even the animals had been touched by the presence of Sargeras. The huge cats of the party had eyes that were crimson and fierce. They would have attacked any of their own kind who was not a part of the royal stables, lustily tearing and biting their foes to bloody shreds.

"The captain and I will continue on alone for a few minutes."

Neither the night elves nor the demons looked pleased with this . . . save

Varo'then, of course. He looked back at his men and growled, "By the order
of the queen!"

Unable to argue with such a fact, the retinue held its place while the pair
slowly rode on.

Azshara did not speak until they were far out of earshot from the rest.
Smiling at Varo'then, she said, "Does it all go well?"

"All what?"

The queen glanced to the horizon. "The cleansing of my realm. I thought
it would be done by now."

"Archimonde will see to it that it comes to pass, my queen."

"But I would like it done *before* Sargeras comes! Wouldn't that make for a
tremendous gift . . . for my intended?"

It was all Varo'then could do to hold back. Swallowing his jealousy, he
managed to say, "A tremendous gift, yes. It'll all come to pass."

"Then what delays it?"

"There are many things. Logistics, chance—"

She leaned toward him, granting the veteran fighter with a striking view
of her form. "My dear, dear Varo'then! Do *I*, in any manner of the imagination, look like a hardy, muscular soldier such as yourself?"

His cheeks darkened. "Nay! Nay, Vision of Perfection!"

"Then please . . . do not use such military terms. I would prefer you
simply show me." Azshara raised her hand palm up; in it appeared a small
crystal sphere the size of a pea. However, as Varo'then watched, it grew to
the dimensions of a large piece of fruit. Even despite the dimness, it glowed
as he recalled the full moon once had.

"Will you do me the pleasure, dear captain?"

Taking the globe, the scarred soldier concentrated. While hardly at the
level of a Highborne sorcerer, he had his skills with the arts. The view globe
immediately reacted to him, turning his thoughts into visions.

"You ask me what delays matters, my queen? I would say that these are
some of the reasons."

From his memory, he first dredged up the image of a red-haired creature
like nothing Azshara had ever seen. She peered closely, eyes glittering.

"Handsome in his . . . foreign ways. *Definitely* male."

"A wizard. Powerful." The face twisted like putty, altering in shading and
shape. An older, wise figure appeared.

"Gracious! Is this a corpse you show me?"

"Nay. Despite his coloring—or lack of it—this creature lives. He was little
danger to us when we encountered him, but I suspected then that he suffered
some malady . . . and since that time, my spies have reported that he was seen
in the company of a dragon—"

Now this impressed the queen. "A *dragon*?"

"Aye, and between him and the beast, they caused no end of trouble for Archimonde's warriors. Both've vanished, though I suspect this one'll be back."

"Perhaps not so ghastly after all," Azshara commented, eyeing the pale figure so akin to a night elf. "And it's only these who keep my world from perfection?"

Captain Varo'then scowled. "There are some of our own, of course, my lady. Misbegotten or misguided. I've learned of two Your Glory might find of interest. You will forgive me if the images are indistinct, but they are from the minds of others passed on to me."

Azshara gazed at the new figures. One had his hair tied back and wore black, the other let it hang loose and seemed to be in drab-colored garments. Both faces were so akin to each other that she at first thought them one and the same.

"Twins, my queen," he clarified. "Brothers."

"Twins . . . how delectable." She ran her fingers over the shifting images. "But so young . . . surely not leaders."

"Powerful of magic, it seems, but, nay, neither they nor the others lead the resistance. That falls, of course, to the esteemed Lord Ravencrest."

"Dear Kur'talos . . . I always thought him my most cherished servant, and this is how he rewards me."

Captain Varo'then dismissed the queen's globe. Eyes overshadowed by his dark brow, he said to her, "Black Rook Hold has ever envied the palace, Light of Lights."

She pouted briefly. "I've decided that Lord Ravencrest has displeased me, Varo'then," Azshara finally declared. "Can you remedy that?"

He showed no sign of surprise. "The cost will be great . . . but it can be done, if that is your wish."

"My fondest one, darling captain."

Azshara stroked his cheek ever so slightly, then abruptly turned her mount around and headed back to the waiting guards. Her long, translucent gown fluttered behind her.

Pulling himself together, the officer contemplated the desires of his mistress. Kur'talos Ravencrest had displeased her, and there was no greater crime in all Kalimdor.

"It will be done, my queen," he muttered. "It *will* be done."

They left Suramar far behind and pressed the demons in the direction of Zin-Azshari. Rhonin's master spell had begun the push, but now Illidan's Moon

Guard and the soldiers on the line took over in earnest, crushing the demons wherever they attempted to make a stand.

Rhonin did not let up despite his success. Although he gave himself moments to recuperate, he, too, took advantage of the situation to wreak new havoc on the Burning Legion. Every demon who fell the human imagined as the one who might harm his family if he failed. Rhonin no longer cared what effect his presence in the war had; if the Burning Legion was utterly destroyed here, then neither they nor the Undead Scourge would ever scar the world in the future.

Brox, too, had long gone past any hesitation. He was an orc warrior and orc warriors fought. Brox let others worry about repercussions. He only knew that he and his ax thirsted for the blood of demons.

The night elven host drove a wedge deeper into the center of the demon lines. On the flanks, the Moon Guard chopped away at the enemy. The Eredar and Dreadlords still struck back on occasion, but with nothing that Illidan's forces could not handle.

"We're pushing them up into the hills of Urae!" Jarod called to Rhonin. "Beyond that lies only Zin-Azshari herself!"

"A good thing that we've whittled them down so much!" the wizard returned grimly. "If they had enough reinforcements or organization, this would be a foul place to have to fight them! They'd have the upper ground!"

"Once we reach the other side, though, the hills will be ours to take advantage of!"

"Then the sooner we reach them, the better . . ."

The demons continued to back into the hills in chaotic masses with little direction. Of Archimonde, Rhonin saw no sign. If the demon lord had been in control, then surely the Burning Legion would have fought better than this. Unless . . .

Could it be? he wondered, startled by the mere possibility.

"Jarod! Brox! I need to find Ravencrest!"

"Go!" growled the orc as his ax cut through the armor of a Fel Guard, then the demon himself.

Feeling guilty about leaving his comrades at such a time, Rhonin nonetheless felt certain that he had to find the commander and quickly. A horrible notion had occurred to him, but only the noble could verify or repudiate it.

But locating Lord Ravencrest was no simple task. His night saber pushing slowly through the advancing soldiers, the wizard surveyed the area left and right with no success. His quarry could be in a thousand places, possibly even under Rhonin's very nose.

Anxiety growing, he finally managed to locate someone who might know Ravencrest's whereabouts. Lord Desdel Stareye's armor looked absolutely spotless and his own cat was still well-groomed. Rhonin wondered if he had even gotten close to the battle, much less participated in it. Still, Stareye had the ear of Lord Ravencrest, and that was all that mattered for the moment.

"My lord! My lord!" shouted the red-haired wizard.

The night elf gazed at him as if seeing something unsettling. Stareye reached into his pouch and took a bit of powder, which he sniffed. His sword remained sheathed.

"This is a most inopportune time, spellcaster!" he chided. "What is it you want?"

"Lord Ravencrest! Where is he? I need to speak with him!"

"Kur'talos is quite busy enough right now. Shouldn't you be back up front casting something?"

Rhonin had met this night elf's type often in his own time. Leaders like Desdel Stareye were not only ineffective, but they were dangerous if put in command. Born to leisure, they had no true concept of war, treating it like a game.

"This is highly important, my lord—"

"Concerning what?"

The wizard had no time for this, but saw that he would get nowhere unless he convinced Stareye of the seriousness of the situation. "I have to find out if Ravencrest's had any outriders return of late! I want to know if any-one's been beyond the hills!"

The night elf snorted. "You'll be able to see beyond the hills yourself in a few short hours."

Rhonin regretted that he had not forged some sort of magical link to the commander, but Ravencrest had forbidden such communication with him. It was the night elf's belief that, despite their powers, the spellcasters were more susceptible to invasion of their thoughts. He did not wish to risk his own plans, in turn, being read.

The notion was a laughable one to the human, but he had long given up arguing for such a link. Now that surrender had come back to haunt him.

"Lord Stareye . . . *where* is he?"

A brief look of contemplation crossed the noble's haughty countenance. Finally, he answered, "Follow me, then, wizard. I'll lead you to where I last saw him."

Exhaling in relief, Rhonin rode up behind Stareye. To his surprise, how-ever, the night elf began steering away from the battle. Rhonin almost objected, then saw that by doing so they would make better time crossing from one end of the host to the other. Here there were less soldiers causing a living barrier.

But even with this maneuver, precious time slipped away as they wended their way to where Stareye said that he had most recently recalled Ravencrest. Meanwhile, the night elves pushed farther up to the hills, the demons now forced through ever-narrowing passes.

Maybe Stareye was right, the wizard thought dourly. *By the time we do find Ravencrest, the elves'll be over the hills and almost on the path to Zin-Azshari . . .*

"There!" his companion finally shouted. "You see his banner?"

Rhonin did not. "Where?"

"*There,* you fool! It—" Stareye shook his head. "Gone from sight now! Come! I'll lead you to it, then!"

But if Stareye thought to soon rid himself of the wizard, he was sorely mistaken. Rhonin watched carefully as he and the night elf now forced their way through the tightly-packed throng, but not once did he make out Lord Ravencrest's banner. With the host moving so swiftly, the bearded commander had to constantly shift position, and that made Rhonin's task all the more daunting.

"Blast!" uttered the night elf after a time, wiping a bit of mud from his immaculate armor. "He was there! I saw him!"

They cut across the advancing lines, yet still there was no sign of Ravencrest. Rhonin peered at the hills, so close now. They loomed like savage teeth. He could make out demons moving among them, their retreat much slowed by the climb. In some places, the Burning Legion had even ground to a halt.

Or *had* they?

Stareye raised a gloved hand to point ahead, but just at that moment a speck of dirt got into the wizard's eye. Rhonin turned his head from the direction it had come and sought to blink it out.

The banner of Black Rook Hold greeted his startled eyes.

"There he is!" the human yelled.

"No, I think this—" Stareye cut off as he followed Rhonin's gaze. "Yes, of course! There!"

Not bothering to wait for the noble to follow, Rhonin urged his mount toward Ravencrest's position. Riding against the elven tide proved harder than any part of the long trek so far, but Rhonin would not be denied. There was still a chance. All he had to do was reach—

An uproar rose from the front. Horns sounded. Drums beat. Faces around the wizard looked aghast.

"What is it?" he shouted at a soldier. When the soldier did not answer, Rhonin looked back.

"No . . ." he uttered in horror.

The hills now swarmed with demons heading *toward* the night elves. That alone would not have stopped Rhonin dead, but there were also demons pouring around the edge of the hills—a veritable flood of fiery, monstrous figures. Worse, in the hazy sky above, he saw a shower of huge rocks dropping toward the defenders. They were not rocks, of course, but another deadly rain of Infernals.

The portal could not have supplied Archimonde's force this well. As Rhonin watched the monstrous warriors swell to numbers greater than during any previous part of the struggle, he realized why the demon commander had let such a rout take place. He could only have been drawing fighters from other areas of Kalimdor, rightly seeing the night elves as the main opposition to the Burning Legion's triumph.

And now Archimonde had his adversaries exactly where he wanted them.

The voices in Neltharion's head whispered eagerly. The black dragon listened to each of them with the same rapt attention even though they all said the same thing.

It is time . . .

It is time . . .

It is time . . .

He clutched the Dragon Soul tight and held it high in his forepaw. Gaze sweeping across those of the other Aspects, he thundered, "It is *time*."

Bowing their heads in acknowledgment, they departed one by one from the cavern. Only when he was alone—save for the voices, of course—did Neltharion say anything more.

"*My* time . . ."

Mere minutes later, from every chasm, every cave mouth, they began to emerge. Some crawled out from beneath the ground while others leapt off the high mountain peak. Wherever there was an exit to the outside world, the dragons issued forth.

It was time to act.

Never before in the history of the world had there been so many assembled in one place. Now, as they took to the air, their combined magnificence awed even most of them. Red flew beside bronze who flew beside green. Blue and black darted up in the air, the five great flights now one.

There were dragons whose wings seemed to spread across the heavens, others who in comparison were but like gnats. Whether ages old or new to the air, all had been included. The word of the Aspects had demanded it be so.

The first dragons to leap into the heavens did not immediately head toward the realm of the night elves, however. Instead, they circled high above the mountains, gliding on thermals and waiting for their brethren. They filled the sky, many flying under or over one another to avoid collision.

And the legendary behemoths continued to emerge from the mountains. To any who saw them, it looked as if the end of the world had come . . . and perhaps it had. The dragons understood the evil of the demons and that no one could stand idle in the face of such a threat. Dragon after dragon roared lustily as they stirred their blood in preparation for battle.

Then the Aspects themselves appeared. Alexstrasza the Red, the Mother of Life. Malygos the Blue, the Spellweaver. Green Ysera, She of the Dreaming. In the absence of Nozdormu, the Timeless One, the eldest of his consorts took upon herself his part.

Only when they were assembled did Neltharion the Black, the Earth Warder, present himself.

The tiny disk gleamed so very bright, dazzling the dragons despite its otherwise plain exterior. Neltharion roared as he launched into the air, his cry echoing over and over throughout the chain.

As Neltharion soared off, the other dragons followed. The time of reckoning was at hand. They had given of themselves to create the mightiest of weapons for use against the mightiest of foes, and if that proved not enough, they had claws, teeth, and more with which to still assail the demons.

And if all *that* would not prove enough . . . then surely nothing would.

Tyrande heard the cries, heard the horns. She knew immediately in her heart what they meant. Again the struggle had taken one of its mercurial shifts. The demons had struck back, and clearly hard.

With a blurted apology to the unfortunate whom she had been healing, the new head of the order leapt atop her night saber. Shandris, already astride, made quick room for her, and the two rode off to find the other sisters.

Most were already waiting for her. They included not only those who had originally been assigned to Tyrande, but many of the elder priestesses as well. All knelt or bowed their heads as she neared.

"Please! Stop that!" Tyrande begged, clearly uncomfortable. "It's not necessary!"

"We await your orders," Marinda respectfully said.

Tyrande had been dreading this moment. It was one thing to organize aid for the refugees and wounded soldiers, another to fling the entire sisterhood into the heat of battle.

"We must—" She stopped, silently prayed to the Mother Moon for guidance, and continued. "We must divide up evenly and support those areas weakest along the front lines . . . but not all of us! I want . . . I want a third of us to keep to the back and do what can be done for any of the injured or wounded."

Some of the sisters looked disturbed, clearly desiring to be up front alongside the fighters. Tyrande understood that, but also recognized that just because the battle was desperate, this was not the time to put aside the other skills the temple taught.

"We need healers among the soldiers. Any soldier able to come back to fight aids our cause. Consider this also: There must always be a Sisterhood of Elune. Should we all stand and fight—and perhaps die—who will be left to spread her word and her love among our people?" Tyrande tried not to think about the possibility that there would be no people to teach about Elune if the demons won here.

"We hear and obey," one of the senior priestesses said. The rest nodded.

"Marinda, I leave those caring for the wounded in your hands."

"Aye, mistress."

Tyrande considered further. "And if I should perish, I wish you to take over."

The other night elf looked aghast. "Tyrande—"

"The chain must be unbroken. I understand that. I hope you do, too."

"I—" Marinda frowned. "Yes, I do." Her eyes briefly measured some of the other sisters. As Tyrande had done, she already considered who would be best to lead if she fell.

The new high priestess exhaled. Perhaps her decisions had been rash ones, but she could not be concerned about that now. They were needed. Elune was needed.

"That's all I have to say . . . except, may the serene light of the Mother Moon illuminate your paths."

The ancient farewell said, Tyrande watched as many of the sisters left. Those who would follow her began mounting.

One of them glanced toward Tyrande. "Mistress . . . what about her?"

"Her?" She blinked. Having grown so accustomed to Shandris riding with her, Tyrande had forgotten that the younger female could not possibly come with her now.

Likely knowing what was to come, Shandris tightened her grip. "I'm going with you!"

"That is not possible."

"I'm good with a bow! My father taught me well! I'm probably as good as any of these!"

In spite of the looming situation, her defiance caused many of the sisters to smile.

"That good?" one gently mocked.

Tyrande took Shandris's hand. "No. You stay here."

"But—"

"Dismount, Shandris."

Her eyes tearing, the orphan climbed down. She stared up at Tyrande with huge, silver orbs that made the high priestess feel guilty.

"I'll be back soon, Shandris. You know where to wait."

"Y-yes . . . mistress."

"Come," Tyrande ordered the others. If Elune had thrust her into this role, she had to accept it and do her best to live up to her calling. That included keeping as many of her sisters alive as the Mother Moon allowed.

Even if she had to sacrifice *herself* to do it.

Shandris watched them vanish. The orphan's face was tear-stained, and her hands were balled into fists. Her heart pounded in time to the beating of the war drums and the cries of the dying.

When she could stand it no longer, Shandris ran after the priestesses.

NINETEEN

Although he had told Malfurion that Korialstrasz would arrive before long, Krasus insisted that he and the elf begin heading in the general direction of the battle. He did not do it because he felt that it would cut down the trek. Hardly that. The distance they covered could be flown by an aged, ill dragon in barely a few minutes. Healed by the druid's miraculous spell, Korialstrasz would take only one.

No, they walked because the dragon mage needed to walk in order to keep his impatience in check. He wanted so much to do something to hasten their journey, but he dared not create another portal to reach their destination, not after the last disaster. That left it to waiting for his younger self, but even with a fleet dragon coming to pluck them up, Krasus felt as if he had no more time remaining. Events were coming to a head, and he was out of options.

If Korialstrasz could get them to the struggle swiftly, then things could still be salvaged. If not—

"Master Krasus! I think I spy something behind us!"

Praying that it was not another of Neltharion's hunters, he peered back. A single huge shape moved determinedly toward them. There could be no mis-taking that it had seen them.

Krasus suddenly felt a tingling in his head. He allowed himself a smile. "It is Korialstrasz . . ."

"Praise be!"

The red leviathan's wings beat hard, each stroke seeming to eat away another mile. Korialstrasz grew rapidly, his expression finally visible. Krasus thought his younger self looked extremely relieved.

"There you are!" thundered the behemoth, landing a short distance behind them. "Each second of flight felt like an hour even though I flew my fastest!"

"You are a welcome sight," the mage told him.

Korialstrasz lowered his head and eyed Krasus most curiously, as if puz-zled by something concerning him. "Is it truly so?"

The way he asked made Krasus start. Korialstrasz knew exactly who and what the spellcaster actually was.

"Yes," he replied to his other self, "it is."

"And you," the dragon said, turning to Malfurion. "I am forever in your debt, night elf."

"There's no need for that."

The behemoth snorted. "So *you* say. You were not the one dying."

Krasus's eyes narrowed. "You were attacked, were you not?"

"Aye, two of the Earth Warder's own! They were filled with a horrid mad-ness! I slew one, but the other caught me. He, too, is dead now, though."

"It is as I feared." The mage could say no more, the spell preventing him. Frustrated, he turned to a subject he could discuss. "We must return to Rhonin and the others. Are you prepared to take us there?"

"Climb aboard and we will be on our way."

The two did as the dragon bade. Once they had settled at his shoulders, Korialstrasz stretched his wings, then gently took off. He circled the field twice before heading toward the direction of the battle.

As they flew, Krasus constantly glanced behind them. He was certain that they were fast approaching the point when the dragons would be com-ing, but so far he noted nothing. That gave him hope that he could devise a plan to deal with Neltharion's betrayal before it took place. If the evil of his creation could be stopped or, better yet, wielded by one not tainted, then the demons could be defeated, and his own kind saved from their slide to near-extinction.

"We must be getting near," Malfurion called. "The sky is growing hazy!"

Sure enough, the foul mist that pervaded wherever the demons had marched soon met them. Korialstrasz tried to keep low, but in order to avoid flying blind, he had to practically let his torso scrape the ground. When that effort finally proved unmanageable, he said, "I must fly higher! Perhaps there we will find a limit to this murk!"

Through the mist the trio rose. Krasus squinted, but saw nothing beyond his younger self's nose and sometimes not even that far. With visibility so poor, he knew that Korialstrasz had to rely on smell and other senses to make headway.

"There *must* be an end to it!" the red dragon snapped. "I will find it even if it takes me—"

A winged figure suddenly appeared in their path. The Doomguard darted back into the mist the moment he saw the dragon.

Korialstrasz immediately gave chase, forcing Krasus and Malfurion to hold on tight.

"Leave him!" the mage shouted. "We must get to the battle!"

But the fierce wind created by Korialstrasz's swift flight carried away his words. Krasus beat on the dragon's neck, but the heavy scales prevented the other from noticing.

"What about a spell?" Malfurion cried. "Just something to attract his attention!"

Krasus had wanted to do that, but knew better. "If we startle him at all, he may jolt and drop one or both of us! In this thick mist, it would be impossible for him to catch us before we hit the ground below!"

Forced to let Korialstrasz continue his pursuit, the two could only lean low and hope that the dragon either caught the demon quickly or gave up. However, recalling exactly how determined he had been when younger, Krasus knew that Korialstrasz would not turn back so soon. His own stubbornness now worked against all of them.

Again the demon flickered into sight. The fearsome, horned warrior flew as fast as his fiery wings could carry him. Even he understood that he could not stand against such a giant.

The mage frowned. The Doomguard had their share of cunning, and could see through this mist far better than their foes. The demon should have been able to figure out a way to lose Korialstrasz, who was clearly having trouble locating him. If not for the almost straight line the demon flew—

The truth suddenly dawned on Krasus. "Malfurion! Prepare yourself! We are about to be attacked!"

The druid looked around, seeking a foe in the fog.

A second later, he and Krasus were greeted by many.

The winged warriors came at the trio from all angles. At least half a dozen rose up under Korialstrasz, striking at the dragon's chest and stomach. Others dropped down, seeking to either slay or knock off the two riders. Several more fluttered about in front of and behind the leviathan.

Korialstrasz roared, sending out a flood of fire at those in front of him. Most of the demons scattered, but one he caught dead center, reducing the horned warrior to ash.

The red's massive tail swung like a mace, battering three of the Doomguard away. The others darted in, slashing with their horrific blades and even managing a few cuts in the scales.

Atop him, Krasus and Malfurion were harried. The dragon mage managed to cast a quick spell that created a glowing orange shield above them, but the demons battered relentlessly at it, quickly weakening his work.

The night elf reached into a pouch at his side. He took from it some small particles, then cast them at those demons most immediate. As they touched each of their targets, the particles blossomed into huge tendrils—creeper vines. Malfurion muttered under his breath, and the vines expanded in every direction.

The demons began tearing and slashing at the plants overwhelming them, but the vines grew at a swifter pace than they could cut.

Several encircled and tightened around one demon's throat. There was a crackling sound, and the horned warrior slumped . . . then plummeted from sight.

Other demons found their limbs and, most important, their wings, entangled. Two fell screaming to their deaths.

Krasus cried out as a Doomguard who had gotten under the shield cut him on the shoulder. Eyes blazing, the mage took out much of his frustration with a single word of power. The demon howled as his flesh melted like wax, dripping over and through his fiery armor. That which passed for bones clattered in a heap before spilling groundward.

Yet still there seemed Doomguard everywhere. Krasus could not help but feel that they had been set there to await either the return of the one dragon that had aided the night elves or any other of the great beasts. The irony that the demons might have delayed Neltharion's betrayal long enough for Krasus to do something about it did not escape the mage.

Hindered by the fact that he carried riders, Korialstrasz could not dive about as he normally would have, but the dragon nonetheless made good use of his other skills. One demon came too close. With a snap of his jaws, Korialstrasz crushed the attacker, then spat out the remains.

Shaking his head, he uttered, "Horrible taste! Horrible!"

Krasus continued to look around. The Burning Legion never came in one assault. They always had another attack waiting for the proper moment.

He spotted four Doomguard flying side by side. After a moment, he realized that they all held onto what at first seemed a long, thick rope. As they neared, however, he saw that it was not a rope, but rather some sort of flexible metal line.

He jerked his gaze in the opposite direction. Sure enough, four more demons carried a similar object, and both groups appeared headed for Korialstrasz's wing area.

"Malfurion! Look there!"

The druid did, his expression turning perplexed. "What do they plan to do with that?"

"Tangle or bind his wings, likely! Korialstrasz is too distracted! We must do what we can to stop them!"

Even as he spoke, the elder mage sighted two more groups likewise armed. The demons wanted to ensure they accomplished their dire task.

As those carrying the lines neared, the other Doomguard fought with more frenzy. Krasus and the night elf tried focusing on the true threat, but the Burning Legion would not permit them.

A huge gust of wind abruptly scattered many of the hellish warriors above. Malfurion exhaled, the spell—with all else—taking something out of him. However, he had bought Krasus time to act.

Borrowing from one of the druid's most potent attacks, the one that had slain Hakkar, Krasus eyed the first group. The demons nearly had the impossibly-long wire over a distracted Korialstrasz's left wing. If they succeeded in looping it around, the dragon would be forced to try to stay aloft with the right—an insurmountable task.

The bolt struck only one of the demons, but the very line they carried sent the shock through to the others. The monstrous attackers shook and screamed, then, as the lightning faded, their limp hands released the metal bond. The four plummeted into the mist.

Although he had stopped one set, Krasus now saw that there were at least five others. The other winged fighters closed again, bedeviling the three.

"I must ask of you the greatest of favors!" thundered the red dragon. "Cling to me as if your lives depended upon it, for they certainly will!"

The two smaller figures immediately obeyed. Krasus shouted, "Hook your feet under the scale, Malfurion! Quickly!"

Just as they both did what he suggested, Korialstrasz spun on his back.

The tactic took the Burning Legion by complete surprise. Korialstrasz's huge, leathery wings struck demon after demon. Two of the groups carrying the metal lines went floundering, their burdens vanishing into the mist below.

As he spun, the red behemoth also unleashed three quick but stunning bursts of flame. The first two utterly ravaged a pair of Doomguard. The last missed, but scattered several more attackers.

"Look out!" Malfurion cried.

A huge missile barreled into the dragon's chest. Krasus's footing slipped, and he suddenly dangled by his hands. The druid could do nothing to help him, barely holding on himself.

The fiery figure bounded away from its victim. The Infernal dropped into the mist unconcerned about the tremendous distance it would fall. Even from up here, the demon would survive a crash below unscathed.

The other attackers used the moment to close. Krasus kicked at the blade of one as he pulled himself back onto the red dragon's back. Malfurion threw some more particles from his pouch, but the now wiser Legion forces all but avoided them. Only one Doomguard fell prey to the vines, but with so many others around, the loss was negligible.

As Krasus seated himself again, one of the groups began winding the long line around Korialstrasz's right wing. Jabbing his fingers at the four, he spoke another word of power.

His fingernails snapped off, flying at the demons. As the nails flew, they stretched to more than a foot long each. In rapid succession, all four demons froze where they were as the sharp missiles bored through them. Krasus rubbed his fingers—where new nails were already growing—and watched as the demons dropped.

"Korialstrasz!" Krasus shouted. "We must break free! We cannot stay here and fight like this!"

This time, his younger self heard him, and, although clearly he did not like to leave the battle unfinished, he deferred to Krasus. "That may be more difficult than you think!"

Krasus understood exactly how difficult it would be. There were Doomguard everywhere and the dragon, mindful of his riders, had to move with care. That was what the Burning Legion now counted on.

But they had to leave. They had already delayed too long.

The leviathan paused to incinerate a careless Doomguard. "I have one notion! It worked before! Hold tight again!"

Neither Krasus nor the night elf had ceased holding tight since nearly being tossed earlier. Still, they both gripped the dragon by the scales as best they could.

And no sooner had they done it than Korialstrasz's wings ceased beating.

The dragon sank like a rock, leaving the startled demons hovering high above. By the time they started after, Korialstrasz was far, far out of reach.

Malfurion shouted. Krasus gritted his teeth and recalled too late that this had been a favorite strategy of his when younger. Most opponents, even other dragons, expected his kind to stay aloft. Vaguely Krasus remembered experiencing something like this when Korialstrasz had fought the two blacks.

Down and down they fell, the dragon using his wings only to keep from flipping over. It seemed impossible that his passengers would hold on, but somehow they did.

It occurred to Krasus that, with the mist so thick, his younger self might not see the ground soon enough, but then a strange thing happened—the mist simply *vanished*. It was as if some great being had cut a wedge out of the haze. A faint touch still remained, but visibility was so good that Krasus could see hills far, far away.

"*Ha!*" roared a triumphant Korialstrasz. He beat his wings, jostling his companions slightly. The dragon caught the wind and eased smoothly into flight again. Of the Burning Legion, there was no sign.

Korialstrasz did not wait for them to catch up. He flew on toward their original destination, moving at a speed that none of the demons could possibly match.

Behind Krasus, Malfurion gasped, "May I never have to do *that* again! Night elves were surely not meant to fly as much as I have!"

"After this journey, I would hardly blame you for such feelings . . ." Krasus suddenly eyed the path ahead. "Once again, I am having a sense of déjà vu. Most disturbing."

"What is it? What's wrong now? More demons?"

"That would be a simple situation, druid. This appears far more complex."

"What do you mean?"

"Look at this swath of clarity in what has been one continuous blanket of evil since the Burning Legion's arrival."

"Maybe my people are defeating them and this is the first sign."

Krasus wished that he could share Malfurion's optimism. He raised his head to the air and, as Brox often did, sniffed for a scent. What the mage sensed nearly overwhelmed him and confirmed his fear.

"Korialstrasz! Smell the air! Tell me what you detect!"

The dragon immediately obeyed. What Krasus could see of his expression turned startled. "I sense . . . I sense our own kind . . ."

"Only one?"

"No . . . there are so many, they overlap . . ."

"What does it mean?" Malfurion asked Krasus.

The dragon mage hissed. "It means that the demons we fought have done us more harm than I could have imagined!"

"But . . . we escaped virtually unscathed . . ."

Krasus would have preferred a few new wounds to what they had instead suffered. Even the minutes used to fight their way free of the trap had been too much. The others would be far ahead by now.

There was so much that he wanted to relay, but the spell cast on him prevented it. To Malfurion, Krasus could only utter one thing, but it was enough.

"The other dragons are ahead of us, druid . . . and *he,* no doubt, is at the head of the flight."

Krasus saw that Malfurion had grasped the essence of his words immediately. The dragons were heading for the battle, certain that they wielded a power sufficient to destroy the Burning Legion.

They could not know that Neltharion, the one who led them to that battle, would there betray them . . .

Miles ahead and swiftly approaching their destination, the dragons flew ready for battle. Neltharion had led them along a route low to the ground, using the might of the Dragon Soul to eradicate the mist. That in itself had impressed the rest, including Alexstrasza and the other Aspects. No one doubted the amazing properties of his creation.

And as he soared toward his impending triumph, Neltharion's head filled with the whispering voices. *Nearly there, nearly there!* they said. *Soon, soon!* they promised.

Soon all would bow before his glory, and the world would be made right.

"What do you wish of us?" Alexstrasza called to him.

I wish you to bare your throat to me . . . the Earth Warder thought, but instead answered, "I have described the array! I need all set in the sky as I asked! The Dragon Soul will do the rest!"

"As simple as that?"

I want to make it easy for you to bow to me . . . "Yes, as simple as that."

She asked no more questions, for which Neltharion was grateful. His mind raged, and her nattering had nearly caused him to give himself away.

The Dragon Soul—*his* Dragon Soul—continued to clear the way for their eyes. As Neltharion peered ahead, he caught a glimpse of movement on the ground, movement like thousands of ants.

They had come upon the battle. He could scarcely contain his glee.

Patience . . . murmured the voices. *Patience . . .*

Yes, the black dragon could afford to be patient a little longer. He could be magnanimous. The prize was so great, a few more minutes would not matter.

Just a few more minutes . . .

Brox saw them first. Wiping the sweat from his brow after having dispatched a felbeast, the orc happened to glance up and see the first of the leviathans arrive over the battle scene. He gaped for a moment, almost losing his head to a Fel Guard for his stupidity. Brox traded blows with the demon, cut the creature into three pieces, then stepped back and looked around. Unfortunately, that one was not near.

The orc snorted. Rhonin might not know of the dragons yet, but surely it would not be long before *everyone* became aware of their presence.

The struggle, Brox decided, had just grown a lot more interesting.

Rhonin had never reached Lord Ravencrest. The noble stood within sight of him, but the sudden shift in the fight had forced the wizard to concentrate instead on keeping the front line from collapsing before him. Several quick spells of short duration had helped stabilize it, but he could not save the situation all by himself. Unfortunately, the Moon Guard was already stretched thin in some places and in others Illidan had them focusing on him so that he could cast his grand spells.

Malfurion's brother had grown more and more reckless, and not simply because of the circumstances. He flung spells left and right as if they were pebbles, not caring that he came precariously close to hitting his own people.

Another area threatened to buckle. Prodded on by the Doomguard, three Infernals collided with the soldiers there, tossing them everywhere. Fel Guard poured through, chopping and thrusting at anything that still showed life.

The red-haired wizard gestured, but just as he finished the last bit of his spell, an explosion rocked the region in question. The Infernals shattered and the monstrous warriors behind them fell, their armor and most of their flesh torn away.

Had that been the only result, Rhonin would have cheered. However, among the demon dead were many night elves who had suffered the same horrible fate. Survivors cried out for aid. Blood splattered everything.

Rhonin cursed, but not because the fault had been his. His spell remained uncast.

His furious gaze fell upon Illidan. The sorcerer had finally done it. He had killed his own, and the most horrific part was that he had either not noticed or not cared.

The Burning Legion forgotten, Rhonin began shoving his way toward Malfurion's twin. Illidan had to be taken to account; this could not happen again.

The subject of his righteous ire turned and saw him approaching. Illidan gave him a smile of triumph, which did nothing to alleviate the wizard's anger.

But then Illidan looked up past Rhonin. Both his eyes and his smile widened as he pointed.

Despite wanting nothing to distract him, Rhonin had to look.

His eyes, too, widened . . . and a curse escaped his lips.

There were dragons in a suddenly-clearing sky. *Hundreds* of dragons.

"No . . ." Rhonin growled at the high-flying figures. He made out one at the forefront, a black so large that he could be only one dragon. That, in turn, meant that this could be only one particular event in history . . . the very worst of events, as far as the defenders could be concerned. "No . . . not now . . . not now . . ."

TWENTY

There was little that could dismay Archimonde. He attacked every situation with an analytical mind—night elves, magic, even dragons. But now his composure had been shaken. He had not expected the dragons to come in such numbers. All he had learned of them indicated that they remained out of worldly matters, so aloof that they could not see the end of their world coming. A few, of course, had been expected to act as mavericks, rogues. Archimonde had planned for those, countless Doomguard hiding in the mists and ready to take them on.

But not only had he been outmaneuvered by the beasts . . . they had *all* come.

The demon commander quickly composed himself. Sargeras permitted no failure at this point. Archimonde reached out with his thoughts, touched the minds of every Eredar and Dreadlord, and ordered them to turn their magics on the approaching flights.

Confident that the sorcerous might of the Burning Legion would deal with these interlopers, Archimonde returned his attention to the battle. The Nathrezim and warlocks would eliminate the dragons. The latter were only creatures of *this* world, after all, their power limited to its laws. The Legion was so, so much more.

Yes, there was definitely nothing even the dragons could do to prevent his glorious victory.

Tyrande's sisters had been pushed toward a hilly region upon which stood a few gnarled and dead oaks. The surprise swarming of the demons had left all night elves stunned, and regardless of the sisterhood's attempts to rally those around them, even they had a hard time keeping hopeful under such a crushing blow.

The new high priestess now fought on foot, her night saber having sacrificed itself against blades meant for its mistress. Tyrande had slain the demons who had killed it, and now went to help another sister wounded badly in the same assault. Tyrande pulled the bloody figure up to the trees, where she hoped that the priestess could be left without being noticed by the attackers.

From her higher vantage point, the struggle took on an even more ominous tone. Everywhere Tyrande looked, she saw a sea of fiery figures pressing her people. Night elves fell left and right, mercilessly slaughtered.

"Elune, Mother Moon," she suddenly muttered. "Is there nothing more you can do for your children? The world will end here if something cannot be done!"

But it seemed the goddess had given all that she could, for death continued to come to the night elves. Tyrande leaned down, hoping to at least aid her fellow sister, while at the same time wondering if she should even bother.

Then, the odd sensation that someone watched her made the high priestess pause in her healing. She looked over her shoulder, certain that she had glimpsed a shadow. However, when she peered close, Tyrande saw only the dead trees.

She almost returned to her work, but then something else caught her attention. Tyrande looked up to the sky and her crestfallen expression changed to one of hope.

Dragons filled the air, dragons of every flight.

"Praise Elune!" she gasped.

Her determination renewed, Tyrande focused on healing the other priestess. The Mother Moon had answered her prayers again. She had sent a force with which even the Burning Legion could not reckon.

Surely now there was nothing more to fear . . .

The dragons spread through the sky as Neltharion had dictated, alternating by their various colors so as to spread the particular talents and traits of each flight as evenly as possible. Near the Earth Warder, Alexstrasza, Ysera, Malygos, and the bronze female poised. Had Neltharion glanced at the red dragon, he might have noticed that Alexstrasza's eyes darted here and there, as if seeking someone. In his madness, the black had not even registered the absence of her youngest consort.

Far below, the tiny figures had begun to notice the dragons' overwhelming presence. A great, toothy smile spread across Neltharion's reptilian features. His audience was ready.

"Now," he rumbled, "let the Dragon Soul be revealed to our enemies below!"

The tiny disk flared so bright that every behemoth save the Earth Warder had to turn their eyes from it. Neltharion ignored the burning sensation in his orbs, so captivated was he.

The Dragon Soul struck.

Its attack came as a flash of the purest golden light, purer than the sun and stars, purer than the moon. It swept down across the demon horde and utterly vaporized the Burning Legion wherever it touched.

The demons howled. The demons shrieked. They spilled away from the killing light, fleeing as they had done before no foe, not even the night elves. Fear was a thing little known to their kind, but they felt it now.

The defenders at first watched in abject awe, so silent that one might have mistaken them for stone. Even the haughtiest among the nobles could not but gape at such power unleashed, power that made their command of the Well's energy laughable at best.

Among the night elves, Rhonin shook his head, repeating, "No . . . no . . . no . . ."

Farther away, Illidan watched the epic destruction with the utmost envy, realizing that all he had learned was nothing compared to what the dragons wielded.

And on the other side of the battle, Archimonde frowned as his monstrous force collapsed like straw before a single power. Already he could sense Sargeras's displeasure and knew that *he,* not Mannoroth or the Highborne, would suffer the brunt of his master's wrath.

The Burning Legion did fight back, however ineffectively. The Eredar and Nathrezim focused their dark magic on the disk and its creator, casting spells that should have melted the Dragon Soul and stripped Neltharion of hide, flesh, and bone. They assailed all the dragons, seeking a swift end to this attempt to crush them.

"It is time!" roared the Earth Warder, barely able to suppress his madness. "Let the matrix be set!"

The other leviathans linked themselves by mind and power. Already tied into the disk by their earlier contributions, they had little difficulty in feeding the Dragon Soul yet more of their strength.

With a mocking cry, Neltharion unleashed the disk's energies on the attacking spellcasters.

Eredar by the scores crumbled to dust, their screams short but telling. Dreadlords fluttering in the sky fell as light burned through them, reducing the fearsome demons to skeletal pieces. In other places, warlocks perished by a hundred different and horrific manners as the disk turned their very spells back upon them.

In the end, even the most cruel of them fled in panic. This was no power with which they could deal. Even their fear of Sargeras could not keep them from routing.

And when the Fel Guard, Doomguard, and others saw how their brethren fell to the power of the dragons, the last of their courage melted away almost as literally as many of their comrades had. Archimonde found himself a commander without anyone to command. His threats went unheeded, even when he slaughtered several of those around him to prove how much he meant them.

Astride his night saber, Lord Ravencrest gave out a bellow and pointed at the retreating horde. "The moment is at hand! For Kalimdor and Azshara!"

His call was taken up by the soldiers. The host pressed forward. At last, the war would be won.

Only Rhonin hesitated. Only he knew the truth. Yet, how could he argue with all that the others had witnessed? The dragons' creation had done the task for which it had supposedly been created.

He looked around desperately for the one other who would have realized the threat, who could have told him what they might do.

But still there was no sign of Krasus.

Neltharion roared in triumph, watching as the puny demons scattered. He had proven to all the might of his Dragon Soul and, therefore, his own superiority.

Then, one of those he knew would betray him dared interrupt his moment of glory.

"Neltharion!" called Alexstrasza, her voice strained. "The demons are on the run! The Soul has done its work magnificently! Now is the time for us to break the matrix and assault them from all sides—"

"No!" He glared at her, no longer able to or desiring to hide the madness within. "No! *I* will say what will be done from here on! I, not you, Alexstrasza!"

The other Aspects suddenly stared at the Earth Warder as if seeing him for the first time. Malygos, in particular, appeared troubled as he tried reasoning with the black leviathan. "Good friend Neltharion! She meant no disrespect! It's just that we can now be more effective if—"

"Be silent!"

The disk flared.

As one, the assembled flights stiffened, their wings caught in mid-flap. They did not plummet, however; the monstrous power of the Dragon Soul instead kept them frozen in the air. Their eyes were the only sign that they still had any consciousness, and all save those of the blacks held horror at the revelation that one of their most powerful had turned upon them.

"There will be no betrayal of me! I will do what is my right! My destiny is at hand! This land, *all* lands, will bow before my might! I will remake the world as it *should* be!"

His terrible gaze fell upon the battle, but not at the Burning Legion. The black behemoth held out the golden disk and hissed at the advancing night elves. "Let all see that they live by *my* choosing!"

And the power of the Dragon Soul was cast upon the defenders.

Caught up in what should have been their moment of victory, the night elves had even less of a chance to defend themselves against the disk's power, not that it was likely they could have done anything. The brilliant light flashed across the foremost ranks . . . and they vanished, only their brief shrieks marking their passing. Riders atop night sabers perished in mid-run, their mounts dying with them. Scores of foot soldiers fell in the blink of an eye.

The grand assault splintered as the horror registered. Night elves now fled away from their retreating enemy, leaving a vast area of baked earth and a few gory fragments.

Chaos reigned. Neither the night elves nor the demons knew what to expect. All eyes turned to the fearsome black shape that wielded such death.

The Earth Warder's voice overwhelmed all other sounds as he spoke to the tiny figures beneath him. "Know me, vermin! Know me and pray! I am Neltharion! I am your god!"

The voices in his head had risen to a crescendo, urging him to more mayhem. However, for once Neltharion ignored them. He now wished to savor his triumph, make the puny creatures bow to his magnificence, and acknowledge his supreme power. He could, after all, decimate them whenever he pleased.

Which he would do as soon as he had tired of them.

"All must kneel before me! Now!"

Many did, while others stood in confusion and uncertainty.

The Dragon Soul eradicated that reluctance, its deadly light flowing once over the demons, then over the night elves. The lesson was a powerful one, and the rest fell to their knees in rapid succession.

"I have watched," the insane leviathan snarled. "I have seen my world *ruined* by you pitiful insects! There must be order! I will have my world perfect again! Those who are not fit to serve me will be slain!"

A slight hiss from behind him made Neltharion whirl. Despite being unable to move save at his command, Alexstrasza had managed to give one hint of her anger and contempt.

"And *you . . .*" the black uttered, those below momentarily forgotten. "You, the rest of these traitorous 'friends' of mine, you will live by my sufferance alone! For your conniving, your plotting, you deserve nothing better!"

Alexstrasza struggled to speak. Deciding to be magnanimous, Neltharion granted her that ability.

"What have you wrought, Neltharion? What evil have you perpetrated? You call us traitors, but I see only one for whom that title is deserved!"

"I give you permission to speak, dear Alexstrasza, but you should use it to plead for mercy for your crimes! *You* dare condemn *me*?"

She snorted at such words. "There is no one here among us who has committed more horrendous crimes than you!" Alexstrasza hesitated, then her tone abruptly softened. "Neltharion . . . this is not you! You always sought to make the world one of peace, of harmony . . ."

"And I *will*! When all obey my dictates, there will be no more chaos, no more war!"

"And no more death? How many must die to create your 'peace,' my old friend?"

"I—" The voices grew insistent, demanding that he put an end to her words, and to her. The black dragon shook his head, trying to clear his thoughts. "Alexstrasza . . . I . . ."

"*Fight* what madness has overwhelmed you, Neltharion! You are strong! Recall what you once were . . . and destroy that abomination before it's too late for all of us!"

She had said the wrong thing. The Earth Warder's crimson orbs hardened again and he clutched the disk protectively. "No! So, your betrayal worsens! You would take what is mine, what I've created, for yourself! I knew it! I knew that none of you could be trusted!"

"Neltharion—"

"Be silent again!"

Alexstrasza's jaws froze. She clearly struggled to speak, but the power of the Dragon Soul was too much.

Dismissing her as of no more consequence, the dark giant again stared down at the throngs held still by utter fear of him.

"I have decided!" he told them. "I have decided that this place is best with none such as you befouling it!"

He held out the Dragon Soul.

The disk flared—

And a crimson juggernaut suddenly crashed into him.

They had arrived to find a scene of utmost horror—wholesale destruction below and, above, the dragons snared in a trap set by one of their own.

Krasus swore. "It is too late! Neltharion has committed his betrayal!"

No sooner did he say it than the mage realized the geas the Earth Warder had placed on him no longer existed. Why should it? Neltharion himself had revealed his treachery; there was no point to the spell anymore.

"This is monstrous!" roared Korialstrasz. "He has Alexstrasza prisoner! How dare he? I will slay him for that—"

"You must calm yourself!" Krasus interjected. "Neltharion is too powerful now that he has unleashed the Demon Soul!"

" 'Demon Soul'? Aye, a better name than that which he called it! Truly it is a demonic creation, more befitting the foul creatures of the Burning Legion!"

Krasus had not meant to say the name by which the disk would become known later in time, but it was too late. Perhaps this had even been the way the name had changed. The mage no longer knew what was a part of the original history and what had been altered by his interference. At this point, it hardly seemed to matter anymore. What *did* matter was that Kalimdor was in danger from a threat that made even the demons seem insignificant by comparison.

"What can we do?" asked Malfurion.

"The Dra—Demon Soul is not invulnerable! Neltharion is the key! He is its creator, and its weakness!"

"Do you mean to destroy it? We could use it to save my people!"

Krasus grew grim. "Druid, any other path to survival would be better than wielding that abomination! It is a corrupting influence! Surely you can sense that even from here!"

The night elf nodded. Anyone but apparently Neltharion could likely sense the evil within when the disk was in use.

Korialstrasz shook his head. "I can stand this no longer!"

Without warning, the red dragon descended toward a hilly region behind the defenders' lines and out of sight of the insane black. He dropped down with such swiftness that neither rider could protest.

Only when Korialstrasz had landed and his two riders dismounted did Krasus have the chance to say anything. "What is it you intend?"

"You know me as well as anyone. You know what I intend."

Krasus did and vaguely recalled that decision now. Yet, what had once been set in stone no longer was. Korialstrasz had all but died once; a second time might prove permanently fatal.

Yet, even knowing that, he could no longer argue against the dragon's action. The love Korialstrasz had for his queen and mate was one that Krasus also felt.

"Strike low and to the back, then," he told his other self. "And do your utmost to break his grip on the disk."

The behemoth dipped his head in appreciation. "I take your wisdom to heart."

With that, Korialstrasz took to the air once more, wings beating rapidly as he sought to quickly gain speed before attacking. The two watched the dragon depart, Krasus particularly keeping his eyes on the red until the latter had flown off.

The moment it became evident to him that the die had been cast, the mage turned, saying, "Come, Malfurion! We must make with all haste for your people!"

Krasus raced along the landscape, all sense of dignity forgotten. Dignity was for those with both time and patience, commodities not available to him and his companion. All that mattered was reaching Rhonin and the others.

Of course, then the question would be . . . exactly what could they do?

On and on they ran, but to the mage it seemed that the night elves were as far away as ever. "This goes much too slow!" Krasus snapped. "By the time we make it there, it will be too late!"

"I could try to summon something! Perhaps Cenarius will be able to send hippogriffs again!"

"I doubt very much that we shall be so fortunate as previous! Perhaps . . . perhaps if I can reach Rhonin . . ."

He paused. Taking a deep breath, Krasus tried to reach out to his former protégé. But although he sensed the human, there was too much turmoil going on. Krasus doubted that Rhonin even noticed his touch.

"I have failed," he finally said. "It seems that we must keep running."

"Let me try. Surely it can't hurt at this point."

Krasus eyed the druid. "Who do you think to contact?"

"My brother, of course."

The slim spellcaster considered the choice, then said, "May I suggest another? Tyrande, perhaps?"

"Tyrande?" Malfurion's cheeks darkened.

Trying not to embarrass the night elf more, Krasus added, "When we sought you in the palace, it was through *her* that the link became quickly established. I think, with my aid, you can do it again. Besides, she is more likely to have transportation for us."

Malfurion nodded, accepting the logic. "Very well."

Still facing each other, the two seated themselves. Krasus stared into the night elf's eyes as both concentrated.

"Tyrande . . ." Malfurion whispered.

Krasus felt him reach out to her. The druid and the priestess touched minds almost instantly, verifying his assumptions. They might not yet realize it themselves, but he could sense the deep feelings between the two as Malfurion again called to her. *Tyrande . . .*

Malfurion? She sounded both startled and relieved. *Where—*

Listen carefully! I can't explain much, he replied, stressing the urgency as best he could. *Krasus and I need mounts! Can one of your sisters head toward the south-ern hills?* He envisioned them as best as he could for her and felt her acknowl-edgment of the location.

I will come myself! the priestess said.

Krasus broke in before Malfurion could protest. *She will be able to follow the link directly to us. Another might ride around this area too long and still miss where we are.*

The dragon mage sensed her agreement and, finally, Malfurion's submis-sion.

I must find mounts first, but I'll be there quickly! With that, Tyrande receded from the link. She remained bound to Malfurion, but in a manner that would permit her to act on the situation without being distracted by his thoughts.

"Praise the Aspects!" Krasus announced as he severed himself from their connection. Helping Malfurion up, he declared, "We have a chance now."

"But how much of one? First the demons and now this! Surely Kalimdor is doomed!"

"Perhaps, perhaps not. We do what we can do." The mage suddenly looked up to where Korialstrasz had flown. The hills prevented the pair from seeing the upcoming struggle. "As do others," Krasus added bleakly. "As do others . . ."

TWENTY-ONE

K orialstrasz collided with Neltharion as hard as he could, aiming for the areas least protected by scales. At the same time, the red unleashed a burst of flame toward the insane Aspect's eyes.

He succeeded in startling the Earth Warder, but Neltharion did not lose the disk as Korialstrasz had hoped. The black dragon had a death grip on it. Even as Neltharion went rolling through the air, he kept enough presence of mind to prevent the loss of his cherished creation.

Korialstrasz hissed at his failure. Alone, he stood no chance against the much larger dragon. Worse, the red felt the pull of what Krasus had more rightly dubbed the Demon Soul and knew that, as he had done with the rest, the Earth Warder would be able to make Korialstrasz, too, a slave.

But still Alexstrasza's consort refused to back away. He had committed himself and he would fight until he died, if only to perhaps save his mate.

Before Neltharion could recover, Korialstrasz slammed into him again, this time driving his head into the black's torso. The Aspect gasped as the air was driven from him. His paw jerked open, and this time the disk slipped free.

"Nooo!" thundered Neltharion. With a frenzied show of force, he shoved back the other dragon, sending Korialstrasz hurtling. The Earth Warder dove quickly after the piece. Wings pressed behind him, Neltharion dropped so quickly that he managed to grab the Demon Soul before it had fallen very far.

Pulling up, the black behemoth roared in rage at the smaller beast. "How . . . *dare* . . . you?"

Korialstrasz tried righting himself, but moved too slowly. To his horror, he saw Neltharion hold the disk toward him.

"You will bare your neck to me!"

The flash of light overwhelmed Korialstrasz. It burned as nothing he had ever before experienced. It felt as if his scales melted, his bones seared. He cried out in agony.

But still the red forced himself *forward*, not back. He fought against the pain, closing in on Neltharion. The Earth Warder bellowed his frustration. In his madness, Neltharion had sought to destroy, not enslave, and that now worked against him.

They clashed. So close, the Soul did not prove as useful as Neltharion might have imagined. Both dragons were momentarily reduced to claws and teeth, and Korialstrasz held his own.

Neltharion snapped at his throat. The red inhaled, sending a full blast of heat into the Earth Warder's face. This time, the attack proved more successful. The black dragon spun back, his head smoking.

But Korialstrasz's victory proved short-lived. Fluttering just beyond his reach, Neltharion pressed the Demon Soul to his heaving chest and grinned madly at his opponent.

"You are no longer amusing, young Korialstrasz! You are a gnat to me, an insect which must be squashed! Enslavement is too good for you . . ."

As he spoke, the disk glowed bright. Its golden aura spread out, encompassing Neltharion. His laughter held no more sanity. The Earth Warder's eyes blazed, and he seemed to swell out of proportion.

"An insect!" he repeated almost merrily. "All of you, nothing but insects to me!"

The black dragon now shook as if almost ready to explode. He held out his free paw and pointed at the distant ground.

The earth buckled. Demons and night elves scattered farther from one another as volcanic eruptions began. Magma and fire shot high in the sky, raining down on those unfortunates not swift enough to escape. The very power of the earth that he had sworn to wield wisely, Neltharion now used to kill indiscriminately. Before Korialstrasz's eyes, the Earth Warder perverted his role, transforming himself from an Aspect of the world to its antithesis.

As he committed his latest atrocities, Neltharion changed further. A rip appeared in his torso, scales torn apart as if made of paper. Yet, blood did not flow from the wound, but rather pure fire. Another tear formed on his chest, and a third on the opposite side of the first.

As if the unleashing of a plague, horrific rips materialized all over Neltharion. The high scales on his back tore into pieces. Even to see all this caused Korialstrasz pain, but the huge black seemed not to notice. If any-thing, Neltharion appeared to revel in what was happening to him. His eyes burned bright with power reflecting that of the disk, and he continued to laugh as he unleashed devastation.

Steeling himself, Korialstrasz tried one more time to stop the hideous leviathan. He soared toward Neltharion, already preparing for his own death. Korialstrasz silently apologized to an absent Krasus, who would surely die the moment that he did.

Although caught up in his murderous work, Neltharion still managed to notice his adversary's return. With as close to a sneer as his reptilian visage could produce, the black dragon pointed the Demon Soul at Korialstrasz.

Its power hammered the red, thrusting him down toward the ground. Korialstrasz tried to slow his descent, but the disk's power proved relentless.

With an ear-shattering thud, he crashed. Even then, Neltharion would not let up; he was determined to crush the other giant into the earth.

Then a crackling field of blue energy surrounded Neltharion, causing him to hiss and draw the Soul back to his chest. The black behemoth roared angrily as he sought the source of his captivity.

Through watery orbs, Korialstrasz saw a wave of motion heading toward Neltharion.

The other dragons were free. Between his battle with Alexstrasza's con-sort and the havoc he had unleashed on the night elves and demons, Nelthar-ion had not focused enough attention on the spell holding the rest as slaves. Now that mistake gave Kalimdor hope.

One group quickly detached itself from the rest. A flight of blue furies cir-cled wildly around the caged Aspect, at their head one who had, until the betrayal, championed the Earth Warder's cause more than any other.

"Neltharion!" roared Malygos. "Friend Neltharion! Look what you become! The thing that you've created will destroy you! Give it to me so that I can put an end to its corruption!"

"No!" Neltharion shouted back. "You want it! You all want it! You know how powerful it can make you! It can create a god!"

"Neltharion—"

But Malygos got no further. The black dragon hissed and his body grew more fiery. The golden aura spread from both him and the disk, burning away the cage the blue had cast.

"You leave us no choice, old friend!" Malygos hissed as he dove for the other Aspect. Around them, the other blues positioned themselves to strike Neltharion from all sides with their power. Of all flights, the blues knew the intricacies of magic as none of the others. Here at last, a weak Korialstrasz thought, Neltharion would fall to defeat.

Like a pack of wolves closing in on the kill, the blue dragons swarmed around their foe. An aura of deep cobalt surrounded Malygos.

"That obscenity should never have become reality," the spellweaver informed his counterpart. "And as I've become instrumental in encouraging its creation, 'tis only fair, old friend, that I *erase* it!"

What seemed an arc of pure white flew at the disk. As it neared, it revealed that Malygos had spoken the literal truth when he had said he intended to "erase" the Demon Soul. Wherever it touched, an emptiness existed. No mist. No *sky*. A pure white emptiness remained. The effect on the heavens proved momentary, of course, but for the sinister disk the fate would certainly be permanent.

Or rather . . . *should* have been permanent. Neither the watching Korialstrasz nor any of the others would ever know whether Malygos's spell would have destroyed the Soul. Before it could touch the disk, Neltharion spat. His spit became a black, blazing sphere that met the arc but seconds before the latter would have touched his creation. A blinding series of sparks marked their collision . . . and then there was nothing.

With a savage cry, Malygos signaled for his flight to attack.

But Neltharion acted more quickly. Even before the white arc vanished, he held forth the Demon Soul. Instead of the golden light that had decimated so much of the land below, a gray one shot forth in every direction.

Malygos created a shield of smoke, but plain smoke it might as well have been. The gray light caught him, threw him back hard. He sailed over the hills, over the horizon, roaring in agony all the way.

For his consorts and followers, however, the fate that Neltharion had in mind was much more horrific.

As one, the dragons *shriveled*. They deflated like draining water sacks. Their cries were terrible to behold. Though they struggled, none could escape the grasping gray illumination.

The other dragons sought to come to their rescue, but it was already too late. Reduced to dry husks, their magic and their life force drained by the Demon Soul, the dying blue dragons faded at last to dust that scattered in the wind.

"No . . ." gasped Korialstrasz, trying to rise up. His head spun and he collapsed again, shattering what was left of the hillside he had landed upon. "No . . ."

"Fools!" rumbled the Earth Warder without the least bit of regret for what he had just done. "You have been warned time and time again! I am supreme! All that *is* belongs to me! All that lives, lives because I allow it!"

And with but a glance their direction, the fiery behemoth sent a hurricane wind that tossed about the other dragons as if they were nothing. Even Alexstrasza and Ysera could not stand against it, the two other Aspects blown back as easily as the rest. Along with the others, they tumbled far, far out of sight, all the while spinning haplessly. Not one dragon out of hundreds escaped Neltharion's spell.

His body swollen out of all proportion, blazing rips covering his torso, the monstrous dragon turned to again survey the night elves and their foes. "And you! You have not learned yet! You will! You will!"

He laughed again, his free forepaw clutching at one of the tears in his hide. For the first time he seemed to notice the terrible changes wrought upon his form, and his expression shifted momentarily to one of awe. Then, to the onlookers below, Neltharion shouted, "We will see who is worthy of my world! I leave you to your little war . . . you may *fight* to see who will be permitted to live and worship me!"

And with one last insane laugh, the black behemoth turned and flew away.

Korialstrasz gave thanks that the Earth Warder had not been able to continue on his mad path of destruction, but knew that the reprieve was only temporary. While he had gloried in the transformation wrought by the disk, Neltharion had finally realized that something had to be done about the forces ripping his body asunder. The weakened red had every confidence that the black would soon enough find a solution . . . and then Neltharion would no doubt return to claim his "world."

Again Korialstrasz tried to rise, but his body still would not obey him. He gazed up hopefully at the murky heavens, but of his people, of his Alexstrasza, the injured red saw no sign. A fear coursed through him, the fear that they had suffered a fate akin to that of Malygos's flight. Imagining his queen limp and lifeless atop some harsh mountain, a sizzling tear slipped from his eye. Yet, try as he might, even such images failed to enable Korialstrasz to rise.

Rest . . . I must rest . . . I will find Krasus, then . . . he will know what to do . . .

The red giant let his head fall back. All he needed was a few minutes. Then he could take to the air again.

But it was at that moment that a new and harsh sound assailed his sharp hearing. It took Korialstrasz only a second to recognize it.

The sound of battle.

The demons were attacking again.

A nightmare. Krasus found himself in the midst of a terrible nightmare. He and Malfurion had reached a point that, while it had not given them a view of the battle, it had at least allowed the pair to witness what took place up in the sky.

And so Krasus had watched as his kind fell to one insane creature.

He had seen his younger self bravely—if foolishly—attempting to confront an Aspect. The struggle had gone as the mage had expected, even though his memories of the time were all but gone. A chill had coursed through him when Korialstrasz had finally fallen, but although Krasus felt his pain, he also felt that the red lived . . . a minor victory at this point.

But worse to him, worse even than the knowledge that so many night elves had perished at Neltharion's hand, was what had happened to the other dragons. With Malygos's flight virtually decimated, now the spellweaver would begin to slip into his own madness as his kind became all but extinct. Gone would be the merry giant, and in his place would loom the ominous, reclusive beast.

And beyond that, the attack that had sent all the others tumbling far over the horizon rattled Krasus to his core. He kept telling himself that Alexstrasza would be all right, that most of the dragons would survive the epic winds that threw them half a world away. History told him so, but his heart kept insisting otherwise.

He tore ahead of Malfurion, trying in desperation to transform. He was older, wiser, and more skilled than his younger self; Krasus could have taken on Neltharion with better hope of success. The dragon mage struggled to change, to become what he should be . . .

In the end, however, he only succeeded in first stumbling, then falling. Krasus dropped face first into the earth, where he lay for a moment, all of his failures rising up to overwhelm him.

"Master Krasus?" Malfurion lifted him up.

Ashamed of his display, the mage buried his emotions under the mask he generally wore. "I am fine, druid."

The young night elf nodded. "I understand some of what you're going through."

Krasus almost snapped that the druid could not possibly understand, but realized almost immediately how harsh and stupid such a caustic remark would have been. Of course Malfurion understood; at this very moment, his people, possibly those he cared for, were dying.

Suddenly, his companion looked up. "Praise Cenarius! We're in luck!"

Luck? Following his gaze, Krasus spied a welcome sight. Tyrande rode toward them, two other sisters accompanying her. She also led along a pair of extra mounts, obviously for the two spellcasters.

Pulling up, she leapt from the night saber and hugged Malfurion without any sense of shame. The other sisters politely looked down; Krasus noted that they seemed very respectful of Tyrande despite clearly being elder.

"Thank the Mother Moon!" she gasped. "With all that happened and Korialstrasz appearing like that, I feared that you—"

"As did I, you," the druid replied.

Krasus felt a slight ache in his heart that had nothing to do with either his or Korialstrasz's condition. In the place of the two night elves, he imagined himself and another.

But that would never come to pass unless they stopped both the Burning Legion and Neltharion.

"We must move on," he told them. "We must stop the demons if we have even a hope of stopping the Earth Warder."

With some reluctance, Malfurion and Tyrande separated. When everyone had mounted, the band turned back, heading toward the site of the struggle.

They heard the cries and shouts long before they saw the first bloodshed. The battle had shifted position entirely, even surprising Tyrande and the sisters, who had just left it.

"It should not be this close!" blurted one of the latter. "The lines are collapsing completely!"

The other nodded, then turned to Tyrande. "Mistress, we need to find another path. The one we took is overrun."

Both Krasus and Malfurion noted the term used, but neither understood what it meant. Tyrande added to the mystery by accepting the suggestion in a manner befitting one in command: "Lead on where you think best."

They rode on, seeking another way to the host. A path opened up before them, but it brought the group precariously near the fighting. Still, it seemed their only route left unless they wanted to ride completely behind Ravencrest's army, which would add wasted hours to their trek.

As the party rode, Krasus eyed the battle nearby. The demons fought as if they still intended to take the world for their lord when they were, in fact, as likely to be wiped out by Neltharion as the night elves. Archimonde could only be assuming that he would somehow gain the upper hand quickly and then take on the black dragon. How he hoped to accomplish that, Krasus could not determine, but he put nothing past the demon commander. The future was no longer assured; anything could happen.

"Down this way!" called the priestess in the lead. She steered her mount around a descending trail, then vanished briefly around the edge of a hill that they had been skirting.

The others followed suit, aware that each second counted. But as they came around the hill, Malfurion shouted, "Look out!"

Coming seemingly out of nowhere, the battle flowed into them. Desperate soldiers fell back as grinning demons chopped into their weakening lines. The riders just barely missed colliding with the former. Worse, the fluidity of the line brought them face-to-face with the enemy.

The sister in the lead tried to deflect the burning blade of a demon, but she moved too slowly. The monstrous sword ripped through her shoulder and neck and she dropped like a stone. Her mount tore into the demon immediately after the attack, but there was nothing that could be done for its rider.

"Mistress!" the remaining sister shouted. "Get back!" She shared blows with a Fel Guard, beating him away from Tyrande.

Malfurion's childhood friend did not shirk from the battle, though. With a fierceness that reminded Krasus of one of his own, she came to her companion's aid, driving her blade under the demon's armor. The Fel Guard crumpled and briefly the defenders' line reformed.

"We need to reach Rhonin and Lord Ravencrest!" Krasus urged.

Yet, despite their best efforts, they found themselves pushed back by the sea of bodies. Krasus cast a spell that sent the fallen weapons of other demons flying into those monstrous warriors in the forefront. Beset by both the night elves and the enchanted blades, many demons died.

The effort pushed Krasus more than he had expected. Again, Korialstrasz's weakness affected him, too. His younger self had expended himself against Neltharion, and the link between the two had evidently even let him draw from Krasus.

Malfurion proved more effective. He whipped up a dust storm that blinded only the Burning Legion, forcing the demons to swing recklessly in the hopes of finding some target. Soldiers picked off the confused warriors with ease.

Focused on the encroaching invaders, Krasus paid no attention to the sky; thanks to Neltharion, he saw no reason why anyone would need to look up anymore.

But when he heard the screaming sound and noted the growing shadow, Krasus finally did look up, just in time to curse his failing.

The two Infernals struck . . . and chaos overwhelmed all.

The hurtling demons hit the ground with devastating results. A tremendous quake overwhelmed everyone. Soldiers were sent flying. Others screamed as huge chunks of stone and earth—tossed up by the Infernals' landing—crushed them.

Tyrande's mount was struck by one such missile and fell, tossing the priestess into the fray. The other sister reached for her, but a fiery blade caught her through the heart. Malfurion, too, attempted to grab Tyrande, but one of the Infernals rose from the pit it created and barreled into his night saber.

He received no aid from Krasus. The dragon mage hung half-conscious in the saddle, the side of his head bruised by what must have been a huge rock. Worse, Krasus's mount, panicked by the tremors, ran off with the stricken figure.

The druid finally leapt from his night saber. The Infernal ran past him, the brutish demon interested only in general carnage.

Fighting through the mob of disheartened soldiers, Malfurion caught sight of Tyrande. One hand pressed against her head, she half-knelt in the mayhem. Her helmet lay at her feet, one part severely dented. The druid marveled that she was alive.

"Tyrande!" he cried, stretching a hand out to her. She stared blankly at it a moment before taking it. Malfurion dragged her back from the worst of the fighting.

With Tyrande leaning on him, the druid headed for somewhere to momentarily hide. All he cared about was getting her away from this area. Malfurion felt guilty for having asked her to come, even though there was likely no part of the battle where anyone could be considered safe.

He half-dragged her up the hillside. Even up here, it was not so safe, for night elves and demons already fought at the base. At the moment, however, it was the only possible choice.

A few green plants still hung to life on the hill. The druid touched one and begged of the plant its moisture. He brought the green leaves to Tyrande's lips, letting precious water drip into her mouth.

She moaned. He readjusted her position, letting her head rest in the crook of his arm. "Easy, Tyrande. Easy."

"M-Malfurion . . . the others . . ."

"They're all right," he lied. "Take a minute to clear your head. You struck it when you fell."

"Hel'jara! She—it went right through her!"

Malfurion quietly swore; if she recalled the one sister's death, then she would soon rec: ll too much more. "Try to relax."

But even as he asked that of her, Malfurion himself tensed. He felt certain that someone watched them.

Quickly peering behind him, the druid thought that he caught sight of a shadow. One hand immediately twisted into a fist. Had one of the attackers slipped through?

"Tyrande," he whispered. "I'm going to talk to Krasus. He's not far. You rest more."

She gazed at him with an expression that indicated she found something wrong with what he said, but could not identify just what. Hoping that her mind would not clear too quickly and make her remember that the mage had become separated from them, Malfurion gently let her rest against the hill, then slipped away.

As he cautiously wended his way toward where he thought he had seen the shadow, the druid focused on spells utilizing what existed around him. The land here would be only too eager to aid him if he sought to destroy a Fel Guard or other demon.

Someone or something had been here. He saw a slight depression in one area, but it was smaller than he would have imagined from one of the fearsome warriors. The print indicated either a very short figure or some animal, though he could not say which. There also seemed to have been more than one creature.

Pushing past a tree, he halted. Ahead came the sound of something scraping against rock. Malfurion rushed ahead, already prepared to attack.

However, as he came around another tree, he saw not a demon, but a slighter, more familiar figure. Another night elf.

She scrambled out of sight, slipping away too fast for him to follow without leaving Tyrande dangerously alone. The young female had not been wearing armor or robes of the temple, but rather garments such as many of the refugees wore. In one hand, she had been carrying something long and wooden, but his brief glimpse had not given him enough of an image to guess just what.

It was not so surprising to find a refugee wandering about. The ordinary people were now likely scattering in fear. The host was being decisively beaten back, and nothing seemed capable of saving the night elves this time.

Malfurion turned and hurried back toward where he had left Tyrande. She was all that mattered to him now. He could do nothing for any young refugee who had gotten so far from the rest.

The druid scrambled among the trees, eyes already searching for Tyrande. Malfurion had wasted precious time chasing after the young figure; he had to get Tyrande and himself away from here quickly, before the fight rose to where she lay.

As he came around the last of the trees, Malfurion gave a sigh of relief. The sounds of combat were still some distance away. Tyrande would be safe—

He stopped dead as he came upon the prone figure of his childhood friend . . . and an ominous figure hovering over her.

It should have been impossible for the creature to hear him, but it turned to Malfurion nonetheless. Hooves kicked at the rocky earth as the goatlike figure confronted him. The upper half resembled one of his own kind, save for the wicked horns curling high above. The all-too-night-elven face leered at the druid as the newcomer's taloned fingers stretched in anticipation.

But what was most terrible, even more so than finding this creature looming above his Tyrande, was the fiend's face.

Malfurion knew that face. He had told no one, but it haunted his dreams. Even though there were some changes in the features, he could never have forgotten the eyes . . . the black and crimson crystal eyes.

Lord Xavius had risen from the dead.

TWENTY-TWO

The lines of the night elves proved so fluid now that everyone's position shifted continuously. That notwithstanding, Lord Ravencrest did what he could to keep order, to keep morale. For all that he had argued with the noble in the past, Rhonin now felt thankful that the master of Black Rook Hold had the sway over his soldiers that he did. The wizard could not imagine someone like Desdel Stareye doing the same.

Ravencrest finally caught sight of the human. Riding toward him, he shouted, "Wizard! I need you up there, not back here!"

"One of us should remain near you, my lord!" In truth, Rhonin wanted to stay nearby to hear any reports that might come, but protecting the commander of the host had also become a priority with him.

"I'd rather you be up by the Moon Guard and Illidan!" For the first time, Ravencrest betrayed a secret. "I'd feel much better if you took the lead at this moment! The lad's good, but we need control now, not mayhem! If you'd please!"

Pointed out like that, Rhonin could hardly argue. Already he had sensed Illidan drawing ever more wildly from both his comrades and the Well itself. After witnessing the madness of the black dragon, Rhonin could easily imagine Illidan becoming likewise the more he freely immersed himself in his magic.

"As you say, my lord!" Urging his mount forward, the wizard looked for Illidan. It was not hard to locate the young sorcerer. Like a beacon of silver light, Illidan stood out among the defenders. The aura he wore about him nearly blinded those closest, but of course, Malfurion's twin was too blinded by his own might to realize how he affected the rest.

Even as Rhonin neared, the black-garbed figure unleashed a series of explosive bolts at the oncoming horde. Demons were tossed everywhere, scorched body parts even raining down near the wizard. Unfortunately, a few soldiers, also caught in the fringe of the spell, perished in the same horrible manner.

One of the Moon Guard collapsed. Illidan snarled at the rest and the much more experienced spellcasters sheepishly realigned themselves so as to remove the fallen one from their magical matrix.

What does he think he's doing? thought Rhonin to himself. *At this rate, they and everyone around him will be dead!*

Illidan started casting, then noticed the wizard. The night elf grinned at Rhonin, so pleased with his work that he failed to notice that the rest of the army was collapsing.

"Master Rhonin! Did you see—"

"I've seen everything! Illidan! Ravencrest wants me to take over! We need to coordinate our attack and bring back some semblance of order!"

"Take over?" A dangerous look flashed across the night elf's expression. "From me?"

"Yes!" Rhonin saw no reason to placate Malfurion's brother; the fate of an entire people—an entire world—might very well hang in their hands.

With clear bitterness, Illidan acquiesced, then asked, "What do we do?"

The mage had already thought that out. For the time being, he wanted to remove Illidan from the matrix completely, giving the Moon Guard the opportunity to recuperate. With Rhonin at their head, they would be able to assist while still recovering.

"I've tried contacting Krasus, but to no avail! So much magic might be making it difficult! Your link to your twin should be stronger, more inherent! I need you to find the two of them for us! We need their aid in this, too!"

The sorcerer's eyes narrowed, a clear sign that he recognized what Rhonin was doing. Nonetheless, he nodded again. "I'll find my brother. We wouldn't want to be without *his* powers, would we?"

Illidan moved away before Rhonin could say anything. The wizard frowned, but knew that he could expect no better understanding from the hot-headed youth.

A few of the Moon Guard looked almost relieved when Rhonin joined their efforts. They no longer cared that he was an outsider; they just knew that he would lead them well.

"We need to sweep away their front line much the way we did once before," he informed the group. "Bind with me and we'll begin . . ."

As he prepared for his spellwork, Rhonin took one last glance at Illidan. The sorcerer still wore a look of aggravation, but appeared to be doing as told. Eventually, the wizard thought, Malfurion's brother would learn to appreciate what Rhonin had done.

At least, the fiery-tressed mage *hoped* so.

Illidan felt anything but appreciative after the clear dismissal. All his life he had been told that he was destined for greatness, for legend, and here he had thought that his time had come. His people were in panic, with nothing standing between them and genocide. Surely *now* was the moment when he became a part of epic history.

And perhaps he would have, if not for two of those he trusted most. Lord Ravencrest had taken him under his wing, raising Illidan up from nothing to a sorcerer of noble rank in the blink of an eye. His master had given him control of the remaining Moon Guard, and the twin believed that he had done well in the role of lead spellcaster.

Now, though, Ravencrest had removed him, replaced Illidan with one who was not even a night elf. For all the respect that Illidan had for Rhonin, this was too much. The wizard should have seen that, too; had Rhonin had any true confidence in him, the outsider would have refused the role.

His moment of greatness had been stolen from him . . . and in its place he was now reduced to calling for his so-admired brother.

The dark thoughts that had of late invaded his mind returned in full force. Although he worked to open the link that Rhonin had requested, Illidan half-hoped to discover that the reason Malfurion was still missing was that he had fallen victim to the Burning Legion. Illidan expected his twin to go down fighting heroically, of course, but beyond that he found that he was not at all that shaken by the image of a dead Malfurion. Tyrande would be upset, obviously, but the sorcerer would comfort her . . .

Thinking of Tyrande scattered away much of the darkness. Illidan felt regret for any pain that the actions he imagined would cause her. How could he *think* of putting her through that, even for him? She had chosen Malfurion, and that was that.

Forcing himself to focus on his twin, Illidan concentrated. First he would deal with this situation, then make a decision about his future. He had thought it lay with Ravencrest and Tyrande, and in both matters he had been wrong.

Now Illidan had to decide just *where* he belonged . . .

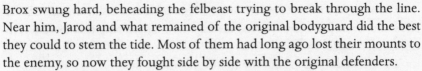

Brox swung hard, beheading the felbeast trying to break through the line. Near him, Jarod and what remained of the original bodyguard did the best they could to stem the tide. Most of them had long ago lost their mounts to the enemy, so now they fought side by side with the original defenders.

A half-torn banner carried by a mounted fighter fluttered past the orc's field of vision. Brox grunted in surprise, recognizing it as one generally positioned near Lord Ravencrest's. Had the defenders been shoved and pushed so to the brink that there was no more organization?

He looked to his left and had his fear verified; the black, avian banner of the Hold flew not all that far away. Brox could not even recall having moved so much, and yet here was absolute proof.

Ravencrest himself rode into sight. Unafraid to risk himself, he slashed at a Fel Guard, then kicked the wounded demon in the head. Flanked by his personal bodyguard, the lord of Black Rook Hold was impressive to behold even to the veteran warrior. Originally, Brox had had little respect for the night elves, but Ravencrest had proven a fighter born, one worthy of even being called an orc.

Other night elves swarmed around the noble, taking strength from his stalwart appearance. Ravencrest did what even the spellcasters could not— he literally strengthened his followers just by standing with them. The faces Brox saw were determined, proud. They expected to die, but they would do what they could to prevent the demons from winning.

With so many crowded around him, there were times when the night elven commander appeared almost in danger of being cut by his own soldiers. More than one blade came within inches of him, but he ignored them all, concerned only with the weapons of the enemy.

Then one mounted soldier drew much closer to Ravencrest's back than Brox thought necessary. The night elf had a grim look that did not quite fit with those of the others, and his gaze was on the commander, not the demons.

The orc suddenly found himself moving toward Ravencrest.

"Brox!" called Jarod. "Where do you go?"

"Hurry!" rumbled the green-skinned warrior. "Must be warned!"

The captain looked to where Brox pointed, and although he clearly did not see what the orc did, he nonetheless followed.

"Away! Away!" Brox roared at the night elves before him. He leapt up and saw the rider positioning himself. In one hand, the soldier held his sword and the reins of his mount. The other had slipped to his belt . . . where a dagger useless against the Legion hung. He drew it and leaned toward his commander.

"Beware!" shouted Brox, but Ravencrest did not hear him. The din of battle was too great for any warning.

The assassin's mount shifted, forcing him to readjust. Shoving several soldiers out of his path, Brox waved his huge ax high, hoping that Lord Ravencrest would notice it.

The noble did not . . . but the traitorous soldier did.

Eyes narrowing and the desperation in his face growing, the assassin lunged forward.

"*Look out!*" Brox called.

Ravencrest started to turn toward the orc. He frowned, as if annoyed at this untimely interruption.

The assassin drove the dagger into the back of his neck.

The night elven commander jerked in the saddle. He dropped his sword and reached for the smaller blade, but the soldier had already withdrawn it. Blood poured out of the wound, spilling onto the noble's regal cloak.

Most of those around Ravencrest had not yet registered what had happened. The assassin threw away the dagger and tried to ride off, but now the sea of bodies worked against him.

With a loud battle cry, Brox used the flat side of his ax to clear the way for him. Night elves gaped at what seemed a warrior gone insane. The orc no longer sought to tell them what had happened; all that mattered was reaching the betrayer.

Shuddering, Lord Ravencrest fell forward. His followers began to notice. Several reached up to grab hold of the commander before he could topple from his mount.

Brox finally managed to battle his way to where Ravencrest was. "There! There!"

A few of the night elves looked at him in confusion. Two finally followed after the orc.

The assassin could not maneuver his beast through the throng. He looked over his shoulder and saw the pursuit nearing. A fatalistic look crossed his dark features.

He shouted a command to his night saber. To Brox's dismay, the cat swatted a soldier who had been standing in the way. As the unfortunate fell, the night saber bit at another. Soldiers hurried to clear out of the path of what they perceived to be a maddened animal.

Calculating the distance, Brox leapt. He landed short, just behind the night saber. Reaching out, the orc swung wildly at the creature's flank.

The blow landed soft, barely scraping the fur, but it was enough to snare the giant cat's attention. Ignoring the commands of his rider, the animal turned to attack the newcomer.

Brox barely deflected its savage claws. The night saber spat, then lunged.

Bringing the ax up, the orc buried it under the cat's jaw. The sharp blade tore into the dark fur, and blood splattered Brox. He fought to keep the beast from falling on him as its own momentum drove it onto his weapon.

A sharp pain coursed along the orc's left arm. He glanced at the arm and saw a ribbon of open red flesh.

The assassin pulled back for another strike, but as he swung, another sword met his.

Jarod grunted as the downward force of the other's attack almost sent him to one knee. The traitorous soldier kicked at the captain, but Jarod stepped out of reach.

The captain did not count on the dying night saber. Flailing furiously, its life fluids spilling over the ground, the cat slashed out at anything near. It batted Jarod with the back of one paw, bowling him over.

Feeling its struggles ease, Brox quickly drew the ax from the cat. With a gurgling sound, the night saber stumbled forward. Its forelegs collapsed underneath and the animal fell in a heap.

The night elf leapt as his mount dropped, coming at Brox with his blade before him. The veteran warrior fell back as the two collided. Surprise on his side, the assassin landed on his feet while the orc fought valiantly to keep his balance.

"Stinking monster!" sneered the night elf. He thrust, nearly cutting off Brox's ear. Brox kicked at the other's legs, but the soldier nimbly jumped.

The orc caught him with the ax while his feet were still off the ground.

Giving Brox a startled look as the ax cut through both his armor and torso, the betrayer tumbled back, still clutching his sword. Brox pushed himself up and met the wounded assassin head-on.

Gasping, Brox's adversary straightened. He held the sword ready and all but challenged the orc to take him.

Brox swung.

. . . And to his surprise, the assassin dropped his weapon and cried out, "For Azshara!"

Unhindered, the ax cut through its target at the chest. The night elf slumped forward, dead before his body collided with the blood-soaked earth.

Panting, Brox stepped toward the corpse. He nudged it with his foot, but the soldier did not stir.

Jarod came up to him, the captain holding his arm as if it were sore, but otherwise looking unharmed. One soldier who had followed them aided the officer. "You slew him!" Jarod called. "Excellent! Well done!"

But the accolades fell on deaf ears. The orc turned back and eyed the scene surrounding Lord Ravencrest. Several of the noble's followers held him up above the chaos as they carried him back from the battle. Ravencrest's eyes were closed, and he looked as if he slept, yet Brox could see that he did not. The night elf's jaw hung slack, and one arm that had escaped the hold of his loyal troops hung limply in a manner the aged fighter recognized all too well.

Brox had failed. The master of Black Rook Hold was dead.

The host was leaderless.

The hooved figure tilted his head in amusement. "Have you no lust for surprises, Malfurion Stormrage? Or have I become so much more that your limited mind cannot fathom who I once was?" He performed a mock bow. "Permit me to reintroduce myself! Lord Xavius of Zin-Azshari, late of her majesty's service . . . and late of life."

"I . . . I saw you die!" the druid snapped. "Torn apart—"

"You *killed* me, you mean!" Xavius said, the humor momentarily gone from his expression. "Scattered me to the sky!"

He took another step toward the druid, which was exactly as Malfurion had hoped. The farther the abomination that had once been Azshara's advisor moved from Tyrande, the better.

Malfurion vaguely recalled from legend the creature whose shape the dead night elf now wore. Satyrs, they had been termed, magical demons of cunning and deadly mischief.

"You killed me," Xavius continued, once more leering menacingly, "and condemned me to a worse fate! I had failed the exalted one, the great Sargeras . . . and as was his right as a god, he punished me most severely . . ."

Having seen the horrors perpetrated by the Burning Legion, Malfurion could well imagine that Xavius's punishment had been "severe." Mercy was a concept utterly foreign to the demons.

The monstrous artificial orbs flared as the satyr continued. "I had no mouth, yet I screamed. I had no body, yet I felt pain beyond comparison. I did not blame my lord and master, however, for he only did what had to be done." Despite saying that, the horned figure shivered briefly. "No, even throughout my ordeal, I kept in my mind one thing; I remembered over and over who it was that had led me to such terror."

"Hundreds died because of you," the druid argued, trying to draw the satyr even closer. If he wanted to attempt any spell at all against this more horrific Xavius, then he needed Tyrande at a safer distance. "Slaughtered innocents."

"The imperfect! The tainted! The world must be made pure for those who will worship Sargeras!"

"Sargeras will destroy Kalimdor! The Burning Legion will destroy *everything!*"

Xavius grinned. "Yes . . . he will."

His sudden declaration caught Malfurion off-guard. "But you just said—"

"What fools like to hear! What those like the good Captain Varo'then or the Highborne assume . . . what *I* once assumed! Sargeras will make the world pure for his worshippers . . . and then he will destroy it for the crime of having *life*. See how simple it all is?"

"How bloodthirsty, how insane it is, you mean!"

The satyr shrugged. "It all depends on your perspective . . ."

Malfurion had heard enough. His hand went to one of his pouches.

Without warning, strong arms wrapped around his, holding him tight. The druid struggled, but his captors were too powerful.

The other satyrs dragged him toward Xavius. The lead creature leered more, his terrible eyes mocking the night elf.

"When the great lord Sargeras cast me back onto this plane, he did so in order that I would bring to him the one who had caused the first portal to cease, and therefore delayed his glorious arrival."

Malfurion said nothing, but continued to fight against the two satyrs holding him.

Xavius leaned close, his breath washing over the night elf's face in stench-ridden waves. "But he left it to me as to *how* I would bring you back to him for punishment. I thought to myself, will it suffice simply to turn you over to the Great One?" He chuckled. " 'No,' I told myself! My Lord Sargeras wishes Malfurion Stormrage to suffer as much as possible, and it is my cherished duty to see that you do . . ."

To Malfurion's horror, the grotesque figure turned back to Tyrande, whose rest seemed oddly deep. The satyr bent low, his mouth coming so near to hers.

"Keep away from her!" the druid roared.

Xavius turned his head just enough to look at Malfurion. "Yes, I thought. He must suffer . . . but how? A resolute young male, no doubt willing to sacrifice himself . . . but what about *others*? What about those *dearest* to him?"

With one clawed hand, the satyr stroked the priestess's hair. Malfurion strained to reach him, wanting to throttle Xavius. He had never hated another creature—the demons not included—but right there and then, the druid would have happily crushed in the former advisor's throat.

His fury only amused Xavius. Still leaning close to Tyrande, the satyr added, "I discovered quickly that Malfurion Stormrage had two for whom he cared. One was like a brother to him—wait!—he *was* a brother, a twin! Close as youths, they now had grown separated by interests and yearnings. But, of course, Illidan was still beloved by his dear sibling, Malfurion . . . even if Illidan himself began to harbor envy for the one to whom *she* looked with favor . . ."

"You have me! Leave them be!"

"But where would be the punishment in *that*?" asked Xavius, rising. His aspect became cruel. "Where would the vengeance be? How greater your pain when you lose not just one, but both." He laughed. "Your brother is *already* lost to you, even if he doesn't know it, Malfurion Stormrage! This delectable one, on the other hand, was more trouble to seek out. I thank you for your assistance in drawing her to us . . ."

As the satyrs pinning his arms laughed with their master, Malfurion cursed himself for having asked Tyrande to help Krasus and him. By doing so, he had given her to these monstrosities.

"No! By Elune, I'll not let you!"

"Elune . . ." Xavius spoke the name with contempt. "There is only *one* god . . . and his name is Sargeras."

He snapped his fingers, and the others pushed the druid to his knees. Xavius walked toward him again, hooves clattering. Each step echoed in Malfurion's pounding head.

Then, a voice suddenly cut through the fog of his mind, a voice so much like and unlike his own. *Brother?*

"Illidan?" he blurted before he could stop himself.

"Yes," replied Xavius, taking the question for his captive's desperate need for more explanation as to what the satyr had done to the twin. "He was quite easy. He loves her as much as you, Malfurion Stormrage . . . and that she has chosen you over him he cannot accept . . ."

Illidan loves Tyrande? The druid was aware that his brother had cared for her, but not to that extent. *But she loves—me?*

Too late did he recall that his brother now sensed his thoughts. Illidan's fury and shame at this revelation suddenly enveloped Malfurion. He rocked backward from the force of his twin's emotions.

Again, Xavius misread what was happening. "Such surprise? How wonderful to hear that you've gained her love, and how terrible to know that because of it she will suffer as no one but you shall!"

Illidan! Malfurion called to his brother. *Illidan! Tyrande is in danger!*

Instead of concern, however, he felt only contempt from the sorcerer. *Then will she not turn to you, brother—the powerful, the magnificent master of nature? What help can she desire from a cursed buffoon, a misfit condemned by the color of his eyes to have false dreams, false hopes?*

Illidan! She will be tortured! She'll die a horrible death!

From his twin he received only silence. Illidan seemed to have receded from him. The link was still there, but just barely.

Illidan!

Malfurion was jarred from the inner conversation by the visage of Xavius filling his gaze. The unnatural eyes appeared to be boring through his own, as if wondering what was going on inside the druid.

"*This* is what condemned me to more than death?" the satyr hissed. "If you are my nemesis, then I see even more that I deserved everything the Great One did to me . . ."

He snapped his fingers, and from Malfurion's right came a half dozen more of the foul creatures. Xavius pointed at Tyrande's prone body, at the same time glancing in the direction of the battle. "They will soon be upon this place. Let us leave before it becomes . . . unruly."

Xavius returned to Tyrande while three of the satyrs—clearly also once Highborne—held high their hands and began casting. Malfurion recognized immediately what they planned. The creatures could not hope to escape by any other methods save a portal. Having created one that stretched beyond time and space, they could surely devise one for travel to Zin-Azshari.

And, once there, all hope for either Malfurion or Tyrande would be gone.

Illidan! Yet, even with the urgency he tried to convey, the druid felt no response from his twin. He was alone.

The raucous sounds of fighting crept closer. A blackness formed in the empty air among the three casting satyrs.

Xavius himself reached for Tyrande, his grin wider and more malicious than ever. "She will enjoy the Great One's company," he taunted, "before she dies . . ."

The portal stretched wide and tall, large enough to admit the demonic creatures and their captives. Xavius picked up the priestess as if she weighed nothing to him—

And a feathered bolt suddenly buried itself in the satyr's shoulder.

TWENTY-THREE

Black thoughts overwhelmed Illidan. He had done as Rhonin had asked and sought out his brother, only to be reminded again of his inadequacies and failures. Never mind that both his brother and the female that they loved had been caught in some terrible predicament; all that mattered was that Malfurion had lorded it over him that he had gained Tyrande's favor without even realizing there had ever been a contest. His innocuous brother had blundered into the greatest prize of all while Illidan, who had fought for her, had nothing to show for his efforts but an empty heart.

A small part of him nagged at the sorcerer to overlook that and help them. At the very least, he should have done something for Tyrande. Some dire force serving the Burning Legion had her in their clutches.

The Burning Legion. At times Illidan wondered how much better he might have fared if he had been one of those serving Queen Azshara and the Highborne. They now looked destined to reap the benefits of their alliance with the demons. Krasus and Rhonin claimed that the Legion would destroy all life, including the queen's people, but surely that was not the case. Why, then, would Azshara join with them? All the Highborne had to do was close the portal and the threat was past. If they kept it open, it was because they knew better.

Illidan snarled. His head pounded from contradictory thoughts and notions that but a few days ago would have revolted him. He looked to the side, where Rhonin commanded the Moon Guard in their efforts. The wizard did not look like the type to give up such a position once he had gained it. Illidan swore. Now, in addition to his brother, both Rhonin and Lord Ravencrest had betrayed him . . .

Illidan! came Malfurion's voice again, this time more despairing.

The sorcerer shut his mind to the cry.

Tyrande slipped from the satyr's grip, but landed safely against the earth. She hardly stirred, which convinced Malfurion again that the priestess had at some point been bespelled by Xavius.

The former advisor clutched his shoulder where the shaft had buried itself deep. Blood poured from the wound, but Xavius was more angry than injured. He tugged at the shaft, but when it would not come out, he snapped off the end in frustration.

Even as the attack registered with the other satyrs, one of those holding Malfurion shook violently, then fell forward. An arrow identical to the first stuck out from between his shoulder blades.

Using his now free hand to grab from one of his pouches, the druid threw the contents in the face of his other guard. With a cry, the satyr clutched at his eyes, where one of the ground herbs that Malfurion had gathered under the guidance of Cenarius burned the soft tissue there. He stumbled to the side, no longer at all concerned about his captive.

Malfurion did not look back for his rescuer, instead drawing a dagger and slashing at the neck of the blinded creature. As the satyr slumped, the druid used the wind to guide his blade as he tossed it at Xavius.

Although wounded, the former Highborne dodged it with ease. Gaze shifting briefly to where the three others sought to solidify the portal, Xavius leered and grabbed for Tyrande again.

A third shaft sank into the ground inches from his hoof. Eyes blazing, Xavius waved at the satyrs not occupied by the spellcasting.

Two charged at Malfurion, the other after the unknown archer. The druid reached into his pouches again, then tossed a small, spherical seed toward one of the oncoming creatures.

The satyr drew back, letting the seed drop before him. However, as the grin started to stretch over his face, the pod opened and a burst of what appeared to be white dust engulfed him. The satyr began hacking and sneezing to such a degree that he finally fell to his knees. Even then, his suffering did not ease.

Malfurion threw another seed at the second, but the toss went wide. The abomination leapt upon him, clawed hands grasping for his throat. Behind his attacker, Malfurion saw Xavius try to lift Tyrande, but the wound had finally begun to tell; the satyr at last had to use only his good arm to start dragging her to the portal.

Fearful that Xavius would succeed despite his handicap, the night elf searched his mind quickly for some spell with which to remove his immediate threat. The satyr laughed mockingly as his nails scraped the skin under Malfurion's chin. Words spilled from the horned creature and the druid sensed a horrible heat rising around his neck, as if a suffocating collar had formed there.

And at that moment, the battle swept over the hill.

Night elves and demons locked in combat pushed up and into the area. Soldiers backing up collided with Xavius and his burden. The satyr growled, and with only his nails, beheaded one unfortunate fighter from behind.

But even Xavius could not stem such a tide by himself. Chaos swept over everything. The satyrs opening the portal struggled to keep it alive.

As for Malfurion, he was fast losing breath. The grinning satyr atop him raised a clawed hand with the obvious intention of ripping the druid's chest open. Fumbling for his pouch, Malfurion grabbed the first thing he found, then thrust it into his adversary's open mouth.

Eyes widening, expression turning fearful, the horned creature pulled away. As he did, the sensation of strangulation left the night elf. The satyr stumbled back, his eyes continuing to swell. Malfurion felt an intense heat radiate from the fiendish figure.

The struggling creature burst into flames that quickly and efficiently engulfed him. He shrieked as his body blackened and the fire ate away at his flesh.

Gagging, the druid covered his nose and mouth. During their last encounter, Cenarius had shown him how to harness the heat contained within the seeds and fruit of some plants, and magnify it a thousandfold. One of those prepared seeds had evidently been what Malfurion had thrust into the satyr's maw.

Mere seconds after swallowing the seed, the creature collapsed, his remains but a few charred bones. Malfurion had never truly appreciated some of the teachings of his *shan'do,* but now he saw that everything Cenarius showed him had power to it. Truly, there seemed no force stronger than that which nature itself wielded.

Looking past the dead satyr, he spotted Xavius again. One of the others had come to help their leader, and now the two carried Tyrande between them. However, when Xavius looked back and saw the druid racing toward him, he left the effort to his minion and turned on the night elf.

The satyr slammed one hoof against the ground, and a tremor sent Malfurion and several combatants falling. A crevice opened up, racing swiftly toward the druid. Malfurion barely had time to roll away before it would have swallowed him.

The path to his adversary cleared, Xavius approached. His bleating laughter, so monstrous in tone, shook the night elf to the core.

"To be the hero again, you must do something right," the fearsome figure mocked. "You should not be crawling around in the dirt, breathlessly awaiting your death."

Malfurion reached for his pouch, but Xavius acted first. He made a sweeping motion with his claws, and everything from the druid's belt went flying away.

"No more of that, if you please." Xavius seemed to grow as he neared, taking on a more animalistic appearance. "The great Sargeras desires you alive, but in this I think I will dare disobey him. He will find satisfaction in your brother and the female . . ."

Cenarius had taught Malfurion to care for all life, but only revulsion filled the druid now. He leapt at Xavius, snatching at the satyr and trying to bring him to the ground.

With his one good hand, Xavius readily caught his foe by the throat. He let Malfurion dangle above him, taking special delight in the night elf's frustrated grasping. "Maybe I will still leave just the hint of life in you, Malfurion Stormrage . . ." he teased, "if I can contain my full vengeance, that is."

Visions of Tyrande and Illidan in the clutches of the Burning Legion made Malfurion struggle harder. He kicked out as hard as he could.

His heel caught Xavius in the wounded shoulder, driving the broken bolt deeper.

This time, the lead satyr howled. His hand opened and the druid dropped. Malfurion rolled to the side, then managed to come up again.

"You've betrayed too many," the druid told Xavius. "You've hurt too many, lord advisor. I won't let you hurt anyone, anymore." He knew what he had to do. "From you, there'll only come *life* from now on, not death."

Xavius's black and crimson orbs flared. His smile held only malevolence. Dark power radiated around him—

But the druid struck first, the wooden shaft giving him an idea.

The broken piece suddenly healed, then sprouted *roots*. Whatever spell the satyr had intended, he now stopped as he again tried to remove the arrow from his shoulder. However, Malfurion's casting had done more than simply keep it embedded; roots also grew *within* the wound, the wood feeding from the satyr's very life fluids.

Xavius's body bloated like that of a dead fish. He cried out in fury, not pain, and his blazing hand touched the growing wood, seeking to burn it free. Instead, the satyr only screamed again, for the roots were now so much intertwined with his system that whatever *they* felt, so, too, did Xavius.

As the former Highborne stared, his claws turned gnarled, becoming tiny branches with burgeoning leaves. The satyr's horns spread out, growing into thick, higher branches from which foliage then sprouted. Xavius was not so much becoming a tree—rather, his body was providing Malfurion's creation with the nutrients and building blocks to make itself.

"This will not end it between us, Malfurion Stormrage!" Xavius managed to cry. "This . . . will . . . not!"

But the druid refused to be shaken. He had to complete the spell despite the strong will of the satyr fighting it and the distractions of the battle around them.

"It will," he whispered, more for himself than Lord Xavius. "It *must*."

With one last bestial howl, all trace of the satyr vanished as the tree that the druid had created from the wooden shaft took full bloom. Xavius's skin mottled, then became thick bark. His mouth, still howling, turned into an open knot. Combatants around him scattered as the roots stretching down to his hooves burrowed deep into the ground and sealed his position.

And in the midst of so much devastation and death, a huge, proud oak spread a canopy of rich, green leaves over the hillside, the triumph of life over the mockery of it.

With a gasp, Malfurion dropped to his knees. He wanted to stand, but his legs would not permit him. He had drawn so much out of himself to force his spell against Xavius's powerful will. Despite the battle going on around him, all Malfurion wanted to do at that moment was curl up under the tree and sleep forever.

Then Tyrande's face filled his mind.

"Tyrande!" Struggling against what felt like a thousand iron chains wrapped around his body, the night elf pushed himself up. At first, Malfurion saw only soldiers and demons, but then finally caught sight of the three spell-casting satyrs. Mere feet away, the fourth carried Tyrande toward the ominous gateway.

"No!" He called on the wind to help him and it swirled around the lone satyr, battering him as he tried to approach escape. Still far too exhausted, Malfurion struggled toward the priestess and her captor.

Then, yet another arrow caught the satyr in the chest. He teetered for a moment, finally falling toward his comrades. Tyrande slipped from his grasp, but the wind, mindful of the druid's desires, let her land gently on the ground.

Again giving thanks to both the wind and his unseen comrade, Malfurion gathered himself for one final run. He pushed his way toward Tyrande, each step a battle, but one whose reward kept him going.

As he neared her, however, one of the three satyrs broke away from the others. The portal shimmered, grew unstable.

The hooved figure scooped up Tyrande.

Letting out a wordless cry, the night elf lunged, but came up short. Something whistled past the satyr's head, nicking his ear and sending blood dropping on his shoulder. In spite of the wound, the monstrous creature held tight his prey as he leapt into the gateway—

He and Tyrande vanished.

The last two satyrs followed him even as the portal began its final collapse. As the third disappeared through, the black gap faded away as if it had never been.

And in doing so, it cut off any hope that Malfurion had of still rescuing Tyrande.

It was too much for him. The night elf collapsed where he was, ignoring the fearsome struggle closing in on him. He had defeated Xavius again, made certain that the one who had instigated the arrival of the Burning Legion would nevermore lend his nefarious hand to such vile causes . . . but all that meant nothing now. Tyrande was gone. Worse, she was the captive of the demons.

Tears rained down his cheeks. The sky darkened ominously, but the druid did not notice. All that mattered to Malfurion was that he had failed.

Failed.

Droplets fell from the heavens, matching his tears. They began to pour down at a more tremendous rate. Oddly, Malfurion remained the only one untouched by the sudden storm. Lightning flashed and thunder rumbled, mirroring his turbulent but darkening mood. Nothing was of importance without Tyrande. He knew that now . . . for what little good it did him.

The wind howled, mourning his loss. The new tree that perched atop the hill shook and swayed as tornado-strength gales battered everything but the distraught night elf . . .

Finally, a voice managed to cut through his despair. It came first as an irritation in the back of his mind, then an echoing sound in his ears. Malfurion put his hands to his ears, attempting to shut it out and return to the blackness overwhelming his thoughts. However, the voice would not be drowned out, growing more insistent with each call of his name.

"Malfurion! Malfurion! You must pull yourself free of this state! Hurry, lest you drown everything and everyone!"

He knew that voice, and although so much of him wanted to ignore its intrusion, just enough rallied. The warning in the tone forced the druid to at last look not within, but *without*.

Malfurion discovered himself amid an impending natural disaster.

The rain came down in such velocity and force that nothing much stood in it way. Curiously, other than him, only the new tree seemed somewhat immune to the raging storm.

"What—?" blurted Malfurion. But as soon as he spoke, the storm abruptly assailed him as well. He dropped to the muddy ground as he was hammered repeatedly by the hellish downpour.

Then, despite the incessant rain and shrieking wind, a huge form fluttered over him. Looking up, the night elf spotted a winged giant swooping down. He recalled the demigoddess Aviana, and wondered if this was her in the form of death. But he was no creature of hers, and the druid doubted that she would make an exception simply for him.

A booming voice identified the gargantuan figure. "Night elf! Stay exactly as you are! It is hard to focus in this chaos, and I do not wish to crush you by accident!"

Korialstrasz seized him in one gigantic paw and pulled Malfurion into the air. The dragon fought valiantly against the storm, but clearly every inch up took strenuous effort. The night elf sensed that the red was not at his best. In truth, it surprised him that Korialstrasz had even survived the encounter with Neltharion.

As they climbed, Malfurion made out some of the landscape below. Both armies were in flight, the demons heading back over the terrain that Neltharion had ravaged. The night elves scurried the opposite way. Both sides battled a new and deadly foe—the rain creating mudslides and treacherous trails. A high hill collapsed, pouring over a band of Fel Guard. A night saber slipped off a ridge as its claws sank uselessly into soft, wet soil. The cat and its rider tumbled to their deaths.

In the midst of the carnage, Malfurion located a small figure trying to make its way down the very hill from which he had been snatched. Mud poured around the young female night elf, half burying her. Higher up, a large portion of the hill looked ready to break loose, surely her doom.

In her hand she still clutched a bow.

"Wait! There!" he cried to Korialstrasz. "Help her!"

Without hesitation, the red dragon veered earthward, heading for the stricken female. So caught up in her desperate struggles, she did not notice the leviathan until Korialstrasz's talons wrapped around her. She shrieked as the dragon pulled her from the life-threatening muck and carried her aloft.

"I will not hurt you!" Korialstrasz roared. The young female obviously did not believe him, but she quieted. Only when she saw Malfurion clutched in the other paw did the female finally speak.

"Mistress Tyrande! Where—?"

The druid shook his head. Her expression turned crestfallen and she leaned forward, weeping. Even then, she held the bow in a tight grip.

Returning his attention to the storm, Malfurion realized that it could not be natural. It had materialized too abruptly. Yet, it hardly appeared the work of the Burning Legion nor did it seem the efforts of his own people. Even Illidan would not have let something like this grow so out of control.

He peered up, expecting to find that the black dragon had returned. However, there was no sign of Neltharion or the dreaded disk. What, then, was the cause of the catastrophic tempest?

He broached the question to the dragon, but it was not Korialstrasz who answered. Instead, a figure grasping tight to the behemoth's neck and shielded somewhat from the elements by a shimmering golden glow, responded, "It is *you*, Malfurion! It is you who brings this down upon all!"

He stared up at Krasus, whom he had last seen taken away by a frightened mount. The mage did not look at all well, the welt on the side of his head still bright red, but he appeared as determined as ever to be a part of all things.

Still, his words sounded addled to the druid. "What do you mean?"

"This storm's birth is the result of your misery, druid! It radiates your despair! You must put an end to it and your hopelessness if anyone is to survive!"

"You're mad!"

Yet even as he said it, Malfurion could sense a familiarity about the storm. He reached out and touched it as Cenarius had taught him to touch all parts of nature and what he discovered repelled the druid. It was not the storm that so disgusted him, but that part of it which he knew was indeed himself. He had created this monstrosity, somehow utilizing his sadness and dismay. In turn, it had beset not only his enemies, but his comrades, too.

I am as terrible as the demons or the black dragon! the druid thought.

Krasus must have sensed some of his companion's thinking, for the dragon mage uttered, "Malfurion! You must not let such feeling drown your reason! This was accidental! You must transfer the power of your emotions to *aid*, not destroy!"

For what reason, though? Again, the druid thought of Tyrande, lost to the master of the Burning Legion. Without her, he saw no reason to go on.

It was, however, Tyrande who finally shook the blackness from his mind. *She* would not want this destruction. She had done everything she could to keep her people alive. Malfurion had failed her; if he let this storm continue, he would be failing her memory.

He glanced over at the young female who had clearly risked herself in order to save the priestess. Of too few seasons to be a novice, she nonetheless had used her skill with the bow to do anything she could regardless of satyrs and demons alike.

Thinking of that and watching her weep, Malfurion felt all his emotions concerning Tyrande swell up again. Without hesitation, he stared into the storm, pressing his will on the wind, the clouds . . . every part of nature that combined to create such bedevilment.

The wind shifted. The rain still poured down, but it seemed to lessen where the night elves fled and worsen where the Burning Legion scrambled over Neltharion's ruined lands. Malfurion's head throbbed as he fought the weather's tendencies and made it focus all effort where the demons were.

The rain overhead ceased. The storm moved with obvious intent in the direction of Zin-Azshari.

Malfurion let out a gasp. He had done it.

The night elf slumped in the dragon's grasp. From above him, Krasus called out, "Well done, druid! Well done!"

He should have been astounded by what he had accomplished not once, but twice. Certainly, even Cenarius would have been. Yet, all Malfurion could think about was that he had failed to save Tyrande.

And that made all the difference.

The storm lasted three days and three nights. With the relentlessness with which it had been imbued by its creator, it drove the Burning Legion on and on. By the time it had dissipated, they were but two days from Zin-Azshari.

Unfortunately, the night elves could not rally enough to follow them far. On the other side of the volcanic region created by Neltharion, the defenders tried to mend their own wounds and regroup. To many, the destruction caused by the storm, the Demon Soul, and all else paled when compared to the death of Lord Kur'talos Ravencrest.

Unable to give him a proper burial ceremony, the night elven commanders did what they could. At Lord Stareye's demand, a wagon pulled by six night sabers was driven through much of the host. Atop it lay the dead noble, his arms crossed and the banner of his clan placed in his hands. Garlands of night lilies encircled the body. Ahead of the wagon, a contingent of soldiers from Black Rook Hold kept a path open. Behind, another group made certain that members of the weeping crowd did not seek to touch the body, lest it spill to the earth. All along the route, heralds let loose with mournful horns to alert those ahead of the sad display approaching.

When that had been done, Ravencrest's corpse was set along with those of all who had perished in an area separated by some distance from the living. It fell to Malfurion to ask of Korialstrasz a terrible favor, one to which the dragon readily agreed.

With hundreds standing near enough to see but not be in any danger, Korialstrasz unleashed the only fire certain to burn despite the dampness pervading everything.

As the bodies of Lord Ravencrest and the other dead became an inferno, Malfurion sought seclusion. However, one figure would not leave him, that being the young female who had attempted to rescue Tyrande. Shandris, as she called herself, constantly pestered him with questions concerning when he would go after the priestess. Malfurion, sadly, had no answers for her, and finally had to get the other sisters to take her under their wing if only to keep from tripping over her.

Lord Stareye, proclaimed commander by his counterparts, had scoured the army for other traitors. Two soldiers associated with the assassin had been executed after fruitless questioning. Stareye now considered the matter closed, and moved on to the next stage of the struggle.

Krasus and Rhonin, accompanied by Brox and Jarod Shadowsong, tried to convince the host's new leader of the need to turn to the other races to create a combined force, but their pleas fell on ears deafer than ever.

"Kur'talos laid down his edict on this subject and I will honor his memory," the slender noble said with a sniff of white powder.

That ended the discussion, but not the concern. The Burning Legion would not be long in recovering, and Archimonde would quickly send them back against the night elves. There was no doubt in anyone's mind that the demon commander would unleash a fury even more terrible than any the defenders had thus far faced.

And even if the night elves held the invaders in check or pushed them back to the very gates of Zin-Azshari, none of their success would matter if the portal stayed open and the Highborne and demons managed to strengthen it further. A thousand thousand demons could perish and the night elves could storm the palace itself . . . but all would be for naught if Sargeras stepped through to their world. He would sweep away their army with a wave of his arm, a glare of his eyes.

That, in itself, made the decision for Krasus. The others gathered with him, he declared the only thing that might be done to stave off what appeared almost inevitable.

"Ravencrest was wrong," he insisted, defying the memory of the dead, "and Stareye is blind. Without an alliance of all races, Kalimdor—the *world*— will be lost."

"But Lord Stareye won't speak with them," Jarod pointed out.

"Then *we* must do it in his place . . ." The mage eyed each of them. "We cannot count on the dragons for now . . . if ever. Korialstrasz has gone to see what has become of them, but I fear that as long as Neltharion holds the disk, they can do nothing. Therefore, we *must* go to the dwarves, the tauren, the furbolgs . . . and we *must* convince them that they should help those who disdain their assistance."

Rhonin shook his head. "The other races may see no reason to ally themselves with ones who'd almost as much as the Burning Legion prefer to see them all wiped out. We're talking *centuries* of enmity, Krasus."

The thin figure nodded grimly, his gaze shifting to the direction of the unseen capital. "Then, if that is the case, we will all die. Whether by the blades of the Burning Legion or the malevolent power of the Demon Soul, we will all surely die."

No one there could argue with him.

Malfurion was the only one of the group not in attendance; these past few days, he had been on a hunt. It had started with a plan, a desperate plan, and there had been only one he could consider mad enough to join him on it. The druid wanted to go after Tyrande, still perhaps rescue her from the demons' evil. Only one other among the thousands in the host might see the matter in the same light as he and Malfurion had spent all this time searching for his intended partner in this suicidal quest of his.

But of his brother, Illidan, he could find no sign.

At last, he dared approach the Moon Guard. Pretending to merely ask for his twin's counsel on the upcoming advance, the druid sought the audience of the most senior of the sorcerers.

The balding night elf with the thin beard looked up as Malfurion neared. While the Moon Guard still did not trust his calling, they respected the terrifying results of his spells.

"Hail, Malfurion Stormrage," the robed figure said, rising. The sorcerer had been sitting on a rock, reading a scroll that no doubt contained some of the arcane knowledge of his own craft.

"Forgive me, Galar'thus Rivertree. I come seeking my brother, but I can't locate him."

Galar'thus eyed him uneasily. "Has word not been passed on to you?"

Malfurion's tension mounted. "What word?"

"Your brother has . . . disappeared. He went riding to investigate the volcanic regions created by the dragon . . . but never returned."

The news left the druid incredulous. "Illidan rode out there alone? No bodyguard?"

The sorcerer bent low his head. "Can you think of one of us who could stop your twin, master druid?"

In truth, Malfurion could not. "Tell me what you know."

"There is little. He rode out the night after the storm settled with the promise that he intended to return before daylight. Instead, two hours after night ended, his mount returned without him."

"Was there—how was the beast?"

Galar'thus could not look at him. "The night saber looked ragged . . . and there was some blood on him. We tried to trace it to your brother, but much magic still radiates the area. Lord Stareye said—"

"Lord Stareye?" Malfurion grew more upset. "He knows, and yet *I* wasn't told?"

"Lord Stareye said that no time could be wasted on one certainly dead. Our efforts must be made for the living. Your brother rode out of his own accord. I'm sorry, Malfurion Stormrage, but that was the commander's decision."

The druid no longer heard him. Malfurion turned and fled, stricken by the new loss. Illidan dead! It could not be! For all the differences between him and his twin, Malfurion had still loved his brother deeply. Illidan could not be dead . . .

Even as he thought that, a shiver ran down his spine. Malfurion halted, staring not at anything nearby, but rather *inside* himself.

He would know if his twin was dead. As sure as he felt the beating of his heart, Malfurion felt certain that if Illidan had perished, the druid would have known. Despite the evidence, Illidan had to be *alive*.

Alive . . . The druid eyed the smoldering lands, trying to sense beyond them and failing. If Illidan *was* out there . . . then where exactly was he?

Malfurion had the horrible feeling that he knew . . .

TWENTY-FOUR

The stench of the ravaged city did not in the least disturb the cloaked and hooded rider as he rode slowly along the ruined avenue. He eyed the overturned tree towers and crushed homes with mild, analytical interest. The corpses so very slowly rotting away he looked at almost with disdain.

His mount suddenly growled and hissed. The rider immediately clutched the two tentacles he held tight, forcing the felbeast to move on despite its reluctance. When the huge, demonic hound did not do so at a sufficient pace, the rider unleashed a wave of black energy that, instead of feeding the vampiric creature, filled it with awful pain. The felbeast quickened its pace.

On and on through the dead city, the hooded figure traveled. He sensed many eyes watching him, but chose to do nothing. The guardians were of no interest to him; if they let him be, he would do the same.

His reluctant mount, which he had seized two days outside of the city, slowed again as it came to a crossroads. This time, however, the rider knew that the felbeast slowed not because of reluctance, but because it knew that its brethren were closing.

They would not leave him be. They intended a trap.

They were fools.

The three Fel Guard charged him from in front. With their brutal, horned visages and blazing weapons, the giants presented a formidable sight. But they were not, he knew, the true threat.

From the ruins on each side of him, a felbeast eagerly leapt at the supposedly distracted prey. Their tentacles reached out hungrily as they prepared to feast on this naive spellcaster.

He sniffed, disappointed with their ambush. With one quick tug, he tore a tentacle from his mount, ensuring that it would understand not to join the effort. As the felbeast howled, he tossed its appendage at the three warriors.

The bloody tentacle stretched out as it flew at the trio, turning into a sinewy noose that snared all three around the waist. The bestial warriors tumbled forward, ending in a pile of limbs.

Even as the tentacle left his hand, the rider glanced at the felbeast coming from his right. The demon suddenly howled and burst into flames. It dropped several yards short, its burning corpse quickly adding to the thick odor permeating the area.

The second monster collided against his mount. The new felbeast's tentacles adhered to the chest and side of the rider and the creature began to feast.

Rather than devour the hooded figure's magic, however, the felbeast instead found itself *feeding* its prey. It frantically tried to remove its suckers from his body, but he would not permit it to do so. The felbeast began to shrivel, its skin sagging on its very bones. A creature of magic, it was almost entirely composed of energy that the rider now absorbed.

In but a matter of seconds, the deed was done. With a mournful cry, the tattered felbeast collapsed in a mangled heap. The rider plucked the still-adhered tentacles from his torso, then urged his frightened mount on without another glance at either the dead hounds or the struggling Fel Guard.

He sensed others near, but no one else had the audacity to bar his way. With the path clear, it did not take long to reach his goal—a tall, gated wall upon which dour night elven soldiers glared down at him.

Reaching up, the rider removed his hood.

"I come to offer my services to my queen!" Illidan shouted, not to the guards but rather to those well within the palace itself. "I come to offer my services to my queen . . . and to the lord of the Legion!"

He waited, expression unchanging. After almost a minute, the gates began to open. Their creaking echoed through Zin-Azshari, the sound almost like that of the ghostly moans of the city's dead.

When the gates had ceased moving, Illidan calmly rode inside.

The gates closed quickly behind him.

The Sundering

To my nephew, Brandon

PROLOGUE

A primal fury raged all about him, relentlessly ripping at him from all sides. Fire, water, earth, and air—all tinged with raw, uncontrolled magic—spun around him in madcap fashion. The strain to simply remain in one place threatened to tear him asunder, yet he held. He could do no less.

Past his gaze soared countless scenes, countless objects. An endless, wild panorama of time assailed his senses. There were landscapes, battles, and creatures even he could not name. He heard the voices of every being who had, did, and would exist. Every noise ever caused thundered in his ears. Colors unbelievable blinded his eyes.

And most unsettling, throughout it all, he saw himself, himself in each moment of existence, stretching forth from almost the birth of time to beyond its death. He might have taken heart from that save that every aspect of him was posed in the same contorted manner as he was. Every existence of him struggled to keep not just his world—but all reality—from collapsing into chaos.

Nozdormu shook his head and roared his agony and frustration.

He wore the form of a dragon—a huge, golden-bronze leviathan who seemed as much made of the sands of time as he was scaled flesh. His eyes were gleaming gemstones the color of the sun. His claws were glittering diamonds. He was the Aspect of Time, one of the five great entities who watched over the world of Azeroth, keeping it in balance and protecting it from danger within and without. Those who had formed the world had created him and his counterparts, and of Nozdormu, they had granted particular powers. He could see the myriad paths of the future and delve into the intricacies of the past. He swam the river of time as others did the air.

Yet, now Nozdormu barely held disaster in check, even though he had the aid of himself countless times over.

Where does it lie? the Aspect asked of himself not for the first time. *Where is the cause?* He had some general notion, but still not any specifics. When Nozdormu had sensed the unraveling of reality, he had come to this place to investigate, only to discover that he had barely arrived in time to prevent the destruction of everything. However, once caught up in that task, the Aspect realized that he could do no more on his own.

To that end, the behemoth had turned to one who whose power he dwarfed a thousandfold, but whose ingenuity and dedication had proven him as able as any of the great five. Nozdormu had contacted the red dragon, Korialstrasz, consort of the Aspect of Life, Alexstrasza, in a fragmented vision. He had managed to send the other leviathan—who wore the guise of the wizard, Krasus—to investigate one of the outward signs of the growing catastrophe and perhaps find a way to reverse the terrible situation.

But the anomaly that Korialstrasz and his human protege, Rhonin, had searched for in the eastern mountains had instead engulfed them. Sensing their sudden nearness, Nozdormu had cast them into the time period from which he suspected the cause. He knew that they survived, but, beyond that, what success they had managed appeared negligible.

And so, while the Aspect hoped for their quest, he still searched as best he could himself. Straining his powers to their limits, the massive dragon continued to follow every manifestation of the chaos. He fought past the swirling visions of orcs on the rampage, kingdoms rising and declining, violent volcanic upheavals, but still could find no clue—

No! There was at last something different . . . something that seemed to be influencing the madness. Power subtilely radiating from a nexus far, far from him. Nozdormu pursued the faint trace as a shark would its prey, his senses diving through the monstrous maelstrom of time. More than once, he thought he had lost it, but somehow managed to pick up the trail again.

Then, slowly, a vague force coalesced before him. There was a familiar sense to it, one that almost made him reject the truth when at last it was revealed. Nozdormu hesitated, certain that he had to be mistaken. The source could not be this. Such a thing could not be possible!

Before Nozdormu emanated a vision of the Well of Eternity.

The black lake churned with as much turmoil as the rest of the Aspect's surroundings. Violent flashes of pure magic battled over its dark waters.

And then he heard the whispering voices.

At first Nozdormu took them for the voices of demons, the voices of the Burning Legion, but he was well familiar with such and quickly dismissed that line of reasoning. No, the evil he felt dripping from these whisperers was more ancient, more malevolent . . .

The primal forces continued to rip at his very being, but Nozdormu ignored his pain, caught up in his discovery. Here, at last, Nozdormu believed, the key to the catastrophe lay. Whether or not it was still within his power to affect matters, he could not say, but at least if he was able to discover the truth, there might be a chance for Korialstrasz to yet succeed.

Nozdormu probed the lake further. He was better aware than most that what appeared a body of water was, in fact, so many things more. Mortal creatures could not comprehend the full scope of it. Even his fellow Aspects likely did not understand the waters as well as Nozdormu did and he knew that there were secrets hidden to him.

Visually, it was as if he flew over the black depths. In actuality, however, Nozdormu's mind plied a different realm. He battled a labyrinth of interlocking forces that shielded the core of that which was called the Well from revelation. Almost it was as if either the waters themselves were alive or something had so insinuated itself into the Well that it now was part of it.

Again, Nozdormu thought of the demons—the Burning Legion—and their desire to use the Well of Eternity's power to open the way and eradicate all life on Azeroth. Yet, this was too shrewd for them . . . even their master, Sargeras.

A sense of unease swelled within him as he wound his way through. Several times, the Aspect almost became trapped. There were false paths, alluring trails, all designed to forever bind him to the Well and devour his power, his essence. Nozdormu moved with utmost caution. To become trapped would not only mean his demise, but perhaps also the end of *all* things.

Deeper and deeper he dove. The intensity of the forces making up the Well astounded him. The power the dragon sensed brought back memories of the creators, whose ancient glory made Nozdormu the equivalent of slug climbing out of the mud. Were they somehow tied to the Well's secrets?

The visual image still remained of him hovering just above the shadowed surface. Only he and the Well had any stability in this place beyond the mortal plane. The waters floated in space, a bottomless lake stretching worlds across.

He drew closer to the violent surface. On the mortal plane, it should have reflected at least some of his image, but all Nozdormu saw was blackness. His mind reached deeper yet, burrowing along, closing in on the core . . . and the truth.

And then tendrils of inky water stretched up and seized his wings, limbs, and neck.

The Aspect barely reacted in time to keep himself from being dragged under. He struggled against the watery tentacles, but they held him fast. All four limbs were trapped and the tentacle around his throat tightened, cutting off his breath. Nozdormu understood that these perceptions were only illusion, but they were powerful ones representing the truth. His mind had been snared by that which lurked in the Well. If he did not free himself quickly, he would be just as dead as if the illusions were real.

Nozdormu exhaled—and a stream of sand turned the Well into a glittering display. The tentacles jerked, slackened. They withered, the magic that had created them worn and old.

But as they collapsed, others darted forth. Expecting this, Nozdormu flapped hard, rising swiftly. Four black limbs slashed futilely, then sank.

But the dragon suddenly jerked, his tail snagged by a tendril from behind. As Nozdormu turned to deal with it, more shot out. They jutted up from every direction, this time so many that the Aspect could not avoid them all.

He swatted away one, then another, then another—and then became trapped by more than a dozen, each binding him with monstrous strength. The dragon was inexorably drawn toward the swirling Well.

A maelstrom formed beneath him. Nozdormu felt its horrific suction even from above. The gap between the Aspect and the waters narrowed.

Then, the maelstrom changed. The waves rushing around its edges grew jagged, then hardened. The center deepened, yet from it issued forth what at first appeared another, albeit different, tendril. It was long, sinewy, and as it rose up toward him, its tip blossomed into three sharpened points.

A mouth.

Nozdormu's golden eyes widened. His struggles grew more adamant.

The demonic maw opened hungrily as the tentacles forced him toward it. The "tongue" lashed at his muzzle, its very touch searing harshly his hide.

And the whispers from within the Well grew more virulent, more eager. Distinctive voices that sent a chill through the Aspect. Yes, these were more than demons . . .

Again, he breathed the sands of time upon the tendrils, but now they cascaded off the black limbs as if simple dust. Nozdormu twisted, attempting to get even one of the tendrils loose, but, they held onto him with a vampiric passion.

This did not sit well with the Aspect. As the essence of Time, he had been granted by his creators with the knowledge of his own demise. That had been given as a lesson, so that he would never think his power so great and terrible that he had to answer to no other. Nozdormu knew exactly how he would perish and when—and this was not that moment.

But he could not free himself.

The "tongue" coiled around his muzzle, tightening its grip so much that Nozdormu felt as if his jawbones were cracking. Again, he reminded himself that this was all illusion, but knowing that did nothing to stop either the agony or the anxiety, the latter eating away within him in a manner he had never experienced.

He was almost at the teeth. They gnashed together, clearly in part to unnerve him—and succeeding. The strain of also holding together the bonds of reality put further stress to his thoughts. How much more simple just to let the Well take him and be done with all the effort—

No! Nozdormu suddenly thought. A notion came to him, a desperate one.

He did not know if he had the power to make it pass, but there was little other choice.

The Aspect's body shimmered. He seemed to withdraw into himself.

The scene turned backward. Every motion made reversed itself. The "tongue" unrolled from his muzzle. He inhaled the sands, the tendrils undid themselves, drawing back into the black waters—

And the moment that happened, Nozdormu halted the reversal, then immediately withdrew his mind from the Well.

Once more, he floated in the river of time, barely keeping reality cohesive. The titanic effort took even more of a toll now that he had expended himself in his disastrous search, but somehow the Aspect found the strength to continue. He had touched upon the evil corrupting the Well and knew more than ever that failure would bring worse than destruction.

Nozdormu now recognized them for what they were. Even the horrific fury of the entire Burning Legion paled in comparison.

And there was nothing the Aspect could do to stop their intentions. He barely could keep the chaos in check. He no longer even had the will to reach out to the others, assuming he could have even done so.

There was no other hope, then. Only the same one as ever and yet that seemed so slight, so insignificant now, that Nozdormu could barely take heart in it.

It is all up to them . . . he thought as the raw forces tore at him. *It is all up to Korialstrasz and his human* . . .

ONE

They could smell the stench in the distance and it was difficult to say which was strongest, the acrid smoke rising from the burning landscape or the incessant, almost sweet odor of the slowly-decaying dead lying sprawled by the hundreds across it.

The night elves had managed to stem the latest assault by the Burning Legion, but had lost more ground again. Lord Desdel Stareye proclaimed it a retrenching maneuver enabling the host to better gauge the Legion's weaknesses, but among Malfurion Stormrage and his friends, the truth was known. Stareye was an aristocrat with no true concept of strategy and he surrounded himself with the like.

With the assassination of Lord Ravencrest, there had been no one willing to stand up to the slim, influential noble. Other than Ravencrest, few night elves truly had experience in warfare and with the dead commander the last of his line, his House could present no one to take his place. Stareye clearly had ambitions, but his ineptitude would see those ambitions crushed along with his people if something did not happen.

But Malfurion's thoughts were not simply concerned with the precarious future of the host. Another, overriding matter ever caused him to look in the direction of distant Zin-Azshari, once the glittering capital of the night elves' realm. Even as the dim hint of light to the east presaged the cloud-enshrouded day, he went over and over again his failures.

Went over and over again the loss of the two that mattered most to him—fair Tyrande and his twin brother, Illidan.

Night elves aged very slowly, but the young Malfurion looked much older than his few decades. He still stood as tall as any of his people—roughly seven feet—and had their slim build and dark purple complexions. However, his slanted, silver eyes—eyes without pupils—had a maturity and bitterness cast in them that most night elves lacked even under such diversity. Malfurion's features were also more lupine than most, matching only his brother's.

More startling was his mane of hair, shoulder-length and of a unique, dark green—not the midnight blue even his twin had. People were always eyeing the hair just as they had once always eyed the plain garments to which his tastes turned. As a student of the druidic arts, Malfurion did not wear the garish, flamboyant robes and outfits considered normal clothing by his race. Instead, he preferred a simple, cloth tunic, plain leather jerkin and pants, and knee-high boots, also of leather. The extravagant garb worn by his people had been a telling sign of their jaded lives, their innate arrogance—something against his nature. Of course, now, though, most night elves save Lord Stareye and his ilk wandered as ragged refugees in muddied, blood-soaked clothes. More to the point, instead of looking down their noses at the peculiar young scholar, they now eyed the green-haired druid with desperate hope, aware that most of them lived because of his actions.

But what were those actions leading him toward? Not success, so far. Worse, and certainly more disconcerting, Malfurion had discovered that his delving into the natural powers of the living world had begun a physical change.

He rubbed his upper head, where one of the two tiny nubs lay hidden under his hair. They had sprouted but a few days ago, yet had already doubled in size. The two tiny horns chilled Malfurion, for they reminded him much too much of the beginning of a satyr's. That, in turn, reminded him too much of Xavius, the queen's counselor who had come back from the dead and, before

Malfurion had finally dealt with him, sent Tyrande into the clutches of the Burning Legion's masters.

"You've got to stop thinking about her," someone coming up behind him urged.

Malfurion glanced without surprise at his companion, although most others in the host would have stared even harder at the newcomer than they did the druid. There was no creature in all Kalimdor like Rhonin.

The hooded figure draped in dark blue robes, under which could be seen similarly-colored shirt and pants, stood more than a head shorter than Malfurion even despite boots. But it was neither his height nor his garments that raised eyes and comments. Rather, it was the fiery, shoulder-length hair spilling out from the hood, the rounder, very pale features—especially the nose that bent slightly to one side—that so unsettled other night elves. The eyes were even more startling, for they were a bright emerald green with utterly black pupils.

Despite his comparative shortness, Rhonin was built stronger than Malfurion. He looked very capable of handling himself in combat—which he had—an unusual ability for one who had proven himself quite versed in the magical arts. Rhonin called himself a "human," a race of which no one had heard. Yet, if the crimson-tressed traveler was an example, Malfurion wished that the host had a thousand more just like him. Whereas his own people's sorcery, so dependent upon the Well of Eternity, now often failed, Rhonin wielded his own power as if the offspring of a demigod.

"How can I stop? How do I dare?" Malfurion demanded, suddenly growing angry at one he knew did not deserve such malice. "Tyrande has been their prisoner for too long and I've failed over and over again to even see within the palace's walls!"

In the past, Malfurion had used the training he had received from his mentor—the demigod, Cenarius—to walk a realm called the Emerald Dream. The Emerald Dream was a place where the world looked as it would have had there been neither civilization nor even animal life. Through it, one's dream form could quickly reach locations all across the world. It had enabled him to pass through the magical barriers surrounding Queen Azshara's citadel and spy upon her Highborne and the commanders of the Burning Legion. He had used it to disrupt the plans of Xavius, the queen's counselor, and, after a harrowing imprisonment, temporarily destroy the portal and the tower containing it.

Now, however, the great demon, Archimonde, had strengthened those barriers, cutting off even the Emerald Dream. Malfurion had continued to try to pierce the barriers, but he might as well have been physically battering himself against a real wall.

It did not help that, in addition to awareness that Tyrande was within, the druid also suspected that Illidan might be.

"Elune will watch over her," Rhonin replied steadfastly. "She seems very much a favorite of the Mother Moon."

Malfurion could not argue with that reasoning. But a short time ago, Tyrande had been a young novice in the service of the lunar goddess. Yet, the coming of the Legion seemed to have precipitated in her a transformation as great as in him, if not more so. Her powers had grown strong and, to her immense surprise, when the high priestess had been mortally wounded in battle, she had chosen Tyrande as her successor over many much more experienced and high-ranking sisters. Regrettably, that newfound status had ultimately led to her kidnapping by a transformed Xavius and his satyrs. Xavius had finally paid the price for his actions, but that had not saved Tyrande.

"Can even Elune stand up to the darkness of Sargeras?"

Rhonin's thick brow arched. "Talk like that won't help any, Malfurion," He glanced behind himself. ". . . and I'd especially appreciate it if you'd not speak so around our new friends."

For a moment, the druid forgot his misery as the shadowed forms rose up from the direction the wizard had come. Immediately it was clear that they were of more than one race, for some dwarfed the night elf in both height and girth while others came up short even to Rhonin. Yet all who strode up to where the pair stood moved with determination and a sense of strength that Malfurion had to admit his own people had just begun to find.

A musky scent wafted past his nose and he immediately tensed. A furred figure clad in loincloth and wielding a massive spear paused to gaze down at the night elf. The giant's breath came in heavy snorts which caused the ring through his nose to jingle slightly. His muzzle was more than a foot long and at the skull met two deeply-entrenched, black eyes that burned with determination. Above the harsh, wrinkled brow, a pair of treacherous-looking horns thrust ahead of the muzzle.

A tauren . . .

"This is—" Rhonin began.

"Know that Huln Highmountain stands before you, night elf," rumbled the shaggy, bull-headed creature. "Huln of the eagle spear!" He raised the weapon, displaying the sharp, curved end forged to resemble the raptor's beak. From the lower end of the metal head to the bottom tip of the shaft, a tightly-bound skin had been wrapped, upon it markings in the language of Huln's people. Malfurion knew just enough about the tauren to understand that here was marked the history of the weapon, from its forging through the epic feats of its owners. "Huln, who speaks for all the tribes gathered."

The bull nodded his head brusquely, accenting his words with his gestures. His coat had more than two dozen braids in it, most of them dangling from under his jaw. Each was recognition of a kill in battle.

The squat but muscular figure below the tauren's right arm snorted. Vaguely, he looked like some kin of Rhonin's, at least in features. However, there any resemblance ended. His build made it seem as if some powerful force—perhaps either the tauren or the ursine brute behind him—had taken a war hammer and pounded the heavily-bearded figure flat.

More astounding, he was made of stone, not flesh.

His rough-hewn skin appeared to be a gray granite, his squinting eyes glittering diamonds. The beard was actually an intricate series of mineral growths that even made it look as if the figure was graying with age.

The dwarf—for that was as Malfurion knew his kind—reached into one of his many belt pouches and removed a clay pipe and tinder box. As he lit the pipe, the fire briefly outlined the grizzled face, especially the huge, round nose. Whether or not the "gray" in the beard marked advanced age, he showed no infirmity. Despite being of stone, the dwarf wore a hooded outfit, wide, flat boots, and had the pants and shirt a miner might wear. Across his back hung an ax nearly as big as him with one extremely sharp edge.

"Dungard Ironcutter, speaking for the clans of the Earthen," was all he said, dwarves not much on conversation.

The Earthen. Malfurion made certain to remember the last. "Dwarf" was a night elven word, a derogatory one at that.

The bearlike thing behind Dungard suddenly growled. Neither the dwarf nor the tauren paid the fearsome utterance much attention, but Malfurion instinctively backed up a step.

The creature lumbered forward. It resembled a bear, yet moved more like a man. In some ways it reminded Malfurion of the twin gods, Ursoc and Ursol, but was clearly a primitive creature. It wore a pale, brown loincloth and a necklace made of claws. The three-toed beastman raised a club in one hand. The other four-fingered paw formed a fist.

The creature roared again, its tone slightly different from the first time.

"The furbolg Unng Ak says that he speaks for the packs," Rhonin translated readily.

There were others behind them, but they did not choose at this time to step forth. Malfurion gazed at the unique gathering and eyed Rhonin with some admiration. "You convinced all of them to come . . ."

"Brox and I helped, but it was mostly Krasus."

Malfurion looked among the throng of creatures, but did not see Rhonin's mentor. Taken at a glance, the tall figure in the cowled, gray robes looked the most like a night elf of any of the outsiders. Certainly much more than Brox, the hulking, green-skinned warrior who called himself an orc. Yes, Krasus could have passed for a night elf—but one long dead, for his skin was very, very pale and much of his hair was a brilliant silver. The mage's features were also more hawklike than any of Malfurion's kind. In addition, his eyes somewhat resembled Rhonin's, but were long and narrowed and held in their dark pupils a fire borne of ancient wisdom.

The ancient wisdom of a being who was in truth a *dragon*.

A figure stalked toward them. Not Krasus, but Brox. The orc looked weary but defiant, as he always did. Brox was a warrior who had battled all his life. The tusked orc had scars everywhere. He vied with the tauren in musculature. Lord Stareye dismissed Brox as a beast no better than Huln or the furbolg. Yet, everyone respected the orc's arm, especially when he wielded the enchanted wooden ax Cenarius and Malfurion had created just for him.

The druid continued to seek out Krasus, but the latter was nowhere to be found. Malfurion did not like that. "Where is he?"

Pursing his lips, Rhonin sourly answered, "He said he had something else that had to be done quickly, regardless of the consequences."

"And that means?"

"I've no idea, Malfurion. In many matters, Krasus trusts only himself."

"We need him . . . *I* need him . . ."

Rhonin put a hand on the night elf's shoulder. "I promise you . . . we'll rescue her."

Malfurion was not so convinced, just as he was still not convinced that Lord Stareye would accept such allies as these. The mission that Rhonin and his companions had undertaken had not been sanctioned by the host's commander, but Krasus had been convinced that once the noble was confronted with such aid, he would see reason. But convincing Desdel Stareye would be a much more difficult quest than talking sense to furbolgs.

The druid finally surrendered to the fact that there would be no new and immediate attempt to rescue Tyrande. In truth, they had already tried everything they could, at least for now. Still, even as he turned again to the matter of the new arrivals, Malfurion's thoughts ever worked to devise some manner by which to save his childhood friend . . . and, at the same time, discover the truth concerning Illidan's fate.

The dwarf puffed stolidly on his pipe, while Huln waited with a patience belying his brutish form. Unng Ak sniffed the air, taking in the different scents and clutching the club tight.

Rhonin, eyeing their potential allies, remarked, "Of course, damned if I wouldn't prefer Krasus here right now myself. I can hardly wait to see Star-eye's face when this bunch stands before him . . ."

The noble's jaw dropped. His eyes bulged as much as was possible for his kind. The pinch of snuff almost to his nostril crumbled to the floor of the tent like ash as his fingers twitched.

"You have brought *what* into our midst?"

Rhonin's expression remained calm. "The one chance we have left of staving the losses and perhaps even winning."

Lord Stareye angrily flung aside his richly embroidered cloak. A flurry of intertwining green, orange, and purple lines marked its passage. In contrast, his armor was the more subdued gray-green common among the night elves, although its breast plate was decorated in the center by his House symbol, a multitude of tiny, gem-encrusted stars in the center of each of which a golden orb had been set. Lying on a table used for mapping out strategy was his similarly-decorated helm.

The haughty night elf stared down his lengthy, pointed nose. "You have disobeyed a direct order, yes! I shall have you clapped in irons and—"

"And I'll dissolve them before they lock. Then, I'll leave the host, as, I sus-pect, will some of my friends."

It was simply stated, but all there understood the threat. Stareye stared at the three other nobles who had been with him when Rhonin and Malfurion had come to announce the arrival of allies. They returned his stare blankly. None wanted to take the responsibility of urging the commander to rid his force of its most prominent fighters.

The senior night elf suddenly smiled. Malfurion resisted shuddering at that smile.

"Forgive me, Master Rhonin! I speak in haste, yes, in haste! Certainly I would not wish to offend you and yours . . ." He reached into the pouch, removed some more of the white powder, and inhaled it in one nostril. "We are all reasonable. We shall deal with this in a reasonable manner, however unjustly it was thrust upon some of us." He gave a negligent gesture toward the tent's flap. "By all means, show the—them in."

Rhonin went to the entrance and called out. Two soldiers stepped through, followed by an officer very familiar to Malfurion. Jarod Shadowsong had been a captain in the Suramar Guard when he had had the misfortune to take as a pris-oner Krasus. In the ensuing events, he had become a reluctant part of their band and had even been placed in charge of keeping watch over them by the late Ravencrest. Stareye had left Jarod in such a role even though it had long become clear that no one could keep the band in one place, especially the elder mage.

In Jarod's wake came Huln, the furbolg, and Dungard. Behind the trio rushed in a full dozen more soldiers, who quickly took up strategic positions in order to protect their commander.

Stareye's nose wrinkled. He did little to hide his contempt. Huln stood as if a rock. Unng Ak grinned, showing many sharp teeth.

Dungard smoked his pipe.

"I would prefer that you douse that instrument," the noble commented.

In response, the dwarf took another puff.

"Insolent! You see what beasts and refuse you expect us to ally ourselves with?" Stareye growled, already forgetting his words to Rhonin. "Our people will never stand for it!"

"As commander, you must make them understand," the wizard calmly returned. "Just as these three and those representing the others had to do so with their own kind."

"You prissy night elves need some folks who know how to fight," Dungard abruptly muttered, the pipe still in the corner of his mouth. "Someone to teach you real livin' . . ."

Unng Ak let out with a loud bark. It took Malfurion a moment to realize that the furbolg had laughed.

"At least we understand the intricacies of civilization," another noble snapped back. "Such as bathing and grooming."

"Maybe the demons'll let you live to be their handmaidens."

The night elf drew his sword, his companions following suit. Dungard had his ax out so swiftly that the movement was but a blur. Huln gripped his spear and snorted. Unng Ak swung his club once in challenge.

A flash of blue light abruptly burst to life in the center of the tent. Both sides forgot their argument as they attempted to shield their eyes. Malfurion turned away to protect himself, noticing only then that Rhonin was unaffected by it all.

The human stepped between the parties. "Enough of this! The fate of Kalimdor, of your loved ones—" He hesitated a moment, his eyes looking into the distance. "Of your loved ones . . . depends on overcoming your petty prejudices!"

Rhonin glanced at at Huln and his companions, then at Stareye's nobles. Neither side seemed inclined to have him repeat his blinding display of power.

He vehemently nodded. "Good, then! Now that we understand, I think it's time to talk . . ."

Krasus struck the floor of the icy cavern with a painful thud.

He lay there gasping. The spell to transport him here had been a chancy one, especially considering his condition. The cavern was far, far away from where the elven host lay—almost half a world away. Yet, he had dared risk the spell, knowing not only what it might do to him but also that it might already be too late to do what he desired.

He had dared not tell even Rhonin of his intentions. At the very least, the wizard would have demanded he accompany him, but one of the pair had to maintain control over the situation with the night elves' potential allies. Krasus had full faith in the human, who had proven himself more adaptable, more trustworthy, than nearly any one else the former had known in his long, so very long life.

His breathing stable, Krasus pushed himself up. In the chill cavern, his breath came out in narrow clouds that drifted slowly up to the high, toothy ceiling. Stalactites vied with jagged ice formations and frost covered the rocky floor.

The mage mentally probed the immediate area, but found no trace of another presence. The news did not encourage him, but neither did it surprise Krasus. He had been there to witness the catastrophe first hand, the vision of Neltharion the Earth Warder—the great black dragon—in his madness turning upon his race still seared into Krasus's memory. Every one of the four other flights had suffered, but the inhabitants of this cavern had paid for their resistance most of all.

The children of Malygos had been slaughtered to a one, their lord cast far away. All this by the power of the Earth Warder's treacherous creation, which the dragons themselves had imbued with power.

The Dragon Soul . . . known better to him as the *Demon Soul.*

"Malygos . . ." Krasus called, the name echoing through the glittering chamber. Once, despite its chill, it had been a place of merriment, for the blue flight were creatures of pure magic and reveled in it. How hollow the cavern was now, how dead.

When he had waited long enough for the great Aspect to respond, Krasus strode cautiously over the slippery, uneven ground. He, too, was a dragon, but of the red flight of Alexstrasza, the Mother of Life. There had never existed animosities between the blues and reds, but, nonetheless, he took no chances. Should Malygos dwell somewhere deeper within the cavern system, there was no telling how the ancient guardian would react. The shock of seeing his kind decimated would throw him over the edge into madness from which it would take centuries to recover.

All this Krasus knew because he had *lived* those future centuries. He had struggled through the betrayal of Neltharion, who would later be called—more appropriately—*Deathwing.* He had watched as the dragons had fallen into ruin, their numbers dwindling and those of his own kind, including his queen, forced to be the beasts of the orcs for decades.

The dragon mage again probed with his higher senses, reaching deeper and deeper into the caverns. Everywhere he sought, Krasus found only emptiness, an emptiness too reminiscent of a vast tomb. No significant aura of life greeted his search and he began to despair that his sudden urge to come here had been all for naught.

Then . . . very, very deep in the bowels of Malygos's sanctum, he noted a vague life force. It was so faint that Krasus almost dismissed it as a figment of his own desire, but then he sensed another, similar presence near it.

The cowled figure wended his way through the treacherous, dark passages. Several times Krasus had to steady himself as the path turned precarious. This was a realm used by creatures a hundredfold larger than he presently was and their massive paws easily spread across cracks and ravines he had to climb through.

Had it been his choice, Krasus would have transformed, but, in this time period, that option was not available. He and a younger version of himself existed here simultaneously. It had enabled the pair to accomplish great things together against the Burning Legion, but demanded also limitations. Neither could transform from the shapes they wore and, until recently, both had been vastly weaker when away from the other. While that latter problem had been solved—for the most part—Krasus was condemned to remain in his mortal body.

A shriek overhead made him press against the wall. A huge, leathery form fluttered past, a wolf-sized bat with a feline face, thick fur, and incisors as long as a finger. The creature spun around for a second dive at the mage, but Krasus already had one hand up.

A ball of flame met the beast in mid-air. The bat flew directly into it.

The fiery sphere swelled, then quickly imploded.

Cinders—the only remnants of the creature—briefly showered Krasus. That he had not sensed the bat perplexed him. He caught a few of the ashes and probed them with his senses. They revealed that the beast had been a construct, not a true living thing. A sentinel, then, of the Master of Magic.

Wiping away the last of the bat, Krasus continued his daunting trek. It had cost him heavily to transport himself by spell to such a faraway place, but for this task, no effort was too great.

Then, to his surprise, he was suddenly greeted by a warmth from ahead. It grew as he continued on, but not to the levels that the dragon mage would have expected. A deeper frown cut into his narrow features as he neared what looked to be a second major cavern. By his calculations, the level of heat should have been several times what it was.

A faint, blue radiance from the cavern illuminated the last bit of passage. Krasus blinked once in order to adjust his eyes, then entered.

The eggs sat nestled everywhere. Hundreds of blue-white eggs of varying size, from as small as his fist to almost as large as him. He let out an involuntary gasp, having not expected such a bounty.

But no sooner had Krasus's hopes risen, then they crashed hard. A more detailed examination revealed the awful truth. Savage cracks lined many, but they were signs of decay, not birth. Krasus placed a gloved hand atop one larger egg and sensed no movement inside.

He went along from clutch to clutch, and as he did, the dragon grew more bitter. History appeared destined to repeat itself regardless of his decision to so flagrantly defy it. The future of the blue dragon flight lay spread before him, but it was a future as devoid of hope as originally. In the time line of which Krasus was familiar, Malygos had been unable to rouse himself from the catatonic state Neltharion had left him until after the magic maintaining the egg chamber—magic bound to the great Aspect—had long failed. Unprotected from the cold, the eggs had perished, and, with them, all hope. In the far future, Alexstrasza had offered to aid Malygos in slowly recreating his flight, but even at the time of Krasus's departure into the past, that plan had barely even begun.

Now, despite everything he had initially preached to Rhonin, Krasus had been attempting perhaps the most precarious change yet to the future of his world. He had hoped to salvage the clutches and bring them to a place of safety, but the constant battle against the demons and the need to force allies onto the foolishly-reluctant night elves had delayed him too much.

Or had it? Krasus paused hopefully over a half-developed egg. Life still yet grew within it. A bit sluggishly, but well enough so that the mage felt certain that new warmth would keep it going.

He checked another and found it, too, a viable candidate. Eagerly, Krasus moved on, but the next several eggs revealed no aura. Gritting his teeth, the robed figure rushed to the next clutch.

He discovered four more salvageable eggs. With one finger, he marked each of those and the ones discovered earlier with a soft, golden glow before continuing his survey.

By the end, there were far fewer eggs than Krasus had hoped to find, but more than he deserved. The dragon mage eyed the ones marked, their glow letting them stand out wherever they were in the vast chamber. He knew with absolute certainty that there were no more. Now, though, what mattered was keeping the select few from perishing as the rest had.

The other dragons, even his beloved Alexstrasza, were invisible to his senses. He could only conclude that they had secluded themselves somewhere in an attempt to recover from Demon Soul's horrific power. His own memories of this period were scattered, the result of his journey and his injuries. Eventually, the other flights would return to the battle, but, by that time, it would be too late for Malygos's kind. Even his younger self was not available to him. Korialstrasz, badly beaten in his heroic struggle to distract Neltharion, had gone to find out what had happened to the other leviathans.

And so it was left to Krasus to decide what to do. Even before he had left for Malygos's lair, he had tried to think of a place he considered secure enough for dragon eggs. Nothing satisfied him. Even the grove of the demigod, Cenarius, had proven unworthy in his eyes. True, the antlered deity was the trusted mentor of Malfurion Stormrage and might very well be the offspring of the dragon, Ysera, but Krasus knew that Cenarius had far too many matters with which to deal already.

"So be it, then," the cowled spellcaster murmured.

With one gloved finger, Krasus drew a circle in the air. Golden sparks accented the tracing his finger made. The circle was perfect and looked as if it had been cut into the very atmosphere itself.

Touching his fingertips to the center, the dragon mage *removed* the circle. A white gap floated before him, one reaching beyond the mortal plane.

Krasus muttered under his breath, The circle's outline flared red. There was a moan from within it and small, loose stones began rolling toward the gap. Krasus muttered more, and, although the suction grew more intense, the stones slowed to a halt. Instead, the eggs began to shake slightly, as if even in the cold, dead ones, something moved.

But it was not so. One of the viable eggs nearest to Krasus's creation suddenly rose. It drifted almost serenely toward the small gap. A second marked egg did likewise, then the rest followed. The dead eggs continued to quiver, but remained where they were.

And as he watched, the future of Malygos's flight lined up before the hole and started to enter.

Curiously, as each egg approached, it seemed to shrink just enough to fit through. One by one, in constant succession, Krasus's valuable find disappeared into the gap.

When the last had vanished, the cowled spellcaster sealed the opening. There was a brief, golden spark, and then all trace of the gap vanished.

"Enough to survive, but not enough to thrive," Krasus muttered. It would take centuries for the blues to reach secure numbers. Even supposing every egg hatched, there would still not be that many blue dragons even by the time period from which he had come.

Still, some were better than none.

A sudden wave of nausea and exhaustion overtook Krasus. He barely prevented himself from falling. Despite having for the most part solved the puzzle of the original malady striking him when he had entered the past—that being that both he and his younger self had to share their life force—there were limits yet.

But he could not rest. The eggs were secure, placed in a pocket universe where time ran so slow as to be negligible. Long enough to pass them on to one he could trust . . . assuming he survived the war.

Thinking of that war, Krasus began mustering his strength. Whatever his confidence in Rhonin and Malfurion, there were too many question marks about the certainty of the outcome. The time line had forever shifted; it was possible that the Burning Legion, who had originally lost this struggle, would triumph. Whatever his own meddling with the line, Krasus was well aware that now he had to do everything he could to assist the night elves and the rest. All that mattered now was that there *had* to be a future.

As he began the spell that would carry him back to the host, Krasus eyed the scores of dead eggs. There would also be a future if the demons won. This would be it. Cold, dark, no life. An eternity of emptiness.

The dragon mage hissed vehemently and vanished.

TWO

Zin-Azshari. Once the glorious epitome of the night elf civilization. A sprawling city at the edge of the basis of the night elves' power, the Well. The home of the revered queen, Azshara, for whom her adoring subjects had renamed the capital.

Zin-Azshari . . . a ruined graveyard, the launching point of the Burning Legion.

Lupine felbeasts sniffed through the rubble, ever seeking the unmistakable smell of life and magic. Twin tentacles jutting up from near their furred shoulders darted around as if with minds of their own. The toothy suckers at the end of each opened and closed hungrily. Felbeasts savored draining a sorcerer dry of both his power and his life, but the rows of sharp teeth displayed in the scaly monsters' mouths gave warning that flesh was a tasty tidbit to them, too.

Two demonic hounds rummaging through the collapsed wreckage of what had once been a five-story tree home quickly gazed up at the sound of marching feet and the clatter of arms and armor. Rows upon rows of fierce warriors churned past, their destination the night elven defenders days away.

The Fel Guard were the backbone of the invaders, their numbers dwarfing all
the rest combined. They stood nine feet high, but while broad at the shoulder
and chest, were oddly narrow, even gaunt, in their midsection. A pair of huge,
curled horns thrust up from their almost fleshless heads. Their bloodred eyes
warily watched the devastated landscape. Although they marched with precision, there was a general impatience among the Fel Guard, for they lived only
for carnage. Now and then, one of the fanged warriors would jostle another
and the threat of anarchy would break out.

But a quick flash of whip from above ever kept the warriors in line. Fiery-
winged Doomguard fluttered above the ranks of every regiment, watching
for disorder. Slightly taller, they differed little else from their brethren below,
save in their lesser numbers and greater intelligence.

Though a dread mist covered Zin-Azshari now, the monstrous armies had
no difficulty maneuvering through it. The mist was as much a part of them as
the swords, axes, and lances they wielded. Its sickly green tint matched exactly
the color of the fearsome flames that radiated from each demon.

The skulls of night elves watched mournfully from the ruins as the Burning Legion marched. They and countless others like them had perished early
on, betrayed by the very queen they worshipped. The only night elves still
alive in the capital were the Highborne, the servants of the queen. Their
secluded quarter of the city, surrounded by gargantuan walls, kept the visions
of the slaughter from their delicate sensibilities. Clad in the garish, multicolored robes of their elite rank, they tended to their needs while awaiting the
commands of Azshara.

The warriors of the palace guard still lined the walls, their eyes filled with
a fanatic glare worthy of the Legion. They were commanded by Captain
Varo'then—more a general these days than a simple officer, despite his title—
who acted as the eyes and mouth of his monarch when she could not be troubled from her recreation. Given the order, the soldiers would have stood side
by side with the demons against their own people. They had already watched
without emotion the massacre of the city's inhabitants. As with most all within the palace, they were both Azshara's creatures and servants to the lord of
the Burning Legion.

Sargeras.

One who was neither the queen's nor the demon's puppet hung in a cell deep
beneath the palace, trying to stifle the gnawing fear in her gut by constant
prayer to her goddess.

Tyrande Whisperwind had woken to a nightmare. The last that she could
recall, the priestess of Elune—the Mother Moon—had been in the middle of

a terrible battle. Tossed from her dying mount, she had struck her head. Malfurion had dragged her to safety . . . and then from there everything had turned muddled. Vaguely, Tyrande recalled horrific images and sounds. Goatlike creatures with leering mouths. Clawed, furred hands clutching her. Malfurion's desperate voice and then—

And then the priestess had awakened here.

Long, elegant eyes of silver surveyed her prison for the thousandth time. Graceful lips parted in regret and grim acknowledgment of her situation. She shook her head, her long, dusky blue hair—the silver streaks in it more prominent now that she did not wear her war helmet—flowing in waves with each change of direction. Nothing had altered since last Tyrande had looked around. Had she really expected anything to do so?

Chains did not bind her wrists and ankles, but she might as well have been held by such. A shimmering, green sphere floating a foot or so above the dank, stone floor surrounded her from head to toe. In it, she stood with arms stretched over her head and her legs sealed tightly together. Try as she might, the recently-anointed high priestess could not separate her limbs. The magic of the great demon, Archimonde, ever proved too powerful in that regard.

But if his magic had imprisoned Tyrande utterly, Archimonde had failed in his ultimate intention. There had been no doubt as to his desire to torture her, to bend her to his will and, thus, to that of his own master. At his hand, Archimonde had not only had his own terrifying imagination, but the dire skills of the Highborne and the sadistic satyrs.

Yet, the moment that the demon had attempted to harm her physically, a faint aura the color of moonlight had draped around Elune's acolyte. Nothing Archimonde or his minions could do could penetrate it. Against such evil effort, the plated armor surrounding her lithe form would have proven as useful as the thin, silver cloak that they had ripped from her early on, but the transparent aura acted like an iron wall a mile thick. Archimonde had battered himself against it time and time again to no avail. In his rage, the giant, tattooed figure had finally seized an unsuspecting fel guard by the neck, crushing in the other demon's throat without the least effort.

Since then, they had left her alone, their efforts to eradicate the night elf host more important than a lone priestess. That did not mean that they did not have future intentions for her, for the satyrs who had carried her through the magical portal at the battle site had informed their master that she was close to one whom Archimonde had marked . . . Malfurion. At the very least, they would use Tyrande against him, and that was the basis for much of her present fear. Tyrande did not want to be the cause of Malfurion's downfall.

Marching feet alerted her to newcomers in the dungeon corridors. She glanced up in apprehension just as someone unlocked the door. As it swung open, a figure she dreaded at least as much as Archimonde stepped inside. The scarred officer wore armor of a glittering emerald green with a bright pattern of golden sunbursts across the chest. Behind him fluttered a flowing cape that matched the sunbursts in color. His narrow eyes never seemed to blink and when they alighted on her, their intensity was such that Tyrande could not look directly into them.

"She is conscious," Captain Varo'then remarked to someone behind him.

"Then, by all means," responded a languid, feminine voice. "Let us see what Lord Archimonde so prizes . . ."

With a bow, Varo'then swept aside for the speaker. Tyrande bit back a gasp, even though she had expected who it was.

Queen Azshara was as beautiful, as perfect, as the storytellers said. Luxurious silver hair cascaded down her back. Her eyes were golden and half-veiled, her lips full and seductive. She wore a silken gown that matched her hair, one so thin that it gave ample hint of the sleek form beneath. Jeweled bracelets hung on each wrist and matching earrings hung almost all the way to her exquisite, bare shoulders. The arched tiara in her hair held a ruby that reflected the dull light from the torch a guard carried to almost blinding effect.

Behind her followed another female, one who would have also been considered quite beautiful, but who, in the presence of Azshara, paled in comparison. The handmaiden dressed in garments similar to her mistress, save that their quality was more than a step below. She also wore her hair as much like the queen as possible, although the silver in it had clearly come from a dye and did not even approach the intensity of Azshara's mane. In truth, the only thing that stood out were her eyes—silver as with most night elves, but with an exotic, feline curve to them.

"*This* is her?" the queen asked with unconcealed disappointment as she studied the captive.

In truth, in Azshara's presence, Tyrande felt even mousier than the handmaiden. She wanted to at least wipe the grime and blood away from her face and form, but could not. Even aware that the queen had betrayed her people, the priestess felt the desire to kneel at Azshara's slim, sandaled feet, so charismatic was the monarch.

"She's not to be underestimated, Light of Lights," the captain replied. When his eyes fixed upon Azshara, they did so with burning desire. "She appears favored by Elune."

The queen did not find this at all impressive. Perfect nose wrinkling, she asked, "What is Elune to the great Sargeras?"

"Spoken so wisely, your majesty."

Azshara approached closely. Even her least movement appeared calculated for maximum impact on her audience. Tyrande again felt the urge to kneel before her.

"Pretty, in a coarse way," the silver-tressed figure added offhandedly. "Perhaps worthy to be a handmaiden. Would you like that—what was her name again, captain?"

"Tyrande," Varo'then replied with a brief bow.

"Tyrande . . . would you like to be my handmaiden? Live in the palace? Be a favored of mine and my lord? Mmm?"

The other female started at this suggestion, the feline eyes seeming to flay the priestess. There was no attempt to hide intense jealousy.

Gritting her teeth, the young night elf gasped, "I am sworn to the Mother Moon, my life and my heart hers . . ."

The queen's beauty was suddenly marred by a brief look that rivaled Captain Varo'then's for its evil. "Ungrateful little trollop! And such a liar, too! Your heart you actually give rather easily, don't you? First to one brother, then another brother! Are there others besides?" When Tyrande did not respond, Azshara continued, "Are males not delightful to play with? It is so fun to have lovers fight over you, isn't it? So tasty to see them draw blood in your name! Actually, I must commend you! Brothers—especially *twins*—are such a splendid touch! Peeling away their familial bonds until they wish to rip out each other's throats, betray each other . . . all for your favor!"

Varo'then chuckled. The handmaiden smiled darkly. Tyrande felt a tear slip from her eye and silently cursed her emotions.

"Oh, dear! Have I brought up tender subjects? I do apologize! Poor Malfurion and Illidan . . . those were their names, weren't they? Poor Illidan, most of all. Such a tragedy, what happened to him. Small wonder he chose to do what he did!"

Despite herself, Tyrande blurted, "What about Illidan? What do you mean?"

But Azshara had turned back to Varo'then and the handmaiden. "She needs her rest, don't you agree, captain? Come, Lady Vashj! Let us see if there is any progress on the portal! I want to be ready when Sargeras crosses over . . ." The queen practically preened at mention of the demon's name. "I want to look my best for him . . ."

The guards stepped aside as Captain Varo'then led Azshara and the Lady Vashj to the door. Just out in the hall, the ruler of the night elves glanced over her shoulder at the captive priestess. "You really should reconsider whether to be my handmaiden, dear girl! You could have had *both* of them alive and yours to play with . . . after I'd grown tired of them, of course."

The slamming of the iron door echoed the dying of Tyrande's hopes. She saw in her mind both Malfurion and Illidan. Malfurion had been there when she had been kidnapped and Tyrande knew that he was grief-stricken by his failure to protect her. She feared that such emotions would make him reckless, an easy target for the demons.

And then there was Illidan. Just before the last battle, he had discovered which direction her feelings lay and had not taken it well. Although Azshara's remarks had certainly been designed to further cut down her resolve, Tyrande could not help put some credence to them. She knew Illidan well and knew how wild he could become. Had that streak, fueled by her rejection, made him do something terrible?

"Elune, Mother Moon, watch over them both," she whispered. Tyrande could not deny that she was concerned most of all for Malfurion, but she still cared for his twin. The priestess also knew how horrible Malfurion would feel if anything befell his brother.

Thinking of that, Tyrande added, "Mother Moon, whatever fate should take me, please save Illidan, at least for Malfurion! Give them one another! Let not Illidan—"

And at that moment, she sensed another presence near her, one certainly within the castle walls, so close it felt. The encounter was brief, so very brief, yet, for all that, the priestess knew exactly who she had sensed.

Illidan! Illidan in Zin-Azshari . . . in the palace!

The discovery shook her to the bone. She imagined him a prisoner, tortured horribly since he did not have the miraculous love of Elune protecting him as it did her. Tyrande saw him screaming as the demons flayed him alive, their magic ensuring that he remained fully conscious through each agonizing moment. They would torture him not just because of what he had done against the Legion, but also for Malfurion's efforts, too.

She tried again to touch his thoughts, but to no avail. Yet, as she made the attempt, something about the brief contact began to bother her. Tyrande puzzled over it, delving deep within herself. She had sensed something about Illidan's emotions that did not sit well, something very wrong—

When she realized just what it was, Tyrande grew cold with dread. It could not be! Not from Illidan, whatever the past!

"He would not become so . . ." Tyrande insisted to herself. "Not for any reason . . ."

Now she understood some of what the queen had said. Illidan—as impossible as it was to believe—had come to Zin-Azshari of his own desire.

He wanted to *serve* the lord of the Burning Legion.

The southernmost tower of Azshara's palace was ablaze in sorcerous energies, be it day or night the work of the Highborne never ceasing. Sentries on duty nearby tried not to stare in the direction of the tall structure for fear that the powerful magicks might somehow engulf them.

Within, the Highborne, their hooded, elegantly embroidered robes of turquoise hanging on their gaunt forms, stood alternating with sinister, horned figures whose lower halves resembled that of goats. Once, they, too, had been night elves, and even though their upper torsos still showed some indication of that, through guile and witchery they had become something more. Something that was now a part of the Burning Legion, not the world of Azeroth.

Satyrs.

But even the satyrs looked weary as they struggled with their former brethren on the spell taking place within the hexagonal pattern. Floating eye-level over the design, the fiery mass had as its center a darkness that seemed to go on forever, giving witness to how far beyond their plane of existence the spellcasters had reached. They delved beyond the edge of reason, beyond the limits of order . . . and into the chaos from which the demons had come.

Into the realm of Sargeras, lord of the Legion.

A huge shadow loomed over the sweating spellcasters. The winged monstrosity moved on four tree-trunk legs. His froglike face included great tusks. Beneath a thick brow ridge, blazing orbs glared at the tinier figures. The top of his scaly head nearly scraped the ceiling.

His massive tail sliding back and forth across the floor, Mannoroth rumbled, "Keep it stabilized! I'll rip off your heads and drink your blood from your necks if it fails!"

Despite his words, however, he sweated as much as the rest. They had attempted a new spell in the hopes of making the portal larger and stronger—enough so that Sargeras himself could enter through it—but had, instead, nearly lost control. Such a failure would mean execution of some of the sorcerers, but it also might mean Mannoroth's own horrific demise. Archimonde brooked no more mistakes.

"If I might be permitted?" asked a voice from near the chamber entrance.

With a snarl, Mannoroth glanced at the puny night elf. His unsettling amber eyes aside, he saw little of interest in this distrusted newcomer called Illidan Stormrage. Archimonde suffered the creature to live because of some potential he sensed, but Mannoroth would have preferred nothing more than to hang the arrogant ant by hooks through his eyes, then slowly dismember him a limb at a time. It would be some vengeance against Illidan's brother, the druid who had caused Mannoroth so much disaster and shame.

But such entertainment would have to wait. For no reason other than to perhaps watch Illidan fail miserably, Mannoroth indicated with one huge, taloned paw that the night elf should proceed. Illidan, clad in black leather jerkin and pants and with his hair bound tight in a tail, strode past the great demon with utter disregard as to Mannoroth's station. It was worse than dealing with Azshara's pet soldier, Varo'then.

Illidan stopped at the circle, surveying the work. He nodded after a moment, then, with a relaxed wave of his hand, opened up a space for himself between a startled satyr and a Highborne.

The portal rippled. Mannoroth ground his yellowed fangs. If the night elf caused the portal to fail, Archimonde could not fault his second in command for splattering the culprit against the wall.

Illidan made a single gesture toward the fiery gap—and it suddenly held. The fraying that the demon had sensed vanished. If anything, the portal was now stronger than before.

Mannoroth's green brow furrowed. Could this puny creature have the power to—

Before he could follow the notion further, a presence suddenly filled the chamber, a presence whose point of origin lay far, far inside the portal.

"To your knees!" the four-legged demon quickly roared.

Everyone—spellcasters and guards alike—immediately dropped.

Everyone . . . save Illidan.

He calmly stood before the portal despite it being impossible that he did not sense the overwhelming presence reaching out from it. Illidan stared into the blackness, almost expectant.

You are the one . . . came the voice of Sargeras.

The torches flickered wildly. In the dancing shadows they caused, one almost appeared more alive than the rest. It rose not only to the ceiling, but across it, coming to a head exactly above the fiery gap.

Illidan noted the manifestation with the same seeming indifference he had all else. Mannoroth could only mark him as the biggest fool the demon had ever encountered.

You are the one who has done what others could not . . .

Finally, the night elf showed some sense by lowering his head slightly in deference to the voice. "I deemed it necessary to act."

You are strong . . . Sargeras said from the beyond. There was a moment of silence, then, *but not strong enough* . . .

Meaning that, despite his power, Illidan did not possess the wherewithal to enable the portal to allow the lord of the Legion through to the mortal plane. Mannoroth found his own thoughts in conflict, frustrated that the way was still not open for Sargeras, but pleased that the night elf had come up lacking.

"I might know of a method, though," Illidan unexpectedly remarked.

Again, there was complete silence. Mannoroth grew troubled as it stretched long, for he had never witnessed Sargeras so quiet.

Finally . . . *Speak.*

Illidan held up his left palm. In it, the illusion of an object formed. Mannoroth stretched up so as to better view it. He felt quite disappointed. Instead of some intricate amulet or blazing crystal, all the night elf revealed was a rather plain golden disk whose greatest aspect was that it filled the palm. Had the actual piece lain before him, the winged behemoth would have trampled right over it without pause.

He expected Sargeras to punish Illidan for wasting his time, but instead, the lord of the Legion responded with obvious interest. *Explain . . .*

Without preamble, the renegade sorcerer said, "This is the key. This has the power. This is the *Dragon Soul.*"

Now Mannoroth and the others paid much more attention. They had all witnessed its fury, felt its overwhelming power. With it, the black dragon had slaughtered demons and night elves alike by the hundreds. He had churned up the earth for miles around and even cast out the other dragons when they had sought to stop him.

All this from so humble-looking a piece.

"You have seen it, even from where you wait," Illidan went on. "You've sensed its glorious might and you rightly hunger for it to be yours."

Yes . . .

"It could slay thousands simply through your will. It could sweep clear a land of all resisting life . . . all life, period."

Yes . . .

"But you didn't consider that it might be the source of power you need to reach this world, did you?"

Sargeras did not answer, which was answer enough. Mannoroth grunted. The night elf was too clever for his own good. The Burning Legion coveted the artifact, but it was still in the possession of the black dragon. Eventually, the demons would have the strength and resources to hunt the beast, but not while they had Illidan's people to still slaughter.

It has the power, the lord of the Legion at last declared. *It could open the way . . . if it was ours . . .*

"I have the means by which to track its location, to know where the dragon's hidden it."

Another telling pause, then, *the black beast has shielded himself well . . .* Sargeras responded. *Even from me . . .*

Illidan nodded, the smile on his face one that, had it been on anyone else's, the lord of the Legion would surely have ripped it—and every bit of flesh and sinew attached—off even from the beyond.

"But he's not shielded from me . . . because I know how to track him . . . with this."

The night elf gestured and in his left hand there suddenly appeared an almost triangular, ebony plate the size of his head. Mannoroth leaned forward. At first he believed it a small piece of armor from one of the world's defenders, but then he saw that it was not metal.

A dragon's scale.

The black dragon's scale.

"A very tiny bit, easily missed by so large a beast," Illidan remarked, turning it over. "He was struck several times in the combat with the red. I knew there had to be at least one broken scale . . . and so I rode out and searched for it. Once I found what I wanted, I then continued on to here."

Mannoroth glared. Was there no end to the sorcerer's audacity? Unable to keep silent any longer, he growled, "Why? Why not bring it back to your friends? Your brother?"

The night elf looked over his shoulder. "Because I deserve power, reward."

The demon expected more, but Illidan was finished. The sorcerer turned back to the portal.

"I need unrestricted access to the Well's energies. The dragon is mighty, especially with the artifact. But, with the Well to fuel me, I'll find him no matter where he is!"

"And then you'll just take it from him, mortal?" The tusked demon sneered. "Or will he simply give it to you?"

"I'll relieve the beast of it one way or another," Illidan casually replied, still staring into the raging abyss. "And bring it here."

Mannoroth started to laugh—then cut off as a pressure tightened around his throat. It vanished almost immediately after, but the message was clear. Whatever the winged demon's own thoughts, the lord of the Legion was interested in the miscreant's words.

You would bring the dragon's creation to me, Sargeras declared to Illidan.

"Yes."

And you will be rewarded greatly for your efforts, should you succeed.

The night elf bowed his head. "Nothing would please me more than to stand before you with the Dragon Soul in my hand."

Sargeras seemed to chuckle. *Such loyalty deserves a mark of favor, a mark that will at the same time aid in the fulfillment of your quest, night elf . . .*

Illidan looked up. For the first time, the barest hint of uncertainty graced his narrow features. "My Lord Sargeras, your crossing to Azeroth will be favor enough and I need no other aid in my—"

But . . . I insist.

And from out of the portal shot forth twin tentacles of dark green flame.

Mannoroth immediately shielded his eyes. Illidan—the focus of Sargeras's spellwork—had no such opportunity, not that it would have done him any good to do so.

The flames poured into his eyes.

The soft tissue was seared instantly. Illidan's scream echoed throughout the chamber and likely well beyond the palace walls. All trace of arrogance had left his expression. There was only agony, pure and unadulterated.

The flames intensified. Arms spread wide, Illidan was dragged up above the floor. He arched backward, nearly breaking in two. Supernatural fire continued to pour into his blackened sockets even after the last bit of the eyes had long burned away.

The Highborne and satyrs dared not leave their task, but they cringed and tried to shy away from the struggling night elf as much as they could. Even the guards shifted a step or two farther back.

Then, as suddenly as they had shot forth, the flames withdrew.

Illidan fell to the hard stone floor, somehow managing to land on his hands and knees. His breath came out in pained gasps. His head hung nearly to the floor. There remained, at least outwardly, no hint of his earlier brashness.

The voice of Sargeras filled the minds of everyone there. *Look up, my faithful servant . . .*

Illidan obeyed.

There was no sign of the eyes. Only the sockets remained, sockets scorched black and fleshless. Around the rims could be seen parts of the skull itself, so absolutely had Sargeras removed the orbs.

But if he had taken away the night elf's eyes, the lord of the Legion had replaced them with something else. There now burned within twin flames, fiery balls the same vicious hue as that which had wreaked such havoc on the sorcerer. The fires burned wildly for several more seconds . . . then faded until they seemed but smoky remnants. The smoke, however, remained, neither dwindling away nor growing stronger.

Your eyes are now my eyes, night elf, their gifts to serve me as well as you . . .

Illidan said nothing, clearly too distraught from pain.

Sargeras suddenly reached out to Mannoroth in particular. *Send him to his rest. When he is recovered, he will set forth to prove his devotion to me . . . and seize the artifact . . .*

At Mannoroth's gesture, two Fel Guard strode up and seized the shaking Illidan. They all but dragged him out of the chamber to his quarters.

The moment the night elf was out of earshot, Sargeras's lieutenant rumbled, "It's a mistake to leave this mortal to his own devices, even so humbled!"

He will not journey alone . . . there will be another. The night elf called Varo'then may be spared for this.

The demon's broad wings flexed at this news. Mannoroth grinned, a macabre sight at best. "Varo'then?"

Azshara's hound will keep good watch on the sorcerer. If Illidan Stormrage fulfills his promise, the sorcerer will be granted a place among us . . .

Such an elevation Mannoroth disliked. "And if the sorcerer proves treacherous?"

Then Varo'then will instead be granted the favor I would bestow upon the druid's twin . . . once the captain has delivered onto me the dragon's creation . . . and Illidan Stormrage's beating heart . . .

Mannoroth's grin grew wider.

THREE

The Burning Legion renewed its attack with undiminished fury. While the defenders ever needed to sleep and eat, the demons did not have any such weaknesses. They fought night and day until cut down, only retreating when the odds were too great. Even then, they did so making each foot of land retaken paid with much blood.

But now they again found their adversaries refreshed. Now, instead of merely the night elf host, there were others who fought. Almost doubling the host's strength, the tauren, dwarves, and other races added a new and desperately-needed edge to the defenders' strength. For the first time in days, it was the Legion that failed, pushed back within a night's ride of ruined Suramar.

Yet, despite this success, Malfurion felt little renewed hope. It was not just that he had come to see his devastated home as the constant barometer of victory and defeat, the battle continuously ebbing and flowing within sight of the once-beautiful settlement. Rather, it was the very core of the host's new power that bothered him. True, Rhonin had managed to force upon Lord Stareye the new allies, but the prejudiced noble had made what should have been a common cause a reluctant truce. The night elves did not truly fight alongside the others. Stareye kept his people to the left and middle flanks, the others to the right. There was little communication and almost no interaction between the various groups. Night elves dealt only with night elves, dwarves with dwarves, and so on.

Such an alliance, if it could laughingly be called that, was surely doomed to defeat. The demons would compensate for the new numbers and attack harder than ever.

What coordination there had to be had been foisted upon the unfortunate Jarod Shadowsong. The druid wondered that the guard captain did not hate the outsiders, for they had brought him nothing but calamity. Yet, Jarod took on his new tasks with the dour dedication that he had the previous ones, for which Malfurion had to admire him. In truth, whatever the benefit of Rhonin's, Brox's, or Malfurion's presence, Jarod's work matched it. He coordinated all matters between the factions—by necessity filtering out dangerous arguments and slurs—and creating something cohesive. In truth, the captain now had at least as much to do with the host's strategy as the pompous Stareye.

Malfurion only prayed that the noble would never realize all this. Ironically, it appeared Captain Shadowsong certainly didn't. In his mind, he was merely obeying orders.

Rhonin, who had been resting atop a rock overseeing the battlefield, abruptly straightened. "They're coming again!"

Brox leapt to his feet with a grace his hulking form belied. The graying orc swung his ax once, twice, then started for the front line. Malfurion leapt atop his night saber, one of the huge, tusked panthers used by his people for travel and war.

Horns sounded. The weary host stiffened in readiness. Different notes echoed along the ranks as the various factions prepared.

And moments later, the battle was again joined.

The defenders and the demons collided with an audible crash. Instantly, grunts and cries filled the air. Roaring a challenge, Brox severed the head of a Fel Guard, then shoved the quivering torso into the demon behind. The orc cut a bloody swathe, quickly leaving more than half a dozen demons dead or dying.

Atop another night saber, Rhonin also battled. He did not merely cast spells, although, like Malfurion, he constantly kept watch for the Eredar, the Legion's warlocks. The Eredar had suffered badly during past campaigns, but they were ever a threat, striking when least expected.

For now, however, Rhonin utilized his magic in conjunction with his combat skills. Astride the night saber, the human wielded twin blades created solely from magic. The blue streams of energy stretched more than a yard each and when the wizard brought them into play, they wreaked havoc on a scale with the orc. Demon armor made for no resistance; Fel Guard weapons broke as if fragile glass against them. Rhonin fought with a passion that Malfurion could well understand, for the red-haired figure had let slip of a mate and coming children whose fate also rested in defeating the legion. As Malfurion was with Tyrande and Illidan, so, too, was Rhonin with his faraway family.

The druid fought no less powerfully, even though his spells sought communion with nature. From one of the many pouches on his belt, he brought forth several spiny seeds, the type that clung to one's garments when passing among the plants. Holding his filled palm up, he blew gently on the seeds.

They rushed forward into the air as if taken by a wind of hurricane strength. Their numbers multiplied a thousandfold as they spread out over the oncoming demons, almost turning into a dust storm.

Roaring, the horrific warriors plowed through the cloud without care, their only interest the blood of the defenders. However, only a few steps later, the first of the demons suddenly stumbled, then clutched his stomach. Another imitated him, then another. Several dropped their weapons and were immediately cut down by eager night elves.

Those who were not suddenly grew extremely bloated. Their stomachs and chests expanded well beyond proportion. Several of the tusked figures fell to the ground, writhing.

From inside one still standing, scores of sharp, daggerlike points burst through flesh and armor. Ichor drenched the screaming demon's form. He spun around once, then collapsed, dead. His body lay pincushioned . . . all from the swelling seeds within.

And around him, others fell, dozens at a time. All suffering the same dire fate. Malfurion felt some queasiness when he saw the results, but then considered the merciless evil of the enemy. He could ill afford any compassion for those who lived only for mayhem and terror. It was kill or be killed.

But despite the many demons who perished, there were always more. The night elves' lines began to give in as they were especially hammered. They had fought longest against the Burning Legion and so were most weary. Archimonde was too clever not to make use of the weak point. More and more tusked warriors poured into the crumbling area. Felbeasts harried the lines and from above the Doomguard dropped down on distracted soldiers, crushing in skulls or burying lances in chests and backs. Oft times, they would take a night elf or two, drag them up high, then drop the helpless figures among the host. Falling among their fellows, the soldiers became missiles slaying those on the ground as well as themselves.

An explosion threw several night elves yards into the air. From the gaping crater arose a blazing Infernal. Powerful of body but weak of mind, the demon lived only to crush anything in its path. It barreled into a line of soldiers, tossing them aside like leaves.

Before Malfurion could act, Brox met the Infernal head on. It seemed impossible that even the orc could hold back such a giant, but somehow Brox did. The Infernal came to a dead stop and, from his roar, the demon found this quite frustrating. He raised a fiery fist and tried to pound the orc's skull into his rib cage, but Brox held the staff of his ax up, the thin handle somehow blocking the deadly blow without cracking. Then, moving faster than the Infernal, Brox shoved aside the demon's hand and jammed the ax head into his adversary's chest.

For all his vaunted might, the Infernal was no less protected against the magical weapon than his comrades. The blade sank in several inches. From out of the gaping wound, green flames shot out. Brox grunted as he shifted to avoid the flames, then removed the ax for another strike.

Although wavering, the Infernal was not yet defeated. Roaring, he slammed both fists together, then struck the earth with them. The thundering smash sent tremors toward Brox, throwing him off his feet.

Immediately the demon charged, intent on trampling the orc to death. But as he neared, Brox, who had managed to keep his weapon, positioned it against the ground like a pike.

The Infernal impaled himself. He struggled to reach Brox, but the veteran warrior kept his position. In his fury, the Infernal only worsened matters. The ax sank deeper, causing a new gush of fire that came within an inch or two of the orc.

With a shudder, the huge demon finally stilled.

But despite such personal victories, the Burning Legion relentlessly pushed forward. Malfurion tried to summon up some of the emotion that had enabled him to push back the horde in the past, but could not. Tyrande's kidnapping had left that part of him drained.

He saw Lord Stareye far to the left, the noble berating the struggling soldiers there. Stareye was a far contrast to his predecessor. Ravencrest would have been as blood- and grime-soaked as his troops, but Stareye looked immaculate. He was surrounded by his personal guard, who let nothing unseemly near him even at such a critical moment.

Then, to the druid's surprise, a shaggy figure charged past him, heading for the near-breach. Another and another followed, gargantuan tauren moving up to the weakened line and adding their astounding strength. With a gusto worthy of Brox, they attacked the demons, cutting down several of the tusked warriors in the first strike. Among them, Malfurion made out Huln at the head, his eagle spear impaling one Fel Guard with such force the tip broke through the back. Huln shook off the dead demon with ease, then parried a wild swing by another. The lead tauren grinned wide.

And with the tauren came an unlikely figure. Jarod Shadowsong, blade already blooded, shouted to the huge beastmen with him. To Malfurion's surprise, the group shifted as if obeying some command. They spread out, enabling the night elves to rebuild their own lines and come to the aid of their rescuers.

Priestesses of Elune also materialized, the warrior maidens a striking group, especially in contrast to their peaceful ways before the coming of the Legion. Their appearance stung Malfurion, though, for it increased again his guilt that he had not managed to keep Tyrande out of the demons' clutches.

Astride their animals, the priestesses used sword and bow against the enemy. However, among those most proficient was one not truly a priestess. Shorter than the rest, young Shandris Feathermoon lacked a summer or two before she should have been officially able to become a novice. But drastic times demanded drastic measures. Marinda, the sister acting in Tyrande's absence, had granted Shandris a place in their depleted ranks. Now, clad in slightly-oversize armor taken from a fallen compatriot, the newest of the Mother Moon's daughters fired off three bolts, all of which scored perfect strikes in the throats of demons.

The Legion's progress halted. The defenders began to push back. Malfurion and Rhonin added their powers to the task and the night elves retook ground.

In the midst of the sisterhood, there was a sudden shriek. Two of the armored priestesses fell, their bodies contorted and crushed by their very armor. Even dead, their expressions revealed the agony that the compressing metal had put them through.

Malfurion's eyes narrowed and he gasped. One of them was *Marinda*.

"Eredar!" snarled Rhonin. He raised a hand toward the northwest.

But before the wizard could strike back, a fount of flame erupted from that very direction. Malfurion sensed the distant warlock's own agony as the flames engulfed him.

"My sincere regrets for so delayed a return," muttered Krasus, the source of that retribution. The dragon mage stood a short distance behind the pair. "I was forced to make the return in stages," he added with bitterness.

No one condemned him, not after all he had done. Still, it was clear that Krasus would not so easily forgive himself.

"We've pushed them back again," declared Rhonin. There was no enthusiasm in his words. "Just like we did the time before and the time before . . ."

The battle retreated from them. Now that matters were once more in the hands of the defenders, the sisters of Elune turned to their true vocation—dealing with the wounded. They moved among the soldiers and a few even went to tend the tauren, albeit with some clear reservations.

Battle horns made the trio look to where Lord Stareye rode. The noble waved his sword around, then pointed at the Burning Legion. It was clear that he was taking full credit for the host's latest advance.

Krasus shook his head. "Would that Brox had reached Ravencrest in time."

"He did his best, I'm sure," Malfurion responded.

"I have no quarrel with the orc concerning his effort, young one. It is fate with whom I ever battle. Come, let us take this reprieve to see if we can aid the sisterhood. There are plenty of wounded to go around."

There were, indeed. Malfurion put to good use another aspect of his training. Cenarius had taught him much concerning those plants and other life that could ease pain and heal wounds. His talents were not so proficient as that of most of the priestesses, but he left his charges in much better condition than he found them.

Among the wounded, they located Jarod. The captain sat near his resting night saber as a sister looked to a long gash in the officer's arm.

"I've tried to convince her it's nothing," he remarked sourly as they approached. "The armor protected me fairly well."

"The Burning Legion's weapons are often poisoned," Krasus explained. "Even a slight wound might prove treacherous." The pale mage dipped his head toward the officer. "Quick thinking out there. You saved the situation."

"I only pleaded with the tauren, Huln, to give me a few of his people to save mine, then asked the dwarves to make sure I hadn't weakened the tauren lines."

"As I said, quick thinking. The night elves and the bullmen fought well together, when it came to it. Would that our erstwhile commander saw that. The moment I arrived, I perceived that there was no true cohesion among the allies."

Rhonin smirked. "Could you expect any better from Lord Stareye?"

"Alas, no."

They were interrupted by the arrival of a senior priestess. She was tall and moved like a night saber herself. Her face was not unattractive, but her expression was severe. The sister's skin was a shade paler than most of her people. For some reason, despite that, she reminded Malfurion of someone.

"They said they saw you," she commented blandly to Jarod.

He looked at her blankly, as if not certain she actually stood there. "Maiev . . ."

"It's been long since we saw one another, little brother."

Now the physical resemblance became more apparent. The captain disengaged himself from the other priestess's efforts and stood to face his sibling. Even though he stood taller than her, somehow Jarod seemed to look up at Maiev.

"Since you entered the moon goddess's service and chose the temple in Hajiri as the place for your studies."

"It's where Kalo'thera ascended to the stars," Maiev countered, referring to a celebrated high priestess from centuries past. Many in the sisterhood considered Kalo'thera almost a demigoddess.

"It was far from home." Jarod suddenly seemed to recall the others. He looked to them, saying, "This is my older sister, Maiev. Maiev, these are—"

The senior priestess all but ignored Malfurion and Rhonin, her gaze strictly on Krasus. Like the rest of the sisterhood, she evidently saw that he was special, even if she did not understand why. Maiev went down on one knee before Jarod could continue, declaring, "I am honored in your presence, elder one."

Expressionless, Krasus answered, "There is no need to kneel before me. Rise, sister, and be welcome among us. You and yours were timely in your appearance today."

Jarod's sibling stood with pride. "The Mother Moon guided us well, even if it meant the sacrifice of Marinda and some others. We saw the line breaking. We would've arrived before the bullmen if not for the greater distance we had to cover." She glanced in the direction the tauren had gone. "Adept reaction for their kind."

"It is your brother who coordinated all," the mage explained. "It is Jarod who may have saved the host."

"Jarod?" Maiev's tone indicated some disbelief, but when Krasus nodded, she buried that disbelief and tipped her head to the captain. "A simple officer of the city guard playing commander! Fortune was with you this time, brother."

He simply nodded, his eyes cast to the side.

Rhonin, however, did not let Maiev's slight pass. "Fortune? Good, common sense, is what it was!"

The priestess shrugged off the incident. "Little brother, you were introducing us . . ."

"Forgive me! Maiev, the elder mage is Krasus. To his side is the wizard, Rhonin—"

"Such illustrious visitors are welcome in this time," she interrupted. "May the blessing of Elune be upon you."

"And this," the captain continued, "is Malfurion Stormrage, the—"

Maiev's eyes burned into the druid's. "Yes . . . you were known to one of our sisters, Tyrande Whisperwind."

Considering that Tyrande had become high priestess, albeit for only a short period before her kidnapping, the remark was not one Malfurion found respectful. "Yes, we grew up together."

"We mourn our loss. I fear her inexperience betrayed her. It would've been better for her if her predecessor had chosen one more . . . seasoned." There was a subtle implication that Maiev referred to herself.

Biting back his anger, Malfurion said, "There was no fault by her. The battle had spread everywhere. She came to my defense, but was injured. Unconscious. During the chaos that followed, servants of the demons took her." He met the other priestess's steely gaze. "And we *will* get her back."

Jarod's sister nodded. "I will pray to Elune that it is so." She looked to the captain. "I'm glad you weren't injured too badly, little brother. Now, if you'll forgive me, I must attend to the other sisters. Marinda's loss means we must quickly decide on a new leader. She had not yet chosen one herself." With a bow that extended mostly to Krasus, Maiev ended, "Again, may the blessings of Elune be upon you."

When she was far away, Rhonin grunted and said, "A cheerful, friendly sort, your sister."

"She's very dedicated to the traditional teachings of Elune," Jarod responded defensively. "She's always been very serious."

"One cannot fault her for her dedication," Krasus remarked. "Providing it does not blind her to the paths taken by others."

Jarod was saved from further defense of Maiev by Brox's return. The orc had a satisfied grin on his wide face.

"Good battle! Many deaths to sing of! Many warriors to praise for the blood they've spilled!"

"How lovely," muttered Rhonin.

"Tauren're good fighters. Welcome comrades in any war." The hulking, green warrior came to a halt, resting his ax on the ground. "Not as good as orcs . . . but almost."

Krasus eyed the direction of the battle. "Another temporary reprieve, at best, even with the joining of the other races. This cannot continue. We must turn the tide once and for all!"

"But that would mean the dragons . . ." his former protege interjected. "And they don't dare do anything, not so long as Deathwing has the Demon Soul." Rhonin saw no reason to call the black dragon by his original name, Neltharion, anymore.

"No, I fear they dare not. We saw what happened when the blue dragons tried."

Malfurion frowned. He thought of Tyrande. Nothing could truly be done for her unless the Burning Legion was thwarted and they would need everyone, especially the dragons, to accomplish that. But the dragons could not face the Demon Soul, so that meant—

"Then, we've got to take it from the black," he suddenly announced.

Even from Brox, ever willing to leap into any battle, the druid received a wide stare. Jarod shook his head in dismay and Rhonin eyed Malfurion as if he had gone completely mad.

Yet, Krasus, after his initial surprise, gave the night elf a speculative look.

"Malfurion is correct, I am afraid. We must do it."

"Krasus, you can't be serious—"

The dragon mage cut off the wizard. "I am. I had already vaguely considered it myself."

"But we don't even know where Deathwing is. He's shielded himself even better than the other dragons."

"That is true. I have considered some ancient spells, but none so far that I believe will have much success. I will attempt them, and if they fail, I will then have to—"

"I think I can do it," Malfurion interrupted. "I think I can find him through the Emerald Dream. I don't believe he's sealed himself off from it as the palace has done."

Krasus looked quite impressed by the druid. "You may very well be right, young one . . ." He considered further. "But even if he has made such an error, there is, of course, the danger that Neltharion will still sense you. He did, as you mentioned earlier, try to track you inside the Dream."

"I've learned to be more careful. I'll do it. It's the only way to save her—to save us."

The cowled figure placed a gloved hand on Malfurion's shoulder. "We will do what we can for her, too."

"I'll start immediately."

"No! You need rest first. For her sake as well as yours, you need to be at your best. If you make a mistake or are discovered by him, all will be lost."

Malfurion nodded, but in his disappointment, there was now some hope, however slight. True, Neltharion might be prepared, but the dragon was obsessive, single-minded. His megalomania might work against him.

"I'll do as you say," he told the mage. "But there's also one other thing I've got to do, then. There's someone I need to speak with who may better my chances."

Krasus bowed his head in agreement and understanding. "Cenarius. You need to speak with the forest lord."

FOUR

She had not been fed, but Tyrande did not yet feel hunger. Elune still filled her with the moon goddess's love, nourishment enough for anyone. How long that would last, however, was an important question. The dire forces raised by the demons and the Highborne grew with every passing moment and, in addition, the priestess sensed some other, darker presence as well. It did not seem a part of the Burning Legion's plan, but worked alongside it.

Perhaps such a notion was only the first sign of coming madness, but Tyrande could not help wondering if the demons were being manipulated just as they were manipulating the queen.

Someone worked on the door. Tyrande's brow furrowed. She had heard no marching. Whoever was out in the corridor had come in utter silence. Moreover, she realized that the guards had grown extremely quiet over the past several minutes.

The door slid open. Tyrande tried to think who would come in such secrecy.

Illidan?

But it was not Malfurion's brother who slipped inside. Rather, it was the noble who acted as Azshara's chief handmaiden. The other night elf glanced up with guarded eyes at the captive, then turned to make certain that the door closed without a sound. As she did, Tyrande could not but help notice no guards visible outside. Were they simply out of sight or entirely gone?

Looking at her, the handmaiden smiled. If it was meant to comfort Tyrande, it did not entirely succeed.

"I am Lady Vashj," the newcomer reminded her. "You are a priestess of Elune."

"I am Tyrande Whisperwind."

Vashj nodded absently. "I have come to help you escape."

Tyrande instinctively thanked the Mother Moon. She had misjudged Vashj, thinking her a jealous sycophant of the queen.

Stepping as close as she could, Vashj continued, "I've taken a talisman that can open the sphere around you and release you from the demon's spell. You can also use it to ward off their notice, as I have."

"I . . . am . . . grateful. But why risk this?"

"You are a priestess of Elune," returned the other female. "How could I do otherwise?" Vashj revealed the talisman. It was a grotesque, black circle with tiny, cruel skulls lining the edge. From the center thrust up a six-inch point with ebony jewels at the base.

Tyrande sensed both its magic and its evil.

"Be prepared," the handmaiden commanded. "Obey me in all things if you hope to no longer be the demons' prisoner."

She reached up and touched the point to the green sphere.

The jewels flashed. The diminutive skulls opened their macabre jaws and hissed.

The sphere was sucked into the tiny maws.

Tyrande felt the spell holding her dissipate. She suddenly had to twist in the air to keep from falling face first. The priestess landed on the stone floor in a crouched position. To her surprise, Tyrande felt no pain from the landing, Elune's touch still protecting her.

Vashj glanced with frustration at her. With the sphere gone, Tyrande now faintly glowed with moonlight arising from *within*. The handmaiden shook her head.

"You must not remain like that! It will give you away once out of this cell!"

Closing her eyes, Tyrande prayed to her goddess, thanking the Mother Moon for her protection but assuring her that this was now for the best. At first, however, it seemed as if Elune paid her no mind, for she felt the protective spell remain fixed.

"Hurry!" Lady Vashj urged.

Eyes still shut, Tyrande tried again. Surely the Mother Moon understood that now the very gift she had bestowed upon her servant risked the priestess.

At last, Elune's presence began to recede—

And a sense of imminent threat overwhelmed Tyrande.

She opened her eyes to see Vashj thrusting at her throat with the sinister talisman. The daggerlike protrusion would have ripped a wide, lethal gap—if not for the war training all priestesses received. Tyrande's hand came up just in time to shove the point aside. She felt a stinging on her skin, but had managed to keep Vashj from even drawing blood.

Azshara's servant, her expression as monstrous as those of the skulls, sought to tear out Tyrande's eyes with her free hand. The priestess raised her armored knee, catching Vashj in the stomach. With a gasp, the other night elf fell back, the talisman rolling to the side.

Tyrande leapt at her, but Vashj was also swift. She rolled over to where the talisman had landed. Tyrande, crouching, tried to pull her back, but the treacherous handmaiden already had the demonic artifact in her clutches.

She spewed unintelligible words of an overt dark tone as she pointed the talisman.

The sphere suddenly reformed around Tyrande. At the same time, the priestess felt Elune's protection return, though small good it did to help her escape the bubble. Tyrande beat against the sphere, but to no avail.

Rising, Lady Vashj glared bitterly at her nemesis. "It would have been better for you if you had taken the point! You will never be *Her* most favored! I am and always will be!"

"I don't want to be favored by the queen!"

But Vashj seemed not to understand this. Eyes on the talisman, she hissed, "I thought this would work, but I will have to think of something else! Perhaps words in the Light of Light's ear, convince her that you are not to be trusted! Yes, that might do the trick!"

Tyrande ceased trying to convince the handmaiden of her lack of desire to serve Azshara. Clearly, Vashj was quite mad and would hear nothing that contradicted her notions.

A sound from without made Vashj spin to the door. "The guards! They will be back from their 'distraction'!" Looking back at the prisoner, she pointed the talisman again. "Everything must be as it was!"

Once more, Tyrande's arms rose, invisibly binding at the wrist. Her feet clamped tight together.

"Would that I knew more about this piece!" Vashj spat. "I know it could likely slay you with but the right command . . ."

The sounds without drew nearer. Secreting the talisman in a fold in her garments, Azshara's attendant made for the door. As she slipped out, she looked one last time at Tyrande.

"Never hers!" And with that, Vashj vanished into the hall.

The guards reappeared barely moments later. One peered through the mesh grate in the door and eyed her for far longer than necessary. What she could make of his expression indicated that he was disturbed by her presence. Vashj had clearly not acted alone.

As for Tyrande, she could do nothing but berate herself for a chance lost. It should have been obvious to her that Vashj could not be trusted, but Elune had taught that one should look for the best in others. Yet, if Tyrande had acted with more caution, perhaps she could have caught the handmaiden off-guard. Instead of being again trapped here, at least then the priestess could have tried to sneak out of the palace.

"Mother Moon, what do I do?" She was aware that there were limits to the goddess's ability to intervene. It was miracle enough that Elune had protected her so.

Malfurion's visage came to mind, both comforting Tyrande and making her fret. He would *not* give up trying to save her. He would come for her, regardless of the danger to himself. In fact, she was well aware that Malfurion would be willing to sacrifice himself if it meant her freedom.

And it seemed, Tyrande Whisperwind thought with growing despair, that there would be *nothing* she in turn could do to prevent him from doing so.

The small copse of woods was the best Malfurion could do in terms of finding a peaceful place from which to try to reach Cenarius. The druid sat cross-legged on the ground, glancing again at the pitiful foliage around him. The Burning Legion had not reached this place, but their taint had stretched for enough to affect the life here. The trees already sensed the doom approaching and slowly prepared for it. Most of the wildlife had fled. Silence reigned.

Trying to ignore all that, Malfurion shut his eyes and fixed on the demigod. He reached out, calling to Cenarius and trying to picture the deity in his thoughts.

And to his surprise, the demigod responded immediately. An image formed of the forest lord, a huge figure who towered over night elves, tauren, furbolgs, and even the demons. At first glance, he had some similarity to Malfurion, for his face and torso were like those of a night elf, albeit much brawnier and more weathered. Yet, beyond that, Cenarius was a creature like none other. Below his waist, he had the body of a gigantic, magnificent stag. Four strong legs ending in hooves supported his ten-foot frame. They gave him the speed of the wind and a nimbleness no animal could match.

Cenarius had eyes of pure gold and a moss-green mane flowing down his shoulders. In both it and his full beard grew twigs and leaves. Atop his head— and exactly, Malfurion noted with a start, where his own nubs grew—the forest lord had a glorious pair of antlers.

I know why you've summoned me, the demigod said.

Is there anything I can do to counteract and outmaneuver the black dragon's magic?

He is cunning, insanely so, Cenarius replied, his mouth never moving. He was but an vision upon which the druid could focus, nothing more. The true forest lord was miles away. *But there are things I know of dragonkind that he may not realize.*

Malfurion did not press on how Cenarius might know these things. From what he had learned, the deity was likely the offspring of the green dragon, Ysera—She of the Dreaming—whose kind most inhabited the Emerald Dream. That the great Aspect might have taught her son its innermost secrets would not have surprised the night elf.

The Emerald Dream has layers, Malfurion. Levels upon levels. She of the Dream-

ing discovered these through experience. The Earth Warder likely will not know of them. You may be able to use such a path to circumvent his defenses and keep from his attention for a time.

This was something unexpected. Malfurion's hopes rose. Should he succeed in this, perhaps he could use such a method to infiltrate the palace.

But he had to concentrate on one matter at a time. While his heart yearned to rescue Tyrande, the fate of all his people—and the tauren, Earthen, and others—was of far more consequence. She would have been the first to tell him so.

It did not make his feeling of guilt any less.

Can I learn quickly how to do this? he asked of the demigod.

You, yes. It is all only a matter of perspective . . . see . . .

The image gestured . . . and around the pair an idyllic landscape appeared. It was without imperfection. Malfurion recognized hills and valleys that in the mortal plane had been ravaged beyond recognition by the Burning Legion. The Emerald Dream was as the world had been upon its creation.

The druid looked, but saw nothing he had not already experienced previous.

You note the culmination, but even perfection comes in stages. Behold . . .

Cenarius reached down, his hand gigantic as it touched the pristine world. The forest lord seized a bit of field—and seemed to flip the entire landscape over.

It vanished as he released his grip and in its place was again a primitive Kalimdor, but a Kalimdor in which some new, subtle differences from the previous landcape could be seen. Hills were not as large in some places and a river Malfurion knew did not flow into quite the same region as before. There was a small mountain chain where plains should have existed.

Before the creation, there was the growth, the testing, the earlier stages. This is one.

It was and was not the Emerald Dream. The druid recognized immediately that this was a place of limited scope—and, therefore, use—a Kalimdor that would not enable him to reach every location existing on the mortal plane.

Yet . . . Cenarius believed it could help him with the black dragon.

The looming figure of the woodland deity pointed off in the distance. *Walk it as you would the other, Malfurion, but remain clear of its edges. It is an incomplete place and to wander off it could mean being lost in an endless limbo. I speak of this from dread experience.*

Cenarius said no more, but his meaning was clear. If Malfurion lost his way, there would be no rescue.

Despite that dread knowledge, the night elf was determined to continue on. *How do I return?*

As you always have. Seek to follow your way back to your physical self. The path will become known to you.

All so simple . . . providing one had the training as he did.

Cenarius's image began to fade. Malfurion stopped him.

The others, he said, referring to the forest lord's fellow demigods. *Have you been able to convince them?*

Aviana has spoken alongside me. The die is cast. We must now only decide how.

Malfurion barely checked his disappointment. He had been pressing for the demigods to take a more active part in the host's desperate efforts and, while Cenarius had just indicated that his fellows had agree to do so, now they would debate the manner. With such beings, that debate might last long past the struggle. Kalimdor could be an empty, dead shell before then.

Fear not, Malfurion, the forest lord said, smiling knowingly. *I shall endeavor to hasten their decision.*

The druid had left open his innermost thoughts, a beginner's mistake. *Forgive me! I meant no disrespect! I—*

Cenarius, already fading, shook his antlered head. He pointed a finger—a finger which ended in a gnarled talon of wood—and concluded, *There is no disrespect in trying to urge those suffering from sloth to fulfill their duties . . .*

With that, the stag god vanished.

The druid had expected to return to his body and inform the others of what he had learned, but the unfinished landscape Cenarius had revealed to him already lay open. Malfurion feared that if he took the time to first return to the mortal plane, it might prove more difficult than the demigod believed for him to find his way back to this version of early Kalimdor.

Unwilling to check his impulse any longer, he leapt. As with the path Malfurion usually took, the hazy, emerald light still pervaded everything. In truth, he could not tell any difference between one place and another save for the occasional variation in features.

Over hills and valleys and plains, Malfurion flew. From Krasus he knew the general direction where the dragons tended to live. Obviously, the Earth Warder would not maintain his sanctum so near the others, but Krasus had assured him that the ancient race were creatures of habit. If the druid began his hunt near the ancestral grounds, there was a good chance he might discover something.

The land below became more mountainous, yet, these peaks were neither the perfectly pointed ones of his past journeys into the dream realm nor were they the weathered ones of the mortal plane. Instead, they were, as Cenarius had hinted, *unfinished.* One peak literally lacked its northern face, the earth and rock looking as if some great knife had sheered it off. Malfurion could see the veins of minerals and bits of cavern within. Another peak had a peculiar crown that made it appear as if someone had been molding it like clay but had lost interest.

Tearing his eyes from such fascinating displays, the druid inspected the area as a whole. This was definitely part of the dragon lands. Now all he had to do was find some trace of Neltharion.

As with from the other level, Malfurion probed with his senses for the black dragon's particular trace. He detected others and quickly identified Ysera and one he believed to be Alexstrasza. Other, fainter traces Malfurion determined to be from lesser dragons and, therefore, not of interest.

Moving slowly along, the druid searched in every direction. With each failure, he began to wonder if perhaps Neltharion had not been so naive after all. Perhaps, the black leviathan was more familiar with this plane than Cenarius knew and had shielded himself. If so, Malfurion could wander forever and not find a single hint.

He suddenly halted. A trace that he had offhandedly rejected as belonging to a minor dragon suddenly caught his attention again. It had a familiarity to it that should not have been possible. Malfurion focused on it . . .

The facade peeled away almost immediately. Neltharion's trace lay revealed to the druid. Spells that likely would have kept the Earth Warder hidden from anyone on either the mortal plane or even in the Emerald Dream had proven almost laughably weak here. However, Malfurion tried not to grow overconfident. It was one thing to track the black dragon, another to keep from his notice no matter on what plane. The madness inflicting Neltharion had given him an extreme paranoia that had augmented his higher senses. Even the slightest mistake by the druid might mean discovery.

With the need for utmost caution in mind, Malfurion followed the trace. It took him further on, toward a region where the landscape became more vague, more undefined. Recalling Cenarius's warnings concerning the edges, the druid slowed.

The black dragon was near. Malfurion sensed him just where the mountains began to blur. He also sensed something else, a foul taint that permeated the region and felt far older than anything else. It reminded the druid of what he had felt when probing deep into the Demon Soul. It had not only been imbued with Neltharion's madness, but something more sinister. Then, though, it had only been a trace and he had thought little of it.

What could it be?

Deciding that he could not worry about it now, Malfurion ventured closer. The landscape rippled—and suddenly his dream form reentered the mortal plane.

The huge cavern surrounding him was like a scene out of some nightmare. Noxious-looking clouds of green-gray gas shot up from huge, molten pits dotting the floor. The pits bubbled and hissed and now and then their steaming contents boiled over, spilling across the already-scorched stone. The volcanic activity filled the cavern with a fiery, bloody light and created macabre, dancing shadows. Truly a fitting home for the beast that had slaughtered so may with so little regard.

Malfurion suddenly realized that, in addition to the bubbling and hissing, another sound constantly ranged in the background. Hammering. The more he concentrated, the more the druid realized that it was not simply one hammer, but many, and that there were other sounds of activity as well. Voices, constantly-jabbering voices.

Drawn by it, Malfurion's dream form flew through solid rock yards thick. The sounds reverberated through the mountain. It became an incessant barrage of work-related noises, as if a huge smithy existed within the mountain.

Then the rock gave way to a scene that made the volcanic pits tranquil in comparison.

Goblins. The wiry creatures ran about everywhere. Some worked at huge vats and ovens, pouring steaming, liquid metal into massive, rectangular molds. Others beat with well-worn hammers on hot plates that looked almost like armor for some gargantuan warrior. Scores more hammered out huge bolts. All the while, they all jabbered with one another. Everywhere Malfurion looked, goblins worked on some project or another. A few in grimy smocks wandered about, directing efforts and now and then urging on the slothful with flat-handed slaps on the back of their green, pointy-eared heads.

Aware that this could not be a task with good intentions behind it, he floated closer. Yet, despite what he saw, Malfurion could not figure out what the goblins planned.

"Meklo!" roared a thunderous voice suddenly. "Meklo! Attend me!"

The druid froze in mid-air, briefly overcome by panic. He knew well that voice, as did anyone who had survived the first use of the Demon Soul.

And a moment later, from another cavern corridor, the black dragon himself emerged.

Malfurion quickly moved behind one of the ovens. While he should have been invisible even to Neltharion, past experience had proven that the mad beast could still sense him at times. The path Cenarius had shown Malfurion had enabled the druid to slip past Neltharion's protective spells as planned, but in order to properly search for the artifact, the night elf unfortunately had to stay as close to the mortal plane as possible.

After a brief hesitation, the goblins continued their work, albeit with not quite so much chattering. Neltharion surveyed the area, seeking out the "Meklo" he desired to see.

If anything, the leviathan looked even more monstrous than when he had flown from the scene of destruction. His body was distorted, bloated, and his eyes held a more horrible madness than ever. More shocking, the rips and tears in his scaled flesh had only grown, fire and molten fluids constantly gushing from each pulsating wound. It almost looked as if eventually Neltharion's body would tear itself apart.

But all thought of the terrifying transformation wrought upon the black dragon vanished from Malfurion's thoughts when he saw what the giant held tight in one huge paw.

The Demon Soul . . .

Malfurion wanted to fly up to the dragon and steal away the golden disk, but that would not only have been impossible, it would also have been suicidal. All he could do for the moment was watch and wait.

"Meklo!" Neltharion roared again. His tail came down with a massive thump, causing several of the goblins to jump in fright.

But one who appeared unperturbed by this display was a spindly, elder goblin with a tuft of gray fur atop his head and an extremely distracted expression. As he passed where Malfurion hid, the druid could hear him muttering about measurements and calculations. The goblin nearly walked up to Neltharion's lowered head before finally glancing at his master.

"Yes, my Lord Neltharion, yes?"

"Meklo! My body screams! It cannot contain my glory by itself anymore! When will you be ready?"

"I have had to recalculate, recalibrate, and reconsider every aspect of what you need, my lord! This will require much caution, or we may bring further disaster upon you!"

The dragon's snout thrust against the goblin, almost bowling Meklo over. "I want it ready! Now!"

"By all means, by all means!" Meklo stepped out of biting range. "Please let me look over the latest plate—" The goblin squinted, gazing at Neltharion's paw. "But, my lord! I did warn you, I did, that holding the disk while in this present state amplifies the effect on you! You really need to put it elsewhere until we've made you over!"

"Never! I'll never let it leave me!"

Meklo stood his ground. "My lord, if you don't put it aside, your present condition will consume you and then *anyone* could take it from your burnt bones."

His words finally registered with the dragon. Neltharion snarled . . . then reluctantly nodded. "Very well . . . but the plates had better be ready, goblin . . . or I'll be having a snack!"

His head bobbing up and down quickly, Meklo blurted, "Most assuredly,

Lord Neltharion, most assuredly!" Daring his master's further wrath, he added, "Remember! It must remain on the mortal plane! Your initial use of it unbound the spells more than we expected! The new spellwork needs several more days to bind to the physical shell before we can guarantee that such a thing will never happen again!"

"I understand, gnat . . . I understand . . ." With a hiss, the black leviathan angrily turned about and headed back into the corridor.

Malfurion tensed. The dragon was going to secrete the Demon Soul somewhere. Now was the druid's opportunity to discover the location.

Ignoring the goblins, Malfurion carefully drifted after the Earth Warder. Neltharion's great girth filled the tunnel, allowing the druid no manner by which to see what might lay ahead unless he chose to fly around or through the dragon. Aware of the risks in that, the night elf forced himself to be patient.

That patience wore thin as Neltharion wended his way through a labyrinth of tunnels. The sense of ancient evil the druid had earlier felt only increased as they journeyed. Where Neltharion went was clearly shunned by others. Only once did the Earth Warder pass one of his own flight, that much smaller dragon prostrating himself before his master. Beyond that, no life, not even an earthworm, appeared. The Earth Warder was taking no chances. His obsession with the Demon Soul included distrust of even his own followers—not entirely surprising considering the power the disk granted its wielder.

Malfurion gradually moved nearer, finally ending up just above the dragon's sweeping tail. He all but urged the leviathan to haste.

The giant abruptly paused, his head twisting to look over his shoulders. Malfurion instinctively flew into the nearest wall, sinking deep into the stone. He waited for several seconds, then, dropping to a lower point, thrust his head out to look.

Neltharion was already on his way. Cursing his overreaction, the druid gave chase.

Scarcely had he caught up when the Earth Warder suddenly veered into a narrow cavern. It was all Neltharion could do just to fit into it, the sides of his huge torso scraping the walls.

"Here . . ." he muttered, apparently speaking to his creation. "You'll be safe here."

The sense of dread had grown more so, but Malfurion fought down the desire to flee. He almost knew where and how the dragon hid the Demon Soul.

With great delicacy, Neltharion reached up and took hold of a tiny outcropping. As he did, it flashed—and the piece he removed left behind in its wake a gap clearly gouged out by some great creature, likely the dragon himself.

Neltharion eyed the Demon Soul. Then, with much hesitation, he gently set it into the hole. The moment he had, he thrust the false rock back in front.

Again, there was a flash and now the area looked completely normal. Had he floated directly in front of it, Malfurion could have never guessed that it was not. The false covering had fashioned itself perfectly to fit its surroundings.

Of more interest than even that, however, was that Malfurion could now not sense the disk. Its foul energies were invisible to even the most careful search. The dragon might not have been able to hide it beyond the mortal plane, but clearly had devised the next best thing.

Neltharion paused, eyes still fixed on the spot where he had secreted the Demon Soul. One great paw reached up again, the sharp claws but inches from the false front.

With another frustrated hiss, the black leviathan suddenly lowered his paw and began backing out of the cavern.

The druid sank into the stone again, waiting until he was certain that he had given Neltharion enough time to depart. Seconds passed like hours. Finally satisfied that the dragon had to be gone, the night elf peered out. Seeing that the cavern was empty, Malfurion then drifted toward where the Demon Soul lay.

Even almost pressed up against the false front, he felt nothing. Despite his desire to be away from this cursed place, Malfurion decided to take one look at the disk to make certain that he knew everything necessary concerning it and its whereabouts. Krasus would have questions.

He leaned forward, his dream form slipping through Neltharion's camouflaged vault.

A savage roar filled the cavern.

The Demon Soul forgotten, Malfurion flung himself deep into the walls, soaring several yards through before daring to pause.

He felt an intense, monstrous force probe the area, seeking whatever did not belong. Though it had not so far touched Malfurion, the night elf already recognized the black dragon as its source.

Neltharion had evidently detected something amiss. However, from the vague, sweeping movement of his search, he did not know what it was. The druid stood frozen, uncertain whether it was better to try to leave or to remain where he floated.

The magical probe swept closer, but again passed the night elf by. Malfurion started to relax—then suddenly felt the dragon reaching out directly at him.

The druid immediately pulled back farther. Neltharion's search retreated. The dragon had again missed him.

But the night elf dared not risk himself anymore. He had discovered the whereabouts of the disk. As for the Earth Warder, he might be suspicious, but it was doubtful that he realized someone had actually been nearby.

Malfurion retreated from the caverns, from the mountains. As he left the latter, he sought for the unfinished world within the Emerald Dream. Only when he had reentered it did the druid feel any sense of security.

That sense of security vanished as he once again felt Neltharion's overwhelming presence.

The dragon knew of the Dream realm's layers . . .

The night elf desperately concentrated, focusing all his will on his mortal shell. He imagined returning to it even as he felt the Earth Warder reach out his direction—

And just when he thought the mad beast had him . . . Malfurion awoke.

"He's shaking!" Rhonin blurted from the night elf's left. "And drenched with sweat!"

"Malfurion!" Krasus filled the druid's gaze. "What ails you? Speak!"

"I—I'm all right . . ." He paused to catch his breath. "Neltharion—he—he almost noticed me, but I evaded him."

"You have already gone in search of him? You were not to do that!"

"The—the opportunity arose . . ."

"Now, he'll be warned," Rhonin muttered.

"Perhaps, perhaps not," the human's former mentor returned. "More likely, he will chalk it up to the many shadows he thinks surround him." To Malfurion, the mage asked, "Did you discover the Demon Soul?"

"Yes . . . I know where it is." The druid managed to answer. He saw again Neltharion, the savage draconian face giving him chills. "I'm only afraid that we might not be able to take it from him."

"But we have to," Krasus said, nodding understanding over Malfurion's concern. "But we have to . . . no matter what the cost."

FIVE

Soft hands touched Illidan's face as they washed his burnt, wasted flesh. The scent of lilies and other flowers wafted over his nostrils. He began to stir at last, rising up from the self-induced coma he had used to escape his pain. The latter had finally subsided to something tolerable, but Malfurion's brother doubted that it would ever completely fade.

But as full consciousness returned, his world was suddenly filled with a maddening display of colors and violent energies. The sorcerer gasped and put his arms across where his eyes had been, for there were now barely even lids to cover them. Even that, though, did nothing to keep the swirling energies and constantly-shifting colors from almost driving him mad. This was Sargeras's gift to him, a demonic, magical view of the world.

Then, Illidan Stormrage recalled the words of Rhonin, the human wizard. *Focus,* the powerful spellcaster had so often insisted to him. *Focus and it all comes together. That's the key . . .*

Forcing back his initial shock, Illidan tried to follow through. It was nigh impossible, at first, for there seemed an endless chaos, much too much for a mere mortal like him to control.

But, with the same resolution that had propelled him up so quickly among the Moon Guard, Illidan forced order upon matters. The colors began to organize, the energy to flow with regularity and purpose. Shapes began to form from the natural energies inherent in all things, alive or inanimate.

He realized at last that he lay upon a stuffed couch, its fabric so smooth and soft it was almost sensual. There were three figures standing nearby—all female, Illidan belatedly realized. The more the twin focused, the more he could detail features. Night elves all, they were young, exquisite, and clad in rich but alluring gowns.

More distinctions appeared as he fixed on the one who had been washing his injuries. Illidan sensed the silver coloring of her hair—silver that was not natural—and the feline appearance of her eyes. In truth, his perceptions were more acute than ever. The sorcerer could read minute variations in strands of hair. He could sense the level of power each of these Highborne wielded—and knew that, of all three, the one cleaning his wounds was by far the strongest. Even then, though, her skills were nothing in comparison to his.

The lead handmaiden recovered first. Putting aside the damp cloth, she brought forth what, through the energies surrounding it, Illidan knew was a silken scarf the color of amber.

The color of his lost eyes.

"This is for you, lord sorcerer . . ."

He understood exactly what it was for. This new, sharper sense of sight had momentarily made him forget how he must look to others. With the sort of bow he would have given Lord Ravencrest, Illidan accepted the scarf and wrapped it over where his eyes had been. Not at all to his surprise, the scarf in no manner inhibited his new abilities.

"So much better," murmured the female. "You should look your best for the queen—"

"Thank you, Vashj . . ." came Azshara's voice suddenly. "You and the rest may retire for now."

Vashj clamped her mouth shut, then bowed as she and the other two retreated from the chamber.

Illidan caught his breath as he turned his senses to the queen. A brilliant radiance surrounded Azshara, a silver glow he finally recognized as indication of the power she wielded. Illidan would have blinked if he could. Although Azshara had been beloved by all her people, some, such as him, had assumed that her skills in the arts were negligible. He had always believed that she had required the might of the Highborne for the casting of spells. Illidan wondered if even the late Lord Xavius or the erstwhile Captain Varo'then had ever understood just how accomplished their monarch was.

"Your majesty." Moving from the couch, the sorcerer went down on one knee.

"Please . . . rise up. There is no need for such formality in private." Somehow she moved right up to him without Illidan noticing her do so. The queen guided him back to the couch. "Let us be more comfortable, my darling sorcerer."

As they sat, Azshara leaned toward Malfurion's twin. Her touch set his soul on fire. Her very presence felt almost hypnotic.

Hypnotic? Illidan studied her.

The glow around Azshara had intensified, so much so that it even overlapped him. How Illidan had missed it revealed much about the queen's control.

Even with that knowledge, it was all he could do from being overwhelmed by her.

"I've been most impressed by you, Illidan Stormrage! So very clever, so very powerful! Even our Lord Sargeras sees that or else why would he grant you such a precious gift?" Long, tapering fingers caressed the scarf. "Such a shame to lose the beautiful amber eyes, though . . . I know it hurts much . . ."

Her face was enticingly close to his and, at the moment, it was impossible not to want it closer. "I—I endured it, your majesty."

"Please! For you, I'm merely Azshara . . ." Her fingers ran from his eye sockets to the rest of his face. "Such a handsome face!" She touched his shoulder, pushing aside part of his clothing. "So strong, too . . . and with the mark of the Great One there as well!"

Frowning, Illidan glanced down to where her hand lay.

An intricate pattern of dark tattoos enshrouded his shoulder. Beneath them and well-shielded, the night elf sensed an unearthly magic—the magic of Sargeras—that permeated his flesh. That he had not felt any of it until now stunned Illidan. With a quick glance to his other side, the sorcerer saw that a similar pattern marked his body there. Sargeras had truly claimed Illidan as a creature of the Legion.

Ignoring the queen for a moment, Malfurion's brother gingerly touched one. Immediately he felt a surge of power. It coursed through him. His body radiated primal energy that he knew took as its source that which fed the Well. He realized that the demon lord had amplified his abilities by marking him so.

"Truly you are favored by him . . . and, thus, favored by me," Queen Azshara whispered, drawing close again. "And there are many favors I can grant you, which even he cannot—"

"Forgive this untimely intrusion, Light of Lights," a figure at the door almost growled.

Illidan tensed, but Azshara coolly straightened, brushing back her luxurious hair and eyeing the newcomer with misleading, languid eyes. "What is it, dear captain?"

In contrast to the seductive brilliance surrounding the queen, Captain Varo'then emitted a darkness that reminded Illidan of the demons. He had only a hint of ability in the sorcerous arts, but Illidan already understood that the soldier was possibly as deadly in his own way as Mannoroth.

Perhaps deadlier at times, at least where it concerned his jealousy against real and imagined rivals for his queen. Varo'then all but seethed as he took in the sight of Azshara and Illidan on the couch. She did not help matters by reaching out and caressing the sorcerer's cheek as she rose.

"I've come for *him,* your majesty. This one's made promises and our lord expects those promises fulfilled."

"And I *will,*" Illidan returned strongly, staring back at the officer despite the scarf. Varo'then's eyes narrowed dangerously, but he nodded.

"Then, by all means," Azshara interjected, coming between the pair and glancing at both coyly. "I'm certain between the two of you that no *dragon* stands a chance! I very much look forward to hearing of your exploits—" She ran a hand across the captain's breast plate, causing his eyes to light up in lust. "—*both* of your exploits, that is!" the queen added, doing the same over Illidan's bare chest.

Despite knowing that she played games with the pair of them, the sorcerer could not help reacting slightly. Steeling himself against her wiles, he replied, "I will not disappoint you . . . Azshara."

His use of her name without any title before or after it—and the close familiarity such use hinted at—did not sit well with the soldier. Varo'then's hand slipped to the hilt of his sword, but he wisely let it pass without actually gripping the blade.

"We must first find the beast—which you claim you can do."

Illidan took hold of the dragon scale. "I make no claim; I speak the truth."

"Then, there is no need to wait. It is nearly nightfall."

Turning to the queen, Illidan executed the sort of bow he had witnessed in Black Rook Hold. "With your permission . . ."

She gave him a regal smile. "And you may go, too, dear captain."

"Most gracious, Light of Lights, Flower of the Moon . . ." Varo'then also bowed, his action crisp and military. He then indicated the doorway to Illidan. "After you, master sorcerer."

Without a word to the armored figure, Illidan marched out. He sensed Varo'then follow right behind him. It would not have surprised Malfurion's twin if the captain tried to knife him in the back, but Varo'then evidently had more control than that.

"Where do we go?" he asked his escort.

"You can do your casting once we're away from Zin-Azshari. Our Lord Sargeras wishes this mission to be finished as soon as possible. He itches to set his feet upon Azeroth's soil and give our world his blessing."

"Fortunate is Azeroth."

Varo'then eyed him for a moment, trying to find fault with his answer. Unable to do so, he finally nodded, "Aye, fortunate is Azeroth."

The captain led him through the palace, eventually descending. As they neared the stables, Illidan asked, "So you're to be my companion throughout all this?"

"You should have someone to watch your back."

"I'm gratified."

"Our great lord puts much stock into this notion of the disk fulfilling his needs. He will have it."

"I welcome your company," the sorcerer remarked. At that moment, however, they entered the stables. What Illidan saw there made him stop dead. "And what's this?"

A dozen Fel Guard stood waiting near the night sabers, their monstrous faces eager for bloodshed. Two Doomguard flanked them, clearly there to keep order on their wingless brethren. Another pair of Fel Guard kept tight rein over a slavering felbeast.

"As I've said," Captain Varo'then answered with possibly a hint of sarcasm. "You should have someone to watch your back. These . . ." He indicated the fiendish warriors. ". . . will watch you very carefully. Of that, I make my utmost promise, sorcerer."

Illidan nodded and said nothing.

"We will make haste, I promise you, Rhonin."

"Promise me nothing, Krasus," the human returned. "Just be careful. And don't worry about Stareye. I'll deal with him."

"He is the least of our worries. I trust you and the good Captain Shadowsong to keep the host together."

"Me?" Jarod shook his head. "Master Krasus, you've got much too much confidence in me! I'm a Guard officer, nothing more! It's as Maiev said, fortune smiled on me! I'm no more a commander than—than—"

"Than Stareye?" smirked Rhonin.

"I am afraid we must count on you, Jarod Shadowsong. The tauren and the others, they see the respect you give them and give it back in turn. There may come another time when, as you did earlier, you must make a decision to act. For the sake of your people, I might add."

The night elf's shoulders slumped in defeat. "I'll do what I can, Master Krasus. That's all I can say."

The mage nodded. "And that is all we ask of you, good captain."

"Now that we have that little matter settled," the human commented. "How do you plan to reach the lair?"

"The gryphons are no longer available to us. We shall have to take night sabers and urge them to their swiftest."

"But that'll take too long! Worse, it'll leave you more vulnerable to the Burning Legion's assassins!"

Archimonde had demons constantly shadowing the host, seeking to slay Krasus and his band. Malfurion had been especially marked by Archimonde after the druid's astounding reversal of certain Legion victory, but the dragon mage had no doubt that he was also high on the demon's list.

"A spell would be too risky a manner by which to travel to where Deathwing awaits," Krasus returned. "I have no doubt that he is on guard for such things. We must journey by physical means."

"I still don't like it."

"Nor do I, but it must be so." He looked to his companions for the trek. "Are you prepared to depart?"

Malfurion nodded. Brox replied with an impatient grunt. While it was true that between the druid and the mage they had exceptional abilities at their disposal, Krasus understood the need for the company of a skilled warrior such as the orc. Spellcasters could be incapacitated in many ways. Brox had also proven himself a trustworthy ally.

"Give us an hour before alerting Lord Stareye," Krasus reminded the human as he mounted.

"I'll give you two."

Seeing that the druid and the orc had also mounted, Krasus urged his beast forward. The graceful cat quickly picked up speed, the mounts of the mage's companions right behind. It did not take long for the animals to leave the night elven host far, far behind.

No one spoke as they rode, all three riders intent not only on the path ahead, but any sign of threat lurking around them. However, the night passed without any danger and they made good distance. When the sun began to rise, Krasus finally called for a halt.

"We rest here for a time," he decided, eyeing the sparsely-wooded hills ahead. "I would prefer to enter those when we are more recuperated."

"You think we might be in danger there?" asked Malfurion.

"Perhaps. While the woods are thin, the hills themselves offer many crevices and such for possible ambushes."

Brox nodded his agreement. "Would use hill to north for that. Best view of path. We should avoid that one when riding."

"And with that expert opinion, I agree." The mage looked around. "This area here by these two tall rocks is best-suited for our camp, I think. We shall have a good view of the surroundings while giving ourselves some protection."

They tethered the night sabers to a crooked tree nearby. Bred for generations, the cats obeyed every command immediately and without argument. Brox volunteered to feed the animals from the supplies they had brought with them. There would be enough for three days, but after that they would have to let the cats hunt. Krasus hoped that by then the party would be in a better location, wildlife clearly sparse here.

The trio ate from their own rations. To a dragon like Krasus, eating salted, dried meat was hardly satisfying, but he had long ago steeled himself to such necessities. Malfurion ate some fruit—also dried—and nuts, while Brox ate the same as Krasus, albeit with more gusto. Orcs were not discriminating when it came to food.

"The cats are already at rest," Krasus declared after their meal. "I suggest we do the same."

"I take first watch," Brox offered.

With Malfurion volunteering for the second, the matter of security was quickly settled. Krasus and the druid found places to rest near the taller of the two stones. Brox, proving more agile than his frame suggested, easily climbed up to the top of the steeper rock and sat. Ax resting in his lap, he surveyed the landscape like a hungry carrion bird.

Despite intending to only allow himself to doze, the dragon mage fell deep asleep. He had pushed himself far beyond his limits. What little rest he had gotten earlier was not enough to make up for so much strain.

Dragons dream and Krasus was no exception. For him, it was the everpresent desire to fly free again, to spread the wings he did not have and take to the air. Here, he was once more Korialstrasz. A creature of the sky, he chafed at being bound to the earth. The dragon had always been comfortable in his mortal form, but that had been when he had understood that with a single thought he could transform to his true self. With that taken from him, he often found himself frustrated with the frailty of his present shape.

And in his dream, that curse suddenly took hold, the weaker mortal flesh binding to his body, squeezing him into a smaller and smaller shape. His wings were crushed into his back and his tail severed. His long, toothy maw was shoved into his skull, replaced by the insignificant little nub of a nose he wore in the guise of a spellcaster. Korialstrasz became again Krasus, who plunged earthward—

And who woke up bathed in sweat.

Krasus half expected to discover that the party was under some attack, but the day was silent save for Malfurion's rhythmic breathing. He rose and saw that Brox continued vigilant watch. The mage gazed at the sun, estimating the time. Brox had gone long past his appointed watch. It was nearly Krasus's turn.

Leaving the druid to sleep, the slim, robed figure grabbed hold of the rock and quickly scurried up in the fashion of a lizard. As he reached the top, Brox leapt to his feet and, with reflexes worthy of the dragon, readied his ax.

"You," the orc grunted, helping him up. Both sat atop the rock, watching while they talked. "Thought you asleep, Master Krasus."

"As *you* should be, Brox. You need rest as much as either of us."

The green-skinned warrior shrugged. "An orc warrior can sleep with eyes open and weapon ready. No need to wake the night elf. He must sleep more. Against the dragon, he'll be more use than this old fighter."

Krasus eyed the orc. "An old fighter worth twenty young ones."

The veteran warrior looked pleased with the compliment, but said, "The day of glory is past for this one. There will be no more tales of Broxigar the Red Ax."

"I have lived longer than you, Brox; I know, therefore, of what I speak. There is much glory left in you, much heroic battle. New tales of Broxigar the Red Ax are still to come, even if I must tell them myself."

The orc's cheek's darkened and he suddenly bowed his head low. "Honored by your words I am, venerable one."

Like Malfurion, Brox had learned the truth concerning Krasus's identity. To the dragon's own surprise, the tusked warrior had already long known. As an orc who had learned some of the shamanistic traditions, Brox had sensed the incredible power and age of his companion and, watching Krasus deal with dragons, had come to the logical conclusion that so escaped most others. That Krasus and the red dragon Korialstrasz were one and the same had been beyond him, but even that the orc had accepted with but a mild furrowing of his brow.

"And speaking as a 'venerable one'," Krasus returned. "I will insist that you go and take your turn in slumber. I will watch for the rest of Malfurion's time—however little left there is—and then my own."

"Would be better if you—"

Krasus stared into the orc's eyes. "I assure you, my stamina is far greater than yours. I need no more sleep."

Seeing that he would lose any further argument, Brox grunted and rose. But as he did, Krasus, glancing past the hulking warrior, stiffened.

"Doomguard . . ." he whispered.

Brox immediately dropped flat. They watched as three fiery-winged demons slowly headed toward the hills. The demons were armed with long, wicked blades. The Doomguard watched the vicinity with equal wariness, but clearly had not noticed the party so far.

"They're heading toward where we must pass," Krasus realized.

"Should stop them now."

The mage nodded agreement, but added, "We need to know if there are more. We dare not take these three if it means giving warning to others in the area. Let me try to discover the truth, first."

Shutting his eyes, Krasus let his senses spread out toward the demons. Immediately he felt the darkness radiating from each, a darkness so repulsive that even the dragon was affected. Nonetheless, Krasus did not hesitate to delve deeper. The truth had to be known.

He saw within each the savageness and chaos that he had felt during previous incursions. That such evil could exist in any creature the mage still found hard to believe. It was a madness of sorts on par with that which had taken the once noble Neltharion and had created of him the foul Deathwing.

In the monstrous thoughts of the creatures he finally found what he needed to know. The three were scouts out on their own, seeking places of weakness of which the Legion might make use. They intended to not just confine the war to the battlefield, but also create fear behind the defenders.

Such tactics did not at all surprise Krasus. He was certain that Archimonde already had other plans in motion, which was why the quest to seize the Demon Soul was so important.

He scanned the area for other warriors, but found no trace. Satisfied Krasus ceased his probing.

"They are alone," he announced to Brox. "We will deal with them, but I think it best done with magic, this time."

The orc grunted in satisfaction. Krasus slipped down to wake Malfurion.

"What—" the night elf began. Krasus signaled him to silence.

"Three of the Doomguard," the elder mage whispered. "They are alone. I intend to take them, with your help."

Malfurion nodded. He followed Krasus around the stones to where they could see the hovering demons inspecting the hills.

"What should we do?" the druid asked.

"It would be best if I struck down all three simultaneously. However, their constant maneuvering means I might miscalculate. I leave it to you to deal with any who escapes me."

"All right." Taking a deep breath, Malfurion prepared. Krasus watched the Doomguard, waiting for the moment when they were nearest to one another.

Two of the demons paused to relate information to one another, but the third continued his observations. The mage silently swore, aware that he now had the best opportunity to destroy the pair. Yet, the third was so far away, Krasus feared that his attack would enable that one to flee.

Malfurion must have sensed his hesitation. "I won't let him escape, Master Krasus."

His words brought the mage much relief. Krasus nodded, concentrating.

Unlike Illidan—and even Rhonin at times—he had lived too long to waste effort creating elaborate displays out of his spellwork. The Doomguard were a threat and had to be dealt with. That was all. Thus it was that first one, then the other winged demon just *exploded,* their remnants quickly raining down on the landscape.

But as he had feared, the third escaped his trap. However, the demon's reprieve proved short-lived. As what was left of the first two creatures plummeted, Malfurion held up a single leaf and muttered to the wind. An intense breeze suddenly arose near the druid, a breeze that quickly took up the single leaf and carried it unerringly toward the remaining Doomguard.

The leaf suddenly became many leaves, hundreds of them. They whirled around in the wind, spinning faster and faster. They closed on the already-fleeing demon.

As each touched the Doomguard, they adhered to him. Scores and scores soon clung tightly to the demon, yet the numbers still swirling about looked no less. The horned warrior fought against the wind, but the ever-increasing weight upon him made his efforts falter.

In but seconds, the demon became a mummy wrapped in green. The wings slowed, unable to battle against that which so weighed them down.

Finally, the last of the Doomguard dropped like a rock.

Malfurion did not watch the demon strike the hard ground. He had done what had needed to be done, but never savored it.

"The way is clear," proclaimed Krasus. "But we must hurry, for it will take long to traverse the hills—"

From atop the rock, Brox suddenly called, "Something else in the sky! Above us!"

And mere seconds later, a shadow briefly covered them . . . a shadow sweeping over the entire area. The winged form moved so fast that it was lost among the clouds before any could identify it. The orc held his ax ready, while Krasus and Malfurion prepared spells.

Then the gargantuan form burst into the open again, diving directly for the trio. Its huge, leathery wings beat easily as it descended.

Krasus exhaled, his generally-somber expression breaking into a brief grin. "I should have known! I should have felt it!"

Korialstrasz had returned.

The mage's younger self landed just before the trio. The red dragon was magnificent to behold. His crest ran all the way to his tail. He was large enough to have swallowed the trio in one gulp, yet, despite his toothy maw, one had only to look into his eyes to see his intelligence and compassion.

Perhaps it was a bit narcissistic of Krasus to admire his earlier incarnation, but he could not help it. Korialstrasz had proven himself much more adept than the elder version ever remembered being. It was as if that they were two distinct creatures despite being one and the same.

Letting the dust settle, Korialstrasz greeted the three with a nod of his huge head. His eyes focused most on Krasus.

"A stroke of luck that I sensed some spellwork as I passed near," he rumbled. "My thoughts have been so caught up in other matters, I otherwise would not have noted your presence." To the mage, he added, "Not even yours."

That did not bode well. "You speak of your search for the others?"

"Yes . . . and I found them. They are seeking some manner by which to evade or deal with the Earth Warder's foul disk, but have not come up with any answer as of yet. Even my queen dares not face Neltharion unless they have some defense. You saw what happened to the blues! Slaughtered to extinction!"

Krasus thought of the eggs he had salvaged, but decided that this was not the time to deal with that matter. "Alexstrasza's concern has merit. There is no honor or purpose in flying out to simply be destroyed."

"But if we dragons do not aid the mortal races, there will be no hope for any of us!"

"There may be hope, though. You have not asked why we are to be found here." Krasus indicated the druid. "Young Malfurion has located the Earth Warder's hidden lair and knows where the Demon Soul is."

The crimson giant's reptilian eyes widened. "This is true? Perhaps an all-out assault while he slumbers—"

"Nay! This must be done with secrecy, cunning. We hope to slip in and steal the disk. Otherwise, Neltharion may take it first and then we are all dead."

Korialstrasz saw the wisdom of this, despite the perils inherent in the plan. "Where must you go?"

Malfurion described what he had seen in the Emerald Dream. Krasus had vaguely recognized the region and so it came as no surprise that his younger self did, also.

"I know it! A foul place! There is an evil there older than dragons, although what it might be I cannot say!"

"That is of no consequence at the moment. Only the Demon Soul is." The tall, pale figure eyed the hills. "And if we hope to even have an opportunity to steal it, we had best begin our journey. It will take the night sabers some time to traverse those hills."

"The night sabers?" Korialstrasz looked bewildered. "Why should you need them now that you have *me*?"

"You face the greatest risk of all," Krasus pointed out to the dragon. "You cannot change shape; therefore you remain a very visible target. More to the point, you are very susceptible to the Demon Soul. With one whim, the black could make you his slave."

"Nevertheless, I will do what I can. You need to reach his lair in a timely manner. The cats are not swift enough and you dare not attempt it by spell."

Arguing with oneself was pointless, Krasus saw. Korialstrasz would indeed enable them to reach their goal much sooner. However, once there, Krasus would insist that his younger version leave and leave quickly.

"Very well. Brox, prepare to turn the night sabers out. I will prepare a short missive for mine to carry. They will return to the host on their own and, hopefully, Rhonin will receive my word of our progress. Take what we can carry. No more."

It did not take them long to shift their belongings to the massive red. After the mage had secured the message to his cat, they sent the animals away. Krasus and his companions then mounted near the dragon's shoulders. Once they were all aboard, Korialstrasz shifted back and forth to make certain that his passengers were secure, then spread his wings.

"I will make haste . . . but with care," he promised them.

As they rose into the sky, Krasus grimly eyed the landscape ahead. Korialstrasz was a boon to them, but the success of their quest was in no manner assured now. Neltharion—Deathwing—would be on the watch for enemies, imagined or otherwise. The party would have to watch their every step once they reached his domain. Still, at least there was one thing in their favor.

So close to the dread one's lair, they certainly would not have to worry about any more demons.

SIX

Lord Desdel Stareye had a wonderful plan.

That was how he stated it to all concerned. He had designed it all himself, so it was foolproof. Most of his fellow nobles nodded eagerly and cheered him with goblets of wine held high while the rest simply kept their peace. The soldiers on the lines were too weary to worry and the refugees only cared about surviving. The few critics Stareye might have had now numbered but a handful, Rhonin chief among them. Unfortunately, the constant departures of Krasus had made even the commander's healthy fear of the outsiders dwindle. The moment it had even appeared that the human had been about to find fault with the grand design, Stareye had politely suggested that the council could manage its own efforts and that the wizard had other duties to which he should be attending. He had also doubled the guards in the tent, making it clear that, should Rhonin refuse his suggestion, they would act.

Not desiring a confrontation that would only threaten the stability of the host, Rhonin abandoned the tent. Jarod met him near where the tauren camped, Huln walking with the officer.

The night elf read his expression. "Something bad . . ."

"Maybe . . . or maybe I've just become too cynical where that pampered aristocrat is concerned. The overview of his plan sounds too simple to work . . ."

"Simple can be good," offered Huln, "if it is drawn from reason."

"Somehow, I doubt Stareye has reason. I don't understand why Ravencrest and he got along so well."

Jarod shrugged. "They are of the same caste."

"Oh, it all makes so much sense, then." When the night elf failed to note his sarcasm, Rhonin shook his head. "Never mind. We'll just have to watch out and hope for the best . . ."

They did not have to wait long. Stareye set his plan into motion before the sun set. The night elves redistributed their forces, creating three wedges. Following their lead, the tauren and other races did the same. The noble pulled back much of his cavalry, sending them around to the left flank. There they waited a short distance from the main host.

The front of each wedge was made up of pikes, followed by swords and other hand weapons. Behind those and protected from all angles were archers. Each wedge also included evenly-distributed members of the Moon Guard. The sorcerers were there to protect against the Eredar and other magic wielders.

The wedges were to drive forward as hard as they could, cutting into the Burning Legion's lines like teeth. Those demons caught between the wedges were to be the focus of the archers and sword wielders. The night elves were to move in concert, no wedge outreaching another. The cavalry were held in reserve to cover any weak points that developed.

There was some skepticism among the Earthen and the tauren, but, having no experience with large-scale military strategy themselves, they bowed to what they assumed was the night elves' superior knowledge.

Jarod rode beside Rhonin as the host moved forward. The demons had been uncommonly hesitant, an action that Stareye took as a good omen, but that the other two believed meant a need for more caution.

"I've talked to the Moon Guard," the wizard informed his companion. "We've a few tricks in mind that may make certain his lordship's plan comes to fruition. I'll be coordinating them."

"Huln promises that there will be no weakening from the tauren and I *think* the furbolg indicated something of the same," the captain replied. "I worry, though, if Dungard Ironcutter's people are enough to hold his part of the line."

"If they fight anything like a dwarf I know called Falstad did," commented Rhonin, thinking back, "they'll be the least of our problems."

At that moment, the battle horns sounded. The soldiers ahead immediately steeled themselves, increasing their pace.

"Be ready!" shouted the wizard, his cat picking up the pace.

"I wish I was back in Suramar before all this . . ."

The landscape ahead sloped downward, finally giving them a clear view of what lay ahead.

A sea of demons stretched all the way back to the horizon.

"Mother Moon!" Jarod gasped.

"Keep a grip on yourself!"

A trumpeter signaled the attack. With a lusty cry, the night elves started running. Deep roars from the right marked the tauren and furbolgs. A curious, wailing blast noted the Earthen's advance.

The battle was joined.

The Legion's front line almost immediately buckled under the intense assault. The wedges drove right into the demons. Scores of horned warriors fell to the pikes.

Jarod grew excited. "We're doing it!"

"We've got momentum, but it'll slow!"

Sure enough, after several yards in, the Burning Legion began to get its bearings. They did not completely stop the onslaught, but every new foot was bought slowly, painfully.

And yet, the night elves did continue to move forward.

That was not to say that there were not dangers or bad losses even in the beginning. A few Doomguard fluttered overhead, trying to get past the pikes and strike the archers. Some were brought down by their very targets, but others managed to keep aloft over the defenders. Armed with long maces and other weapons, they dove down, smashing skulls or gutting night elves occupied with other shots. However, under the onslaught of the archers and Moon Guard, they soon retreated.

At another point, the demon lines opened up to unleash a pair of Infernals against the wedge there. The soldiers attempting to block them were crushed and the wedge blunted, almost inverting. One Infernal was brought down by the Moon Guard, albeit not before several archers had perished. The other continued to wreak havoc among the night elves even after they managed to seal the break behind him.

Rhonin tried to focus on the lone demon, but there were too many soldiers around the creature. Every time the wizard thought that he could cast a spell, he took a risk of slaying several night elves.

From nowhere came three of the Earthen. The dwarves barreled their way through the ranks until they came upon the Infernal. Each of the squat but muscular figures carried war hammers with huge, steel heads.

The Infernal made a lunge, but missed. One dwarf slipped under and battered the stone monster's legs. Another came at the demon from the side. The Infernal managed a back-handed slap at his second attacker, but what would have killed a night elf, shattering his bones in the process, only shook the Earthen for a moment. The Infernal had finally come up against creatures with as hard a skin as his.

Now all three dwarves brought their hammers into play. Wherever they struck the demon, the heavy weapons left cracks and fissures. The left leg collapsed, forcing the Infernal down on one knee.

And the last Rhonin saw of the demon was all three Earthen bringing their hammers down on his head.

The wizard noticed Jarod Shadowsong riding back to him. Rhonin had not even known that the captain had disappeared. "Did you summon them?"

"I thought that they might have a better chance!"

Rhonin nodded his approval, then surveyed the battle again. Recovering from their brief setback, the host was once more pushing the Burning Legion back. The demons maintained a defiant look despite their forced retreat, but everything they did only briefly halted the night elves' determined progress.

"The damned thing's working after all," muttered the spellcaster. "Looks like I've underestimated his lordship."

"A good thing, Master Rhonin! I shudder to think what might've happened if it had failed!"

"There is that—" Rhonin let out a howl as an intense force seemed to try to crush his very brain. He tumbled off his mount before Jarod could grab him, striking the ground hard enough to jar his bones. Leaping down after him, the night elf tried to help the wizard rise.

Horrific pounding filled Rhonin's head. The sounds of battle faded in the background. Through bleary eyes, he saw Jarod speaking, but no voice reached him.

Harder and harder the pounding grew. Through his agony, Rhonin understood that he had been attacked by some spell, yet this one had hit with more stealth than any in the past. Briefly the wizard thought of the Nathrezim, whose power had animated the dead, yet this did not feel like their work.

The agony became overwhelming. Rhonin struggled against the crushing sensation, but already knew that he was losing. He was near to blacking out and, if that happened, he feared he would never wake again.

In the midst of the attack, an emotionless voice echoed in his thoughts, *You cannot stand against me, mortal.*

The wizard needed no one to tell him who spoke. As Rhonin's strength at last failed and the blackness took him, the demon's name echoed through his fading senses.

Archimonde . . .

Jarod Shadowsong quickly dragged the still body back behind the lines. The night elf frantically studied Rhonin for some wound, but found nothing. The human was completely untouched, at least on the outside.

"Sorcery," he muttered. Jarod grimaced. A person of little talent in that direction, he had a healthy respect for spellcasters. Anything that could affect Rhonin had clearly originated from a powerful source. To him, that meant only the most powerful of the demons they so far faced, the one called Archimonde.

The fact that Archimonde had found the opportunity to seek out the wizard disturbed the captain very much. Archimonde should have been frantically busy trying to keep order among his retreating forces. Everywhere Jarod had looked, the Burning Legion had been close to crumbling. Lord Stareye's plan had proven a grand success—

The night elf's eyes widened.

Or *had* it?

Brox held on as tight as the others as Korialstrasz flew them toward their destination. The orc had lived in the time when the red dragons had been ruled by his people, but he had never flown on one himself. Now he reveled in the sensation and for the first time truly sympathized with the dragons who had been enslaved. To be so free, to live in the skies, only to be forced to die like dogs for the will of another . . . it was a fate to make any orc shudder. In fact, Brox felt some kinship with the dragons, for, in truth, his people had been slaves of a sort also, their most basic instincts twisted into something grotesque by a demon of the Burning Legion.

Once, Brox had simply wanted to die. Now, he was willing to face death, but death with purpose. He fought not just to defend his people in the far-off future, but to defend all whom the demons sought to crush. The spirits would decide if his life needed to be sacrificed, but Brox hoped that they would wait long enough for him to strike a few more decisive blows . . . and, especially, see that this quest was fulfilled.

The hills gave way to mountains, which at first reminded him of those near his home. However, the mountains soon changed and with them changed something in the air. The landscape turned desolate, as if life was afraid or unwilling to be in this place. Korialstrasz had mentioned an ancient evil and the orc, perhaps more attune to the world than most, felt that evil permeate everything. It was a foulness worse than that spread by the demons and made him want to reach for the ax strapped to his back.

The dragon suddenly descended between a pair of dank, sharp peaks. Korialstrasz effortlessly glided through the narrow valleys, seeking a proper landing place.

He finally landed in the shadow of a particularly sinister mountain, one that reminded Brox of a monstrous warrior raising a heavy club for a strike. The harsh upper edge of the peak added to the already-prevalent feeling of being watched by dark powers.

"This is as close as I dare fly," the dragon informed his passengers as they dismounted. "But I will still follow along for a time."

"We aren't far," Malfurion commented. "I remember this area."

Krasus eyed the same peak that had so caught the orc's attention. "How could one not? A very appropriate abode for Deathwing."

"You've said that name before," the druid said. "And Rhonin, too."

"It is how we know the Earth Warder where we come from. His madness is well documented, is it not so, Brox?"

The veteran warrior grunted agreement. "My people also call him *Blood's Shadow* . . . but, yes, Deathwing is known to all living creatures, much to their dismay."

Malfurion shuddered. "How do we avoid being noticed? I only escaped detection because of what Cenarius had taught me, but we can't all journey to the Emerald Dream."

"Nor would there be any point," replied Krasus. "We could not touch the Demon Soul from that plane. We must be in this one. I know him best. I should be able to guard us from any warning spells. However, that will mean it will be up to you and Brox to do the rest."

"I'm willing."

"I, too." The orc hefted the magical ax. "I will cleave the black one's head from his neck if I must."

The mage chuckled, if briefly. "And there would be song to sing, would there not?"

At first, Korialstrasz led the way, the dragon making the finest defense of all, even in Brox's eyes. However, before long, the path grew narrower, until finally it was all the leviathan could do to squeeze through.

"You shall have to remain here," Krasus decided.

"I can climb up and around the mountains—"

"We are too close. Even if we manage to avoid the spells, I would not put it past Deathwing to post sentinels. They would see you."

Against this logic, the dragon could not argue. "I await you, here, then. You have but to summon me at your need." His reptilian eyes narrowed. "Even if it is to face *him*."

At first, the loss of Korialstrasz made a marked difference in the mood of the party. The trio moved on with more care, watching every corner and shadow. Malfurion pointed out more and more landmarks, indicating just how near they had come to their goal. Brox, who now led the way, stared at every rock in their path, determining whether or not it hid some foe.

Day gave way to night and although now Malfurion could see better, they paused to sleep. The druid felt certain that they were nearly at the lair, which made rest an anxious time even for Brox.

As the orc settled in for first watch, Krasus admonished him. "We take our turns fairly, this time. We will need all of us at our peak of strength."

Reluctantly agreeing, the graying orc hunkered down. His sharp ears soon registered the even breathing of his companions, a sign that slumber had quickly taken them. He also registered other sounds, although few in comparison to most places he had visited during his hard life. This was truly an empty land. The wind wailed and now and then bits of rock crumbled free from some mountainside, but, beyond that, there was almost nothing.

In that stillness, Brox began to relive the last days of his first war against the demons. He saw his comrades cheerfully speaking of the carnage they would cause, of the enemy who would fall to their axes. Many of them had expected to die, but what a death it would be.

No one had expected the events that followed.

For long after, Brox had believed that he was haunted by his dead companions. Now, though, the aging fighter knew that they did not condemn him, but rather stood at his side, guiding his arm. They lived through him, every enemy dead another honoring their memories. Someday, it would be Brox who fell, but, until then he was their champion.

That knowledge made him proud.

Long used to such tasks as he performed now, Brox knew exactly how much time passed. Already half his watch was over. He contemplated letting the others sleep, but was aware of Krasus's warning. For all the orc's experience, he was an infant compared to the mage. Brox would obey . . . this time.

Then, a sound that was not the wind caught his attention. He focused on it, his expression hardening as he recognized what it was. Chattering, high-pitched voices. They were far away, only a chance shifting of the wind enabling him to hear them. The orc quickly straightened, trying to identify exactly where the speakers were.

At last, Brox eyed a small side passage some hundred paces or so to the north. The voices had to come from somewhere farther in. With the silence of a skilled hunter, he left his post to investigate. There was no need as of yet to wake his companions. In this unsettling place, it was still possible that what he heard was only an effect of the wind blowing through the ancient mountains.

As he neared the passage, the chattering ceased. The orc immediately paused, waiting. After a moment, the talk continued. Brox finally had a fair notion of just what he was listening to and that only made him more cautious as he continued on.

With practiced ears, the orc tried to count the speakers. Three, four at the most. Better than that, he could not say.

Other sounds assailed him. Digging. There would be no dwarves here.

Brox crept up slowly and silently to where the unknown party had to lurk. Clearly, whoever they were, they did not expect others in the region, which gave him a distinct advantage.

A small light illuminated the area just ahead. Brox peered around a bend . . . and beheld the goblins.

Compared to an orc, they were tiny, bony creatures with big heads. Other than their sharp teeth and small, pointed nails, there was little about them that seemed any threat. However, Brox understood just how dangerous goblins could be, especially when there was more than one. They were cunning and quick, their wiry frames able to dart past a larger opponent with ease. One could not trust a goblin to do no harm unless that goblin was dead.

Malfurion had mentioned goblins—scores of goblins—working on something for the black dragon. They had even apparently been integral in Deathwing's creation of the Demon Soul. Brox could only assume that these were a part of that group, but, if so, what were they doing out here?

"More, more!" muttered one. "Not enough for another plate!"

"The vein's tapped out!" snapped a companion who was almost identical to the first. To a third, he argued, "Gotta find another, another!"

The digging came from a small tunnel in the nearest mountain. The goblin version of a mine. Even as Brox watched, a fourth creature joined the others. In one hand, he held a covered oil lamp and behind him the newcomer dragged a sack almost as large as his body. Goblins were small but extremely strong for their size.

Unlike the others, he seemed in a good mood. "Found another small vein! More iron!"

The rest brightened. "Good!" said the first. "No time to go hunting! Let the others do it!"

Brox's first instinct was to go charging in, but he knew that was not what Krasus would want. The orc eyed the goblins. They looked as if they would be busy for some time. He could return to the mage and tell him what he had found. Krasus would know the right thing to do, be it capture the goblins or avoid them completely—

A heavy force battered him on the back of the skull, sending the orc to his knees. Something landed on his back, clutching his throat. Again, Brox was struck hard on the back of his head.

"Intruder! Help! Intruder!"

The high-pitched voice cut through the fog of his pain. Another goblin had come up from behind. Goblin fists were not that large, so Brox could only assume that he had been hit with either a hammer or a rock.

The orc attempted to rise, but the goblin continued to pound at him. Blood trickled down Brox's head to his mouth. The taste of his own life fluids stirred the warrior to urgency. Still kneeling, he rolled over.

There was a squawk and then the heavy orc landed on something that squirmed. The beating finally halted. Brox continued rolling and felt the goblin lose the last of his grip.

As he pushed himself up, the warrior heard other goblin voices near him.

What he assumed was another rock hit his shoulder hard. Brox heard metal drawn and knew that the goblins had knives.

He blindly reached for his ax, but could not find it. Before the orc could clear his sight, a shrieking figure leapt on his chest, almost throwing him back. With arm and legs, the goblin clutched him tight while trying to bury a blade in his eye.

As Brox battled to keep the knife from him, a second attacker landed on his shoulder. The orc grunted as a blade edged his ear. Managing to reach up, Brox tore the creature from his shoulder and threw him as far as possible. As the goblin's scream trailed off, the fighter sought again to pull the one away from his chest.

He almost had it done when both his legs were seized. Brox raised one foot, bringing it down hard. With immense satisfaction, the orc heard bone crunch. The grip on that leg ceased. Unfortunately, when he repeated the maneuver with the other, the goblin there shifted position while still holding tight.

The one on his chest managed to sink his knife into Brox's shoulder. The fiendish creature giggled as he raised the weapon.

Enraged, the orc swung a meaty fist, hitting the goblin square in the side of the head. The giggle cut off, replaced by a short gurgle before the goblin went tumbling away.

But, again, Brox received no reprieve. A new attacker crashed into his stomach, driving the air from his lungs. Brox fell back. The only benefit to his disaster was marked by a squeal from the goblin on his leg. Half-crushed by the weight of the warrior's limb, the creature lost his hold.

A second goblin leapt atop the fallen orc, beating at him with a rock. This was hardly the noble death in battle Brox had imagined for himself. He did not recall any orc in any of the great epics being brought down by goblins.

Then the pair on his chest shrieked as a red light threw them across the area. One collided with another goblin, ending in a tangle of limbs, while the second smashed hard against the rocks.

"Make certain that we have them all!" the orc heard Krasus demand.

Shaking his head, Brox managed to focus in time to see the two tangled goblins suddenly sink into the once solid ground. Their cries were cut off the moment their heads vanished beneath.

Another of the creatures, either smarter or more arrogant than the rest, threw a rock with unerring aim at the side of the mage's head. Already aware that it was too late, Brox still opened his mouth to warn Krasus—and watched the rock not only not strike the slim figure, but bounce back with such velocity that when it hit the goblin, it cracked his skull.

The hair on the back of the orc's neck rose. Reacting instinctively, Brox swung behind him. The goblin about to stab him in the back tumbled to the earth.

Krasus remained fixed, eyes now shut tight. Brox gingerly got to his feet, trying not to make any sound that would disturb the spellcaster.

"None escaped . . ." Krasus murmured after a moment. His eyes opened and he studied the carnage. "We caught them all."

Locating his ax, the orc bowed his head in regret. "Forgive me, elder one. I acted like an untrained child."

"It is over, Brox . . . and you may have given us a shortcut to our destination." His hand glowing, Krasus touched the warrior lightly on the shoulder, healing Brox's wounds as if they were nothing.

Relieved that he had not entirely shamed himself, Brox looked at the mage in curiosity. Malfurion, too, eyed Krasus, but with more understanding.

"They know how best to reach the dragon's lair," Krasus explained, hand glowing again. "They can show us the way."

Brox gazed around. Of the goblins he could see, all appeared dead. Then he saw the one who had struck the rocks rise awkwardly. At first, the weary orc wondered how the creature had survived such an impact—and realized swiftly that he had not.

"We are the servants of Life," Krasus whispered with clear distaste, "which means we know Death equally well."

"By the Mother Moon . . ." Malfurion gasped.

Muttering a prayer to the spirits, Brox stared at the animated corpse. It reminded him too much of the Scourge. Without realizing it, he kept his ax tight in case the goblin should attack.

"Rest easy, my friends. I am only resurrecting the memories of his path. He will walk it, then that will be the end of the matter. I am no Nathrezim, to relish in the binding of corpses to do my will." He gestured at the dead goblin, who, after performing a haphazard turn, began shambling north. "Now, come! Let us be done with this distasteful business and prepare ourselves for entrance into the sanctum of the dark one . . ."

Krasus calmly walked behind his macabre puppet. After a moment, Malfurion followed. Brox hesitated, then, recalling the evil that they all faced, nodded approval at the mage's necessary course of action and joined the others.

SEVEN

Archimonde watched his warriors forced back on all fronts. He watched as they died by the dozens on the blades of the defenders or ripped apart by the night elves' feline mounts. He noted the scores more perishing under the brute force of the other creatures who had allied themselves with the host.

Archimonde watched it all . . . and smiled. They were without the wizard, without the druid and the mage . . . even without the brawny, green-skinned fighter whose base fury the demon found admirable.

"It is time . . ." he hissed to himself.

Jarod continued to try to wake Rhonin, but the wizard would not respond. The only response that the human had given thus far had been to open his eyes, but they were eyes that did not see, did not even hint of a mind behind them.

But still he tried. "Master Rhonin! You must stir! Something's amiss, I know it!" The captain sprinkled water over the red-haired spellcaster's face. It trickled off with no effect. "The demon lord's up to something!"

Then, a peculiar noise caught his attention. It reminded Jarod of when he had used to watch flocks of birds landing in the trees. The fluttering of many wings echoed in his ears.

He looked up.

The sky was filled with Doomguard.

"Mother Moon . . ."

Each of the flying demons carried a burden in their arms, a heavy pot from which smoke trailed. The pots were far larger and heavier than any night elf could have borne and even the Doomguard appeared hardpressed to keep them, but keep them they did.

Jarod Shadowsong studied the swarm, watching how they flew as hard as they could for the defenders' lines . . . and then went beyond. Below, it was doubtful that many even noticed them, so ferocious was the fighting. Even Lord Stareye likely saw only the dying demons before him.

The noble had to be warned. It was the only thing that made sense to Jarod. There was no one else. Krasus was gone.

Seizing Rhonin's body, the captain dragged it over to a large rock. He positioned the wizard on the opposing side, away from the view of the battlefield. Hopefully, no one would see the robed figure there.

"Please . . . please forgive me," the soldier asked the unmoving form.

Jarod leapt onto his mount and headed for where he had last seen the noble's banner. But just as he left the area where he had secreted Rhonin, the foremost of the Doomguard suddenly hovered over the night elves. The captain saw the first one tip over his pot.

A boiling, red liquid poured down on the unsuspecting soldiers.

Their screams were awful. Most of those upon whom the deadly rain had fallen dropped writhing. From the single pot, nearly a score of night elves had been burned and maimed, some mortally.

And then the other winged demons began turning over their own containers.

"No . . ." he gasped. "No!"

A deluge of death washed over the defenders.

Rank upon rank of soldiers broke into utter chaos as each fought to protect themselves from the horror. They had stood up to blades and claws—dangers that could be battled with a weapon—but against the scalding horror unleashed by the Doomguard, there was nothing to be done.

The cries ringing in his head, Jarod urged his mount to its swiftest. He sighted Stareye's banner, then, after a few tense moments, the noble himself.

What Jarod saw gave him no heart. The slim night elf sat atop his cat, his expression aghast. Desdel Stareye sat as if dead in the saddle. He watched the destruction of his grand plan with no obvious intention of doing anything to try to salvage the situation. Around him, his staff and guards stared helplessly at their commander. Jarod read no hope in their faces.

Managing to maneuver his night saber closer, the captain pushed past stunned guards and a noble with shaking hands to reach the commander. "My lord! My lord! Do something! We need to bring down those demons!"

"It's too late, too late!" babbled Stareye, not looking at him. "We're all doomed! It's the end of everything!"

"My lord—" Some inner sense caused Jarod to look skyward.

A pair of demons hovered above, their pots still filled.

Seizing the noble's arm, Jarod shouted, "Lord Stareye! Move! Quickly!"

The other night elf's expression hardened and he pulled his arm away in disdain. "Unhand me! You forget yourself, captain!"

Jarod stared incredulously at Stareye. "My lord—"

"Away with you before I have you clapped in irons!"

Knowing he could do nothing to convince the noble otherwise, Jarod reined hard, forcing his mount away.

It was all that saved him.

The torrent that washed over Stareye and the others seared flesh and melted metal. In its death throes, Stareye's night saber threw his sizzling body off. The noble landed in a monstrous heap, his arrogant features now a mangled horror nigh unrecognizable. His companions and guards fared little better; those that were not horridly slain lay twitching, their bodies ruined, their screams enough to chill the soul.

And Jarod could do nothing for them.

The Doomguard flew overhead all but untouched by the defenders. Sporadic fire from an archer here and there brought down a few, and some perished in manners that clearly had the touch of the Moon Guard on them, but there was no cohesive effort. Jarod found the lack of organization stunning, then recalled that Stareye had replaced all of his predecessor's officers with his own sycophants.

More incomprehensible, there were even some elements of the night elf forces not yet in play. They anxiously stood by, awaiting commands that would never be given. Jarod realized that they did not know that Lord Stareye was dead and likely thought the noble would be calling upon them at any moment.

He quickly rode up to one contingent. The officer in charge saluted him.

"How many bows do you have?" Jarod asked.

"Threescore, captain!"

Hardly enough, but at least a start. "Get every bow set! I want them trained on those Doomguard now! The rest create a defensive square for them!"

The other night elf gave the order. Jarod looked around desperately for something else to use. Instead, another rider came racing up to *him*. The newcomer saluted in a manner that indicated immediately that Jarod was the first thing resembling an officer that he had seen.

"The wedge is flattened, the line barely holding by us!" He pointed behind himself to a location near the middle. "Lord Del'theon is dead and we've only a subofficer in charge! He sent me to find out someone to strengthen us!"

By this time, the troops that Jarod had taken over had already arranged themselves. Even as the captain considered what to do about the new problem, he saw almost a dozen Doomguard drop from the sky. It gave him a slight hint of hope, at least.

To the newcomer, he finally suggested, "Ride to the tauren! Tell them Captain Shadowsong asks of the people of Huln for some warriors to come with you and strengthen the wedge!" Jarod recalled something else, "Ask also for their their best archers . . ."

When he had finished, the other night elf, his own expression slightly less distraught, rode off to obey. Jarod barely had time to refocus his thoughts before two more came. The captain could only guess that he had been seen organizing resistance and that someone had foolishly believed he spoke in the name of the dead Stareye.

But despite knowing better, Jarod could not simply turn them away. He listened to their needs and battled to find some solution, however temporary.

To his surprise, one of the Moon Guard arrived shortly after. Although clearly one of the senior spellcasters, the robed figure looked relieved to confront Captain Shadowsong.

"The archers are slowing the damage the winged fiends have been causing! We've been able to reorganize, though three of our number are dead and two more are incapacitated! We are trying to deal with those above and the warlocks in the distance, but to do so we'll need more protection!"

Jarod tried not to swallow. Hoping to avoid showing the sorcerer his uncertainty, he pretended to glance farther down the left flank. There he saw several rows of soldiers milling about as they tried to reach the oncoming demons. The press of bodies in front of them prevented those in back from being of any benefit and, in fact, often shoved the ones ahead into the blades of their foe.

He pulled one soldier from the square. "You! Ride with him over there and take a squad from those ranks! Tell the rest to keep back a step and shore up the front lines as needed!"

On and on the demands came. They never allowed Jarod to catch his breath. There came a point when even the Earthen and the other allies began requesting his assistance. Jarod, never able to find someone of greater authority, ever answered their questions and prayed that he had not sent innocent lives to the slaughter.

At any moment, the captain expected to see the horde overwhelm his people, but somehow, the night elves held. The combined efforts of the Moon Guard and archers at last proved too decimating for the winged demons and they fled back, many still with the pots full. The host's casualties had been high, but as matters quieted a little, Jarod hoped that something he had done had kept them from being higher yet.

When the captain finally had the opportunity to return to Rhonin, it was with half a dozen subordinates in tow. He had not asked for them; various officers in the host had insisted they stay with Jarod in case he needed to alert them to some need. The former Guard officer found their presence unsettling, for they treated him as if he were on par with either Ravencrest or Stareye. Jarod Shadowsong was no noble and certainly no commander; if the host had managed to recover from the near disaster, it was due mainly to the fighters themselves.

To his tremendous relief, the wizard was alive and untouched. Unfortunately, he still did not seem to see or hear anything despite looking as if awake.

Jarod tried once more to give him water, but to no avail. Frustrated, he turned to one of the soldiers and snapped, "Find me one of the senior Moon Guard! Hurry!"

Yet, it was not one of the sorcerers who came back with the rider, but rather a pair of figures clad in the armor of the Sisterhood of Elune. Worse, the senior priestess was none other than Maiev.

"When I was told that the officer in command needed a spellcaster, I never dreamed he was speaking of you, little brother!"

Captain Shadowsong had no time for his sister's dominant tone. "Spare me the wit, Maiev! The wizard's caught in some spell that I think one of the master demons cast! Can Elune help free him?"

She eyed him curiously for a moment, then knelt beside Rhonin. "I've never dealt with one of his kind, but I assume he's similar enough to us that the Mother Moon will grant me the chance. Jia, assist me. We shall see what we can do."

The second priestess stepped over to Rhonin's other side. The two raised hands to chest level with the palms out, then pressed their fingertips together. The moment the priestesses touched one another, a faint, silver glow arose from their hands. It quickly spread along their arms and around the rest of their bodies.

Maiev and her companion began chanting. Their words made no sense to Jarod, but he knew that the Sisterhood of Elune had a special language of their own that they used to commune with the lunar deity.

The glow surrounding the females flowed over the wizard. His body jerked slightly, then relaxed.

Another rider joined the group. "Where's the commander?"

Several of the past messengers had called Jarod by that very title despite his constant insistence that they do no such thing. Angered by the interruption at so delicate a time, he spun around and blurted, "You'll keep your mouth shut and wait until I tell you it's the right time to speak—"

The mounted figure's eyes widened. Only at that point did the captain see the gold and emerald trim on the shoulders or the emblem on the breast plate.

Jarod had insulted a noble.

But instead of taking offense, the rider nodded in apology and quieted. In an attempt to hide his shock, Jarod quickly turned back to watch his sister's work.

Maiev was sweating. The second priestess shook. Rhonin's body quivered and his already-pale flesh looked as white as the moon.

The wizard jolted to a sitting position. His mouth opened wide in a silent scream—and then, for the first time since being struck down, Rhonin blinked.

A groan escaped the human. He would have slumped back against the rock, possibly striking his head, but the captain acted, managing to thrust a hand in between.

With a sigh, the wizard closed his eyes. His breathing grew regular.

"Is he—?"

"He's free of the demon's hold, brother," Maiev replied somewhat shakily. "He will rest as long as he needs." She rose. "It was a hard struggle, but Elune was generous, praise be."

"Thank you."

Again, his sister eyed him with curiosity. "No thanks are necessary from *you* of all people. Come, Jia. There are many in need of healing."

Jarod followed Maiev's departure, then turned his attention back to the noble. "Forgive me, my lord, but—"

The rider waved off his words. "My troubles can wait. I failed to see that you sought aid for the foreign sorcerer. I am Lord Blackforest. I know you, don't I?"

"Jarod Shadowsong, my lord."

"Well, Commander Shadowsong, I, for one, am grateful you didn't perish along with Lord Stareye and the others. There were reports you tried to save him even in the end."

"My lord—"

Blackforest ignored his interruption. "I'm trying to gather some of the others. Stareye's strategy was clearly inept, may the Mother Moon forgive any slight toward the dead. We hope to come up with something better—if we're to survive. You'll want to be there, of course. To guide matters, I assume."

This time, Jarod could not speak. He nodded, more out of reflex than anything. The noble apparently took this as determined agreement and gratefully nodded back.

"With your permission, then, I'll have things arranged at my tent and begin gathering the rest." Blackforest nodded once more, then turned his mount around and rode off.

"Looks—looks like—you've come up in the world," a voice rasped.

He glanced down to see Rhonin conscious. The wizard still looked pale, but not so much as before. Jarod quickly bent down and gave him water from a sack. Rhonin eagerly drank.

"I'd feared that the spell had done damage to your mind. How fare you, Master Rhonin?"

"I feel as if a regiment of Infernals are battering my skull from the inside . . . and that's an improvement." The human sat up straight. "I gather there was trouble after I was struck down."

The captain told him, keeping it as brief as possible and downplaying his role. Despite that, however, the wizard looked at Jarod in obvious admiration.

"Looks like Krasus was right about you. You did more than save the day, this time. You likely saved the world, at least for the moment."

Cheeks darkening, the night elf vehemently shook his head. "I am no leader, Master Rhonin! All I did was try to survive."

"Well, nice of you to help the rest of us survive while you were at it. So, Stareye's dead. Sorry for him, not so sorry for the host. Glad to see some of the nobles have come to their senses. Maybe there's hope yet."

"Surely you don't think I'm going to meet with them?" Jarod had a vision of Blackforest and the others surrounding him, their eyes all staring. "I'm only a Guard officer from Suramar!"

"Not anymore . . ." The wizard tried to rise, finally signaling his companion to help him. As he straightened, Rhonin met Jarod's gaze. The human's unique eyes seized his. "Not anymore."

Korialstrasz had not yet learned the patience of his elder counterpart, Krasus, and so it was that he began to fidget. The red dragon knew well that it would be some time before the party would return—assuming that they *did* return— and although he tried to find peace during his wait, he could not. There were too many things running through his thoughts. Alexstrasza, the Burning Legion, the implications of Krasus's presence, and more. He also recalled too well the punishment he had taken at Neltharion's paws. Now his other self was fast approaching the sanctum of that fiend and there was more than a little concern that Krasus might fall prey to the Demon Soul.

In frustration, the red giant began scratching at the mountainside with one talon. Massive chunks of stone and earth that were no more than pebbles to the dragon dropped into the valley below. This, however, entertained Korialstrasz only for an hour. More agitated than ever, he started eyeing the dark sky and wondering if perhaps it was safe to take to the air for a few minutes.

A low roar echoed through the mountains.

All frustration thrust aside, a now alert Korialstrasz slipped down from his perch, planting his huge body on the side of the peak. He peered up, seeking the source of the sound.

A dark form slowly flew overhead. A small black dragon. The pace at which the other leviathan flew marked him as a sentinel.

Korialstrasz quietly hissed. Had the other simply been flying off somewhere, there would have been no cause for worry. However, that the black prowled this particular region meant danger to the plan.

Yet, he was crossed up as to whether he should remain hidden or seek out the guardian. If the others had not been noticed, then attacking the black might prove a fatal mistake. The sentinel could escape and warn his master. Then again, if left alone, the other dragon might discover Krasus and the rest, anyway, on his return flight.

Korialstrasz clutched the mountainside tight as he attempted to come to some quick conclusion. If the black flew too far away, the red might not be able to catch up to him—

The rock face under his claws gave way.

Caught unaware, Korialstrasz tumbled from the mountain as the entire side collapsed. The dragon instinctively spread his wings and righted himself, suffering only a few hard pelts from the massive avalanche he had inadvertently caused. He shook his head, clearing his tangled thoughts.

The roar in his ears was the only warning he had before the black struck him from behind.

Despite being slightly smaller, Korialstrasz's attacker hit with powerful fury. The red was thrust toward the jagged ground at a ferocious speed. His left wing scraped painfully against the rocks.

Korialstrasz managed to stretch one forepaw against another peak, digging his claws deep. His momentum tore tons of rock from the other mountain, but slowed his descent enough to give him time to think. The red dragon tipped to one side, startling his foe and causing the black to lose hold.

As the second dragon tumbled back, Korialstrasz righted himself. He tried to rise up again, but his adversary still had one pair of claws on his back. The added weight made the strain terrible, but Korialstrasz would not give in.

Flapping as hard as he could, he twisted in mid-air. Using his tail, the red swung his rival against the nearest peak.

The black collided hard, sending a storm of rock below. His claws came free, but not before tearing off several scales. Korialstrasz roared. He felt blood trickle down his leg.

For a moment, both giants forgot the battle as they recovered from their injuries. Then, Korialstrasz's foe made a lunge for his neck. The larger dragon got his wing up in time, literally batting away the black.

The strike knocked the last bit of fight out of Neltharion's servant. With a last defiant roar, the ebony leviathan veered away from Korialstrasz.

"No!" Now that they had joined in battle, he dared not let the other dragon flee. The sentinel would alert his master, who would, in turn, suspect that more than a single red dragon lurked in the vicinity.

The black was smaller and, therefore, very swift, but Korialstrasz was sleek and cunning. As his adversary slipped around a passage, Korialstrasz took a different route. He had spent enough time staring at the landscape while he waited to know where some of the different valleys remerged.

Through the mountains, he flew. Ahead, the left side of a fork offered an enticing turn, but Korialstrasz knew that it was the one favoring the right that would lead him back to his quarry.

In the distance, he heard the hard flapping of his enemy's wings. The red dragon grew concerned. He should have passed the other by this point, but the sound gave indication that the black one was instead widening the gap.

Pushing himself to his limits, Korialstrasz neared the point he had been seeking. Only a short distance more. He could not hear the flapping, but felt certain that he had finally gotten ahead.

He crossed back into the other valley—

There was a near collision of wings. Both dragons roared, more from surprise than fury. Korialstrasz spun around twice and the black dragon rammed sideways into a small peak, shattering the top.

But momentum was now with the smaller of the two. The black pushed ahead, regaining precious air.

Shaking his head and damning his poor luck, Korialstrasz pursued. He *would* catch the other dragon, no matter what it took. Too much had already been lost in this struggle . . .

His determination hardened, Korialstrasz roared once more and continued the chase.

But in pursuing the obvious, the red leviathan had missed something smaller below. Eyes watched—those who had eyes, that is—as the two huge beasts vanished in the distance.

"An impressive aerial display, don't you think, Captain Varo'then?"

The scarred night elf snorted. "A fair enough fight, though too short."

"And not enough bloodshed for you, I'd wager."

"Never enough," responded Azshara's servant. "But more than enough prattle, *Master* Illidan. Is *this* proof we're close at last?"

Illidan casually adjusted the scarf across his ruined eyes. For him, the battle between two such titans had been far more interesting, for these great creatures were of magic origins and so the sky had been filled with astonishing energies and brilliant colors. Malfurion's brother had come to admire his new senses, they revealing to him a world such as he had never realized existed.

"I'd think that obvious, captain, although don't you find it interesting to have not only a black dragon but a red one near here? Why do you suppose the second was in this area?"

"You said it yourself. This is a place where the beasts live."

The sorcerer shook his head. "I said this was where we'd find the lair of the huge black one. That red was here for a specific reason."

Varo'then's marred face grew uglier as he realized just what his companion meant. "The other dragons want the disk! Makes the only sense!"

"Yes . . ." Illidan urged his mount along, the officer following. Behind them marched the demon warriors. "But they'd be so easily caught. You saw how they were beaten." He considered further. "I think I recognized the markings on that red."

"What of it? All those beasts are the same!"

"Spoken like a Highborne." Illidan rubbed his chin as he mused. "No, I think that *is* the one I've met . . . and if that's so, we might just have some familiar company ahead."

EIGHT

Malfurion watched the goblin wend his way through the narrowing cracks and while he understood that Krasus had needed to animate the body, it still unnerved him. Even the mage's reassurance that this was a spell little used and even less desired by his kind did not completely assuage the night elf.

Yet, he gave no outer sign of his emotions save to stand as far as he could from the creature. Curiously, the goblin's movements grew more adept as time passed, almost to the point where he seemed to have actually come back to life.

To the druid's surprise, it was Krasus who first mouthed what the others had been long thinking.

"How much farther?" muttered the pale, robed figure. "This abuse of the tenets of life disgusts me more and more . . ."

As if in answer, the goblin suddenly bent over. Malfurion glanced at Krasus, thinking that perhaps the mage had become so sick of what he had been doing that he had finally just released the body from the spell. However, the contemplative expression his companion wore said otherwise.

"Watch . . ." Krasus murmured. "Watch . . ."

The animated goblin touched a stone lying near the base of the mountain. To Malfurion's eyes, the stone appeared to be just a random one that had no doubt fallen from the peak some time back.

Yet, as soon as the creature turned it slightly to the right, the entire rock face shimmered—and more than half of it disappeared.

Brox let out a grunt. Krasus nodded.

"Very cunning," he remarked. "Look, where once there was stone, to the left is now a narrow passage cut through the peak itself."

They followed their macabre guide for several more minutes, then Krasus suddenly had the goblin come to a halt.

"Listen . . ."

Somewhere far away, they heard the chitter of goblin voices and the constant hammering of metal.

The druid stiffened. "We've reached it."

"And so we can put an end to this obscenity . . ." Krasus waved his hand and the goblin turned. The animated figure crawled over a rock, vanishing from sight. A moment later, the dragon mage made a cutting action. "He will be found . . . but after we are through here."

Krasus started forward, but Malfurion suddenly seized his arm. "Wait," the druid whispered. "You can't go in there."

He was rewarded with a rare glimpse of the mage caught off guard. Krasus stared deep. "You have a reason for saying this at such a late hour?"

"I didn't think of it until a short time ago. Krasus, of all of us, he'll notice you easiest. You're one of his own kind. He'll be expecting the dragons to try to steal the Demon Soul away from him."

"But my kind is most susceptible and so we would be more likely to stay far from it. Besides, I have shielded myself well."

Nodding, Malfurion continued, "And your kind also has the most to lose while the disk is still his. It behooves the dragons to at least try . . . and that's what the Earth Warder will think, too. Inside, he'll surely be on guard for any dragon magic, especially such shields."

"And he is an *Aspect* . . ." The slim figure pursed his lips. Malfurion expected Krasus to eloquently explain why the night elf's thinking was incorrect, but, at last, the robed mage replied, "You speak the truth. We would try and he would expect us to try. I know him well. It is something I should have considered earlier, but I suspect I wanted so badly to ignore it. I am fortunate enough to have come this far, but his lair will surely be arranged so as to trap any dragon other than his own."

"As I thought."

"Which does not mean that you and Brox will have it any easier," Krasus reminded him. "Yet, the audacity of two of the lesser races sneaking through his very sanctum might slip by him, if just barely."

"Brox should stay with you."

"No, the orc is better suited to assisting you. There are many physical dangers, least of which are far more goblins than what we've come across. You will need to concentrate on securing the Demon Soul and, while I will assist as much as I can from out here, someone must watch your back inside."

"No one will harm him," rumbled Brox. He hefted the ax and grinned. "Make me a good song, elder one?"

Krasus gave a rare smile. "I will begin composing it the moment we are rid of this place."

Unable to come up with any other argument as to why he should enter alone, Malfurion accepted the orc's company. In truth, the night elf was glad to have him. Brox's sturdy demeanor and powerful arm made stepping into the dragon's lair a little less daunting.

A little.

But Malfurion knew that it had to be done and he believed that he had the best chance. It was no sense of ego that drove him, only some feeling that all he had studied somehow made him the proper choice.

It was decided that Brox would initially lead the way, with Malfurion taking over when he began to recognize his surroundings. Brox harnessed his ax for the beginning, the passage too narrow for proper use of the huge weapon. Instead, the orc drew a long dagger, which he wielded with clear expertise.

"I will keep watch from here," Krasus promised as they departed. "I can at least do that without the black one noticing."

It was fortunate for them that the goblins used the tunnel to bring raw materials in or else even Malfurion would have had trouble fitting inside. As it was, Brox had to keep his arms close to his body most of the time. The orc held the dagger in front of him, watching and listening.

The sounds ahead grew more incessant. Malfurion hoped that such a racket would work to their advantage. If the goblins were distracted by the noise they created, they might not notice the pair.

A dim light ahead finally illuminated the curving tunnel. Brox visibly tensed. Malfurion put a hand on his shoulder.

"If I'm correct," the druid whispered. "When we entered the caverns, the passage that the dragon took should be to the left."

Brox grunted understanding and led on. Their path grew brighter and the noise began to reach manic levels.

The sight that met their eyes was even more chaotic than what Malfurion had earlier witnessed. There were at least twice as many goblins as before and all scurried about as if their very lives depended upon it . . . likely the truth. Several worked to break down huge piles of raw ore, while others tossed fuel into the towering furnaces. Through a system of massive pots on moving chains, an unceasing flow of molten metal poured into gargantuan molds. Beyond that, vast vats of water awaited those molds that had already been filled. Sweating goblins bathed in steam worked to secure one mold already set in a vat.

Far to the pair's right, two massive plates already forged lay discarded, previous attempts that had failed. There were fine cracks in the metal, making them useless for whatever task the dragon desired them.

"I still don't understand what they want with all this," muttered Malfurion. "Does the dragon plan a suit of armor for himself?"

The orc's brow crushed together. "With that one, could be anything . . ."

Tearing himself from the enigma, the night elf studied their left. Sure enough, a path ran along the edge toward a gargantuan passage, the same one he recalled Neltharion using.

"There! We follow along there!"

Brox nodded, but kept Malfurion from stepping out of the tunnel. "Goblins below. Must wait."

The creatures in question toiled at removing rubble left over from the ore. The druid studied the progress of the work and quickly realized that the goblins would be there much too long.

"We need them away or distracted, Brox . . ."

"Spell, maybe."

Malfurion considered the contents of his belt pouches, then studied the cavern. There were a couple of things that might just work—

But as he reached into one pouch, the monstrous voice of Neltharion shook the huge chamber. "Meklo! I have returned! This next shall work or I will dine on every miserable one of your kind . . . with you as my appetizer!"

From the far side of the chamber, the aproned goblin whom Malfurion had seen previous suddenly came running. He kicked several of those working, urging them to greater speed, then trotted toward the tall passage. All the while he muttered to himself what Malfurion's sharp ears thought were more calculations.

But even before Meklo could reach the tunnel, from out of it burst the black dragon.

An oath escaped Brox—who had not seen how the transformation had even more consumed Neltharion—but, fortunately, it was drowned out by the giant's bellowing.

"Meklo! You misbegotten get of a worm! My good patience is at an end! Have you the new plates or not?"

"Two! Two, my lord! See? See?" He gestured to where several workers toiled to remove a pair of the gargantuan pieces of metal from their molds. Despite the water vats, they still sizzled with residual heat, enough to burn someone badly.

"Stronger than the last, I hope! They failed miserably!"

His head bobbing up and down, the grizzled goblin declared, "The finest blending of metals! Stronger than steel! And imbued with the energies you presented, they'll last up to any strain even though they will feel as light as a feather!"

As if to emphasis this last, the goblins working on the first of the plates easily carried it about even though Malfurion would have expected that they would need ten times their number.

Neltharion eyed the plate with eagerness. His breath quickened as the still-red metal passed near.

"All we need do is set it in the water tank for a short time, then—"

"NO!" burst out the Earth Warder.

The goblin quivered. "B-beg pardon, my lord?"

Eyes manic, the dragon continued to stare at the plate. "I want it sealed on *now!*"

"But the remaining heat will only add to the stress on you! The bolts already have to be hot out of necessity! It would truly be prudent to wait—"

The ebony leviathan stomped the floor with one paw—coming within inches of Meklo. "Now . . ."

"Yes, my Lord Neltharion! At once, my Lord Neltharion! Move you sluggards!" Meklo blurted the last at the goblins still trying to maneuver the plate.

As they turned about, the dragon headed toward a large, open space against the far wall. While Malfurion and the orc watched in curiosity, the leviathan settled down, exposing his right flank in the process. The great, gaping rips continued to burn with fire.

"Secure it!" Neltharion roared. "Secure it!"

"What do they mean to do with that?" the night elf muttered.

Brox shook his head, as bewildered as him.

"Get the bolts ready, the bolts ready!" Meklo ordered. "As hot as possible!"

Two crews of a dozen goblins began maneuvering a huge pair of tongs into a furnace. As the druid watched, they plucked from it a massive bolt at least as large as the orc.

"Hammer crew! Ready the machine!"

A groaning noise came from the right. A score of goblins pulled what at first looked like a peculiar catapult toward the dragon. Yet, this machine had no cup, but rather a gigantic metal head that was flat on one end. There were chains and pulleys attached to it whose purposes Malfurion could not in the least fathom.

"The plate!" Neltharion's impatience grew. "Set it in place, I say!"

With frantic effort, the goblins obeyed. They swayed back and forth several times as they neared the dragon's flank—not because of the panel's weight, but rather Neltharion's breathing, which apparently made the spot they sought shift more than the tiny creatures could handle. Finally, at a signal from Meklo, they leaned forward and let the plate fall against the scaled hide.

The two onlookers stepped back in shock as metal and flesh collided. A searing sound echoed through the cavern. The terrible rip underneath caused the plate to shake, but it did not slip off.

"It's holding so far!" Meklo announced to all. "Quick! The first of the bolts!"

Malfurion could scarce believe what he was witnessing. "They—they're actually going to seal it to his very flesh! That's madness! Madness!"

Brox said nothing, his eyes narrowed, his hand clutching the dagger so tightly that his knuckles were white.

The Earth Warder had a look almost like bliss. His great mouth was twisted into a reptilian smile and his crimson eyes were half veiled. His chest rose and fell faster and faster in anticipation.

Those goblins working the tongs brought the gigantic bolt toward one of the several holes located around the edge of the plate. At a quick glance, the night elf counted at least a dozen such holes. Were each intended for a bolt that would be driven deep through the scales?

Again, the rocking motion of the dragon's body caused the goblins some difficulty. On their third try, they managed to catch one of the upper holes. The bolt slid partway in, the creatures using the long tongs to keep it there as best as possible.

Meklo immediately waved to the other crew. "Get the hammer in place! Ready it for immediate striking!"

With more grunts and groans, the goblins pulled the device in front of Neltharion. The giant's half-veiled eyes watched eagerly as the dragon's servants adjusted the machine's position.

Meklo leapt atop it with an agility surprising for his age, then peered down at the bolt. He had the crew correct slightly before leaping off.

"Pull!" the goblin leader called.

The same group that had guided the machine now seized the chains and tugged on them in various fashion. How exactly the goblins' creation worked was beyond the druid, but the results of their actions was not.

The flat end of the massive metal head came down hard on the bolt.

The collision sent forth a bone-shattering sound. The bolt sank in deep, almost to its own head.

Neltharion roared, but whatever pain was in his cry was mixed with clear satisfaction.

"Again!" the dragon roared. "Again!"

Meklo climbed up, studied where the bolt lay, and once more had his underlings move the machine. Satisfied, he leapt off, crying as he landed, "Pull!"

The other goblins tugged on the chains. The various pulleys turned here and there—and the hammer came down again.

Neltharion's cry this time drowned out the actual strike. The bolt sank deeper.

"It's in!" the chief goblin called out.

The only response to his words was a tremendous laugh by the black dragon.

"Hurry on with the next bolt!" Meklo ordered. "Hurry on with it, I say!"

In the tunnel, Malfurion, still shivering, dropped against the wall. "He means to have *all* those plates attached to his body! Why? Why?"

"Defense . . ." replied the orc. "Strong, but light. You saw that." Brox shrugged. "Also maybe to keep from ripping apart . . ."

"But the pain! You saw how deep that one went! And the plate itself . . . it's still hot, too!"

"He is mad . . . but maybe his madness will help us, druid."

He had Malfurion's interest. "What do you mean?"

Brox pointed into the cavern. "The eyes of the goblins . . ."

At first, the druid was not certain as to what the orc referred, but then he noticed that every one of the creatures had halted in what he was doing to watch the astounding events unfold. They could scarcely be blamed for doing so, yet, it did indeed offer the pair the chance for which they had been looking.

"We need to time it for when they get the next bolt ready," Malfurion realized.

"Aye. That'll be soon, too, druid."

Already the goblins with the tongs had returned to where the bolts were made. They seized one and brought it to the furnace. Even from where Malfurion stood, he could feel the heat from within and it did not surprise him when the creatures quickly removed the bolt, which now glowed red-hot.

"Must be ready," Brox urged.

They watched as the goblins brought the bolt toward Neltharion. The dragon only had eyes for the work being done upon him. He looked at the bolt as if at a lover.

"Hurry . . . hurry . . ." the Earth Warder rumbled.

As the bolt was raised up to a location on the opposite end of the plate, Malfurion and Brox braced themselves. Much too slowly, the piece of metal neared the hole . . .

As it slipped partway in, they started forward. Switching to his ax, Brox led the way, the orc ready should some goblin happen to enter the cavern from the great passage. Below them, Meklo barked at those working the machine. The creaking of the device as it was moved covered any noise made by the intruders.

They had nearly made it halfway along the path when the goblins got their creation in place. A sudden silence filled the chamber, causing Malfurion and his companion to freeze.

The druid kept one hand by the pouch he had chosen earlier. If the goblins noticed them, he had items within for one spell that would, he hoped, keep the creatures and their master busy while the pair fled.

But Meklo began shouting orders again and things resumed as hoped. As the hammer was readied, first the orc, then the night elf, reached the end of the pathway.

From behind them, the lead goblin's high-pitched voice once again called, "Pull!"

The crack of the hammer vibrated in Malfurion's head as he and Brox rushed down the passage. The foul images of what the dragon was having done to himself reverberated even more. Madness had truly consumed Neltharion and the name by which Krasus and Rhonin especially called him seemed far more apt.

Deathwing.

Brox slowed down, allowing Malfurion to catch up. "Druid . . . the way here is yours now."

The night elf already recognized parts of the passage, enough so that he felt he could indeed locate the disk's hiding place. That hardly meant that the pair were well on their way to success, for the lair of the Earth Warder would certainly have other dangers.

Behind them, there came another clang, followed by the chilling laughter of the black leviathan. The last especially urged Malfurion to greater swiftness.

It took far longer than he expected to reach the first turn. Malfurion had not taken into account either the dragon's much longer stride or his own ability—when in dream form—to easily glide with enough speed to keep up with the beast. That meant that their journey was going to take much more time.

He told this to the orc, who, typical of him, merely shrugged and replied, "Then, we run faster."

And so they did. Even then, it seemed forever before the first turn and even longer before the second. Yet, Malfurion took heart from the fact that he recognized more and more features. They were by now at least midway to their goal . . .

Brox suddenly grabbed the night elf's shoulder, throwing him to the side of the tunnel. Malfurion started to speak, but the warrior shook his head.

The druid heard thundering steps, the cause of the orc's concern. As the pair pressed themselves into the curved wall of the towering tunnel, a murky form stepped from another passage into theirs.

It walked on two legs and had a shape vaguely akin to the two intruders. Protrusions jutted out from all over its body and it walked with a peculiar gait. The head was distorted and at first, Malfurion could see no eyes.

As it drew nearer, the night elf nearly gasped.

The creature was formed from rock, but not in the manner by which either the Earthen or the Infernals were. Rather, what stood before them looked as if someone had piled boulders one on top of another, forming a crude statue of sorts. Yet, despite its appearance, it moved quickly enough for Malfurion to realize that, if it saw them, they would be hardpressed to escape.

The stone figure paused, seeming to scan the area. It did indeed have eyes, if two black gaps in what passed for its head counted. They looked with special interest toward where the duo hid . . . then moved on to study another part of the path.

The guardian—it could be nothing else—took two more steps, which brought it directly even with the druid and the fighter. As tall as any dragon, it dwarfed the night elf. Watching one blocky foot rise and fall, he imagined being crushed flat.

For several anxious moments, it studied its surroundings. Malfurion began to grow certain that it suspected their presence, but at last the giant moved on, heading in the direction from which the two had come.

When it was far from sight, the druid and his companion crept out of their hiding place.

"Do you think it'll come back?" Malfurion asked.

"Yes . . . so we must hurry."

They continued down the winding passages, the night elf pausing more than once to collect his bearings. Once, the two went several yards down one tunnel, only to have Malfurion discover that he had gone the wrong direction.

At last, however, they came across a narrow cavern that Malfurion could never forget. He paused at the entrance, stunned that they had finally reached their destination.

"It's up there." The night elf pointed up at the false protrusion. "Right where that sticks out. Just to the left of that crack."

Brox clearly did not see it, but as he harnessed his ax, he said, "Will take your word, druid."

There remained, however, the difficulty of reaching it. Again, what had been so easy to deal with when in his dream form was now high, high up. The Demon Soul's hiding place required a sturdy—not to mention, dangerous—climb.

In the background, they could still hear the hammering and the dragon's occasional roars. Urged on by that, the pair began climbing. Malfurion, being more nimble, at first took the lead, but Brox's strength and endurance soon had them moving at more or less the same pace.

"There—there's a small cave just below and to the left of the spot," the druid called. "We can use—use it for rest."

"Good," grunted the green-skinned warrior.

Neither looked down, aware how that could throw them off balance. The tiny cave, likely just large enough to hold both of them, beckoned.

Without warning, a familiar voice filled his mind. *Beware the trolls!*

It took the night elf a moment to register the mental warning from Krasus. That the elder spellcaster had kept a link with him did not surprise Malfurion, but the mage's warning made absolutely no sense. Trolls? What did he mean?

A slight powdering of dust sprinkled his face. His eyes stinging, Malfurion blinked it away.

Through watering eyes, he saw a long, cadaverous head with ears akin to those of a night elf and a shock of hair dangling over the forehead. Two yellowed tusks jutted up from his jowls. A black, glowing gem had been embedded in the middle of the forehead, no doubt Deathwing's method of keeping such guards under his sway. The creature was much taller than a goblin, even a bit taller than Malfurion. His ruddy, dark gray skin blended in well with the rock face.

"Hello, supper . . ." sneered the troll. He reached down with the clear intention of pushing Malfurion off the wall.

The druid pulled back as best he could, the troll's sharp nails coming within a hair's breadth of his face. Malfurion tried to steer around the cave, but the troll grabbed hold of the rock face and, much like a spider, came crawling down after his prey.

He heard an angry growl from Brox and saw, out of the corner of his eye, that another troll was coming up from underneath the orc's position. Worse, a third and fourth had emerged from other holes, one heading for each of the intruders.

"You'll make a pretty splat, supper . . ." the first troll taunted. "Eat your brains raw and cook your liver for something special!"

He snatched at Malfurion again, this time managing to get a hold of the druid's wrist. With amazing strength, the troll attempted to tear him free.

None of the spells the night elf had been taught seemed of any use to Malfurion. He fought hard to maintain his remaining grip, digging his fingers in so hard he was certain he would scrape off all the flesh.

Then, a shriek from below distracted the troll. Brox had put his dagger to good use, burying it in his own attacker's shoulder. The troll toppled off the wall, falling to his death. Unfortunately, he took the orc's blade with him.

With a snarl, the one who had seized the druid's wrist tugged even harder. As Malfurion battled to hold on, he noticed the second of his foes coming up underneath, no doubt intending to knock the night elf's foot loose. There would be little chance for Malfurion to maintain his hold if that happened.

The druid noticed a small beetle moving along the wall just above where the troll clung. Malfurion quickly concentrated, praying that his grip would last long enough.

As he hoped, the beetle turned and headed toward the night elf's fiendish adversary. More important, others began coming out of the rock, all of them congregating underneath the troll.

At first, Malfurion's foe did not notice anything amiss, but then the cannibalistic creature began to squirm uncomfortably. He tried to ignore what was happening, but finally it proved too much of an annoyance. With a frustrated hiss, the troll released his grip on Malfurion and began swatting at the insects now crawling on his chest.

Malfurion swung his fist. He only grazed the troll on the arm, but it was enough. Already forced to an awkward position by the beetles, the last of the troll's grip readily gave way.

With a cry, the creature slipped. Luck was with the druid, for the troll collided with his companion below. Unable to withstand the weight crashing down on him, the second troll also lost his hold.

Malfurion looked away as they struck the floor, his gaze turning to the orc.

"Go!" roared Brox, maneuvering against the last of the trolls. "The disk! Get it!"

After a moment's hesitation, Malfurion reluctantly obeyed. He had seen Brox fight demons under worse circumstances. The orc could handle the remaining troll.

Be wary . . . came Krasus's voice. *I have removed some of the protective spells, but there are others with which you must deal!*

The druid already sensed them. Some were fairly obvious, others well-hidden. He studied the nature of each's creation and, through that, either removed or nullified them. It surprised him that this part of his quest should be so swiftly accomplished. Malfurion had expected more from Deathwing.

There was another scream, a troll scream. The night elf did not even bother to look, for he already heard Brox grunting as the orc ascended.

The false front awaited Malfurion. He probed it with his mind—finding new spells, but nothing he could not counter.

Glancing down, he saw that Brox had reached the cave that they had originally sought. The orc peered inside.

"Wind . . . maybe way out, druid."

Anything that would shorten their time here was welcome. Nodding, Malfurion returned his attention to the false front. They had been fortunate so far that the distraction caused by Deathwing's mad work had buried the sounds of the trolls' deaths, but fortune would not smile on the two forever . . .

He delved past the last of the protective spells, then tugged at the false rock. It was heavy, as he had expected, but he managed to pull out the side nearest to him enough so as to be able to slip inside.

"I'll be quick!" he called.

Brox nodded.

Malfurion had expected darkness within, but what greeted him instead was a brilliant light that at first burned his sensitive eyes, then, somehow, soothed them.

And when his eyes adjusted, the night elf saw that but a few scant yards from him lay the Demon Soul. It rested upon a regal, red cloth the size of a ship sail, nestled in it like a newborn infant. The disk was so small that even Malfurion could wield it in one hand. It looked rather plain despite the magnificent glow radiating from it. Yet, knowing what power dwelled within, the night elf treated the dragon's creation with the utmost respect and caution.

The druid studied the forces in play around the Demon Soul and saw none that would endanger him. Clearly, Deathwing believed his prize so safe here that he had not bothered with any further spells inside.

Malfurion leaned over the disk. So much power in something so little. It had seemed larger in the dragon's paw, yet, he knew it had not changed size.

"Druid!" he suddenly heard Brox cry. "Something comes! The stone one, I think!"

With visions of the monstrous golem rushing through his head, Malfurion wasted no time, scooping up the disk in one easy motion.

Only then did he realized his terrible error.

What sounded like the screams of hundreds of dying dragons filled the chamber. Malfurion fell to his knees as the cries momentarily overwhelmed him. He felt as if the essence of every dragon who had contributed to the Demon Soul's creation now screamed for release—but knew that what he actually heard was a last, cunning alarm secreted around the disk in so subtle a fashion as to be invisible to his most acute senses.

And as the first cries died away, a worse sound echoed throughout the caverns.

The furious, frenzied roar of Deathwing.

NINE

The pain was a pleasure to Neltharion, for each bolt hammered into his scaled hide meant one step closer to godhood. With the armor and the disk, he would be invulnerable to any threat . . .

"Hurry!" the dragon demanded again. "Hurry!"

The goblins almost had the hammer machine in place. Meklo clung to the device, directing the last adjustments before the new strike—

And then a sound that the Earth Warder thought never to hear resounded through the caverns, a sound that so horrified the leviathan that he kicked out without thinking, sending the machine, Meklo, and the rest of the goblin crew flying.

"My disk! My Dragon Soul! Someone tries to steal it!" He let out a fearsome roar that sent the rest of the goblins retreating from the massive work chamber.

Neltharion rose. Only partially secured, the third of his metal plates dangled back and forth as he spun toward the passage. The black giant's feet and tail sent tables, forges, and molds scattering across the cavern. Fires broke out and one furnace exploded, bombarding everything with burning missiles.

To Neltharion, none of the chaos and destruction mattered. Someone had dared attempt to take that which was most precious to him. He would not permit it! They would be caught and they would be slain . . . but slowly, agonizingly. It was the least that they deserved for such an affront.

That any intruder had gotten past all his various traps, guardians, and spells utterly outraged the Earth Warder. This had been a concerted effort and one that had to have been attempted by the other dragon flights. He would make them all suffer, as he had done to the blues.

Roaring again, the dragon hurried into the tunnel.

He comes! Krasus warned needlessly. *He comes!*

Then, the link between the pair was unexpectedly severed. Malfurion feared that something had happened to Krasus, but he knew that he could not concern himself with his friend. What mattered most was to escape with the Demon Soul.

"Druid! Come! Hurry!"

He slipped the disk into a pouch, the light fading as Malfurion sealed the bag. Climbing out, he saw Brox waiting anxiously by the nearest edge of the first troll's cave. Moving swiftly, the night elf made his way to the other opening. Brox pulled him inside. Allowing Malfurion no time to catch his breath, the orc dragged his companion deeper into the cave.

"May be a way out! Wind may mean exit."

The troll's lair lay littered with bones and refuse. Malfurion tried not to look at the former, even if they were likely from goblins.

But their hopes for a path to freedom were quickly dashed. The two other chambers that they found led nowhere and the air current that Brox had felt came from small cracks.

"It would make sense that the dragon wouldn't leave such a route open even to his enslaved trolls," the night elf muttered. "We're trapped . . ."

They heard heavy footsteps outside, but not the kind that a dragon would make. Malfurion peered around the edge of the chamber and made out the hulking form of the stone golem as it passed.

"Deathwing can't be far behind . . ." No other title suited the black dragon anymore, not after what the druid had witnessed.

"We stand and fight, then," Brox replied stoically. "Let them see we have no fear."

The disk . . . use the disk . . .

Malfurion started. The voice vanished so quickly that he had no time to identify it, but it obviously had to be that of Krasus. The night elf still hesitated, though, aware of the dark powers of the Demon Soul. He had seen what wielding the disk had done to the dragon; might it not affect him in some similar manner?

A roar shook the cave. Rocks fell from the ceiling, some of them large enough to cave in a night elf's skull. There was no more time left to think . . .

"Druid, what do you plan?" Brox asked anxiously as he saw Malfurion bring out the Demon Soul. Its light filled the chamber and, unfortunately, spread well beyond. If the golem did not know where they were before, certainly it knew now . . . and so, very soon, would Deathwing.

"It's our only hope . . ." Malfurion raised the disk toward the largest of the air passages. He had no idea how the Demon Soul functioned, so he simply tried to imagine it creating for them an opening large enough for the pair to escape.

Nothing happened.

You must meld with it . . . let it be you and you it . . .

Again, the link vanished, but at least now the night elf had a clue. Focusing on the disk, Malfurion delved into it with his thoughts.

Immediately, he felt its unnerving nature. This was not an object that belonged of the mortal plane. The forces that Deathwing had summoned came in great part from *elsewhere*. The druid almost withdrew, but knew that he dared not.

Meld with it, Krasus had said. Malfurion tried to open himself up to the Demon Soul, let its power touch his own.

And just like that . . . he succeeded. The strength flowing through the night elf filled him with such confidence that it was all he could do to keep from marching out to confront Deathwing, the golem, and every other dragon in the lair. Only the knowledge that his own death would surely mean the end of hope for those he cared about prevented Malfurion from doing that.

The orc studied him warily. "Druid . . . are you well?"

"I'm fine," he nearly snapped. Taking a deep breath, Malfurion gave Brox an apologetic look, then refocused the Demon Soul on the air passage.

"Open the way . . ." the night elf whispered.

The glow around the disk brightened . . . and suddenly the rock above melted away to vapor. It left no rubble, no trace whatsoever. The Demon Soul burned away stone and earth without any effort. Although they could not see the magical forces in play, the duo marveled at the effects. Farther and farther up went the new tunnel, disappearing from sight.

"It'll continue until the path is completely cleared," Malfurion said, although how he knew that, he could not say. "We should start up."

What felt like thunder shook their tiny cave. Brox quickly looked around the corner. "The stone one's trying to dig in!"

They wasted no more time. Malfurion leapt up into the magically-created passage, with Brox at his heels. The mountain continued to quake from the malevolent guardian's efforts.

Worse, the two had only managed a few steps when they heard the dragon's rumbling voice. "Where are they? I will peel the flesh from their bones, drive pins through every nerve! Away!"

The last word was followed by a tremendous crash, which Malfurion could only assume was the golem being shoved aside by its master.

"This mountain will be your tomb!" Deathwing bellowed into the cavern.

There was a great sound—like a geyser that a younger Malfurion had once seen erupting—followed by a horrific increase in the temperature.

"Get in front of me!" the druid cried. As Brox leapt past, he pointed the Demon Soul behind them and threw his entire will into the sinister disk.

A savage gust of icy air shot down the tunnel . . . meeting only a short distance away a fiery flood of molten earth racing up. The monstrous flow slowed to a crawl . . . then halted less than a yard from Malfurion.

Gasping, the night elf scrambled back. Brox, eyes wide, carefully helped

Malfurion up the path. The orc appeared overawed by the forces his comrade had wielded, overawed and not a little concerned.

"Be careful with that, druid. I trust not such might in so misleading a form."

"I—I agree wholeheartedly." And yet, it had felt exhilarating unleashing such power. Perhaps Malfurion had been wrong; perhaps he should have turned back to face the black dragon. Had he defeated Deathwing, one of the major threats to Kalimdor would have been removed. After that, the Burning Legion would hardly have seemed like so terrible a danger. With the Demon Soul, Deathwing had handled them quite easily.

The magicks of the disk continued to amaze them as they climbed. All along the way, they found the ground beneath them molded for proper footing. Thanks to that, the pair more than doubled their earlier pace.

"I feel wind," Brox uttered carefully. "Stronger wind."

Their hopes raised, they pushed on harder. Malfurion heard a sound which he at first took for hissing, but then realized was the very wind the orc had mentioned.

"There!" the night elf rasped. "The opening!"

Indeed, the Demon Soul had done exactly as asked. They emerged on the sloping edge of the mountain, a cool yet welcome breeze greeting their exit from the hellish lair.

They were not safe, yet, however. Sooner or later, Deathwing would realize that they had gotten outside. He and his flight would come in pursuit.

"Best put that away again," the aging warrior suggested. "The glow will be seen."

Malfurion did not bother to mention that Deathwing might be able to sense the disk even when it was in the pouch. Still, at least putting it away would give them a little better chance. His fingers reluctantly bidding the Demon Soul farewell, the druid tied the pouch tight.

Once more, it was Brox who led the way. The orc tested each step down the snowy slope, more than once finding spots where they would have ended up tumbling to their deaths. For now, Brox kept his ax secured. One stumble could cost him the valuable weapon.

Fortunately, the need for the dragon's metalwork had meant that Deathwing had made use of caverns located lower in the mountain. While the way was dangerous, they at least did not have to try to descend an entire peak. Malfurion had hopes that they would reach the bottom well before first light.

But their luck seemed to again sour when a great form high above swooped past. Brox and Malfurion immediately fell into the snow, trying to cover themselves up as the dragon flew by.

It was indeed Deathwing and perhaps the only thing that had saved the two was the dragon's own madness. Deathwing searched the area in a manic anger, disgorging massive shots of molten earth at the various peaks as he passed. Each struck with such force that whole parts of mountains went flying off, huge chunks raining down on the landscape. He did not seem to be probing the area with his magical senses or else surely he would have noticed them by now.

Malfurion raised his head. "I think he's flying to the—"

Deathwing abruptly veered, coming back their direction.

"Move!" growled Brox.

They leapt up from their hiding places, making for a large outcropping ahead. Over his shoulder, the night elf saw the rapidly-growing form of the huge black. It was impossible to tell from the dragon's expression whether or not he had seen the pair, but he was certainly coming far too close for comfort.

As they leapt around the outcropping, the druid heard the same horrific sound that presaged each of the molten blasts.

"Here!" The orc pointed at an overhang. A lip on one side gave them some protection, but would it be enough?

The mountainside exploded.

The outcropping vanished utterly, the fragments everywhere. The temperature rose so high that snow melted. Great chunks of ancient ice slid off, crashing below. Sizzling puddles dotted the side of the peak.

Deathwing fluttered above the area, eyeing the devastation. The great beast moved in closer, then snorted in disgust. With a savage roar, he turned around and headed away again, this time winding around the mountain that housed his lair.

Behind what remained of the lip and half-buried in dirt and wet snow, Malfurion and Brox dug themselves free. The night elf coughed several times, then immediately checked the pouch. When his fingers touched the familiar shape of the disk, he sighed in relief.

Brox was not so cheery. "Deathwing'll be back, druid. Must be away from here before then."

Shaking off residual mud, they started down again. Every so often, they heard the dragon's outraged roar, but the black leviathan did not make a reappearance. Nevertheless, the pair did not lessen their pace.

As they neared the bottom, the night elf peered into the valley below. "I don't recognize where we are. I think we're far from Krasus." He closed his eyes. "I can't sense him, either."

"The elder one may be shielding self, with the black one out and angry."

"But *we* have to find him, somehow."

They agreed to wait until they were at the mountain's base before worrying any more about it. Krasus was likely better off than they were.

The valley was a place of perpetual dark, the tall peaks keeping it in shadow. The night elf led the way, but Brox kept close. They were near enough to Deathwing's domain to have to be concerned about goblins.

They needed to wind around to the left to reach where they had separated from Krasus, but after only a few yards that direction, the duo found themselves confronted by the edge of an overlapping mountain. Malfurion considered using the Demon Soul, but suspected that such a spell would certainly attract Deathwing's attention. Besides, each time the druid used the disk, it proved harder to put it away again.

"It looks like if we head around the other way, it might just lead us all the way around," suggested Malfurion.

"Agreed."

Their new path forced them to climb over some of the rubble left by the dragon's fury, but, fortunately, there were gaps here and there that worked to their advantage.

Another roar warned them of Deathwing's return. Malfurion and the orc pressed themselves against the mountain base, watching as the giant flew directly overhead. Deathwing scanned the region carefully, but still missed them. They remained hidden until the dragon was well out of sight.

"Odd that we've only seen him. Where are all the other dragons?"

Brox had an answer immediately. "They find the disk; they may try to become leader."

So it was the black's paranoia that now served the two fleeing figures. Deathwing did not dare let another of his flight find the Demon Soul first. Even from what little Malfurion knew of its power, it might have very well been enough for a lesser dragon to defeat the powerful creature.

They quickly moved on, but again the path played tricks with them. Despite their best efforts, the night elf and the orc were forced farther away from their goal.

The druid grew frustrated. "I should just use the damn thing to bring us to Krasus!"

"And the black one will come right behind."

"I know . . . it's just—"

A monstrous, armored figure collided with the orc.

At the same time, a lupine creature the size of a night saber leapt at the druid. From its back thrust a pair of vicious, wriggling suckers that immediately sought for the spellcaster's chest.

A felbeast.

The clang of weapons quickly informed Malfurion that Brox would be of no immediate assistance to him. The druid struggled as the horrific demon atop him tried to snap off his head. Malfurion nearly choked, so overwhelming was the stench of the felbeast's breath.

Row upon row of yellow fangs filled the night elf's gaze. Drool from the monster splattered him, each drop burning like acid. Malfurion used one hand to keep the full weight of the creature off of him, while with the second he batted away at the two hungry suckers.

One, however, finally slipped past his defenses. With the sharp teeth lining the inside of the sucker, it adhered to his flesh.

Malfurion cried out as he felt it begin to drain him of his power. It mattered not whether a spellcaster was a sorcerer, wizard, or druid, the magic that they used quickly became a part of them. By draining it out of its victims, the felbeast also devoured their life force. Given time to finish its unholy meal, the felbeast would leave only a dried husk.

The night elf had no time to consider spells. Even as the pain multiplied, he fumbled for a pouch—*any* pouch.

Taking advantage of his distraction, the demon managed to get the second sucker adhered. Malfurion nearly blacked out, but knew that doing so would mean his terrible demise.

His fingers grazed one bag—the disk's bag—and voices began whispering in his head.

Take it, use it, wield it . . . they said. *Your only hope, your only chance . . . take the disk . . . the disk . . .*

One of them reminded him of the voice that he had earlier thought to be Krasus. Malfurion desperately gripped the pouch, squeezing the Demon Soul out into his hand.

Immediately, he felt his confidence grow. The night elf glared at the fiendish visage above him.

"You want magic—I'll give you magic!"

He touched the Demon Soul to one of the tentacles.

The felbeast's eyes bulged. Its body swelled like a sack suddenly filled to bursting. In desperation, it removed the suckers from Malfurion's chest.

A moment later, it exploded.

Gobbets of demon flesh splattered Malfurion, but he scarcely noticed. Rising to his feet, the druid used the disk's power to instantly clean away the filth. He looked around and saw Brox still in combat against not one, but two Fel Guard. One was wounded, but clearly the orc was still at a disadvantage.

Malfurion casually pointed the Demon Soul at the one he could most clearly see.

A streak of golden light shot out, enveloping the demon warrior. He roared—then dissolved into a pile of dust.

The other Fel Guard hesitated. That was all the opening that Brox needed. The orc's enchanted ax cut deep into the demon's chest, armor and all.

As the second attacker fell, Brox spun about. Malfurion, a very satisfied smile on his face, started toward his companion.

"That went well," he commented.

But Brox did not look so pleased. His eyes shifted to the disk.

The gaze filled Malfurion with sudden distrust. The voices returned, stronger than ever.

He covets the disk . . . he would have it for himself . . . it belongs to you . . . only you can use it to put the world in order . . .

"Druid," the orc said. "You shouldn't use that anymore. Evil, it is."

"It saved both our lives just now!"

"Druid—"

Malfurion stepped back, holding up the Demon Soul. "*You* want its power! You want to take it!"

"Me?" Brox shook his head. "I want nothing from it."

"You lie!" The voices urged him on, telling him what to say. "You want to take over the Burning Legion from Archimonde and his master! You want them to conquer Kalimdor for you! I won't let that happen! I'll see the world in flames before I let you do that!"

"Druid! Do you hear yourself? Your words . . . there is no reason to them . . ."

"I won't let you have it!" He pointed the disk at the orc.

He must be destroyed . . . they all must be destroyed . . . any who would desire the disk . . . who would take it from you . . .

Brox stood steadfast. He did not charge the night elf, did not even raise his ax in attack or defense. He simply watched and waited, leaving his fate in Malfurion's hands.

And, at last, the druid realized what he had been about to do. He had been about to slay Brox just to keep the Demon Soul.

In disgust, Malfurion dropped the sinister disk and backed away from it. He looked again at his companion, seeking some manner by which to properly apologize to Brox for what had nearly happened.

The graying warrior shook his head, indicating that he placed no blame on the night elf.

"The disk," he growled. "It is the disk."

Malfurion did not like the notion of touching it again, but they had to take it with them. Krasus would surely know how best to handle the black dragon's monstrous creation. All they needed to do was find him.

Locating a loose piece of cloth, Malfurion bent down to retrieve the Demon Soul. He knew in his heart that the cloth was no true protection against its enticements, but it was all he could do. To fight it—and the insidious voices that seemed to follow the disk—the night elf tried to concentrate on those dearest to him. If he fell victim to the Demon Soul, they would all pay with their lives. First and foremost, Tyrande, already a victim, appeared in his mind. Malfurion doubted very much that wielding the Demon Soul would somehow save her. Instead, it was more likely that the druid would end up slaying her as he nearly had Brox.

He gave thanks to Cenarius, whose wise, gentle teachings had helped give him the strength to turn from the voices. The Demon Soul was an abomination to the natural world and, therefore, an abomination to the druidic path.

"We've got to flee this place, Brox," he said, straightening. "There's no telling just how many more demons might be in this area—"

His eyes widened as grotesque hands formed from the hard ground at his feet. With astounding speed, they seized Malfurion's ankles, pinning him in place.

The orc let out a growl and started forward to help him. Brox, however, barely took a step before his own feet were similarly grabbed. Undaunted, he swung at one hand holding him, shattering it. That, though, gave him only a single step before two new ones resecured his freed limb.

Meanwhile, Malfurion found himself caught between using the Demon Soul—which still lay wrapped in his palm—and calling upon the natural forces which Cenarius had taught him to use. That hesitation cost him, for a veil of darkness abruptly covered his eyes and what felt like an iron clamp bound his mouth shut. The Demon Soul slipped from his startled grasp, clattering on the ground.

He heard Brox roar with outrage and the sound of the ax beating at stone. Then, there was harsh thump and the orc grew frighteningly silent.

A heavy breathing that Malfurion recognized as that of night sabers first warned the druid that their attackers drew near. The Burning Legion, though, did not use the panthers. As far as he recalled, only his own people did.

Someone from the *palace*?

"You let them live. Why?" asked a voice that was indeed that of a night elf, but had the emotion of a demon.

"These two will be of great interest to our lord . . ."

Malfurion started at the second voice. *Could it be?*

He heard something land lightly on the ground, followed by footsteps coming toward him. There was a scraping sound as the nearby figure picked up what could only be the dragon's foul creation.

"Not much to look at," the one standing near Malfurion commented. Almost as an afterthought came the words that verified the druid's worst fears. "Hello, brother . . ."

TEN

K rasus cursed when he sensed the disaster erupting in the black dragon's lair. He had tried his best to detect every intricate spell Deathwing had cast over the Demon Soul's hiding place and knew that Malfurion had done likewise, but, despite everything, they had been outwitted.

Worse, his link to the druid and the orc had been severed and not by any magic cast by the black dragon. Some force in its own way as terrible as Deathwing's had come between the mage and his companions . . . and Krasus believed that he had some inkling as to just what it was.

The Old Gods existed only as legend even to most dragons, who had been born in the dawn of the world. Krasus, through his eternal inquisitiveness— or, as Rhonin put it, his eternal *nosiness*—knew them to be much more.

As the tale went, the three dark entities had ruled over a bloody chaos of which even the demon Lords of the Burning Legion could not imagine. They had ruled over the primal plane until the coming of the world's creators. There had been war of cosmic proportions and, in the end, the Old Gods had fallen.

The three had been cast down into eternal imprisonment, the place of their confinement hidden from all and their powers bound until the end of time. That should have been the final line of the saga, but now Krasus suspected that the Old Gods had somehow found a manner by which to reach out to the mortal plane and seek that which would free them.

It all begins to make sense, the mage realized as he climbed over the rocky landscape in search of his friends. *Nozdormu . . . the rip in Time, the coming to the era of the night elves and the Burning Legion . . . the Well of Eternity . . . and even the forging of the Demon Soul . . .*

The Old Ones were creating the key that would open the gates of their prison . . . and if that happened, even Sargeras would find himself pleading for the peace of death.

Rip Time apart and they would unmake their prison. Perhaps they even plotted to reverse their own earlier defeat. It was difficult for him to guess exactly the exte:t of the Old Gods' plans, for they were as much above him as he was to a worm. Still, at least their initial goal was understandable.

I must warn Alexstrasza! Krasus instinctively thought. The Aspects were the most powerful creatures on all the mortal plane. If anyone had a chance against the Old Gods, it was them. He cursed the madness that had turned Neltharion the Earth Warder into Deathwing the Destroyer. Combined, surely all five of the Aspects represented a force capable of defeating the elder beings. If not for Neltharion—

Krasus slipped, nearly falling from the ridge he had currently been navigating. How labyrinthine were the plots of the Old Gods! *They* were the ones who had turned the Earth Warder! They were the ones who had twisted Neltharion's mind—and with more than one intention! The Old Gods had made of him a puppet who would aid their escape, but they had also divided—and thereby weakened—their one potential nemesis. Without Neltharion, the other four Aspects were not nearly as much a threat.

Worse, they also had Nozdormu occupied, no doubt another layer of their planning. Krasus paused, falling back against the mountainside. It was too overwhelming. The dark elders had spent too much time and effort. Set too many pawns in place and covered their machinations too well. How could anyone—let alone, *him*—undo their malevolent designs?

How?

So caught up was Krasus in such overwhelming realizations that he failed to notice the massive, black shadow until it had long enshrouded the region around him.

Deathwing filled the sky. "YOU!"

The monstrous dragon exhaled.

Had it been any other, the chase would have ended there with a small pile of charred bones quickly engulfed by a steaming torrent of molten earth. But, because it was Krasus, who knew Deathwing far too well, the mage reacted in time . . . just barely.

As Deathwing's manic fury spilled down upon him, the robed figure brought up a wall of pure golden light. The black dragon's blast pounded the seemingly-delicate shield without mercy . . . and yet the latter held. Krasus strained, fought to keep his balance, and sweated from effort. Every fiber of his being screamed for him to give in, but he did not.

Finally, it was the winged terror above who paused, but only to summon up another horrific discharge. That, however, was all the hesitation that Krasus needed.

The focus of Deathwing's ire raised his arms—and vanished.

He could not face the dread behemoth one against one. The outcome of such a struggle was all too obvious. Even at his strongest, Krasus was merely a consort to an Aspect, not actually one of the five great dragons. Valor was a worthy thing, but not in the face of such impossible odds.

The mage reappeared near the mountain south of the one from which he had fled. Collapsing against a rock, Krasus gasped for breath. The effort of deflecting his adversary's assault *and* transporting himself by spell had taken much out of him. In truth, he had expected to materialize much farther away from the other dragon.

"I'll find you!" called the black leviathan, his shout echoing. "You'll not escape me!"

The one thing Krasus knew was in his favor was that Deathwing had grown so wild with anger that he did not focus his powers as he should have. The mage felt his adversary's magical probe of the surroundings, but it was cursory, sweeping by so fast and wide that the one it hunted was able to shield himself easily.

Forcing himself up, Krasus wended his way down. The nearer to ground level, the better he would be.

What had happened to his companions, the mage could not say. He felt certain, though, that they had escaped Deathwing, or else the black would not have bothered with him. Clearly Deathwing still hunted for his precious disk and now believed Krasus had it.

So much the better. If it cost him his life so that the others could bring the Demon Soul back, so be it. Rhonin would know what to do.

He scrambled down the mountainside, even exhausted as he was moving far more nimbly than any night elf or human. All the while, Krasus listened for Deathwing, noting with expert ears where the raging titan flew.

At one point, Deathwing flew directly overhead, but the robed figure quickly flattened against an outcropping and the winged giant passed him by. Deathwing loosed random shots at the landscape, unaware that his own fury continued to work against him.

Then, the dragon did what Krasus had feared he might. Apparently deciding that the area had been scrutinized well enough, Deathwing banked and started heading back toward his mountain sanctum. Krasus doubted very much that the black had given up searching so soon . . . which meant that Deathwing now hunted the Demon Soul elsewhere.

Fearing for Malfurion and Brox, Krasus eyed the departing form and concentrated.

From every direction, the rubble caused by some of the black's previous blasts flew up, bombarding Deathwing. Massive chunks, some as large as the dragon's head, struck hard. Deathwing gave out a startled roar as he veered madly toward a mountain, only just at the end avoiding a collision.

Krasus turned and ran.

The cry thundering from behind gave ample proof that Deathwing had taken the bait. Krasus did not bother looking behind him, his senses already warning the mage as to the black's swift coming.

Everything had to be timed right for what Krasus planned. He had to nearly feel the foul Aspect's breath on his neck . . .

"I will burn you to ash!" bellowed his monstrous foe. "Burn you to ash!"

Deathwing did not fear harming his precious creation, the Demon Soul designed to withstand such horrific elements. The irony was that it would be a scale from the dragon's hide that would prove the weakness of the disk . . . a physical part of Deathwing the only thing that could destroy his monstrous toy.

Krasus had considered finding some manner by which to cause the Demon Soul's destruction here in the past, but he feared that such an act might be too much for the already-stressed time line to take. Better to let the dragons have it as he planned and hope that history followed its proper course—assuming that was still possible.

Deathwing drew closer . . . closer . . . The black clearly wanted to make certain of his blast.

Any moment now, the mage thought, tensing and preparing his own action.

He heard the telltale sound of his pursuer about to unleash another wave of molten earth.

Krasus gritted his teeth—

There was a gushing sound . . . and the area where the robed figure had been was drowned in steaming lava.

The Earth Warder rose high into the air, his laughter well-matching his madness. He circled the region, now lit up by the blazing, orange rock. Raw magical forces that were an inherent part of the fiery mass he had disgorged made it impossible to locate the disk, but Neltharion could wait.

He savored the horrific demise of the mysterious dragon mage, the pet of Alexstrasza's who had nearly upset his plans early on. It was a shame that there would be nothing left of the creature, for the black would have liked to carry some reminder with which to present his fellow Aspect before he made her his concubine. Neltharion had sensed the closeness of the two, almost as if this Krasus had been as favored as her consorts, especially the insipid and irritating Korialstrasz.

Still, all that truly mattered was that the creature was dead and the disk would be his again. He simply had to be patient. The Soul was surely near him, buried under the magma and awaiting reunion with him.

But then . . . a nagging little thought disturbed his reverie. Neltharion considered the guileful ways of his quarry and how he and his companions had managed to steal away the disk in the first place.

The dragon dropped lower, trying to sense his beloved creation through the chaotic energies only just beginning to die down. He could still not sense the disk, but it *had* to be somewhere in there. It *had* to be . . .

Krasus materialized some distance away, the overbearing heat of Deathwing's attack still with him. He sprawled on the ground, aware that once again he had not gotten as far away as he would have liked.

It was his hope that the black thought him dead now, the Demon Soul buried with him. As a dragon himself, Krasus was aware of the energies each of his kind emitted during attacks and believed that Deathwing's would delay the Aspect from searching for the night elf and orc. Each precious minute would further the pair's chances of success.

As for Krasus himself, now that his foe thought him no more, he could rest long enough to gather the strength to transport himself to his companions. The mage gave thanks that his plan had worked, for he doubted that he would have had the ability to do much else if Deathwing had discovered the ruse. In fact, Krasus suspected that, at the moment, he would have been fortunate if he even retained the power to light a candle, much less defend himself against an insane Aspect.

Depleted, the robed figure lay stretched out against the rocky soil. The first rays of light stretched up over what little of the horizon he could see. In this benighted place, they would do little but mark the vague differentiation between eve and day. Yet, Krasus welcomed them, for as one of the red flight, he was a being of Life and Life flourished best in the sun's light. As his eyes adjusted to the new illumination, the mage finally allowed himself to relax, at least for a moment.

And that was when the deep voice from above rumbled triumphantly, "Ah! I have found you after all!"

Hunger began to gnaw at Tyrande's stomach, not a good sign at all. The Mother Moon had sustained her for a long time, but there was so much need for Elune throughout Kalimdor that she could not concentrate so much on a mere priestess. Priestesses expected always to make the sacrifice first, should the need arise.

Tyrande felt no betrayal. She thanked Elune for all that the deity had done. Now it would be up to too-fragile mortal flesh, but the training of the sisterhood would help her.

Each eve, at the time when the sun set, one of the Highborne would bring a bowl of food. That bowl and its contents—some gruel that Tyrande suspected was the old leftovers from her captors' own meals—sat untouched on the floor near the sphere. All Tyrande had to do was tell one of her captors that she was hungry and the sphere would magically descend. It would then allow the ivory spoon always accompanying the bowl to pass with its contents through the barrier.

Considering that the Lady Vashj wanted her dead, Tyrande was doubly grateful that she had not eaten anything so far. Now, however, the cold, congealing substance in the bowl looked very appetizing. A single bite was all that the priestess would have needed to maintain her strength for another day; the full bowl would have aided her for a week, maybe more.

But she could not eat without another's assistance and she had no intention of asking. That would be a sign of weakness the demons would surely exploit.

Someone unlocked the door. Tyrande quickly glanced away from the food, not wanting to give away any hint of her deteriorating state.

With a grim expression, a guard swung open the door. Through it came a Highborne whom the captive had not met before. His gaudy robes were resplendent and he clearly was aware of his handsome features. Unlike many of his caste, he had a rather athletic build. Most arresting, though, were his pale, violet skin and, especially, his hair—auburn with streaks of *gold* in it, something Tyrande had never seen. Like all Highborne, however, he wore a look of complete disdain, most prominently when addressing the guard.

"Leave us."

The soldier was only too willing to depart the sorcerer's presence. He locked the door behind him, then marched off.

"Holy priestess," the Highborne greeted, with only a hint of the condescension he had granted the guard. "You could make this situation much less uncomfortable for yourself."

"I have the Mother Moon to comfort me. I need and desire nothing else."

His expression shifted subtilely, but in it Tyrande caught a glimpse of something that she almost thought remorse. It was all that she could do keep from being startled by this. She had assumed that the Highborne had all become slavelike minions of the demon lord and Azshara, but her companion revealed that this might not be so.

"Priestess—" he began.

"You may call me Tyrande," she interjected, trying to open him up. "Tyrande Whisperwind."

"Mistress Tyrande, I am Dath'Remar Sunstrider," the Highborne returned, not with a little pride. "Twentieth generation to serve the throne . . ."

"A most illustrious lineage. You've reason to be proud of it."

"As I am." Yet, as Dath'Remar said this, a shadow momentarily crossed his face. "As I should be," he added.

Tyrande saw her opening. Dath'Remar clearly wanted something. "The Highborne have always been the worthy keepers of the realm, watching over both the people and the Well. I'm sure that your ancestors would find no fault in your efforts."

Again, the shadow came and went. Dath'Remar suddenly looked around. "I came to see if I could urge you to eat something, holy priestess." He picked up the bowl. "I'd offer more, but this is all they permit."

"Thank you, Dath'Remar, but I'm not hungry."

"Despite what *some* may desire, there is no poison nor any drug in here, Mistress Tyrande. I can assure you of that." The well-groomed Highborne brought the tip of the spoon up to his mouth and ate a little of the brown substance. Immediately, he made a face. "What I can't assure you of is the *taste* . . . and for that I apologize. You deserve better."

She considered for a moment, then, deciding to take a desperate chance, said, "Very well. I'll eat."

Reacting to her words, the sphere descended. Dath'Remar watched, his eyes never leaving the priestess. Had her heart not been elsewhere, Tyrande would have found the Highborne very attractive. He had little of the foppishness that she had seen in so many others of his caste.

Scooping up a spoonful, Dath'Remar brought the food toward Tyrande. The utensil and its contents shimmered slightly as they pierced the green veil surrounding her.

"You must lean forward a bit," he instructed her. "The sphere will not permit my hand to pass through."

The priestess did as requested. Dath'Remar had spoken true when he had said that the food lacked much in taste, but Tyrande was nonetheless secretly happy to have it. Suddenly her hunger seemed to grow tenfold, but she was careful to hide this from her captor. The Highborne might be sympathetic to her situation, but he still served the demon lord and Azshara.

After the second mouthful, he dared speak again. "If you would only cease resisting, it would go so much easier. Otherwise, they'll eventually tire of having you around. If that should happen, mistress, I fear your fate would not be a pleasant one."

"I must follow as I believe the Mother Moon intends me to, but I thank you for your heartfelt concern, Dath'Remar. It is warming to find such in the palace."

He cocked his head to the side. "There are others, but we know our place and so don't speak unwisely."

Watching him carefully, Tyrande decided that it was time to press deeper. "But your loyalty to the queen is without question."

The tall figure looked affronted. "Of course!" Then, growing more subdued, he added, "Though we fear her judgments not as it has been. She listens not to us, who understand the Well and its power so thoroughly, but rather to the outsiders. All our work has been cast aside simply for the task of bringing into the world the lord of the Legion! There was so much we strove to attain, I—"

He clamped his mouth shut, finally realizing the tone of the words spilling from it. With grim determination, Dath'Remar silently fed her. Tyrande said nothing, but she had seen enough. The Highborne had come here more for himself than her. Dath'Remar had sought a confession of sorts so that he could relieve himself of some of the turmoil going on in his mind.

Before she knew it, the bowl was empty. Dath'Remar started to put the container back, but the priestess, seeking a few more moments, quickly asked, "Might I also have some water?"

A small sack had been brought in with the meal, but, like the food, Tyrande had never touched its contents. With an eagerness that hinted of his own desire to not yet put an end to their encounter, Dath'Remar quickly grabbed the sack. Opening the end, he brought it toward her, only to have the barrier keep the sack from her lips.

"Forgive me," he muttered. "I had forgotten."

The Highborne poured some of the water into the bowl, then, as he had with her meal, fed her a spoonful. Tyrande took a second before daring to speak again.

"It must be strange working beside the satyrs, who were once as us. I must confess to being a bit unsettled by them."

"They are the fortunates who have been elevated by the power of Sargeras, the better to serve him." The answer came so automatically that the priestess could not help feeling that Dath'Remar had repeated it many times . . . perhaps, including, to himself.

"And you were not chosen?"

His eyes hardened. "I declined, though the offer was . . . *seductive*. My service is to the queen and the throne first and foremost. I've no desire to be one of those th—one of them."

Without warning, he put away the bowl and spoon. Tyrande bit her lip, wondering if she had guessed wrong about him. Still, she had little else with which to work. Dath'Remar Sunstrider represented her only chance.

"I must leave now," the robed figure declared. "I've already stayed too long."

"I look forward to our next visit."

He vehemently shook his head. "I'll not be returning. No. I'll not."

Dath'Remar spun from her, but before he could depart, the priestess uttered, "I am the ear of Elune, Dath'Remar. If there's ever anything you'd like to say, it is my role to hear. Nothing goes beyond me. Your words will be known to no other afterward."

The sorcerer looked back at her, and although at first he said nothing, Tyrande could see that she had affected him. Finally, after much hesitation, Dath'Remar answered, "I will see what I can do about bringing you something more palatable next time, Mistress Tyrande."

"May the blessings of the Mother Moon be upon you, Dath'Remar Sunstrider."

The other night elf dipped his head, then departed. Tyrande listened to his footsteps fade away. She waited then for the guards to check on her, but when they returned, they simply took up their positions, as usual.

And at that point, for the first time since her captivity, Tyrande Whisperwind permitted herself a brief smile.

ELEVEN

To an orc, blood was the ultimate tie. It bound oaths, commanded allegiances, and marked the true warrior in combat. To taint a blood bond was one of the worse crimes imaginable.

And now the druid's brother had done just that.

Brox eyed Illidan Stormrage with a loathing he had granted few other creatures. Even the demons he respected more, for they were but true to their nature, however perverse and evil it was. Yet, here was one who had fought beside Brox and the others, who was twin to Malfurion and, therefore, should have shared his love and concern for his comrades. Illidan, however, lived only for power and nothing, not even his closest kin, could change that.

Had his arms not been tightly bound, the orc would have gladly sacrificed himself tackling the sorcerer and snapping his neck. Whatever faults he considered himself to have, the orc would have never willingly betrayed others.

As for Malfurion, the druid stumbled alongside the graying warrior. Their arms tied behind their backs and ropes around their waists tugging them after the night sabers, the pair could barely keep up. Illidan's brother had an even worse disadvantage, for the treacherous twin had not yet removed the spell of blindness. Eyes covered by small black shadows that no light could pierce,

Malfurion continued to flounder and fall, scraping and cutting himself constantly and even once nearly smashing his head on a rock.

From the blindfolded sorcerer, there came no sign of regret. Each time Malfurion tripped, Illidan merely tugged on the rope until the druid managed to right himself. Then, the guards behind the prisoners would prod them forward and the trek would continue.

Brox eyed his ax, now hanging from the cat ridden by the scarred officer. The orc had already marked this Captain Varo'then as the other prime target, should circumstance enable Malfurion and him to free themselves. The demon warriors were dangerous, true, but they lacked the devious cunning Brox saw in the other night elf. Even Illidan was second in some regards. Still, if the spirits blessed him, Brox would slay them both.

Then, if it was at all possible, something would have to be done about the Demon Soul.

Curiously, it was not Illidan who carried it now. But moments after the sorcerer had retrieved it from his brother, the captain had walked up to the treacherous twin, stretched out a gauntleted hand, and demanded Illidan give it over. Even more curious, Malfurion's brother had complied without so much as a word of protest.

But such mysteries could not concern the green-skinned fighter. He only knew that he had to slay the pair, then take the Demon Soul from Varo'then's body. Of course, to do that, all the orc had to do first was break free of his bonds and likely battle his way through the demons.

Brox snorted in self-derision. The heroes in the epics always managed to accomplish such things, but it was doubtful that he would. Captain Varo'then had a clear talent for tying rope. He had secured his prisoners all too well.

On and on they trudged, leaving the lair of the black dragon farther behind. However, Brox did not travel with the confidence of Illidan and the captain. He was certain that Deathwing would find them. It was a puzzle that the giant had not appeared already. Had something distracted him?

Eyes widening, he suddenly grunted at his own ignorance. Yes, the orc finally realized. Something had. Something . . . or, rather, someone. *Krasus.*

Brox understood well the sacrifice the mage might be making. *Elder one, I wish you well. I will sing of you . . . for what little time I still live.*

"Ungh!"

Brox looked just in time to see Malfurion fall again. This time, though, the druid managed to twist. Instead of landing on his face, he did so on his side. The action saved him from a bloody nose, although clearly Malfurion had still shaken every bone in his body.

Try as he might, the orc could do nothing to aid the fallen night elf. Gritting his teeth, he glared at Illidan. "Give him his sight! He'll walk better, then!"

The sorcerer adjusted the scarf over his own eyes. Brox had seen just enough to know that something terrible had happened to them.

"Give him his sight back? Why should I?"

"The beast has a point," Captain Varo'then abruptly interrupted. "Your brother slows us down too much! Either let me slit his throat here and now or give him eyes so that he can see the trail!"

Illidan gave him a sardonic smile. "Such tempting choices! Oh, very well! Bring him forth!"

Two of the demons pushed Malfurion forward at the points of their weapons. To his credit, the druid straightened as best he could and marched defiantly toward his twin.

"From *my* eyes to yours," Illidan murmured. "I grant you what I no longer need."

He pulled up the scarf.

The hair on the back of the orc's neck stiffened as he saw for the first time what lay underneath. Brox uttered an oath to the spirits. Even the monstrous guards next to him shifted uneasily.

The shadows faded from Malfurion's own orbs. He blinked, then saw Illidan. The druid, too, gaped in horror at what had befallen his brother's eyes.

"Oh, Illidan . . ." Malfurion managed. "I'm so very sorry . . ."

"About what?" The sorcerer contemptuously replaced the scarf over the ungodly sockets. "I've something much better now! A sense of sight you could only dream of attaining! I've lost *nothing,* do you understand me? Nothing!" To the officer, Illidan disdainfully commented, "He should be good to travel now. We can even pick up the pace, I think."

Varo'then smiled, then gave the command to continue on.

Malfurion stumbled toward the orc. Brox guided the night elf to a more staid pacing, then muttered, "Sorry I am about your brother . . ."

"Illidan's chosen his path," the druid said in a much more gentle tone than the orc would have used.

"He betrays us!"

"Does he?" Malfurion stared hard at his twin's back. "Does he?"

Shaking his head at his companion's wishful thinking, the orc gave up.

They moved on, the shrouded day aging. Their captors rode with little concern, but Brox kept glancing back at the mountain chain, certain that Deathwing would make his appearance at any moment.

"Tell me, sorcerer," the scarred officer suddenly said after more than an hour of silence. "This disk. It does everything you've told us?"

"Everything and more. You know what it did to the Legion and the night elves . . . and even against the dragons."

"Yes . . ." The orc could hear the avarice in Varo'then's voice. Only now did he notice the way the captain's hand kept caressing the pouch containing the Demon Soul. "All true, eh?"

"Just ask Archimonde, if you like."

Varo'then's hand pulled from the pouch. The soldier had enough sense to respect the power of the great demon.

"It should be powerful enough to transform the portal to Sargeras's desire," Illidan continued. "The rest of the Legion will then be able to enter Kalimdor . . . with Sargeras himself at their head."

Malfurion gasped and even Brox grunted in revulsion. They looked aghast at one another, well aware that no force would be able to withstand both the demon lord and his full host.

"Must do something . . ." Brox quietly urged, testing his muscles against the ropes and, regrettably, finding the ropes still the stronger.

"I have been," the druid whispered back. "Since Illidan gave me my eyes back. I couldn't concentrate before that because I kept falling . . . but now that's no problem."

Making certain that the demons still paid them no mind, Brox growled, "How?"

"The cats. I've been talking with them. Convincing them . . ."

The orc's brow furrowed and he recalled how Malfurion had mentally spoken with animals in the past. "I'll be ready, druid. Is it soon, you think?"

"It's been harder than I thought. They—they've been tainted by the Legion's presence, but . . . I think . . . yes . . . be ready. They should act any moment now."

At first, there was no obvious sign of success . . . but then Captain Varo'then's mount balked. The captain kicked at the animal, but the night saber would not move.

"What's the matter with this damned—"

Varo'then got no further, for the panther abruptly reared. Caught by surprise, the officer rolled off the creature's back.

Illidan started to look over his shoulder, but then his own mount did as the first. However, the sorcerer was better prepared and although he slid from his seat, he was not toppled.

"You fool!" Illidan blurted, although to who, it was impossible to say. "You stupid—"

Brox acted the moment the cats turned on their riders. He ran toward Captain Varo'then's mount, seeking his ax. The night saber obliged him by turning its flank toward the orc . . . surely a command given by Malfurion.

Spinning around, Brox presented his bound limbs to the ax head. The ever-sharp edge severed the ropes easily and only nicked the warrior's right arm.

Brox seized his weapon. "Druid! To me! We can ride this beast out—"

But the night saber bounded past him. With its head, it rammed a Fel Guard seeking to run Malfurion through. The other demons back away, momentarily uncertain what to make of the mad situation.

The cat, meanwhile, began gnawing on Malfurion's ropes. Gazing at Brox, the night elf shouted, "Never mind me! The pouch, Brox! The pouch!"

The orc looked to where Varo'then had landed. The palace officer sat rubbing his head, the pouch holding the Demon Soul still dangling from his belt. He did not seem aware of the nearby presence of Brox.

Raising his ax high, the orc charged the captain. However, the scarred night elf recovered quicker than Brox hoped. Seeing the huge green form barreling at him, the slim fighter immediately rolled away. As he came to his feet, Varo'then drew his sword.

"Come, you lumbering brute," he taunted. "I'll carve you up and feed you to the cats . . . if they can stomach you!"

Brox brought down the ax . . . and had he struck the elf, Varo'then would have been cut in twain. The captain, however, moved like lightning. The orc's weapon cleaved the hard earth, leaving a trench more than a yard long.

Varo'then leaped forward, jabbing at his foe. The sword cut a crimson line across Brox's left shoulder. Brox ignored the stinging as he hefted the ax for another attempt.

Out of the corner of his eye, he saw Malfurion direct the riderless night saber at the Fel Guard. The first demon retreated, uncertain as to whether to attack Varo'then's mount. That hesitation cost him, the huge panther bringing down the armored figure a moment later and tearing into his throat.

Brox tried to spot Illidan, but the need to keep track of his own adversary made that impossible. He hoped Malfurion was watching his brother. One spell by the sorcerer and they were doomed.

He roared as Captain Varo'then managed a nastier cut on the same shoulder.

The night elf grinned. "The first rule of war is to never be distracted . . ."

In response, the orc swung his ax in a fearsome arc which narrowly missed decapitating the soldier. Varo'then, his demeanor now more serious, backed away.

"Second rule," growled Brox. "Only fools talk so much on the battlefield."

His body suddenly tingled. Brox's movements slowed down, each action growing more and more ponderous. It felt as if the very air around him solidified.

Sorcery . . .

Malfurion had not dealt with Illidan, just as the veteran warrior had feared. The familial bond had made the druid hesitant and now that hesitation would cost them.

Captain Varo'then's grin returned. He moved with more confidence toward his slowing foe. "Well! I usually don't like things so easy, but, in this case, I'll make an exception." He pointed his sword at Brox's chest. "I wonder if your heart's in the same place as mine . . ."

But as he approached, a dark shadow enveloped both of them. Brox wanted to look up, but his movements had slowed so much now that he knew that the night elf would gut him before he could lower his head again. If this was to be his death, the orc wanted to stare his slayer in the eyes as a warrior should.

But Queen Azshara's servant was not looking at the orc anymore. He, it was, who now gazed high into the heavens, his mouth twisting angrily.

"Away from him, miscreant!" bellowed a voice from above.

As a helpless Brox watched, Varo'then, eyes wide, leapt away from the orc. A mere eyeblink later . . . and the area where the treacherous night elf had stood was bathed in flame.

Most astounding to Brox, the fire came with such precision that he barely felt the heat. That puzzled him further, for he had assumed, rightly, that a dragon soared overhead . . . and surely not just any dragon.

Deathwing.

But if it had been the sinister black, he would have scarcely avoided endangering Brox. With that in mind, the orc could only imagine one other dragon with such interest in the party . . . Korialstrasz. In all the chaos since escaping Deathwing's lair, he had forgotten the red, but, it seemed the red had not forgotten Malfurion and him.

"Be ready!" shouted Korialstrasz. "I come!"

Brox could do little, but he braced himself as best he could for what he knew would come, relying on Korialstrasz's skills.

A moment later, the great claws wrapped around his body and he was torn into the air.

The rush of wind in his face, Brox felt his limbs unstiffen. Either by the red's action or some quirk of circumstance, Illidan's spell had lifted.

He also noticed for the first time that Malfurion hung in the leviathan's other paw. The druid looked exhausted and also a bit upset. Malfurion pointed down at the ground far below, shouting something to both the orc and the dragon.

Brox finally made out his words. "The disk!" Malfurion cried. "They still have the disk!"

The orc started to respond, but Korialstrasz suddenly arced, heading back toward the site of the struggle. The dragon dove toward the party, eyeing each figure.

"Which one?" the giant roared. "Which one?"

He need not have asked. Captain Varo'then, his hand already in the pouch, pulled free the Demon Soul. Brox recalled the troubles Malfurion had first suffered trying to make the disk work and hoped that the scarred officer would have the same problem.

And it seemed that fortune was with them, for Varo'then raised the disk with evil intent clearly in mind . . . but the Demon Soul did nothing.

Roaring, Korialstrasz closed on the captain. Varo'then's expression grew dismayed.

But then, against all logic, the disk flared bright. Another voice called from above the dragon's head, "Away! Quickly, or else we are all—"

What struck the red was clearly but a fraction of the Demon Soul's might, but it was enough. Brox himself felt the repercussion of the shock wave that hit Korialstrasz dead on. The dragon quivered, moaned . . . and ceased flapping his wings.

The leviathan veered back toward the peaks. The ground rushed up. Brox began reciting the names of his ancestors, calling on them to ready themselves for his coming.

The unyielding side of a granite mountain filled his gaze . . .

"What did you do?" Illidan snapped.

"I used the disk . . ." Captain Varo'then replied, his tone initially filled with awe. Then, awareness returned and he studied both the piece and his companion. "You were right! It's everything you said and more! One could become an emperor with it . . ."

"And one could be flayed alive by Sargeras for even thinking such."

The temptation crossing the officer's face vanished. "And rightly should they be, sorcerer. I trust you've not entertained such a foolish notion."

Malfurion's twin smiled ever so briefly. "No more than you would, dear captain."

"The queen will be most pleased by the results of our quest. The Soul secured, its power proven on a full-grown red dragon, and the end of two of those most responsible for the delays thus far."

"You could have used the disk differently," the sorcerer pointed out, "and saved the pair for questioning."

Varo'then scoffed. "What could they tell us that we need to know now? This—" He thrust the disk toward Illidan. "—is all that is required for victory." The other night elf leaned forward, his mouth bending down cruelly.

"Unless you've some remorse concerning your brother? Some disloyal regret?"

Adjusting his scarf, Illidan snorted. "You saw how I treated him. Does that look like brotherly love?"

"A point well taken," his companion said after a time. The captain thrust the disk back into the pouch. As he did, his brow furrowed slightly.

"Something else wrong, captain?"

"No . . . just thought . . . there were voices . . . no . . . nothing." He did not notice Illidan's studious expression, which vanished the moment the officer looked at the sorcerer again. "I think it nothing. Now, come. The cats are under control again. We need to get the disk back to Zin-Azshari as soon as possible, don't we?"

"Of course."

Varo'then secured his animal and mounted. Illidan did likewise, but, as he climbed up, he took the moment to briefly look back at the mountains.

Look back and frown bitterly.

They should have been back by now, so Rhonin thought as he stared in the direction that Krasus and the others had ridden. They should have been back. Somehow, he knew something had gone wrong. When the night sabers had returned with the elder mage's note, the human's hopes had risen. Korial-strasz should have enabled the party to make much quicker time. They should have reached their destination long ago and surely Krasus would have wasted no time in attempting to secure the Demon Soul.

Yes, something had gone terribly wrong.

He mentioned none of this to Jarod, who had his own mountain of troubles. It was not that the meeting in Blackforest's tent had gone awry; on the contrary, just by being himself, Shadowsong had cemented his position as commander. At some time during the last battle, the former Guard captain had reached a point where he could not stand by and let foolish orders, whatever the caste of their source, pass as wise council.

When another noble had suggested a flanking maneuver that would have likely ended with the host fragmented, Jarod had started in, explaining why such would only create a debacle that would destroy the night elves. That he had to make this clear to what should have been the most learned of his race astounded the human. In the end, Jarod had managed to turn every noble there into his loyal followers, so relieved were they to have someone who appeared to have an instinctive grasp of tactics.

Rhonin had, at first, assumed that he would have to secretly guide Jarod, but the young night elf *did* know what he was doing. The wizard had seen

Jarod's kind before—born with an ability the greatest learning could not surpass—and gave thanks to Elune and whatever other deity might have been responsible for granting the defenders someone to take Ravencrest's place.

But with the quest for the disk in jeopardy, would even Jarod be enough?

Jarod joined the wizard. The reluctant leader of the host wore a newly-polished set of armor given to him by Blackforest, one that bore no crest, but did have red and orange arcs running down both sides to the waist. The cloak was likewise colored and flowed about him like a possessive lover. He now also had a crested helmet, the fiery tail—made from dyed night saber hair—dangling below his neck.

Behind him came his ever-present retinue, subofficers and liaisons for the varying noble leaders. Jarod paused to wave the group away from him before finally speaking.

"Once, I'd have dreamt of no greater honor than to rise to a rank of privilege and wear the fine garments appropriate to my new station," Jarod remarked dourly. "Now, I just feel like I look like a buffoon!"

"You won't get much argument from me," Rhonin admitted. "But it impresses the lot, so you'll have to make due with it, at least for now. When your authority's stronger, you can begin dispensing with the trappings, piece by piece."

"I can hardly wait."

The wizard led him farther away. "Cheer up, Jarod! It won't do if your people see their new hope looking so bleak. They might fear for their chances."

"I fear for our chances, especially with me in command!"

The human would not permit him such talk. Leaning close, Rhonin snapped, "Thanks to you, we live! Yes, that includes me, too! You *will* come to terms with this! We've heard nothing yet from the others, which means that you, I, and those dying in battle may be the only hope for Kalimdor . . . the only hope for the future!"

He did not elaborate, for it would have been beyond even the erstwhile officer to come to grips with the truth . . . that Rhonin was from a period perhaps ten thousand years later. How could the wizard explain that he fought not only for those who lived, but for those *yet* to be born, including the ones he loved most.

"I never asked for this . . ." protested Jarod.

"Neither did the rest of us."

The night elf sighed. Removing the garish helmet, he wiped his forehead. "You're right, Master Rhonin. Forgive me. I'll do whatever I can, even if I can't promise it'll be much."

"Just keep doing what you're doing . . . the right thing. You turn into another Desdel Stareye and we're all lost."

The new commander gazed down at his finery, sneering at its impeccable state. "Little enough chance of that, I promise."

That brought a smile to the wizard. "Good to hear—"

A horn blared. A battle horn.

Rhonin looked over his shoulder. "That's coming from far down the right flank! There shouldn't be any Legion force there! They could never get around without us knowing it!"

Jarod clamped on his helmet. "But it appears that they have!" He waved the soldiers back over to him. "Mount up and bring me my own cat! The wizard's, also! We need to see what's happening over there now!"

They brought the animals with an efficiency that Rhonin had not noted under the leadership of Stareye. These soldiers truly respected Jarod. It was not merely that he now had the backing of so many important if impotent nobles. Word had already spread of his deeds and how he had taken the reins in the moment when everyone else had believed the cause lost.

As the captain—no, *former* captain, the spellcaster had to remind himself— mounted, a new transformation seem to overcome him. A grim determination spread across his once-innocent countenance. He urged his night saber on, quickly pushing ahead of Rhonin and the others.

The horn sounded again. The wizard noted that it was a night elven horn. One of Jarod's first commands and the one that had proven he had the nobles' backing was to blend the host and its allies better. No longer were Huln's and Dungard's people off to the one side. Now, each element of night elf military had its own contingent of outsiders whose skills augmented, not detracted. Even the furbolgs had their part to play, strengthening wedges and using their clubs to crack the skulls of any Fel Guard who tried to reach the valued sorcerers and archers farther back.

Many of the changes were simple or subtle and it amazed Rhonin that he had not thought of them himself. However, now something had come to truly test the revamped host. A ploy no one could have expected from Archimonde.

Yet, as they neared, it was not quite a battle that they confronted, but rather a confusion. Night elves sought to bring weapons into play, but the tauren and Earthen that Rhonin saw appeared to have no interest in playing any part in their own defense. They stood idly by as their allies frantically tried to fill the gaps that they created by their inaction.

"What by the Mother Moon are they doing?" Jarod demanded to the air. "They'll undermine everything! I finally had the nobles convinced of their necessity."

Rhonin started to answer, but just then he became aware of something far beyond the line. The enemy was even closer than he could have imagined.

The wizard made out hulking forms, winged creatures, and a vast variety of ominous shapes that he, who had faced the Legion in the future, still could not identify.

Oddly, they moved almost at a walking pace and from them Rhonin heard no bloodcurdling calls. There were giants among them, too, giants that dwarfed any demon of which the wizard was familiar. The winged forms did not remind him of Doomguard and although there were other flying horrors among the Burning Legion, he could not recall any matching those approaching.

Jarod reined his night saber to a halt near a tauren that turned out to be none other than Huln. "What's the matter? Why aren't you fighting?"

The tauren leader blinked and looked at Jarod as if the questions made no sense. "We will not fight these! It would be unthinkable!"

A pair of Earthen nearby echoed his words with stern nods. Jarod at first looked dismayed, then his expression turned resolute.

"Then, we will fight them ourselves!" he growled, riding past the tauren.

But Rhonin had grown very suspicious concerning the reasons for the allies' reticence. "Wait, Jarod!"

"Master Rhonin, not you, too?"

The oncoming horde was now close enough that the wizard could make out some individual features . . . enough to verify for him that he had been correct in calling the night elf back.

"They're not the Legion! They've come to join us, I'm sure of that!"

He was even more certain when he saw that which lead them, a towering creature moving on four swift legs and atop whose shaggy head was a rack of magnificent antlers. The gargantuan being was followed closely by scores of creatures resembling satyrs in that their upper torsos were like those of night elves, but their lower bodies were instead those of fauns and they were all young, beautiful females. They seemed almost as much plant as animal, their skin covered in sleek, green leaves. While more delicate-looking in some ways, there was that about their demeanors that made him suspect that any foe would regret confronting them.

Already caught up in their preparations, the soldiers paid this figure no mind. Rhonin realized that a catastrophe of great proportions would quickly take place if he did not put a stop to things.

"Jarod! Ride up with me, quick!"

With the night elf in tow, the crimson-tressed wizard urged his mount past startled soldiers. Jarod caught up to him, shouting, "Are you mad? What are you doing?"

"Trust me! They *are* allies!"

The figure in the lead suddenly loomed over them. Startled, Rhonin barely reined in time.

"Greetings, Rhonin Redhair!" boomed the antlered being. The female figures eyed the wizard with curiosity. "We come to join the fight for our precious realm . . ." He studied Jarod Shadowsong. "Is this the one with whom we must coordinate our actions?"

The human glanced at his companion, who sat open-mouthed. "He is. Forgive him! I find myself a little astounded by your coming as well . . . Cenarius."

"Cenarius . . ." muttered Jarod. "The forest lord?"

"Yes, and I believe he's brought some august company with him." Rhonin added, peering beyond the mythic guardian.

It was as if the tales of his childhood had come to life . . . and, indeed, perhaps that was the most apt description. Rhonin and the night elf gazed up— often *high* up—at giants known only from the dreams of mortals. For all his height, the forest lord was dwarfed by some of his companions. A pair of twin, bearlike creatures like veritable mountains flanked Cenarius, one eyeing Rhonin with particular interest. Beyond them and only slightly smaller, a being resembling a wolverine with six limbs and a serpentine tail eagerly surveyed the distant battlefield. His breath came in hungry pants and his massive claws raked the ground, creating massive grooves.

Towering over almost everything else was a humongous, tusked boar with a mane of sharp, even deadly thorns. A name came unbidden from Rhonin's early studies . . . *Agamaggan* . . . a demigod of primal fury . . .

Some were not so overwhelming, but were no less stunning. There was a beautiful yet dangerous-looking bird woman around whom flocks of avians abounded. A tiny red fox with a sly yet gnomish visage scurried between the legs of the giants and darting around many of the demigods were minute, sword-wielding men with butterfly wings . . . pixies of a sort.

A shape pure white flashed by at the edge of the wizard's gaze. He immediately sought out the source, but found nothing. Yet, an image remained burned in his thoughts, that of a huge stag with antlers that seemed to reach the heavens . . .

And on it went. Male figures with hooded faces and whose flesh—what little there was visible—was oak bark. Hippogriffs and gryphons fluttered in the air and creatures resembling giant stick bugs with humanoid forms swayed patiently in the wind. Further on, there were scores of *other* unique figures, some of whom the wizard would have been hard-pressed to describe even while staring at them—but all of whom bore marked resemblance to some particular aspect of the natural world.

And even from where he stood, Rhonin could sense the energies surrounding each, the natural forces of the world embodied by those created first to protect it from harm.

"Jarod Shadowsong . . ." the wizard managed. "May I introduce to you the demigods of Kalimdor . . . *all* of them."

"At your command," Cenarius added respectfully, his front legs falling to a kneeling position. Behind him, the others followed suit in their own manner.

The new leader of the host swallowed, unable to speak.

Rhonin took a quick look behind himself. Everywhere, soldiers, tauren, furbolgs, Earthen, and more watched the tableau in awe. Most now recognized that these newcomers were beings of tremendous age and power . . . all of whom were now acknowledging Jarod as the one from whom they would take their cues in battle.

Cenarius rose, eyeing the night elf as one did an equal. "We await your word."

And to his credit, the former Guard captain straightened, replying, "You are all very welcome, elder one. Your strength is greatly appreciated. With any luck, we have a chance, a good chance, of surviving."

The forest lord nodded, his eyes looking beyond Jarod to the other mortal defenders. A determined expression steeled Cenarius's bearded countenance. "Yes. You have it right, Lord Shadowsong . . . we have a *chance . . .*"

TWELVE

As Malfurion stirred from unconsciousness, pain struck him over what seemed every inch of his body. It was almost enough to send him back to the darkness, but a sense of urgency pushed him on. Slowly, the druid began to register sounds and, just as significant, the lack of sounds.

He opened his eyes and was greeted by the soft shadow of night. Thankful for once to avoid the glare of daylight, Malfurion pushed his aching form up to a sitting position, then surveyed the region.

He let out a gasp.

Some yards beyond and half-buried in a crater no doubt caused by the collision, the dragon Korialstrasz lay still.

"He—he lives . . ." managed a rumpled figure rising like a specter from the grave. "I—I can readily assure you of th-that."

"Krasus?"

The mage stumbled toward him, looking more gaunt and pale than ever. "Not . . . not the circumstances I had planned for our reunion."

Taking hold of the elder spellcaster, Malfurion guided him over to a rock and made Krasus sit. "What happened? How do you come to be here?"

Taking a deep breath, the robed figure explained how he had led the black dragon on a chase, trying to buy time for the night elf and the orc. As he spoke, Krasus seemed to recover much of his strength, something the night elf attributed to the other's amazing background.

Then, Malfurion recalled mention of their other comrade. "Brox!" he blurted, looking around. "Is he—"

"The orc lives. I think his hide and skull even stronger than a dragon's. He came to me just as I stirred. I believe he is out trying to locate food and water, our own destroyed in the crash." Krasus shook his head and continued, "We may also thank Korialstrasz for our relative health. He did what he could to protect us—including a hasty spell—at cost to himself." The mage said the last proudly.

"Shall I try to heal him as I did once before?"

"No . . . the last time, you drew upon the strength of a healthy land. Here, you might have to draw too much on yourself. He would understand. There is another way." Krasus did not explain what it was, though, instead saying, "As to how the two of us came to be together, Korialstrasz found me as I lay recuperating from a narrow escape from the black one. He had slain a guardian of Deathwing's, then feared—rightly, as it turned out—that something had gone wrong with our plan to steal the disk."

With Krasus astride, they had taken a circuitous route to avoid both Deathwing and any other sentinels he might have stationed, then had followed as best they could the telltale trace magic Krasus detected from the Demon Soul. Unfortunately, they had not found the pair until after those from the palace had captured them and taken the disk.

"That was your brother with them, was it not, Malfurion?"

The druid hung his head. "Yes. He . . . I don't know what to tell you, Krasus!"

"Illidan bears their taint," the mage said pointedly. "You would do best to remember that and remember well." There was something in his tone that hinted of more knowledge in respect to Malfurion's twin, but Krasus did not elaborate.

"What do we do now? Do we go after the Demon Soul?"

"I think we must . . . but first, you need to tell me everything you can about what transpired before my arrival."

Nodding, Malfurion detailed his and Brox's capture, the taking of the malevolent disk, and the arduous journey. Each time it was necessary to mention Illidan, Malfurion nearly choked.

Krasus listened stone-faced, even when the night elf described as best as he could recall for what purpose they hoped to utilize the Demon Soul. Only when Malfurion had finished did the mage respond.

"It is an even more foul scenario than I had imagined . . ." he muttered, half speaking to himself. "They will have planned this . . . and yet . . . and yet, in it there may be some hope . . ."

"Hope?" Malfurion could hardly see any hope in what he had told the other.

"Yes . . ." Krasus rose. Steepling his fingers, he rested his chin on them as he considered further. "If we can only make them *listen*."

"Who?"

"The Aspects."

The night elf was incredulous. "But we can't! They've shut themselves away, even from you! If Korialstrasz were conscious, then—"

"Yes," interrupted the dragon mage. "And it is Korialstrasz who, in part, may aid us in bringing them out . . . if I know She Who is Life as I do."

His words made little sense to Malfurion, but the druid had gotten used to that somewhat. If Krasus had some plan in mind, the night elf would do whatever he could to help.

The rattle of loose rock presaged Brox's return. Unfortunately, the orc returned empty-handed.

"No stream . . . no puddle. No food . . . not even insects," the warrior reported. "I have failed, elder one."

"You have done as best as you could, Brox. This is a dismal land, even so far from Deathwing's domain."

At mention of the black scourge's new name, Malfurion tensed. "Do you think that he might still come after us?"

"I would be astounded if he did not. We must attempt something before that happens." Krasus peered over his shoulder at the unmoving form of Korialstrasz. "I give thanks that this Captain Varo'then used the Demon Soul in haste, or else we would all be ash. Korialstrasz can recover—and I know that—but, it is up to us to make contact first. And by us, I mean *you*, night elf."

"Me?"

As Krasus's eyes narrowed, Malfurion noticed for the first time how reptilian they were. "Yes. You must walk the Emerald Dream again. You must find its mistress, Ysera."

"But we've already attempted that since the dragons were driven off by the Demon Soul and she's refused to respond."

"Then, this time you must tell her that Alexstrasza must know that Korialstrasz is dying."

Aghast, Malfurion looked at the huge body, but Krasus immediately shook his head. "No! Trust me . . . I would be the first to fear that. Just tell Ysera. She cannot but help alert She Who is Life of this."

"You want me to *lie* to the mistress of the dream realm?"

"There is no other choice."

Thinking about it, the druid saw that his comrade made sense. Only a warning of such magnitude might gain one of the Aspects' attention. They would not think Malfurion so foolish as to risk their wrath with a false story.

There remained only the question as to what would happen when the dragon discovered that he *had* lied.

But Malfurion could not think about that. He trusted in Krasus's judgment. "I'll do it."

"I will try to watch over you. Brox, I leave it to you to protect both of us, if necessary."

The orc bowed. "My honor, elder one."

As he had done in the past, Malfurion sat with legs folded and cleared his mind first of all outside disturbances, then worked on easing the aches of his body. As the pain receded, he focused on the mythic realm.

Even despite his present condition, the night elf discovered it easier than ever to enter the Emerald Dream. The only unsettling sensation was a warmth at the points where the two small nubs on his forehead were located. Malfurion wanted to reach up and touch them in order to see if there had been any change, but knew that his first priority was finding Ysera.

He considered searching for her across the elemental landscape, then realized that, being who she was, all he had to theoretically do was call out to her. Whether or not the Aspect responded was another matter entirely.

Lady of the Emerald Dream, Malfurion called in his mind. *She of the Dreaming . . . Ysera . . .*

The druid sensed no other presence, but knew that he had to continue. She was here, somewhere . . . or everywhere. Ysera *would* hear him.

Ysera . . . I bring dire news for She Who is Life . . . the consort of Alexstrasza . . . Korialstrasz . . . is dying . . . Malfurion pictured the scene, trying to give the one he sought to contact some notion as to where the male dragon lay. *Korialstrasz is dying . . .*

He waited. Surely *now* the mistress of the dream realm would appear. How could she not at least investigate such potential tragedy?

Time was a nebulous thing in the Emerald Dream, but it still passed. Malfurion waited and waited, yet of the green dragon, he sensed nothing.

There came a point when at last he knew that to hope any longer would simply prove folly. Deflated by his failure, the druid returned to his body.

Krasus's anxious gaze met his own. "She responded?"

604 Richard A. Knaak

"No . . . there was nothing."

The mage looked away, frowning. "But she should've responded," he muttered half to himself. "She knows what it would mean to Alexstrasza . . ."

"I did as you said," the druid insisted, not wanting Krasus to find fault with his effort. "Said everything as you suggested."

The robed figure patted him on the shoulder. "I know you did, Malfurion. Of you, I have the utmost faith. It is a—"

"Dragon!"

Brox's warning cry came just before the behemoth materialized through the clouds. Malfurion focused on those clouds, hoping that he could urge them to some effort against the attacker.

But not only was it not a black dragon who approached, its very appearance made Krasus laugh heartily. Both the night elf and the druid gazed with some concern at their senior comrade.

"*She* comes! I should have realized that *she* herself would seek to discover the truth about such dire news!"

A crimson dragon the size of Deathwing hovered overhead. As Malfurion studied her, he recognized certain traits and knew that he had seen this particular giant before.

Alexstrasza, the Aspect of Life, landed anxiously next to the body of Korialstrasz. Even despite her reptilian appearance, the night elf recognized the all too common traits of fear and concern.

"He cannot be dead!" she bellowed. "I will not permit it!"

Krasus strode up next to the prone male, displaying himself before the red female. "And he is *not,* as you can so plainly see, my queen!"

Her consternation changed to confusion and then to anger. Alexstrasza thrust her head down toward the tiny mage, her maw coming within arm's length of his body.

"You of all who know me know what a bitter jest that was! I feared that—that you—and he—"

"Not for the lack of the Demon Soul's trying," he returned. "If its current wielder had not been so unversed in its usage, you would see four dead here."

"You will explain yourself in a moment," the dragon snapped. "But first I must see to him."

She leaned over Korialstrasz, spreading her wings wide so as to encompass the male's entire form. As she did, a golden radiance surrounded the great Aspect, one that quickly enveloped Korialstrasz as well. A gentle warmth touched Malfurion, easing his troubled mind. It occurred to him that here was a being as much a part of his calling as Ysera, possibly more. Druids worked with the natural life forces of the world and who better represented that than Alexstrasza? "He has suffered much," the dragon stated, her expression softening. "The Demon Soul, as you have rightly declared that abomination, caused him great harm . . . but, yes, he will recover completely . . . given the opportunity, that is."

The golden aura receded. Turning her massive head to the sky, Alexstrasza let out a great roar.

To the party's surprise, two more gargantuan reds dropped through the clouds. They circled once, then alighted near opposite ends of Korialstrasz. Once near, they still proved to be smaller than their queen, but on par with the unconscious male.

"Your command, my queen?"

"Take him back to the lair and place him in the Grotto of the Shadow Rose. He will mend better in mind and soul there. Treat him gently, Tyran."

The larger of the two newcomers bowed his head respectfully. "Of course, I shall, my queen."

"You will find there will be some more memory loss," Krasus interjected, not at all overawed by the presence of so many dragons. But then, he was one, also, Malfurion had to remind himself. "Those shall never be recovered," the mage added.

"Perhaps that is for the best," she returned, gazing at the tiny figure with the utmost fondness.

"As I thought."

Krasus stepped back as the two males—Alexstrasza's other consorts, apparently—carefully seized Korialstrasz, then took to the air. The Aspect, meanwhile, turned her full attention to the cowled figure. The fondness had become mixed with annoyance.

"It was not a particularly pleasant trick you played! Ysera alerted me immediately and although it was against my better judgment, I immediately came to investigate—as you *knew* I would!"

"If I have been remiss," Krasus answered, bowing deep. "I accept your anger and your punishment."

The huge dragon hissed. "You have me here and you speak of the Demon Soul in another's grip! How does this all come to pass?"

Without preamble, the mage went into the tale. Alexstrasza's expression changed several times and some of her anger faded. By the end of the story, disbelief dominated her emotions.

"Into the sanctum of Neltharion himself! It is a wonder that any of you live!" She cocked her head as she studied Krasus. "But, from you, I am growing less surprised by such actions. It is only a shame that after so much effort, the disk ends up in the clutches of those as monstrous in their own way as the Earth Warder has become."

"Yet, this seeming disaster offers us potential for salvaging at least some part of Kalimdor, my queen. The greatest goal they have is to bring into our world their master, Sargeras . . ."

"And they will use the Demon Soul to do that!"

"Yes . . . which means that they can wield it for no other purpose during that attempt." Krasus met her gaze defiantly. "The dragons will have nothing to fear from it. This is the moment when the Legion will be at its most vulnerable . . ."

"But the disk—"

"This is the one chance when you might seize it, as well," he pointed out. "And if you cannot destroy it, you can certainly bind it so that Deathwing will never be able to wield it again."

"Deathwing," she growled. "So appropriate for him now. There is no more Neltharion, no more Earth Warder. Truly, he is Deathwing . . . and you are right, this is our one chance to make certain that his foul creation troubles us no more."

Although it clearly slipped past Alexstrasza's attention, Malfurion noticed Krasus's expression briefly darken. In some manner, the mage had not been entirely honest with the dragon. The night elf said nothing, trusting that whatever secret Krasus held back, he held it back for good reason.

"Malygos will be of no use to us, I regret to say," the gigantic red murmured. "And the Timeless One is still missing, but his flight stands with us. Ysera's flight and mine will fly united, also . . ." Alexstrasza nodded. "Yes, it is possible. You are correct. I will speak with her and the consorts of Nozdormu. I should be able to convince them."

"Quickly, I hope."

"I can only promise to try." She spread her wings, but before the dragon could take off, Krasus signaled again for her attention. "You have more to say?"

"Only this. The Old Gods seek to use the disk, too, and they manipulate the Legion."

Her eyes widened so much that Malfurion was taken aback. Alexstrasza caught herself, then demanded, "You are certain of this?"

"There is question . . . but, yes."

"Then I must make doubly certain of convincing the rest. Is that all or do you have another surprise?"

Krasus shook his head. "But it is paramount that we return to the host and try to convince their commander to coordinate with the flights. All can still easily go awry if we do not. Can you aid us in our journey? I fear my powers untrustworthy at this time."

The queen considered. "Yes, I have something I can quickly do. Stand far back, all of you."

As Krasus and the others quickly obeyed, Alexstrasza once more stretched her wings. At the same time, the golden radiance returned a hundredfold stronger, yet, now it concentrated most behind the dragon. So bright was it that Alexstrasza's shadow lay well-defined before the trio, covering the landscape where once Korialstrasz had lain.

The dragon queen uttered words that made no sense to Malfurion save that he felt the power that each syllable contained. Alexstrasza cast a spell of terrible potency . . . but for what purpose?

The ground before the night elf rumbled. Brox grunted, eyeing the earth as if it were a foe. The hard surface started to rise . . .

And with a grinding sound, one vast piece broke free. Something about it struck the druid as familiar, but, only when another, similar portion tore loose farther away did Malfurion understand.

They were *wings*. The rising earth perfectly matched the outline of the Aspect's shadow. Even as the rock wings flapped once, another, more sinewy section joined them in life—and immediately opened its maw to unleash a cry identical in tone to that earlier uttered by Alexstrasza.

A stone replica of the dragon queen pulled itself free of the ground.

In all ways, it looked like a perfect carving of the great red, save in color. Even the eyes bore the same wisdom, the same care, that he had seen in hers.

The two giants stood side by side, the reproduction watching the original. The glow faded from Alexstrasza and she focused on Krasus.

"She will do for you as I would do for you."

The mage looked humbled. "I am not worthy of you, my queen."

Alexstrasza snorted. "If you were not, I would not be here."

The stone version raised its—her—head in what was recognizable as mirth, then also looked down at Krasus.

"I go now to convince the others," the red added. "I feel certain that all will be as we hope."

"Beware! Deathwing will still desire his abomination!"

She gave him a knowing look. "I am familiar with him of old. We will keep him from interfering."

With that, Alexstrasza leapt into the air. She circled over the party once, her gaze upon Krasus in particular. Then, with a last sweep, the Aspect soared up into the clouds.

"If only I could tell her . . ." the cowled figure whispered.

"Tell her what?"

Krasus frowned as he eyed the druid. "Nothing . . . nothing that I dare change." His expression shifted back to determination. "We have the means by which to return swiftly to our comrades! Let us not waste it . . ."

But Malfurion was not finished. "Krasus . . . who are 'The Old Gods' of whom you spoke?"

"A terrible evil. I will say no more, but know this. To defeat the Legion is to defeat them . . ."

Malfurion doubted it was all that simple, yet the night elf chose not to pursue his questioning any further . . . at least for the time being.

The stone dragon bent low as the three approached. Malfurion marveled at the fluidity of the creature, the grace with which such a thing could mimic true life. It showed the power of the Aspect, that she could create such a wondrous imitation of herself.

With Krasus in the lead, the trio climbed atop near the shoulders. Once aboard, the size difference between Alexstrasza and Korialstrasz became even more apparent.

"You will find that the scales will shift as readily as on a true dragon," Krasus explained. "Slip your feet in behind them to secure yourself better, then hold on as you generally do. She will be faster than Korialstrasz."

Their mount waited until all three had settled in, then, with a roar worthy of the dragon queen, she flapped her heavy wings and took off. Krasus had not been exaggerating. Even before the golem leveled out, she had already flown some distance.

The miles quickly raced by as they flew. The night elf gazed over the stone leviathan's shoulder, still not used to flying, especially so *high*.

"Couldn't we have followed Illidan and the others and taken the disk back?" he asked the mage.

"Even if we had caught up with them, it is most likely that we would have suffered a similar, if not more lethal, fate than previous. If they are not well into the Legion-held lands already, I would be surprised. As frustrating as it is for me to say this, our chances greatly improve once they deliver the Demon Soul to the palace."

Malfurion grew silent. Everything that Krasus said made sense, but the very notion of just letting the demons have the disk—if only to distract them for a time—repelled the druid immensely.

Yet, it did not repel him as much as the fact that it was his own brother who had personally made such a dire event possible.

You have pleased me very much . . . the voice from within the portal grated. *So very much* . . .

Illidan and Captain Varo'then knelt before the fiery hole, Malfurion's brother revealing none of his thoughts as he listened to the demon lord's praise. He and Azshara's underling had left the rest of their party behind once they had entered the ravaged regions conquered by the Legion. Illidan had not wanted to dare a spell transporting them until that point, for he highly respected the black dragon's own skills. The Earth Warder might have seized upon their spell and brought them to him, not a fate at all enticing.

The duo had materialized in this very chamber before the startled gaze of Mannoroth, the high-ranking demon's disconcerted expression a bonus for not only the sorcerer but apparently Varo'then, too. However, before Mannoroth's surprise could fully transform to outrage, Sargeras had reached out from the beyond to demand if his servants had accomplished their mission.

Informed that they had, Sargeras now lavished praise on them. Such only further frustrated the demon lord's lieutenant, but his devotion—and fear—of Sargeras obviously outweighed any animosities. However, clearly trying to gain some bit of glory for himself, Mannoroth immediately rumbled, "Very well done, indeed, mortals!" He stretched out one meaty paw toward Varo'then. "I'll take that now so that I can prepare the spell for the portal."

Although he showed nothing on the outside, Illidan's heart jumped. Now, of all times, the sorcerer had no desire to give over the disk to a demon. Still kneeling, he gazed up at both the waiting giant and the portal. "With all due respect, Lord Mannoroth, the intricate magicks of the dragon's creation are better wielded by myself, who now understands them best thanks to our master's gift."

To emphasize his point, Illidan raised up the scarf. Even Mannoroth grimaced at the sight.

"He makes a valid point," the captain interjected. "But as the current bearer of the disk, I respectfully suggest it is the great one who shall decide who wields it in order to strengthen the portal."

Both the sorcerer and the demon glanced with annoyance at the soldier, who stared straight into the abyss and paid neither any more attention.

"Of course, it's Sargeras who decides," Malfurion's twin quickly agreed.

"None other," echoed Mannoroth.

There can be but one wielder, the demon lord's voice declared. *And that one shall be . . . me . . .*

His pronouncement caught all of them offguard, but, especially Illidan. This was not—this could not *be*—the outcome. Everything hinged on his manipulating the disk.

Almost the instant he thought that, Illidan immediately checked the mental shields that he had built around his innermost thoughts. Secure in the knowledge that Sargeras could not have possibly detected anything, he focused on this new problem. There had to be some way . . .

"With all due respect, great one," the sorcerer dared interrupt. "The portal is a night elven creation and so in the manipulation of it with the disk—"

The portal is no longer a concern . . . not now that I have the dragon's toy . . .

The words reverberated in the heads of each. Illidan, Captain Varo'then, and Mannoroth stared uncomprehendingly at the monstrous gap. Even the Highborne, who continuously strained to keep the portal together, almost paused, so stunned were they.

The disk shall open the way, as planned, but through a medium more trustworthy than this pathetic little hole . . . The gap pulsated. *One more powerful, more certain to hold when bound with the power of you have brought me . . . I speak, of course, of the Well itself . . .*

THIRTEEN

Jarod Shadowsong did not feel like a legend, but the eyes of everyone he passed gazed at him as if he was one. His reputation, already built up far beyond what it deserved for his minuscule successes on the battlefield, had grown a hundred times greater with the coming of such mythic beings as Cenarius and the other ancient protectors of the world. The story of the intentional public acknowledgment of him as commander by Cenarius had been retold over and over throughout the camp until some variations had him clad in gold and accepting the forest lord's service by knighting the latter with a gleaming, magical sword. Despite the outrageousness of such tales, few among the defenders seemed to scoff at them. Even the council of nobles eyed the low-caste officer with something resembling reverence.

There was no one Jarod could talk to about his concerns, either. Rhonin was the closest thing to a confidant, but the human kept insisting that the night elf live with the changes in his life.

He dared not even go to the priestesses and seek some sort of confession by which to unburden himself of his anxieties. With Maiev all but high priestess, word would certainly get back to his sister . . . and that was the last thing the officer wanted.

For one of the few times since having command thrust upon his back, Jarod rode alone through the camp. He had told his adjutants that he would not be long and so there was no need for them to follow. Besides, everyone already knew who he was. All they had to do was ask and he would easily be located.

He received constant salutes and more than a few grateful expressions. Some sisters of Elune working among the wounded looked up at his pacing, even they nodding respectfully. Thankfully, Maiev was not one of them.

One slightly shorter priestess adjusted her helmet, saw him, and immediately came running. Jarod reined his mount to a halt, fearful that she bore some message requiring a meeting with his sister but aware that he could hardly turn tail.

"Commander Shadowsong! I was *hoping* to see you again!"

Jarod scrutinized the priestess's face. Attractive, although a little younger up close than he had first supposed. The face was familiar, but where—

"Shandris . . . it's Shandris, isn't it?" The orphan that Mistress Tyrande had taken under her wing before her kidnapping.

Her eyes widened appreciatively at his remembrance of her. Jarod suddenly felt very uncomfortable under that intense gaze. Shandris was a year or two away from being old enough for a suitor and while he was not that many years ahead of her, it was still a gulf the size of the Well of Eternity.

"Yes! Commander, have you heard anything about her?"

Now, he recalled their last conversation . . . and each one previous. Her missing rescuer had been a focal point of each and every one of their encounters. Jarod had been polite with her, but never could give her the answer she sought. There had been no attempt to rescue the high priestess. How *could* there be? She had surely been taken to the palace and, if so, had likely been slain shortly thereafter.

But Shandris refused to believe that Tyrande would not return. Even when Malfurion, the most logical one to attempt to rescue her, had gone off on his mission, Shandris had half believed that when he returned, the druid would somehow have Tyrande with him. Jarod had kindly tried to convince her otherwise, but the young female had a stubborn trait worthy of a tauren. Once she set her mind on something, she kept to it—which was also why when the novice had first begun to look at him with personal interest, the soldier had started to worry.

"Nothing. I'm sorry, Shandris."

"And Malfurion? He's back?"

He frowned. "There's been no sign of him, either, little one, but I must remind you, his mission leads him elsewhere. What he and the others attempt means more to our people than even rescuing the high priestess means to you and, especially, the druid. You know that."

"She's not dead!"

"I never said that she was!" he snapped back. "Shandris, it would be a dream of mine for her to be rescued, but even Mistress Tyrande would understand why that's not come to pass!"

Her expression froze for a moment, then softened. "I'm sorry! I know you've got so much to do! I shouldn't bother you with this, Jarod."

Oblivious to her use of his first name, the former Guard captain tried to placate her. "I've always time for you, Shandris . . ."

Her eyes took on a sudden glow that warned him that he had taken his placating one step too far. Again, the novice looked at him in a manner females did not generally look at Jarod Shadowsong.

"I really must go now, Shan—" But the rest of what he planned to say died on his lips, for the all-too-familiar cry of the battle horns sounded just then and Jarod knew that, this time, they were no mistake actually announcing the arrival of welcome additions. No, these sounded from the front lines and the roar that followed accented all too well the fact that the bloodshed had started once more.

As he turned his mount, a slim hand touched his knee. Shandris Feathermoon called, "Commander! Jarod! May the blessings of Elune be upon you . . ."

Despite himself, Jarod smiled gratefully, then urged his beast on. Although he did not look back, he felt with complete certainty her eyes on his back.

Reports came at him left and right the moment he reached his tent. There were demons on the southern ridge, others coming over the river to the north. The main horde pressed the center, a massive wedge of their own already cutting into the defenders' lines without any sign of slowing.

"The scouts report a second massing just behind the first!" shouted a rider just arriving. "They swear it's as large, even *larger*, than the main body!"

"How many of the damned monsters are there?" growled a noble. "Haven't we made a dent in their army yet?"

The answer came not from Jarod, but rather Rhonin, and it was not an answer any of them wanted to hear. "Yes, we have . . . but it's a very, very small dent."

"By the Mother Moon, outsider, how can we possibly win, then?"

The wizard shrugged and gave the only response he could. "Because we must."

They all looked to Jarod. Trying not to swallow hard, he looked over the party, then, in his sternest voice, said, "You all know what you need to do at your positions! We need this new wedge broken up! Let's get to it!"

He surprised even himself with how determined he was. As the others dispersed, the night elf turned to Rhonin. "I think they're saving that second massing for when that wedge breaks through!"

"Send the tauren in," suggested the wizard.

"Huln's people are needed where they are." Jarod tried to think, but, unfortunately, the only notion he had was one he could not imagine implementing. Yet . . . "I must find Cenarius!"

And, with that, he ran off.

It was time to end this farce.

So Archimonde thought as he used his senses to survey the battle. The news had come to him that a thing of power had been delivered to his lord, the disk utilized by the mad dragon to create such admirable carnage. Sargeras himself felt certain that this disk would open the way for him. Having seen it—and coveted it for the battlefield—Archimonde could well believe his lord correct.

But if the entrance of Sargeras into Kalimdor was now an imminent event, it behooved the demon commander to make certain that the world was ready . . . and that meant that he had to present Sargeras with a victory. His lord had to see that Archimonde could be trusted, as always, to deliver a conquered world.

And so, with the swiftness and cunning that had made him the one to ever sit at the hand of Sargeras, Archimonde had devised a new battle plan that would ensure the final annihilation of the miserable creatures defending this backwater realm. There would be no escape, no last minute reprieve. He knew that he now pitted himself against a much untried, untested adversary whose only virtue was that he had a grain more sense than the buffoon commanding prior. This new leader had momentarily entertained Archimonde with his good fortune, but good fortune was nothing in the long term.

I will bring you a new trophy, my lord, he thought to himself, already imagining the wailing survivors brought in chains by the hundreds to the lord of the Legion. *I will bring you much sport,* Archimonde added, imagining the horrible, tortured demises Sargeras would grant each prisoner.

I will bring you this world . . .

The demons' wedge continued to cut through despite the night elves' best efforts to halt it. Even the assistance of the Earthen and other races already mixed among the defenders did nothing to even slow it.

A line of Infernals formed the point of the wedge, barreling through with monstrous efficiency. They were guarded well by Eredar, who created around them a shield that let no mortal weapon through. Even Earthen war hammers made only a spark and that but a moment before their wielders were crushed under the massive onslaught of the stone demons.

While those in the center attempted in vain to at least hinder the wedge, the demon horde doubled its onslaught on those just beyond the edge of the Infernals' charge. Already shaken up, the soldiers there fell easy prey.

Slowly at first, then with much more certainty, the Burning Legion began to cut the host in two. No one doubted that if they succeeded, the day—and the world—would be lost.

Rhonin and the Moon Guard did what they could, but they were mortal and suffered exhaustion more than the Eredar and other spellcasters of the Legion. Worse, they had to watch out for their own lives, for Archimonde focused on them more than ever.

A night elven sorcerer to Rhonin's right suddenly shrieked and shriveled as if all moisture had been sucked out of his body. A second passed in the same gruesome manner before the wizard could register the first death.

Then, Rhonin felt an intense dryness spreading within his own body. Gasping from instant dehydration, he barely managed to throw up a shield against the spell.

One of the Moon Guard caught him as he fell, dragging the stricken wizard from the battle.

"Water . . ." Rhonin called. "Bring water!"

They brought him a sack, which he emptied without a drop spilt. Even then, Rhonin felt as if he had not drunken a thing in more than a day.

"Kir'altius is dead now, too," reported the sorcerer who had come to his aid. "It happened too swiftly to do anything . . ."

"Three here . . . how many elsewhere?" The crimson-haired spellcaster grimaced. "We've no choice! We can't do anything for the soldiers if we're all dying like this . . . and yet, if we're occupied, the Legion's sure to break through the last lines!"

The night elf with him shrugged helplessly. They both knew that there was nothing that they could do change the situation.

"Help me up! We have to create a matrix! It might be enough to at least shield ourselves better! Maybe then we can—"

From behind him sounded horns calling the host to battle. Rhonin and the sorcerer looked back in puzzlement, they, like everyone else, aware that every night elf was already on the front line.

And then . . . there came a charge like none witnessed in the life of Kalimdor. It consisted of no cavalry, no regiment of hardened soldiers. There was only one night elf even among them and that was Jarod Shadowsong, leading the charge astride his cat.

Rhonin shook his head, scarcely able to accept the sight. "He's leading the guardians of Kalimdor against the wedge!"

Cenarius followed closely behind the night elf, the two bear lords—Ursoc and Ursol, if Rhonin remembered correctly—behind him. Above them flew what from Krasus's account had to be Aviana, Mistress of Birds. After that came a being like a winged panther with hands almost human and beyond that a reptilian warrior with a shell reminiscent of a turtle's. They were but the first wave of several score beings, many of whom Rhonin could not even recall having seen earlier. The wizard knew none of the names or titles, but he sensed better than others their full power focused on the oncoming demons.

And sensing that power, the spellcaster smiled in hope.

"We need to ready the Moon Guard!" he commanded. "Forget the wedge! Concentrate only on the Legion's spell attacks!" Rhonin grinned wider. "Damn that Jarod! Only he'd be naive enough to order demigods into battle behind him and get away with it!" Then, his mood darkened as he recalled all that the Legion threw at the defenders. "I hope even they're going to be enough . . ."

"Forward!" shouted Jarod needlessly. His view filled with Infernals and other demons. He silently gave himself to Elune and prepared to die. All he hoped was that his insane act would somehow stave off the enemy's advance long enough for some miracle.

The Infernals were the embodiment of primal force. They were creatures that existed only to crush, pummel, or crash through whatever obstacles— living or not—lay in their path. The spells of the warlocks and other dark sorcerers of the Legion made them a force nigh unstoppable.

Until, that is, they collided with Jarod's charge.

The shield spell of the Eredar was nothing to Cenarius and his kind, for they had been wielding the natural magic of their world since nearly its birth. They tore through the shield as if it were air . . . then did the same to the Infernals behind it.

Agamaggan it was who sped past the rest, the boar proving far more impenetrable than the stonehard demons as he plowed up both the ground and them in one sweep. Great tusks skewered Fel Guard, then tossed the remains aside. Doomguard fluttered up ahead, trying to lance the gargantuan boar, but those that attempted to get through the deadly forest of thorns covering Agamaggan's back instead ended up impaled.

Dead demons still hanging from his mane, the demigod swung around, bowling over other Infernals. The Infernals scattered in utter confusion, this not at all the delicious devastation that they generally wrought. Their rout in turn created further bewilderment among the Fel Guard, who had never faced a situation where their advance force had been so utterly brought to ruin.

Doomguard whipped them on, but all the Fel Guard did was to continue to be crushed under the demigod's hooves or be mangled atop his tusks.

Agamaggan welcomed all such foolhardy foes with a gleeful snort. His eyes burned bright as he cleared the path before him, leaving an awful spectacle of his might behind him. The warriors of the Burning Legion lay piled high. Agamaggan paused only when he had so many corpses caught on his thorns that it proved time to shake a few off. The boar shook like a wet dog, flinging ragged pieces of demons left and right. His coat cleared for more, the demigod lustily returned to his entertainment.

Yet, despite such a horrific debacle, the demons kept coming. Jarod's sword cleaved through the head of the first demon to survive Agamaggan's passing. Cenarius seized another Infernal, raised the struggling monster high over his head, and *threw* him back among his brethren. For the first time, Infernals discovered what it was like to be rammed by one of their kind. The force with which the demigod tossed his missile sent his targets tumbling back into others, creating a chain reaction that went on several lines deep.

The twin bears were much more direct. With heavy paws, they raked across the demons' ranks, bowling aside Infernals and Fel Guard as if brushing leaves off their arms. Several felbeasts leapt through the crumbling wedge and adhered themselves to the foremost of the pair. He laughed and tore off the Legion's hounds from his torso one by one, breaking their backs and sending the corpses flying into the deeper ranks of Archimonde's warriors.

The wedge disintegrated. Doomguard flew in from above to hold back the chaos, but from the sky there came what seemed every bird in all the land. The demons spun about in panic as tiny finches and gigantic raptors tore at their flesh. And among the birds flew their mistress, Aviana, her delicate face now transformed into that of a hungry predator. The demigod's talons ripped through wings, sending Doomguard spiraling to their deaths. Others she seized in an inescapable grip, then used her sharp beak to tear out their throats.

A bearded warrior clad in brown leather and but half the height of a night elf rode into the fray atop a pair of white wolves he guided by the reins in one hand. In his other, the laughing figure wielded what first appeared a sickle. This he threw among the demons with as equally deadly an effect as any other weapon there, if not more so. The spinning sickle flew through the Legion, beheading one demon and cutting open the chest of another before returning to the hand of its master. Over and over this was repeated, the squat warrior reaping a bloody harvest each time.

The demons faltered as they had previously only under the onslaught of the black dragon's disk. This was a foe on par with any that they had ever faced and even their fear of Archimonde briefly evaporated. Fel Guard began to do the unthinkable . . . turn from a battle.

But those first to make that mistake did so at the cost of their lives. Archimonde brooked no retreat, not now, not ever, save as it suited his strategy. The demons upon whom he turned his wrath *melted*, their armor and flesh sliding off their bones like soft wax. Their shrieks became gurgling sounds and in seconds all that remained were bubbling puddles with a few fragments floating within.

The message was clear enough for those who would have followed their path . . . death came in many forms, some more terrifying than others. Daunted, the fleeing warriors turned back to face the demigods, the former's strength now fueled by Archimonde's dark incentives. Aware that one way or another they would perish, the demons fought without regard to safety.

Their manic fighting at last had its effect on Jarod's astounding force. The blades of a score of Fel Guard finally proved too much for the wolverine guardian Rhonin had earlier seen. Yet, as his life force drained from a hundred deep thrusts, he still tore apart each of his attackers, be it by tooth or claw. When this first of the demigods finally fell, his burial mound consisted of Legion bodies piled higher than his head.

There were others that soon joined him, chief among them the Mistress of Birds. Guided by the will of Archimonde, Doomguard with lances fought their way through the flocks toward the one they sought. Two dozen demons perished along the way, but too many more achieved their goal, surrounding the guardian of all winged creatures of Kalimdor and piercing her with their long, barbed spears.

But even the blood of the demigoddess fought for her, dripping down the lances of her slayers and pouring onto their hands. As she fell, lifeless, her assassins tore at their own hides, her blessed blood now infesting their unholy bodies. In the end, the Doomguard died to a one, rending themselves to pieces trying to escape what they could not.

Lances and blades now stuck out of the hides of both bears and Cenarius had wicked cuts all over his body. Every other demigod bore similar marks of the Legion's brutal strength, but still they pushed on.

With them came the night elves, the tauren, the furbolgs, the Earthen . . . every mortal race that had become part of the host. All sensed that now was the defining point of Kalimdor's struggle.

But Rhonin feared that the defining point still favored the Legion. Even with the world's guardians at the forefront, the host had made no actual inroads. If the defenders could not utterly defeat the Burning Legion with such allies, what hope was there?

"We still need the dragons . . ." he muttered as he repelled a warlock's attack. Three more sorcerers had died before he and the Moon Guard had recovered enough and even though the spellcasters now held their own again, they did little other than keep their counterparts occupied.

"We still need the dragons . . ." Rhonin repeated almost like a mantra. But there had been no word from Krasus and even the wizard, who knew well the mage's tremendous skills and cunning, began to wonder if perhaps his former mentor had indeed perished in the lair of Deathwing.

Then a huge, dark shape soared over the battle and Rhonin's worst fears were realized. Deathwing was here! That could only mean that Krasus and the others *were* dead and now the black sought to wreak vengeance upon all his imagined enemies.

But as the huge, winged beast turned back, the wizard noted a peculiar thing about it. The dragon was not black, but a dusky *gray*, like rock. There were also many differences in its face and form, differences that, for some reason, had a familiarity to Rhonin. It almost reminded him of another dragon from his days fighting the orcs. It almost looked like—like—

Alexstrasza?

The gray dragon landed among the demons, crushing several underneath. With one wing, it swept aside a dozen more. The giant let out a roar and seized a mouthful of the enemy, crushing them between its jaws before letting their bodies drop.

Only then did Rhonin see that the dragon had no gullet.

It was *literally* made of stone.

With ruthless abandon, the great golem tore through the Legion. Seeing what it alone could do, the wizard again wished for the true dragons to return.

Then, it occurred to him to wonder just what had brought this false Alexstrasza to the host's aid.

"Krasus?" he blurted, turning around. "Krasus?"

And there, just coming up over a ridge, strode the tall, pale form he knew so well. Beside Krasus walked Malfurion and Brox, both clearly weary, but intact.

Cautiously breaking off from the battle, Rhonin ran to meet the others. He almost hugged them, so grateful was he to see such familiar faces.

"Praise be, that you're all alive!" He grinned. "The Demon Soul! You've got it!"

No sooner had he spoken then Rhonin saw that he was wrong. He looked from one to the other, trying to read the story from their eyes alone.

"We had it," Krasus replied. "But it was stolen by agents of the Legion . . ."

"Including my brother," added Malfurion, shaking his head at Krasus, who had clearly wanted to avoid telling Rhonin that part. "It's no use to hide that! Illidan's thrown his lot in with the palace!" The druid shook from frustration. "The palace!"

"But . . . that dragon! What does that mean . . . and where's Korialstrasz? You said in your message that you'd met up with him!"

"There is no time for that! We must prepare!"

"Prepare for what?"

Brox suddenly pointed his ax past the others. "Look! The stone one!"

They followed his gaze to see the animated effigy of Alexstrasza aswarm with demons. They chopped at it—her—much the way the Earthen had earlier the one Infernal. Others attacked her legs with blades, chipping away as best they could at the false dragon's foundation.

The wizard could scarce believe what was happening. "Why doesn't she fly away?"

"Because the time of her enchantment is almost at an end," Krasus remarked with clear sadness.

"I don't understand . . ."

"Look. It happens already."

The golem's movements grew sluggish, this despite the fact that the damage done to the body had to be superficial at worst. The stone dragon managed to shake her wings free of several of the demons, sending them flying far into the sky. However, that effort proved her last major one.

"What's happening, Krasus?"

"She was meant to bring us here at the desire of the one of whom she is only a shadow. But shadows fade, Rhonin, and her task is done. We can give thanks that enough remained for her to do such damage as we have witnessed."

Despite the clinical tone of his words, the mage's eyes gave indication of a regret far deeper. Rhonin understood. To Krasus, even seeing this effigy of his beloved queen and mate suffer was a strain.

The false dragon roared mournfully. Demons now practically covered the entire body save the head. The left legs defiantly straightened, but from the right ones there was no movement.

"It's over—" Krasus began.

Then, without warning, the false Alexstrasza leaned into her right. Her wing on that side folded in and her left rose into the sky.

Midway up, all animation ceased. The eyes of the golem grew lifeless.

And under the stress of so much weight, the right wing collapsed. The demons atop the statue clung helplessly as the dragon queen's creation tipped over . . . and crushed every demon still hanging onto the back.

Krasus's chest swelled with pride. "Every inch worthy of my queen, even if only her shadow!"

Dust rose from where the gargantuan statue lay. Even as they watched, the legs and the left wing joined the right in collapsing. Demon warriors scattered as huge chunks of rock fell among them.

"What now, though?" demanded the human. His hopes had grown with the arrival of his companions, but if they had neither the disk nor this magical construct as reward for their efforts, then their entire journey had been for nought.

He was not encouraged by Krasus's next words. "What *now,* young Rhonin? We fight as we have fought and we wait. We wait for my good queen to rally my kind and bring them to the fight. The Demon Soul is going where it will be, for a time, no threat to them. They will *have* to act."

"And if they don't? If they hesitate too long, as before?"

His former mentor leaned close so that only the wizard would hear. "Then Sargeras will have at last the means by which to enter Kalimdor . . . and once he has entered our world, the demon lord will unwrite the history of ten thousand years."

FOURTEEN

The storm raged over the Well of Eternity, the black waters whipping into a frenzy. Waves higher than the palace crashed on the shore. A howling wind tossed any loose debris through the air like deadly missiles.

Lightning illuminated the coming of the party from the towered edifice. Even the queen herself—accompanied by her handmaidens, of course—had journeyed with, although she was borne on a silver litter carried by Fel Guard.

Mannoroth led the way, followed by Illidan and Captain Varo'then. A number of Highborne sorcerers and satyrs—the two groups purposely separate from one another—followed in their wake and, behind them, came a contingent of the palace guard. At the end of the grand procession marched twin ranks of demon warriors a hundred strong each.

Mannoroth stood at the edge of the Well, stretching forth his brutish arms and drinking in the chaos beyond. Through the "gift" granted him by Sargeras, Illidan marveled at the forces in play above and within the vast body of water. Nothing he had experienced so far, not even the power of the demon lord, compared to that which the sacred Well contained.

"Truly, we never tapped more than a shadow of its greatness," he murmured to the captain.

Varo'then, blind to such glory, merely shrugged. "It'll now serve us well by bringing to us our Lord Sargeras."

"But not immediately," the sorcerer reminded him. "Not immediately."

"What does that matter?"

They grew silent as the winged demon turned. He reached out to the officer, grating, "The disk! It's time!"

Expression masked, Varo'then removed the Soul from his belt pouch and handed it over. Mannoroth momentarily eyed the dragon's creation with open avarice, then likely thought better of trying to keep it for himself. Glaring at the Highborne and the satyrs, the tusked demon snapped, "Take your places!"

The spellcasters wended their way over fragments of homes and broken bits of bone. The carnage that had taken much of Zin-Azshari had spread even to the very edge of the Well. Illidan learned that a few defiant night elves had tried to make a stand here on the shore, hoping that their nearness would enable them to draw better from the source of their people's magic. That hope had not panned out and the demons had gleefully torn them apart on this very spot.

The irony was, at least to Malfurion's twin, that they had been correct in their assumption, if not the execution of their plan. He could see the myriad ways in which to manipulate the Well's immense potential and understood more than ever what the lord of the Legion intended.

The sorcerers and satyrs formed the pattern dictated by Sargeras. Mannoroth studied their positions carefully, threatening into their proper places those who had erred. When at last the scaled behemoth was satisfied, he stepped back from the group.

"Do I understand we won't see our Lord Sargeras just yet, dear captain?" Azshara languidly asked from her litter.

"Not at this time, no, Light of Lights . . . but it shall not be much longer. Once he has the way stabilized, he will step through."

Eyes veiled, she nodded. "I trust I will be notified of his arrival, then."

"What can be done will be done," Varo'then promised.

Illidan wondered if the queen truly believed that she would become the consort of the demon lord. He doubted very much such a notion fit into Sargeras's designs.

But thought of Azshara's desires faded quickly as he watched the spellcasters begin. A crackling ball of blue lightning formed within their pattern. Now and then, a tiny bolt would dart toward one figure or another, but although the Highborne or satyr in question started slightly, they never faltered in their task.

Muttering filled the air, each voice speaking minutely different words of power. The combination of their distinctive incantations began to summon forth energy from the Well. Illidan watched as those energies, as individual as their summoners, coalesced around the sphere. With each addition, the bolts cast off by it grew brighter, stronger . . .

Then, within the sphere . . . the all-too familiar gap appeared.

The spellcasters had reopened the portal to the Legion's nether realm close to the Well of Eternity so that Sargeras could better draw upon the latter. Illidan sensed the sudden nearness of the demon lord's presence.

Let it be cast out . . . the voice in all their heads commanded.

"Do it!" reinforced Mannoroth, looming over the night elves and satyrs.

As one, those making up the pattern ceased their muttering and clenched their fists.

The sphere—and the portal within—soared out over the storm-tossed waters, quickly vanishing from sight.

Now . . . the disk . . .

Illidan's heart leapt. He wanted to grab the dragon's creation from Mannoroth, but common sense kept his countenance still and his hand by his side. There would be no taking the Dragon Soul—or *Demon Soul,* as he had heard his brother call it—at this time.

But at another opportunity, however . . .

As before, Illidan immediately buried such thoughts. Fortunately, even Sargeras was likely far too intent on the events at hand to pay any attention to the sorcerer's duplicitous intentions, even had Illidan's mind been unshielded.

He watched intently as Mannoroth held the disk high. The winged demon muttered words lost in the wind.

Green fire surrounded the golden piece. The *Demon* Soul—yes, that name was far more appropriate, Malfurion's brother decided—rose above Mannoroth's palm . . . and then, like the sphere containing the portal, flew out over the churning waters of the Well.

"Is that *all?*" Azshara asked somewhat petulantly.

Before the erstwhile Captain Varo'then could soothe her, the wind abruptly died. The storm, too, appeared to pause, although the dark, menacing clouds continued to twist and turn like a thousand serpents coiling around one another.

Illidan it was who sensed first what was coming. "I'd recommend that your highness have her bearers retreat up to the top of the ridge down which we earlier came."

To prove that he meant what he said, the sorcerer turned and started back.

The captain glared at him, as if suspecting some ruse, then ordered his own soldiers to do the same.

With a graceful wave of her hand, the queen had her Fel Guard follow suit.

A sound like the roar of a thousand night sabers issued forth from somewhere near the center of the Well. Illidan glanced over his shoulder at the black waters, his pace doubling.

The sorcerer and satyrs finally fled, their task no longer demanding that they stay so near the shoreline. Only Mannoroth remained, the demon again stretching forth his arms as if to embrace a lover.

"It begins!" he roared almost merrily. "It begins!"

And a wave as large as any dragon swept over the area where the demon stood.

The entire shoreline vanished under a relentless, ripping tide that did not flow inward, but rather *sideways*. Ruined structures were washed away as if they were nothing. The horrific waves washed over the land again and again, more and more stripping it bare. Stone obelisks were torn from their foundations and paved pathways scattered in chunks. The dead, who had remained unburied, were taken to a deeper, darker place beyond Zin-Azshari where Illidan knew that they would find no better rest than before.

As he finished climbing the ridge, the sorcerer saw at last what was truly happening to the Well and even he stood stunned at the magicks wielded so easily by the distant Sargeras.

A vast whirlpool now engulfed the entire body of water.

He could not, of course, view its full extent, but the very fact that it stretched from the shore of the capital for as far as he could see in *any* direction gave ample evidence of its mammoth proportions. Illidan saw that, for once, the frenzied energies of the Well now moved in uniform purpose . . . and all were drawn toward the center.

Below and awash in the forces at the edge of the Well, Mannoroth laughed. Fearsome waves that continued to rip away chunks of stone and earth larger than the demon did not even bother the winged being in the least. Mannoroth drank in the glory of his lord's power, urging Sargeras on with shouts.

Secure on shore, Illidan dared probe deeper into the spell. His higher senses brought him seemingly bodily over the water, moving him along so swiftly that he soon left all land behind. At the same time, the sorcerer's mind also soared higher, taking in a better overall picture of what Sargeras had wrought.

He had guessed right when he had believed that the whirlpool encompassed the whole of the Well of Eternity. Even yet only able to see a portion of the entire panorama, it was already obvious to the night elf that no part of the Well had been left untouched.

Then, a shimmering light ahead caught his attention. Stretching his senses to their limits, Illidan took in the Demon Soul itself floating high above the surface. The simple-looking disk radiated a golden light that focused most on the waters below. Illidan already knew enough about the Demon Soul to understand that Sargeras wielded it as no one other than the black dragon could have, possibly more so. Even from the distant realm where he waited, the lord of the Legion manipulated the incredible power of the disk perfectly in conjunction with the primal forces of the Well.

But where was the portal? Try as he might, Illidan could not sense it around the Demon Soul. Where, then had Sargeras—

Cursing his ignorance, the sorcerer looked down into the center of the maelstrom.

Looked down . . . and stared into a pathway beyond reality, a pathway to the realm of the Burning Legion.

Illidan had thought that most of the demons had passed through already, but he saw now that what had come had been but a fraction. Endless ranks awaited in the beyond, savage, tusked warriors hungry for destruction. They spread on forever, as far as he could tell, and among them were fiends such as he knew Kalimdor had yet to experience. Some were winged, others crawled, but all were filled with the same intense lust for blood as those he had faced.

Then . . . Illidan sensed the demon lord himself. He felt only the least bit of Sargeras's presence, but it was more than enough to make the night elf flee from his glimpse of the nether realm. What Illidan had previously experienced of Sargeras's will had been, he realized belatedly, the tiniest mote of what there truly was. Here, where the lord of the Legion physically existed, no shield could possibly keep the demon from knowing all that Malfurion's brother thought.

And if Sargeras knew what Illidan planned, the sorcerer's fate would make that which had befallen the citizens of Zin-Azshari a pleasant and peaceful way to die . . .

"What ails you, spellcaster?" grated Varo'then's voice.

Illidan forced himself not to shake as his mind returned to his body. "It's . . . overwhelming . . ." he said honestly. "Just overwhelming."

Even the captain did not argue with him there.

Mannoroth plodded up the ridge, his four trunklike legs making craters in the already much-damaged ground. His monstrous orbs held a fanatical look such as Illidan had never seen in the demon prior. Although he had been drenched in the Well, the fearsome figure was completely dry. Such was the truth of the Well, for although it resembled liquid, it was far more.

"Soon . . ." Mannoroth nearly cooed. "Soon, our lord will pass through into Kalimdor! Soon he will come . . ."

"And then he will remake Kalimdor into paradise!" Azshara breathed from atop her litter. "Paradise!"

The demon commander's eyes grew fiery with anticipation, anticipation . . . and something else that Illidan quickly focused upon. "Yes . . . Kalimdor will be remade."

"How soon?" the queen pressed, her lips parted and her breath quickening. "Very soon?"

"Yes . . . very soon . . ." Mannoroth answered. He trudged past her, heading back to the palace. "Very soon . . ."

"How wonderful!" Azshara clapped her hands together. Lady Vashj and the other attendants mirrored her glee.

"We're done here, then," snarled Captain Varo'then, who seemed caught between his desire for Sargeras to arrive and his jealousy against any being who would steal the queen's emotions from him. "Back to the palace!" the officer commanded the soldiers and demon warriors. "Back to the palace!"

The Highborne and the satyrs needed no such commands, most already following Mannoroth. Only Illidan lagged behind, his thoughts torn between what he thought he had read in the latter's words and expression and the glimpse the sorcerer had managed of the demon lord's realm.

Malfurion's brother looked back at the roaring whirlpool that was now the Well of Eternity . . . looked back and, for the first time, felt his extreme confidence in himself slightly shaken.

Tyrande was aware that something was taking place, something of tremendous magnitude, but what it might be, she certainly could not tell from her cell. Elune still provided her with some defense against her captors, but little more. The priestess was blind to what happened in the outside world. For all she knew, her people had been crushed and the Burning Legion now marched unhindered across Kalimdor, razing to the ground what remained of the once-beautiful land.

They had taken the guard from her door, the insidious Captain Varo'then deciding that such were wasted on a prisoner clearly going nowhere. Tyrande could hardly blame the officer for his decision; she had certainly revealed herself to be of no threat to the palace.

The sound of sudden footsteps caught her attention. It was hardly the time to bring her food and water. Besides, since the one time she had accepted both from Dath'Remar, Tyrande had neither eaten nor drunk anything more. The Highborne had begged her on both his successive visits to do so, but she took only what she needed, not wanting to risk becoming accustomed to depending upon those who had imprisoned her.

The door slid open with a short-lived creak. To her surprise, it was Dath'Remar and another Highborne. The latter glanced inside only once, took stock of the prisoner, then slipped back into the corridor.

"Dath'Remar! What brings you—"

"Hush, mistress!" He surveyed the cell as if expecting to find it filled with Fel Guard. Seeing that they were alone, Dath'Remar approached the sphere.

From his robes, he removed the sinister artifact that Lady Vashj had used to briefly free her. Tyrande bit back an exclamation, at first wondering if perhaps the sorcerer intended the same fate for her as Azshara's attendant had.

"Prepare yourself," Dath'Remar whispered.

He repeated the same steps Vashj had. The sphere lowered and the invisible bonds vanished.

Stiff, Tyrande nearly fell. The Highborne caught her in one arm, the artifact held close to her throat.

"My death will avail you little," she told him.

He looked startled, then glanced at the thing in his hand. With utter repugnance, the other night elf tossed it away. "I have not come to perform such a foul deed, mistress! Now, keep your voice low if you wish to have any hope of escaping this place!"

"Escape?" Tyrande felt her pulse race. Was this some new, cruel jest?

Dath'Remar read her eyes. "No trickery! This was discussed long and hard by us! We cannot stand this obscenity any longer! The queen—" He almost choked, clearly caught between his devotion to Azshara and his repugnance for all that had occurred. "The queen . . . she is mad. There can be other explanation. She has turned her back on her people for a being of depravity and carnage! This Sargeras promises a perfect world where we, the Highborne, would rule, but all some of us see is the ruination of everything! What paradise can be built from blood-drenched stone and parched earth? None, we think!"

She was not entirely astounded by his confession. There had been hint of his concerns in their prior conversations. It had originally surprised her that there was any independent thought left in the palace—the demon lord surely desiring absolute devotion—but perhaps Sargeras had finally spread his will in too many directions.

Whatever the reasons, the high priestess gave thanks to the Mother Moon for this opportunity. She felt certain that she could entrust herself to Dath'Remar.

"This is our only chance," the sorcerer emphasized. "The demon lord's minions are out near the Well performing some spellwork. They'll be occupied long enough. The others are waiting below, in the stables."

"The *others?*"

"We can stay here no longer, especially if you are discovered missing. This was decided. I arranged so that most who would leave would not be included in the demons' present task . . . and those who had to be will be honored for their sacrifice for the rest of us."

"May the Mother Moon watch over them," Tyrande whispered. The fates of those others would not be pleasant ones when Mannoroth and his lord discovered the night elves' duplicity. "But what about the guards?"

"There are a few of them among us, but most are the dogs of Captain Varo'then! We will have to be cautious about them! Now come! No more questions!"

He led her out into the corridor where the second Highborne waited. Tyrande hesitated at first, suddenly startled to actually be out of her cell. Dath'Remar, glaring impatiently, pulled her along.

Up a long flight of stairs they rushed, Dath'Remar's companion taking the lead. There were no signs of sentries, which the priestess assumed had to mean that the sorcerers had done their best to clear the path ahead of time.

The stairway ended at an iron door upon whose center had been framed the beatific face of Azshara. Seeing her made Tyrande involuntarily shake, a reaction which stirred a sympathetic look from the two Highborne.

"Through here is the hall that will lead us directly to the stables. The others should have the mounts ready. When the gates open, we charge like the wind."

"What about . . . what about the demons?"

He straightened in pride. "We are the *Highborne,* after all! We are the finest spellcasters in all the realm! They will fall before our might!" Then, with less hubris, Dath'Remar added, "And, likely, many of us will fall as well . . ."

"I sense the way is clear," interjected the second sorcerer, smiling arrogantly. "The distraction spell still holds Varo'then's little curs."

"But not much longer, I suspect." Dath'Remar gently pushed aside the door. Sure enough, the hallway beyond was devoid of the grim-faced soldiers.

"We are nearly at the stables," the other Highborne remarked, his own confidence growing. "You see, Dath'Remar! So much worry about a worthless pack of—"

His words ended in a gurgle as a bolt pierced his neck, the end coming out the opposing side. Blood sprayed Tyrande and Dath'Remar.

As the dead sorcerer tumbled to the floor, several guards filled the corridor.

"Halt right there!" ordered a subofficer with a plumed helm.

In response, Dath'Remar angrily waved one hand to the side.

An invisible force bowled over the guards, sending them flying against the walls like leaves in the wind. The clatter of their striking echoed throughout the hall.

"That will teach them to dare attack a Highborne of the Elite Circle!" he snapped.

"Someone will come to investigate the noise," the priestess counseled.

To his credit, Dath'Remar seemed to acknowledge his overzealous assault. With a grimace, he pulled Tyrande along.

They entered the stables but a short time later, where Tyrande found herself confronted with an amazing sight. She had assumed from her companion's description that there would be a fair number of Highborne, but not so many as she saw before her now. Surely a good third of the caste awaited, including entire families.

"Where is—?" began one female, but, a look from Dath'Remar immediately silenced her on the subject of the dead sorcerer.

"We heard the struggle above and sensed the shifting of magical forces," added another male. "The demons will have sensed it, also."

"It was necessary." Dath'Remar led Tyrande forward. "You've a swift mount for the priestess, Quin'thatano?"

"The swiftest."

"Good." The sorcerer turned to her. "Mistress Tyrande, we will need you to speak for us when we reach the host. We are aware of the ill-feelings the rest will have toward our kind—"

"We will make them listen!" urged the female Highborne. "We have the power to do so—"

"And likely get ourselves all slain!" growled Dath'Remar. To Tyrande, he added, "You will do this for us?"

"Such a question! Of course, I will! I swear, by the Mother Moon!"

This seemed to satisfy him, if not some of his fellows. Yet, it seemed that everyone here deferred to Dath'Remar Sunstrider when it came to decisions.

"Well enough, then! The word of the high priestess should be sufficient for all!" He indicated the night sabers. "Mount up! We've not a moment more to lose!"

The fleeing Highborne brought little with them, a mark of the urgency. Well-accustomed to the fineries of life, Tyrande would have expected them to have nearly brought their entire homes.

Another sorcerer handed the reins of a sleek, lean female panther to the priestess. Hanging from the animal's side was a long, sturdy sword no doubt stolen from Captain Varo'then's soldiers. Nodding her gratitude for this welcome gift, she climbed up and waited.

Dath'Remar looked to make certain that everyone was ready, then pointed at the two huge, wooden doors leading out. "We ride together! No breaking off! Those that do shall suffer the consequences of their careless-ness. The demons are everywhere. We must fight and ride at the same time, possibly for days." He straightened. "But we are the *Highborne,* the foremost wielders of the Well's bounty! With it, we shall tear open the path ahead and leave in our wake the bodies of those who would seek to prevent our passing!"

Tyrande kept her expression neutral. Even the Highborne had to know that many would die and die brutally. She silently prayed to Elune to guide her in aiding her new companions. These Highborne sought redemption for their part in bringing the Legion to Kalimdor; Tyrande would do whatever necessary to see to it that they were given the opportunity to receive that for-giveness.

Dath'Remar pointed at the entrance. "Let the way be open!"

The huge doors exploded outward.

"Ride!"

Tyrande urged her mount after his.

The first of the Highborne burst through the shattered doors, their night sabers leaping over the wreckage with ease. The corpses of a few demons lit-tered the immediate area, apparently caught up in the devastation.

"Mannoroth and the others should still be at the Well!" shouted Dath'Remar. "Therein lies our hope of success!"

Mention of the Well brought Illidan into Tyrande's thoughts. How she wished that he was among these trying to escape the demon lord's evil rather than embracing it.

The sinister mist pervading Zin-Azshari did not slow the riders, the High-borne likely very familiar with it by now. The priestess focused on following her rescuers and waiting.

Waiting for the first threat to their flight.

And when it came, it came in the form of felbeasts, who leapt upon riders in the middle of the pack, bringing down two and nearly eviscerating another. The demons' tentacles adhered to the bodies of the victims, draining them with gusto.

A female spellcaster threw what at first appeared a tiny stick. However, by the time it reached its target, it had stretched out into a full lance, which pierced the felbeast in the chest.

The other demonic hounds perished in similar fashion, the last of them fleeing off with loud, dismayed howls. Dath'Remar sent a bolt of lightning down on the survivors, obliterating two and sending their body parts raining down on the fleeing Highborne. A third felbeast escaped.

"We are surely known now!" the sorcerer snarled. "Faster!"

A deep, mournful horn blared. Moments later, several others from far ahead of the party responded. Tyrande prayed fervently to Elune, aware that the night elves would very soon be fighting for their lives.

"Sarath'Najak! Yol'Tithian! To me!" The pair in question rode up beside Dath'Remar. Each raised a fist ahead and began chanting.

A sharp, continuous flash of crimson energy formed before the lead riders. Even Tyrande sensed the tremendous forces summoned from the Well.

Then . . . out of the mist materialized a wall of gargantuan, tusked warriors framed by the greenish flames radiating from their armored forms. The Fel Guard poured toward the renegades with weapons nearly as long as Tyrande.

But the first to meet the crimson barrier *burned*. Their own flames took on the same cast as the sorcerers' creation, then engulfed the demons. Monstrous warriors shrieked and fell to the wayside. In only a heartbeat, nothing remained of those stricken save a few scorched pieces of armor.

But the demons continued to press and soon they surrounded the escapees. Individual sorcerers began casting their own spells, with mixed success. They could not concentrate on every demon present and those that managed to slip past wreaked havoc on the night elves. A female went down as her mount, its throat severed, collapsed beneath her. Before she could rise, the Fel Guard who had slain her cat beheaded her. Another Highborne was stripped from the saddle, his body impaled through the back before being tossed without care under the trampling paws of the night sabers.

One huge warrior managed to slip in behind Dath'Remar. Gasping, Tyrande drew her blade and prayed for Elune to guide her hand.

The sword took on the pale, silver glow of her patron. It cut through the demon's armor as if through air.

With a grunt, the Fel Guard started to turn toward Tyrande—and the top half of his body slid off. The demon crumpled, the priestess's blessed strike so fine that its victim had not at first realized that he was dead.

Unaware of his near-fatal brush, Dath'Remar shouted something to his two comrades. Tyrande could not see what they did, but the shield that they had created not only spread farther afield, but also shifted to an intense blue.

There was a crackling sound and the first demon to run into the new spell flew back as if tossed by a catapult. He crashed among his fellows, his body crumbling to dust.

This new spell proved far more effective. Slowed down by the demons' initial onslaught, the escaping Highborne now regained speed. Yet, behind them they left more than a dozen of their number, most ripped apart by the savage blades of the Burning Legion. Riderless night sabers, their backs soaked in blood, kept with the pack.

A younger Highborne female near Tyrande screamed, then rose up and vanished into the mist. A second later, her scream cut off with a terrible finality and her broken body dropped among the fleeing figures.

Night elves began looking up and around in consternation. Tyrande looked over her shoulder—and saw, too late, the clawed hands that seized an older male and dragged him up out of sight.

"Doomguard!" she shouted. "Beware! Doomguard in the mists above!"

Another pair of claws came down near her. Tyrande slashed. She heard a savage growl and the Doomguard retreated . . . minus one hand.

Two robed spellcasters raised their arms. What seemed like a halo formed first over them, then spread out over much of the rest of the party.

But before they could finish whatever spell they sought to unleash, an explosion rocked them. Their night sabers reeled and the two Highborne were thrown.

From the center of the explosion arose an Infernal. How the demon had fallen among the riders without being either seen or detected, Tyrande did not know, but, at the moment, that hardly mattered. The Infernal began rampaging among the night elves, crashing into full-size panthers without so much as losing a step.

Even as that happened, two more Highborne were stolen from their seats by Doomguard above. The priestess looked to Dath'Remar, but there was no help or guidance from that direction. The lead sorcerer was already hard-pressed to keep back the thickening ranks of Fel Guard, who appeared to be trying by sheer numbers to overwhelm the spell he and the others had concocted. With each step, the escape slowed and by Tyrande's estimation, it would not be long before the Highborne came to an utter halt.

Pulling up, she raised her sword to her face and called again upon the powers granted her by the Mother Moon. Whether or not she survived, Tyrande could not stand idly by while others perished.

"Please, Mother Moon, hear me, Mother Moon . . ." the priestess muttered.

The glow about her blade spread to her, at the same time intensifying. Tyrande thought of the cleansing light of the lunar deity, how, under it, everything was revealed for what it was.

The silver aura flared bright.

Under Elune's light, the mist melted away. Demons on the ground and in the sky found nothing shielding them. More important, they suddenly cringed and looked away, unable to withstand the divine illumination.

And in faltering, they opened a way for the riders.

"There, Dath'Remar!" Tyrande shouted. "Ride that way!"

He did not have to be encouraged. Dath'Remar and his two comrades blazed the path the priestess's prayer had revealed. Mostly blinded, the few demons before them proved minor obstacles readily crushed.

"Ride through! Ride through!" the leader of the Highborne encouraged. Their attackers fell away, none strong enough to resist the light.

Her heart emboldened, Tyrande enthusiastically followed with the rest. The glow about her extended some distance beyond the fringes of the group. She thanked Elune over and over again for this miracle . . .

But, just as Tyrande herself cut past the Legion's lines, clawed hands seized her, ripping the priestess from her night saber. With a startled cry, she flew up and away from her companions.

Straining, Tyrande looked into the contorted visage of a Doomguard. The demon's eyes were all but shut and his ragged breathing indicated just how much the illumination around her pained him.

Without hesitation, she cut at the armored figure. Her blow landed sideways, but it startled her attacker. One hand lost its grip. Tyrande had no opportunity to look down to see how far away the ground was. She could only pray that Elune would cushion her fall.

With grim determination, the priestess drove her blade through the Doomguard's chest.

His jerking movements tore the sword from her grip. The last bit of the demon's hold vanished.

Tyrande clutched his dead body, hoping to pull it under her before she hit the earth. Unfortunately, in his death throes, the Doomguard twisted out of her reach.

She shut her eyes tight. Her prayers were to her goddess, but her last focused thoughts were on Malfurion. He would blame himself for her death, if that was now to be, and she wanted no such burden upon his shoulders. What happened to her would be fated by the gods, not his actions. Tyrande understood that Malfurion had done all he could, but that the fate of their people far outweighed her meager self.

But if only she could have looked into his face once more . . .

Tyrande struck the ground . . . and yet, the collision was not at all as she expected. It barely even shook her, much less broke all her bones and split open her skull.

Her fingers touched dirt. She *had* landed . . . but, if so, why was she still in one piece?

Rolling to a sitting position, Tyrande looked around. The aura about her had faded, leaving her surrounded by mist and alone save for the broken bodies of night elves and demons.

No . . . not alone. A tall, so very familiar figure emerged from the resurging mist and, at sight of him, her cheeks flushed.

"Malfurion!"

But almost the instant that Tyrande uttered the name, she knew that she had chosen the wrong one.

Illidan, his mouth fighting a frown, leaned over the fallen priestess. "Stupid little fool . . ." He reached down a hand. "Well? Come on with me . . . if you'd like to live long enough to see me save the world!"

FIFTEEN

Above the center of the Well of Eternity, the Demon Soul flared bright. Within the abyss formed by the Sargeras's spell, forces set in play by both the Soul and the Well churned, slowly building up into the creation of a stable portal. From his monstrous realm, the lord of the Legion prepared for his entrance into this latest prize. Soon, so very soon, he would eradicate all life, all existence, from it . . . and then he would go on to the next ripe world.

But there were others waiting in growing expectation, others with dire dreams far older than even that of the demon lord. They had waited for so very long for the means to escape, the means to reclaim what had once been theirs. Each step of success by Sargeras toward strengthening his portal was a step of success for them. With the Well, with the Demon Soul, and with the lord of the Legion's might, they would instead open up a window into their eternal prison.

And once open, there would be no sealing it again.

The Old Gods waited. They had done so for so very long, they could wait a little longer.

But only a little . . .

And with the entrance of Sargeras surely imminent, Archimonde threw everything into the battle. He stripped warriors from all other directions, knowing that the defeat of the host would be the defeat of the world.

The host, in turn, fought because it had no choice but to fight. Night elves, tauren, and others knew only that to give in meant to bend their necks to demon blades. Fall they might, but not without giving everything they could.

⎯⎯⎯

Malfurion struggled to do his part. His spells summoned whirlwinds that carried aloft warriors and beasts, then dropped them from deathly heights. Seeds cast by him into those winds sprouted full-grown in the demon bellies, ripping their hosts to shreds. The lifeless corpses then dropped down upon the Legion, causing further havoc.

Deep below the earth, Malfurion found the burrowers, the worms and such, who had managed so far to hide from the evil. Urged on by him, they churned away at the ground, making it unstable. Tusked warriors suddenly sank beneath as if in quicksand, while others, bogged down, fell easy prey to archers and lancers.

In the sky, the demons held sway, but they held it with much cost. Jarod had archers almost fully concentrating on the Doomguard and their like. Whatever the carnage caused by the winged furies, many paid for it with bolts bristling out of their necks.

The Moon Guard fought valiantly against the Eredar, the Infernals, and, worse, the Dreadlords. The night elves were strengthened not only by Rhonin and Krasus, but also the shamans of the tauren and furbolgs. The shamans worked in much more subtle manners, but their results were proven by warlocks who fell over dead or simply vanished.

And yet, there were always more demons to replace those who perished.

Brox stood at the forefront with Jarod and Kalimdor's legendary guardians, the orc seeming as astounding a creature as the beings by whose side he fought. Brox laughed as he had not since that day of battle when he and his comrades had expected to die valiantly. Indeed, the graying warrior expected to die now, but still his ax proved the superior, cutting through foe after foe as if it hungered for demon flesh. It was not merely the magic instilled in the weapon that caused such damage to the enemy, but the skill with which the orc wielded it. Brox was a master of his art, which was why his chieftain, Thrall, had chosen him in the first place.

Then, a pack of felbeasts caught one of the bears by surprise, leaping atop their victim and quickly bringing down the giant. Before their gargantuan adversary even hit the ground, a score more joined the first pack. Their suckers immediately adhered to the furred body and the monsters drank lustily of the guardian's inherent magic . . . and, thus, life.

The fallen one's twin roared angrily when he saw what had happened. Pummeling aside Fel Guard, he threw himself upon the horrific leeches. One by one, the demigod tore them away from the unmoving form, ripping off heads and breaking backs in the process.

But when he had reached his twin, it was immediately evident that rescue had come too late.

Raising his head high, the forest guardian roared his pain, then turned on the ranks of demons and began rampaging through their lines as if they were made of paper. Despite lances and other weapons constantly pincushioning him, he dug deeper into the Burning Legion, swiftly leaving behind his other companions until he could no longer even be seen. Brox and Jarod, closest to the front, heard his last, unrepentant roar . . . and then noted grimly the silence that followed.

Bodies lay littered for as far as the eye could see and it was not uncommon for combatants to duel one another standing atop the corpses of their predecessors. Demigods fought besides night elves who fought beside tauren who fought beside furbolgs, Earthen, and more and all wore the same grim expressions.

It was Cenarius who still led Kalimdor's epic guardians and he tore at the demons with a violence that shocked even Rhonin and Krasus. His gnarled talons stripped through armor and flesh, spilling the monstrous warriors' innards upon the field. The forest lord fought as if one possessed and with the death of each fellow guardian, his efforts grew more terrifying, more relentless. He seemed determined to make up for all those who had fallen, no matter the cost to himself.

And fall they continued to do. With Fel Guard clutching him like hounds worrying their prey, the great boar, Agamaggan, finally teetered. He rammed into several felbeasts, tossing them up or goring them with his tusks, but then, at last, the weight of so many demons proved too much. The demigod dropped to his knees, where his tenacious adversaries began chopping in earnest at his torso. The huge beast shook off some of those clinging to him, but that proved his last effort. Blood dripping from a hundred deep wounds, he groaned . . . and then stilled. Even after, the savage attacks on his body did not cease, the demons so caught up in their butchery that they did not yet realize that they had slain him.

This latest death spurred Cenarius yet further. He fell upon the demons hacking away at the boar's mangled corpse, crushing their throats or impaling them on the other demigod's thorny mane. Such was his fury that at last he became the prime focus of the Burning Legion's onslaught. The invisible hand of Archimonde guided the most powerful of demons toward the forest lord.

Already battling for their own survival, there was nothing Krasus or any of the others could do. More and more the fearsome warriors surrounded Malfurion's mentor until even Cenarius's antlers could barely be seen.

Then . . . just as it seemed he, too, would fall, there was again the flash of white once seen by Rhonin. A gargantuan, four-legged form struck the swarm of demons head on. A rack several times more massive than that of the forest lord threw fiery warriors by the score from the faltering Cenarius. Huge hooves crushed in hard skulls or caved in armored chests. Teeth snapped off limbs or ripped open throats.

And only at last did the astounding creature come into focus. There, towering over the weakened Cenarius, a magnificent, pure white stag held the demons at bay. So much did his coat gleam that the minions of the Burning Legion were half-blinded, making them easy prey for the massive animal.

Again and again, the stag used his antlers to clear the bloody field before him of foes. Nothing, not even Infernals, could slow his efforts. He cleared the Burning Legion not only from the area of the fallen forest lord, but even from that of other defenders nearby.

Brox and Jarod suddenly found themselves under the overwhelming gaze of the stag. Words did not pass from the gigantic creature to them, yet, somehow they knew that they were to drag Cenarius back from the battle. This they did even as a new wave of horror charged forward. Yet, before the stag, nothing long stood. Row upon row of demon rushed up with weapons drawn, only to be torn to shreds moments later.

But if the Legion's blades could not bring down this new champion, the horde had other, more sinister tools at their disposal. From the sky there abruptly came black lightning, which burnt and baked the ground around the stag. In the lightning's wake erupted dark, green fires that scorched the pristine coat of the demigod. Charred earth rose up and, forming clawed hands, seized the four legs tight.

Then, the ranks of demons parted . . . and through the ominous gap strode Archimonde himself.

With each step toward the stag, Archimode swelled in size until he stood as tall as his adversary. In contrast to his manic warriors, the demonic commander remained stone-faced, almost analytical. He held no weapon, but his clenched fists radiated the same monstrous fire that burned around the stag.

The demigod shook, breaking away the earthy claws. Then, with a challenging snort, the demigod lowered his antlers and met the archdemon.

Their collision was marked by thunder and a tremor that toppled fighters for some distance around. Demons and night elves alike fled the awesome fury of their duel. Where the stag's hooves struck the harsh ground, sparks flew up into the heavens. Archimonde's own feet dug deep, creating ravines and tossing up new hills taller than his warriors.

Bloody scars traced the paths of the demon's claws in the stag's hide. Sharp, glistening dots from which burst green fire showed where antlers had pierced Archimonde's seemingly impervious skin. Demon and demigod wrestled and no other living creature dared come in their path.

Farther back, Jarod and Brox, joined midway by Dungard the Earthen, brought the stricken Cenarius to where Krasus stood. Risking an attack by the Eredar, Krasus pulled himself from the battle to investigate the forest lord's condition.

" 'Tis some bad wounds he's suffered," muttered Dungard, taking out his pipe.

"He is badly struck," the mage agreed after running his hands across Cenarius's chest. "The poison that is a part of all demons affects him much more than most, possibly because of his affinity to Kalimdor itself." Krasus grimaced. "Still, I *think* he will live . . ."

At that moment, the demigod muttered something. Only Krasus knelt close enough to hear his words properly and when the robed figure looked up, he wore an expression of sorrow.

"What is it?" asked Jarod.

But before Krasus could answer, from the battlefield came a terrible cry. As they all turned toward its source, they witnessed Archimonde with one arm around the giant stag's neck, his other hand twisting his foe's muzzle to the side. Already the stag's head turned at an awful angle, hence the cry.

Krasus leapt to his feet. "No! He must not!"

It was already too late. The demon, his expression still indifferent, tightened his hold further.

A tremendous cracking sound echoed through the region, one that, for just a brief moment, caused all other noises to cease.

And in Archimonde's grip, Cenarius's valiant rescuer fell limp and lifeless.

With an almost flagrant detachment, the archdemon tossed aside his adversary as one might discard a piece of refuse. He then wiped his hands and gazed at the stunned defenders.

Suddenly, creeping vines rushed up from the otherwise lifeless soil, seizing Archimonde's limbs and squeezing tight. Undaunted, Archimonde tore off one set of vines, but as he attempted to throw them away, they instead wrapped around his wrist. At the same time, others grew to take the place of those removed.

Malfurion Stormrage stepped forward, facing the distant demon with eyes as dead as when he had first told the others of Tyrande's kidnapping. A static aura surrounded him and he constantly muttered over a small piece of what Krasus was the first to recognize as a leaf similar to those of the vines.

Archimonde's expression never shifted, but his movements became more frantic. The vines now covered three-quarters of his immense body and appeared all but certain to drape the rest imminently.

Perhaps realizing this, the archdemon ceased his attempts to remove the strangling plants. Instead, eyes narrowed, he freed his arms enough to bring his hands together.

And as Archimonde clasped his fingers . . . the Legion's terrifying commander vanished in a blaze of green flame.

Malfurion gasped. The druid went down on one knee, shaking his head.

"I've failed him . . ." Brox and the mage heard him mutter. "Failed my shan'do when I most shouldn't have . . ."

The orc and the Earthen looked to Krasus for some explanation. The robed figure pursed his lips for a moment, then, quietly explained, "The great Green Dragon, the Aspect called Ysera, is the mother of Cenarius, the forest lord."

Dungard, who had been puffing on his pipe, furrowed his brow, then said, "My people always thought it to be Elune who birthed the forest lord . . ."

"The true tale is quite complicated," replied Krasus.

Brox still said nothing, aware that there was more to come.

"His father . . ." the mage continued, "his father is the ancient woodland spirit, Malorne . . ."

After a moment, the orc finally asked, "And so?"

"Malorne . . . also called the White Stag."

Dungard almost dropped his pipe. A sharp intake of breath marked Brox's sudden understanding. He looked out to where the huge, torn body of the beast lay sprawled ignominiously among the other dead. The father had come to save the son at cost of his own life, something any orc easily understood.

"I failed him . . ." Malfurion repeated, forcing himself up. He glanced at Krasus. "From you, I learned that Ysera was my shan'do's mother—which was surprise enough—but I already knew the truth concerning Malorne. Cenarius made it known to me during my studies that he was seed of the White Stag . . ." The night elf clenched his fist. "And when I saw what Archimonde had done to the father of he who's been like a parent to me, I wanted nothing more than to squeeze the life out of the fiend."

Krasus put a comforting hand on the druid's shoulder. "Have heart, young one. You have briefly driven Archimonde from the battle, no light thing . . ." The mage's eyes narrowed as he glanced past his companion to the field of carnage. "It at least buys us time . . ."

Malfurion shook himself from his sorrow. "We're losing, aren't we?"

"I fear so. With all we throw against them, the demons still prove too strong. I had been certain—had thought—" Krasus spat. "I dared turn Time on its head, did everything despite my own warnings . . . and the results are nothing but calamity after calamity!"

"I don't understand . . ."

"You need understand only this—unless the dragons come and come soon, we shall fall, if not by the blades of the Burning Legion, then by a darker, more ancient evil that manipulates even the dread Sargeras! You know of that which I speak! You felt their awful presence! You know what they would wish of this world! They—"

A howl erupted from Krasus.

"What—" began the druid.

Krasus bent low to the ground. The others watched in horror as his limbs began to turn to stone.

"Eredar!" shouted Malfurion. He felt his own limbs begin to contort in what he knew presaged the same dire fate as that striking the mage. "Brox! Seek out Rhonin—"

But the orc was in no better state than the night elf. Wounded though Archimonde had to be, it was clear to all that he had orchestrated this insidious spell that struck only them. Sargeras's lieutenant knew well that to slay Krasus and his band would be to put an end to the last major hurdle preventing the Burning Legion's victory. Even Jarod lay stricken.

Then, just as each felt the growing stone constrict their lungs and force out their last breath, they heard in their minds a feminine voice that both comforted and steeled them. *Fear not,* it said, *and breathe easy . . .*

As one, Krasus, Malfurion, Brox, and Jarod gratefully inhaled. At the same time, they noticed the rising of the wind and the tremendous shadow passing overhead.

"She has come!" roared Krasus, lifting his hands to the heavens. *"They have come!"*

The sky filled with dragons.

They were red, green, and bronze, the flights of Alexstrasza, Ysera, and the absent Nozdormu. The two Aspects dominated the array, their tremendous wings alone spanning distances several times that of the dragons next nearest in size.

As one, the leviathans dove down toward the demons, who were still focused on their earthbound foes.

"Jarod!" called Krasus, spinning on the host's commander. "Get those horns roaring so loud and so long that there will be no mistaking their intent! The day can still be ours!"

Jarod seized the nearest night saber and rode off. As he vanished in the distance, the dragons began their attack in earnest.

A line of crimson giants opened their mighty maws and unleashed an inferno. Fire swept over the Legion's front lines, several hundred demons burnt to ash in the blink of an eye.

Bronze dragons swept over the demon ranks . . . and as they passed, the monstrous warriors moved in reverse. Yet, while Time had turned about for them, it had not for those behind. Chaos ensued as a collision of titanic proportions created utter mayhem among Archimonde's fighters.

One of the bronzes fell—twisted beyond recognition—as the Eredar and Nathrezim sought to hold back this imposing attack. But their spells faltered and their focus turned on one another as the flight of Ysera hovered above. The closed, dreaming eyes of the green dragons put nightmares into the minds of the susceptible spellcasters. Warlocks looked at one another and saw only the enemy about them.

They reacted accordingly. Eredar slew Eredar and Nathrezim gladly joined in the slaughter. Trapped in the dark daydreams created by the greens, the demons were merciless against their own kind and even Archimonde could not rouse them from their lethal mistake.

Back behind the mayhem, Alexstrasza descended to where Krasus and the others awaited her. Ysera began to do the same—but then, to the astonishment of those who knew of her, the Aspect's eyes opened wide at the horrific sight that lay in the midst of the battlefield. Beautiful, glistening, jade orbs drank in the vision of the white, antlered corpse.

Malorne's corpse.

The dragon let out a wail—not a roar, but a very *pitiful* wail—and flew to where the giant stag lay. The demons still in the area fell victim to her immediate outrage. Ysera snapped up several, crushed others, and sent the rest flying with a slap of one massive wing.

When there was no one else upon which to vent her sorrows, She of the Dreaming descended next to the stag and rested her chin upon his broken head. Her body shook from what could only be sobs.

"We had known we would be late . . ." Alexstrasza managed, eyeing her counterpart with much understanding. "But not so late as this . . ."

"Cenarius still lives," Krasus pointed out. "She must be made aware of that."

With a nod, the Aspect of Life momentarily shut her eyes. A moment later, Ysera lifted her head and looked their way. The two giants gazed at one another, then Ysera fluttered up from Malorne's body.

The others stepped back as she landed next to the unconscious Cenarius. With remarkable delicacy, Ysera took the prone forest lord into her forepaws.

"They will suffer such nightmares that whatever they have for hearts will explode . . ." she grated. "I will bring upon them demons of their own, who will drive them mad until all they can think about is death . . . but I will not permit them to wake long enough to achieve it . . ."

She would have gone on—and also made good her promise—but Krasus dared interrupt. "Render onto the Legion what fate it deserves, She of the

Dreaming, but recall that the fate of Kalimdor—that which Malorne and Cenarius fought well for—still hangs in the balance! Sargeras seeks entrance into the mortal plane . . . and the Old Gods seek to manipulate the demon lord for their own escape!"

"And well aware we are of this," Alexstrasza interjected before a still-distraught Ysera could snap back at the mage. "What is it that must be done?"

"The struggle must go on here, but it also must come to Zin-Azshari . . . and the Well. It will take both dragon and mortal, for there are many elements to confront there."

"Tell us what you plan." Ysera almost objected to her sister's acquiescence, but Alexstrasza would brook no delay from even her. "You know him! You have but to see within him to understand that he must be listened to!"

The emerald dragon finally bowed her head. "So long as the demons suffer."

"We will *all* suffer," the cowled mage went on. "If we do not stop the portal from reaching full bloom . . ." Krasus faced the direction of far-off Zin-Azshari. "A thing that cannot be too far-off, if what I sense means anything . . ."

Sargeras felt Archimonde's hidden dismay. The demon lord was disappointed with his most trusted servant—who had never failed before—but there would be time to punish Archimonde later. The portal was nearly finished. Sargeras wondered why it had taken so long for him to consider this plan. It had all proven so *simple.*

Still, in the long run, such things did not matter. All that did was that soon *he* would step into Kalimdor and when that happened, not all the dragons in that world would be able to save it from him . . .

They felt the nearness of their freedom quickly approaching. How ironic that it would be one who had once been one of the hated Titans who would prove the instrument of their release! It had taken the combined might of many Titans to even force them into captivity; after their triumphant return, there would be little effort needed to eradicate this single, arrogant creature and turn his warriors to serving *their* cause.

The portal strengthened. The time when to usurp it fast approached. Most amusing, the pathetic little beings who fought the fallen Titan's warriors thought that they could take back the disk. Even now, the imprisoned entities could sense the dragons—the Titans' hounds—approaching the Well.

They would be in for a very fatal surprise.

SIXTEEN

Astorm raged over the Well, one that from even such a far distance Malfurion could detect all too easily. It was no normal storm, not even in the sense of those that frequented the mystical waters. This one touched upon powers that were not a part of the mortal plane, powers all too akin to those unleashed by the Burning Legion.

The Burning Legion . . . and something more.

The druid did not quite understand just who or *what* the Three were even after having been touched by their ancient evil. In truth, Malfurion did not *want* to know more. What had insinuated itself into his mind during the quest into Deathwing's lair had been enough to make him determined that such beings could never be allowed to enter Kalimdor . . . if that was any more possible to achieve than stopping the entrance of the lord of the Legion.

He glanced up and around him at the hope of his world. A dozen dragons, Alexstrasza and Ysera at their head. Another female who represented the bronzes followed close behind. Three others of each flight flew in their wake, all of them consorts of one of the Aspects, including this Nozdormu spoken of earlier by Krasus.

The mage himself rode astride the giant red's shoulders, seeming to drink in the wind as they sailed. Knowing him for what he was, Malfurion suspected that Krasus tried to imagine himself as one of the dozen leviathans, his own wings sending him coursing through the heavens.

Brox rode the bronze leader and Rhonin one of Alexstrasza's mates. The red Aspect's senior consort—Tyranastrasz—oversaw the dragon efforts against Archimonde, but the rest were with her, save the stricken Korialstrasz. As for Malfurion, the night elf had the honor to have as his mount Ysera. She had, in fact, insisted upon his being the one she carried.

"You are his pride," she had told the druid, speaking of Cenarius, "and for what you sought to do for him and Malorne, I owe you this . . ."

Unable to articulate any worthy reply, Malfurion had simply bowed before her, then climbed up near her shoulders.

And off they had flown, as simple as all that, to face the terrible might of the demon lord and those manipulating him.

As simple as that . . . all knowing that they might very well perish.

Yet, for Malfurion, it was even more complex than that. At this point, he had little fear concerning his own death—any sacrifice he made worth it to stop such menace—but there were others on his mind as well. Somewhere near their destination, somewhere near or within vast Zin-Azshari, he hoped to find Tyrande and Illidan.

He still could not forgive himself for what had befallen Tyrande and could not blame *her* if she could not find it in her heart to forgive him, either. He had let her fall into the Legion's clutches, a most unthinkable fate. No, if, as he hoped, Tyrande lived, Malfurion expected nothing but hatred and contempt from his childhood friend.

What he expected from himself if he came across his *brother,* the druid could not even imagine, but something would have to be done about Illidan.

Something . . .

"Illidan, please! You must listen to me!" Tyrande blurted as the sorcerer dragged her along with him. It was not her first such outburst, but she hoped that this time he might heed her words. "This is not the path you should take! Think! By embracing the power of the Legion, you more and more draw yourself toward their evil!"

"Don't talk nonsense! I'm going to save Kalimdor! I'll be its beloved hero!" He turned on her. "Don't you understand? Nothing else has worked! We fought and fought and the Legion just keeps coming! I finally came to realize that the only way to deal with demons was to understand them as only they can understand themselves! We must use what they were against them! That's why I came here and pretended to join their ranks! I even fooled their lord into granting me his greatest gifts—"

"Gifts? You call what he did to your eyes *gifts?*"

Malfurion's brother loomed over her, looking at that moment more like one of the demons than any night elf. "If you could *see* as I do, you'd know how amazing the powers are he gave me . . ." With an unnerving smile, Illidan allowed her again to see the pits where once his eyes had been. He paid no mind when Tyrande, just as she had upon her first view of the horror wrought upon him, involuntarily pulled back. Replacing the scarf, he concluded, "Yes, the greatest gifts imaginable . . . and the greatest weapons against the Burning Legion . . ."

The sorcerer pulled her along again and although it was within the priestess's power to struggle free of him, in truth, Tyrande did not exactly wish to leave Illidan. She feared for him, feared for his heart and mind and wanted to do what she could to try to save the misguided spellcaster. The teachings of

Elune only in part guided her; Tyrande Whisperwind still recalled vividly the younger Illidan, the Illidan full of dreams, hope, and goodness.

She only prayed that some part of that younger Illidan still existed within this more jaded, highly-ambitious figure eagerly dragging her through a demon-benighted land.

Thinking of the armored horrors she had already fought, Tyrande glanced around as they wended their way through the fallen city. Each moment, the priestess expected one of the monstrous warriors to pop up from among the ruins and attack. Surely, Mannoroth knew of Illidan's treachery by now.

Perhaps noticing her glances or even reading her thoughts, the black-clad sorcerer slyly informed Tyrande, "The spellwork over the Well has Mannoroth's full attention and he thinks little of me as it is. I've cast the illusion that I've returned to my quarters and am meditating." He grinned wide. "Besides that, the flight of several of the Highborne—the priestess of Elune with them—has also taken their focus elsewhere."

In the distance, they heard Legion horns again sounding the chase. Tyrande prayed to Elune to watch over Dath'Remar and his comrades. They had a long, long way to ride and so many demons to fight through.

Oblivious to her concern for the Highborne, Illidan grinned and added, "Yes, this should give me just enough time for what I planned!"

"And what is that?" Even as she asked, Tyrande saw in the distance the black, foreboding waters. "Why are we headed toward the Well?"

"Because I intend to turn Sargeras's portal into a full-fledged maelstrom, one that will *suck* the demons back out of Kalimdor and into their nether world! I'll utterly reverse the effect of the dragon's disk! Think of it! With one spell, I'll save not only our people, but *everything!*"

His expression shifted, now almost seeming hopeful of her approval. However, when Tyrande did not immediately show such emotion, Illidan quickly became his harsher self again.

"You don't believe I can do it! Maybe if I was your precious Malfurion, you'd be jumping up and down, clapping your hands at my cleverness!"

"It isn't that at all, Illidan! I just—"

"Never mind!" He peered around the stormy landscape, seeking something. His monstrous gaze alighted on a fallen tree home. The angle of the dead oak meant that they could climb inside and get a perfect view of the Well of Eternity. "Just Perfect! Get in there!"

Practically tossed forward, the priestess wended her way into the ruined domicile. The sorcerer followed right behind, all but shoving her as they went.

As she climbed into the overturned structure, Tyrande's foot kicked something.

A skull.

She found herself standing amidst a pile of bones from at least five or six figures. No skeleton was complete and most of the bones had long, telling scratches and gouges in them. Tyrande shuddered, hoping that the felbeasts had feasted on dead carcasses, not living, helpless victims, but from experience fearing the worst.

"You can pray over them once I've saved all of us," Illidan remarked disdainfully. "Just ahead looks like the best—"

A monstrously-familiar form leapt out of the shadows.

It took down Malfurion's twin before he could react. Tyrande screamed, then immediately called upon the power of Elune.

But before she could do anything, the felbeast, its tentacles already seeking Illidan's chest, howled painfully. The demon hound writhed as the sorcerer calmly rose. Illidan's right hand held both suckers together.

"I could use the magic you've been gorging yourself on . . ." he commented almost blithely to the creature.

The night elf planted his left palm against the suckers. However, unlike times past, this felbeast showed no interest in trying to drink from its intended victim. Instead, it fought—however futilely—to pull its vile appendages back.

Illidan's left hand glowed an eerie green that Tyrande recognized as the same color as the horrific flames surrounding the demons. Malfurion's twin inhaled—and Tyrande watched in horror as the demon literally crumbled to dust from end to front, whining to the last. Its very essence was sucked into the sorcerer's palm.

As the horrific vision unfolded, Illidan's aspect became something frightening to behold. Even though he had replaced the scarf over his eye sockets, she could see the terrible fires burning within. The sorcerer wore a wide, almost drunken grin and around him flared green flames as potent as those surrounding any demon. Illidan seemed to swell—

Then, the flames abruptly died away and the sorcerer instantly returned to his normal appearance. He wiped clean his hand, then kicked a little at the ash that was all that remained of the felbeast. Smoothing his hair, Illidan gave Tyrande another confident smile. "Well! Shall we proceed?"

The priestess hid her shock as best she could. This was no longer the Illidan with whom she had grown up. This figure reveled in carnage as much as the demons themselves did. Worse, that he could so eagerly accept into his body the taint of the Legion stirred within her a disgust that Tyrande had never experienced.

Mother Moon, guide me in this! Tell me what to do! Can I still save him?

"Up here," her companion ordered. "I can focus on the center of the Well from that point on the roof."

Moving past the bones, they climbed up to what had once been an elegant roof terrace. Broken rails originally shaped from living wood lay scattered on the ground below and a pearl statue of Azshara—still amazingly whole—lay tangled in the dead foliage of the tree that had supported the house.

Illidan propped himself against what had once been the mosaic floor. Bits of the forest pageantry that decorated it still remained, revealing bits of fanciful animals, bucolic scenery, and lush trees.

Queen Azshara's beatific countenance still made up the center. Malfurion's brother rested his head against her full, if now cracked, lips.

"Nearly time," he murmured, speaking to himself more than her. From a pouch on his belt, Illidan removed a long, narrow vial. Although the crimson glass hid exactly what was within, Tyrande sensed just enough about its contents to feel her anxiety rise.

"Illidan . . . what's in that bottle?"

His shrouded gaze did not shift from the container. "Just a bit of the Well itself."

"What?" His words, said so lightly expressed, shook her to the core. Illidan had dared *take* from the night elves' source of power? "But—no one—it's forbidden—even the Highborne would never think—"

The sorcerer nodded. "No . . . even *they* wouldn't. That is so interesting about our people, wouldn't you say, Tyrande? Surely, though, the notion occurred to *someone* before me . . . perhaps that's where our legends of our greatest spellcasters comes from. Maybe they secretly borrowed from the Well for a special casting or two! Probably did." Illidan shrugged, his countenance stiffening again. "But even if no one else ever did, I don't see any reason why I should hold back. It just came to me, as if out of the blue. Take some of the Well for myself and there will be nothing too great for me to achieve!"

"But the Well—even a drop of it—" Tyrande had to make him see sense! Dabbling with the waters of the Well in such a way courted disaster on par with his acceptance of the Legion's dark magic.

"Yes . . . imagine what forces this entire vial contains . . ." Had Illidan still had true eyes, they would have lit up with anticipation of the results he expected. "Should be enough to enable me to save the world!"

But the priestess was not so convinced. As an acolyte of Elune, Tyrande was far more aware of the Well's legends and history than Illidan could possibly be. "Illidan . . . to use the Well against itself in such a way . . . you could be opening the doors to utter chaos! Remember the tale of Aru-Talis . . ."

"Aru-Talis is only that. A myth."

"And is the gaping crater, so many generations overgrown now by new life, also a myth?"

He waved off her warning. "No one knows what happened to that city or even if it really existed! Spare me your stories of wisdom and fear . . ."

"Illidan—"

The scarved face contorted in growing anger. "I want you to be quiet . . . *now.*"

"—" No sound escaped Tyrande's mouth despite her best attempt to create even the slightest noise. Even when she coughed, it was in utter silence.

Standing again, Illidan eyed the center of the Well. The storm had grown so intense that the ruined tree home now shook from the rising winds. Over the waters, unsettling, almost ghostly lights flashed.

The priestess shook her head. It bothered her that, despite Illidan's own confidence in his abilities, they had not been noticed. Surely Mannoroth was not so blind as Malfurion's twin believed. Yet, other than the hound, they had come across no demons save a pair of Fel Guard early on that Illidan had misdirected with a simple wave of his hand.

Illidan touched a finger to the stopper, which only now Tyrande saw was a tiny, crystalline facsimile of the queen from head to foot. Azshara spun around three times as if dancing for the sorcerer, then the stopper popped off. Illidan caught it with ease.

"Watch, Tyrande . . . watch while I do what your precious Malfurion could not . . ."

And he promptly poured the contents over himself.

But the waters of the Well did not act like normal waters, at least not where Illidan was concerned. They did not drench him and, in fact, only momentarily even made him damp. More ominous, wherever the waters touched Malfurion's twin, he briefly shimmered an intense black. Then, the unsettling aura sank within the sorcerer, filling him much as the felbeast's stolen energies had earlier.

"By the gods . . ." he whispered. "I knew I would feel something . . . but this . . . this is *wonderful.*"

The priestess vehemently shook her head, but her silent protest was lost on Illidan. She started toward him, only to discover that he had also sealed her feet in place.

Mother Moon! she thought. *Can you not help me?*

But there was no sign that Elune responded and Tyrande could only continue to watch Illidan.

He stretched his arms toward the Well and began muttering under his breath. Now the black aura returned, concentrating itself in his hands and intensifying more with each second.

Beneath the scarf, his eye sockets glowed like fire. The material even looked as if it had begun to singe.

But as Illidan began his spell, Tyrande's own highly-attuned senses felt another presence stir. The priestess sought again to give warning, but Illidan faced away from her.

She felt the invisible presence enshroud the unsuspecting sorcerer and, as it did, Tyrande realized it was not the touch of *one* being, but rather *several*.

And as that awful knowledge sank in, so, too, did the sensation that the entities were of a nature as dark as—no!—*darker* than even that she had felt when touched by the foul mind of Sargeras.

It astounded her that Illidan did not also sense them. Tyrande, certain that somehow this was yet another vile element of the Burning Legion, waited for Malfurion's brother to be horribly struck down.

But, instead, she noted in amazement that the mysterious entities now *augmented* Illidan's spell, transforming it into something far more formidable than it would have been. The sorcerer laughed as his work drew near to fruition, Illidan clearly certain that all the effort was his and his alone.

The priestess suddenly understood that the lack of encounters along the way to the Well had not been entirely due to Illidan's cunning.

More frantic now, she prayed over and over to Elune for aid. Illidan had to be warned that he was being duped. She was certain that his grand spell would somehow only trigger a worse disaster.

Mother Moon! Hear my pleas!

A blessed warmth filled Tyrande. She felt the spell that Illidan had put on her suddenly fade away. Her hopes rose anew.

"Illidan!" the priestess immediately cried out. "Illidan! Beware—"

But even as he started to look her way, the sorcerer brought his palms together . . . and a beam of black light burst forth, racing out into the storm-rocked heavens above the Well of Eternity.

Tyrande felt the presences withdraw. Worse, as they faded away, she also sensed their immense satisfaction.

Her warning had come too late.

Sargeras felt the last vestiges of resistance suddenly fall away. The portal that he desired began to fully form. Soon, he would gain entrance into this life-befouled world . . .

Krasus jolted.

"What is it?" called Alexstrasza.

The cowled figure eyed the tiny vision of Zin-Azshari lying far ahead . . .

and the colossal tempest spreading out over the Well of Eternity. He shuddered. "I fear we have even less time than I calculated . . ."

"Then, we must make even greater speed!" With that, the huge red dragon beat her wings harder yet, her muscles straining from effort.

Peering behind them, Krasus saw the other dragons follow suit. Everyone sensed that, more than ever, time was against them. The mage silently swore. This should not have happened. Even his own kind had taken far too long to debate the merits of what should have been obvious. If they had only listened . . .

Yet, Krasus could also not help thinking that, if he and his comrades failed, the doom befalling not only the night elves but unborn generations ahead would be in tremendous part his fault. He himself had hesitated to toy with Time, then, when the decision had finally been made to do so, he it was who had suggested attempting no pursuit of Illidan's band. Of all who had crossed its path, Krasus knew most the cursed way of the Demon Soul. If he had tried to track down those who had taken it from Malfurion, then perhaps there would have still been a chance to retrieve the disk.

But that was neither here nor there. What mattered now was to make amends, to still return history to its former course.

"We must be prepared!" he called out to Alexstrasza. "Even though we will bypass the palace, neither the Highborne nor Mannoroth can be taken lightly, even by our ancient line! They will attack from Azshara's stronghold! Nor must we forget what else seeks use of the portal the Well and the Soul create! They will also do everything within their power to keep us from the disk."

"If sacrifice ourselves we must to save Kalimdor, then we but fulfill our sacred duty!" she responded back.

Krasus gritted his teeth. The future he knew so well was still a possible thing, but just as likely was one—supposing that they succeeded—where any or all of them perished here. For himself, that was something he could accept. To see his beloved queen die, though . . .

No! She will not! The mage prepared himself. Whatever it took, he would do his best to see that Alexstrasza lived . . . even if without him.

The dragons came upon the outskirts of Zin-Azshari and Krasus, who had expected the carnage wrought by the Burning Legion's initial entrance into the mortal plane, was still highly repelled by all he saw. Memories of that second war, when Dalaran and other nations had fallen before the demons and their dread allies, stirred.

Below, endless ranks of demons looked up at their coming and roared challenge. The dragons ignored most, the Fel Guard and their like bound to the ground and, therefore, of little threat. Of more interest were the Doom-guard, who came up in great numbers, fiery lances and blades at the ready.

Alexstrasza watched a massive group converge on them, then, pulling her head back, she released a fount of flame.

Cries arose and burning Doomguard plummeted. With that single breath, the crimson leviathan had cleared the sky of almost a hundred demons.

"Gnats . . ." she muttered. "Nothing but gnats . . ."

Then, one of the green dragons in the back roared in surprise as he was pummeled by several huge, round missiles. Krasus did not have to see them close to know that they were Infernals. Even the scales of a huge dragon were not entirely impervious. The wounds the green suffered were superficial, but repeated strikes would eventually take their toll.

"Let us make some use of these foul creatures!" Ysera hissed. She focused her closed eyes upon the next wave.

The new band of Infernals slowed. They continued to descend, but far from their intended targets. Krasus calculated their new path and smiled grimly. The palace was about to learn firsthand of the sort of devastation that they had permitted into Kalimdor.

But Krasus's earlier warning of the dangers that both the Highborne and Mannoroth represented proved all too prophetic in the moments following, for suddenly the stormy sky unleashed a barrage of horrific, black bolts. Caught in the center, the dragons and their riders were forced to break forma-tion just in the hopes of surviving.

Not all did. Perhaps slowed by the earlier barrage of Infernals, the green male hesitated. More than a dozen bolts struck him hard. Lightning scorched through his left wing, then seared him horribly in his tail and chest.

But although the lightning ceased, the worst was yet to come. Each of the wounds burned bright, and, as Krasus watched, their damage rapidly spread along the dragon's body. Weakened further, the green made an all too easy target for more of the Highborne's lightning. Six more bolts caught the male as he fought to stay aloft. The dragon roared in agony, his death knell echoing in Krasus's ears.

The green dropped from the sky.

His huge form hit the Well's dark waters hard. Yet, even for so gigantic a creature, the dragon's collision was as a pebble to the swirling maelstrom. Barely a ripple marked the green as he sank into the foreboding lake.

A foreboding rumble filled their ears.

"Hold on tight!" commanded Alexstrasza, turning.

A new, frenzied attack swarmed the dragons. Black lightning shot down everywhere and, this time, no dragon survived unscathed. Even Alexstrasza shook as one bolt caught her on the right hip.

"It does not burn!" she exclaimed. "It is so very cold! It chills to the bone!"

"I will see what I can do for it!"

"No!" She glanced back at him. "We must preserve our strength for attack—!"

The Aspect of Life abruptly banked, barely avoiding a pair of bolts that would have struck not only her dead-on, but Krasus as well. All over the heavens, dragons twisted about in a macabre ballet. Krasus looked about and saw that all his companions still held tight. He had feared that the necessity of avoiding the magical lightning might make it impossible for the dragons to keep their riders aloft, but even under such circumstances, the ancient leviathans kept watch over their charges.

But this could not go on forever. Eyes narrowed, Krasus peered toward the center of the Well. Yes . . . he could detect the Demon Soul. He could also sense that the portal was nearly complete.

"To the center!" the cowled spellcaster shouted. "We have little time!"

Alexstrasza immediately veered that direction. Krasus leaned forward. As vast as the Well of Eternity was, it still proved only a few beats of Alexstrasza's vast wings to bring them within sight of their objective.

Sure enough, there, high above the gaping maw of the maelstrom, the Demon Soul floated almost serenely. Surrounded by an unholy black aura, it was unaffected by the fearsome magical storm.

"It will be protected!" Krasus reminded her.

"Ysera and I will work in conjunction with Nozdormu's prime consort!"

He nodded. "Rhonin and I will watch for reaction from Sargeras or the Old Gods!"

The riderless dragons withdrew to watch for attack from Zin-Azshari. The three female dragons encircled the sinister disk, their previous encounter with it making all extremely wary. Alexstrasza looked once at her counterparts, then nodded.

From each burst forth a golden light.

Their spells touched the Demon Soul simultaneously, enveloping it. The foul aura about it was smothered by their power. The disk began to tremble . . .

Without warning, their spells were suddenly repelled. The backlash was so terrible that all three dragons were tossed backward for some distance. It was all that their riders could do to maintain hold.

Barely clinging to his queen, Krasus shouted, "What is it? What happened?"

Alexstrasza managed to right herself. Her eyes stared wide at the Demon Soul, now some distance off. "The Old Gods! I *felt* them! But from within the disk! The Demon Soul not only bears a part of our existence, but *theirs* as well!"

The news did not entirely surprise Krasus. Yet, clearly their addition to the disk's creation did not hinder the Elder Gods as it did the dragons. They obviously hoped to wield it, something that the other dragons could not do. Deathwing had evidently crafted it differently where they were concerned . . . if he had even realized their intrusion.

"Can you penetrate their spellwork?"

"I do not know . . . I honestly do not know!"

Krasus swore. Once again, he had underestimated the Three.

He saw Rhonin trying to signal him. The wizard pointed in the direction of Zin-Azshari. Krasus turned his gaze toward the fabled city—

—And watched as more than a score of shadowy abominations, each as large as a dragon, soared toward them.

SEVENTEEN

Azshara had been primping herself.

Oh, it was not that she was not already perfection incarnate— even *she* knew that much—but that for once the queen had found someone worthy of more effort.

My Lord Sargeras is arriving! At last, one fit to be called my husband!

Not for a moment did Azshara question the sanity of her convictions. She who had mesmerized her subjects was herself mesmerized by the lord of the Legion.

At that moment, a tremor shook the palace. It was not the first to do so. Pulling herself from the splendid view in the mirror, the queen spun around. "Vashj! Vashj! What is responsible for that awful racket?"

Her chief handmaiden came rushing in. "A feeble attempt by rabble to stop the inevitable, so reports Captain Varo'then, oh Light of Lights!"

"And what is the dear captain doing about this insult to my ears?"

"Lord Mannoroth has given to him and his hand-picked soldiers appropriate mounts. The captain is already on his way to deal with the miscreants."

"So, all is proceeding as it should? There will be no delay of our lord's arrival?"

Lady Vashj bowed elegantly. "None that Lord Mannoroth foresees. The rabble batter uselessly at the spell."

"Splendid . . ." Queen Azshara went back to admiring herself in the mirror. There was really nothing else she could do to further enhance her beauty. The silken gown trailed behind her over the marble floor, its gossamer design leaving very little unrevealed. Her luxurious hair was piled high and glittering star diamonds—illuminated by their own inner light—decorated it in strategic locations.

Another tremor struck, this one much nearer. Azshara heard cries from the direction of her handmaidens' quarters and saw cracks spread across the wall there.

"See if anyone is injured, Vashj," she commanded. As the latter moved to obey, the ruler of the night elves added, "And if so, please relieve her of her duties and send her back to her family. I will accept nothing but utter perfection from those who would surround me."

"Aye, Light of Lights!"

A distasteful frown greeted Azshara as she looked again to the full-length mirror in the opposing wall. The queen immediately imagined greeting her Lord Sargeras. That brought back the smile.

"There . . . now we just have to wait a little longer . . ." She continued to survey herself, dreaming of the world that she and her new mate would create. A world as perfect as her.

A world *worthy* of her.

Malfurion shook his head, trying to clear it of the vertigo he had suffered during Ysera's tumble. It amazed him that he even had a head left to shake, considering that more than once the druid had been hanging by his hands over the gaping hole at the center of the darksome Well.

"What happened?" he asked, not realizing that he repeated Krasus's own query.

Ysera told him much the same as Alexstrasza had the mage. The night elf listened with sinking heart. To come so close, only to have their hopes dashed so quickly . . .

Then, he, like Rhonin and Krasus, saw the horrific forms rising up from the city. Malfurion saw that soldiers rode astride the abominations, which resembled bats formed from shadow. He knew without a doubt that Captain Varo'then would be leading the sinister band.

Sure enough, a moment later, the druid made out the familiar figure of the scarred officer. Sword out, Varo'then shouted something to those behind him. Immediately, the soldiers broke up into three groups, one for each flight. Only then did Malfurion see that he had terribly underestimated their numbers. There had to be at least three beasts for every dragon.

Alexstrasza wasted no time. The red dragon unleashed a stream of fire— which went through the foremost monster and continued on, finally fading. Even the soldier riding the beast looked unfazed.

"That's impossible!" Malfurion gasped.

"Impossible . . . yes . . ." Ysera's eyes moved back and forth rapidly beneath her shut lids. "There is . . . a fault in our perspective of these fiends . . ."

"What do you mean?"

"That they are not quite as they appear to be nor are they *where* they seem."

Yet, if that was the case, Varo'then and his soldiers made for very tangible illusions. Two of the shadow creatures fixed onto Brox's mount, tearing at her wings. The bloody scores that they made in her hard, scaled hide were proof enough as to their deadliness. Yet, when the bronze sought to strike back, her attacks went for naught.

Ysera, too, fell prey to them. One flew past her throat, raking it with curved, black claws that were a part of the wing. Blood dripped from the red wounds. Ysera snapped at the wing, but her bite found only air.

"I know where they must be!" growled Ysera, for one of her rare times losing her patience. "But when I wish to strike, they are no longer there!"

To make matters worse, one in particular now fixed upon Malfurion and the Aspect . . . the beast carrying Captain Varo'then himself.

"I thought I spied you!" sneered the scarred night elf. "As slippery as your brother! I warned them! I knew he couldn't be trusted!"

Malfurion had no opportunity to ask what Varo'then meant by his words, for the next second the captain and his unholy mount were upon the druid and the dragon. A fetid smell engulfed Malfurion and even Ysera wrinkled her nose. Intangible to their attacks this horror might be, but its stench was so powerful that the druid felt as if struck by a fist.

A mocking laugh was all that warned Malfurion of the captain's lunge. Varo'then's blade stretched impossibly, darting for the other night elf's unprotected chest.

Tipping to the right, Malfurion avoided the sword, but nearly lost his grip. As he clutched tight, Varo'then attacked him again.

Ysera could do nothing, for the inky form of the bat creature all but enveloped She of the Dreaming. At the same time, a second monster snagged the dragon's hind legs.

Something that Cenarius had taught him suddenly came to mind. Reaching into a pouch, the druid removed a small, prickly seed. Unlike those he had used against the Burning Legion in the past, this one had points too delicate to wreak any havoc on the foe. However, they were especially adept at sticking to anything with which they came into contact.

He tossed out two to the heavens and through his casting the two became four, then became eight, sixteen, and doubled accordingly in rapid succession.

Within a heartbeat, hundreds filled the air, then thousands. They did not, as they should have, cling to the dragons or Malfurion's comrades, for that was not the druid's desire. Rather, he sought to use them to find out the truth about their adversaries.

The first ones passed through the bat creatures, but, curiously, others began sticking to empty space. More and more quickly followed suit. Shapes began to form, shapes creating quite a revelation.

The secret of the shadow bats finally lay revealed. The monstrous mounts of the soldiers shimmered constantly, disappearing from sight every few seconds and reappearing elsewhere almost instantly. To fight them would still prove tricky, but now the defenders had a far better idea of where to strike and that was all that they needed.

Perhaps because the bronze female was part of the Aspect of Time's flight, she reacted quickest. With great gusto, the dragon seized upon one bat who materialized just within reach. Her swiftness astounded Malfurion, as did her savageness. She ripped through what passed for a stout neck on the creature, then sent it and its frantic rider hurtling into the black void below.

"Damn!"

At the angry epithet, Malfurion looked over his shoulder to find Captain Varo'then almost upon both his and Ysera's back. The scarred night elf thrust and this time managed to scrape the druid's leg. His thigh stinging, Malfurion threw the first thing that he could pull from a pouch.

His adversary sneezed—and so did his hideous mount. Taking advantage of the distraction, Ysera dove into the monster, biting and tearing with such abandon that no semblance of her superior intellect remained apparent. She was pure beast, fighting with the same primal fury as her foe.

But the shadow creature was not defenseless. Its claws were still as sharp as the dragon's and its long fangs looked more than able to pierce hard scale. With a strange keening cry, it met Ysera eagerly.

At first, the two riders could do nothing but hold on for their lives. Malfurion tried to concentrate on a spell, but the jarring movements of the two combating behemoths made that impossible.

Ysera batted with her tail at the second creature near her hind legs. A lucky strike sent the beast flying back, giving the dragon, at least for the moment, a more even combat with Varo'then's mount.

The captain had sheathed his sword and now drew a dagger. Suspecting that Varo'then was quite skilled at tossing such a blade, Malfurion kept low. The officer grinned darkly, patient despite their dire situation.

Ysera's body jerked. The druid looked down and saw that the second beast had returned . . . and a third followed close behind. He shouted a warning to the dragon.

With a roar, the green leviathan used her incredible wings to throw herself from her opponent. The act caught both the monster and Varo'then by surprise. It also enabled Ysera to turn on her second attacker. Wings still, she dropped upon the bat and rider, catching both under her immense girth. Her claws ripped to shreds the seed-coated wings and she bit deep into the squat neck.

With a harsh squeal, the monstrosity went limp in her claws. Ysera immediately discarded the carcass, letting it fall toward the Well. Of the soldier, Malfurion could see no sign and the druid had to assume he had been slain when first the dragon had landed atop the pair.

As the green leviathan pulled away in order to orient herself, the night elf caught brief glimpses of the others. Three bat creatures harassed Brox and the bronze. Even as Malfurion watched, the orc buried his ax in the shoulder of the nearest with remarkable effect. The enchanted weapon cut through whatever bone and sinew there was and exited the other side.

The monster veered off awkwardly, barely able to stay aloft. The bronze, however, did not let it escape. She breathed once at the fleeing figures . . . and both rider and mount transformed from menace to decayed corpses that a moment later crumbled to dust. The mad wind quickly scattered the decomposing fragments over the dark waters.

But if several of the bats were gone, so, too, were some of the dragons. Only one other green male still flew and one of the bronzes was also missing. Others among the survivors had bleeding wounds that, with what they had suffered from the lightning barrage, had to be be debilitating.

But, worse, Malfurion knew that so long as they had to deal with their foes, they could do nothing about the Demon Soul and the portal. Already, the vast maelstrom below had taken on a noticeable greenish hue at its edges, one too akin to the flames of the Burning Legion to be coincidence.

"The Demon Soul!" he shouted. "We have to do something about it! The portal's nearly complete!"

"I am open to suggestions, mortal—if you can also tell me how to be rid of these pests at the same time!"

A fiery burst briefly illuminated their surroundings. Malfurion caught the last vestiges of a burning bat dropping into the Well. Directly above it flew Alexstrasza and Krasus. The druid could sense the mage's handiwork in the devastation. Given time, the band *would* defeat Varo'then's fighters, but by then it would be too late. Even if it would not be, they had already seen that the combined might of Ysera and Alexstrasza was not enough to break the defenses surrounding the disk. Something else would have to be done . . . but *what?*

Dragons and bats continued to swoop past. The odds were more even than before, but still not enough to enable them to concentrate at all on the Demon Soul. The shadow bats continued to harass each of the dragons. One of the reds, already dripping from several bites, fell under assault by a pair of the fiends. Another bronze bit through the wing of her assailant, but the monster had its fangs deep in her shoulder. Rhonin and Krasus continued to cast spells of varying success and Brox cut expertly at whatever foe came within reach.

An ebony form darted past. Malfurion thought it one of the bats, but then saw the familiar, reptilian outline of a dragon. He glanced away—then, jaw dropping—looked back again.

It was indeed a dragon . . . but a dragon as black as the demonic creatures that they fought and with iron plates bolted to his hide.

Deathwing . . .

They had thought that they could keep his beloved creation hidden from him. They had dared think that he would not eventually find out where it had been taken. Their audacity enraged him. Once Neltharion had his glorious disk back, he would punish *all* of them. The world would be better off with no one but dragons . . . and only dragons who understood matters as he did.

Called by the Soul, Neltharion had flown across the swirling Well totally oblivious to what was happening. Everything else was of secondary importance. All that existed for the black dragon was the disk.

He flew past both Ysera and Alexstrasza, giving them but cursory glances. With the disk, he would bring them down, then add them to his consorts. Their power would add to his, as was only right.

The Soul floated serenely ahead, as if waiting patiently for him to rescue it. Neltharion's monstrous visage stretched into a wide, anticipatory grin. They would soon be reunited . . .

Then a force struck the black with such might that Neltharion was tossed back among the combatants. He collided with one of the bat creatures, sending its rider screaming to his death. Neltharion roared in outrage at the unexpected attack. Seeking a focus for his intense anger, he seized the stunned bat and tore it to shreds. When that did not assuage him, he turned his baleful gaze on the disk, searching with his heightened senses for that which held him from his prize.

The spellwork he detected around the Soul was intricate, very intricate . . . and vaguely familiar in some aspects. Yet, Neltharion could not put together the voices in his head with that which now confronted him. Even when those same voices now began urging him away from his desire, the dragon could not conceive that he had been someone's dupe.

Neltharion shook his head, driving away the voices. If they spoke against taking the disk, then they were no more to be trusted than Alexstrasza and the others. Nothing—absolutely nothing—mattered other than retrieving the Soul.

And so, the huge black dove in again.

But, like before, he was repelled as if nothing of consequence. The dragon fought not merely the power wielded by the voices, but also that of the lord of the Legion. With a roar mixing outrage and pain, Neltharion spun far beyond the battle, finally coming to a halt at the very northern edge of the Well. Fighting his agony, the furious giant glared at the storm-wracked center.

He would not be rejected again. Whatever spells his enemies had cast around the Soul, he would tear through them. The disk would be his . . .

And then *all* of them would pay . . .

The Burning Legion struggled against the overwhelming might of both the dragons and the host. Doomguard swarmed the leviathans, seeking to bring them down by lance. Nathrezim and Eredar cast monstrous spells, but they were caught between defending against the dragons and fighting the Moon Guard. The warlocks could not do both. They perished more often than they slew, mostly under the unyielding flame of a leviathan's breath.

Yet, throughout it all, Archimonde revealed no uncertainty. He understood that what happened here now had no relevance save that the mortals and their allies would be distracted until the coming of his Lord Sargeras. Archimonde accepted that he and Mannoroth would be punished for their failure to prepare Kalimdor properly for their master, but that was as it should be. All that mattered now was to play the game a little longer. If that meant the deaths of more Fel Guard and Eredar, then so be it. There were always more, especially waiting to march in behind Sargeras.

But that did not at all mean that Archimonde simply watched and waited. If he was to be punished, he would vent some of his well-hidden fury on those who had caused it. The giant demon raised his hand, pointing toward a bronze dragon hovering above the Legion's right flank. The dragon had been systematically ripping apart warriors below, digging through them the way a burrowing animal would soft earth.

Archimonde made a grasping gesture. The distant dragon suddenly quivered . . . and then every scale *tore* from its body. Blood spilling from everywhere, the flayed giant bellowed in shock, then dropped among its victims. Demon warriors immediately flowed over the unprotected body, thrusting with their weapons until the dragon lay lifeless.

Unsatisfied, Archimonde looked for another victim. How he wished the night elf, Malfurion Stormrage, had been among the host. The druid had cost him much in their previous encounter, but Archimonde sensed that Malfurion was one of those who had flown toward the Well. Once Sargeras came through, the druid would suffer a far worse fate than even Archimonde had planned for him.

Still, there were so many others upon which to vent himself. Expression cold and calculating, the archdemon fixed upon a band of the bullmen he had heard called tauren. They had the potential to become splendid additions to the Legion's ranks, but this particular group would never survive to see that glorious day . . . or the end of their world, either . . .

They were winning . . . they were winning . . .

The dragons had made the difference. Jarod knew that. Without them, the host would have fallen. The demons had come across the one force that they could not defeat. True, some dragons had perished—one just in a most grisly manner—but the host pushed forward and the demons fought in more and more disarray.

Still, he was bothered. The demons' confusion was no trick this time, that he knew. Yet, he would have expected something more from Archimonde. Some masterful regrouping. Archimonde, though, seemed to be attempting nothing more than a holding action, as if he awaited something . . .

The night elf cursed himself for a fool. Of *course*, Archimonde awaited something . . . or rather *someone*.

His lord, Sargeras.

And if the archdemon believed that the arrival of the Legion's master was still imminent, that did not bode well for those who had gone to take the Demon Soul and seal the portal.

For a moment, Jarod's nerve failed him, but then his expression hardened and he fought with even more fervor. It would not be due to any lacking on his part if the defenders failed. His people—his *world*—would certainly fall if the host faltered now. Jarod could only hope that Krasus, Malfurion, and the others would somehow still succeed in their mission.

Overhead, dragons continued to soar past in search of the enemy or to aid those in the host under the most stress. To the commander's right, Earthen chopped their way through demoralized Fel Guard. A furbolg battered in the skull of a felbeast.

It all looks so hopeful, Jarod thought, aware that it was anything but. He saw a band of Huln's people slicing their way through the opposition. With them rode a party of the priestesses of Elune and Jarod noticed his sister, Maiev, at their head. It did not at all surprise him to see her up at the front. Although he quietly worried for her, there would be no dragging her from the battle. He had concluded that Maiev was trying to prove herself to the rest of her sect so that they would correct what she clearly thought an oversight and make her high priestess. Whether or not such ambition was permitted in the moon goddess's order was debatable, but Maiev was Maiev.

Astride the third night saber he had ridden this day, Jarod gutted a tusked warrior. His own armor hung ragged on him, so damaged had it gotten from the blows of his adversaries. There were at least half a dozen wounds spread out over his body, but none, thankfully, life threatening or even overly-draining. Jarod could rest when the battle was over . . . or when he was dead.

Then . . . cries broke out from the direction of the tauren. The night elf watched in horror as several of Huln's kind burned as if some virulent acid had been poured over them. Their hair sizzled and their flesh melted away in clumps.

The priestesses tried to aid them, but a surge of Fel Guard barreled over the foremost females. The demons cared not whether an adversary was male or female. They impaled tauren and beheaded priestesses with utter savagery.

Jarod knew that he should stay where he was, but Maiev, whatever her faults, was his only family. He cared for her far more than he dared show. Quickly making certain that his own area would not fall victim once he departed, the commander forced his mount around and headed for the horrific scene.

A few tauren still stood, some of them badly injured but able to wield their spears and axes. They and the survivors of Maiev's band stood all but encircled by demons. Even before he had ridden halfway, Jarod watched two more of the defenders perish under the onslaught.

Then, Maiev slipped. A looming Fel Guard swung at her. She managed to deflect his attack, but just barely.

With a howl, Jarod rode his mount into the struggle. His cat took down the demon attacking his sister. Another demon slashed at him, instead catching the animal on the shoulder. Jarod ran his blade through his foe's throat.

The demons suddenly focused on Jarod. It had not occurred to him that they might know who he was, but their determination suggested just that. They ignored other viable targets just to reach the commander.

His night saber took down two more, but then suffered several deep wounds from lances. On foot, Jarod would have a great disadvantage over so many towering figures, yet, there was nothing he could do. Three more lances finished the noble animal and it was all Jarod could do to leap off or be trapped underneath its carcass.

He landed in a crouching position next to his sister, who, for the first time, seemed to realize the identity of her would-be rescuer.

"Jarod! You shouldn't have come! They need you!"

"Stop commanding for once and get behind me!" He shoved his sister unceremoniously to the rear just as two horned figures closed on him. Despite his good fortune so far, Jarod Shadowsong had little belief that his small sword would be any match for their two massive blades.

But as he readied himself for his final battle, a horn sounded and the area was suddenly aswarm with soldiers and tauren. Huln crashed into the two demons, beheading one and crushing in the chest of the other before the pair could realize that they were under assault. A cloaked figure rode past, one Jarod belatedly recognized as Lord Blackforest.

There could only be one explanation for their sudden arrival. They had seen Jarod riding into struggle . . . and believed in him enough to come to his aid.

The reinforcements shoved back the Burning Legion, buying Jarod and Maiev time. He dragged her farther from the fight, the remaining sisters following close behind.

Jarod made her sit on a rock. Maiev, eyes speculative, studied her younger brother.

"Jarod—" she started.

"You can reprimand me later, sister!" he snapped. "I won't stand behind while those who followed me face the enemy in my name!"

"I was not going to reprimand—" was as far as the priestess got before he was out of earshot. With his sister at least temporarily secure, Jarod concerned himself only with his comrades. Even Blackforest, one of the most prominent of the nobles, fought hard. He and his ilk had managed to learn from Lord Stareye's mistakes. This was a battle for survival, not a game for the amusement of the high castes.

Coming up on Huln, Jarod lunged at a demon seeking the tauren's side. Huln noticed the action and gave the night elf an appreciative snort.

"I will carve your name on my spear!" he rumbled. "You will be honored by generations of my line!"

"I'd be honored just to live through this!"

"Ha! Such wisdom in one so young!"

A female dragon of Alexstrasza's flight swooped down, laying a cleansing blast of red flame that forever doused many green ones. The action further eased the situation for Jarod's contingent. The commander of the host began to breath just a little easier.

But a second later, the same dragon went careening back beyond the night elves' lines, her chest a sizzling mass of ruined scale and torn innards. The earth shook as she collided with it and a furtive look by Jarod gave him ample enough evidence to know that she would not fly again.

And in the wake of the leviathan's death, a dozen soldiers also flew back, their bodies charred. Demons, too, tumbled, as if whatever attacked did not care who perished so long as nothing stood in its path.

Huln put a protective arm across Jarod's chest. "What comes is no Infernal or the work of the Eredar! I believe it seeks—"

Then a massive wind tossed fighters from both forces aside as if they were nothing. Night sabers were no less immune, Blackforest and his mount thrown with the rest. Huln managed to stand his ground a second longer, but even the stubbornness of a tauren could not hold against the incredible gale. He went flying past, the warrior striking at the wind in frustration as he vanished from sight.

Yet . . . Jarod Shadowsong felt *nothing,* not even a breeze.

And so he found himself alone when the giant strode out of the dust raised by the wind, the giant with dark skin and intricate tattoos that even the unskilled Jarod could sense radiated sinister magical forces.

"Yes . . ." mused the figure, eyeing the night elf up and down. "If I cannot have the druid, I shall amuse myself on what pathetically passes as the hope of this doomed host."

Jarod readied his blade, aware that he had no hope against this opponent but finding himself unwilling to surrender to the inevitable. "I await you, Archimonde."

The archdemon laughed.

EIGHTEEN

B rox was only a simple warrior, but he knew when a battle was going bad. It was not that he and the others could not defeat these armored night elves and their fiendish mounts, but that each second wasted so brought the portal nearer and nearer to completion. Already, a sinister green aura had formed around the gullet of the whirlpool. The orc understood magic well enough to know that soon the passage would be strong enough for whatever evil desired to come through, be it Sargeras or the "Old Gods" Krasus had mentioned.

A barbed lance flashed by his head, scraping away a few bits of skin but otherwise doing the hardened orc no harm. The scowling soldier wielding it steered his shadow bat to the side, hoping to get in past the bronze dragon's claws for another thrust at the green warrior.

The dragon caught hold of the shadow bat. The two struggled, upsetting the night elf's aim. Instead of impaling Brox, he caught the orc at the shoulder. Brox growled as the barbed head tore a thick piece of flesh from the spot. Despite the pain, he managed to lean forward and chop the lance in two.

With a curse, the soldier drew his sword. However, Brox, throwing caution to the wind, rose from his seat and *leapt* at his opponent.

He landed in a crouching position, gripping one of the bat's ears for support. The outrageous act so startled the night elf that he sat openmouthed as, with one hand, the orc buried his ax in his foe's armored chest. The soldier collapsed, tumbling off the back of his mount.

But Brox's impetuous action nearly cost him his own life. He had thought to use the bat's back to leap back atop the dragon, but the creature's hide proved oddly slick. As he let go of the ear, the orc lost his footing. Still gripping his ax tight, he slid toward the tail, following the night elf's corpse.

The burgeoning gateway far below filled Brox's eyes. He sensed the evil swelling within—

Then, a pair of claws caught him just as he fell free and Rhonin's voice shouted, "We've got you, Brox!"

The red dragon acting as the wizard's mount twisted so as to allow the orc to climb atop. Rhonin gave the orc a hand up, letting the graying warrior slide in behind him.

"That was just a little foolhardy even for an orc, wasn't it?"

"Maybe so," Brox admitted, thinking of the portal. Brave as he considered himself, he was grateful that he had not fallen into it. The farther away he got from it, the better.

The wizard suddenly stiffened. "Watch out! Here come two more!"

The shadow bats converged on their position. Rhonin's hand flared bright as he readied a spell. Brox hefted his ax, prepared to be as much help as he could. He welcomed the new adversaries, if only because they took his mind off the portal.

The portal and an evil that stirred fear even in an orc.

The sight of Deathwing rebuffed by the spell surrounding the disk both astounded and disheartened Malfurion. If even the black dragon could not penetrate the dark magic, then what could the druid and his companions hope to do?

But Malfurion had no more opportunity to worry about the disk, for, at that moment, a menacing form dropped upon Ysera. The green dragon roared as the bat's fangs sank into her shoulder near the spine. The night elf slid to the side, trying to avoid being buried under the beast.

A sword cut at his head, narrowly missing his ear.

"Slippery little fool!" hissed Varo'then, once more wielding his favored weapon. Azshara's officer thrust again, this time nicking Malfurion on the cheek. Varo'then drew the sword back for another strike. "The next one'll take your head!"

The druid thrust his hand into a pouch. He knew what he sought and prayed he would find it. The familiar feel reassured him and he pulled out the seeds.

Captain Varo'then adjusted his position. The evil grin spread wide. The demons had found a perfect subordinate in the sadistic soldier.

As the blade came down, Malfurion threw the seeds into the bat's maw.

The monster convulsed immediately. The sword point, fixed on the druid's throat, instead cut a bloody but shallow line across his collarbone. Malfurion grunted from the pain, but held on.

A fiery glow erupted from within Varo'then's mount. The captain tried to maintain control, but to no avail. The bat flailed around, shrieking.

A moment later, it burst into flames.

Malfurion had used the seeds' inherent heat during earlier battles. However, with only a few left, he had not thought to wield them up here, where they might not be utilized well. Only because the shadowy creature had been right on top of him had the night elf managed to make certain that all reached their target, the throat.

The fiery spectacle was so bright that Malfurion had to look away. He heard Varo'then shout, but the words were lost.

With one last shrill cry, the incinerated beast dropped from sight.

Gasping for breath, Malfurion clung to Ysera. The dragon could do nothing for her rider, for another of the bats already had her attention. The druid held on as tight as he could while he tried to regain his composure. The pain from his wounds stung terribly and the knowledge that the disk was still untouchable drained him further.

A sharp pain coursed through his calf.

Malfurion cried out. He nearly lost his hold. Blood trickled into his boot as he wildly kicked at the source. He turned watery eyes toward his leg and the cause of his agony.

Captain Varo'then clutched tightly to Ysera's lower back, the scarred soldier grunting as he made his way up a scale at a time. The cause of Malfurion's new pain—the officer's curved dagger—was clenched between Varo'then's teeth. Malfurion's blood dribbled unnoticed down the other night elf's pointed chin.

How Varo'then had managed to snag hold of Ysera as his burning mount had dropped, Malfurion did not know, but once again he had underestimated the officer. He kicked again as hard as he could, but the captain easily avoided his foot. While it was all Malfurion could do to hold on as Ysera fought, the more battle-hardened Varo'then moved with practiced skill toward his foe. His narrowed eyes sized up Malfurion like a fat animal ready for the slaughter . . .

The druid reached for a pouch—and, at the same time, Varo'then's left hand came up.

"Aaugh!" A crimson flash blinded Malfurion. Too late he recalled that the captain had some minor talent with sorcery. Not enough to be a true threat in that manner, but certainly enough to put his enemy off-guard while the officer moved in for the kill.

Malfurion put up his free hand, an act which likely kept him from being slain. A heavy, metallic form fell upon him—Varo'then's armored body—and the druid felt the other night elf's hot breath in his face.

"The Light of Lights will reward me greatly for this!" the captain uttered maniacally. "Mannoroth fell afoul of you! Archimonde fell afoul of you! Such an insipid creature and you outwitted them both! Lord Sargeras's grand commanders! Ha! I'll not only again be her favored for this, but *his* as well! Me! *Lord* Varo'then!"

"Sargeras means to destroy Kalimdor, not remake it!" Malfurion blurted, trying to make his foe see sense.

"Of course! I realized that long ago! Pfah! What do I care for this little patch of dirt? So long as I can serve the queen and command warriors in her name, I care not where I do it! Who knows, perhaps for this Sargeras will make *me* his supreme commander! For that and the adoration of Azshara, I'll gladly see Kalimdor a cinder!"

Varo'then's madness truly consumed him. Malfurion suddenly grew outraged that one of his own kind could so blithely speak of the end of all things, especially the cherished world that had birthed their kind. It went against everything Cenarius had taught him and what Malfurion had always believed.

"Kalimdor is our blood, our breath, our very existence!" the druid shouted, his fury rising. "We are as much a part of it as the trees, the rivers, and the very rocks! We are its children! You would be slaying the mother that birthed us!" His forehead started to burn.

"You *are* pathetic! We live upon a tiny rock that's one of many rocks! Kalimdor is nothing! Through the Legion and my queen, I will cross a thousand worlds, all of whom will be crushed under our feet! Power, druid! Power is my blood, my breath, do you understand?" Captain Varo'then twisted his dagger-wielding hand out of Malfurion's grasp. "But if the coming death of Kalimdor troubles you so, I'll grant you the favor of sending you to the after-life to be there to welcome its shade firsthand!"

But Malfurion's anger had reached its limits. Eyes on fire, he stared into Varo'then's own. "You want *power?* Feel the power of the world you would betray, captain!"

It flowed through the druid as naturally as his blood. He felt it rush from its source . . . Kalimdor. The world itself was not sentient, but it was a living thing, nonetheless and, through Malfurion, it at last struck back.

From the druid erupted a soft, blue light that hit Varo'then full in the chest. With a cry, Malfurion's attacker was battered from his mount. Dagger knocked from his flailing grip, the captain helplessly soared up high over the Well of Eternity. The light not only now bathed Varo'then, it burned right through him. His flesh, his sinew, his organs, and his skeleton were all visible beneath his glowing armor. The officer's screaming head was a skull under transparent skin.

Varo'then had rejected everything about Kalimdor . . . and now, through Malfurion, Kalimdor rejected everything about him. Still enveloping the cap-tain, the light made an arc over the center of the Well, then descended sharply toward the gullet of the whirlpool. As it did, it suddenly faded.

Like an Infernal dropping upon the victims of Suramar, what was left of Captain Varo'then plummeted into the solidifying portal.

As suddenly as it had come, the power surging through Malfurion ceased. He felt a loss and yet, at the same time, a comfort that the world had not yet become entirely defenseless. Still dangling from Ysera's back, he eyed Varo'then's ultimate destination.

"Let us see if the lord of the Legion still rewards you after *this,* captain . . ."

A jolt nearly sent him falling after Varo'then. Ysera had a bat in each forepaw and although the dragon had just ripped out the throat of one, the second had torn through her wing.

Malfurion struggled to a more stable position, then took from another pouch a tiny bit of salve he had earlier mixed. The salve had been made from selected herbs, but although the druid had tested it on the battlefield, he was not at all certain that it would be strong enough to aid such a giant as Ysera.

Yet, from the moment Malfurion rubbed it on the base of her wing, the results prove far more than he could have anticipated. The tiny amount of salve spread beyond where he touched, quickly covering the entire appendage. The rips in Ysera's wing quickly and completely mended, not even scars remaining to mark the savage wounds.

"I feel invigorated!" roared She of the Dreaming as she tore apart the second of the creatures. Ysera turned her head to Malfurion. Despite the shut lids, he felt the intensity of her gaze. "Cenarius has taught you well—" She suddenly stopped. Her eyes flickered open, if just for a second. "But perhaps *much* of the credit must still go to your natural tie to that which you wield. Yes, much, indeed . . ."

The druid realized that her brief glimpse had been focused at the top of his head. He reached up . . . and discovered that the nubs now thrust out a good three inches.

He had begun to grow antlers just like those of his shan'do.

Before this newest revelation could take hold in his mind, a fearsome roar shook the area, drowning out even the storm.

Out of the storm clouds dropped Deathwing.

The black leviathan hurtled himself once more at the impenetrable spells. His body erupted continually where plates had not yet sealed the tears in his hide. His eyes were wide with utter rage. He flew toward the Demon Soul with a swiftness that took Malfurion's breath away.

The air around the disk abruptly crackled, flashes of yellow and red giving warning as to the power bound to the dragon's stolen creation. Malfurion sensed new forces at play, power instilled into the spell matrix in order to amplify its hold on the Demon Soul.

Deathwing struck the matrix head-on. The sky around him exploded with raw energy that should have seared the insane Aspect to death, but, although his flesh and scales clearly burned, Deathwing nevertheless pushed forward. He roared defiantly at the mighty forces set in array against him. His mouth twisted into an insane, reptilian grin that grew with each push closer to his goal.

"There are no boundaries to his obsession . . ." Ysera said, marveling at the other Aspect.

"Do you think he might actually make it?"

"The true question is . . . do we wish him to?"

Scales tore from the black's already savaged body. The crackling bolts now focused fully on the giant, scorching him again and again. Yet, although he would now and then flinch under their intensity, Deathwing did not slow.

A red dragon flew past Malfurion and he saw both Rhonin and Brox astride. In a voice amplified by a spell, the wizard called, "Krasus warns that we have to be prepared! He thinks that Deathwing may yet manage to break the spell! We have to be ready to take on the black the moment that happens!"

"Deathwing . . ." Ysera muttered. "Seeing him now, how true that name rings . . ." To Rhonin, she roared, "We shall be ready!"

They would have to strike immediately and in concert. It was the only chance they had . . . and only a slightly better one than attempting to take the disk from the spell themselves. The night elf did not like their chances, but he would summon whatever he could of Kalimdor into him.

Aware that this might be the last hope for everything he loved, his heart instinctively went to Tyrande. Not Illidan, but Tyrande. He wanted to speak to her one last time, to know that she might live . . . even if he did not.

Malfurion?

The druid nearly slipped from Ysera's back. At first he believed the voice in his head only illusion or perhaps some sinister ploy by the dark powers against which they fought, but, in truth, Malfurion sensed that this could be none other than Tyrande who contacted him now.

He recalled how she had been the one who had helped summon him back when he been unable to return to his body. Her link to the druid was far greater than he could have ever imagined and in the instant that he thought that, Malfurion sensed that she had noticed it, also.

Malfurion! she repeated with more hope. *Oh, Malfurion! It is you!*

Tyrande! You live! Are you—have they—

The priestess was quick to reassure him. *The Mother Moon watched over me, praise be, and I was aided by Highborne seeking return to our people! I know that you did what you had to do! But listen! Your brother—*

My brother . . . No sooner did she mention Illidan, then the druid sensed that presence once so much like his own very near Tyrande. So near, in fact, that they had to be *touching*.

Brother—began Illidan.

You! Something surged within Malfurion, something that he realized he had to check immediately. Yet, despite his best efforts, the druid was not completely successful.

Malfurion! came Tyrande's plaintive call. *Cease! You'll kill him!*

He had no idea exactly what it was he was doing to Illidan, but Malfurion concentrated, trying to draw back what he had released. To his relief, he felt Illidan recover quickly.

Never . . . never knew you had that in you . . . brother . . . While the tone held consistent with Illidan's usual condescension, there lay in his mind a more stunned knowledge that the sibling he had felt weak was not.

You've much to answer for, Illidan!

If we all live, I will face my accusations . . .

His words held merit. What use was there to condemn Illidan if they were all to perish? Besides, Malfurion realized he wasted valuable power on his brother.

Putting thought of Illidan aside, the druid touched Tyrande again. *You're well? He's done nothing to you?*

Nothing, Malfurion. I swear by Elune . . . but we hide now in the ruins near the Well and dare not even attempt to cast a spell! The demon Mannoroth has warriors everywhere! I think they suspect where we are despite both Illidan's sorcery and my prayers . . .

He wanted to go to her, but, once again, that was not possible. Malfurion swore. *If we can succeed in—*

But before he could relay more, Deathwing unleashed a horrific bellow. The raw emotions in the dragon's cry shattered the links with Tyrande and Illidan and erased from Malfurion's thoughts any other matter.

He found himself looking upon a dragon tortured beyond comprehension but yet who was so obsessed with what he sought that no pain could daunt him. Some of the plates sealed to the black were nearly slag and several portions of his body had been stripped clear of scale. Revealed underneath was raw flesh burnt or ripped away. The leviathan's wings were torn in several places and it amazed Malfurion that the mad Earth Warder could still fly. Deathwing's claws were gnarled and ruined, as if he had been scratching at some impervious object.

Then, Malfurion saw how near the black hovered from his prize.

"By the creators!" Ysera roared. "He will let nothing stop him!"

The druid silently nodded, then realized how dire her words truly were. It looked as if, at any moment, Deathwing would do the impossible . . . and then it would be up to those hoping to steal the disk from him to do the same.

Away . . . away . . . demanded the voices that had once encouraged the dragon in everything he did. Now, they, like all the others, had proven themselves to be treacherous. Truly, there was no one Neltharion could trust but himself.

"I *will* have it! The Soul is mine! No one else's!"

He sensed their outrage that he would not obey them. They savagely attacked his mind even as through other means they fueled the Burning Legion's spells that also battled him. Never had the black dragon suffered so, but it would all be worth it. Even though he only inched forward, he still made progress. The disk was almost within his grasp.

Away . . . they repeated. *Away . . .*

Under their outrage, however, Neltharion also noted growing anxiety, even *fear.* The voices, too, saw that he had almost reached the his creation. Perhaps they understood that when it came back into his possession, he would punish *them* along with all the rest.

Then, another factor came more into play. The demon lord reached out from his own realm, magnifying the horrific forces already bound into the

spell matrix. Neltharion bellowed again as the torture he had suffered previous proved but a fraction of what he now felt.

But, if anything, it only drove him on. Mouth stretched back in a dragon's
version of a death grin, the leviathan laughed loud at all those who would
deny him his right. He laughed and pushed the final few yards to the disk.

"It is mine!" he roared in triumph. "Mine!"

His paw wrapped around the Demon Soul.

"It must be now!" Krasus warned Alexstrasza. "It must be now, if we are to—"

The world exploded.

Or so, at least, it seemed to the cowled figure. A mad cornucopia of colors
overwhelmed Krasus. He heard Alexstrasza roar in surprise and agony. A
tremendous force buffeted the two. Krasus tried to hold onto his queen, but it
was too much of a strain for the mortal form he wore.

He was thrown.

Things hurtled past him. A squealing, charred shadow bat. A small form
that might have been its rider or one of his own comrades. Several pieces of
dragon scale, their own color burnt away.

Krasus rolled over and over, unable to slow his momentum despite
attempted spells.

We have lost! he managed to think. *Surely, this is the end of all!*

Then, a huge paw scooped him up and he heard Alexstrasza's hoarse voice
cry out, "He has done it! He has done it!"

Through his tears, the mage managed to peer at Deathwing and the
Demon Soul.

The black dragon roared at the top of his lungs as he ripped the disk free
of the spell. Deathwing's body blazed and it amazed Krasus that even a being
as powerful as the Aspect could survive such damage. The leviathan raised his
creation high, laughing triumphantly despite his clear agony.

And then, from the depths of the Well, a black force shot out and struck
Deathwing head-on.

It threw the dragon back, hitting him with such ferocity that he was hurtled far, far beyond the vast Well. Far beyond even the shore. A tumbling
Deathwing flew from sight into the clouds . . .

In his wake, the Demon Soul—lost from his grip—plunged toward the
whirlpool.

"We must seize control before either Sargeras or the Old Gods can restore
it to the portal's matrix! I think that, despite Deathwing's spell on it, I can hold
it, at least long enough for our purposes! But we must reach it first!"

"I will try my best . . ." gasped Alexstrasza.

Only then did Krasus see how much his queen had been burnt by the forces unleashed by Deathwing's mad actions. The Aspect of Life could barely keep aloft.

But another massive dragon suddenly flew past them, a familiar green leviathan with a most unique night elf astride.

"Malfurion . . ." Krasus murmured, eyeing the druid, who now sported a small pair of antlers akin to those of his teacher. "Yes, it *has* to be he who attempts it . . ."

Yet, that did not preclude any effort by the others. Alexstrasza did not slow despite her wounds and from Krasus's right flew Rhonin and Brox on the red male. The bronze female also followed, but without a rider, she could not do anything but watch over the others.

Malfurion's dragon moved in on the plummeting disk, the Demon Soul leaving a bright, golden trail as it dropped. Krasus watched as the druid opened his palm . . . then unerringly caught the foul piece. The night elf clutched it to his chest.

And from within the portal came a monstrous roar that shook the dragon mage's very soul. He peered down, staring in dismay at a horrific green storm brewing in the center.

Sargeras was trying to cross through the nearly-completed gateway.

As a warrior, Brox knew well his limits. This was now a time of wizards and sorcerers. There were no foes with blades and axes up here, not anymore.

Malfurion gazed at the dread device, his eyes wide and unblinking. Brox understood the disk's seductive power and quickly shouted past Rhonin, "Druid! You must not trust it so! It is evil!"

The night elf glanced up, then gave his comrade a determined nod. Brox exhaled in relief—an exhalation that became a choking sound as he, like the rest, heard the fiendish cry erupting from the Well. It was the cry of an angered god.

The cry of Sargeras, lord of the Burning Legion.

"The demon lord seeks to enter Kalimdor!" the crimson male roared. "The portal is all but complete! He may be able to succeed . . . and, if he does, we are all lost!"

Brox stared at the green tempest below. It was contracting, coalescing into a smaller, almost perfectly octagonal gap. "What happens? The gateway shrinks, not grows!"

"Sargeras must further seek to strengthen his chances by localizing the spell! Once through, he will have no trouble stretching it wide again. If anything, he has his chance of success more likely!"

Horrified, the orc pulled his gaze from the monstrous storm . . . and saw that their situation was even more dire. From Zin-Azshari there now rose hundreds, perhaps, *thousands,* of winged forms. "Look! There!"

The demon Mannoroth had allowed Captain Varo'then and his soldiers to attack the party when all it had seemed was needed had been a delaying tactic. Now, though, with what the black dragon had done, the plan had clearly changed. Mannoroth surely realized that there was a true danger to the Legion. He had therefore summoned every Doomguard and other winged demon available to deal with the world's defenders.

Brox itched to sink his ax into the oncoming swarm, but he knew his efforts would be laughable compared to those of Rhonin and Krasus. True, he could ride along as the red male and the wizard fought them, but what good would that do?

Alexstrasza and Krasus, being farther back, had already turned to confront the horde of aerial demons. The red male began arcing away from the center of the Well. That left the wielding of the Demon Soul and the sealing of the portal to Malfurion . . . providing that he was somehow given the time needed. Even Brox could sense the sinister energies building up within the condensed portal. Sargeras had nearly succeeded . . .

The orc could think of only one thing to do. A part of him spoke called it madness, yet, another part insisted it *had* to be done.

"Farewell, wizard!" he roared. "It is my honor to have fought beside you and the rest!"

Rhonin glanced back at him. "What're you planning to—"

Brox leapt.

The red dragon attempted to snatch Brox, but the giant's astonishment made him react far too slowly. The orc fell past his claws, dropping relentlessly toward the center of the Well of Eternity . . . and the blazing storm now reaching its peak.

Howling with anticipation, Brox felt the wind tear at his face as he descended. His grip on his ax so tight that his knuckles had turned white. He grinned just as he had that day when he and his comrades had stood ready to protect the pass at cost of their lives.

As Brox neared the portal, his perspective shifted. He saw movement within. Ranks and ranks of demons, all preparing to follow their lord into the mortal plane. Demons stretching into Forever. Of Sargeras himself, Brox saw no sign, but he knew that the demons' fearsome master had to be very, very near.

And then . . . the orc passed through the gateway.

NINETEEN

alfurion did not see Brox leap, the night elf already consumed by what lay before him. Now that he had the disk, it occurred to the druid just how daunting his task was. Malfurion had hoped one of the others, especially Krasus, would be the one to seize the Demon Soul, but their underestimation of the spell and the black dragon's shocking intrusion into events had turned everything upside down. Now, it was all up to him and he had no idea exactly what to do.

At that moment, he sensed Tyrande in his thoughts again. Instinctively reaching out, Malfurion sensed with horror that she was in danger.

Tyrande! What—?

Malfurion! There are demons everywhere! Illidan and I believe that Mannoroth is trying to get you through us!

He quickly sought the link that he still shared with his twin. His initial contact with Illidan shocked Malfurion, so full of bloodlust was it. Through his brother, the druid felt Illidan strike out at the Burning Legion, the bodies of fiery warriors piled high before the black-clad spellcaster.

Illidan suddenly became aware of his presence. *Brother?*

Illidan! Can you flee?

We are surrounded and Mannoroth no doubt eagerly awaits my use of a spell to spirit us to safety! He would quickly usurp it, bringing us to his loving arms . . .

Malfurion shuddered. *I'm coming! I'll help you!*

But even as he said it, the druid knew that he could not leave the Well. The portal had to be destroyed, even if it meant *sacrificing* his twin and Tyrande.

How Malfurion prayed for a return to the old days, before the Legion. The days when he and his brother would have fought side by side. When they had been youths, he and Illidan had been able to overcome all obstacles because they had been as one.

Would that it could be so one more time, the druid desperately thought. *Would that I could stand next to Illidan and he next to me and together we dealt with this evil . . .*

Only too late, did Malfurion notice the Demon Soul flare.

A peculiar feeling of displacement hit him. His eyes momentarily lost focus. Groaning, Malfurion shook his head . . . and discovered that he now stood next to Illidan in the ruins of Zin-Azshari.

"Malfurion?" gasped Tyrande. She reached out to touch him, but her hand went through the druid.

Yet, when Malfurion put out a hand toward his twin, he felt solid flesh. Illidan flinched, startled.

Malfurion blinked . . . and once again he rode above the Well of Eternity. Only, this time . . . Illidan sat beside him.

The sorcerer gazed at Malfurion from behind his scarf with both suspicion and barely-concealed awe. "What've you *done,* brother?"

The druid eyed the Demon Soul and recalled his desire. The foul disk had granted it.

He and Illidan were in both places simultaneously.

So be it. Whatever its evil, the Demon Soul had given him the chance he needed. "Stand with me, Illidan!" Malfurion challenged. "Stand with me here—" The scene shifted back to Zin-Azshari. "—and here!"

To his credit—and with an old, familiar grin—Malfurion's twin immediately nodded.

In the mist-befouled city, the brothers stood shoulder-to-shoulder as the demons poured over the rubble trying to reach them. Scores perished as Illidan created yard-long swords from black energy and Malfurion channeled the forces of nature into a storm whose raindrops melted armor and demon flesh. Tyrande stood with them, the priestess of Elune calling upon the pure light of her mistress to blind, even burn, the approaching monsters.

And all while this happened, Malfurion and Illidan also sat astride Ysera, struggling with the spell holding the portal together. That Sargeras had not yet stepped forth puzzled both, but they did not question their momentary reprieve.

Yet, even with the Demon Soul, they accomplished nothing. Already the sky was filled with Doomguard, all seeking those who would keep their master from Kalimdor. Krasus, Rhonin, and the dragons destroyed them by the dozens, but still their numbers appeared undiminished. Of Brox, there was no sign, but the druid could not truly concern himself with the orc just now.

Ysera deflected attack after attack, but Malfurion understood that she could not defend them forever. Yet, despite both his and Illidan's attempts to use the Demon Soul against the portal, they continued to fail.

Then, the answer came to him. Malfurion looked into his brother's shrouded eye sockets. "We're doing this all wrong! We're using the disk to enhance our spells!"

"Of course!" snapped Illidan. The scene around them momentarily shifted back to Zin-Azshari, with the sorcerer gutting a Fel Guard. "How else to wield it?"

Their surroundings again became the Well and the demon-filled sky. The druid looked at Deathwing's unholy creation. He loathed what he was about to suggest. "The Demon Soul is still part of the spellwork! Instead of drawing from disk, we should be *giving* to it! We should be working *through* the disk, not treating it like a sword or ax!"

Illidan opened his mouth to argue, then shut it immediately. He saw the sense in his twin's words.

Again, Malfurion's view became Zin-Azshari. He immediately sensed a new force among the demons in the city, one moving with dire purpose toward the ruins where the brothers and Tyrande sheltered. It had a familiar taint . . . and stench.

"Satyrs!"

The goat creatures bounded over the other demons, each of the former night elves already preparing spells. They laughed madly and some even bleated.

But as the abominations converged on the trio, Malfurion once more found himself astride Ysera. The constant shifting distracted him and he suspected that, one way or another, he and his brother's ability to be in two places would soon cease.

"Join with me, Illidan! Do it!"

Despite their enmities, the sorcerer did not hesitate. Their minds linked, fusing almost completely. Malfurion sensed his twin's ill-conceived plans to make himself the hero of Kalimdor and recognized immediately how the sinister forces that had almost seduced the druid into claiming the disk for his own had used Illidan's arrogance to add their own spells into the mix.

He had forgotten the Old Gods, as Krasus called them. So, they had not abandoned their efforts; Sargeras's portal still held the key to their freedom. More than ever, the druid understood that he *had* to use the Demon Soul if they were to destroy the gateway.

Be ready! he commanded Illidan.

Malfurion called upon the inherent energies of Kalimdor, the same forces that had helped him cast out the venomous Captain Varo'then. Now, he would have to demand of them a far greater sacrifice. This would take more than that he had used to save a dragon from death, as the druid had naively done for Krasus and Korialstrasz. In asking of his precious world such power, there was a chance that the druid might bring upon his home the very fate the Burning Legion had planned for it.

As he called upon Kalimdor and asked it to grant him its strength once more, he felt Illidan draw upon the energies of the Well itself. Once both had achieved their desire, the brothers bound the two forces together—making them one—and fed the results into the Demon Soul.

Both Malfurion and Illidan jerked as their magicks melded with that within the disk. The druid momentarily returned to Zin-Azshari . . . just as a satyr leapt upon Tyrande. Without regard for himself, the druid slashed at the horned creature with a sword created from a jagged leaf. The satyr's head went rolling—

And, once again, Malfurion's focus shifted back to his position over the Well. Gritting his teeth, he forced his senses back into the Demon Soul.

He and Illidan became a part of the disk. They *were* the Demon Soul . . .

They flowed toward him, an endless river of utter evil seeking his death.

"Come!" roared Brox, kicking aside the severed limb of another demon foolish enough to get within reach of his ax. He stood atop a mound of dead flesh, his many kills. The orc's body was awash in his own blood, but a strength such as he had not felt in years filled the graying warrior.

A chaotic fury surrounded the lone guardian, the madness of the realm of the Burning Legion. There seemed no ground, no sky, only an insane swirl of fiery colors and untamed energies. Had he not been so completely focused upon his adversaries, the orc suspected that he surely would have been driven insane by now.

Behind him, the portal burned with evil purpose. The green flames danced as if demons themselves and seemed to draw the Burning Legion like the proverbial moth. Brox had expected that he would be overcome immediately, but not only had he so far survived, he had kept not even a single demon from reaching the gateway.

How much longer he could last, the aged warrior did not know. For as long as the portal existed, he hoped. The enchanted ax gave him an edge, one that Brox had utilized to good advantage, but the weapon was only as good for as long as his strength lasted.

A movement of black at his right caught the orc's attention. Instinctively, he shifted to meet it—

And was battered horribly by a force that made the might of the demons before him seem as nothing. Brox's shoulder cracked and he felt several of his ribs collapse into his organs. Sharp, agonizing pains ripped through him.

He tried to rise, but again the veteran warrior was battered relentlessly. His legs were crushed and his jaw broken on the right. Brox tasted his own blood, a not unfamiliar thing. One eye was bruised beyond opening and it was all the orc could do just to breathe.

But his one remaining hand still gripped the ax. Overcoming everything, Brox swung, hoping to hit his attacker.

The blade encountered an obstruction, and, at first, Brox's hopes rose. However, the squeal that immediately followed informed the badly-injured orc that he had only caught an eager felbeast trying to close in on easy prey.

Such a pity . . .

Despite the words, there was certainly *no* pity in the terrible voice thundering in his head. A vast shadow blanketed the orc.

Such a pity to waste such a delicious ability for carnage . . .

With a strained roar, Brox managed to right himself. The ax came spinning around.

This time, he knew that it was no mere demon hound he hit.

A resounding bellow of outrage deafened the injured warrior. Through what remained of his good eye, Brox caught sight of a titanic, horned figure in molten black armor whose thick mane and beard appeared to be composed of wildly dancing flames. The orc could not make out the giant's features well enough, yet somehow knew them to be both wondrously perfect and terribly awful at the same time.

Then, the titan raised one arm and in it Brox beheld a long, wicked sword the upper half of whose blade had been broken off. What remained was jagged and still very capable of slaying.

Through broken teeth, the orc began a death chant.

The jagged tip impaled him, bursting through his spine. Brox's body quivered uncontrollably and the light in his eyes dimmed. The ax slipped from his limp fingers.

With a sigh, the orc at last joined his comrades from the past.

"There're too many of them!" Rhonin shouted.

"We must do what we can! Malfurion must be given time!" Krasus responded from Alexstrasza's back.

"Can he do anything?"

"He is a part of Kalimdor itself! He must be able to! He stands the best chance! Believe it!"

Rhonin said nothing else, merely nodding and sending a score more demons to whatever hell existed for them in the afterlife.

The noise without and even within had grown incessant. Queen Azshara no longer had any patience. Clad in her finest so as to present the great Sargeras a most wonderful spectacle, the Light of Lights strode into the hall, followed by her demon guards. Night elven sentries stood nervously at attention as she passed.

"Vashj! Lady Vashj!"

Azshara's chief attendant came rushing from the opposite direction, quickly prostrating herself before her monarch. "Yes, my mistress! I am here to obey!"

"You are here to answer questions, Vashj! I was assured that nothing was amiss, but, if anything, it sounds so highly chaotic in and around the palace! My sensibilities are offended! I want order restored, is that understood? What will our Lord Sargeras think?"

Vashj kept her face all the way to the exquisite marble floor, each square of which bore the stylized profile of Azshara. "I am but your humble servant, Light of Lights! I have tried to ask of Lord Mannoroth some news, but he ordered me away with threats of peeling my flesh from my bones!"

"Impertinent!" Azshara looked in the direction leading to the tower where the Highborne and demons worked. "We shall see! Come, Vashj!"

With her anxious companion in tow, the queen wended her way up. It was a sign of her displeasure that she had not first summoned the rest of her attendants so as to make a more glorious entrance. For this journey, Vashj and her bodyguards would just have to do.

At the doorway, a pair of Fel Guard and two felbeasts attempted to block her entrance. "Move aside! I command you!"

The hounds whined, obviously desiring to obey, but the two monstrous warriors defiantly shook their heads.

Azshara looked back at her own retinue. Smiling at the demons who had accompanied her, she commanded, "Please remove these from my sight."

Her guards moved without hesitation against their comrades. They had been around the queen long enough to fall prey to her wiles. Outnumbered, the demons blocking the way fell quickly, as did the hounds. One of her own perished in the process, but what was a guard compared to the desires of Azshara?

When the corpses had been cleared from her path, the queen stepped forward. Vashj opened the way, then slipped behind Azshara.

The chamber was a beehive of activity. Gaunt, sweating sorcerers worked frantically under the baleful gaze of Mannoroth. Satyrs, Eredar, and Dreadlords also struggled with spells, the results of which obviously took place beyond the palace walls.

Undaunted by what was clearly a monumental strain on the part of the spellcasters, Azshara approached the gargantuan demon. Mannoroth, sweating not a little himself, did not notice her presence at first, a slight the queen only barely forgave.

"My Lord Mannoroth," she began frostily. "I find myself disappointed with the lack of order taking place before the arrival of Sargeras—"

He spun on her, his toadlike visage filled with astonishment at her audacity. "Little creature, you'd do well to leave here now! My patience is at an end! For even interrupting me at this juncture, I should rip off your head and devour your innards!"

Azshara said nothing, merely gazing imperiously at the demon.

With a hiss, Mannoroth reached one meaty hand toward her. His intention was clear; he had no further use for the night elf's existence.

But though he came close, Mannoroth faltered at the end. It was not because of any sudden notion that Sargeras might still desire the silver-haired creature to live. Rather, Mannoroth discovered that here was a force against which only his lord and Archimonde would prove superior. Try as he might, the demon would have found it easier to throttle himself than the queen.

He finally drew back, caught between his sudden unease around one he had highly underestimated and the present danger to the portal.

"For the sake of our Lord Sargeras," Azshara regally declared. "I shall forgive your outburst . . . this time."

Hiding his unease, Mannoroth quickly turned from her. "I've no more time for this! The portal must be protected . . ."

He did not see her brow arch. "The portal is in danger? How?"

Grinding his yellowed fangs together, the demon rumbled, "The desperate acts of a few last rabble! All will be well . . . but only if there are no more interruptions!"

Azshara pursed her lips at his offensive tone, but saw the sense of his words. "Very well, Lord Mannoroth! I shall return to my quarters . . . but I expect this incident to be settled swiftly so that Sargeras will finally come to me. We are done here, Vashj."

The queen of the night elves departed with regal flair. Mannoroth glanced over his shoulder as she stepped from sight, the demon still incredulous. Then, recalling himself, Mannoroth quickly went back to the task at hand. The rebels would be crushed and the way kept open for the lord of the Legion. Already, he could feel Sargeras nearing the gate, which held despite the stealing of the dragon's disk by the druid and his friends.

Soon . . . very soon . . .

Malfurion and Illidan continued to battle the demons in the ruins. At the same time, they continued to let flow into the disk their very selves. Illidan sought to push full force into the situation, but, fortunately, Malfurion kept his twin in check. This had to be done in a calculated manner, even if seconds were as valuable as one's last breath.

Then . . . at last they were ready to strike.

But as he began the final spell, Malfurion felt a tremendous evil touching his mind, an evil that was not Sargeras. Voices whispered in his head, promising him everything. He could rule Kalimdor, have Tyrande as his queen and the Burning Legion as his army. All would bow to his greatness. He had but to make a slight alteration to his casting.

The druid fought back the whispers, aware of what their speakers truly desired. He pushed on with the spell—

Only to have Illidan suddenly seek to do what the voices had desired of Malfurion. Where the druid had overcome their seductive words, the sorcerer had fallen victim.

Illidan! Malfurion thrust his thoughts at his twin in a manner akin to physically striking him. He felt the dark hold over Illidan break. His twin gasped . . .

I am myself again, Illidan assured him a moment later.

Although not entirely trusting, Malfurion continued with their task. They had little time left. It was a wonder that the demon lord had not already entered. Worse, although the entities had been repulsed, if the portal stayed open, Malfurion had no doubt that they would somehow still follow Sargeras into the mortal plane.

Aware of what would befall Kalimdor then, Malfurion cast the spell. Whatever damage it did, it would be as a light breeze in comparison.

A dead silence filled the air. It was as if no sound existed in all the world. The wind stilled and even the storm-tossed Well emitted not even the least rumble of thunder.

Then . . . a great howl shook the Well, Zin-Azshari, and, possibly, all the rest of Kalimdor. A terrible gale picked up behind Malfurion, but Ysera quickly compensated for it. The new wind rose with a fury matching anything the druid had ever come across before. Caught unaware, the other dragons flew about wildly at first, then, amazingly, righted themselves as if the gale had vanished.

That was hardly the case for the Doomguard and their ilk. The winged demons fluttered about uncontrollably, unable at all to battle against this new and fearsome wind. Several collided, cracking skulls and shattering limbs, but although many demons perished, the wind was so powerful that their limp corpses did not drop but instead spun around over the Well as if performing some macabre dance.

The gale swelled tenfold, a hundredfold, and yet for the dragons and their riders, it was little more than a breeze. Not so for their frantic foes. By the hundreds, the Doomguard swirled around and around and around . . .

And then were sucked inexorably toward the portal.

Those with breath left to them howled and screamed and gnashed their teeth, but they were as dust to the blast. From every direction, the monstrous warriors plummeted relentlessly toward the gateway through which their brethren waited to emerge.

"It's working!" shouted Illidan with a triumphant laugh. "It's working!"

But Malfurion did not ease up, for he felt resistance pressing against the spell. Whether the work of the lord of the Legion or the Old Gods, he could not say at this point. All the druid knew was that if he weakened, all he had achieved would be lost and his world with it.

The unnatural wind continued to grow, sucking demons out of the sky and into the vortex at the center of the Well. Within seconds, the heavens had been cleansed of the Legion's foulness, and yet, the gale did not let up.

Malfurion, still in two places at the same time, now watched in awe as the horde converging on the spot where he, his twin, and Tyrande still stood suddenly slowed in panic. Huge Fel Guard and monstrous hounds began clutching at the ruined earth. A savage Infernal managed two steps toward the trio, then, even the massive demon could go no farther.

Limbs and tail flailing, the first felbeast flew off into the air, its whine pitiful as it vanished over the Well.

It was followed swiftly by another felbeast, then several of the gargantuan warriors. The dam opened wide then, demons by the scores suddenly pouring upward in some bizarre reversed rain. They flowed unceasingly over the black waters and, as they did, Malfurion noted how their bodies grew more fluid, almost insubstantial.

A sense of vertigo shook him and the night elf nearly lost control of the spell. His view of Zin-Azshari vanished. Quickly turning to his side, Malfurion saw that Illidan no longer sat beside him. He still felt the link between his twin and himself, but it was more tenuous.

The druid maintained his concentration. He felt the natural forces of the world feed through him. The trees, the grass, the rocks, the fauna . . . all sacrificed a part of themselves to give him the strength he needed. Malfurion vaguely understood that what he did now went far beyond what Cenarius had taught him and far beyond anything that the night elf had done before. Illidan's magic continued to bind with his, adding its might, too.

He cried out abruptly as what felt like a thousand needles buried themselves in his mind. There was no mistaking Sargeras in this attack. The demon lord's presence filled him, attempted to consume the druid from within.

Malfurion strained, fighting back some bit of the agony. Kalimdor continued to feed him, to give him all it could. It entrusted Malfurion with its future, its fate. He was its guardian now, more so than Cenarius, Malorne, or even the dragons. It was up to him and him alone.

Alone . . . against the Burning Legion and the Old Gods.

"Work, you dogs!" Mannoroth bellowed at the sorcerers and demons. "Harder!"

One of the Highborne momentarily slumped forward. Like the rest, he was almost skeletal. The once-extravagant robes now draped him like a colorful funeral shroud. He coughed, then noticed too late the humongous shadow over him.

"My Lord Mannoroth! Please, I only need—"

With one hand, the demon seized him by the head, crushing the skull and its contents to a bloody pulp. Mannoroth shook the dangling body for the benefit of the cringing night elves and warlocks. "Work!"

Despite their emaciated states, the spellcasters immediately doubled their efforts. Even then, Mannoroth found no satisfaction. He tossed the grisly remnants aside and moved to the pattern. He would have to rejoin the effort if he hoped for it to succeed.

But as he shoved aside those in his path, a peculiar sense of displacement touched him. Mannoroth's movement grew sluggish and when he looked at one of the Eredar, he saw that the same was happening to the warlock. The night elves seemed less affected, but even they moved slower and slower.

"What—is—happening?" he demanded of no one and everyone.

Heavy tail slapping against the floor, Mannoroth tried to return to the spellwork, but as he raised his still blood-soaked hand, his eyes widened. The scaled hide had a translucent appearance. The demon could see his own sinew and bone and even they no longer looked completely substantial.

"Not possible!" the winged behemoth rumbled. "Not possible!"

The tower wall facing the Well of Eternity shattered outward.

A great force tugged at the demons. Those nearest the jagged gap almost immediately followed the massive chunks of stone out over the black body of water, quickly vanishing in the distance. Heavily-armored warriors were lifted as if as light as a feather.

The pattern broke. Despite their fear of Mannoroth, the night elves fled what was clearly catastrophe. Having reached their own limits, the Eredar attempted to follow the sorcerers, only to be swept up in the same awful wind that had ripped away the Fel Guard. With wild howls, the warlocks vanished through the hole.

At last, there remained only Mannoroth. His incredible strength and bulk working for him, the winged demon held his own against the hungering gale. Mannoroth's brutish orbs fixed on the decaying pattern. He started for the center. Enough magic remained in it so that with his own power he could create about him a protective shield in which he could wait out this attack.

Each step proved ponderous, but Mannoroth forced himself forward. One trunklike limb entered the pattern, then another. His wings beat madly, giving him what little push they could. The demon's third foot entered . . . and, with a triumphant grin spreading across his horrific countenance, Mannoroth planted the fourth there as well.

Raising his clawed hands high, he summoned the magic of the pattern around him. Even moving his arms proved nearly unbearable, but the gigantic demon managed.

A fiery, green dome formed around him. The suction ceased. Mannoroth turned to face the shattered wall and laughed hard. Against lesser demons the wind might prove superior, but he was *Mannoroth!* Mannoroth the Flayer! Mannoroth the Destructor! One of Sargeras's chosen—

The flames of the shield bent toward the broken wall . . . and to his dismay, the demon watched as his protection was sucked away.

As he attempted to turn from the wall, the wind seized hold of him. A backward-flying Mannoroth gaped as he was plucked from the floor with ease. The demon roared his frustration as he slammed into the broken stone, sending more huge chunks of the wall tumbling outside.

He managed to grab hold and, for a brief moment, hope filled Mannoroth. But the strain on his thick fingers and heavy claws was too much. His nails scraped uselessly against the stone as he was finally torn from the tower.

Still roaring, Mannoroth was cast out over the Well of Eternity.

TWENTY

B lood trickled down Jarod Shadowsong's face. His left arm was broken, of that he was certain. What was not so certain was whether any of his vital organs had been damaged by the hammering blows that had caved in his breast plate in several places. He had a little trouble breathing, but, for the moment, at least he could stand . . . somewhat.

Struggling to raise his sword, Jarod again faced his adversary.

Archimonde looked none the worse for wear. Jarod had left no mark on the sinister demon, had not even managed to *touch* Archimonde once, save at the receiving end of one cruel hit after another.

What made it all worse was that Jarod understood quite well that the towering demon was merely toying with him. Archimonde could have slain his tiny foe a dozen times over, but the creature was taking a sadistic pleasure in slowly battering the night elf into oblivion. Still, Jarod knew it would not be much longer before Archimonde unleashed the fatal blow. There was only so much more he could do to the beaten soldier.

And yet, some inner force made Jarod stand ready for more punishment.

They stood alone on this part of the battlefield, although there were those in the distance on both sides watching the tableau unfold. The demons, of course, surveyed the sight of their commander thrashing the night elf with horrific glee and constantly yelled their encouragement to Archimonde. Jarod's own followers no doubt saw just how pathetic the former guard captain truly was. They likely wondered how they could have ever seen him as their hope.

A fierce wind swept up, raising dust. Jarod squinted, trying not to be blinded. Archimonde slowed as he approached, the demon expressionless. Jarod imagined that dark giant was plotting how best to pummel his victim.

But if he was to die, the night elf decided that he would do so at least giving the appearance of trying to fight on. Gripping his sword tight in both hands, Jarod let out a cry and charged Archimonde.

Through the rising dust, he caught the demon smiling slightly at his audacity. However, as Jarod neared, that smile slipped away and, to the desperate officer's surprise, Archimonde *stiffened*.

The powerful wind nearly threw Jarod forward. Bearing his teeth, the night elf lunged at his adversary's stomach. It was the only spot he could reach that might—just might—give way to his feeble blade. If he could at least mark Archimonde before the giant crushed him . . .

Dust and tears blurred Jarod's vision, giving the demon an almost ghostly appearance in the process. Archimonde reached a hand toward him and the night elf braced himself for some hideous spell to melt his flesh or turn his bones to oil.

But no such spell came. Instead, crouching slightly, Archimonde took a step *back*. His torso he left completely unprotected.

Jarod thrust, already preparing himself for failure. He had no doubt that either his blade would break off Archimonde's hide or that he would miss entirely.

But he did *not* miss and, to his further astonishment, the sword sank deep into the gigantic demon's stomach. Yet, curiously, there was no resistance whatsoever, almost as if Archimonde was indeed a ghost. Jarod continued pressing, all the while awaiting his own death.

Instead . . . Archimonde went flying back as if struck hard. However, he did not land, as might have been expected, but rather *kept* flying. Arms and legs flailing, the demon commander rose up into the air and only then did Jarod realize that it was the wind that had Archimonde.

All composure finally abandoned Archimonde's expression as he hurtled higher and higher into the heavens. His face contorted into a grotesque mockery more apt for a creature of his evil. The demon let out a cry of fury . . . and then vanished from sight over the horizon.

Even before the weary officer could register that he had survived his incredible duel, he saw that the wind now assailed the *entire* Legion. Demons struggled to keep their positions, but like the dust they were taken up and tossed about. Monstrous hounds leaping forward instead rolled backward, bouncing first over the landscape before soaring after Archimonde. The Fel Guard were plucked one by one from the lines and even though many stood face-to-face with the defenders, not one night elf, tauren, or other creature of Kalimdor joined their astounding fate.

Infernals dropping from the sky abruptly veered off, their flights now mirroring that of their lost commander. One even came within inches of the soil before reversing direction.

The dragons, oddly, were also barely touched by the mad elements. After some minor adjustments, they regained their balance, then, wisely, retreated to the ground. There, they, too, watched the Legion's downfall unfold.

The sky filled with writhing, snarling demons, all struggling in vain to return to the ground. Below them, gaping fighters stared with weapons lowered as the threat to their land, to their world, was simply torn away before their very eyes. Even the corpses of those demons long slain joined the ones above, adding to the spectacle.

" 'Tis a miracle!" someone shouted from behind Jarod. He glanced over his shoulder to discover that several of those who had earlier been tossed back by Archimonde had begun to return. Many continued to watch the sky, but a number of others eyed Jarod as if he alone was responsible for the stunning turn of events.

The ranks of the demons were stripped from Kalimdor line after line until soon a barren wasteland spread out before the defenders. Not one demon remained. In fact, not even one *piece* of any demon remained.

More than a few night elves dropped to their knees in relief. However, despite what had happened, Jarod had the unsettling feeling that the struggle was not quite at an end. It could not be so easy . . .

"On your feet, all of you!" he roared. With his good hand, he seized a dumbfounded herald and commanded, "Sound the horns! I want order in the host again! We have to be prepared to move!"

A priestess of Elune came to his side and inspected his arm. As she did, Jarod continued to collect his thoughts.

"Are we giving chase?" a noble called, looking too eager for Jarod's taste.

"No!" the commander snapped back, unmindful of the difference in caste. "We wait for word from the mage Krasus or one of those with him! Only then do we move . . . and whether it's to advance on Zin-Azshari or flee for our lives, we'll need to be ready to do it as fast this wind!"

As they obeyed, Jarod, allowing himself just enough time for the priestess's ministrations, stared once more in the direction the demons had flown, the direction of the capital and the Well.

It could not end this simply, no . . .

Yet, throughout Kalimdor, the Burning Legion was cast from the ground and tossed helplessly toward the Well of Eternity. Their struggles were as nothing against the wind and as Krasus and the rest watched, they massed over the waters like a gigantic swarm of bees before dropping into the maelstrom.

"Is that it? Is it over?" shouted Rhonin.

"It may be . . . and it may be not!" To Alexstrasza, Krasus called, "To Malfurion!"

She nodded, banking in the direction of the druid and Ysera. Rhonin and the red male followed close behind.

Malfurion and his mount hovered over the whirlpool, the night elf awash in the Demon Soul's golden glow. His normally-dark skin looked almost as pale as Krasus's. He glanced at the cowled mage in anxiousness.

"He's still trying to come through!" The druid's face had aged. Lines traced over it and his eyes had sunken in a little. "I don't know if my spell can hold him!"

Krasus gazed down, his heightened senses enabling him to see deep into the Well.

Deep into the portal . . .

And so it was that he beheld Sargeras, lord of the Legion.

Molten armor clad the titan from neck to foot, its black fury so great that it burned the mage's eyes just to look. Fighting the pain, Krasus dared stare into the face of evil, a monstrous distortion of perfection. Once, there had been a handsome, even beautiful being—a being of the race that Krasus knew had created his world. Now, however, the beauty was tainted. The flesh was that of death and the eyes the fiery emptiness of utter chaos. Sargeras's teeth were fangs. Behind him whipped a long, thick tail with jagged scales jutting out at the tip. His hands ended in wicked, curved talons and in one of those hands, he wielded a monstrous sword cracked midway but with a jagged edge still capable of much mayhem.

Krasus choked, horrified at what he discovered next. On the end of that monstrous weapon, a tiny, green body lay impaled.

Brox.

In all the excitement, the mage had forgotten all about the orc. Now, though, Krasus understood why his party had gained precious—very precious— seconds. The orc had sacrificed himself to delay the Legion.

Sargeras stood at the gateway. Despite the incredible forces driving his horde back into his realm, the lord of the Legion pressed forward. Slowly, surely, he reached the portal . . .

But as Sargeras neared, Krasus noted a stunning thing. The demon lord was *injured,* albeit minutely. A small slash mark decorated his right leg, a mark that Krasus's keen eyes recognized as made by an ax.

Brox's ax. Impossible as it seemed, the enchanted weapon had scratched Sargeras. Not enough to cause him any real harm, of course, but that a wound existed at all opened up a unique possibility.

"Rhonin! Alexstrasza! We must act as one! Malfurion! Be prepared! You will have your chance to destroy the portal, but only barely!"

The others followed his lead. Krasus felt his queen and his former protege allow him to guide their power. The red male added his strength as well, as did Ysera. It left Malfurion open to attack, but if this final effort failed, *none* of them could hope to survive.

Eyes alight with power, Krasus focused the party's combined magic at the gateway. The mage trusted to the demon lord's intense concentration for the success of the spellcasters' desperate venture.

In comparison to Sargeras, both Archimonde and Mannoroth were as fleas. The power of a hundred dragons would have been as nothing to him. Had Krasus sought to strike Sargeras directly, either in the chest or head, the results would have been laughable, at least to the demon lord. That Brox had managed his miraculous attack at all said much for the power imbued in the weapon by the druid and his shan'do.

No, instead, the mage poured all that he was given by the others at the tiny, insignificant wound Brox's ax—a piece of Kalimdor's magic itself—had managed.

And then it happened. Krasus sensed Sargeras's concentration weaken just for a moment. Not from pain—that would have been too much hope for— but rather, simply from *startlement.*

Which was what Krasus wanted. "Now, Malfurion!"

Clutching the Demon Soul tight, Malfurion assailed the portal.

Krasus had gambled that the magically-wrought wound would be just sensitive enough to gain the demon lord's momentary attention if it was struck again. All their assembled might had done had been to create a slight irritation, one upon which Sargeras had instinctively focused instead of the gateway.

The mouth of the maelstrom quivered, then lost cohesion. An explosion of energy erupted from the depths of the whirlpool.

The portal started to collapse.

One side after another, the fiery border surrounding it fell in upon itself. Sargeras attempted to reconstruct it, but by then, it had moved beyond even his power to do so. One precious second had stolen the demon lord's victory.

And then a thing happened that Krasus could never have dreamed possible. Sargeras, refusing to believe his defeat, stepped within the crumbling portal itself, trying both to rebuild it and cross through. His desire to do so proved his undoing. As the portal imploded, the demon lord found himself trapped. He could not flee, could not pull back. Dropping his sword, the titan even battered against the gateway with his fists, but to no avail. The corridor between realms shrank rapidly, at last crushing in on him. Sargeras roared and his voice echoed in the heads of all.

I will not be denied! I will not!

But the gateway continued to condense and Sargeras seemed to condense with it. He struggled to keep the way open, the interior of the gate aflame from his titanic efforts.

And then, with the demon lord still shouting his rage and beating at the walls . . . the portal ceased to be.

Sargeras ceased to be.

"It's done!" gasped Malfurion. "It's—"

But his voice died as, despite the gateway's vanishing, the maelstrom in the center of the Well continued to swirl madly. Worse, it appeared to be growing, swelling. Even as the druid watched, the edges ate away at the shoreline of Zin-Azshari.

The night elf glanced over at Krasus. "What's happening?"

Krasus waved off explanations. "We must be away from here! We must get *everyone* as far from the Well as possible!"

Alexstrasza and the others quickly veered away, heading for land. Raw energy crackled in and around the black waters. The whole of Zin-Azshari shook and as the dragons passed over, the mage spied massive faults beyond the city's limits.

"It's begun . . ." Krasus whispered to himself. "May the creators protect us . . . it's begun and there is nothing we can do to stop it . . ."

A new tempest assailed the party, scattering the dragons despite their might. Compensating for this latest storm, the winged leviathans regathered . . . save for one.

Ysera—and thus Malfurion and the disk—was missing.

Krasus quickly scanned the heavens, but of the Aspect, he could see nothing. Not until his gaze turned groundward did the cowled figure see where she had flown.

Back toward the Well of Eternity.

"No!" Even Ysera did not understand what fate was to befall this region. Worse, there was no telling what would happen to the time line if, instead of being carried away, the Demon Soul was lost to the Well's throes. "We must go back! We must get them!"

To her credit, Alexstrasza immediately banked. Rhonin's red male and the riderless bronze began to follow, but Krasus waved them on. Concentrating, he managed to enter Rhonin's thoughts despite the myriad magical forces interfering.

You must go to the host! You must warn Jarod that everyone has to flee as far as they can from the direction of the Well! Flee to Mount Hyjal!

He did not have to explain further, for, of all of them, the human understood best. A child of the future, Rhonin knew what was to come as well as his former mentor did. The wizard leaned forward, speaking to his mount, and, seconds later, the red turned away. The bronze hesitated, then followed.

Krasus watched the landscape as Alexstrasza pursued Ysera's trail. Near what had once been the gates of the city, a deep crevice as wide as his queen's wing now stretched. Some of the structures that had been left standing despite the demons' initial rampage now shook violently and several tumbled over even as the pair soared over.

It is imminent . . . The dragon mage stared ahead, trying to catch a glance of Ysera and the druid. *The Sundering is upon Kalimdor* . . .

A chandelier crashed on the marble floor, the thousand crystals composing it scattering. Several flew with the sharp speed of missiles. One of Azshara's handmaidens fell, a beautiful, glistening shard through her forehead.

The queen, gripping a pillar for support, eyed the bleeding corpse with frustration. She had enough on her mind without one of her servants sullying her presence so. Yet, clearly no one had the wherewithal to clear the body away. The rest of them, even Vashj, ran around in panic as the walls shook and the floor cracked.

Evidently forgetting the laws against touching the queen's person without permission, Vashj seized Azshara's arm. "Light of Lights! We must flee the palace! Something has gone terribly wrong! None of the Great One's warriors remain and the sorcerers have fled the tower! One I stopped claimed a tremendous wind cast out even Lord Mannoroth over the Well!"

Azshara was already aware of the absence of the warriors of the Burning Legion, her personal bodyguard having been ripped from their positions before her very eyes and sucked through a wall in her chamber. Despite the stunning spectacle, though, the queen refused to believe that Sargeras would not in fact still appear and she intended to be ready when that glorious event took place.

Vashj still tugged on her arm. Azshara's infinite patience had its limits. She suddenly slapped her lady-in-waiting.

The others froze where they were, the fact that their surroundings threatened to collapse upon them forgotten. They fully expected their mistress to now execute Vashj on the spot.

Instead, in her most regal voice, Azshara commanded, "You will all remember your places! I expect you to obey the instructions I have given you! We will continue to prepare for our Lord Sargeras's entrance . . ."

To emphasize her point, she strode to one of her chairs. The first tremor had toppled it over, but Vashj quickly righted it, then dusted off the seat with the hem of her own garment.

Nodding approval, Azshara sat. Her handmaidens immediately took up their positions and Vashj poured the queen a goblet of wine, somehow avoiding spilling it despite the continued shaking of the palace.

"Thank you, Lady Vashj," the queen of the night elves said graciously. She sipped a bit, then posed herself in expectation. No matter how long it took for Sargeras to arrive, she would be ready for him. He would step before her and be dazzled by her perfection, as all were.

After all, she *was* Azshara.

As Ysera reached the shore, Malfurion, the Demon Soul pressed against his breast, eyed the grand capital of the night elves with horror. Attuned to the natural forces of Kalimdor, he recognized immediately imminent disaster. Recognized it and realized that he had to act fast.

"My brother and Tyrande! They're still in Zin-Azshari! Please! I can't leave them!"

"You know where they are?"

"I do!"

The massive green dragon nodded. "Guide me, but make it quick!"

They turned off without alerting the others. Malfurion peered across the shoreline. Ysera had flown so swiftly that they had been forced to backtrack some distance, but the druid sensed that they were finally near the other night elves.

There! Tyrande waved to him, the sight of her so wonderful that Malfurion momentarily forgot that he was also here for his twin. Only after recalling that did the druid suddenly note that Illidan was nowhere to be seen.

Ysera landed. As ever, the Aspect gazed around with eyes shut, but Malfurion understood by now that, despite appearances, she could see far better than most creatures.

He leapt off. Tyrande met him, clinging to Malfurion with such intensity that he momentarily could think of nothing else than doing the same. Only when the dragon cleared her throat slightly did the two reluctantly separate.

"Malfurion—" the priestess began.

He put his fingers over her lips. "Hush, Tyrande. Where's Illidan?"

Her eyes widened briefly. She looked over her shoulder. "By the very edge."

With a curse, the druid ran past her. Illidan surely knew that the land was crumbling about him. How could he be so mad?

As he scrambled around a ruined tower, Malfurion nearly collided with his twin. Illidan somehow managed to stare at him with his covered eye sockets.

"Brother . . . a timely return . . ."

"Illidan! The Well is out of control—"

The sorcerer nodded. "Aye! It's been twisted and turned by too many spells! That fuss we—especially you—made with the Demon Soul was too much! The same spell that sent the Burning Legion back into their foul realm now works on the Well! It's devouring itself and taking its surroundings with it!" He turned back to the black body of water. "Fascinating, isn't it?"

"Not if we're caught up in it! Why weren't you running?"

Illidan wiped his hand. Only then did Malfurion see the slight glimmer of power surrounding it. He also noted the moisture.

"What've you been doing with your hand in the Well, Illidan?"

At that moment, a tremendous tremor sent both night elves to their knees. Illidan shouted, "If you've a way out of here, we should probably use it! I've tried casting Tyrande and myself out of here, but the Well is too much in flux!"

"This way!" Malfurion grabbed his brother by the arm and dragged Illidan back to the others. Tyrande already sat upon Ysera. She aided Illidan up, then Malfurion.

At that moment, a huge form hovered overhead. The druid instinctively expected some demonic horror, then saw that it was none other than Krasus and Alexstrasza.

"The Demon Soul!" the mage shouted. "You have it still?"

The night elf slapped one of the pouches at his waist. He had secreted the disk in it just before Ysera had landed.

Krasus nodded in relief. "Hurry, then! We must fly fast and far! Even the air will not be safe!"

Well aware by now that the mage knew so much more than he had yet admitted, Malfurion held on tight. Ysera rose from the rubble just as another crevice opened up beneath her paws.

"Zin-Azshari is going . . ." the cowled spellcaster cried, "and it is only the beginning!"

The two dragons beat their wings as hard as they could, but they moved as if flying through tar. Malfurion looked behind and saw that the sky above the Well no longer even existed. A huge funnel cloud enshrouded everything. Illidan had spoken much of the truth, it seemed. Between the spellwork of the demons, that of the elder gods, and the defenders' own efforts, the Well of Eternity had been torn asunder once too often.

Had he and his friends saved the world, only to destroy it?

What first he took for deafening thunder rattled the druid. He clutched his ears, waiting for it to pass.

"Look!" cried Tyrande, her lips near enough to him for her voice to still be heard. "The city!"

They watched . . . watched as the ground beyond Zin-Azshari broke apart. A great canyon miles deep opened. The entire capital literally began sliding toward the Well.

"The . . . pull . . . grows . . . greater!" Ysera roared.

The Well was drawing the surrounding regions into its maw, literally devouring Kalimdor. Zin-Azshari now floated in the black waters, an island bobbing about like so much flotsam. Ironically, the palace still stood mostly intact, although the tower where the Highborne had moved after the destruction of their previous sanctum leaned precariously.

Ominous bolts of energy played around the city as it neared the maelstrom's gullet. Unlike much of what the Well tore loose from Kalimdor, Zin-Azshari headed straight for the center. Malfurion felt Tyrande's grip on him tighten to the point of pain.

"It's going . . ." she whispered. "It's going . . ."

Around her, Azshara's handmaidens screamed. Vashj clung to her leg. The queen held her empty goblet, refusing to accept what was happening to her palace. She was *Azshara,* Light of Lights, supreme ruler of her people! She had not permitted this!

Sargeras would not be coming. Azshara understood that, although she had not said so to her followers. It would not do to let them know that she realized that she had erred. Somehow, the rabble had kept him from coming to Kalimdor . . . from coming to her.

The rumbling grew louder. A darkness in which even night elves could not see suddenly enveloped the palace. The only illumination came from the untamed forces of the Well. Black water began pouring into the palace, washing away two of her servants. Their screams were quickly drowned out.

I am Azshara! she silently insisted, her expression constant. With but a thought, the queen created a shield that surrounded her and those still remaining. *My desires are absolute!*

Her power kept the water at bay, but the pressure of maintaining her shield quickly grew troublesome. Azshara's brow furrowed and beads of sweat—the first sweat of her life—appeared on her forehead.

Then . . . voices whispered from the gloom, voices calling to her, promising her escape.

There is a way . . . there is a way . . . you will become more than you ever were . . . more than you ever were . . . we can help . . . we can help . . .

The queen was no fool. She knew her shield would not last much longer. Then the Well would claim her and her followers and the glory that was Azshara would be lost to the world.

The silver-tressed night elf nodded.

"Ungh!" The goblet fell from her hand. Her body was wracked with pain. She felt her limbs twisting, curling. Her spine felt fluid, as if much of it had instantly melted away . . .

You will be more than you have ever been . . . promised the voices. *And when the time comes, for what we grant you . . . you will serve us well . . .*

The last vestiges of her shield spell failed. Azshara shrieked as the waters overwhelmed her. In the background, she heard other cries as well . . . her handmaidens, the guards, and the rest of the Highborne who still served her.

The Well filled her lungs . . .

But . . . she did not drown.

Krasus, too, watched as the vast city, the epitome of the night elf civilization, was sucked whole into the throat of the maelstrom. He shivered, not only because of the destruction before him, but of the knowledge that he had of the future. The dragon mage had hoped to see Zin-Azshari torn apart before it sank, but that part of history had remained true. The city would sink to the depths . . . and, over the centuries, begin to birth a new horror.

There was nothing he could do about that now. Krasus looked away from the Well, looked away from the devastation spreading rapidly in all directions.

Huge chunks of Kalimdor continued to be torn into the Well with no sign of the terror lessening. Already several miles of land beyond Zin-Azshari had vanished. The only good thing was that the Burning Legion had long ago sent fleeing any life that had remained. So far, only parched soil and the bones of the dead fell victim . . . but if the catastrophe did not slow soon, Krasus wondered if anything would remain.

It has to, though! he insisted. *History says it must be so!*

But he knew too well that Time had already unraveled far too much . . . and that he was, in great part, responsible.

Krasus could only pray . . .

TWENTY-ONE

R honin thanked the stars that he saw little in the way of life before reaching the host. It would have been impossible for two dragons and a weary wizard to save anyone still so near the region of the Well. The only people he discovered was a large band of Highborne riding for their lives toward the host. Fortunately, they had nearly made it by the time he and the dragons came upon them.

A quick descent and an even quicker conversation revealed the surprising truth. Their leader, one Dath'Remar Sunstrider, told the story of their attempt to flee with Tyrande. Dath'Remar's regret over losing her was clear and Rhonin, who had sensed Malfurion's contact with her, informed the sorcerer that she had survived the escape. He could not promise that Tyrande still lived, although the wizard doubted that Malfurion would let anything happen to the female night elf once he had been reunited with her.

Rhonin and the dragons guided the Highborne to the host, preventing, in the process, any fight breaking out between the two factions. With the bronze dragon guarding the Highborne—for their own safety—the human and his mount sought out Jarod.

They found the commander already astride his night saber and anxiously awaiting word. Rhonin smiled in relief as he realized that the night elves and their allies were already prepared to move.

Still atop the red, he quickly greeted Jarod, then said, "We have to get the host moving! All the way to Mount Hyjal! The portal's been destroyed, but all that spellwork around the Well has caused chaos! It's eating itself up and taking everything around it with it!"

"Gods . . ." But Jarod's shock quickly subsided as his inherent sense of responsibility took over. He summoned a herald who Rhonin realized the former guard captain had kept handy just for such news. "Give the signal to reverse direction!" Calling up two more riders, Jarod added, "Send word to the officers and nobles! We move at swiftest pace to Mount Hyjal! No stopping! Those who need assistance will be granted it, but no one hesitates and no one stays behind! Go!"

"We'll keep watch from above," the wizard said.

"What about . . . what about those who might be other directions?"

Rhonin was grim. "The Burning Legion cleared the way for us there. I would say that any survivors are as far from the Well as we hope to get. We were the strongest resistance, after all."

"We can only hope for the best for those, then."

"And pray for ourselves at the same time."

As if to emphasize that point, a distant rumble caught the attention of both. Both the wizard and the soldier looked in the direction of the sound . . . and saw utter blackness just at the horizon.

"Get them moving, Jarod! Fast!"

The host started toward Mount Hyjal mere minutes later, but still not swift enough for Rhonin. Each time he glanced back, the darkness appeared to have swollen. The human swallowed, aware just what was happening and wondering if the catastrophe had already taken Krasus and the others.

A short distance into their desperate trek, the night elves and others began to realize their danger. It would have been impossible to keep them ignorant and neither Rhonin nor Jarod had any desire to do so. What did matter was to maintain some order and Jarod Shadowsong proved adept at that. The dragons, too, aided, swooping down and guiding back to the throng those who began, in their panic, to turn off.

Rhonin kept looking back, seeking some sign of Krasus and the others, but finding nothing. The darkness continued to encroach at an incredible pace and the ominous rumble grew more and more strident.

It's catching up to us! The wizard looked ahead. Mount Hyjal stood in the distance, enticingly close and yet still so far.

Would even reaching it be enough? Krasus thought so and Rhonin's recollection of history agreed . . . but so *much* had been altered.

Vereesa . . . I did what I could . . .

The darkness drew nearer. The roar as the ground miles back was torn and sucked into the Well pounded in his head. Below, many started to run and scream . . .

And still there was no sign of Krasus and the others.

Hillsides were ripped away. Entire lands simply crumbled into the churning, hungry whirlpool, quickly vanishing into its center. High above, Krasus watched whole settlements—fortunately long emptied by the war—vanish in a heartbeat. Nothing could stand before the onslaught of the Well's death throes. The carnage caused by the Burning Legion paled . . . no . . . it could not even *compare* to what now took place.

The first hint of Mount Hyjal appeared at the horizon. From high above, the mage could make out the desperate mass of bodies moving toward it. Providing that he had not guessed wrong, they would just *barely* make it to safety.

If there were any survivors of the war in the other directions, Krasus could do nothing for them. He could only again thank the stars that so little of worth remained in the areas over which the demons had marched.

He still had hope that the destruction would soon cease, that in this instance, at least, things would go as history recalled. They had the Demon Soul, an important factor in that, and—

He suddenly had a premonition of danger. Krasus quickly looked back.

A monstrous, black tendril arose from within the gargantuan Well . . . a tendril darting up toward an unsuspecting Ysera and the trio astride her.

The Old Gods! I should have known!

"Turn! The Old Gods still seek the Demon Soul for their use! This is their last chance before they are sealed off again!"

Alexstrasza veered around. Ysera noted their sudden action, but at that moment, the tendril reached her . . . and plucked the druid from the dragon's back.

"Malfurion!" cried Tyrande. The priestess tried to grab him, but he was already well out of her reach.

Frowning, Illidan also stretched a hand toward Malfurion. From his fingertips, a claw of crimson energy formed that immediately sought to snare the druid by the arm. Unfortunately, the claw only made it midway to his twin before abruptly fading, the violence of the Well disrupting the sorcerer's handiwork.

Malfurion gaped in horror as the tendril swiftly drew him back. Alexstrasza beat her wings hard. Krasus concentrated, trying to focus on Malfurion and the disk. At the very least, the dragon mage knew that he had to try to retrieve the Demon Soul. It was not a cold decision; the loss of the druid would be a tremendous one . . . but the loss of the Demon Soul to the dread elders would be calamitous.

Wild, rampaging magical forces battered Krasus and his queen. The spells he sought to cast went awry. The foul tendril brought Malfurion to the Well's gullet.

Then . . . what Krasus had prayed for but had, at this point feared would not pass, saved the night elf. The Well of Eternity had, *finally,* reached the end of its struggles. Now, it no longer devoured Kalimdor, but only itself. With a rapidity against which even the dark entities could not match, Krasus watched the vast, black body fall in upon itself. Even the storm surrounding them sank into it. Alexstrasza flapped furiously, barely able to keep them from following it.

The black waters receded, pouring into the Well's own gullet. The tendril tried to retract faster, but before it could . . . the very last of the Well of Eternity sank down into its own throat.

The tendril faded away like so much smoke. Krasus sensed the malevolent presence of the Old Gods vanish with it.

Flailing, the druid suddenly tumbled loose over a new threat. Below, filling the abrupt void left by the Well's apocalyptic hunger, came the seas of Kalimdor. Great waves a thousand feet high crashed against one another, hundreds of tons of water pouring each second into what had been the middle of the continent.

Krasus watched, awestruck, as the Sundering came to a crashing end and the *Great Sea* formed.

Yet, although taken by the sight, he did not forget Malfurion and the Demon Soul. With the Well had gone the last of its untamed and turbulent energies. Now, Krasus had full command of his power . . .

But before he could use it, a magnificent giant of bronze appeared from nowhere, a huge male dragon who glittered despite the remnants of the gloom still overshadowing the sky.

"Nozdormu!" the mage uttered.

The Aspect of Time swooped down, catching both the night elf and the disk. He soared quickly toward Alexstrasza and Ysera, but his golden gaze was for Krasus alone.

"Just in Time . . ." was all the male rumbled. Then, he flew past them, heading toward Mount Hyjal with Malfurion and the disk still clutched in one huge paw.

The other Aspects immediately banked, following. Krasus watched Nozdormu fly on as if nothing at all had happened to the world.

The mage finally shook his head and, for the first time since being cast into the past, breathed easier.

The survivors of the host did not breathe easier, not yet, for although they began to recognize the end of the danger, they also knew that their world had been forever altered. Many simply stared hollow-eyed at the new sea. The waters were already stilling, the waves beginning to lap *gently* at the ravaged shoreline.

So many had lost loved ones. The repercussions would only just begin materializing over the weeks and months—even years—to come. One of those who understood it best was Jarod Shadowsong. Despite his own shaken soul, he kept on a face of determination for his people. Even the nobles for the most part turned to him in need of reassurance. From those who seemed more steadfast, such as Blackforest, he appointed commanders to oversee the requirements of the host.

Mount Hyjal became a rallying point, for it remained untouched by the war and disaster that had followed. Jarod ordered banners made with the peak as their centerpiece, a new flag for a new beginning.

Aid came to the night elves from the tauren and others less affected by the ruination of Kalimdor. All had suffered, but no one's home had been so utterly destroyed as had that of Jarod's race. He gratefully accepted the help of Huln's people and was glad to see that there were few incidents of prejudice from the other night elves toward outside assistance. How long that would last would depend on the future of the refugees. They no longer had their elegant and extraordinary cities—their cities with the huge, living tree homes and magically-sculpted landscapes reserved only for themselves—from which to look down upon all else. In fact, most no longer even had roofs over their heads, the number of tents in very short supply. Jarod had donated his own tent to younger refugees orphaned by the ordeal.

Unfortunately, it did not take long for the first threat to the stability of the host to rear its ugly head. With the Well no more, the rest of the night elves did not fear the Highborne as they once had. Muttering began to grow among the refugees, muttering which intensified the more the Highborne made themselves visible.

"You'll have a new war on your hands," Krasus advised him. "You need to quell this now."

"Some will never forget the horrors wrought upon us by their actions." Jarod's gaze shifted off toward the new waters. Below it lay the ruins of his own lost Suramar. "Never."

The pale figure confronted him. "You *must* put aside the differences, Jarod Shadowsong, if you wish your people to survive!"

Steeling himself, Jarod summoned the nobles and other ranking members of the host. He also called forth Dath'Remar Sunstrider and the seniormost Highborne. The two factions met him under the old banner of Lord Raven-crest, which Jarod used as a substitute until the new ones could be finished. Kra-sus had suggested this last, both of them aware that the reputation of the late noble was one that had been respected by both the aristocracy and palace alike.

"We are here under protest," Blackforest growled, eyeing the robed fig-ures. His gauntleted hand rested on the pommel of his sword. "And will not long abide such foul company . . ."

Dath'Remar sniffed disdainfully, but said nothing. His opinion of the nobles was clear enough.

"Haven't you learned anything from all this?" snapped Jarod. He gestured toward the sea. "Isn't that enough to put an end to animosities? Do you both intend to finish what the demons began?"

"And what these willingly assisted in!" pointed out another noble.

"We make no excuses for what we did," Dath'Remar returned defiantly. "But we tried to make amends. Did you never wonder why the full portal took so long to come to fruition? We risked ourselves to keep it from doing so under the very eye of the demon lord! We sought to rescue the high priestess of Elune and many of us perished fighting the Burning Legion ourselves!"

"Not enough!"

"May I speak?"

A group of Elune's followers joined the fray, Tyrande Whisperwind and Jarod's sister at the forefront. Maiev looked uncommonly subdued in the high priestess's presence and Jarod could understand that. There was something about the young female that immediately eased his heart.

Everyone bent down on one knee, but Tyrande, an embarrassed frown appearing, gestured for them to rise. Jarod bowed slightly, then said, "By all means, the voice of the Mother Moon may speak whenever she so desires."

Tyrande nodded gratefully, then, to the assembled parties, she said, "Our world will never be the same. That which we were we are no more." Her expression grew solemn. "We are in flux. What our people are to become, I cannot say, but it will likely be nothing akin to what we once were."

Uneasy rumbling rose from both the nobles and the Highborne. The words of the high priestess were not to be taken lightly.

"We have survived this struggle, but, if we do not come together, we may not survive our own evolution. Consider this before you begin resurrecting old enmities . . ."

And with that, Tyrande turned. Maiev eyed her brother with what Jarod realized was confidence in him.

As his sister followed Tyrande, he saw that Shandris Feathermoon had been standing behind her. The departing novice gave Jarod an unabashed smile that made him more uncomfortable than the presence of the nobles and the sorcerers, yet, at the same time added to the lightening of his heart.

Blackforest cleared his throat. Jarod quickly returned to the matter at hand. "You've heard the voice of the Mother Moon and I couldn't agree more with her words. What say you?"

Blackforest opened his mouth, but Dath'Remar managed to answer before the armored aristocrat could utter a sound. "We greatly respect the word of the high priestess and will do what we can to make further amends for our past transgressions . . . if we will be permitted the opportunity by our august companions."

The lead noble let out a grunt. "We will do no less. If the Highborne have seen the error of their ways, we will accept their return to the fold and welcome their effort as we all seek to rebuild our home."

Both answers were spoken with some lingering animosity, but it was the best that Jarod could hope for at this point. There would be confrontations ahead, but perhaps none that would drag his people down to oblivion.

"I thank you all for coming and for seeing reason. Let us now begin to consider how best to take advantage of the miracle that's let us survive."

Several voices from both factions began speaking at once, each trying to come up with better ideas than the others. Jarod grimaced, then started trying to pick out the best ones.

One immediately caught his attention. "Water!" he interrupted. Something that had been reported to him by a scout came to mind. A lake at the very top of Hyjal. It was worth investigating. He decided to do so himself, though, if only to gain some reprieve from all his other responsibilities. "Lord Blackforest! I'd like three volunteers from among you! I've a short excursion in mind . . ." To Dath'Remar, he added, "From your group, too . . ."

As they chose from among themselves, Jarod congratulated himself. The excursion would also be a good opportunity to force the parties to work together. It was a safe, quiet event, but one, because of the importance of water, that would resound well among his people. If the nobles and sorcerers reported the findings together, the rest would see that cooperation *was* possible.

Jarod fought back a smile. Perhaps he was finally learning about leadership after all . . .

"Malfurion . . ."

The druid tore his gaze from the new sea. "Master Krasus."

The dragon mage grimaced. "Equals need no title between one another. Please, for the last time, I am merely *Krasus.*"

"I will try." Unconsciously, Malfurion took a step back from his friend. "Did you want something?"

"No . . . but *they* do."

A great beating of wings filled the night elf's ears. Dust arose around him and suddenly three gargantuan forms alighted behind the cowled figure.

Alexstrasza. Ysera. Nozdormu.

"You know why we have come," the red female said softly.

Malfurion's hand slipped to the pouch at his side. "You want it. You want the Soul."

"The *Demon* Soul," Krasus corrected. "You forgot to give it over to the Aspects once we landed. The heat of the moment, no doubt."

"Yes . . . yes . . ." The druid's hand thrust into the pouch. His fingers encircled the disk, caressing it in the process. Why did he have to give it up? Had he not proven that he had the right to it? Had he not singlehandedly used it to rid Kalimdor of not one menace, but two?

"Malfurion . . ."

If they felt that they deserved it more than him, why did he not just make them try to take it? Between his own skills and the power of the Soul, he could surely slay them all—

Disgust filled the druid. He quickly drew the damnable disk from its hiding place, then held it out for the mage to take.

Krasus nodded. "I knew you would make the correct decision." Yet, he did not accept the Demon Soul directly, instead pointing to the ground. "Please place it there."

Brow arched in curiosity, Malfurion obeyed. The moment that the disk left his grasp, he felt as if a tremendous weight lifted from his back.

"Step away, please."

When the night elf had obeyed, Krasus faced the three Aspects. "Will your power be enough?"

"It will have to be," replied Nozdormu.

The trio arched their necks, bringing their colossal heads within inches of the Demon Soul.

"We cannot bind it completely," Alexstrasza uttered. "That is beyond even all of us put together. Yet, we can ensure that Neltharion—*Deathwing*—cannot wield it any better than us."

"A wise maneuver, as I said," Krasus responded. Yet, Malfurion sensed again that the cowled figure, the dragon in mortal form, held back important information from even the queen he so obviously adored. What it was, the night elf could not even hazard, but there was a sadness in Krasus's ancient eyes that the mage quickly hid whenever the leviathans glanced his way.

The three giants stared at the tiny object, the simple golden disk that had caused so much calamity. They stared at it . . . and the Demon Soul was suddenly engulfed in a rainbow of energies. Dominating were red, green, and the brilliant bronze of the sandy Nozdormu. The Demon Soul rose several inches off the ground, hovering just before the Aspects. The magical forces unleashed by the dragons circulated around it, in the process turning the disk over and over.

Then . . . one by one, those energies sank into the black dragon's abomination. Red, then green, then bronze, followed by the myriad colors accompanying each.

The spellwork ceased. The Demon Soul dropped, clattering on the hard ground. It looked unchanged, undiminished.

"Did it work?" he asked.

"It has." Krasus met the druid's eyes. "Malfurion, I ask you to pick it up again."

Loathe as he was to touch the piece, the night elf acquiesced. Oddly, Malfurion discovered that he had no more desire to keep the Demon Soul. Either the dragons had made that so or his will had grown stronger.

The mage glanced at the Aspects, who nodded in unison. To Malfurion, he respectfully said, "There is a place we know. A place the black one would not. With your permission, we will show it to you in your mind . . . and then I ask that you call upon your own skills to send that foul thing there."

Although he felt capable of doing as Krasus asked, Malfurion frowned. "Can't you do it?"

"Before, I alone might have been able to carry the disk, albeit with difficulty. The others, they could not because of Deathwing's handiwork. Now, this new spell has made it impossible for the black one or *any* other dragon to touch the Demon Soul, much less use it. That is why we need you for this."

Nodding, the druid held out the disk. "Show me."

Krasus and the Aspects stared deep. Malfurion shook momentarily as they entered his thoughts.

The image they created was so vivid that he almost felt as if he had visited it himself. Eager to be rid of the Demon Soul, the druid quickly said, "I have it."

With much relief, Malfurion sent the golden disk away.

Krasus exhaled. "Thank you."

The Aspects nodded their heads in gratitude. Then, Alexstrasza looked to the sky. "The clouds . . . they are beginning to part . . ."

Sure enough, for the first time since the Burning Legion had come to Kalimdor, the sky finally started to clear. It began as small gaps here and there, then large, thick clouds broke into much smaller, thinner ones. Those, in turn, became silken wisps easily scattered by soft winds.

Malfurion felt a sudden rising of hope, of renewed life . . . and realized that it was not only his own, but that of the land itself. Kalimdor *would* survive, of that he was certain.

A warmth touched his forehead, a pleasant warmth. He reached up and realized that his antlers had grown more. Now small ones jutted from the main stems.

Ysera, her eyelids shut but her eyes moving rapidly underneath, stretched to her full height, then turned to face her fellow Aspects.

"The world will heal, but there is much more work to do. We should return to the others . . ."

Nozdormu nodded. "Agreed."

Malfurion opened his mouth to thank the dragons for all that they had done . . . then hesitated as a sense of unease swept over him. He looked around suddenly, as if seeking someone. Only after doing so did the druid at last realize just *who* it was he sought so desperately, although the reason why still escaped him.

Where was Illidan?

Rhonin eyed the sea, thinking of all the deaths he had witnessed—both in his own time and in this period—at the hands of the Burning Legion. Many of them had affected him deeply, for, if several had not been friends, they had at least been parts of his life.

He knew that Krasus felt the same, perhaps even more so, for the dragon mage had lived long enough to lose generations of loved ones and companions. The wizard understood his former mentor well enough to realize that the centuries had not made Krasus immune to sorrow. The cowled spellcaster suffered deeply with each death, however much he hid those emotions at times.

And now, there was yet another to add to the losses. Rhonin had never thought to mourn an orc, but he did. Brox had become a stalwart comrade, a noble companion. Only belatedly had the human understood the warrior's sacrifice. The orc had dropped himself through the portal knowing that horrible doom awaited him there, yet, Brox had not hesitated. He had been aware that Malfurion needed time and time the orc had granted the druid.

Rhonin knelt by the edge of the sea, the creation of which he saw in some ways as a tribute itself to Brox. It would not have existed without the orc's action. Undelayed, Sargeras likely would have stepped through the gateway, then slaughtered everyone.

Did Brox bring history back to what it should be or was he part of it all along? the wizard wondered. Perhaps Nozdormu knew, but the Aspect of Time was not about to tell anyone. He had not even spoken of his own ordeal save that it had involved the Old Gods. Now, with the portal gone, even that threat had been removed.

Standing again, the wizard eyed the flotsam still flowing toward the shore. The tide brought in a variety of things, bits of plants, mostly, but also wreckage from the night elves' realm. Shreds of clothes, broken pieces of furniture, rotting food, and, yes, there were bodies. Not many, thankfully, and none at this spot. Jarod had parties scanning the shore, seeking any dead so that they could have swift but proper burials. It was not just a matter of propriety, but safety, too. The dead might carry with them disease, a very real fear for the refugees.

Something floated near the wizard, bobbing up and down twice before settling just under the surface. Rhonin would have ignored it, but sensed something unusual. The thing had a touch of magic to it.

Stepping into the water, he reached down.

Brox's ax.

There could be no mistaking it. Rhonin had seen the astonishing weapon in action enough times. Despite its tremendous size, the double-edged ax fit perfectly in his grip and felt as light as a feather. It did not even feel wet.

"This isn't possible," he muttered, eyeing the sea suspiciously.

But no spirit arose from the depths to give a reason for the amazing discovery. The wizard looked down at the ax, then at the sea, and lastly at the ax again.

Finally, Rhonin stared off into the direction of the lost portal. An image of Brox standing atop slaughtered demons and challenging more to come to him filled the human's thoughts.

The wizard suddenly raised the ax high in what he recalled from his own time as an orcish salute to fallen heroes. Rhonin brandished it three times, then lowered the ax head-first.

"They'll sing of you yet," he whispered, recalling Brox's words to both him and Krasus. "They'll pass songs of you down for generations to come. We'll see to that."

Hefting the ax over his shoulder, he went to find Krasus.

TWENTY-TWO

Illidan dismounted, his wrapped eyes surveying the thick forest for any threat. Of course, even had there been one, he had no doubt as to his ability to deal with it. The Well might be gone, but he had learned enough from Rhonin and the Burning Legion to make up for much of its loss. Besides, in a few minutes, even that consideration would be of no consequence.

The sorcerer tied his mount to a tree. Jarod Shadowsong and the others in charge of the host were busy arguing about mundane matters such as food and shelter. Illidan was more than happy to leave such petty things to others. He had come to this place for a far more important reason, one that he felt outshone all others.

He intended to salvage the lifeblood of the night elves.

They were all naive, so Malfurion's twin had decided, if they did not believe that the demons would someday return. Having tasted Kalimdor once, the Burning Legion would be eager for a second bite. Next time, they would strike in a far more terrifying manner, of that he was certain.

And so, Illidan planned to be prepared for that coming invasion.

The pristine lake buried deep atop Hyjal's highest peak had survived the onslaught undiscovered by either the defenders or the demons. A green, idyllic island lay at the very center. Illidan saw it as fate that he had been the one to come across the body of water first. It suited his desires perfectly.

He touched the thick pouch at his waist. The precious contents within called to Illidan. Their siren song assured the sorcerer that he had made the right decision. His people would fall over themselves in their gratitude and he would stand among them as one of their greatest heroes, possibly even more so than Malfurion.

Malfurion . . . his twin was honored by all as if he alone has saved the world. The people gave Illidan some crumb of recognition, but many misunderstood what the sorcerer had attempted to do. Rumors swelled that he had gone to the demons to truly join them and that only his brother had saved his soul from damnation. All Illidan's own efforts went unappreciated. His eyes— his *glorious* eyes—were only seen by the rest as a mark of his supposed pact with the lord of the Legion.

His so-perfect brother spoke pretty words about him to the public, but that only made Malfurion look magnanimous. Even the antlers sprouting from his twin's forehead did not disgust the dainty night elves. They embraced it as a sign of divinity, as if Malfurion now stood as one of the demigods . . . the same demigods who had perished so easily in battle while Illidan had survived and thrived.

It'll all change, though, he told himself, not for the first time. *They'll see what I've done . . . and thank me a thousand times over.*

Anticipation spreading across his face, the sorcerer opened the pouch and removed from it a vial identical to the one that Tyrande had seen him use earlier. In fact, not only was the vial the same, but so were contents.

The Well of Eternity might be gone, but Illidan Stormrage had saved a small bit of it.

It'll work! I know it'll work! He had felt the Well's astonishing properties himself. Even so minute an amount would be potent.

The stopper shaped like Queen Azshara once more danced for him before popping off. Letting the stopper fall to the grass, the night elf held the open container over the lake.

He poured the contents into the water.

The lake shimmered where the drops of the Well touched it. The water, originally a calm blue, suddenly glowed intensely where the drops hit. The change spread rapidly, first cutting across to the island, then around it. In but seconds, the entire lake had taken on a rich azure hue that no one could mistake as other than magic.

To Illidan's heightened senses, the spectacle was even more breathtaking. He had expected a reproduction of the Well, but this was fascinating in itself.

Yet . . . it could still be so much more.

He reached into the pouch and removed a second vial.

This time, the sorcerer simply tore off the stopper and dumped the contents into the lake. As he did, the blue intensified further. Tendrils of raw energy began to play on the surface and Illidan felt a wonderful radiance that he had not experienced since the Well.

His lips parted. He wanted to throw himself into the water, but managed to hold back. His hand slipped to the pouch.

What would a *third* vial do?

He undid the stopper and started to pour.

"What by the Mother Moon are you doing there?"

Illidan had been so caught up in his efforts that he had failed to notice the approach of others. He spun about, the last vial still in his hand, to face a party of mounted figures, Jarod Shadowsong chief among them.

"Captain . . ." the sorcerer began.

One of the Highborne glanced past Illidan. "He's done something to the lake! It—" The spellcaster's expression grew awed. "It feels like the *Well*—"

"Elune preserve us!" bellowed a noble next to Jarod. "He's resurrecting it!"

The commander dismounted. "Illidan Stormrage! Cease this immediately! If not for your brother, I'd—"

"My *brother* . . ." An imperious fury arose, fueled by his nearness to the enchanted lake. Once more, the power surged through him. He was capable of anything . . . "Always my precious brother . . ."

The others dismounted, following Jarod Shadowsong. Their wary expressions made Illidan tense. They wanted to keep him from the lake's power! He eyed the Highborne, who would certainly attempt to usurp it for themselves . . .

"No . . ."

One of the nobles hesitated. "By Elune! What sort of eyes does he have that glow beneath that veil?"

Illidan glared at the Highborne.

Their leader raised a hand in defense. "Look out—"

Flames erupted around the other sorcerers. They screamed.

Jarod and the nobles charged him. Illidan sneered at the paltry threat and gestured.

The ground beneath them exploded. Jarod was tossed back. The lead noble, Blackforest flew high in the air, finally striking a tree with a resounding crack.

"You stupid fools! You—"

His feet suddenly sank into the earth. As he looked down, tree branches wrapped around his body, pinning his legs together and his arms to his torso. Illidan tried to speak, but his mouth filled with leaves that adhered to his tongue. The sorcerer could not even concentrate, for a buzzing echoed in his ears, as if a thousand tiny insects nestled in them.

Gasping, Illidan slumped to his knees. Through the buzzing, he vaguely sensed someone else approaching. The sorcerer knew without a doubt who it had to be . . .

"Oh, Illidan . . ." Malfurion's voice cut perfectly through the buzzing. "Illidan . . . why?"

The druid stared at the lake, its blazing blue color a clear sign of its contamination. No one could drink from it now. Like the Well of Eternity before it, it was now a fount of power, not life.

"Oh, Illidan . . ." he repeated, eyeing his bound twin.

"Dath'Remar is still alive," reported Tyrande, kneeling beside the Highborne leader. "One more also, but the others are dead." She shuddered. "They were burned in their skins . . ."

Malfurion had intended to come alone, only the dragons and Krasus with him, but, like the druid, Tyrande had somehow sensed that Illidan was up to something. With several of her priestesses in tow, she had ridden after the dragons, but had arrived too late.

As had Malfurion.

"Lord Blackforest is dead. The others, I think can be saved," announced another priestess.

"My . . . brother *lives*," managed Maiev. She and Shandris both attended to an unconscious Jarod. He had bruises all over his face and his armor was even more battered now. Dried blood caked several wounds already healing thanks to the prayers of the priestesses.

Jarod's sister rose and her countenance was one terrible to behold. She started for Illidan, at the same time drawing her weapon.

"No, Maiev!" Tyrande commanded.

"He almost slew my brother!"

The high priestess met her. "But failed. His fate is not yours to decide. Jarod will do so." She glanced at Malfurion. "Is that not so?"

He nodded sadly. "It's his right and I'll not argue it." The druid shook his head. "So, this is why he stayed so near the shore of the Well."

"I didn't know that he had gathered more," Tyrande added apologetically.

With a sudden hunch, Malfurion knelt near his brother. Illidan's breathing was even, but he stiffened when he sensed Malfurion near. The druid searched the pouch.

"At least four more vials . . . he would have turned this lake completely into another Well."

"Can anything be done to change it back?"

Krasus had remained in the background, watching the events unfold. Now, however, the cowled mage muttered, "No . . . nothing. What has been done cannot be undone."

Alexstrasza, however, added, "We can do something to make of it a different force. One not as treacherous in nature as the Well became."

The mage's eyes momentarily widened. "Ah! Of course!"

Malfurion forced himself from his brother's side. "And what's that?"

The three dragons glanced at one another, each nodding agreement. Alexstrasza turned back to the night elves. "We are going to plant a tree."

"A tree?" The druid looked to Krasus for some sort of clarification.

But the mage, his own expression guarded, simply answered, "Not a tree. *The* tree."

They quickly turned it into a ceremony so as to lessen the impact of Illidan's misdeeds. The sorcerer was hidden away in order to prevent further trouble and Jarod's sister volunteered to guard him until a final fate could be decided. Jarod, healed by Shandris and Maiev, insisted that, when that time came, it would not be only his choice, but Malfurion's.

Other than Krasus, Rhonin, and the dragons, there were only night elves at the gathering. What the Aspects intended was for their race, which had suffered so much and feared for its continuance. Nobles, Highborne, and representatives of what had once been the lower castes assembled. The rest of the survivors gathered as they could down below, unable to see the spectacle but aware that it would influence the course of their lives.

Malfurion and the rest who had been invited journeyed to the island at the center of the lake. Despite Hyjal's tremendous height, the top of the peak was fairly warm, perhaps even more so now that the lake had become touched by magic.

"It's beautiful," Tyrande whispered.

"Would that it was only that," Malfurion replied morosely. Illidan continued to be in his thoughts. He already had some suggestions as to what to do about his twin and it pained the druid to imagine them being put into action. Yet, Illidan clearly could not longer be trusted. He had slain others out of madness. His notion that the night elves needed a new Well in order to protect themselves against some possible future attack by the Burning Legion was not sufficient reason for his heinous crimes.

Although still creatures of the dark despite having been forced to adapt to daylight battles, Jarod had agreed with the dragons to assemble at noontime. Alexstrasza explained that the sun's zenith would be essential to what they planned and the night elf was not about to argue with the giants.

Despite the island's reasonable size, only tall grass covered it. At its center, the group positioned itself as requested by Alexstrasza. The dragons took up a prime location near what they said was the *exact* middle, leaving a small place open between them.

The Aspect of Life began the ceremony. "Kalimdor has suffered greatly," she rumbled. As those in the group nodded, Alexstrasza continued, "And the night elves most of all. Your race was not completely innocent in all of this, but the trials and tribulations through which you have passed forgive that."

There were a few uneasy glances toward the Highborne, but no one argued.

The red dragon lowered her palm. In it, nestled like an infant, a single seed similar in appearance to an acorn rested. Malfurion felt a tingle as he stared at it.

"Taken from G'Hanir, the Mother Tree," she explained.

The druid recognized the home of the dead demigoddess, Aviana.

"G'Hanir is no more, having perished with its mistress, but this seed survives. From it, we shall raise a new tree."

Nozdormu dropped one paw to the ground and, with a single swipe, created a hole perfect for planting the seed, Alexstrasza gently placed the seed in it, then Ysera pushed the dirt over the hole.

The Aspect of Life gazed up at the sun. Then, she and the other two dragons bent their heads low over the buried seed.

"I give Strength and Healthy Life to the night elves, for so long as the tree stands," Alexstrasza proclaimed.

From her, a soft, red glow flowed to the mound. At the same time, the sunlight over the mound intensified, spreading all the way across the lake in every direction. Some of the night elves stirred, but all remained silent.

A wonderful warmth spread over Malfurion and he instinctively took Tyrande's hand. She did not pull away, but rather tightened her grip.

And from the mound, there came movement. As if a tiny creature burrowed to the surface, the dirt pushed up and away.

From the seed had sprouted a tiny sapling.

It rose until a yard high, small branches sprouting. Lush, green leaves burst from the branches, creating a delicate canopy.

As Alexstrasza pulled back slightly, Nozdormu spoke, a slight hiss in his voice. "Time will be on the night elvesss' side once again, for I grant them continued Immortality, forever a chance to learn, for asss long asss the tree stands . . ."

From him issued forth a golden bronze aura that joined with the sunlight as the red had. Flowing through the sapling, it sank into the mound.

The tree grew again. As the onlookers gaped, it rose to more than twice the height of a night elf. Its foliage grew dense, green, and full of promise. Branches thickened, showing the health and strength of the tree. The roots began to come up above ground like many legs. A space almost large enough for several seated night elves formed underneath.

Nozdormu nodded, then, like his counterpart, withdrew. There remained only Ysera.

Eyes lidded, the green leviathan studied the tree. Despite its swift growth, it was still dwarfed by the dragons.

"To the night elves, who have lost their hopes, I give forth the ability to Dream again. To Dream, to Imagine, for in that is the best hope of rebuilding, of recovering, of growing . . ." She looked ready to do as the other Aspects had, then paused. Her head swung toward Malfurion. "And to those who follow the path of one held special by me—and mine—I grant him and the other druids to come the path into the Emerald Dream, where, even in their deepest sleep, they may cross the world, learn from it, and draw upon its own strength . . . the better to guide Kalimdor's health and safety throughout the future."

Malfurion swallowed, unable to otherwise respond. He felt the eyes of everyone upon him, but, most of all, felt Tyrande's proud touch.

Ysera looked again to the tree . . . and from her issued a green mist. Like the two before, her offering bound with the sunlight, then settled over the tree.

As the last of it vanished into the soil, the assembled onlookers felt the ground shake. Malfurion led Tyrande back a few steps and, as if this was a cue, the rest followed suit. Even the dragons moved back, albeit not near as much as the tinier creatures.

And the tree *grew*. It grew twice its previous height, then twice that. It rose higher and higher into the heavens, until the druid felt certain that even those well below the peak could at least see the huge, burgeoning canopy. So massive was the canopy that the entire region should have been bathed in shadow, but somehow the sunlight continued to focus on the area, even the lake.

The roots also expanded, stretching taller and bending to best support the gigantic tree. They spread so high that now it seemed all of Lord Ravencrest's lost Black Rook Hold could have fit underneath . . . and still the roots—the entire tree—grew.

When at last it ceased, even the dragons looked like no more than birds who could perch upon one of the branches and hide in the foliage.

"Here stands before you *Nordrassil*. The *World Tree* is brought into existence!" intoned the Aspect of Life. "For as long as it stands, for as long as it is honored, the night elves will thrive! You may alter, you may follow different paths, but you will ever be an integral part of Kalimdor . . ."

Krasus suddenly stood behind Malfurion. In a whisper to the druid, he added, "And the tree, whose roots go deep, will keep this lake as it is. The sun will always be a part of this well. The black waters will not run here."

Malfurion took this in with much relief. He glanced down at Tyrande, who met his gaze with an expression that left his cheeks darkening. Before Malfurion realized what was happening, she kissed him.

"Whatever this long future our people have been promised holds," his childhood friend murmured. "I wish to see it with you."

He felt more blood rush to his cheeks. "As I do with you, Tyrande."

Malfurion kissed her back, but as he did, another's face intruded into his thoughts. There would be a period of rejoicing, of spreading the word concerning the Aspects' gifts to their people, but for Malfurion, those events suddenly mattered little. There was still Illidan to deal with.

Tyrande pulled away, her mouth twisted into a frown. "I know what it is that suddenly fills you with sorrow. What must be done must be done, Malfurion, but don't let his crimes steal your heart away."

He took strength from her words. "I won't. I promise you, I won't."

Over her shoulder, Malfurion noticed Krasus and Rhonin quietly retreating from the gathering. He glanced at the dragons and saw that Nozdormu was also missing. Just like that. Somehow, the Aspect had simply vanished without anyone noticing.

There had to be a connection.

"Malfurion, what is it now?"

"Come with me, Tyrande, while no one's looking."

She did not argue. The two night elves followed after Krasus and the wizard.

The voice echoed in Krasus's head. *It hasss been delayed far too long. It mussst be done now.*

Nozdormu.

"Rhonin—"

The human nodded. "I heard him."

They slipped out while the night elves were still babbling over the tree. Krasus would have liked to have spoken with Malfurion a little more, but the mage *was* eager to return home.

Before the ceremony, Nozdormu had come to him. The Aspect of Time had caught Krasus alone. "We owe you a debt, Korialstrasz."

By "we," Nozdormu did not just mean the other Aspects and him. He referred also to his various selves spread through Time itself. Such was his unique nature.

"I did what had to be done. Rhonin—and Brox—too."

"I alssso speak to the wizard at this very moment," the Aspect had commented offhandedly. It was nothing for him to be in two places at the same time, if he so desired. "I tell him, asss I tell you, that I will sssee to it that you reach home."

Krasus had been very grateful. It had pained him to still be around an Alexstrasza who did not know the fate to befall her and the other dragons. "I am—thank you."

The bronze giant had given him a solemn look. "I know what you hide from her, from usss. It is my fate and curssse to know such things and be unable mysssself to prevent them. Know that I now asssk for forgiveness for the wrongs I will caussse you in the future, but I mussst be what I am destined to be . . . as Malygos is."

"Malygos!" Krasus had blurted, thinking of the eggs secreted in the pocket dimension. "Nozdormu—"

"I know what you did. Give them over to me and I will pass them to Alexstrasza. When Malygosss is well enough, he will be presssented with the young. Compared to all elssse that has happened, it isss a sssmall change to the time line and one of which I approve. The bluesss will fly the skies again, even though their numberss will not be great even after ten thousand yearsss. But better sssome, than none."

Krasus had also wished to see his beloved queen once more, but it had been agreed that he might let slip something even she should not know. Now, though, as he and Rhonin stood ready for the bronze dragon's reappearance, the mage regretted not having sought her out, anyway.

Rhonin studied him. "You could still run to her. I'd understand."

The gaunt figure shook his head. "We have twisted the future enough. What will be will be."

"Hmmph. You're stronger than I am."

"No, Rhonin," Krasus muttered with a shake of his head. "Not in the least."

"Are you prepared?" Nozdormu suddenly asked.

They turned to find the Aspect waiting patiently.

"How long have you been there?" snapped the cowled spellcaster.

"Asss long as I chose to be." Foregoing any other answer, Nozdormu spread his wings. "Climb atop. I will take you to your proper period in the future."

Rhonin looked dubious. "Just like that?"

"When the lassst of the Well devoured itself, the Old Gods were again ssssealed away. Their reach into the river of Time vanished with it. The tearsss in the fabric of reality vanished. The way forward is now sssimple enough . . . for me."

From the ground, Rhonin lifted up Brox's ax.

"What isss *that* doing here?" asked the Aspect.

Both spellcasters looked defiant. "It comes with us," Krasus insisted. "Or we stay here and meddle more."

"Then, by all means, bring it with."

They mounted quickly, but as they did, Krasus spied a pair of forms hiding in the woods. He sensed immediately who they were.

"Nozdormu—"

"Yesss, yesss, the druid and the priestess. I've known all along. Ssstep out and say your farewellsss, then! We must be gone!"

Although the Aspect took their appearance in stride, Krasus felt far less comfortable. "You two heard—"

"We heard all," interjected Malfurion. "Not that we understand *all*."

The mage nodded. "We could say little and still cannot say more. Just know this, the two of you. We *shall* meet again."

"Our people will survive?" asked Tyrande.

The mage calculated his words before speaking. "Yes, and the world will be the better for it. And with that, I say good-bye."

Rhonin raised Brox's ax, echoing Krasus's farewell.

Nozdormu stretched his wings again. The night elves immediately backed away. They raised hands toward the pair.

But before they could . . . both the dragon and his riders simply vanished.

TWENTY-THREE

R honin awoke to find himself lying in a field of grass.

At first, he feared that something had gone awry, but then, as he sat up, a familiar and very welcome sight greeted his eyes.

A house. *His* house.

He was home.

More important, he sighted Jalia, the townswoman who had been taking care of Vereesa during her pregnancy. She seemed in a fair state, anxious but cheerful. Rhonin unsuccessfully tried to calculate the time passing since he had vanished. He wondered how old the babies would be by now.

Then, to his horror, he heard Vereesa cry out, "Jalia! Come!"

Without hesitation, he leapt to his feet and followed after the woman. For a full-bodied person, Jalia moved quickly. She raced through the doorway, even as Vereesa called out again.

The wizard burst through the door a few moments later, hand already up in preparation to defend his bride and children. He looked around, expecting a home ransacked or burnt, but found everything in place.

"Vereesa? Vereesa?"

"Rhonin! Praise the Sunwell! Rhonin, in here!"

He ran toward the bedroom, fearful of what he would find. A moan set the hair on his neck standing.

"Vereesa!" Rhonin barged inside. "The twins! Are they—"

"They're coming!"

He stared wide-eyed. His wife lay in the bed, *still* very much pregnant . . . but not for long.

"How—" he began, but Jalia shoved him aside.

"If you don't know how, then you'd best just stand back and let her and me handle it, Master Rhonin!"

The wizard knew better than to argue. He fell back against the wall, ready to be of any help should the need arrive, but saw quickly that Vereesa and Jalia had things well in hand.

"The first one's coming," Vereesa announced.

As he watched and waited, Rhonin thought of all the astounding events he had recently been a part of. He had passed through time, survived the first coming of the Burning Legion, and had aided in the effort to save the world and the future.

But none of that, he discovered, was as miraculous as what he was a part of now . . . and for that he gave thanks that he and the others had succeeded.

And in that time so long ago, Jarod Shadowsong presided over a gathering far more dour than the one on the island. Those who now represented the leaders of the host—and their allies, too—stood ready to hear judgment.

Soldiers prodded along the one on trial. His mouth was wrapped shut with a cloth but bonds of metal now kept his arms behind him and his hands from gesturing. Invisible spells cast by Malfurion and others ensured that there would be no repeat of the terrible incident at the lake.

When he stood in the center of the circle that his accusers had formed, Illidan, monstrous eyes scarved, stared arrogantly at the figure before him. One of the soldiers cautiously removed the gag.

"Illidan Stormrage," began Jarod, sounding nothing like the simple Guard captain he had once been. "Many are the times you fought valiantly alongside others against the evil encroaching on our world, but, sadly, too many are the times you've proven yourself a danger to your own people!"

"A danger? I'm the only one who sees honestly! I was planning for our future! I was saving our race! I—"

"Attacked those who disagreed with you—slaying many—and recreated what should have been best forgotten!"

Illidan spat. "You'll all be praying to me as if I were a god when the demons return! I know how they think, how they act! Next time, they won't be cast out! You'll need to fight them as they fight! Only I have that knowledge—"

"Such knowledge, we're better without." Jarod looked around, as if seeking someone. When he apparently did not find that person, the leader of the night elves sighed and continued, "Illidan Stormrage, as it falls to me, I can think of only one thing to do with you! It pains me, but I hereby declare that you shall be put to death—"

"How *original*," sneered the sorcerer.

"Put to death in a manner—"

"Jarod . . . forgive me for being late," interrupted a figure behind Illidan. "May I still speak?"

The armored night elf nodded almost gratefully. "This is yours to decide as much as it's mine."

Malfurion walked around his brother. Illidan's face followed him as the druid stepped between the sorcerer and the soldier. "I'm sorry, Illidan."

"Ha!"

"What is it you want to say, Master Malfurion?" urged Jarod.

"There is some truth in what my brother says about the Burning Legion, Jarod. They may come again."

"And you want us therefore to forget his crimes and his danger?"

The druid shook his antlered head. "No." He glanced at his twin, the other half of him, then briefly at Tyrande, who stood at the edge of the circle with Maiev and Shandris. She had stayed with him all the while he had suffered through what should be done. The high priestess supported his decision, not that it eased his ache.

"No, Jarod," Malfurion repeated, steeling himself. "No. I want you to imprison him . . . even if it means he stays so for ten thousand years . . . if necessary . . ."

As the rest of those assembled suddenly broke out into startled muttering, Malfurion closed his eyes and tried to calm himself. He had his suspicions concerning the future, knowing as he did now about Krasus and Rhonin. The druid prayed he had made the right decision.

But only the future would tell . . .

And, lastly . . .

Thrall had not heard from the two he had sent to the mountains to investigate the shaman's vision. They might still be searching, but the orc leader had the suspicion that the truth was far worse. No good ruler, not even of his race, liked to send loyal warriors to their death without something coming from it.

Night had long fallen and most of his subjects were deep asleep. Only he and the guards outside still stirred. Thrall *should* have been sleeping, but his concern over this unsettling quest had grown with each day since Brox's and Gaskal's departure.

The torchlights flickered, creating shadows that moved as if alive. Thrall paid them no mind until he suddenly noticed that one by the door was solid.

The orc immediately leapt up from his stone throne. "Who dares?"

But instead of an assassin—and there were always plenty of those—a wizened orc wearing wolf skins and bearing a totem with the carved head of a dragon on it shuffled forward.

"Hail, Thrall!" the elder figure called in an oddly-strong voice. "Hail, savior of the orcs!"

"Who are you? You are not Kalthar!" Thrall growled, referring to his shaman.

"I am one who brings news . . . news of a valiant warrior, Broxigar."

"Brox? What of him? Speak!"

"The warrior is dead . . . but dead sending many enemies before him! He has again fought the Legion and cut down so many it would take a day just to count them one by one!"

"The Legion?" The orc's worst fears were realized. "Where? Tell me so that I can gather our warriors and fight them!"

The almost hairless elder shook his head, then gave Thrall a grin without teeth. "There are no more demons! Broxigar and those fighting beside him defeated the Legion and it was your warrior who stood at the pass again, even when faced by their master!" The figure bowed his head respectfully. "Sing songs of him, great Thrall, for he was part of those who saved the world for you . . ."

For a time, the younger orc stood silent, then, "This is true? All of it?"

"Aye . . . and I bring this, all that remains to honor a hero." Despite his seeming infirmity, the shaman brought forth a huge, twin-edged ax. Thrall blinked, somehow not having noticed it earlier.

"I've seen nothing like it."

"It is a weapon crafted by the first druid, formed from the magic of a forest spirit. Fashioned especially for Brox's hand."

"It will have a place of honor," Thrall whispered, gently taking it from the crooked figure. He eyed it in admiration. Light as a feather and, from the look of it, wood from bottom to head—even the blades—but clearly a capable ax. "How is it you have this—"

But the shaman did not answer . . . because he was no longer there.

With a grunt, Thrall rushed through the entranceway. He instinctively gripped the ax, suddenly wary that this had all been some intricate plot to do away with him.

He confronted the two guards stationed outside what passed for his throne room. "Where is he? Where is the old one?"

"There's been no one!" the senior guard quickly answered.

With a frustrated growl, Thrall pushed past them. He hurried out into the open. The full moon well illuminated the surroundings, but still the ruler of the orcs saw nothing.

Not, that is, until he happened to look up at that moon.

And in it, just passing into the night, he saw a huge, winged form.

A red dragon.

Krasus/Korialstrasz veered in the direction of his flight's lair. Rhonin was with his Vereesa and, through the dragon, the legacy of brave Brox had been brought to the orcs.

Now it was *his* turn to at last go home . . . and see tomorrow what the future would bring.

THE END

ABOUT THE AUTHOR

Richard A. Knaak is the *New York Times* bestselling author of some three dozen novels, including the *The Sin War* trilogy for *Diablo* and the *Legend of Huma* for *Dragonlance*. No stranger to the world of *Warcraft*, he has penned, in addition to this, the collected *War of the Ancients* trilogy, *Day of the Dragon* and its upcoming followup, *Night of the Dragon*. His other works include his own *Dragonrealm* series, the *Minotaur Wars* for *Dragonlance,* the *Aquilonia* trilogy of the Age of Conan, and the *Sunwell Trilogy*—the first *Warcraft* manga. In addition, his novels and short stories have been published worldwide in such diverse places as China, Iceland, the Czech Republic, and Brazil. He looks forward to continuing to return to Sanctuary and Azeroth in future stories.